Life Before Death

Abby Frucht

Scribner Paperback Fiction
Published by Simon & Schuster

For Carolyn Frucht, Sylvia LaMar, and Liz Frucht.
And with enormous gratitude to Valerie Jahns.

SCRIBNER PAPERBACK FICTION
Simon & Schuster Inc.
Rockefeller Center
1230 Avenue of the Americas
New York, NY 10020

First Scribner Paperback Fiction edition 1999
SCRIBNER PAPERBACK FICTION and design are trademarks of Macmillan Library Reference USA, Inc., used under license by Simon & Schuster, the publisher of this work.

Designed by Brooke Zimmer
Set in Granjon
Manufactured in the United States of America

1 3 5 7 9 10 8 6 4 2

Library of Congress Cataloging-in-Publication Data
is available.

ISBN 0-684-83507-X
0-684-84627-6 (Pbk)

ACKNOWLEDGMENTS

The library staff at Mercy Medical Center, along with the staff of the Breast Center at Mercy-Oakwood Medical Center, both in Oshkosh, Wisconsin, offered generous guidance during various research activities associated with the writing of this book. As always, my father, Howard Frucht, read the manuscript and provided invaluable medical and anecdotal advice.

The staff at the Oshkosh Public Museum, which suffered a fire similar to that of the museum in this novel, graciously allowed my attendance during some of their recovery efforts. Martha Frankel, friend, neighbor, reader, and curator, was ever willing to answer my questions, share materials, and offer professional insights.

Anne Yang kindly articulated several aspects of the local Hmong culture and society.

A special thanks to Leigh Haber for being there when I needed her.

And to Don Noffke, Valerie Jahns, Mary Grimm, Carolyn Frucht, and Deborah Schneider for their careful reading of the manuscript in progress, and for their friendship and encouragement throughout.

PART ONE

The Shard

1

I am such an insufferable optimist, and for the longest time, not including that awful day five years ago when my parents were killed and I turned thirty-five, life seemed to be moving in such a routine, predictable, responsible way that when I discovered the lump in my breast my first thought was that all sorts of new, unexpected, interesting things would finally start happening to me.

For a while I lay as I was when I'd found it, in bed with the covers kicked off but the sheets still pulled modestly up to my neck and the morning just clinging to the far side of the curtains but not yet slipping in, and a man named—can you believe it?—Hercules, slumbering in the room next to mine.

His mother had named him for the constellation rather than for the warrior, she was fond of insisting. It was what she saw the second he came out of her, not even the whole configuration, just the five or so stars that extended above the horizon as she gave birth in the big outdoors, on a striped sheet spread over a pile of rip-stop nylon sleeping bags. She was squatting. It was nearly midnight, March nineteenth, a northern sky, he should feel lucky she hadn't glanced over just then and hit on Bootes or Triangulum. He said yes, but Lynx would have been nice. If only she hadn't been squatting. Had she been lying down, she might have hit on Lynx.

I said I would call him Lynx if he wanted, but he said no, as I'd hoped he would. We weren't lovers or anything like that, and it wouldn't feel right for me to call him Lynx, in the unquestionable absence of romance. Besides, ever since the day he was born and I took him out of my friend Martha's arms and rocked him, and thought to myself how glad I was not to be jealous of her for having had him, and kissed the narrow, squeezed crown of his head, and thought how awful it would be to have to kiss him if I *were* jealous, and put him back in her arms, and took him away again thinking she looked kind of weary, and buried my nose in the backs of his knees feeling how thankful I was not to be the one to have to change his diaper or climb out of bed to feed him in the middle of the night, and nibbled his ear, and found a little splotch of pasty stuff still on his scalp even though they had already bathed him but I did *not* swab it off, not me—ever since then, I'd liked calling him Hercules while experimenting with the various kinds of affectionate enthusiasm needed to say a name like that without feeling idiotic. A faked Sylvester Stallone accent was one solution. *Hey Herculeeze, get your ass in here pronto. Hey Herculeeze, shut that door or I'll hit you upside the head.*

Hey Herculeeze, get a load on this lump in my tit.

No. I wouldn't tell him, not even when we slipped out of the Stallone skit into more tender regard, when I called him Herk or sometimes Herky. The reason he was sleeping on my guest room floor was that my fold-out couch was being reupholstered and though I'd good-naturedly offered the use of my bed, he said it wasn't necessary. He was six and a half feet tall, I pressed, my bed was king-size; if I couldn't give him someplace to sleep, what kind of hostess would that make me? But thank you, no, he shyly repeated. He was only nineteen. His mother was my closest friend. She lived in Seattle, which is where I used to live before coming midwest. I'd even phoned her to ask, joking, if it was alright with her if Hercules slept in my bed until he found his own apartment or my couch was delivered, whichever came first. She said I could offer whatever I wanted, as long as I didn't invite him to wear one of my nightgowns. This was only half a joke. Despite his size, Hercules was a person of remarkably delicate gestures, who even as a child had a way of pondering even the most functional objects with an intensity that made Martha look at them, too, again and again until she saw their fascination. And though we'd come to the conclusion that it would be *alright* if he was gay—sad, because there would be no grandchildren for Martha, who wanted some, and disappointing because we would never be able to imagine precisely what it might feel like to be the person he loved—but *alright,* now it seemed more likely that he was going to surprise us and be straight. As far as we could tell he was a virgin, anyway. At nineteen. This was one of the things that made him so special. Also he was still as gentle, as meticulous as ever, which was why I had offered him an internship for his fall semester—cleaning, polishing, dating, identifying, and mounting for exhibit the museum's collection of pocket watches. At work, his "office" was the closet off mine. He was entranced with the watches, as I knew he would be. There were a hundred and seventeen of them but only eighty-nine fobs, all of which had for unknown reasons been removed long ago from the watch cases and left to tangle in the bottom of the box. They made a massive knot of chains for which no one had the patience until Hercules, whose giant fingers eased and coaxed the tiny links free. After only two days he had managed to separate thirty-one chains, and through a cursory comparison of the engravings on fob and watch case had tentatively matched them up. He arranged the pairs neatly on the velvet insides of a violin case open on the tiny office floor.

HERCULES didn't play violin, he played bass. The slender case of the smaller instrument was only his version of a lunchbox/carryall. The bass remained at home in my apartment, fully upright in a corner of my bedroom, its vinyl jacket on a hanger in the closet, like a clothes bag. A hard cello case, or coffin, as such a thing is called, costs nearly a thousand dollars, and since Hercules couldn't bear to shut the bass up in one, the instrument stood contentedly in the shadows of the bedroom corner, a spot most suitable for the instrument's womanly shape.

I wasn't checking for lumps when I found mine. I wasn't

performing my monthly breast exam as advised. No. I was caressing myself, having just wakened, my body half asleep beneath
the langorous touch of my fingers. Eye, mouth, chin, buttock,
thigh, wrist, ankle, navel, shoulder, armpit, rib cage, earlobe—
so I suppose you could say I was masturbating even though it
was only foreplay; I wouldn't do the real splendid thing so
long as Hercules lay purring just on the opposite side of the
wall. How frustrating, anyway, that there wasn't a man in the
world I wanted and thus no face to attach to my wandering
fingers. Over the years, not including the months following
the terrible birthday when that tiny plane crashed into my parents' home in Ireland, when I didn't care whether I wanted a
man or not, I just let him have me, whoever he was—but generally, over the years, if there was someone I wanted, and if he
wanted me, too, then whether or not we were lovers already I
could feel his breath on me when I caressed myself, and I
could feel his urgency and desire. I'd open my legs, I'd place a
hand—*his hand*—against the hollow of my throat, I'd let the
hand travel downward as if the touch were new, my body
unexplored, unfamiliar, the surprises still waiting in every
taut, soft, damp, dimpled, muscular spot. But for quite a long
time, months, really, there had been no one I wanted, in fact
there was not even someone in particular I *no longer* wanted,
so my hand was just my hand, and its encounter with the rest
of my body, especially because I wasn't going to do the real
thing, was only casual.

My fingers even a little bored.

My breasts maybe a trifle dejected.

As if without hope for the future of the relationship.

I opened my legs just as little and as quietly as could be so as
not to alert Hercules, I put my hand to the hollow of my throat
and felt it rest there uncertain as to the advisability of continuing, I closed my legs, then parted them again, then let my hand
dart furtively between them but only long enough to cause a
noncommittal jolt.

For a moment my fingers thumped disinterestedly on the

drum of my belly before following the slope along the indentation of my waist. Had there been a man I liked whose face and desire were linked to my touch, I might have swiveled onto the opposite hip in order to indulge the sensuality of that spot, but now I only lay flat and uninspired, resigned to vague indifference, utterly forty, so contentedly middle-aged I could have sat up and mooed about it had I had the inclination.

Between my thighs, the pulse slumbered again. In the room next door, Hercules grunted and shifted position.

I laid the hand palm down on my breast. Unhappily satisfied, the two of them, hand and breast, resigned to snuggling a minute before saying a fond good-bye.

But then under my fingers my nipple grew hard. I offered it a brief, conciliatory squeeze, knowing it was time to get up and dress for work.

There was a pebble in there.

Smaller than a tooth.

Larger than a grain of sand yet with the same chiseled, irregular edges.

The lump was actually sharp to the touch. I remember being careful not to examine it too vigorously for fear it might cut me.

In the corner of my bedroom the shape and posture of the bass resembled that of a solicitous but altogether too-restrained friend, massively silent, so intent on keeping her terrible suspicions to herself that she had swiveled on a single, tapered ankle to face the corner and keep her lustrous gaze averted. I took my hand off that breast and placed it hopefully on the other, squeezing in the corresponding spot, intending to find the exact same sharp thing as if it were to be expected, some common characteristic of nipple morphology that I'd somehow gone my whole life not noticing.

Just then Hercules rose, opened the guest room door and yawned as he'd done every morning before. I didn't know if his desire to warn me of his emergence from sleep was from embarrassment or habit or simply a nineteen year old's view of the etiquette incumbent on someone who has just spent the night in plaid pajamas sleeping in the home of his mother's best friend who also happened to be his boss. In any case it was clear he considered me a quintessential example of respectable single womanhood and that my apparent ease with him had not broken his resolve to remain the polite and studious observer of my enviable, professional demeanor. After all, I was what he believed he wanted to become, a curator, to whose care and attention a whole community of people entrusted the most cherished bits and pieces of their pasts. Family photos, letters home, bicycle horns, enameled cooking pots—all crossed my neat desk in their mute, hopeful passage from dailiness to history. On the very first day Hercules came to work, the grateful wife of an ailing octogenarian delivered to my custody not only her husband's boyhood fishing pole but a carp he had caught in a stream that no longer existed, that had flowed through a woods that was now the pantyhose store at the outlet mall. Lopsidedly mounted and rudely shellacked, the carp was minus one eye but still looked eager for a feature role in *Area Flora and Fauna*.

"What will we do with it?" Hercules asked when the woman had gone away.

"Number it, tag it, hide it in storage," I answered dolefully. "You never know. A fish is just a fish, but sixty years from now even the pantyhose might be collectibles."

"That's what gets me," said Hercules, using one of his favorite phrases. He used it all the time, half with childlike awe and half with adult resoluteness. "That's what gets me," he remarked one night when we were fixing dinner. "Someday," he remarked, grasping the neck of a bottle of raspberry vinegar and lifting it high to admire it, "this very bottle might be a curiosity. People might not even eat salads anymore."

"*We* might not even eat salads anymore if you don't pull yourself together and dry that lettuce. Pronto, *Herculeeze,*" I answered, with an upward flourish of my eyes as if he were my teenage son and I were putting up with his hopeless teenage

antics even though I knew how lucky my parents would be to
have a grandchild as wonderful as Hercules, if only they were
alive.

"Martha's parents, that is. Lucky. To have a grandchild," I
whispered to myself as I sliced a tomato.

"What did you say?" asked Hercules.

"Dry the lettuce, please," I whispered.

"Sorry," he said, never wanting to offend, drying the lettuce
with such scrupulous attention, the tea towel creased and
puckered just so around his fingers, that I wanted to grab the
whole head away from him and shake it furiously out the window and munch it whole. Really I'd like to shake him up, too,
just a little, though it's not his fault that he sees me so precisely,
or rather, that I can be seen so precisely by someone who knows
how to look. From the moment Hercules showed up he was
able to decipher the frugal code of my environment so acutely
that he knew just which door must lead to the guest
room/study and then, seeing that my fold-out couch was not
where it belonged—that there was only my desk and my bookshelves and my gooseneck lamp opposite the spot under the
window where the fold-out couch should have been—he
placed his backpack and duffel and rolled-up blankets exactly
in the space that would have been left to them had the room
been complete. After that, he studied my jade tree a while in
order to satisfy his idea that the tweezers I stored among the
pens and paper clips in a cup on my desktop blotter had the
purpose he guessed I allotted them. They do. I use them to
tweeze off that white, gooey fur that proliferates in small
clumps on the stems of the jade leaves. After that, although I
didn't see him doing it, he must have glanced long enough at
my bookshelves to be able to ask me, later that night, when we
were sitting in the living room all buttoned and sashed in our
bathrobes and pajamas, taking coy sips of wine from ceramic
goblets, if I had been in the same poetry class as his mother
when she and I were in college together.

"That's where we got to know each other," I said.

"I recognize the Elizabeth Bishop," he said, managing to hit on the book containing not his mother's favorite line but my own, *her white disordered sheets like wilted roses.* Try as I might, since the day I first read that and called Martha up to exclaim about it, neither I nor a single one of my lovers has ever been able to cause my sheets to be disordered in such a way that they resemble wilted roses or any other flower. Crumpled paper, maybe, or pleated like a fan but never moist, never fragrant with bloom or with loss. Hercules seemed to know this, too, just by looking at the way I twirled the stem of my goblet as if daring the wine to break free of its meniscus, teasing and twirling but not spilling a single drop. Sometimes, I thought, I'm too stable a person, too much in control. Even my attempts at reckless irresponsibility—taking the day off work, for instance, driving forty miles north or south along the lakefront until I came to a spot I'd never stopped at before—made me only more serene than ever, one of those ladies you see walking alone on beaches, her shoes dangling from her fingers away from the splash of the water as she crouches to examine the whorls in the sand round the tide pools.

Perhaps Martha had talked to him about me. She's always been the kind of mother who is forthright with her son.

Perhaps she'd said to him, "That Isobel! She keeps an iron in her office, next to her teapot and a spare pair of socks. Every year she used to travel to Ireland to visit her parents, and within days of her return she'd break up with whatever fit, healthy, passionate man she'd been seeing, explaining how either the solitariness or the conviviality of her parents' marriage reinforced her idea that she should break up with him sooner or later anyway for his own good, since it wasn't fair to string him along, thinking he was the kind of person she wanted to spend the rest of her life with, when he probably wasn't thinking they would spend their lives together anyway but just taking her as she came, so to speak. After she breaks up with whoever, she goes in for six months of late-night phone calls congratulating herself about how she hadn't allowed herself to slip and get pregnant, after which fol-

lows a period of silence about three months into which she calls
me up and says 'To think I might have been in labor right now,
this minute, when I'm forty years old and have four grants to
write and an exhibit to catalogue, thank God I had more sense
than that.' Which is her way of resigning herself to her idea that
she wouldn't make a good mother. Which is not in the least bit
true. She'd make a wonderful mother," Martha might say.
"Like me."

At once, sitting in my living room with Hercules that first
night he arrived in town, I was embarrassed by the afghans I'd
pulled from the closet in case we felt chilled, the brushed plaid
woolens so clearly of Scottish virtue, and by the coasters I'd laid
on the low table before us depicting miniaturized scenes from
Greek vases, their sexual antics made chaste and archaic. I don't
know that I'd make a good mother, I thought. Anyway, thank
goodness the debate was rhetorical, and that those late-night
phone calls did not persist for six months, and that anyway
more often than not, it was Martha who called *me* to ask if
maybe the reason I congratulated myself so much was to cover
up how much I really did want a baby, to which I'd reply,
"Now, *that's* an idea," so she wouldn't catch on to how crazy I
thought she was for being a single mom. I nearly said all this to
Hercules, out of thin air, along with the fact that of course I could
no longer visit my parents, I no longer even visit their grave. I'd
selected the site myself, in a cemetery close to their favorite
cliffs within sight of their house if only their house were still
there, and upon my return had broken up as usual with the
man I was seeing, which had nothing to do with my parents at
all, obviously, since they were dead and buried in a whole other
quadrant of the planet, but it wouldn't do to say all that to Hercules. To keep myself quiet, I took a deep, thankful taste of my
wine. No sooner had I finished than Hercules fixed on me his
dewey, nineteen-year-old sympathy and said, "What I like best
about my mother is that you can never quite believe anything she
tells you, even though you know she believes it herself."

So Martha and I were right, he did have a streak of clairvoyance, mixed in with his more than ordinary dose of understanding. When long ago I'd first suggested that to Martha, she hadn't believed me even though it was she who was prone to exaggeration. She *had* told me, many times, that Hercules was the most tactful person she ever met in her life. Which I always *did* believe.

"Well," I said after a while, "I'm getting kind of sleepy, Herky. But you stay up a while. *Go drink your wine and go get tight,*" I added slyly, certain that not even Hercules would recognize that as another treasured line from Elizabeth Bishop. I was right. He looked taken aback. His surprise was a point in my favor, though it didn't quite cause him to recast his knowledge of me. On the morning I discovered the lump in my breast, he was careful as always to make his customary detour into the guest room/study where he kept his things stashed out of sight in his duffel. Even his shampoo, his bar of what could only be Ivory soap in its hinged plastic box, his toothbrush, toothpaste, razor, deodorant, all this he fetched from his duffel and carried into the bathroom each morning, wrapped in his towel that never quite got dry because he kept it rolled up in his duffel with everything else, not wanting to assert, on my bare, gleaming towel racks, its velvety, damp intrusion. He must have thought it would annoy me to have to brush up against it in my own nakedness. He couldn't have guessed, at least I hoped he couldn't, that his towel in my bathroom might have made me a little bit lonely, just as he couldn't have guessed that his bass standing face-into the shadowy corner might make me a little bit lonely, too. After all, it was me who had told him to keep it there, in order to remind myself that I wanted to learn to play strings. Nothing fancy. I had no grand aspirations. But the tang of the notes, the discrete, plucked arrangements of melody and harmonic, was a system with which I lacked even rudimentary acquaintance, and though I didn't care to master it, I wanted the access, as if music were a room and I wanted the door to be just cracked open, the faintest glean of its contents barely reaching me. I'd never bothered to make it happen; I only said to myself, now and then, that the sight of a sheet of music open on a stand in my living room would be a welcome diversion. Not that I went in much for diversion, but that was precisely the point. And now here it was every morning, Hercules's burnished, six-foot companion, not like music at all but more like a woman examining surreptitiously the expression on my face as I palpated the lump. I believe I disappointed her; my expression stayed so peaceful, if anything there was only a flicker of excitement before I grew yet more relaxed, more pleased, even. Try as I might, I couldn't imagine what all the interesting things might *be* that might happen to me as a result of having found the lump, but that didn't seem to matter, because I knew things would. Happen, that is. I don't know why they call it a lump, exactly. I'd call it a shard. It lay beneath the aureole, right at the edge where the nimbus of color fades into the paler, surrounding flesh, and if I ran my finger lightly across the smooth dome of the nipple I couldn't feel it at all. For a moment I experimented with just how much pressure was needed in order for my finger to make sense of its presence. Not much, certainly.

"I have a lump," I nearly whispered to the bass, and then, when Hercules's shower roared in the bathroom, I did speak aloud.

"What gets me," I said, mimicking him, "is the unexpectedness of this, the way it changes the order of things. Things will happen to me that I could never have predicted. Life will take turns, life will play tricks, tomorrow will not be the same as today. When I say that until now my world was routine, I don't mean it was dull, only that I knew every brilliant, blinding, breathtaking moment that was coming. Now suddenly, I don't."

I'd never spoken aloud in an empty room, before. It made me feel queerly, calmly elated.

2

Still, what *are* the things that might happen to me as a result of my having discovered a lump in my breast? I asked myself that morning as I drove me and Hercules to the museum.

Well, I thought, rephrasing the question, shifting to third gear, if someone were to tell me I had only a year to live, or something horrible like that, what would I do?

Would I quit my job? I wondered.

Would I finally learn to play strings?

Would I move back to Martha in Seattle? Would I travel to Prague? Athens? Florence? Take up photography? Follow my favorite modern dance troupes on tour around the country?

I didn't think so, knowing me.

Beside me in the car, Hercules reached for the radio, let his fingers hover a second midair above the controls, let them drop again without pushing the button. Would I say to Hercules, if I were dying, if I had only a year to live, that the memory of how I'd once buried my face in the fat baby backsides of his knees and made funny, snorting, tickling, farting noises still beckoned to me as if I imagined it might be repeated, as if I might do it again?

No.

I wouldn't.

It wouldn't do, my prim voice echoed, more faintly than it was accustomed.

I turned the radio on myself, so fast and so loud that Hercules nearly jumped out the window into one of the drying flower beds along Algoma Boulevard, where the overheated petals hung limp as skirts.

In the blast of the music, I remained perfectly still. I only shut my eyes and drove.

3

Not much later that very same week, the museum burned down.

It was a Wednesday. Some welders were up on the roof, repairing copper flashing. From our offices on the third floor, we could hear the clatter and thump of their boots on the fragile black slates, along with the blunt, gassy hiss of the torches. A single yellow rope, knotted to nothing that I could see, hung past the window at the end of our hallway where the water fountains and the rest rooms are, bisecting our view of the park. It was August, so the fruit trees had long dropped their blossoms, and the other shrubs and beds looked by now limply ordinary, a patchwork of fading, drying-out color on the uncommon green of the lawns. But in the distance, past the park where a lane wound into the cemetery at the edge of the river, the tall cottonwoods were spectres of diaphanous white, their fluffed seeds just beginning to dislodge and drift on the breezes. That dangling, yellow, splintery rope was a hindrance to anyone who on her way to the bathroom relished a glimpse of the cottonwoods, but since I heard no one complaining or even grunting with annoyance while pausing at the water fountain, I assumed I was alone in this aggravation and determined to bear it as stoically as I could. I closed the miniblinds, so I wouldn't have to see how the view was obstructed. Not ten minutes later, when I stuck my head out of the office for a look at the sunlight slatted on the hallway floor, somebody had pulled the blinds up again. I made my way down the hall and reclosed them. For nearly an hour, this mute dialogue continued. The blinds went up, the blinds came down, the yellow rope still dangled on the far side of the glass. Why the welders had dropped it to crisscross the window when they might just as easily have sent it over the stone on either side of the pane was a question I could answer only by supposing that they enjoyed this spectacle of me and whoever having it out. I tied the miniblind pull to the lock on the window. My adversary released it in short order. I knew who it was, just as he must have known it was me. David, the museum director, and I were cultivating our own history of political belligerency (he is an arch conservative), and because the autumn elections were starting to rear their heads we took every opportunity to demonstrate the comic irreconcilability of our differences. It was he, for instance, who kept removing from the foyer the statue of Diana, relegating her half-draped nudity to our jumbled basement exhibit about hunting, and it was I who continued to replace her on her rightful pedestal, and then, it was somebody else who, after hours one evening, fitted a plastic carnation over the single offending part of her torso. And so it went. The blinds went up, the blinds came down, in the distance the cottonwoods breathed their impervious sighs. The whole thing made for the usual kind of morning. I was drafting a catalogue for our springtime show, highlighting the growth to international fame of a local clothing manufacturer's line of children's overalls, a manufacturer whose decades-long generosity to the museum recently culminated in a bequest to document its toddling climb to success. Typing, I could just make out, from the closet off my office, above the noises of the workmen up on the roof, the bell-like clink of Hercules at work untangling the pocket watches, while all morning the fragrance of brewing coffee grew strong and then weak and then strong again. In the neighboring office, the copy machine clicked and whirred, the phone rang and rang, and the director's assistant threw her usual fits about how technology insulted her devotion to preserving the artistry of the past. When I returned from my fifth excursion down the hall, having Scotch-taped the bottom slat of the miniblinds to the windowsill, Hercules was standing in the closet doorway toying with one of the watches, his massive height blocking the dimness from behind.

"You're grinning," he said.

"It's a private joke," I answered, in order to embarrass him for having been so importunate as to mention my expression. He obliged, of course. How amusing to watch a person as broad-shouldered as Hercules turn pink in the face. And how very touching to witness his delight when in his awkwardness he wound the watch and held it to his ear.

"It still ticks!" he exclaimed.

"That's wonderful, Herky," I said, and then somebody pulled the fire alarm.

AT FIRST I thought it was David who set the alarm off in hopes of signaling his frustration with our window blind shenanigans. But when the welders, in chorus, shouted *fire!* from the landing, everyone rushed for the exits. By the time we reached the lobby, a thin odor of smoke had descended to greet us.

According to Hercules's pocket watch, it took the fire department no longer than four and a half minutes to get to the museum. But then it took exactly one and three-quarter hours before they managed to turn on the water. The problem, we kept hearing, was insufficient pressure.

So go to the river, we pleaded. It's just down the road. Pump the water from there!

But for reasons that the fire chief has remained unable to explain, they didn't heed our suggestion. Dumb and unyielding, the river flowed stupidly past. The yellow rope still dangled, even after the slates crashed into the attic.

WHAT GETS me, I said to myself as I stood on the sidewalk with the others, all wiping our eyes of smoke and frustration, was how lovely it was, that fire, how sexual, even, the bright flames lapping and tickling. I could practically feel its heat on my skin, most acutely on my right breast above where the lump seemed to tremble and throb. I'd forgotten about it. Well, not really. But my reverie had been touched by panic, and since Monday morning when I'd found the lump, I'd thought of it only in odd little bursts of anticipatory sorrow, that turned quickly to tranquil relief, that turned to panic again before I let it slip out of my mind. Despite its portent of change, or maybe because of it, I was reluctant to face the lump and take that step forward into its pull. First of all, I wondered, in which direction ought I to step? There seemed any number of options. I might pretend to ignore it, for instance, go on as before only bearing its mute uncertainty day after day, month after month until it stopped me in my tracks.

Except I didn't make tracks.

I was not that kind of person.

I was too sedentary. Around me, time and space made tracks but even they were only spiral, concentric, overlapping as the seasons. At age forty, I reflected, I was really quite the same as I had been at thirty, only then I'd still thought of myself as being an "only child" and now, how could I, when my parents were dead? Truthfully my parents would have been pleased, I often thought, to find me so unchanged, so like myself no matter what did or didn't happen around me. I still remember the evening we had our last baby-sitter; I was twelve years old, the sitter thirteen. Anxiously my mother pulled her aside, explaining that though I was old enough and perfectly mature enough to take care for myself, my parents felt more comfortable leaving me with "company." The sitter and I met eyes. Already we'd sized each other up at school in hopes we might be friends, but now that she was being paid to visit me, friendship was out of the question. I sat down to read a magazine. As if to highlight the difference in status between us, company or no company, the sitter went into the bathroom to start my bathwater. There, she yanked the shower door off the tracks and was knocked to the floor by a heavy, glass blow to the head. The glass shattered when it hit her, blood was every-where. She had only a shallow head wound, I reassured her while dialing for the ambulance—head wounds bled copiously and needed stitches but weren't a danger, she'd be fine; I wrapped her tight in a plush towel and rocked her until the ambulance came. It was me who held the gauze against her head to staunch the bleeding as we sped down the streets, and me who phoned her parents when we reached the hospital, and me who realized that we'd left the bathwater running and that my poor parents, upon coming home, would wade through it to discover the blood on the tiles of the bathroom wall, and the blood in the sink and on the bar of soap. "So what did Isobel do?" my mother could be heard to say next day on the telephone. "She phoned the neighbor, she directed the neighbor to the hidden key, she dictated a note to be taped to the front door of the house after the bathwater had been shut off and the porch light switched on so we would see it right off. That Isobel! Always so dependable! Always in control . . ."

Now I watched the flames snake along the charring gutters, through the downspout all the way to ground level. The downspout was choked with last year's autumn leaves. We really should have had it cleaned. Before our eyes it burst gradually, rendingly open, the split metal curling and popping. Hercules had disappeared from where he'd been standing beside me, but soon I caught sight of him among the crew of firefighters donning gear near the truck, helping with masks and oxygen tanks.

I might make a trip to my doctor, I supposed.

I might do it right this minute, swivel backward off the sidewalk and head for my car as if to escape from the roar of the fire.

Or I might simply call the doctor on the phone.

From one of the pay phones down by the docks on the river. Already, half the museum staff had made for those phones to call spouses and lovers and news reporters. It was a beautiful spot, gulls wheeling round the piers in the watery sunlight, and just to the west where the river met the lake, the arched span of the highway overpass heavy as an ancient aqueduct, and the

boats passing underneath, and out of sight in the booth that
housed the operating gears for the drawbridge, my too-laid-
back (even for me!) friend Trevor Close reading through his
entire set of the Encyclopedia Brittanica while listening to Eric
Clapton on his headphones, perhaps just now glancing up, and
then down, and then up again to prepare himself to wonder if
that was smoke or just fog rolling skyward away from the
museum, and thinking maybe he'd catch sight of me one of
these weeks and inquire.

I might walk out to the end of the dock to get a whiff of fish
and motor oil before making for the phones.

But, if I telephoned the doctor, I'd first have to speak with
one of her nurses, whose cheery dispassion would turn scolding
and authoritative when I told her that though I'd already
waited three days to call, I insisted on speaking with the doctor
at once.

"It's my life," I might argue.

"Yes. And your health," the nurse might reply, biting her
tongue on that other, more potent rejoinder. I don't know
where these nurses get their terrible righteousness. It must be
something they learn at school. In any case the Planned Parenthood might be a better bet, the dingy office of fat, frowzy
women leveling me with their meaningful glances, their handfuls of pamphlets, their waiting room coffee with a mug where
you drop in your coins. Years ago, in college, when I went to
Planned Parenthood for a pregnancy test, the doctor was
dressed all in black. I swear I thought she was their resident
politician. Back then, women's bodies were such serious business, like voting. Birth control as ideology. Come to think of it,
I'd never taken an adequate stand. I'd only dabbled in various
doctrines, always proud to display them in my shopping cart
but turning doubtful at home when their ramifications
emerged. This one, too messy. That one, too clumsy. All of
them, too *certain,* I sometimes found myself thinking, wishing
I had enough of a gambling instinct or that I believed enough
in the kindness of fate to rely instead on the rhythm method or

on those eighty-percent effective packets of sponges. No matter what, if I became pregnant, at least I could say to Martha that I'd tried not to, I wasn't stupid or careless or irresponsible and yet look what I'd ended up with, this bundle of chortling nerves, this quivering backside of chubby knees. She, Martha, was the only person who understood what mixed feelings I had, just as I understood she had mixed feelings, too. Just because she'd been impetuous enough to have a baby didn't make us that different from each other. Lately, when there *was* a lately, I'd relied on condoms. A man shows his colors most vividly the second you hand one over. Is he *Old Boy* or liberated, smart or merely savvy, clumsy or stylish? All at once, was he the kind of person I might care about or not? It was a question my friend, Martha, insisted was less important than its opposite, *Was he the kind of person who might care about me?* In love, Martha's spirit has always been more tolerant and thus more adventuresome than mine, because she's happy with the romance even if she's unhappy with the man. In other words, her spirit's flexible. It gives. Mine doesn't. Or hasn't. The problem is I try to love the person, and that kind of feeling is harder to come by. I even tried to love the men with whom my mother set me up on dates. The sons of her friends. The friends of her friends' sons. Goldilocks, Martha used to call me. This one, too hot. That one, too small. But some of them worked out alright. I always loved—still do—the beginnings. We're both so careful and excited. But then the care dies down while the excitement holds fast, or the excitement dies down while the care holds fast, and after half a year or so of compromise, my heart turns inward. In the weeks following the end of a love affair, that's when I cook my most elegant, nourishing meals.

Another thing I might do instead of visiting my doctor, I realized, was to head on a plane for Martha in Seattle. Or maybe drive there. But would I travel through this country, or farther north? Or maybe south . . . Never, before I'd discovered the lump, had I had reason to be so ambivalent. There'd been no prospect of adventure, nothing to be ambivalent about.

Now suddenly the most banal possibilities multiplied kaleido-
scopically. Even dressing in the morning I felt assailed by the
shoes I chose not to wear. Watching the fire was like that, too. I
might find myself staring at the caved-in roof, but if so I wasn't
gazing at the smoke rising out of my collapsed office window, a
smoke that seemed to vibrate with the left-behind cursor on
the screen of my computer. And if I followed the quivery trail
of the smoke, I missed the sight of the hoses tunneling into the
lobby, and of the water gushing out, a falls on the steps, a river
of gift shop offerings. Postcards, rolled maps, replicas of peg
dolls, replicas of pop guns, time charts, place mats, and finally a
rapids of those inch-wide squares of cardboard affixed with
sets of antiqued costume jewelry.

I might wade through it for the doors, make for the lobby
as if in a trance of tears.

Except I wasn't crying. I almost never did. Sometimes I
thought I couldn't even if I wanted, I was too much in control,
even looking at the proud lines of the masonry building threat-
ening to crack and buckle, I couldn't make myself cry. Anyway, somebody had to stay sane, and since it clearly wasn't
going to be anybody else, it may as well be me. No matter
what, I had no intention of behaving like Jayne, David's spas-
modic assistant, who not content to wade, had thrashed and
stumbled up the steps before somebody—David, I think—
caught her and yanked her back. The funny thing was she
wasn't putting on a show. She really meant to risk her life. She
wanted her private collection of marijuana smokers' parapher-
nalia; the pipes, hookahs, hoses, filters, and milky, elaborate
bottles displayed on a set of glass shelves in her office out of
sight of the public. Even though she didn't smoke, she liked
the carvings on the graceful, curved necks of the pipes, the
residue still chalky on the insides of the bowls, the "quaint
decadence" of it, was what I would have said had I had the
opportunity to describe it in a catalogue. But now her smokes
were going up in smoke, and I, seeing how she cringed in
David's arms, tried hard to smell the drug. Just a hint, just an

echo of the fragrance of the sweetness, might have justified the fact that I was high.

I sought out Hercules to see if he would notice, if he would see in my face, the way nobody else could, my suppressed ecstasy at the sight of the firemen clamoring to stifle the flames.

But Hercules was weeping, his arms around the blue-haired volunteer, also weeping, who worked the cash register in the gift shop. Everyone, I noticed, was standing in three-somes or pairs, their arms intertwined, their light, summer blouses limp in the gathering steam.

I went and positioned myself by a tree. I held my body erect and tried to will the yellow rope to lose its hold on the shriveling gutter. It was like me, that rope, basking and felicitous, hardly batting an eye when the photographer stepped forward to snap my picture. I didn't let myself smile, of course. I only wished I had thought to take my sunglasses out of the office. In the afternoon paper there was this caption beneath my portrait: "A devastated Isobel Albright, chief curator of the Fox Valley Historical Museum, watches in shock and brokenheartedness as this morning's twelve-alarm fire lays waste to architect William Water's ninety-one-year-old English Gothic-style building."

"Do I look *shocked*? Do I look *devastated*?" I asked Hercules that evening beneath the premature glare of the floodlights on the museum lawn, where a local restaurant had trucked in pizza free of charge for the stragglers. In fact there were a lot of us milling around, firemen and museum workers alike. Nobody seemed to want to go home. There was too much to do, and though, given the still-present danger, we couldn't yet begin to take stock of the damage, we needed to be there to let it sink in. The air smelled of pastrami and ashes. Someone had delivered a case of warm beer, but no napkins and nothing to sit on. We made a somber picnic, crouched on the damp grass, wiping our hands on sheaves of newsprint. To our surprise the museum, excepting the roof and third floor, was still upright and basically sound, although its insides were ravaged and its brickwork stained with geysers of water and ash. Beyond the fence, along the sidewalk, past where two policemen shouted warnings through their bullhorns, hundreds of onlookers gazed and paused and strolled and pointed, their mouths open in dismay when they saw the tattered rafters poking every which way into the violet sky. From the crowded look of things, even if we wanted to start our cars and drive home, we wouldn't have been able. But that was alright. We all silently hoped that if we clung to the day it might reverse itself and restore to us our usual routine—lunch at our desks, and after that a troop of school-age children, one of whom always managed to donate a half-sucked lollipop to the coin bath in the lobby, and by three a minor crisis like a grant coming in underfunded or a live bat discovered hanging upside down from the shotgun barrel of a fur trader stepping out of his cabin in the *North Woods* diorama.

Still, dusk continued to fall, while David, wagging his head at the sidewalk procession, bemoaned the fact that the fire was our most popular exhibit ever and that if only we charged admission we would be able to offer a two-step pay raise across the board. At this, everyone glanced eagerly in my direction, expecting me to say *Isn't that just like a Republican to think of his own pocket when the universe is crumbling before his eyes?* But I stayed quiet, knowing how much he was hurting. He'd been director for twenty-six years. He was nearly as old as my dead father and had lost all his right-wing pride when he had been unable to refrain from crying in front of a TV camera after the fire was finally out. We all loved him the more for his grief, but it would be days before he believed that, and then only grudgingly. The truth was everyone cried but me. It was this yet unremarked-on, imperfect pearl of a fact that I carried over to Hercules along with the afternoon paper, hoping to learn precisely which of his ideas about me had been further confirmed by my imperturbability.

I found him tinkering with the giant apostles clock that had been rescued early on from the onslaught of water and smoke. It lay dismantled across somebody's treasured quilt outspread on the pavement beneath the bus-port awning, its pendulum detached, its brass chimes loose from their moorings, its heavy, wood, ornamented doors propped here and there upon splintered hinges. But in the center of the quilt the carved, fenestrated tower lay toppled just so, while around it stood the painted, robed statues of the apostles in worried, conversational huddles like those on the picnic lawn. I bit off a tiny triangle of pizza and placed it carefully in one of Judas Iscariot's outstretched, gold-leafed, terra-cotta hands.

"Careful you don't get any mozzarella on his beard," said Hercules, making me laugh aloud. From the awning just above where Hercules crouched fell a runnel of mud-colored water that pooled up along the stitching of the quilt, while nearby, the glass face of the clock lay forlornly splattered.

"Look at this newspaper photo," I said glibly to Hercules. "And read the sensational caption! Does this look like a devastated person to you? Do I really look devastated? Do I look brokenhearted?"

Hercules sat back on his heels and raised his eyes not to the paper but to my face. He took a short while considering, only to be polite, I now realize. At the time I felt a smile playing on my lips, but I did not let it out until just before Hercules finally spoke.

"Yes," he said.

4

The reason I couldn't cry even when the heat made little ping-ing noises inside the bricks of the burning museum was because I was too busy playing with the idea that if I were superstitious, I might believe that the fire was my fault. Had I not found the lump—no, had I not asked myself what new interesting things might happen as a result of my having found the lump—then the welder would not have neglected his torch, the flame would not have crept beneath the copper flash-ing, the sparks would not have scattered and clung and set off their tiny explosions of flame.

And the reason I couldn't cry even while I speculated that the fire was my doing, was because I kept wondering what else might happen that my parents would never know about. Until now I'd been comforted by the fact they hadn't missed anything by dying, as far as I was concerned. I even had the same job. But now I'd found the lump, which they didn't know about. And the fire had burned down my office, and they didn't know about that, either.

What else? I wondered.

What else would they not know about that happened to me next?

What else?

What else?

5

Funny that while it is the pen to which we attach some notion of permanence, it is the pencil that will outlast us, the smudged lead clinging to our memories and dreams while the ink slides free in an oozing bleed or in a wash of pale, smoky, vanishing blue. Perhaps it's the eraser that had us convinced; so easy to flip the pencil on its rump and obliterate, or perhaps it is the paper that in those bygone, heady days of pencil supremacy was rife with acid and deteriorated anyway. Manuscript to dust. Dust to nothing. I had my mammogram on Friday directly following my visit to the doctor whose nurses didn't scold, after all, but in whose restroom I found a McDonald's hamburger squatting unwrapped in the booth behind the little wooden door where you slide the plastic-lidded cups containing the urine samples. It did not have a name tag on it, the hamburger, I was happy to see, but it did have that terrible slather of sauce that made even the urine samples appear less appetizing than usual, not a thing you would like to have to squeeze out of your own body.

I told the doctor about it. Not to complain. Just to have something to titter about while I opened my bra and lay back on the nearly fluorescent paper to wait for the round cold moon of the stethoscope. Why she started with my heart when it was my breast I worried about is a question I'm glad I kept to myself, because she looked so pleased with the way it was beating, a look on her face like the look on Hercules's when he found the watch was ticking. I felt actually proud to be the owner of such a heartbeat, its rhythm so measured and slow that the first time she heard it, the doctor thought I was a swimmer, a runner, an aerobics dancer, anything, until I confessed I got no exercise at all unless she counted walking or intermittent, occasional, languorous sex.

"Power walking?" she asked.

I shuddered resolutely.

"Strolling," I answered.

The doctor shrugged. The more you exercise, the stronger the heart gets, the less frantically it pumps, the more dependable its calm delivery of goods. Kind of like the tortoise and the hare, she explained, pleased with my heart even though I hadn't loved anybody passionately enough to earn it. So why, now, was her satisfied expression giving way, her sing-along demeanor turning off-key and doubtful the moment I guided her hand to the lump? Surely she hadn't thought I was joking, when I'd insisted it was there. Surely she'd expected to find something.

But not *this,* her expression seemed to divulge.

Surely not *this.*

She is not, has never been, the kind of doctor given to personal exchange. Not a nurturing sort, she prefers a distinctly invitational repartee suggesting that though she is determined to reveal precious little of herself, her patients may tell her as much as they like. Ordinarily, her manner is marked by a touch of ironical humor. Her reply to my story about the McDonald's hamburger was to tell me a story about a colleague whose favorite patient was an animal trainer who once arrived for his checkup in the company of a chimpanzee. He'd dressed the animal in a plaid party dress, then sat her down in a chair in the waiting room before allowing her to choose from a fanful of reading material. The chimp chose *Sports Illustrated,* then flipped through its pages of football players with lustful concentration while in the waiting room around her the other patients filled out forms and read their own books and magazines and never once uttered a word about the chimp, not even to the doctor, the nurse, the receptionist. Perhaps the patients were only being discreet, perhaps they thought the chimp was a woman with some terrible ailment they only hoped was not contagious, though most likely, my doctor supposed, they knew quite well she was a chimp but chose not to comment for fear of disrupting the purposeful, carpeted rectitude of the office waiting room which, after all, was one of the few public places in the world incurring no degree of social obligation. They all had their own problems, their own embarrassments, their own chimps only Thank the Good Lord not quite so apparent.

Besides, my doctor added, most people are more sheep than primate, which was her way of making me feel good for having mentioned the hamburger.

So why, now, was she, too, looking away? She'd shifted her fingers to a spot higher up, just under the armpit, and then across to the opposite breast, and then up to that same spot near the armpit again.

"How did you find these?" she finally ventured. "I mean, since you said you weren't doing a breast exam, what were you doing?"

Was this a personal question? Not on the surface. But if I told her I'd been spending each night within snoring distance of my godson Hercules nearly twenty years my junior whose chortles of laughter and delight I had used to elicit by sucking on the backs of his knees and whose long-necked bass in the morning light exhibited such sensual repose that I couldn't help but caress myself even in the absence of a lover, and that all my summer lassitude turned taut and melodic the instant I touched the lump, as if the bass had uttered a solitary, vibrating, expectant twang, then it may as well be a personal question.

Which I didn't want, not wanting to be the kind of person who bursts into tears in the doctor's office even if they were tears of gladness. For the first time ever, I'd thought of Hercules as my godson. Was he, then? Was he, really?

"Oh," I said carefully. "It doesn't matter what I was doing. What matters is what I do now. And what do you mean, *these?*"

The doctor pursed her lips, squinting, and made a quick note in my file.

"There are two of them," she answered, then. "One here, one here."

She placed a finger of one hand on the spot near my armpit, a finger of the other on my nipple. For a moment the doctor and I were like schoolchildren acting out the principles of electric circuitry, so I lay as still as could be and let the current wash through us.

The lump under my armpit was larger than the first, though not quite as sharp to the touch. In response to my prodding it gave my finger a blunt, unmistakable poke, like there was a whole other person in there trying to get my attention. The doctor filled a paper Dixie cup with tepid water and gave it to me. Still prone, I played my game with the meniscus, tilting the cup, teasing the spill, than standing the cup flat on my belly and letting it balance there. Never had it even occurred to me to call Hercules my godson. As far as I knew he hadn't even been baptized, and the notion of God was a thing Martha and I tossed around only during fits of atheistic soul-searching. Now the word settled inside me like an unfamiliar prayer. *I have a godson,* I mused. *I'll have to call Martha and tell her.*

"You know it might just be nothing. Probably it *is* nothing," the doctor finally offered.

"But," I said.

"But," she repeated.

I drank the water lying down, then pulled myself up on the crackling paper, fastened my bra, urged myself to receive that strange glee I'd discovered when I'd first laid my hand on the sharp, unmistakable pebble. Really, once I'd forced it, the feeling no longer seemed strange but only natural again, my jolt of surprise and the way it spread rapturously through me, all the way to the tips of my toes.

"You understand that under normal circumstances at your age I would advise a mammogram in any case," the doctor went on.

"I'd been thinking about that myself," I lied.

"But that in this case I think it would definitely not be a

good idea to hold off for the usual couple of weeks," she said too quickly.

"Maybe not," I agreed.

"So I'm going to phone from my office right now and make the appointment for this afternoon," she concluded, her tone of voice reminiscent of the one I used when I said to a man that though I no longer wanted us to be lovers I still cared a great deal what happened to him.

In trepidation I said, stopping her as she walked out the door, "This is something you can handle, medically? You'll be the one with whom I consult? I won't have to go running around finding a whole new doctor?"

"It's always good to get a second opinion," she answered, and then, softening, "I'll call you as soon as I get the results. Don't worry. It's not healthy to worry. But I guess I can't call you at work, can I? That beautiful museum."

"We still have our phone line, believe it or not. You have to let it ring forever and then wait twenty minutes for someone to track me down. Tell them I'm outside washing and drying the records."

Had she not taken the file out of the examining room I might have snuck a look at what she'd jotted down in response to my refusal to say how I'd found the lump. I'd never peeked in a doctor's file before.

A VISITING conservator, up from Illinois in the startling capacity of disaster consultant, had advised us to wash off the records. In the future, he said, when it came time to sift through the wreckage of the storage facility trapped for the moment beneath the fallen, shattered roof, those scattered papers would be our key to what was lost and what was saved, for they would help us make sense of the snapped bits and pieces, the fragments of cloth, wood, porcelain, and metals. He instructed us to fill some buckets with water, dunk the papers one by one, sponge off the charred flakes, the smeared ashes and mud, then lay them flat among layers of paper toweling to dry.

He said these simple things kindly as if he were speaking to children, as if he knew, from experience, how frightened we all were of losing our heads in this mess. The smallest step, the least move, seemed as risky to the fabric of our years-long rapport as it was risky to the tapestries, the torn costumes and wrecked tatting. He must have known that the washing was just what was needed, disregarding the value of all of those paper records. Washing was something to do. It gave us someplace to gather, around each bucket dipping paper as if roasting marshmallows in a campfire, keeping the warmth of our years of banter and camaraderie sputtering but alive.

The cards written in pencil were still legible, and though it was tempting to read them as they were laid out to dry—*Appliquéd Satin Muff with Swiss Dot Lining # 2946-5, Estate of Helen J. Cotton 1897; Pewter Ladle with Dolphins # 3001-7, Collection of Mrs. Norbert Heinke 1907; Wooden Marble Set # 6, Anonymous Donor 1931*—we didn't let ourselves do it, afraid that by dawdling over the cards we were only avoiding the terrible dishevelment inside the museum. Everything toppled and torn, and all the broken, injured pieces on pallets on the floor like wounded civilians in a makeshift, wartime hospital. Water leaking from the ceiling, the dark puddles spreading and shrinking here and there along the hallways. There was the odor of mold, the glare of storm lights, the serpentine loops of extension cords around each sculpted, crumbling pillar. There were moths, yellow jackets, ladybugs, inchworms, and spiders. There were footprints every which way, and a few paintings still hanging on the walls like splintered, warped reflections of the ones across the gallery. There was the gurgle of a pump in the basement, and the murmur of the Polish workers from above in what had been the attic, where we were not allowed, for we were prisoners of liability law. Beyond a yellow fire ribbon, the stairs were forbidden, and perhaps it was this that made us crave them so much, each of us dreaming of what we might rescue from beneath the fallen timbers. The Tiffany lamps. The player piano. The zippered clothes bags of top hats and spats collected sixty years ago when what is now a local movie theater closed its doors to vaudeville. Under the weight of the glistening ashes, the precarious floor seemed a black sea of buried treasure upon which loose slates still dropped from the cavernous, torn-apart eaves. We all knew we'd sneak up there later and comb the debris. A group of paid, insured workers all of the same Polish-speaking family were already enviably there, tossing slates off the rooftop down to a flatbed while shouting warnings needing no translation. Out on the lawn, dunking and sponging the papers, we were like parents at the bedside of a sick child.

Among the members of the staff, each of us had different ways of dealing with the quaking scenery inside the museum. David tried his best to ignore it entirely. The gift shop cashiers continued taking a kind of inventory, lifting the ruined artifacts one by one as if checking for price tags before laying them back down. The secretaries and cataloguers tried to organize all the artifacts into logical groupings—toys here, pottery there, unidentifiable round things in one box and unidentifiable square things in another. The janitor squatted in a corner polishing the spokes of a wrecked unicycle. Hercules, because of his size, had found it easier than the rest of us to follow the Polish workers up to the roof and assist in the salvage and hauling. Jayne was ushering in and out a bevy of TV and newspaper reporters.

In a way it was touching to witness everyone's helpless longing for order. But I wished they would stop. Of everyone, I alone was in thrall to the beautiful mess I had made. Neatness, good riddance. Order, good riddance. I picked my way through the cascades of sodden drapes and beamed at the chaos.

Now THAT THE museum was off-limits to the public, it seemed to have become incumbent upon us to establish our first dress code. We'd never had one before. Together in a meeting, or spotted intermittently throughout the day, we'd

always been an elegantly dowdy lot, big on stylish idiosyncrasies. There's me in my big-collared, giant-cuffed blouses,
my skirts snug at the hips, flared at the hem around the ever-
present slouch of my spare pair of socks. There's David in his
chinos, Jayne in her leggings and extravagant, handcrafted
tunics. Always, if Jayne and I ran into each other in the rest
room, she'd be rinsing her eyeglasses and frizzing her hair,
while I'd be touching up mascara and fitting my smoothed
twist back into a clip. Neither one of us wore earrings, a disappointment to us both because, otherwise, we might each feel
smug to be the only one without them.

Now suddenly, after the fire, we were all in stiff competition to see who could manage most to look like they'd dressed
blindly in somebody else's castoffs. Kneeling in ashes being the
kind of activity requiring old clothes, I confess that I needed to
go out and buy some. I bought two Fruit of the Loom t-shirts, a
bandanna, a pair of work boots roomy enough for spare socks
and heavy enough for eventual forays up to the treacherous
attic, and two pairs of Levi's. Stonewashed, though not the
kind with the holes already in the knees or the gobs of paint
already on them. I chose a fairly loose fit with a sturdy seam,
perfect for crawling on nails, but taking care that they had
enough hug to establish the fact that, fire or not, I insist on a
sleek pair of panties. But it was my bra to which I'd given the
most thought when I went for my mammogram, finally settling on a peach-colored stretch-lace demi-cup push-up that
would make even Queen Elizabeth feel sexy. I kept thinking
what a good body I had, soft where it should be but with a few
muscular surprises strong enough to stand up to whatever needles, probes, pinches, and rays to which it might be subjected.

To my delight, the mammogram was one of the gentlest,
most intimate exchanges that can be imagined.

The technician, a person younger than I, handled my
breasts with such calm respect that when the two gleaming
plates of the machine closed over them it was only as if I were

lying facedown on warm stone feeling the planet revolve underneath me.

The pressure entered my body like heat, in slow, certain waves that made the rest of my body tremble and keel.

There would be the technician's sure touch on my shoulders, urging me in no uncertain terms to swivel incrementally this way or that and lean ever so forward into the machine, and there would follow a moment during which both of us stood utterly still until the whirring and clicking came to a halt, and there would follow a shared release of tension marked by the technician saying something like "You're a very good patient," to which I'd reply something like "You deserve me," sliding my hand nonchalantly into my back pocket before the technician withdrew it again, with just a tap on my elbow, and repositioned my arm for the next series of images. In my pocket was an index card that one of the recently signed volunteers had fished out of the rinse bucket earlier that morning and thrust at me.

"You take this," she'd commanded in an urgent whisper, her uncommonly glassy, green eyes pivoting to meet my own.

I said fine, took the card, placed it neatly on the toweling next to the others thinking maybe she was one of those volunteers who considered washing and drying to be beneath them and preferred a more romantic assignment. Those, we sent down to the basement to pry up the waterlogged carpet, and if they wearied of that, we told them to get on home. The idea was to weed out the noncommittal do-gooders and let the true samaritans show their colors before the building was stable and dry. Then, we'd take the most careful ones up to the attic and send those less fit to the lower exhibits to remove all items for sorting and cleaning.

"I said *take* it," she repeated. "I didn't mean put it with the rest. I mean keep it," her voice still a whisper but more coaxing, more cajoling, then before.

Then I noticed that her hand that was thrusting the index

card into mine was not a real human hand but a prosthetic, humming and flexing inside a tight rubber skin. So how could I refuse what it was holding out to me? With a feeling of guilt I accepted the offering and slipped it into my pocket, thinking I'd put it out to dry later and tell David we had a nutcase volunteer.

"Look at it," she said.

I didn't let myself so much as sigh. I pulled the card from my pocket and slanted it this way and that. There was nothing on it but a smeared wash of ink.

"It's very nice," I said.

"It really is very special," she declared, scolding me with her glassy eyes again before turning back to the box of paper and ashes and setting to work with great diligence, I saw, taking care to let only her flesh-and-blood hand touch the water in the bucket. But when I left for the doctor's I cornered David anyway behind the big double doors of the storage shed, where he sat gazing in dismay at all the useless junk we kept out there so as not to waste space inside the museum. Having escaped the fire and the water from the hoses, the junk inside the storage shed was fresher than even the trees on the lawn. Stepping past the doors I breathed deeply a fragrance of garden tools, rust, and rotting twine. There was a claw-footed tub in the corner that probably neither one of us had ever noticed before. It was spotted with spiders and the corpses of flies. We both eyed it with greed, its white porcelain unscathed, its toes reproachfully curled as if it knew we'd never taken it half-seriously.

"You know, that might be late Victorian," I said.

"Nineteen twenties," David corrected dismally. Art nouveau was passé with museum folk. "Don't tell me, Isobel. You're here to warn me about the Crazy Volunteer. I saw her accosting you. But she's okay, I think. She's very sincere. Seems to me she was in the museum the day of the fire; it really seems to have upset her. She came running out flapping her apron around like she thought she could fan out the flames. Somehow, she knows her way around. And she'll be a good worker. And anyway, that hand, how could I tell her I didn't want her picking up stuff with that hand . . ."

"So just ignore her." I finished his thought.

"So just ignore her," he affirmed. "Or even be nice to her."

"Easy enough," I said, and while undressing at the doctor's I found my hand slipping once again into the pocket holding the index card, and once again at the clinic when I couldn't bring myself to leave although I knew they wouldn't give me my results right away. For a while I stood in the room with the machine, each of us trying to be more upright and silent and patient than the other, knowing that on the opposite side of the wall or down a hall somewhere stood a radiologist peering at the image of what was inside me. The shard, the pea. To the radiologist's practiced eye, they wouldn't look like lumps, I supposed. To the radiologist's practiced eye, they would look only more insignificant than significant, or more significant than insignificant. If I stood quietly long enough I might hear something—a sigh, a mutter, a casual flutter of laughter, an urgent rustling of plates and flicking of switches—that would give me the answer. Honestly, I couldn't say which I wanted it to be. I said to myself, "If it's bad, if it's significant, then I will comfort myself with the thought that had it been nothing, had it been only, say, fibroids, then I would have to walk out into an unchanged world, as if I'd toiled up a slope and then down again without pausing long enough at the scenic overlook to have gained new knowledge of something different, something new, that was out there."

And I said to myself, "If it's not significant, if they don't even ask for a biopsy, then I will comfort myself with the thought that had it been significant, than I *would* stand long enough at the scenic overlook to see what was out there, but still the view would be unattainable, way in the distance, out of reach of all the bullshit doctor's visits and tests and scars and treatments and insurance forms and afternoon naps and recuperations I'd have to plow through before I could begin to approach it."

So the day seemed very still, all sepia-toned as if removed from time, so the dim coffee hue of the tiles in the long clinic hallway blended with the queer yellow vaporous sky above the parking lot. I drove back to the museum, I took my place at the buckets awaiting, along with everyone else, the arrival of our donated evening meal, a twelve-foot submarine sandwich that David sliced with a bone letter opener, # *617,* that one of the Polish workers had salvaged from the roof. The doctor didn't call. Evening came. The only real excitement was a bevy of Polish shouts from the roof and a sudden fierce grinding of the crane as it bobbed and strained under a cumbersome weight. The Polish workers seemed to be shouting, "Banana! Hey, Banana!" but when we looked up we saw the player piano swaying and wobbling, suspended directly above us to where the crane's arm had shifted. Down it came ever so slowly, so slowly we nearly forgot ourselves and sat there and watched it and didn't get out of the way. The Illinois consultant rushed up with his tape recorder clipped to his belt, the beam off his hard hat sweeping the trembling descent of the piano so when it touched ground he was ready to receive it and steady the legs, keeping it upright and stable before it was raised up again and placed soundly on the flatbed trailer where it belonged, to be delivered into storage and possible restoration. It appeared to be minus some parts, but when the truck trundled off the lawn over the curb to the pavement there was a tinkle of melody, a familiar tune, the phrase that accompanied the words *it would be a pauper's marriage* in the song "Bicycle Built for Two."

So we were all humming *Daisy, Daisy, give me your answer do,* under our breaths by the time we left for home, the sleeves of our denim shirts rolled to our elbows, our hair falling damp, loose, and unruly, ash on our necks, ash dusting our eyelids, ash smeared, somehow, on our bellies and thighs. When I stepped into the bathroom for my shower and stuffed my jeans into the laundry I nearly forgot the index card nestled in the back pocket. I meant to throw it in the trash but somehow it caught my eye, the blue smear of ink no longer quite so smeary and with something hitherto invisible threaded underneath it, a series of barely discernible numbers I had to tilt just so in the mirror's fluorescence in order to make it out. Number 040455, I deciphered.

04 04 55.

It was the year and date of my birth.

6

It was David who discovered the torn-up ventilation shaft in the rear hallway of the museum where the carpeting had come up and the ceiling tiles had been rent apart. Perhaps it was the heat that had blasted the shaft, perhaps the water, perhaps a firefighter trying to get in or out had kicked out the filters and the louvered covers. When David craned his neck and looked up, he found he could see past the workers in the attic, and past the jagged, caved-in edge of the roof, all the way to the sky.

Which upset him terribly, of course.

For the rest of the day, he was our Chicken Licken running around saying the sky is falling, the sky is falling, the sky is falling.

The funny thing is that though I'd always admired the sky when I'd viewed it from a familiar perspective, from my balcony railing, or through a window or during a walk or even in a painting—though I've always found it beautiful and luminous just like everyone else does, it's never really disturbed me the way it did when I saw it through the narrow, upward tunnel of the ventilation shaft. A cloud sailed past, then the faint blue turned gray when the cloud passed under the sun, then the sun reemerged but only in needles and pins. Beyond the ragged opening of the busted-up roof, the whole vastness of space looked raw and stinging, open where it had been closed, as if not just the roof but the sky itself had been splintered.

7

The dolls were perhaps the most glorious of all.

Side by side on their pallet of burlap, beneath the indirect wash of the first-floor Steiger Gallery lighting, not far from the cratesful of curled-up, abbreviated kitchen utensils and a pile of shredded, stinking quilting and a blistered late nineteenth-century children's watering can and a single lace cuff and a square-toed boot fastened with no less than thirty pearl buttons, the dolls lay more alertly than ever, some lashless, some hairless, some without clothing and some without fingers or toes. The missing digits were not lopped but charred to mere remnants. Either that or the whole limb was wounded. Ankles to knees, wrists to elbows vanished entirely or simply blackened like french fries too long in the oil, one ear a brittle shadow but the other still whorled, still delicately listening.

So damaged, so dismayed, the dolls looked more human now than they had looked before.

They look more alive when they're dead then they looked when alive.

"More alive dead than alive," I whispered to Hercules, who'd been sent to recovery to wipe off the soot and blot the dolls dry before delivering them to our emergency annex, across the road in a wing of the mansion that houses the offices and internal collections of the Botanical Society. Under orders from the visiting conservator, not a thing was to be brought from the Steiger Gallery to the annex before being freed of grime and the threat of mold, and then only if it was deemed salvageable by in-house staff. Damaged paintings were shipped to Chicago and farther for restoration, while all items spoiled beyond repair were labeled, boxed, and stored in a trailer to be tallied by the registrar and eventually sent to Insurance. On everybody's lips was the catch-22 of Insurance; after all, it had been their stipulation that led to the delay of the rescue of artifacts trapped in the attic under layers of soaked, smoking rubble, so by the time the Polish workers managed to dig them out, much that was found had been destroyed.

To the Steiger Gallery, Hercules had brought a bag of cotton balls and a carton of ear swabs, but he seemed leery of making the dolls too clean and depriving them of their stoical, ravaged demeanors. His stalled hands lay at rest on one raised, blue-jeaned knee. In one of his pockets, I could not tell which, was nestled the watch he had saved from the fire, its ticking so faint it might as well have been something I only imagined. And maybe it was. Those days, I could make myself hear almost anything I wanted: the serenade of *It will be a pauper's marriage, I can't afford a carriage* as the player piano lurched off on the flatbed, the whir of the X-ray machine at the mammography clinic, Martha's years-ago voice on the phone saying, about life in Seattle just after I'd moved, *As they say, life goes on. But it isn't as fun as before. I have to tell you my heart's not broken, not as it might be if you were a man. Tell me, Isobel. Why do you suppose that is?*

"Actually these aren't the dead dolls. The dead ones are over there. They all lost their heads when the attic caved in," said Hercules, pointing to some heaps of torn clothing and limbs arranged as respectfully as was possible in boxes against the wall, the faceless remnants positioned just so, like dismembered parts in a row of coffins. Stumps to ashes. "The ones here with the faces are the survivors. Poor things," he went on when I'd squatted beside him. "They look so burnt out."

Which was by now an old joke, funny only because it wasn't funny anymore. The dolls that weren't sleeping appeared to be taking in everything at once, the way anyone appears to be doing when they are flat on their back with their eyes wide open, as if the world had been put there for them to observe it. Squatting above them with Hercules, I felt, in light of the doll's supine staring, like the pictures some doctors tape to the ceilings in their examining rooms. A curious, high distraction. On my own doctor's ceiling was a lithograph of a bridge executed with such luminous precision that I believed I might wrap my hand around the arched span if only I could reach it, or pluck a boat off the surface of the river, or a leaf off a tree. The trees lining the inky river were gingkoes. Their leaves were small, golden fans. In my current state, laughing so as not to cry on Hercules's shoulder, exultant with the effort I needed to make in order not to fall apart, I imagined those small fans clutched in the hands of the dolls, their flame-ravaged fingers thrumming the curved, golden stems. Early that morning, Hercules had witnessed my half of a telephone conversation with the doctor, so now he knew how close my laughter was to hysteria. He moved his flannel-soft shoulder an inch or two closer to me, so if I needed I might plunk my head on it and shut my eyes. Having never before been the daydreaming type, now I was training myself to become one. If I could make the world into a more flexible place, a place of mirrors and doorways, access and egress . . . if the dolls fanned themselves with the leaves of the offset gingkoes, then that must mean that the line between animate and inanimate, mortal and immortal, was more liquid than I'd thought. More conciliatory. It might actually be pleasant to be inanimate if you were a doll—so willfully osmotic, the tiny grasp of cupped fingers wanting exactly what hovered beyond its reach. Watching them, I swore I'd never long for my old self back, the one who brewed a cup of tea because she thought the steaming mug contained all that was required of the whole galaxy, a swirling hot eddy of subtle, tart flavor. And nor would I crave my old Scottish afghan, the one I used to wrap around myself every day when I got home from work as if to shrink the boundaries of the universe. No, nothing like that would ever again be enough. Before the onslaught of the fire, of all the artifacts in the museum it was the paintings I admired most, the still lifes of course, the way they framed their own needs, their own

comments. A ripe pear on a plate. A dusky scattering of walnuts and lit candles. Of course I knew that the walnuts could
never be cracked, the candles never snuffed out, the shirt slung
so casually over a chair not a thing that could ever slip off. But
I didn't know until now that their impenetrable deceptions
were precisely what used to appeal to me about them. The
dolls would not put up with still lifes, not when so much as a
moth was flitting about. In their terrible stillness, the dolls
were ravenous creatures, wanting anything that threatened to
pass them by. How acquisitive they were! How possessive!
How their very contemplation lavished on their surroundings
a kind of influential weather, quiet as dawn and determined as
dusk, watching what it changed, changing what it watched.
The dolls, bless their eager, untouchable hearts, knew the vastness of the world and so accepted what it put before them only
provisionally, always eager for the next offering. *Teach me,* I
silently pleaded. *Show me how to want what I can't even see.*
Show me how to beckon it closer to me.

"I wonder if tomorrow is going to hurt," I whispered finally
to Hercules.

"It will," he said. "But they'll give you something for it.
Anyway, you can tell me about the pain and we can talk about
it, and that will make it at least interesting."

"Alright," I agreed, and for the rest of the day before I
drove to the hospital I indulged in a reverie of terms I might
use to describe pain. *Searing* was the word I relied on most.
Either that or *strangely impersonal.* When I'd got off the phone
with the doctor that morning, Hercules had taken the bass
from my bedroom, carried it into the guest room study, and
stood with it in the spot where his blankets would have been if
he didn't roll them up every morning and stow them away. He
didn't begin playing. He only adjusted the tension of the
strings and then positioned the instrument as if for playing, the
fingers of his left hand arrayed precisely on the neck, the fingers of his right poised motionless above the f-holes. I understood he was waiting to see if I wanted him to play or not. If I

stepped into the study and sat myself down on the carpet across from him or even stood at the window near the canopy of the jade plant, he would begin to pluck at the very underside of a melody, draw it forth as if out of the shadows of the room, the hidden places under the chairs and behind the books on the bookcases, that were the bass's territory. But if I remained in the living room or went anyplace else, he wouldn't. Somewhere among the leftover college texts on my bookshelves was a brief description of a school of philosophy proposing that every gesture constructs its own opposite, like a figure eight, so if I pick up a comb and start combing my hair, then the act of not picking up the comb and not combing my hair is in that very moment equally viable. (Or if I tell a man I love him, Martha and I used to ruminate, then won't the opposing declaration hover around us with just as much force, with maybe more possibility, than before?) What Hercules was doing, by just readying himself to play bass, was applying that bit of wacky philosophy to my too-rational apartment. For a long time we hovered, making ourselves late for work, locked on that point where the curves of the figure eight intersected. Would he play, or wouldn't he? Would I sit down, or wouldn't I? Challenging him, I stepped directly onto the threshold of the spare room doorway. He only cocked his head. He flexed his fingers but did not lower them to the strings. When the silence became too suspenseful, I said, "I found a lump in my breast on Monday. On Tuesday I had a mammogram. That was my doctor I was just on the phone with."

Hercules's expression didn't change. It didn't need to. Secretly, it must already have prepared itself for what I was going to tell him. He leaned the bass very gently into the wall.

"I'm going in for a biopsy tonight," I said. "I mean, I go in tonight and they prep me and then they do the biopsy in the morning. That means you can sleep in my bed, Herky. You can spread out as much as you want. They found several spots indicating what they call calcification," I went on. "If a lump contains fluid, then that means it might be cystic, which means it might be okay. But if it's calcified, and if they can't get enough fluid to do a needle aspiration, then they have to take it out and check it. And if there's cancer, then they'll go back in and check some lymph nodes, too, to see if it's spread. But most likely they won't do that right away. Tomorrow, they need to localize the lumps by inserting hooked needles. For this they prefer not to use even a local anesthetic unless the patient insists. Which I absolutely will. Then to excise the tissue they use either local or general, depending I guess on how deep they need to cut, and then the pathologist makes the diagnosis. In about ten minutes. While I'm still flat on the table trying to pretend I'm just having a nap."

"How many lumps turn out malignant?" Hercules asked, without revealing that this was something he must have heard me ask the doctor.

"Around twenty percent," I answered.

"There's no way I'm sleeping in your bed when you're in the hospital," Hercules exclaimed. "I won't even sleep where I usually do. I'll sleep on the kitchen floor, not on the carpet. I'll camp on your front stoop. I'll lay a blanket on the balcony. Or I can sleep in the waiting room if you want someone close by. Probably, really, I won't sleep at all."

"No, you will not spend the night awake in the waiting room," I said, flushing with embarrassed pleasure because I couldn't bring myself to insist that he sleep in my bed, either. The very idea of him tossing and turning outdoors on a bedroll, under the stars that had named him, was a revelation to me. I said to myself, if I am going to call him my godson, then let him be filial. Let him offer his tender regard up to the sky, along with his particular forgiveness of me. For years, since the age of eleven, Hercules had known that aside from his mother I was the only person in the world who knew the name and whereabouts of his father. None of us made a big deal out of this; it was only a fact. When Martha told Hercules that I knew as much as she did, she meant only to reassure him that if anything ever happened to her, there was yet another person from whom he might attempt to coax the information. His forgiveness of me, offered in advance when he was eleven, then twelve, then fifteen, was because he knew I wouldn't tell. He didn't want me to tell, really. He never tested my resolve. All these years, our little triangle of held/withheld knowledge has remained unruffled. But suddenly the prospect of Hercules spending the night on my front stoop filled me with an insane urge to blurt the secret out to him. The very ordinary name of his not-so-ordinary father was the only thing I had that I might offer in return for his consolation. In frustration I asked, when I had packed my overnight bag and stood it near the door where it would be waiting for me when I got home from work, "Herky, do you know *why* your mother doesn't want you to know who your father is?"

"Of course not," he said.

Not *why?*

Not *so, tell me.*

Exactly what would I have told him, had he insisted?

Would I have told him that his mother was simply embarrassed to have slept with the man?

I supposed *maybe,* then *no,* then *possibly,* then *why not?* In any case, having left the apartment and come to the museum, Hercules and I shared a morning of silence in which to reflect on what wasn't being said, before I asked him, in the presence of the dolls' eager curiosity, what song he might have played had I stepped into the spare room and sat down and crossed my legs to listen.

" 'Sittin' on the dock of the bay,' " he answered without hesitation.

Watchin' the tide rollin' away, went the faintly remembered echos of the song inside my head.

"That's because I sing off-key," he confessed. "It's one of the few songs that sounds better when it's flat."

Hercules blushed. Terribly. (For the longest time, I couldn't figure out why. Then it dawned on me; he believed he had made an unintentional, unforgivable pun. About my breast. About what was in store. *Better when it's flat.* Mature as he was, adult, sympathetic, loyal as he was, he was after all only nineteen, with a nineteen year old's sense of what was worth a blush and what wasn't.)

"That's true," I said. "It sounds more mournful and honest, somehow. For a while when I was in high school, I had some friends in a band that played that song. The boy that sang it was named Stanley. Of all of them, Stanley was the most, I don't know—"

"The most homely," offered Hercules.

"Yes," I said. "And the mangiest and the lankiest and by the far the most, I don't know . . ."

"Generous," said Hercules. "The one who showed up with a carton of doughnuts when everyone else got the munchies."

"That's true," I remembered.

"The one whose fly was always only half-zipped," said Hercules.

"Yes," I said, throwing my head back with laughter.

"And he always had kind of a humble, crooked smile," said Hercules.

"Yes."

"Even when he sang."

"Especially when he sang," I amended.

"And his girlfriend, well, there was always the same girl hanging around him but you could never imagine them—"

Here, Hercules paused. I realized he was wondering which term might be most appropriate for use in my still formidable presence.

"Screwing," I said.

Just as I'd hoped, Hercules blushed. Finally he added, "And the two of them were just a little more drugged out than anyone else."

"Just pot," I said.

"But maybe sometimes a little glue, in the van in the parking lot outside the bar during break," said Hercules, nodding sagely, at which I stopped my laughter because of course he knew too much. More than any usual person would be able to surmise or imagine. Not even Martha knew that "Sittin' on the Dock of the Bay" was a song to which I attached particular memories.

"Tell me what kind of clothes Stanley wore," I demanded.

"No," said Hercules, though I could practically see those pants reflected in his eyes—bell-bottoms, too long, the frayed hems catching under the soles of Stanley's awkward, scuffed, wing-tip shoes.

And suddenly, I got it.

I realized what it was that Hercules was doing.

He was doing his best to reveal to me, in case I had forgotten, that he *knew* things.

For instance, he might even know, might have known all these years, the story of Martha's regrettable entanglement with his father.

He might be able to say, at any given instant, exactly where the poor man was and what he was doing.

But that wasn't all.

There was a separate intelligence murmuring under the surface, like what happens in water just before it starts to boil. Hercules wouldn't let it bubble over, however. He intended to keep it steamy but unimposing, so I might figure it out on my own.

The dolls seemed to understand more than I did. They gazed up at my ignorance with amused sympathy verging on annoyance. As if to guide me just a little, Hercules bent nearer to one of their bisque faces and blew at a coating of soot on its eyelid. When Hercules huffed at the coating of soot, the doll's entire eye vanished in a tinkling funnel of painted dust. There was only the horsehair looped underneath, gluey and yellowed with age.

Funny, I thought, the things dolls keep in their bodies. Frayed rope. Sawdust. Bits of loosely knotted cloth.

Hercules blew once again on her face. Her painted lips

came free, the flakes colorless as they drifted away. She did not look surprised. Determined to take her transformation in stride, she was neither shocked nor afraid nor even caught just a little off-guard.

"I don't know what you're trying to tell me," I said to Hercules. "I'm such a blockhead sometimes."

"Only when you need to be," Hercules said.

To PREP ME that night at the hospital, they needed to shave the tiny hairs off my breast. Otherwise, the view through the surgeon's magnifier might resemble a hillside of windswept grasses.

"Will it grow back coarse?" I asked the nurse who arrived with the razor and washcloth, along with a shallow basin of antiseptic-scented water. She placed her cargo on my tray table next to the disappointing array of magazines and word puzzles I'd decided to buy at the last minute in case the night got too long and scary. Needing a boost of morale, I wished I had packed my zippered travel case of makeup and hair accessories. It's not the makeup itself that gives me a boost, but the combing, patting, caressing, and clipping that accompanies its application, and the brief wordless chat I have with my face as I assess it in the mirror. *How are you doing?* I ask my cheekbones. *Oh, we could use a little color. Nothing dramatic. Use the brush, not your fingers. We're in the mood for a few soft swipes.* The pad of letter-writing paper I'd packed very first thing would remain untouched, as would the address book containing the phone numbers of people who really ought to call me, if only they knew where I was. Except for Hercules, I'd told no one what was happening, not even Martha, but still the silence of the phone affixed to the wall above the hospital bed hung over me in an irksome way as if at any moment my mother might call from some Heavenly pay phone after all these sad years of her poised, dead silence, and I would have to tell her I couldn't talk right now, I was having my breast shaved.

The razor didn't tickle. The nurse's touch was not as personal as the X-ray technician's had been, but when she lathered me up she was careful to catch the spare drips with the washcloth, then allowed me to pluck the coarser nipple hairs myself, the way I wanted, by hand, not with the tweezers. There were only a few. When the plucking was done, when the skin surrounding my nipples was smoother than sucked caramels, it was time for me to meet with my surgeon, whose name was Jack Klink. He'd come highly recommended by my GP, and since this biopsy was only the very first step, and since we didn't yet know if there would be any further steps necessary at all, I'd decided to schedule the procedure right away and not make a big deal of choosing a doctor. Anyway, he seemed smart if a little too much on the tennis side. He might have been wearing his sweat guards under his button-down cuffs. Whites under whites. All fit and sparkling, his clipboard swatting the air like a racket. I wondered if surgeons were necessarily competitive sorts, and if Dr. Klink was in the habit of bringing his bottle of Cranapple spritzer into the operating room. He even offered me a sip once he'd pulled the bottle out of his shirtfront pocket, his way of saying that even if I did have breast cancer, he wouldn't catch it.

He palpated the lump near my armpit first, then drifted to the smaller one under my nipple, which he squeezed all around, testing for discharge of which there was thankfully none. At once I didn't want my bodily fluids touching any inch of this man.

"You have absolutely perfect breasts," was the first thing he said to me after his name and how are you.

I gave a snort of hard laughter, dismissive and cruel as could be. But inside, I began to be nervous. I thought maybe some kook had tied up the real Dr. Klink and snuck up on the elevator to hit on the breast ward. He didn't look like a kook—he was a clean-cut Asian American, delicately made. But still. My nurse-call button was out of my reach. I took hold of his bottle of Cranapple spritzer and gave the crotch of his trousers a good, pink fizz.

"You can get out of here, now," I said.

"I'm not going to tell you you're in the angry phase already," he said. "I hate that shit."

"What?" I asked, chastened.

"I hate that *denial, anger, acceptance, grief* crap they lay on people these days. A patient has cancer, she deals with it however she can. And don't let them tell you stress is a culprit. Have you been under stress lately?"

"Never," I answered.

"See?" he said. "Which is not to say that laughter doesn't heal, in a way. Of course it does. It makes the rest of your life more fun, however long or little you've got."

"You say that as if you have a feeling I haven't got much," I said.

"Not at all."

"Really?!"

"I mean I have no idea. Absolutely. That's what we're here for. When I said you have perfect breasts, I meant they'll be easy to look at. They're not fibrocystic. They're not terribly dense. They're not terribly large. They'll be very cooperative, in other words. They'll make my life easy."

"Yeah, but they're making my life a little complicated," I said.

"We don't know that yet. Be optimistic."

I am. I've been wanting a little adventure, I wanted to say. But he was telling me that because the needle aspiration attempted earlier by the resident "was somewhat troubling," I would need to have the surgical biopsy for sure.

"What do you mean, *somewhat troubling?*" I asked. "You mean there wasn't any fluid?"

"There wasn't much, and what there was was inconclusive."

"You mean it wasn't encouraging," I said.

"Right."

"You mean it was discouraging," I pressed.

"I'm not the type to be discouraged. If I was, you wouldn't want me for a doctor," he said. "Now, I want you to think for a minute about where you want your scar."

"Over there," I said, pointing out the window.

"The thing is," he said, "with a breast, with this kind of biopsy, you basically can peel the whole breast away from any incision, and get to the lump, and then put the breast back where it started. I hate to put it that way. I know it sounds awful. I know it's not the kind of thing you want to listen to the night before surgery. But, anyway, yes, you can have the scar wherever you want it."

"Okay then," I said smartly. "Do the incision on the sole of my foot."

He touched the felt tip of his pen to a spot on the outside curve of my breast, raising his eyebrows. I raised mine in return. I was utterly naked, the unbuttoned nightgown having fallen to the sheets around my waist, and as with the nurse, I felt how natural this encounter seemed to both of us, the doctor's brow furrowing only a little as he traced the thin line of green ink on my flesh. It didn't look really awful, that green ink scar. It looked like where a zipper might be on an evening dress. "Were you born in this country?" I asked, although his English was perfect.

"Laos," he said. "I'm a Hmong. There *is* one other thing we need to talk about, Isobel."

"Your family were refugees?" I asked.

"Much of my family was lost in the jungle. Some of them might still be there for all I've been able to find out about them. But yes, I am a refugee. I was brought over here when I was eight."

"You were placed with an American family?"

"I was placed with a Hmong family," he said, closing the cap on the marker, then doing a little backhand with his clipboard before removing from it a pen and a few typed forms.

"But you seem so American."

"I'm a Midwesterner. I'm probably more Midwestern than you are," he reflected. "Tell me, Isobel. With what kind of tradition do you associate yourself? With your family? Your religion?"

"With work," I said, "and books," feeling this was somehow not the sort of answer he was after. "My parents died five years ago, so I don't really have a family, anymore," I added.

"No, you don't, do you? Just to look at you, there's nothing you seem to be part of, somehow. How did your parents die?"

"The house they were living in in Ireland got hit by a small plane," I said, using the simple reply I'd perfected over the years. Only suddenly it didn't seem so simple anymore, and for a moment we both speculated quietly on the chance nature of disaster, a plane from without, a shard from within. Dr. Klink flashed his Asian All-American ironical smile, slipping his Cranapple spritzer back into his pocket before sitting on the edge of my bed with a handful of consent forms and a pen that he eased into my hand. They were standard forms; I didn't want to read them. Basically they gave permission to the hospital to zap me during surgery, and in the case of an emergency or in the soundest, most carefully considered judgment of the team of doctors, to do what was necessary in the interests of my survival.

"You're not knife-happy," I conjectured.

The doctor shook his head.

"You're a compassionate sort," I added.

"I like to think so."

"You're not research-happy. You're not the kind of doctor who performs experiments on your patients hoping to get a paper in the *New England Journal of Medicine*."

"If this were really a time for joking, I would tell you I don't even read the *New England Journal of Medicine*."

"Isn't it?" I asked.

".What?"

"A time for joking,"

"For you, sure. For me, not sure," he said.

I signed the papers. When he left, he seemed entirely unmindful of the splash I'd made on his trousers. I supposed, *parents lost twenty years in a jungle, brothers and sisters and uncles and aunts lost forever in a jungle, you don't worry about looking like you've peed in your pants.* And he was kind enough to close the door behind him, leaving me to wonder how I felt about not looking like I belonged to anything, or anyone. I didn't want it to be true, so I decided it wasn't. I belong to my godson Hercules, I said to myself. I belong to those ravenous dolls. I belong to the Polish workers digging for smashed Tiffany up in the museum attic. I belong to the flatbed that drove off with the player piano. I belong to the future, whatever it plunks down in front of me.

It was an eerie feeling, but liberating, to fall asleep believing I belonged to a thing that had not yet arrived to claim me. I was still ruminating about this in the morning even though they wouldn't let me have my usual, meditative cup of coffee. They swabbed my breast with a wild pink ointment and laid me on a gurney. I said I wanted to walk. They said no. They said they wanted me to feel relaxed. I said I *was* relaxed. They said, "Wonderful, then." It was while they were wheeling me along the hallway that everything hit me at once. Watching the ceiling go by, I felt I was ducking a hailstorm. I pretended to be one of the dolls that could not shut its eyes, above which the ceiling was some altered frame of reference bearing down on me. What I loved about Hercules, I realized at once, was that he seemed to possess an arrow of knowledge that he had released from his bow, that was coming straight at me. But the arrow was soft where it might have been sharp, a dewy, soft-petaled, cool-stemmed thing that wouldn't pierce me so much as enter gently when there was someplace for it to go.

And the place seemed to be there suddenly, a glimmer in my insides, a yellow beckoning pulse that drew the arrow in deep and quivering.

Hercules knows, I said to myself on the gurney. *My godson. My marvelous young wonderful man. My ten o'clock shadow. Martha's son. Herky. Herk. My salad companion. My watch-ticker. My foot-stepper. My too-baggy corduroy pants-wearer.*

My truth-teller.

Hercules knows, I said to myself, whether I am to live or die.

And everything else in between.

He knows my diagnosis.

He knows the prognosis.

He knows how many stitches, how many cuts, how black and how blue, how much fear and what there is to be afraid of.

Another thing. He would tell me if I asked.

"Stop the gurney," I announced.

Not one of the orderlies revealed having heard me.

"I said, *stop the gurney.*"

Still, no stopping. The ceiling tiles jerked by, the wheels shuddered below me. Over the hospital intercom came a call for a doctor named Doctor. I had heard it before. "Doctor Doctor," said the voice on the speakers. "Doctor Doctor."

"Stop the telephone," I pleaded. "I mean, *stop! The telephone! I want to make a call!*"

Still, no stopping. I was reminded of work days I'd placed eleven messages with eleven separate answering machines and received not a single reply.

"Stop!" I insisted. "I need to talk to Hercules!"

No wonder the orderlies didn't stop. This kind of thing probably happened every day. There was probably a rule, *No stopping the gurneys on the way to surgery in order to allow delirious patients to make last minute phone calls to Greek gods.*

Finally, I closed my eyes and let them wheel me in the peace they demanded.

WHAT THEY found in the course of the biopsy was disturbing enough to require that they put me under, and what they found when they put me under and performed the axillary dissection of my lymph nodes was bad enough to require that they do what they did to me next. The thing that seemed most ridiculously unjust, when some hours later I had the strength and the wherewithal to talk to Dr. Klink, was the idea that youth, which I've been treasuring all this decade of my thirties, should have played such a sorrowful trick on me.

"The kind of cancer you have is an infiltrating lobular carcinoma," the doctor was saying. "In women your age, for some reason, in young women, in women in their thirties and early forties, this kind of cancer grows more quickly than it does in older women. We don't really know why. Your tumors were small, as you say, but the one under the nipple showed evidence of necrosis, which indicates an even higher propensity for spread, and there was some evidence of blood vessel involvement . . . Anyway, the incidence of bilaterality in this kind of cancer is thirty percent, which is more than twice as high as that for other cancers. And your particular manifestation is a variant, rather than a pure, *classic* type, which makes treatment a little more complicated. And then, what we found in your lymph nodes . . . I'm sorry, Isobel. It was a decision made in direct consultation with our chief oncologist. The diagnosis, the precise nature of the growth, was incontestable. The treatment, for women your age, is less flexible than it would be if you had, say, a medullary carcinoma. We simply don't have the options. There's simply no room to weigh the patient's thoughts about treatment against the inclinations of the doctors. Believe me, I took this to heart. I did not do it lightly. I'm not asking your forgiveness. It's not my right as a doctor to ask your forgiveness. But I ask for your trust."

"Have you been practicing this speech?" I asked. My words were all slurred together but he leaned close enough to decipher them.

"For a couple of days," said the doctor. "I had an uncomfortable feeling, when I looked at the X-rays. But I hoped to hell I wouldn't have to be sitting here saying these things today."

"Tomorrow maybe," I said.

"No. Not tomorrow, either," said Doctor Klink. He took a sip of his spritzer. He really did look sad. And regardless of his protestations, he really did look as if he wanted my forgiveness as well as my trust.

"We're going to schedule some scans right away," he went on. "The prevailing incidence of spread in this kind of cancer is of two kinds. One is diffuse retroperitoneal spread, which involves the abdominal cavity, and then, what we really have to protect against, which is why we are going to recommend such an aggressive routine of chemotherapy, but we'll get to that later, the second kind of spread we have to protect against is meningeal."

"What does that mean?" I slurred. "Are you using such amazing terminology because you think when combined with your slight accent it will make me admire you? Are you speaking with slightly more of an accent than usual in order to gain my respect by rubbing it in that you're speaking what to you is still a foreign language?"

This, thankfully, was so muffled by the echoes of the anesthesia that he could not decipher it.

"Meningeal means brain. What we have to protect against is spread to the membranes surrounding the brain," he went on.

"And what if you find it now?" I asked as clearly, as distinctly as I could. "What if you do the brain scan and discover the cancer's already there? Won't that mean it was kind of redundant to take off my breasts?"

"We won't find it now," said the doctor. "If it had spread to your brain we'd have evidence of that already, in the way you were behaving, in the way you were speaking, in the things you were able to do and not do. It's not in the brain yet. Believe me."

"You haven't answered my question," I said. "Do you have a prognosis of any kind? Given that you've lopped off two-tenths of my body, can you give me some idea what my chances are? And no matter what my chances are, what if I told you, what if I had told you in advance, that when I fall in love, that whenever I fall in love, the feeling starts in my breasts, it starts in my nipples, without them I'd never be able to be in love with anybody? Would you have done the same thing?"

"Is that true?" he asked.

"Tell me first if you would have done the same thing."

"I honestly don't know," said Dr. Klink. "Probably. Is it true?"

"No, it isn't." I said. "I've never been in love, period."

"Thank God," he said. "I mean . . . I'm sorry . . . I didn't mean it like that, Isobel."

He really did look as though he might cry. I didn't know why I was being so mean to a person who would gladly have taken the pain I was in, morphine or not, psychic or otherwise, and shove it into his own small-boned body and never again play tennis or make love to his wife or read a book or dream of traveling back to the mountains of Cambodia in search of his relatives.

Still, I couldn't bring myself to stop being mean. It seemed too much to give up—this privilege of anger, this license of grief, this enactment of pain. *Searing,* it turned out, was a far more appropriate term than *strangely impersonal,* but still it was nowhere near perfect. It was too objective. It suggested a pain too close to the surface, not mixed with my soul the way this one was.

"Did you at least dispose of them in their favorite bra," I asked, "seeing as they were so cooperative?"

Dr. Klink made a face and took hold of my free hand so suddenly I couldn't pull it away. For a moment it seemed he might kiss my knuckles, a gesture not of courtship or even of gallantry but of simple apology. I wouldn't have minded. To my surprise I found myself poised for the kiss, wanting his guilt laid on thick as could be.

"You asked me what your chances are," he said after a while. "The way we figure it is by blocks of five years. If the scans show no evidence of abdominal spread, with this kind of carcinoma, with the extent of your lymph node involvement, your chance of five year survival is sixty percent."

He slid his fingers through my own and gave a squeeze hard enough that it blocked, for a second, the first impact of that terrible number. Never before had sixty seemed such a paltry figure. On the other hand, it was bigger than half. I envisioned a game of musical chairs. Six chairs. Ten people. If the music was inspiring, I might not want to sit down, I might keep on dancing and circling, out of the room, down the hall-way, across the front steps to the pavement, over the stonewall onto the endless green of the lawn.

"Tell me what my chances are if the scans *do* uncover abdominal spread," I said.

"Something I always like to point out to my patients," said Dr. Klink with another squeeze of my hand, "is that even if you've been diagnosed with a cancer with a high survival rate of, say, eighty or ninety percent, even then I always remind my patients that in the final analysis, the rate is not the issue. Because even if far more people live with it than die with it, that doesn't mean shit if you're one of the people who dies."

"Yes. So what's the survival rate for my kind of cancer if you find spread in the abdomen?"

"Likewise, if a patient has a cancer with a low rate, like yours, they still might be one of the lucky ones," was his reply. I could practically see, in his face, his decision not to kiss my knuckles after all.

"Are you going to answer me or not?"

"No," he said.

"Why not?" I asked.

"Because I can't bear to," he said.

Kiss or not, apology or not, he still had hold of my fingers. Maybe this was simply his *Tennis, anyone?* habit of shaking hands over the net after a game. Not wanting to play the sore loser, I gave in to his grip. I let him raise and lower my hand as if I had no bones to do it myself, practicing passivity, seeing if I liked it in case it was ever demanded of me. Wondering if death was a passive or an active event, I decided to try for a compromise. I held my hand aloft where the doctor brought it. Had he let go, my fingers would have stayed where they were, levitated, alert, so insistently sensate that whatever brushed against them would become my own. My hand was broader than Dr. Klink's. My tumor had been bigger around than his kiss would have been had he finally decided to plant it. But then a nurse poked her head in the room and said I had a visitor who'd been stopped at the nurses' station. Was I dressed? Was I still in consultation?

"Send him in," I said, disappointed with Hercules for not knowing that I wasn't yet ready for visitors. I was not even ready for *him*. When the doctor left, I wanted to be alone with my strange, giddy sorrow, my morphine-laced grief, my pain that beneath the unexpected shock of the bandages felt more surprised than wounded, my hand still poised where the doctor had left it, not having received its apology.

Don't come in! I wanted to shout. *Leave me alone with my stitches! How can it be that a woman gets cancer before she even knows how to ride a bicycle? Teach me before it's too late!*

Never before had I felt the desire to learn how to ride a bicycle. Even as a child I was struck by how proper I'd look on such a contraption, as upright and purposefully balanced as if I'd been born there. No, bicycle riding was too *me*, like wearing a straw hat with a be-ribboned brim, so suitable to who I was that I was embarrassed to do it. To be so much myself would be to admit I was at heart an impassioned Victorian pedaling in a garden, a slip of white eyelet peeking from under my skirt above my spare pair of socks and the endless, perfect rhythm of the spokes. But now it seemed suddenly incumbent upon me to know how to ride a bike, so I could do it the wrong way, maybe, in a way that wasn't *me* at all, down a mountain trail wearing those awful black bicycle shorts that make everyone look like Charlie Chaplin. Maybe I might grow a mustache, too, and stow away on a ship to wherever.

Wherever?

Where *would* I like to go?

Don't come in! I shouted silently to Hercules. I really was disappointed with him, for showing up like this at so exactly the wrong time and interrupting my frantic reverie. *Go away. I'm trying to figure out where I would have liked to go, if only I had had the time to go there.*

It wasn't Hercules, after all.

It was a woman.

At first I didn't know who she was. She moved like a lit fuse. I thought maybe she was the hospital version of the Welcome Wagon Lady rushing to bring me a nail file in case I wanted to saw through the bed frame and escape. Then I knew, it was the Crazy Volunteer, the one who'd given me the smeary index card with my birth date on it. In fact I had the card with me in the hospital room, packed away in a zipper pocket of my suitcase along with a couple of tampons that I was already starting to mourn in the belief that I might never need to use them again. What I knew about chemotherapy was less than nothing except that if the patient were a woman, it was likely to make her reach menopause early and forever in a dry, chafing way. So she couldn't get pregnant even by accident, I found myself thinking. So no matter how much she didn't want it to happen, it wouldn't happen anyway. Ever. Never. At all.

How they'd managed to detain the Crazy Volunteer at the nurse's station I couldn't imagine. She came lurching toward me like a bad in-line skater who didn't know how to put on the brakes.

"How did you know I was here?" I asked, bereft even of civility, wondering if I might inform her she used too much rouge, her cheeks practically aglow with the gummy, red circles.

Something small and rectangular was clutched in her fake hand. She did not seem dismayed by the rudeness of my welcome. To the contrary, it appeared to exhilarate her even further so I feared she might throw herself onto the bed, tackling me and my stitches. To ward her off I raised my arm from under my sheet to reveal the morphine IV and the Reliovac drain, then gave a low moan and shut my eyes.

When I opened them, she was gone.

From the hallway could be heard the muffled footsteps of nurses. The room was filled with a dusky stillness disturbed only by a spot at the foot of my bed where a flat, hinged case had been left lying on a fold of blanket. Through the grimy, blackened surface of the little tooled case escaped the faintest of silvery sheens.

Right away I knew just what it was. Despite the charred complexion I recognized it as having been part of the exhibit in which the player piano might have been displayed had there been enough space, a riverboat exhibit designed to show that this town had once been a place of high, summer society, a place of parasols, brandy flasks, spats, accordion players, even a few entrepreneurial gondoliers who ferried honeymooners back and forth across the river, from willow to gazebo.

The thing on my bed was a cosmetic case that had lain half-in and half-out of a beaded clutch. I'd long coveted the jet fringe of the evening bag, but I'd never thought much of the compact. Inside it, I knew, was a mud-flat of powder as old as the silver itself, and a modern day puff thrown in for effect by the lady who made the donation. What would I want that for? I wondered. Of all things that the Crazy Volunteer might have chosen to bring me, this was the least alluring.

But then I thought of the mirror inside the case, and of my stricken expression framed within as I patted on an incandescent mask of powder.

I reached down to get it.

Not even the morphine could dull that sudden blade of pain. I gave a cry of stunned anger. For a moment I didn't dare even to lower myself back against my pillows, but I was glad that the nurses had not heard my shout. Had they come in and found the compact lying there, they might have whisked it away for fear of infection. How grimy it was, the blanket around it already shadowed with ash. And yet, how I wanted to open it up. I couldn't say why, just as I couldn't say why I'd slid the card with my birth date into my suitcase the day before. What could I possibly want with that? What good could they possibly do me, the purple inkblots of numbers only a little less legible than when I'd first made them out?

With my feet, I was able to maneuver the compact ever so gingerly forward.

The clasp was jammed shut beneath a gummy, black ooze. Unwilling to brave another dagger of pain I decided to bite it free with my teeth.

I was only a little disappointed, when the clasp finally gave, to find what I'd expected would be inside. Just the Maybelline puff and the fissured, dried makeup and in the mirror my face looking vaguely uncertain as to whether it wanted to be illumined, after all.

So I WAITED until the day Hercules was due to arrive to take me home, when the drain that was siphoning my lymph showed an outflow of less than fifty cubic centimeters. When he phoned, I asked Hercules to please bring me a button-down blouse in place of the pullover shirt I'd worn into the hospital. A couple of tentlike button-down dresses was what I should wear for the time being, suggested the Reach for Recovery women who had visited early that morning.

"Washable," they added, knowing I'd be sick with chemo.

"You know what I did?" one of them asked. "I bought a new pink toilet, because I couldn't stand to stick my face in that old white one every minute. And no one was allowed to use it but me."

"Great idea!" said the other.

Ordinarily I wouldn't have stood for their kind of cheer. But now it felt good, having them there. They asked if I'd been able yet to look at my scars, and whether I'd decided on reconstruction. I said no, I hadn't looked and no, I hadn't decided. So they showed me their prostheses and their reconstructions, one keeping watch at the door while the other pulled open her shirt. The one with the prosthesis didn't offer to show me the ropy lines of her scars, but she said the scars felt tingly when anybody touched them, more erotic than her nipples had ever felt.

"I don't have my nipples yet," said the one with the reconstructions. "The nipples always come last, and they won't have any sensation. Every night I try to remind myself of that, so it won't be so weird when it happens, but I can't really imagine what it will be like."

"Like touching the bandage," I offered, putting my hand to my own layers of gauze. "It's not that terrible," I consoled.

"Anyway, it's what I want," she said. "Pure vanity, I guess."

"It's not vanity," the other woman scolded. "It's perfectly natural to want what you're supposed to have. If I don't want breasts for the rest of my life, that's my business, not yours."

"Oh, I know that," said the first.

They both looked a little meek when they buttoned their shirts. All this was new to them, too. When they'd gone I felt so lonely my eyes stung. Why couldn't I cry? Why couldn't I let myself go? Instead, after the nurses had disconnected my IV, brushed my hair for me, and helped me pull my skirt up under my nightgown, I sat primly in the visitor's chair to wait for Hercules, the silver compact nestled in my hand, my face tilted toward a dim light from the window as I patted the ancient powder first on one cheek, then on the other, then on my eyelids and brow. The puff was leathery but supple. My idea was to make myself proud and luminous, the way a person should look when she's managed to let go of the things that have been taken from her anyway. But the powder did another thing entirely, a thing I believed and yet did not believe even as I watched what was happening in the mirror. The furrow between my eyebrows deepened. The soft skin beneath my eyes became fragile half-circles translucent as shadows. Around my lips the tiny creases lengthened and grew, while the flesh on my cheekbones broadened and softened and just barely, nearly immeasurably, sank.

My eyes felt weary but looked joyful all the same. They seemed to have learned things I couldn't quite claim as my own, as the heart knows to pump and the skin knows to sweat and the fingers know grasping and pulling. They were private from me, yet they offered their blend of wonder and grief and caution and exuberance as if they were those of a friend who would let me stare into them as long as I needed.

Was I wiser, suddenly?

Older?

Was that what the powder was doing to me?

The smile on my lips was more crooked than ever, as if over the years its ordinary bias had taken on a willful, playful asymmetry.

Over the years.

Had I said to myself *over the years?*

As if I knew what to do, I crossed the room to my suitcase and bent for the zipper on the outside pocket, pausing just in time for the onslaught of pain.

Which didn't come.

Hercules, when he stepped into the room at that moment, did not say a word until I'd unzipped the suitcase and pulled out the stiffened index card that had my birth date printed on it. The birth date, 04 04 55, was still legible. Underneath it was the number 1999. Four years had passed since I'd put on the powder.

I'm forty-four years old, I told myself in wonder.

Hercules remarked, "What gets me is you're looking so incredibly healthy."

I slid my free hand under the neck of my nightgown. The bandages were gone. There was a stretch-lace spaghetti-strap camisole with no bra and no padding. Beneath it the scars, at the touch of my fingers, gave off a fierce, fine tingling.

8

A hundred days; that's how long an average cancer takes to double. Since the tumor nearer my armpit was larger than the one under where my nipple used to be, and since the one underneath where my nipple used to be measured a centimeter around and thus contained more than a hundred billion cells, then it might be supposed that the cancer was inside my body for four to eight years before I found the lump.

So it's amusing to think of me strolling to my balcony when I got home from work all those years, looking out at the neighborhood, thinking that must be where the action was. The roads, the traffic, the skyline, can't be seen from between the buildings surrounding the courtyard. Only the golf course, and an undeveloped lot where a supermarket has been forever due to go up, and a stretch of residential woods rangy with overgrown maples, are visible from where I leaned against the railing, drinking an iced tea, trying to decide if the evening called for walking or reading. It wasn't me who seemed to decide this question, but the day itself, the way the patches of scenery spread themselves around among the surrounding geometry of brick and sky. I would think to myself, "What's going on today?" and peer between the buildings at a line of European house sparrows perched in a row on the sign advertising the perpetually imminent groundbreaking of the supermarket, and say to myself, "Oh, I could walk along the river on the *way* to the library, and decide when I get there whether to stop for a book or keep walking over the bridge, and maybe sit on the dock a while and watch all the overweight people go by on their boats." Or I would peer past the parking lot at where what seemed to be a red coat was snagged on a telephone line in the woods, and I would say to myself, "I'll walk out on that tiny peninsula behind the American Legion Hall where those two people are always in the middle of breaking up with each other." Then I'd change from my work clothes into my after-work clothes, meaning I'd take off my hose and go barelegged under the same skirt, or unbutton my cuffs and roll the sleeves of my blouse to three-quarter length, or take off my brooch and put on sunglasses. Then I'd set off on the sidewalk, reveling in the late sun on my freshly brushed hair, my anticipation kept in check, pacing itself steadily over the two-mile walk to the lake, not daring even to imagine that the same couple might still be there having their same debate about whether they'd ever see each other again, the woman brooding over cigarettes where she sat on the rocks facing the lake, the man pacing the narrow stretch of mud behind her glaring at a bunch of keys and asking himself aloud whether he ought to throw her house key into the water or give it back to her or just hang onto it in case they didn't break up after all. And lo and behold there they'd be again on the peninsula next time I walked by, only this time it was he who would be smoking on the rocks and she who hung back, crying, nose running into her wind-frizzed hair while she sobbed about never being able to play darts again because the bull's eye would only remind her of *him*. Then, watching my approach along the peninsula, she gave me a look of defiant good humor, snatched a matted-up Handi Wipe from where it was wedged between some rocks having been tossed off God knows what fishing boat how long ago, and blew her nose in it. And that would be my day's adventure, as wild and satisfying to me as if I'd stolen a skiff from the tiny marina, sailed it myself to Washington Island, collected a bucket of steamers for dinner, and cooked them over a fire pit. So removed was I from what was happening in the world that just to watch a woman wipe her nose on somebody else's garbage before she crouched down to wrap her arms around her bull's-eye of a boyfriend provided so much excitement that afterward, it was not only pleasant but necessary to go home and sit with my wine and my book in my living room to unwind. My afghan tucked under my thighs, a few strands of my hair pulled free of their clasp, my bathrobe scented with Victoria's Secret's Encounter shower gel, "a memorable, enticing blend of floral and oriental spice that whispers of romance." My delight at having made my excursion into the fray, then out of it. My unquestioning belief that the only thing "going on" within the walls of my apartment was that the faucet was dripping but that I wouldn't get up and tighten the knob until I had finished reading my chapter.

And not a hint of what was "going on" inside my body.

And all the while the cells of the cancer performing their mathematical paradox, dividing in order to multiply, multiplying in order to divide. I only sat there contented as a nun, which makes sense, it turns out, because nuns get more breast cancer than anyone else.

"Maybe it has to do with their habits," I joked with my doctor, who said, "Actually it has to do with the fact that they don't have children."

Given that my type of cancer grows more quickly than most, and that all tumors receive their blood supply years before detection, neither I nor my doctor were surprised by what he had just told me about the results of my retroperitoneal scan. What did surprise me was that he was telling me over the phone instead of calling me in for a consultation. I suppose he figured we'd be seeing so much of each other anyway it wouldn't make a difference if we skipped the preliminaries. It was only too bad that Hercules was out. I could have used his thoughtful, bashful company. I could have used his way of knowing what I needed when I didn't know it myself. But he was off on a skateboard he'd borrowed from one of the neighbor kids. I'd been fixing my supper when the doctor called—a plate of sliced pears and two deviled eggs—and when I heard what he had to say I dropped some bread in the toaster as well. The cancer had spread to my liver. My chance of surviving the next five years was somewhere between ten and twelve percent. In other words, I supposed it could be said that I was dying. Chemotherapy, intended mainly to keep the cancer from spreading to my brain, would begin in the morning, which was why I was making the toast, so toast wouldn't seem like something I ate only to keep the drugs from making me vomit. On the spice rack in the kitchen stood the silver compact of cosmetic, whose effect on me had worn off by the time I got home from the hospital two days earlier. I had put it on the spice rack telling myself it was to be used only with foresight and care, like the envelope of saffron I so sparingly sprinkled in curries. Still, it wasn't the powder's exoticism that made me cautious. In fact, I was afraid it wouldn't work. Afraid that the wise beatitude of my aging face had all been some trick of the surgery. Afraid that the new year, since disappeared from its sudden place on the index card, had been a side effect either of shock, anesthesia, or the deep, intravenous tide of the morphine. Maybe it was the morphine that did it, that made me dream and imagine myself forty-five, a survivor, a lover of every split second, my smiles crooked with gratitude, humor, and hope. But this evening my scars were in stitches again, and in fresh, astringent pain, as if to warn me that my capsules of painkiller would not do the trick.

Would not transport me.

Would not deliver me.

The doctor said, following a tilting runnel of sound that I assumed was his sip of Cranapple spritzer, "Isobel, as I mentioned before, you'll be undergoing, at least I hope you'll be undergoing, at least I hope you'll *agree* to undergo, a fairly rigorous application of chemotherapy involving use of the drug Ziphrain to combat your nausea. Ziphrain's very expensive. Tomorrow, see if you can find out if your insurance will cover it. If not, I can try to make certain arrangements with the manufacturer. Sometimes, I don't really understand it, but sometimes they cut us a little slack."

"What's it called?"

"Ziphrain. It nearly eliminates the nausea. It also tends to make the patient high."

So there was hope after all for the ancient cosmetic. It might unhinge me again, once I was high on the marvelous Ziphrain. I'd never craved a drug before. Now I wanted it only to give me the courage to pull the silver case off the spice rack and sprinkle my brows with whatever the aged makeup had in store.

Of course, I was afraid that it *would* work, too, and I was frightened as well of the Crazy Volunteer. Not that she wasn't harmless. I kept thinking, when I wanted to think that she wouldn't harm a fly, *she's as harmless as a fly*. For despite her fake hand there seemed to be something six-legged about her. And missing a wing. She was always tripping over her own frantic maneuvering, although she never broke a thing or even dropped a thing unless it was into my outstretched hands. I'd taken to outstretching my hands, palms up, whenever she approached me with one of her less and less sensible offerings—a trapper's glove smelling of hibernating weasel, a telephone not from an exhibit at all but from one of the flooded basement closets where the outdated office equipment was stored, a Victorian valentine with a droopy, stained bow. She must have known from the way I held my hands at the ready that I didn't want to touch her mechanical fingers, which seemed to buzz in their wrapping of vinyl. Once, they pinched my thumb. Another time they closed around my pinkie. Had they belonged to anyone else I think I wouldn't have minded. But she was so sudden and possessive! So like a pair of pincers! There she'd be all at once, always closer than was necessary, her breath ragged with eagerness, her eyelids aflutter, her uneven haircut wiry with glee, her greeting always a variation on what it had been before.

"Take this! It's yours!"

"This belongs to you, Isobel. Take it!"

"Here's your glove, Isobel," with a jerk of her too-plucked eyebrows.

And always that same, abrupt turning away, the return to the work at which no one could fault her; she was so careful, so uncomplaining, so wedded to the task at hand. I took all the stuff home. Not wanting to hurt her feelings by allowing her to find it again in the insurance bin or on the way to the annex, I stashed it away in the trunk of my car.

So it was not until after I'd finished speaking with the doctor and, having eaten all I could of my pears, eggs, and toast, went outside to stand at the edge of the parking lot to wait for Hercules to kick toward me on the skateboard out of the dusk, that I heard the flooded office telephone ringing outrageously in the trunk of my car.

PART TWO

Bald Queen Butterfly

9

On that September evening in the parking lot of my apartment complex, just after Dr. Klink interrupted my dinner preparations to tell me I was dying and that the chemotherapy I would start the next day was intended mainly to keep the cancer from spreading to my brain, when I opened the trunk of my car and lifted the receiver of that bizarrely ringing phone foisted on me by the Crazy Volunteer, that's when the events that I am going to tell about happened to me as if the months were sliding past me over the telephone wires, real and true. October, November, December, January, February, March. The phone was heavy and black as a barbell, and in the moment it took to disentangle the cord and bring the receiver to my ear, over half a year went by in such a langorous way I could feel every second, every gesture, every word. I knew what was happening as vividly as if every second ticked before my eyes on the index card, a langorous rush, a vibrato of memory and recollection that made my heartbeat speed up and slow down all at once, knowing something wasn't right. Knowing everything *was* right. Around me the dusk remained silver and high, just as it had been when I was waiting for Hercules to come skateboarding toward me over the pavement.

Only now, Hercules was nowhere in sight.

Where there had been the sweet, flavorful smell of some neighbor's late summer marinade smoking on a grill, there was now the sharp, coppery scent of fall changing to winter, and where the pavement had been dusted by the end of summer, soon it glittered with frost, then gleamed with the thaw.

And where there had been the distant racket of Hercules's

skateboard, there was now the approaching, departing, circling wind of the passing seasons.

Before my eyes the rising moon practiced each of its phases—at once the quarter moon was full, the full moon a sliver of luminous crescent. I was glad to see they weren't building the supermarket yet, for where there would have been the clamor of construction, the field below me was as unmown as ever, a spindly mixture of blossoming, drying-out weeds.

I stood leaning on the fender waiting for a break in the long-distance static, hoping against hope it would be Martha, who had hurt me very badly in those intervening months, in that half-year that had happened between one moment and the next. October, November, December, January, February, March. "An impulsive heart does not make for dependability," Hercules and I had developed the habit of repeating to each other whenever we found ourselves exclaiming about Martha, knowing all the while that her impulsive heart was what had brought Hercules into this world in the first place. Even Hercules, who didn't know the story behind Martha's troublesome union with his father, knew that. But that's all he knew. He didn't know where it happened—Chicago. Or when—during a break in our junior year in college. Martha had been house-sitting for her older brother. *Tending the mice,* as she said. She told me about it the night after break, seeking me out in my usual fifth-floor corner of the library, my boots side by side under the chair, my brushed hair gleaming in the clasp of a velvet bow, my stockinged feet tucked demurely underneath me as I studied a monograph about the influence of social and economic felicity on the execution of perspectives in landscape painting. What a tranquilly seductive picture I made, until Martha rushed over in a distracted flurry. She never shouted on the fifth floor, she barely so much as whispered, but still the clatter and excitement of her clothing and demeanor managed to cause a stir. She practically vibrated as I gathered my neat stack of books and zipped my pen into the pouch I kept in my notebook. Then she led me to her dorm room, sat me down on her bed, and offered me morsels of torn croissant. She'd been feasting on breads for as long as I'd known her; there was always a loaf, and then there was Martha attached to it, strumming the hard flakes of crust, the spongy insides, plucking at sesame seeds and black, roasted currants. Only after Hercules began to play strings did I understand that Martha might have been a musician, too, had she only had the discipline to match the graceful determination of her fingers. But she was always more self-indulgent than self-regulated. Superstitiously, she hadn't brought her diaphragm along to Chicago, fearing that if she had it, then she'd be less likely to need it. "You want to hear something funny?" she asked. "In some cultures, the gods for agriculture are the same as the gods for marriage. It has to do with the invention of the plow. The earth is the woman. The seeds are the man. When people found a way to drop the seeds into the soil and cover them up instead of scattering them around so they'd get picked up by the wind and taken somewhere else and sown where they didn't belong, the wheat sprouted where it landed. It no longer strayed. It was no longer so promiscuous. It stayed home in the field. That's why in Rome, marriage was solemnized over a plow. Last week, I swear to the god of agriculture, I made the biggest mistake of my life."

It had been a night flight to O'Hare. In the pocket of her skirt were two slips of paper, one a dollar bill and the other a note from a pupil—*which pupil?*—Martha asked herself over and over, in whose third grade class Martha was assigned student-teacher. She'd discovered the note on her own desk chair, folded so compactly she mistook it for a Chiclet. That evening in the dimly humming light of the airplane she read the child's awkward misspelling over and over, feeling more and more protective, more and more chagrined, more and more affection for the child—*which child?*—who had written, *I have no one to play with. Please cum to my house.*

Even as a college student, Martha never traveled light. Her

suitcase was a camp trunk loaded with poetry books, her "carry-on" luggage an army-size duffel bag stuffed so full of woolens, leathers, hard rolls, and scones that the zipper wouldn't close. They'd had to wrest it from her at the gate in Seattle, hold up the plane awhile as they hunted for twine and finally stapled the canvas shut. In Chicago she found a porter to help lug it all out to a cab. She tipped the porter a dollar. Not much later while her cab was still negotiating the maze of outgoing airport traffic, she dug into her pocket to unfold the note once again— *whose lonesome handwriting was it? Was it the girl with the habit of scrunching her eyebrows? The boy with his apple always wrapped in pink tissue paper?*

But the note wasn't there. Only the dollar. She'd tipped the porter with the note instead of with the money! Perhaps it was her misplaced feeling of responsibility for the unhappiness of the pupil who had written the note that propelled her to turn back to retrieve it. But perhaps not, she reconsidered. Maybe it had been her unconscious appraisal of the porter that had caused her to give him the note in the first place. How surprised he was by the message, so sweetly excited when she went back to fetch it that she had no heart to say it wasn't meant for him. From the very beginning there was something *unfamiliar* about the porter, not in the way any unknown person is unfamiliar to another but in the way, as Martha put it, children might seem fundamentally unfamiliar to adults, and men to women, except the porter seemed neither quite man nor child but rather something that borrowed unwittingly from each. The unpopular grade-schooler who had written the note slipped from Martha's conscience. Instead she could think only of the porter's hands, so wiry yet so bashful, and of the way his expression was always intent although he never quite knew what to do or say. At once vague and urgent, with a strange, high, innocent forehead, he wore a single earring in the shape of a timber wolf, looked youthful despite the gray in his hair, and had the air of being always on the verge of writing down something important except he never had pen or paper.

All that week he stayed with Martha in her older brother's house performing menial chores that did not need doing. Once, she found him pulling all the hair balls and fuzz balls and dirt balls from the vacuum cleaner bag and dumping them by handfuls into the trash so that the bag could be reused. Another time she found him polishing the underside of the iron. But he was always so good-natured. Nothing irked him. Nothing piqued him. Nothing even piqued his interest, or his curiosity. Not even Martha herself seemed to arouse him, exactly. In bed she felt like one half of an elderly married couple, patient, forgiving, and now and then pleasantly surprised. It wasn't until her very last hour in Chicago, when he helped her cart her luggage back into the terminal, that she asked him his secret. What kept him so unbothered, so floatingly contented in the face of her apparent, flustered agitation?

"Drugs," she half-expected him to answer.

But unfortunately "drugs" wasn't his reply.

They were standing near the window watching planes come and go. He answered unhesitatingly with neither embarrassment nor apology that as a teenager he had run away from home so many times while exhibiting questionable and maybe even self-destructive behavior that his worried parents, both surgeons, had had him surgically lobotomized.

Outside above the tarmac a plane leveled for landing, its blunt nose nearly teasing the tops of some trees. A lobotomy, Martha understood, involved an incision and a subsequent severing and scraping and clipping and cauterizing of nerves and blood vessels in the frontal lobes of the brain. She raised a shocked finger to the porter's forehead but couldn't bring herself to trace its high pink guileless strangeness below which Martha saw no evidence of the surgeon's scalpel except for a soft, dented memory of shadow.

Even before she knew for certain she was pregnant, she was determined to keep the baby. Over the years it's been a source of some embarrassment to me that Hercules must know how I tried to talk her out of it. My protestations were conventional and thankfully meaningless—she was so close to her degree, she didn't know the family, the baby would be borne of tragedy, the baby would be borne of a comedy of errors. But Martha was too indignant. To dispense with the offspring of a man whose parents had *murdered him alive* was too grievous, too blasphemous, Martha exclaimed all those next nine months, her body lumpy as the earth, her brow furrowed as by a plow. "Wounding is the principle of love, my ass," she often said, quoting her version of Plutarch, when she was too uncomfortable to waddle across campus to her student-teaching job. "Except, I didn't love him. I only thought I did. How could I love someone who didn't have a brain? I only hope I love the baby. Whatever kind of creature it's going to turn out to be."

Of course, the "creature" turned out to be Hercules, who during the long winter that the telephone delivered to me made me a bed in the tub, a cauldron of blankets and books and pillows in which I might stew in self-pity within reach of the toilet. Among all of the things that happened to me that winter—the winter that glided through the telephone in the trunk of my car, the winter that was, but wasn't, the winter that wasn't, but was—among all the things that happened, one was chemotherapy. Chemo was on Fridays; my worst days were weekends. *I have no one to play with. Please cum to my house,* I said to Martha when the therapy began, so wretched and sick I had a vision of her camping in my bathroom just so she could be close to me. Her lap was even bigger around than her heart, a cradle of doughy comfort I longed to lay my head on and let her read me poems aloud while her hands smoothed the weariness out of my brow. She promised she would come, she even bought a plane ticket. Those first long weekends before she was due, to wrap my arms around the plumbing seemed as impatient an embrace as I would ever be in, my knees on the soft fluff of carpet that Hercules kept fresh and aired, my face at rest on the porcelain he scented and scrubbed and refused to use himself, in order to keep things sweet for my rush to the bowl. Even on weekdays when I wasn't feeling so bad he peed outside behind the Dumpster at the edge of the parking lot, facing into the freezing woods, not knowing how I liked to watch him make his way out there so casually you'd think he was only admiring the call of a chickadee. It was something I knew we would do together, Martha and I, if she really came to visit. We would watch him surreptitiously and wonder aloud how we might feel if we were young women in love with him. It was my presence, not being his mother, that would make it safe for Martha to engage in such speculation, just as it was her presence, her *being* his mother, that would make it safe for *me* to do it. It would only be a game, only the two of us clinging to giddy fantasy. Over the years we had watched him turn into a man, and it would be foolish to stop spying now, when the pocket of air between his flannel collar and the back of his neck was suddenly more provocative then ever. No one had warned me about the effects of the chemo, about how one of the drugs, Tamoxifen, has a way of making some women lose their wits a little and do things they might not do ordinarily. Ordinarily I would not climb out of the bathtub trailing nightgowns and half-written letters while stepping onto the balcony wrapped in only a bedsheet in order to watch the nineteen-year-old son of my best friend cross the parking lot, step behind the Dumpster, and pee onto a drift of crackling maple leaves. It wasn't his body that captivated me so, I would say to Martha when she came. It wasn't his clothing, his flannels, his jeans, his lazy corduroys, his soft, open collar, his cinched leather belt. No. And it wasn't his manner exactly either, I'd say, but his posture. It was the fact that from the back when regarded from across the twenty yards separating the balcony from the margin of the woods, the cast of his neck and shoulders when he unzipped his fly and stood there a moment looking into the trees was exactly identical to the cast of his neck and shoulders when he adjusted the tension of the strings on his bass. Cocking his head he seemed even to be listening for the sharps and flats and for the first perfect rapturous notes.

"It *perplexes* me," I would have said to Martha, if only she were there, "that two such different gestures, peeing and tuning a musical instrument, one so primitive and the other so refined, can look so much alike. Maybe it's because he's so unselfconscious."

"Like father like son," Martha might have shuddered if only she had come, her chin at rest on the balcony railing next to my elbow, her ample butt swaying under her skirt. I was lonely for her out there by myself, trying to look regal in my bedsheet-gown. With all the style I could muster I pulled the folds more fashionably around my shivering nakedness, stepped back to the bathroom, dropped to my knees at the basin, threw up for the twelfth time that day and nearly stayed where I was, too weak and exhausted to make it back into the tub. Really, it was nearly as comfortable on the floor and if I looked around I noticed things I would not have seen otherwise. A bobby pin snagged in the weave of the clothes hamper as if to tell me I might someday want to set my hair again. A ladybug nesting in my basket of shampoos as if to suggest that I might someday decide to wash the sour odor of vomit from behind my ears. I wouldn't. I'd wait for Martha to do it. Just to imagine her plump fingers massaging my scalp caused enough of a lathery tingle along the length of my spine that I managed to climb back into my tubful of discarded magazines. How I longed for a glass of iced Pepsi! No sooner had I thought this than in came Hercules bearing a bowl of chilled soup. I'd told him of my fondness for such elegant fare, and not exactly understanding what a chilled soup should be—an icy concoction of oils and herbs and fricasseed fruits, for instance—he'd cooked a can of cream of mushroom and stuck it in the freezer twenty minutes to cool. Seeing how his hopeful ministrations had resulted in a blob of congealed cornstarch made me sad enough that I needed to hide my head again in the gleam of the toilet so he wouldn't see me laughing. I laughed so hard it made me wonder if deep down I was crying. How I hated the chemo, more than I hated the illness. How I wanted to cry!

When Martha showed up I would do it, my tears soaking her offerings of brioche and foccacia, the push and pull of my frustration twisting me up in her skirts.

Even as I imagined this I had a feeling she might not keep her word.

She won't come, she won't come, she won't come, I said to myself all that winter the telephone brought me.

An impulsive heart does not make for dependability, I whispered over and over on the Saturday night she was due to arrive from the airport. Her cab was expected at nine o'clock.

At nine fifty-five, when Hercules went outside and made his way across the parking lot to step behind the Dumpster, his posture as he watched the arc of urine span the edge of the pavement between him and the drift of leaves mimicked precisely the brave disappointment of a person who knows that what he's waiting for is not going to happen.

He must have known I was watching.

He was trying to tell me that his mother wasn't coming.

I'm not saying I know her better than you do, the tilt of his head seemed to whisper across the dark of the lot. *But what you have to believe when you believe anything that she tells you is that she means well. She's never once told a lie, my mother. It's just that her truths are subject to fluctuation. Although at this very moment she's probably headed for the nearest telephone in order to tell you that she didn't catch her flight, something will intervene and she won't end up calling.*

It was after Martha's failure to arrive when she had promised she would—my ear to the phone, my fingers plucking at some dust in the trunk of the car—that I finally gathered the courage to wash my hair. Before I did it I could not have said what made me so afraid. Even while lathering I felt only a vague apprehension—a strange, numbing dread in the tips of my fingers, a tingling alertness all through my head. It must be the astringency of the shampoo, I was thinking. Or maybe general fatigue, weariness, dizziness, that made me feel that something terribly wrong was about to take place. I applied a creme conditioner, then waited a minute for the final rinse. It was when I gathered my hair for it's usual wringing that all of a sudden every lock and tendril of it came free in my hands. I was stunned by the way it lost its grip on my skull, not in taut, rending tears the way I might have imagined but as gently as new shoots plucked from a potful of loam; one twist of my wrists and out the clump came with a sound like a last suck of soil. In my dismay I dropped the handful; it lay coiled on the sieve of the drain as perfect as Rapunzel's—honey-colored, ropelike, fragrant with balsam. For how long did I stand there staring at it when for days I'd barely managed to stand up at all? Perhaps I stared at it so long because I hadn't had a chance to stare at my breasts when *they* were no longer attached to the rest of my body. No chance to inch my weary foot forward, to nudge each sorrowful nipple with the tip of my toe as if in hopes they might still be responsive. Naked, clothed, clothed, naked, over the weeks that the telephone brought, I reached for my hair as if it were still on my head—with a towel as if to dry it, with a comb as if to style it, with my fingers as if simply to indulge in it, but casually, the way you reach for a light switch during a blackout and then pause in the darkness just long enough that you can believe in it again. *I've lost my hair. I've lost my breasts,* I needed always to remind myself, then put the towel, the comb, my fingers back where they'd started. I didn't throw the hair away. Carefully I laid it on the counter, rolled it up in a linen dish towel and when it was dry, plaited it, fastened the braid with my entire collection of hair clips, and hung it in the back of my closet where I would need to look at it only if I wanted.

"It went gentle into that good night," I planned to say to Martha if she ever did come. "You know, the thing about this kind of cancer, well, let me put it this way," I would have gone on. "The thing about an hysterectomy is that they sew you up inside. Your vagina's like the finger of a glove. It doesn't lead anywhere. Where the body was open, now it is closed. How's that for 'wounding is the principle of love'? Well, anyway, thank God I didn't have to have an hysterectomy."

To which Martha would reply, if she ever did come to visit, "Isobel, I think you're the only American in the world who would say *an* hysterectomy."

"Yes, it's an horrendous affectation," I would answer, my round head naked as a newborn on her lap. *My mother would have found a way to caress you ear to ear,* the slope of Hercules's shoulders seemed to be saying weekend after weekend all those endless months of chemo when Martha didn't call, *so that you'd feel not merely bald but elegantly bald, not bereft but bejeweled. If Cleopatra was bald,* said the shrug of his shoulders when he zipped up his fly and turned back toward the lot, *she probably looked like you.*

Cleopatra was desirable and proud, I wanted to argue. Cleopatra wore a halter of hammered gold medallions studded with lapis, not a cotton cardigan sweater incorrectly buttoned over bandages. Besides, she still had both of her pyramids. And she was not menopausal, as I am certain soon to be. She could still be a mummy.

But talk of Cleopatra gave me an idea. One "weak day" when I was tired but not too sick, I took off early from work, drove to the jeweler's and got my ears pierced at last, after all those years of being smug in my refusal of that particular vanity. I waved away the gold training studs the jeweler offered. From the start I wanted only the whole, dangling, glittery array of possibilities; tassels and fringes of lacy filigree and beadwork, ropes of amethyst crystal, loops upon knots upon tiers of faceted color. And not only earrings but collars to match, chokers like whole suns dripping with sparkle and glass. It wasn't camouflage I wanted. It was pure adornment. It was pride. It was a posture replete with flat-chested womanliness, a high bearing splendid with the shock value of hubris. I hid away my blousy wardrobe, my breezy, cool rayons and blustery silks. Beneath ribbed, sleeveless tank tops and spandex bodysuits my torso was mesmerizingly boyish, my bare collarbone draped in petals of silver while above it my baldness rose noble and supreme.

It was shamelessness I wanted.

As opposed, of course, to shame.

The interesting thing about shamelessness being that in order for it to be entirely satisfactory a person needs to be secretly ashamed of *something*.

Which I was.

Not even Hercules knew it.

Only Martha would have known it, if only she had come. My two, shameful secrets, which happened to me in the months that took place in the telephone. Clutching the receiver, I decided I'd confess it to Martha, behind the closed door of the bathroom as I tended the secrets one by one, like a mime, not speaking. My face only inches from the mirror, my hands ever so steady but the rest of me trembling with exactitude lest I do it wrong. One half-circle of false eyelashes. Then the other. A fresh set every week never different from the set before it and always a spare set tucked away in my purse and another in the glove compartment of my car and yet a third in my desk drawer at the museum along with an extra tube of adhesive, hidden away in my spare pair of socks because our desks were no longer private as they used to be. After the fire, what was left of our offices had been carted out to a row of trailers parked on the lawn near the red caboose, so we resembled an unhinged locomotive. Five cars in all, not including the caboose. Two were for storage of artifacts. In the third was a row of folding tables on which had been placed all our salvaged books and papers, in piles and boxes and stacks of envelopes and milk crates and onion crates and a squadron of new accordion files that already stank of leftover smoke. In the fourth were our desks, the floors between them laden with audio-visual equipment, and in the fifth our conference tables and a single cubby of a rest room and a couple of half-size refrigerators. I didn't mind the lack of privacy except as it pertained to my eyelashes. I didn't mind, even, the occasional weekday vomiting I needed to do in public, into the bucket I kept under my desk because the bathroom was too far away for emergency retching. I didn't mind that I occasionally dozed off there as well, my naked head nestled on a pillow I'd bought at Pier One for that purpose. But bald as I was, flat-chested and bejeweled and upright as I was, my pride in the scars and tribulations of chemotherapy did not extend to those fragments of my anatomy. All my resolve to make it through treatment nearly vaporized when I finally saw what was happening. Unlike my hair, the eyelashes didn't come out all at once. No, they were slinky with mischief. Each morning when I washed and creamed and made up my face, there were only a few scattered lashes adhering to the porcelain of the sink and one or two curling impishly around my mascara brush, the molecular bits of white flesh still clinging to the ends. It was the Crazy Volunteer who finally alerted me to what was going on. Instead of gazing off into a middle distance as usual as if at some phantom message, she stared directly at my eyes. Not *into* them. *At* them. And didn't blink. And didn't waver. And stepped even closer than usual as if to astonish me more than ever with the perfection of her skin, not a pore in sight, and no faint growth of hair but an unblemished smoothness except for the two dots of rouge on her cheeks and a funny, sharp dent above one of her eyebrows. She wanted me to tell her the name of one of the attic workers, the one with the Walkman radio.

"Grzadzielewsli's the name on the truck. They're all brothers and cousins, I think, but I don't know their first names," I said. Although a week earlier she had asked me this very same question, I was trying to be patient. "Maybe you could ask him?" I suggested as kindly as I could manage, always conscious of her furious impatience, and of the way she was always bumping into tree trunks and furniture, and of her lack of social grace and etiquette of which she herself seemed desperately aware. Between us existed an unspoken agreement about her deluge of gifts, whose apparent lack of purpose was matched only by my queer sense that I ought to keep them near me, that I ought not to deposit them on the ship-to-insurance shelves in the trailer, that they were in fact absolutely necessary to me in some unexplored way that neither one of us would dare to talk about with anyone including each other.

"Why don't you ask him yourself?" she retorted, spitting the words and turning angrily on her heel with so much gusto that she lost her balance and tipped rather rigidly into a filing cabinet, knocking over a mugful of charred pencils. Finally, before lurching out of the trailer, she turned once again to glare at my eyes. When she was gone I left the trailer, got into my car, drove out of the parking lot, pulled onto a side road where no one would see me, and examined my eyes in the rearview mirror. The lashes weren't yet utterly gone, but of the ones that were left, some poked up and some down. When I grasped some and pinched, out they popped like the legs of a spider. I drove through a red light to get to a drugstore, bought six different varieties of lashes to see which suited me the best, took them home for my lunch break, only to discover I needed to drive right back to the drugstore for the tube of adhesive I hadn't realized was not included.

After the twelve weeks of chemo were over and done, the eyelashes didn't grow back, and perhaps it was this that made me leery of my hair when it appeared like an uneven sprinkling of cinnamon, first on my temples and then on the crown of my head, a clumpy patchwork of filamentous orange-hued light that seemed intent on growing faster than ever before as if to make up for lost time.

But I didn't want to make up for lost time, for to imagine doing so would be to consent to the notion that time had been lost to begin with, there in the trunk of my car, the moon practicing its phases over my head, the months shivering behind it, a halo of static, the weeds brittle, then fresh, in the field.

But time hadn't been lost, there in the telephone. It had been slept through, vomited through, slogged through, sweated through, fumbled through, trembled through, thirsted through, yearned through, fainted through, struggled through, drifted through, and moaned through. But it hadn't been *lost*. No. I refused to regret even the whole Sundays I'd lain in a stupor of indolent self-pity among the quilts and pillows in the bathtub, so consumed by numb loathing of everything around me that the only ounce of strength I was able to muster I spent all at once by grandly slamming the door so I wouldn't have to listen to Hercules practicing scales. There was only the briefest of pauses in his music after the slam of the door, and then in humor he kept on playing, for me, so spiritedly and so sympathetically that I could practically hear my name being called by the notes, *Isobel, Isobel, Isobel Albright!*, and I soon fell delightedly, dreamily asleep.

Even if my hair were growing back smooth as silk and not in mangy, scratchy clumps, I would have preferred to remain bald forever in testament to the audacity my illness had forced upon me. It was Hercules who came up with the idea for the hot wax after hearing my plan to purchase an electric razor, and it was he who bought the wax and heated it up in the microwave. As he waited in the kitchen, I was careful to shut all the blinds on the windows so no one would see when I took off my earrings. Then I washed with a warm, soapy cloth before Hercules dusted my clean skull with talc, and with a few practiced swipes of his fingers wiped the excess talc into the hollow of my throat as if to keep me from feeling goosenecked after the removal of my necklace. Having sampled the temperature by spreading a drop of the melted wax on the inside of his wrist as if it were milk for a baby, he chose the narrowest of rubber kitchen spatulas for its application, along with the pastry brush, which was fitting because there was something delicious and buttery in the sight of the crimped tub of just-melting wax and the way its faint honey odor rose around us. Hercules's strokes were as measured and delicate as if he were painting the hair on rather than off. Because the preparation dried in under three minutes and needed to be peeled off quickly lest it turn brittle, he was careful to complete no more than a tenth of my skull at a time.

It was strange to be touched by Hercules after all of these months of having shared the close walls of my apartment as chastely as if we were fashioned of wax ourselves. I noticed at once that he had an unequivocal fondness for symmetry. If he began by painting a ribbon of wax above my left ear, then he followed by describing a ribbon of identical width above the right, and when he had finished removing the wax from the steep upward slope above the nape of my neck, he applied it next above the more rounded curve of my brow. Though I sat in the swivel chair with the reclining backrest, it was Hercules who moved the most, seeming to enjoy the unfailing fixity of my posture in relation to his continuous inflection. In fact, there seemed from my slightly tilted vantage point to be no end to the ways he could swivel, bend, flex, and innovate; beneath the velvety plaid of his loose flannel shirt he was liquid and solid at once, circling and pausing, his bare wrists poised and eager.

"You're waxing and waning," I joked as he circled.

He frowned, drew back, dabbed the tip of the pastry brush upon the ghost of my fontanel. How alarming it was to be touched by a person whose giant, nimble body seemed fearful of disrupting the fragile, purposeful alignment of the seven bones of my skull! He told me how once in careless ignorance of the correct procedure for tightening new strings on a bass— all the strings are to be threaded through the bridge before any one of them is tightened and then each string adjusted incrementally so that the tension of one never differs too much from that of its neighbors—he'd caused the neck to splinter where it joined the body, and how since then he dreamed periodically of cradling the crumpled instrument in his lap, weeping and rocking with true, fraternal grief. He'd grown up with that bass; he'd had it for nearly a third of his young life. Perhaps here was the reason for his virginity, which I might discuss with Martha if only she'd come. "Your son," I would say to her, "is like someone experimenting for the first time with the proposition that if an egg is squeezed in one hand it won't break. He mistrusts the idea. He thinks there must be some trick. Deep down under all the shy appropriateness of his manner he's afraid he might hurt somebody." At which we'd both frown, because the idea of Hercules hurting anybody even by accident was impossible.

All in all, the hot wax process, including the final massage of baby oil for which Hercules used a moist corner of kitchen sponge, lasted nearly an hour and a half, and we were not quite done when Dr. Klink phoned with the results of my posttherapy scan. That particular phone call from Dr. Klink was perhaps the most amazing thing that happened in those amazing months that passed through the amazing telephone. Because the wax was still gooey around my ears it was Hercules who took the call with his usual "Greetings from the domicile of Isobel Albright!", then held the receiver up to my ear. The scans, announced an ecstatic Dr. Klink, revealed a complete remission of cancer. Gone from the lymph. Gone from the liver. Absent from the pancreas. Absent from the spleen. Not a miracle exactly but miraculous still. I was clean as my new skull. Even after the doctor had spoken I didn't cry. Instead I screamed, my delight so piercing that a house fly clinging to one of the lamp shades lost its grip and plummeted to the floor.

But even then when there was something to celebrate, when the time had passed for my exhausted, nauseated, drug-besotted head to lay itself down on Martha's soft lap and be stroked temple to temple, when the bathroom was no longer boudoir/sickroom but bathroom again, when the toilet was no longer the gleaming imperturbable sphinx toward which I leaned every moment as if to challenge the severity of the human condition, when I might start really living again in some new, unexpected, glorious fashion of which the content still eluded me but the contours beckoned like some secret, shuddering doorway—even then, Martha didn't come or call.

Which wasn't a terrible surprise, of course.

An impulsive heart does not make for dependability, I consoled myself, and tried not to be hurt or angry come that impossible spring, the spring that blossomed on the telephone and moistened the carpet inside the trunk of my car. Freed of the awful cocoon of sickness I donned my in-line skates each morning and set off for work along the path at the edge of the river to celebrate my emergence as *Bald Queen Butterfly,* the silk wings of the scarf I'd looped around my waist flapping iridescently behind me. So courageous I was, so giddy with health and spring fever, that I proposed to Hercules a March night spent in secret in the attic of the museum. The floor had been cleared of debris but the roof wasn't yet completed. We had ordered a shipment of amethyst slate from a quarry all the way in Pennsylvania, but when it finally arrived there weren't enough slates, so in one sloped spot there were only joists and rafters draped with a fluttering of tarps, and though we couldn't see the jagged hole in the sky we could feel it arching above us. I packed a jug of wine while Hercules stowed some chocolates in his pocket. By flashlight we read aloud to each other the silly, contradictory romantic advice offered to readers of women's magazines that we'd bought for a laugh at the supermarket on the way over. *Forget your partner. Be greedy. Lavish your attention only on yourself. Stare into your partner's eyes. Discover what he wants and give it to him. Be coy. Withhold his heart's desire. Be up-front. Dress like a man. Wear a short skirt. Be patient with your lover. If he's not what you want, give him an ultimatum.*

After that we shared the wine from an enameled goblet we smuggled from one of the trailers, and having discovered the violin case of ruined pocket watches we went through that as well. When we pried open some of the lids, small pools of black mud still swirled among the delicate, glommed-up works. But their intricacy was lovely to see, and we bent over it together so our ears touched, our shoulders hunched in unison, our four knees raised above the object of our contemplation exactly as if I were his mother teaching him to tie his shoe.

My bare head buzzed with longing for a premature hot wax.

Hercules, however, appeared unperturbed.

YES, ALL OF that happened, real and true, on that evening I picked up the phone in the parking lot, hoping against hope it would be Martha. It *was*. The very first thing she said, her voice fuzzy with the static as the months flipped forward— October, November, December, January, February, March— was that the reason she hadn't shown up was that she'd been living in Mexico, having boarded the wrong plane out of Seattle on her way to visit me.

Well, not the wrong plane exactly. But she had taken a little side trip, for a momentary thrill, she wistfully explained. Except she'd liked Mexico City too much to leave. The sheer press of the crowds, the jostling, the traffic, the polluted surge of that whirlpool of people caused her to reevaluate what it meant to be part of the human race. The city itself was a throbbing, breathing thing, a corporeal variation of the spiritual Taoism that never quite satisfied her when she'd tried it in Seattle.

"So, are you angry at me?" she asked when she'd finished explaining. "For not calling sooner?"

"Why would I be angry?" I heard myself reply, my voice on the phone as staticky as Martha's. "I was only half dead every day on the floor of the bathroom. Hercules kept it clean. Hercules brought me cans of Pepsi when I was so thirsty from all that endless vomiting I couldn't even wiggle my toes. Hercules drove me to and from the hospital for treatment every Friday, and on Mondays at work when I was still feeling queasy he told everyone to keep the goddamn restoration conservators away from me. Hercules told me I looked beautiful when my hair fell out. Hercules, by telling me I looked like

Cleopatra, gave me the idea for my jewelry. I wear it on my head, draped over my skull. Hercules answered the phone when the doctor called me to tell me I was better. Hercules sponged baby oil on my head so it would glisten along with my jewelry when I in-line skated to the supermarket to buy tulips for my forty-first birthday. Which you missed, by the way. But Hercules didn't. Since Hercules is your son, since you are responsible for having brought him into the universe, how could I be angry at you?"

"Oh, Isobel," said Martha.

"Apparently I've become a real package," I went on, while above me the moon waned, like an eclipse. People made way for me on the streets, I explained to Martha. Maybe they were scared of me. Maybe they were impressed. Maybe, I told her, they thought I was a television star but they couldn't figure out which one. Someone from *Star Wars,* probably. "I feel like a walking sunbeam," I said, moving to the thrill of my own anger, the speedy rhythm of my voice on the telephone as I pressed it to my ear at the trunk of the car. "Except I'm really kind of lonely," I went on. "I can't imagine why, unless it has something to do with the fact that I lost two tenths of my body and made my peace with the stitched-up holes left behind without the company of my supposed best friend to comfort me. You said you were coming, Martha," I scolded, telling her how abandoned I'd felt when Hercules told me he'd found an apartment near the museum, a single room with a big, bare floor and a gusty fireplace with a broken flue. Not being lovers, there seemed no way for me to beg him to stay. I gave him pots and pans instead, I said to Martha through the static, explaining to her about the bands he started playing in over that winter. Rock n' Bones was the blues, Rehab was jazz, they played every Wednesday and Sunday in a club on Route 10. Living with Hercules, I said to Martha, was like putting my ear to a conch shell. There was always this conscientious hush, this delicate, spiraling, fragile echo. "So how could I be angry at you for not coming, when if not for you, there'd be no Hercules?" I concluded.

"Jesus, Isobel," said Martha. "I think you love my son."

"Of course I love him. What friend of his mother wouldn't, if they were still friends, that is," I said, tapping my foot on the fender, my curious fingers tracing the twist of the telephone cord into the open trunk of the car, then out again up to my new bald head of which each plane and indentation felt at once strange and absolutely familiar. How funny it was to be saying these things to Martha. Half-perplexed I was, yet half-accustomed as well. There hadn't *been* any drafty apartment, and yet there *had,* a single room so large and high and bare and drafty that when Hercules found it and took me to see it and we were standing in the middle of it as if standing out on a plain in the middle of Nebraska, I could see the wind ruffling his hair. Couldn't I? And I hadn't been through chemo and yet I had. Hadn't I? And I wasn't cancer-free and yet I—

"And for that you blame me," Martha's voice interrupted.

"For what?" I asked.

"For the fact that you're a middle-aged woman no longer living with your best friend's teenage son who doesn't know you're in love with him."

"*No longer living* with your best friend's son is one thing. *Dying* is another," I answered resolutely. "Martha, you promised you would come. And I expected you to. I wanted so much to lay my skull in your lap. You can't imagine . . . It's not a small thing, you know, to show respect for a person who's sick. I've found a way, on my own, to make my new body worthy of the fact that I want it to survive, but I did it in spite of the fact that you weren't there to stroke me through it the way you promised you would. I had to think my way through wanting your company, and now I'm on the other side. So even if you told me you were coming right now, I don't know how I'd feel. You'd have to shock me somehow, into appreciating your arrival after all this hard time. And I have only to look in the mirror to know I don't shock so terribly easily these days. Every night after my shower I look in the mirror. You know what hot water does to scars? It makes my scars frank as pockets. But still I don't bat an eye. So what I'm saying is, Martha, if you're calling to tell me you're finally coming to visit it's not exactly too late but in order for me not to be entirely blasé about it you'll have to tell me something interesting. It won't shock me just to hear that you're finally coming. I need to hear something else as well. Something I can really wrap my hands around."

I took a deep, wounded breath of fresh, angry loneliness, reveling in the sudden knowledge that that's what I'd been breathing all those impossible months of the telephone. The loneliness meant I was mortal. The anger reaffirmed that just because I was mortal didn't mean that I wasn't alive. There was a fathomless silence on the telephone line, deep enough to make me wonder if we'd been disconnected or if the funny black telephone had finally realized it wasn't plugged in and was far too old to be a cordless model. From the trunk of my car, the phone's black sheen seemed to invite my company as if I might hoist myself into the shadows of the trunk and cuddle next to it while waiting for Martha to speak. There were several things I thought she might be wanting to say. She might tell me I ought not to use the word *skull* in reference to my own head. She might ask me analytically why I supposed that when people were angry with each other they addressed each other by name.

But she didn't say any of those things. She said, when she finally spoke, "Isobel, I'm really sorry."

"That doesn't shock me enough," I said.

"I have a present for you, Isobel," she added.

"Fine," I said. "But not exactly earthshaking."

"Isobel," she continued, "I've kidnapped two babies."

IN THE LIFE of every child there's a ball that gets tossed up into the sky that somehow never seems to come back down. It's just up there. Invisible. Spinning so fiercely as to wrap the sun's glare around its escape. At dusk, the children emerge from their houses to look for it. Among the damp tufts of grass. Among the overturned stacks of terra-cotta flower pots. In the murk of the birdbath. Behind the broken lattice under the porch. But the ball will not be found. And the children will seem to forget it until years later in the midst of some adult crisis of spiritual indifference they remember how it wasn't in the wheelbarrow, wasn't in the watering can, wasn't cradled in the saddle of the swing, and in that recollection they experience just so much as a flicker of awe.

All at once, I was that ball. Up there. Spinning. I couldn't follow Martha's story exactly. There was something about a clinic outside Mexico City at which she'd volunteered to administer vaccines to children, and something about two women struck by a police van as they were crossing the road from the clinic to the liquor store where the mothers often shopped for sodas while their children were being examined by the nurse, and something about a ribbon of cigarette burns on the sole of one tiny foot, and something about two abusively uncooperative fathers, one of whom happened to be the driver of a second police van that failed to arrive in a timely manner at the scene of the accident that killed the two women crossing the road. There was something about a nun who at a crucial hour claimed to have misplaced the document authorizing the release of the children to a church-run orphanage that was rumored to be a dour institution to begin with, and there was something about the obtuseness, not to mention the corruption, of the Mexican courts and something else about the fathers who independently of each other vanished from the steps of the courthouse without taking the babies with them. There was something about the beds in the in-patient wing of the clinic being crowded with North American college students who all had apparently eaten from the same tomato. There was something about the heat. There was something about the sweat, Martha's and all of those students' and that of a journalist she met outside the bathroom they shared in the building where she rented a room. There was something about how the sweat of most babies smelled like milk but how the sweat of these babies smelled bitter as aspirin, and how the sweat of the journalist made her so reckless and impetuous that she had the temerity to rescue them.

"As if I'd never done anything risky or impetuous before," she said.

While Martha was telling me all of this, the tendril of storm cloud thickened and swelled beyond the arching boughs of the distant trees. The April moonlight grew feeble on the hoods of the neatly parked cars. Like the sail of a ship, the storm advanced across the field where the ground had not yet been broken for the construction of the supermarket. Among the swaying, compact buds of the thistle and phlox, rain tumbled in dense, flapping sheets that made the stems sway and keel. I felt the cold, windblown spray of it pelting my bald, naked head. So smooth was my skull after Hercules's fond ministrations, so waxen, that the water rolled off in fine, sliding droplets and fanned out behind me.

"Martha," I shouted, for the wind was growing stronger. "*I want those babies!*"

"I'm headed your way," Martha answered. "I'm still in Mexico but I'm across the Rio Grande from Brownsville, already."

"*Where?*"

"Texas," she said.

We lost our connection.

March, February, January, December, November, October, the months rushed backward, the static disappeared. No sooner had I set the rain-slippery receiver back in its place in the trunk of the car than the April storm vanished and it was September again.

It was 1995. I was forty years old, not forty-one.

I was back where I'd started.

And so was my cancer. And so was my bandage, the stitches, the evening's fresh dose of astringent pain. The blended flavor of sliced pears and deviled eggs was still tart in my mouth.

It was the evening before I was to endure my very first session of chemotherapy.

The air was balmy and sweet with the scent of my neighbor's barbecue. I had a full head of hair. I was wearing no jewelry except for my usual cameo brooch. Hercules had gone inside ahead of me. I took the two flights of stairs, forgoing the elevator as if to save it for the time I might really need it. Still feeling my dread at what the doctor had told me—a ten to twelve percent chance of survival—I had already determined to exercise my strength for as long as I had it. But that wasn't why I was taking the steps, exactly. I needed the time. I needed to put one foot in front of the other so as to step all the more soundly away from my terrible elation at what had happened at the bewildering trunk of my car. From the top of the stairs, I saw Hercules's skateboard propped against the doorjamb along with a bulky valise and a net shopping bag.

It was Martha, of course. I knew it as soon as I saw the second valise alongside the first, and a bakery bag jutting with loaves of rye and sourdough fresh from Seattle. Hercules was in the shower, so when Martha came to greet me, the fragrance of coffee still clinging to the folds of her voluminous skirt, our gingerly embrace was long and private against the press and pull of my stitches.

"Oh Isobel," she said.

"I'm all right," was all I could murmur. No babies, of course. No Mexican shawl. Just my best friend fresh and innocent, exactly on time, neither early nor late, gazing with dismay at the pallor of my skin.

"Does it hurt?" she asked.

"Not really," I said. "It only feels like someone drove across my back while I was laying facedown on a bed of nails."

"What do you want me to do for you the most?" she asked, just as Hercules shut off the water and slid open the shower curtain behind the closed door of the bathroom. He'd been staying here only a couple of weeks, yet already his bath time produced a familiar array of sounds; the rasp of the rings across the metal rod, the way he wrung out his washcloth before rolling it up, the snapping shut of the lid of his soap box, the quiet huff of his towel as he pulled it from its resting place on top of the hamper, the clicking on of the exhaust which he always saved for last, enjoying the leftover steam. When he was gone, there would be no trace of him, nothing but the vapor of a vapor of a vapor scented with Ivory soap. Of course, I thought of his apartment when I thought of this—the room near the museum with the vast, bare floor and the high, narrow, ripple-paned windows and the arched doorways and the fireplace with the broken flue. The acoustics in such a place would be entirely unacceptable even to the most stalwart of musicians, while the furls of damp sky that would creep every night down the chimney would finally pry apart the taut, supple curves of the bass. Hercules would never live in a place like that. Never. Not in a million years. And not in one year, and not in five. I knew that as surely as I knew the address, off Congress Avenue in a row of high-pitched, triangulated roof lines that reminded me of London. But I knew it only halfway, just like I knew, as the telephone had revealed to me, that he *might* someday be living in it.

Mightn't he?

Perhaps he'd leave the bass with me in my apartment, I wondered hopefully, my mind still outside with the bald lady I'd left in the rainstorm in the parking lot, one foot on the fender, one foot off, her giant earrings trembling with the message from Mexico. Was she miserable out there in those guillotines of rain? Had she climbed into the trunk? What was her name? Something something Butterfly? I made my way to the window, watched some moths flutter over the dusky courtyard, dry as leaves. My car was silent and ordinary, just a Saab in a lot, a trifle dusty and forlorn, needing a good washing. I was suddenly exhausted, so weary I wanted to sleep.

"So how was Mexico?" I asked Martha, just testing.

"I've never been to Mexico. You know that," she said.

"Seattle, I mean. Let me lay with my head in your lap," I said.

10

It must have been Trevor, my friend who works the Congress Avenue drawbridge over the river, who told me once when I'd stopped to chat a minute some months before the fire, before the lump, in other words eons ago when I was still effectively a primitive, but after Eric Clapton recorded "Old Love" because that's what I heard the faintest refrain of drifting from Trevor's headphones when he took them off and let them lay loose across his collarbone, that the original meaning of the word *blessed* is "bathed in blood."

"But does it matter whose?" I remember asking, thinking how indiscriminate that all babies are blessed by their mother's blood but so are killers by their victims' blood and so was a man I once dated who served roast beef on a grooved platter in which a deep bowl was carved into the wood so when the meat was all sliced and the blood had gathered in a fatty, red pool, he dipped little pinched-off fingerfuls of buttered baked potato in it. He called it "the juice." I remember realizing that if I loved him, then I would have loved him all the more for this unabashedly beastly recipe, and that the fact that I found it intolerable must mean I didn't love him even if I wished I could. He would make a good father especially on Halloween, I used to say to myself. I remember just sitting there watching him eat, watching him slide the very tips of his fingers into the bowl before sucking them free of butter and blood and potato. He sucked them very thoroughly. He didn't leave any scraps of potato skin or dribbles of hemoglobin in his goatee. I remember wondering, looking at the sharp, trimmed, thoughtfulness of that beard, what it would be like to love such a ghoulish person. What would I do? Would I take hold of his wrist and bring his morsel of blood-soaked potato to my own lips and partake of it? Just how far might love transport me? I remember wondering with a shudder, at once grateful to him for having inspired the question and resentful of him for being unable to answer it.

"Blessing . . . blessing . . . I have a feeling it needs to be a sacrifice. But I'm not sure. We can check," Trevor was saying, opening some reference book or other to the B's and becoming deeply enough distracted by something new he found on the page that I was able to climb the narrow stairway down from the booth and continue along the bridge without seeming to be in too much of a hurry to get away from his too-mellow grin. The trick was to take care never to get stuck shooting the breeze with Trevor when there was a barge approaching, for you might be there a quarter of an hour discussing Winston Churchill's favorite breakfast cereal before the drawbridge descended and set you free. Precisely this had happened once to me, and the scary thing was that I had liked it. I had imagined I might remain there happily forever, like Trevor himself, watching the tangerine-hued waters of the river drift past underneath and wondering why the barge and the current seemed to be moving at different rates of speed. I nearly sat down and looked it up in his reference book. *Rates of speed, barge, river,* I didn't know where to look, maybe there was a section entitled *Physics of Hydraulic Transportation.* Because Trevor's booth is midway down the Fox—not at one end where it opens into Lake Winnebago with its jumping, slapping, glittering fish, or at the other end where it empties into the smaller, grassier Lake Butte de Morts with its hidden, nesting cranes and screeching blackbirds—because his booth is midway along the river right where it skirts the cemetery, he doesn't even need to keep an eye out for boats. If one's coming, then the person in the next booth over gives him a buzz.

If blessedness means bathed in blood, sacrificial or not, then I suppose I am roundly blessed.

But even waking after surgery I never actually saw the

blood, only the dried flakes and unsatisfying postoperative smears already sterile with topical antiseptic, the bandages themselves never wine-red or even rosé but resolutely white and fresh. And the curved blade of the scalpel already bloodless and anonymous inside a drawer in a lab.

They might have thought to reserve just a little of my blood, enough for a sponge bath. Were I to ask him, perhaps Dr. Klink would reassure me that my excised parts at least were resplendent with it.

The doctor's own fingers, I imagine, like slender white candles in their translucent rubber gloves, must have been astral with it.

Though I suppose it wouldn't do.

To ask him to divulge such a thing.

He might be ashamed to have walked off luminously blessed while I lay on the table profane, unconsecrated, blotted too clean, crisscrossed with suture.

On the other hand the very idea might wound him, who having seen so many people tortured and dead in the war, might argue that the only blessing is when the blood is permitted to remain inside the body.

"And friends," he might wistfully add.

"Excuse me?" I'd ask.

"It's a blessing to have friends," Dr. Klink would say knowingly.

NEVER HAD I felt so blessed as when I sat in my living room the night of Martha's arrival with her on one side and Hercules on the other, the trio of us all pressed up against one another on my love seat like people in an airplane, snacking on cheese crisps Martha had brought from Seattle. Upright in a glass they resembled a bouquet of unopened buds shedding a faint, pollenlike dust of paprika.

Martha was doing most of the eating. Her style was to select three cheese crisps at once, offer the handful to me and to Hercules, and when we declined spread them all on a napkin open across her lap so her hands would be free to pour us some wine. The wine we never declined. My idea was to get really drunk for a change in hopes I might be able to ooze real tears like the poetry teacher Martha and I had in college, who wept every time the word *salt* appeared in a poem. *Salt of the earth, salt and pepper,* it didn't make any difference to him. But my tears would be more gratitude than salt. I knew how much they longed to sit together, Martha and Hercules, mother and son, who hadn't seen each other since August when Hercules left Seattle for his internship here. It hadn't been much longer than a month, but I remembered all the times I'd watched them sharing a single armchair, Martha sunk into the seat cushion and Hercules towering lightly and unimposingly above her on the arm, not indecently intimate for mother and son but envi-ably glad to be able to press shoulder to hip if they wanted, Martha burying her nose against the fabric of Hercules's shirt sleeve and Hercules not minding, and not pulling away, and pretending to humor her although we knew he really liked it. And now here they were, knowing how much I needed their comfort, sitting apart from each other on either side of me, not touching each other. It made me gladder than ever to be slen-der enough that they were still only inches apart. If I did start to cry, I wondered, upon whose shoulder would I lay my head? On whose shoulder would I wipe my snot and tears? Martha had gained a little weight since I'd come midwest. She would never be fat, I still believed, for her overeating was only part of a greater hyperactivity, but her flesh these days had a certain quiver that made her clothing flash around it.

"So tell me more about this drug Ziphrain," Martha requested for the third time that evening. Hercules stood up and made for the kitchen where he busied himself in the preparation of a sandwich to be brought out to the balcony. He did this so gracefully that it was impossible to know whether he made himself scarce because he was tired of hearing how Ziphrain combated nausea or because he knew that Martha and I wanted time alone together. It was just as it should be, the two of us watching him step over the balcony threshold as easily as if he didn't know how broad in the shoulders he was, the plaid of his shirt winking as he made for the railing, then leaned into the darkness over the courtyard so his hair parted just so above the whiteness of his neck where the collar revealed it. He was munching a pickle. How contemplative he looked. Both of us could tell he'd be a contemplative kisser, the kind whose face hovered over his kisses and peered meditatively into the eyes of his partner while his mouth bestowed small messages on hers. Both of us knew for certain that his lover, if he ever did break past his amorous reserve and find one, would make us nostalgic for a beauty we'd never had ourselves. Martha was too sloppy to be beautiful, while I was too composed. If I was the horizon, and Martha the precipitous coast, then Hercules's rightful lover would be the cool, deep, radiant water surging in between.

"I can't believe that young man came out of my body," Martha said, and let her head flop toward mine while I inclined mine carefully toward hers. It was difficult to drink our wine in that position without pouring any down the fronts of our shirts but we managed even to loop arms and say cheers and sip from each other's glasses. Then when both our glasses and the bottle were empty we shared Hercules's left-behind wine as well. Each sip was sharp with the flavor of raisins, if we let it pool up on our tongues without swallowing and just waited for it to dissolve. Because Martha was not ordinarily the silent type, I thought she must be getting drunk, she was so quiet, but then she reached forward for the very last cheese crisp and twirled it so craftily between her fingers that I realized she must be pondering something. Or scheming. Yes, she was scheming, I could see it in the tilt of her dark head and in a certain broodiness poised round her temples under the shadows cast by her hair. Pretty soon Hercules came in off the balcony carrying his empty plate as levelly as if there were still a sandwich on it. In the kitchen he hung around rinsing and drying for what seemed like an awfully long time until Martha finally extricated herself from our somnolent embrace and joined him. That's how I knew he was in on it, too. I could practically hear them not-talking in there, not-saying to each other whatever it was they both wanted to be saying and then running the water too long in the sink and rolling shut the top of the bread bag with too much of a crackle so they could whisper their plan. So clumsy was their conspiracy that it insulted me to think that I wasn't expected to be able to notice it.

In exasperation I blurted, "This idea that people with cancer don't want to talk about it is ridiculous not to mention humiliating. Do you think I'll forget the prognosis if only the people around me are kind enough never to mention it? Do you think I'm such a lousy mathematician that I'd believe you if you found something cheerfully optimistic to say about ten percent odds?"

It's not ten percent odds. It's ten to twelve percent, Isobel, I expected them to reply. But thankfully they didn't. Instead they looked so relieved, that I forgave them everything. It seemed my tirade must have been part of their plan all along, and their clumsy secrecy a ploy to make me forego my customary patience at least for a second. Then, having lost my temper, I was ready for the kick and didn't reel with what they said, just leaned back in my love seat and thought about it. They spoke in repetitive, musical cadence, one of them taking the high notes, the other the low, one of them pausing while the other leapt forward, an orchestration intended to allow me to ponder the soulful logic of their position. Anyway I wasn't arguing just yet. My very willingness to hear them out made me wonder if maybe I'd been thinking the same things myself, only too deep down to know it. If with chemotherapy my chances of surviving the next five years were just ten to twelve percent, then did I really want the chemo at all? Wouldn't chemo only disappoint me? If I was so likely going to die anyway, then did I want to spend my last months wallowing in nausea, besieged by fatigue, shot through with armies of pills, injections, spoonfuls, IVs, dashed hopes?

Or, if I was so likely to die anyway, and if death was after all as much a part of life as birth, then mightn't I prefer to proceed in peaceful awareness with only painkillers and sleeping aides to help me through the experience if necessary, and Martha and Hercules to brew me cups of tea and broth, and cheer me with ingeniously mixed drinks—beer mixed with lemonade, iced tea whisked with raspberry nectar along with a half-shot of vodka—so I would remain in normal measures dreamy and practical and dozey but as alert to my own dying as I could possibly be?

I said I didn't know. I said it seemed too early to give up on a cure even for the sake of having *an experience.* I said if they wanted me to commit suicide then why didn't they just get me drunk and hand me a loaded gun and stick me alone in a room with a sad movie. I said I wondered how much their position was influenced by their fear of getting stuck rinsing my bed pans and flipping me over in bed so I didn't get sores. I said I had no intention of allowing them to play Home Care Practitioner, anyway, so they could quit worrying about it. I said if they didn't value me enough to think I should do anything possible to save my life, then what were they doing taking up space in my apartment and why didn't Martha quit eating bread not to mention everything else forever if death was *as much a part of life as birth,* anyway.

When I was done with my tirade I stalked off into the bathroom. Funny to stalk off into the bathroom when there's a whole world out there ready to provide a more adventurous escape, but I had my reasons. It was the bathtub that beckoned me. Though the porcelain still glistened with the left-behind droplets of Hercules's shower, I climbed into it for a moment and shut my eyes. No pillows. No layers of quilting. No magazines. And no nausea, either. How pleasant it would be, to fall asleep there free of nausea, the toilet just a toilet and not a well in which I must throw myself face forward retching and gagging.

At least without the chemo your highs and lows will be yours and not some medical illusion. At least without the chemo you won't be fooled, tricked, deprived of the knowledge of what's really happening to you, their argument continued when I had rejoined them, Martha and Hercules no longer on opposite sides of me on the love seat but on the two chairs facing the coffee table so they might look straight at me, their elbows planted on their knees as they leaned more precipitously into the spiral of their argument and then flopping backward when they relented for a moment and paused as if reconsidering. But they didn't reconsider. Not really. *And at least if you're tired you'll be tired from the illness, not from the drugs, and if you sleep then your dreams will be made of the stuff of your logical, cautious, bemused, romantic mind and of your patient, meticulous heart, and if you waste away then what's left of you will still be human, not Cytoxan, Methotrexate, saline, and Compazine, and if you cry, then your tears will be what you've been waiting for all this time, real sobbing, wrenching grief for the world you'll be missing and for the world that will be missing you, and not just an overflow of synthetically induced anxiety, which by the way is the reason that you haven't been able to cry quite yet, Isobel, because you're not the self-pitying type, you'd rather wait till you're certain it's real sorrow that's making you cry and not indulgence or despair.*

Well into the night we debated. Martha lit some candles in the corners of the room and shut off the lights. Hercules put Cassandra Wilson on the stereo. *Blue Light 'Til Dawn,* just like honey from the bee, the volume high enough that we could make out the lyrics if we wanted but low enough that we could let them fade away. I hadn't realized my room was quite so austere, before Martha and Hercules set to work softening its edges. Martha untied her neck scarf and let it drop in a silk pool onto the carpet. Hercules unbuttoned the front of his shirt, flipped open the book on the coffee table to a painting of a grizzled old man and a straw-haired child drifting companionably in a row boat. Just as Martha and Hercules offered themselves to my room, blurring the boundaries between it and us, so they would offer themselves to my dying, blurring the line between illness and health, between sadness and humor, between sleepiness and wakefulness. They would be my nurses, my angels, my porters, my friends all at once.

"But without the Ziphrain, without the chemo, the cancer is likely to go to my brain. No matter what, I might be cabbage soup in no time," I reminded them, at first dumbfounded and then interested as if from a distance, as if the patient in question were someone other than myself for whom the prospect of a life ravaged by chemotherapy offering only a ten percent chance of survival, must be weighed against a few months of peaceful decline for which the chance of remission was zero.

"We won't let it get as far as cabbage soup," they both answered at once.

"Maybe cream of asparagus," said Martha, tonguing a breadstick.

"Vichyssoise," I ventured.

"Borscht," Martha answered.

"Cascadilla," I suggested.

"What's Cascadilla?"

"Cucumber pureed in yogurt and dill with buckets of cold tomato juice."

"That would be fine," Martha assented.

We fell into a dreamy reverie of menu-planning. If I was too sick to cook, Martha would make the soups. Hercules would learn to bake bread, but I would help with the kneading if I was bed-ridden and needed isometric exercise.

"Pronto, Herculeeze," I said.

But Hercules was scowling. He was timing our digression, tapping his foot impatiently to the too-indulgent rhythms of it, pulling out his pocket watch to see if the hands might by chance have started moving again. So rarely did he show judgment—in fact, I don't believe I'd ever seen him do it before, except in response to his own wrong note on the bass—that Martha and I both quit our imaginary ladling of Cascadilla and went back to the more pressing issue of what I would tell Dr. Klink in the morning when it was time to show up for chemo.

"What do you mean you won't let it get as far as cabbage soup?" I asked. "By what method of euthanasia do you propose stopping it? Smothering me under a loaf of biscuit dough? Weighing me down with books and throwing me into the river? Feeding me one too many glasses of Amontillado and sealing my bedroom with mortar?"

They were silent.

"Or does Dr. Klink advance a more medically palatable method? Have you already discussed this with him?" I asked. "Was it him, I mean he, I mean him, who put you up to this?"

They wouldn't say. Martha only bit her lip to refrain from commenting on my fastidious grammar.

I would have phoned Dr. Klink myself and asked him, if it weren't past three o'clock in the morning. I wasn't angry or chagrined, only curious to know what he and his spectral fingers thought. Maybe he, too, had read the newspaper articles about that woman whose multiple overdose of chemotherapy stripped her body of its insides and robbed her children of their mother. This, at one of the most reputable cancer institutes in the world at the hands of the most respectable doctors whose talents for innovative therapy unfortunately stopped short of the ability to count. Poor beautiful woman. I had seen her picture. Maybe Dr. Klink, too, had stared at it. Gazed at it. Sympathized with it. Hoped to gain some kind of courage from it. How intelligent she looked. How gracefully resolute. But the courage wouldn't come to me. Was it possible to have hope and optimism for a year or two of dying as well as for untold years of living? If death was after all a kind of adventure, then might I step toward it with as much curiosity and zeal and humbling vulnerability as if I were stepping into a love affair?

Maybe, yes, but the thing about love affairs was that when they were over, you were still around to feel safe but sorry about them. If dying were a love affair, then it must be the kind that had always eluded me; sublime, avid, and consuming.

"I do want my death to be my own," I ruminated. "But

reassure me, please. Tell me if I had even a fifteen or twenty percent chance of survival, you wouldn't be telling me not to do the chemo."

We wouldn't dream of telling you to forego the chemo if you had even a fifteen to twenty percent chance of survival, Martha and Hercules assured me over the hours in their accomplished harmony, their attention so focused that they didn't seem to notice we had emptied our third bottle of wine. *If we could make ourselves believe more in your living than in your dying, then we'd be talking you through the drugs rather than out of them. We love you, Isobel. We want you to be comfortable. But most of all we want you to be in possession of yourself, as much as you can be, for as long as you can be. We want to ease you, Isobel. Isn't there a hymn, about carrying someone over the water as if on a wave to the opposite shore? Or is that a Pete Seeger tune? But that's what we want, to be your wave, to be your cradle on the water.*

Hmmm, I responded. *Yes, no, maybe, but, if, what,* until it dawned on me suddenly that Hercules *knew.* Why I needed to be reminded of that over and over I can hardly imagine. There had even been little things in his childhood—the way at age six he rearranged the toys and furniture in his bedroom the week before the Christmas Martha gave him a train set, the way at seven, eight, and nine he sometimes poured us squat glasses of lemonade just at the moment we realized we were thirsty, the way once at age eleven when Martha brought him to visit he headed straight for my refrigerator, slid open the fruit bin, and while digging for a nectarine found one of the embossed leather buttons from my best jacket snagged on a pineapple—moments that Martha had attributed to his willful sensitivity but that by now I considered proof of his clairvoyance.

Of course he *knew,* and he would never urge the rejection of my one chance of survival if there was indeed a chance.

So, there wasn't.

So that was that. Within five years, probably less, I'd be part of the past, a face in an archive, a hand under glass, not ticking.

Chemo or not, Ziphrain or not, like it or not.

"Didn't Shakespeare have a sprite named Zero?" I wondered aloud.

"If he didn't, he should have," said Martha. "Or Naught would be a good name, too, for a sprite. Zero's wife, Naught. You want something to drink, Isobel?" because the sudden, crazy dryness of mortal fear must have flashed across my face. What I wanted was another glass of wine. And another and another. Had I ever been really drunk in my life? No, but it was time. Desperately I upended the bottle and thrust in my tongue as if maybe my eyes were deceiving me. There was only the sharp, woody perfume of raisins. Nothing wet enough to swallow. Zero. Naught. It wouldn't do to jump up for another bottle, not when we were so busy talking about the importance of my being "in possession" of my death. As if I might own it, zip it up in my pocket, walk away with it sober along a straight line. *That Isobel,* they'll exclaim, *she was always in control.*

"What are you thrumming your fingers on your knees about?" asked Martha from across the coffee table. At once it seemed terribly wide, that small table, an uncrossable distance, me on one side and my friends on the other.

"Nothing. Just everything," I answered.

"Everything. Just nothing," mimicked Hercules while taking off his shoes. Of course he didn't simply let them fall. In fact, they didn't touch the carpet, once his feet were free of them. Even while removing the second shoe, he let the first still dangle from his fingers, then laid them side by side across his knees as affectionately as if they were puppies.

"Actually what I'm thrumming my fingers on my knees about is I've never seen anyone petting their shoes," I said. "Also, they touch the carpet when you're wearing them. Why not let them touch the carpet when you're not?"

Hercules blushed. Martha shrieked at the sight of it. All of this was pure nostalgia, a replay of our version of The Three Stooges perfected when Hercules was coming of age, its most fertile moments arising from the slapstick of any boy's awkward adolescence; the broken voice especially, the gangliness, the sullenness, the sanctity and privacy of his bedroom. Most boys his age hung posters of rock stars and sports figures and movie stars on their bedroom walls; Hercules had draped his walls in remnants of crushed velvet to make it look like the inside of a guitar case. The girls would have loved it, if he'd had any over. His sole visitors were a computer whiz named Pete and a wandering, neighborhood dog that seemed to show up every Thursday and stayed the night. That Hercules suffered our amusement unscathed, that he had even sometimes indulged it, was evidence, we three agreed, of his firmness of character. But more than that, and this was something Martha and I didn't quite let ourselves realize until recently, Hercules's endless tolerance for our endless jesting depended on his knowledge of the complexity of our love for him and all its vulnerable understated parts—the hopeless romance mixed with the maternal affection, the mute sexual appraisal mixed with our respect for his changing body, our jealous apprehension of his vanishing childhood.

Hercules carried his shoes into the guest room study, which was still incompletely furnished. No place for Hercules to stretch out except on the floor. And Martha on the love seat. The fold-out couch was still at the upholsterer's, where somehow my instructions as to the alignment of color on the cushions had been reversed. Had Hercules even once consented to sharing my bed, I wouldn't have thought of what he and I were doing as "sleeping together," of course. I would have thought of it as "slumbering together."

From our place in the living room, Martha and I listened to the whine of the zipper on Hercules's duffel bag. It was some time before he came out again, carrying a pack of playing cards. We weren't card-playing types. The only card game I knew was Old Maid, a far cry from Bald Queen Butterfly, to be sure. I put my hand to my head, disappointed, yes, *disappointed,* to discover the hair still in place. Thickly coiled it was, and cool to the touch, and scented, glossy, and thick. But not regal, not a domed crown glittering with pride and silver teardrops. Nothing special, just an ordinary head of extraordinary hair. And the climate out the windows just an ordinary night, open and clear, no sudden pelting rain within hundreds of miles. Had it even happened, then? Had the telephone rung in the trunk of my car? Had the months flipped by? Had I been "in possession" of myself, when I'd had that call from Martha outside Mexico? Or had something else been in possession of me?

It was Solitaire Hercules was setting up to play. After catching my eye and shuffling and cutting the deck and shuffling again he reached for the top card and faced-up a queen, first thing.

It was the queen of hearts. She wore a coy, Mona Lisa smile.

I've never doubted the flexibility of the universe except with my streak of obligatory skepticism. But skepticism can go both ways, can't it? Just because I'm skeptical of the idea that something happened, doesn't mean I can't be equally skeptical of the idea that it didn't happen. Empiricism can go both ways. If you can't see something, does that mean it's not there? Or that it's invisible? "Why," I might ask myself, if I were a skeptic, "why should I suddenly find myself in my own altered future, done up in Rollerblades and false eyelashes with a bottle of Gatorade in one hand and in the other a misplaced museum file flapping in the breeze I kicked up on my bald-headed way to work?"

But just as easily I might ask myself, "Why shouldn't I?" while recalling the philosophic figure eight. If every gesture includes its own opposite, then for every Isobel Albright lying weary and bruised in her bed, thirsty with too much sleep, there's a Bald Queen Butterfly waiting none too patiently for the arrival of two screaming, mewling, diapered, tortilla-scented babies.

But when would it happen again? I wondered. Soon? Weeks? Months? Never? Or had I only to snap open the trunk of the car, or the lid of the compact safely stowed on the spice rack, to find myself inside my impossible future again?

Just then Hercules flipped over a second card with such

determination I felt the gust of air it made. It was the queen of clubs, her eyelids sultry as if with the heat of a summer's day.

The third and fourth cards were queens as well.

Not one of them was bald, but they wore the most elaborate capes like colorful, folded wings.

Martha was oblivious to these oracular cards. She was dozing in her chair, only every few minutes she'd stretch awake in order to implore me once again.

"You'd be wretched with the chemo," she'd plead. "You look so pure tonight, Isobel. You look like Ingrid Bergman in *Casablanca*. You look airbrushed. You're all lit up. You look like a slow dissolve."

"I'm not dead yet, Martha," I finally retorted.

"But you will be," she answered, and fell back asleep.

It was then that I decided to cancel the chemo and enter my friends' truthful embrace.

11

Day after day, the little compact on the spice rack in the kitchen let me down.

The telephone in the trunk of the car did, too.

At lunch break, when the staff and volunteers and visiting consultants gathered for their donated Subway sandwiches on the big lawn beside the burned-out museum, I snuck away from their disheveled picnic, along a flooded, broken hallway where we were not allowed because the hallway hadn't been there the day before the fire; it was a miracle of fallen ceiling panels and heat-blown drywall. Then out I ducked through a side door and behind the straight trunks of the oaks so I might make it unseen to my car. Was I practicing to be a ghost? No. Not exactly. But I didn't want anyone stopping me and urging me to breathe deeply and be human, either, forcing upon me platefuls of food the way they do to a hostess at her own party. I wasn't hungry for food. I only hungered for my future. But while crossing the parking lot to my car I was likely to come upon David weeping in the open doorway of the shed where the air didn't smell of smoke but of ordinary, summery, garden-type rot, his face so openly, beseechingly exposed to the gazes of swallows and spiders and slugs that I nearly told him I was dying but that everything else was going to be perfectly alright. He wouldn't have believed me. In the face of disaster, poor David had no more patience for illness than for hopefulness. To his mind we were in war time and any dream of normalcy was frivolous and doomed, as if half the world were entombed beneath shards of Tiffany lamp, which then would need to be removed carelessly in great shattering handfuls instead of piece by piece as we were removing it now, each col-

ored glass fragment wrapped gingerly in newspaper, num-
bered, labeled, and layered in a wine crate marked *Tiffany* to be
carried off sadly as if there were a little girl named Tiffany
lying splintered inside it. No, were I to tell him what I knew—
that by the time the leaves had fallen we'd be sheltered in a row
of comfortable trailers, and that the smell of smoke at last
would have dissipated and that the intermittent rains of black
confetti would have ceased blowing, and that order, such as it is
when chaos is the order of the day, would have been restored,
he would not have believed me. Very likely he would have
made some of his Republican-sounding noises about commit-
ting me to the mental hospital, on six lakeside acres of yellow-
ing willows and waving, feathery poplars. There was a
locked-up boathouse and a vine-shrouded gazebo left over
from the more romantic days when the hospital had still been
called the Insane Asylum, that I knew about only because I
used to canoe the periphery with a man I wasn't quite dating.
At the time I'd considered these full-moon canoe trips a big
adventure, but now I remembered them for the way the tall
lake grasses whispered against the aluminum side of the canoe
as we drifted past with our eyes closed. Now I wished we'd had
enough gumption to beach ourselves on the rocks, strip off our
clothes, and cavort arm in arm among the thorns of the rose
garden, pretending to be eloping inmates. Looking back, all
the sanest moments of my past were marked by the fact that if
only I'd had the urge, I could have done something at least
impetuous, breaking up with him by tipping over the canoe
instead of never quite getting together with him in the first
place, for instance. Not even yesterday, when I'd driven with
Martha to an American Cancer Society showroom and spent
hours looking at the rows of rubber, fabric, and plastic prostheses—not even then had I managed to be in the least bit daring.
Some of the fake breasts had nipples, some didn't, and though I
could have gone one size bigger just for the hell of it or experimented with a fuller, more matronly model or surprised everyone with something pert and sweetly tilted, designed to be

worn braless under a clingy blouse, I didn't. And though I could have purchased a whole variety of breasts with aureoles in all sizes and hues, like accessorized sunglasses, I didn't. In the end, depressed, I bought nothing at all, so Martha made me two breasts out of a pair of shoulder pads I'd snipped from a dress. For nipples, we sewed on two protruding halves of snaps. I didn't tell her about Bald Queen Butterfly, about the way Bald Queen Butterfly's resolutely flat chest reigned under lycra and jewelry, or what I thought about each day when I snuck home from work—the little envelope of saffron on the spice rack next to the compact—its exoticism, its rarity, its expense, the illogic of the spice's discovery. To think that long ago somebody had plucked the tiny sexual parts off a crocus and crumpled them experimentally onto a bowl of rice or had simply, thoughtlessly, eaten a spoonful of stew onto which the wind had deposited a single, fine orange grain, was enough cause for wonder that I saved myself from having to meditate more directly on the powder in the compact. The more I thought of the makeup, the more magic I expected of it, the less it might deliver. So instead I envisioned spoonfuls of pungently scented curries and raitas, chutneys and steaming pakoras, resolving that no matter how great my disappointment I might still escape from the sickroom into the kitchen and prepare a feast for Martha and Hercules if not for myself.

BUT THE LITTLE compact let me down, and so did the phone in the trunk of the car.

Day after day after day.

Having snapped open the compact and taken hold of the shiny, leathery puff and applied it to my face, I peered into the tiny rectangle of mirror and saw only my expectations wearing thin under too much makeup.

And day after day having snapped open the lid of the trunk of my car and lifted hopefully the receiver of the old black telephone, I heard only a quiet like the quiet of a conch shell and once the tricky buzz of a housefly trapped in the tunnels of the looped, black spiral of cord.

Nothing else.

No thunderstorms, even.

No escape.

And I was getting sicker. Just a hint of fatigue, a suggestion of pain, though the pain wasn't painful, exactly, if such a thing is possible.

I had noticed this before, years ago when I'd sprained my ankle, how the pain spread upward in undulating waves that by the time they reached the top of me weren't waves of pain anymore but waves of endorphin. Pain as its own painkiller. Panic as its own barbituate.

Did this make me a masochist?

I didn't think so.

I hoped not.

When I asked Dr. Klink if he thought I might be in shock, he said not conventionally so. My pulse rate was normal, my blood pressure normal, my temperature only slightly elevated, my skin pale but not drained, my cheeks actually even a little flushed. But he joked there was something electric about me, as if I'd managed somehow to apply my own electroshock therapy.

"During thunderstorms, are you in the habit of attracting bolts of lightening?" he asked.

"No," I said.

"Do you get a jolt from the first thing you touch after walking across shag carpet?"

"Not often. Sometimes in winter."

"Do people wince when you shake their hands?"

"I don't usually shake hands. I realize I should, of course, given my position, at business meetings and such, at conferences; come to think of it I'm always a little embarrassed by the fact that I don't shake hands. Why do you ask?"

"Does your hair stand on end when you wake up in the morning?"

"No."

"Then I guess you're just lucky," he said.

"Under the circumstances, you mean," I said.

"Isobel," he said sternly.

I have mentioned his slightness, the precisely angled shadows of his Cambodian face, but the sudden gravity that seemed to permeate the whole, tiny room when he furrowed his brow in stern supplication was something I'd never noticed. We were in the consultation room of his office. Unlike most doctors he had no desk but a paper-laden table so narrow that when he set his elbows down between us I could have taken a drink of his spritzer—raspberry, this time, not Cranapple as usual. And so often had he been on the verge of touching me when we were not in the process of an examination, so often had his fingers very nearly brushed against mine, that I was not surprised when the lip of his bottle grazed my temple, like the muzzle of a wet gun. "Isobel," he said, "no matter what I say to you, from now on it's always *under the circumstances*. Understood?"

"Understood," I answered, my pulse faintly audible in my temple under the hush of the rim of the bottle that was so like the moist hush of the jungle in which he'd been separated from his parents during the war. Was he thinking about this, too? Was he remembering his fear? Was he giving it—bequeathing it—to me? The dense foliage below the canopy, the damp shadows gnawing on the undersides of the leaves, the story he'd told me about what happened the day his family reached a bridge. It was a high, rickety structure which his grandmother couldn't cross.

"Shoot me," she'd said to her son, my doctor's father. "If you don't shoot me, we'll none of us ever get out."

"I can't shoot you," he'd pleaded.

"Then bury me alive."

"I can't bury you alive."

"Then have the child shoot me."

So Dr. Klink, at age nine, was handed the gun while his

grandmother knelt on the spongy-as-if-weeping ground. I'd waved his words away when he got to this part. It was too horrible to hear. Artifacts I could have handled. A gun, a slender bullet, his grandmother's cloth shoe, even a lock of her bloodied, blessed hair I might have rescued from oblivion and taken pains to honor, preserve, and display. But his story was too fierce to lay at rest behind sheets of glass.

"You had to shoot your own grandmother?" I asked, then gestured at his answer before he could speak it, shooed it off like a bird that now flapped above us. Was he bequeathing them to me, the black wings of that harsh, squawking, predatory animal? My friend, Trevor Close, feared birds, since he'd observed the Caspian terns hunting fish north of the drawbridge. Terns dive bomb, he'd said. They're like winged, mindless daggers. It was the mindlessness that so disconcerted him, he'd said, going back to his book, turning the tissue-thin pages.

"Your circumstances, too," I said to the doctor after a considered moment.

"Excuse me?"

"Everything we say, it's under your circumstances, too, not just mine," I said.

"Game point," said the doctor from across his narrow table.

EVEN SO, it wasn't the bird of fear from which I longed to escape. Or from the gust of its wings, or from the black flapping odor of feathers.

No. There was nothing I longed to escape from, for my escape was not *from* but *to.*

I wanted those babies. I could practically taste the backsides of their knees, the fat, creased milkyways of sweat and baby powder. And I could practically see their two Mexican faces melting in tears and laughter around every corner, at the end of every road. Where were they? When were they coming? Would they have cut their first teeth yet? Would they have started to roll over, sit up, crawl backward the first time, forward the next? Or would Martha let me down again? I longed even to change their diapers, get yellow shit on the tips of my fingers, wipe us both clean on those moist towelettes. I didn't want to be their mother, exactly. No, not me! What would be the point, when my parents weren't around to be the doting grandparents I had always believed they wanted so much to be?

Perhaps, in place of motherhood, finding a new lover would have to satisfy me, I thought.

But even having a lover would miss the point were I not draped in the garb of Bald Queen Butterfly. I needed a man who would lick the whole dome of my skull with little spirals of desire, then plant his wet kisses unflinching along my scars, then slide his fingers tantalizingly among the petals and whorls of my costume jewelry but know enough not to remove it. Also, if he didn't ask where I'd been if I'd decided to go Rollerblading along the river at midnight would be a help. And if he didn't read the sports pages. If there was anything Bald Queen Butterfly didn't want it was the sight of her own boyfriend mouthing the headlines of the sports pages and getting jealous if the only thing she wanted from a basketball game was a good, long, languorous look at Dennis Rodman acting bored and divine in his birthday suit of sweat.

Such a lover would not be spotted on the spur of the moment. Maybe never. In the meantime, just to lift the receiver of the 1940s telephone and hear the Spanish-speaking operator requesting another few pesos would have been enough. Just to feel the bold, new heart of my remission swelling under my flat chest would have been enough, or to feel a single rain drop falling out of nowhere, or to witness a fresh laugh line twitching itself into being on the side of my no longer too-patient mouth.

But there was nothing.

Nothing, except that almost imperceptibly, I grew just a little sicker, just a little more tired. Was that a yellow tinge I noticed in the whites of my eyes?

•   •   •

SEPTEMBER passed in all its ordinary ways. Leaves started turning, geraniums still bloomed on the balconies across the courtyard, flocks of goldeneye paddled the river. I had a terrible fear, that all the time that was left to me might pass in just this way, in the way it had passed for eons—gracefully, methodically—when what I wanted was to cling to a precipice of time, losing hold and regaining it again and again. In a fit of imaginative yearning one day, I even skipped powdering my face, and powdered the soles of my bare feet, instead. My feet were exhausted, with stasis or sickness I didn't know which. I imagined maybe if I dusted them with the strange fairy powder they might take me to a place I'd never been, or at the very least, conjure the neon green wheels of a fresh pair of in-line skates.

But the cosmetic only tickled and left a set of ghostly footprints on the carpet. I followed them. They took me right back to the spice rack in the kitchen and to the little drawer where I stowed the index card of blurred, impossible years. I took the card from the drawer along with a pen and wrote a daring *2001*. That would make me forty-six years old. Nothing happened, except the card seemed to blanch with pale indignation and when I retrieved it a day later the number was gone, a smudge like the others.

So I went back to work, day after day after day, without having eaten a bite of lunch. Working seemed the only thing to do. They needed me there; my famous common sense, my reliable ingenuity. When the crew of autumn gardeners showed up as if we were business as usual, I put them to work erecting a snow fence to keep out onlookers and adventurous children. And it was I who pressed Insurance for money for the trailers and I who determined, in the face of David's pessimism, to write a grant to the city in order to hire a registrar to catalogue the losses from the fire. In preparation I asked Hercules to photograph the salvaged artifacts, beginning with the remnants of doll clothes, the stiffened fragments of velvet and muslin and lace, the stained, rescued aprons and lone, pleated cuffs. So when the Crazy Volunteer cornered me one evening on the flagstone of the entryway where the museum's entire foyerful of ornamental houseplants stood neglected in the torn shade of the awning, and handed me a battered, nineteenth-century, scalloped umbrella, I assumed it belonged to one of the dolls. I popped open the umbrella to shake out the grime, and it was then that the rain started crashing past me in a blinding torrent.

12

The year was 1997. I was forty-two years old. The rain, that sudden deluge, fell with a whooshing, slamming persistence as if with the full weight of the sky chasing after it. Like a shale cliff the gray water broke and tumbled, in great, flat sheets that slammed from above, but thankfully not on me. Somehow the storm seemed cognizant of me and my umbrella, for the water didn't land directly on the threadbare silk webbing among the bent elbows of the spokes but instead cleared a space in which I was safe from the ceaseless pounding.

Even so, dry and upright, I wasn't at peace.

I was looking for someone.

Who?

I didn't know. I tried to stifle my confusion by gazing for a minute at my unfamiliar shoes. They were yellow high-top sneakers with rubbery, fashionable, two-inch heels that stood their ground near the flashing sheets of water.

"Nora! Evvy!" I cried.

Those were the names of the Mexican babies. I knew this as soon as the cries left my mouth. Also, that they were no longer exactly entirely Mexican anymore and not really babies but little square-built, top-heavy toddlers who rocketed to and fro and whirled and rolled and shrieked and giggled and cartwheeled and then suddenly grew limp and warm and fragrant as dumplings before sinking into a mewling sleep while sucking on each others fingers. Watching them somersaulting around I had once remarked to Martha that the only thing that kept our little girls pitching ever forward on the balls of their feet instead of flopping facedown on the ground was the sheer push and pull of their curious desire to run away from each other and then turn around and crash delightedly together before losing contact again, like pool balls. Now they'd dropped into the pockets of the table of the earth, out of sight. Beneath me the black Vibram soles of my sneakers swiveled and turned a full halting circle marked by the spin of the scalloped umbrella. I'd been wrong about the rain. No storm, however fierce, could be the cause of so much water. And behind me was dry—a rough-hewn tunnel with a floor of dense bottle glass tinted a smoky amethyst color on either side of which the walls curved upward into an archway of booming, echoing stone. Nearby a tourist read aloud from a placard announcing that the water falling past the opening of the tunnel reached fifteen feet across from inside to out. A broken dam of wet noise.

Niagara Falls, I realized.

On the Canadian side of the border.

That's how long it took me to figure out where I was.

"Martha!" I cried.

And why we had come there, Martha and me and Nora and Evvy and our twin diaper bags and the two mixed-up bottles of apricot nectar of which the soft twiddle of the artificial nipples still made me so jealous I wanted to cry. Even queenly and bald and glorious as a butterfly, I still turned to mush if I so much as grazed the tip of one of those nipples with my finger. I felt the miniature twang of it all down the length of my spine, at once familiar and forever impossible, for the very peculiar delight of the nipple was something I would never feel again. Still those sweet droplets of juice on the rubbery buds of the bottles reminded me always that I was a mother after all, and that we were a family, strange but true. Martha, who'd found a paying job writing catalogue copy for the museum, had rented the apartment down the hallway from mine, while Hercules, in his drafty apartment on Congress Street, was never far away. But we had left him behind to make this trip to Ontario, where Martha had a yearning to see the shoe museum in Toronto, and I to skate the miles of jagged paved trail along the lip of the Niagara River Gorge. It was a beautiful, precipitous, dangerous trail on which I might lose control at any dip or turn and catapult downward and forever while thinking how glorious it was to be alive. I felt reckless, pure, and invincible. Funny I'd never felt that way before, but now that the cancer was over and done, I felt it again and again, while rocking the babies in their giant stroller, or while cooking a meal or reading a book or having a bath or doing anything that seemed perfect for the moment, like when Martha and I talked about what we missed about men, for neither of us had had a lover in a while. Tongues and desire and company and solace and playfulness and someone who within five minutes of your having told him your dreams when you woke in the morning would forget every one of them, and someone who while you nuzzled into the fuzzy stink of an armpit would sing little off-key bits of BoDeans songs while pretending to be asleep, and someone who watched TV while you read books and who felt so proud after folding the laundry you wanted to pummel him with kisses and hugs. That's what we missed, Martha and I, with a slow, patient thirst that we hoped the abundance of Niagara Falls might begin to satisfy. In the meantime, at least we had Nora and Evvy, and Nora and Evvy had their Uncle Hercules.

Not until we reached Toronto air space had the girls realized Hercules wasn't coming with us, at which Evvy screamed and Nora comforted her by stroking her curls and offering to eat Evvy's granola bar. Evvy said yes. Nora gave her the wrapper for safe keeping, and ate both granola bars, hers and Evvy's in alternating bites, while Evvy watched with perplexed, quiet gratitude. That was the beauty of twinship; they didn't know yet where one ended and the other began. Together, they were delighted by all of the noise and commotion of Niagara. Then, terrified. Then, delighted again.

And now, lost.

Both of them. In my mind, when I tried to see them, tried to imagine where they might be so I might find them and save them, I pictured them winking like soap bubbles, two fragile, bobbing globes in a torrent of twisting wet light.

"Evvy! Nora!" I cried, my voice itself lost in the rush of the falls. No one around me seemed to hear. "Have you seen two baby girls?" I stopped one sightseer after another, each of whom seemed to go out of their way so as not to have to imagine, as I had, the two tiny, pudgy bodies crushed in the gorge. Martha was upstairs in the gift shop looking at linen tea towels, I suddenly recalled. She liked them for lining bread baskets at supper and breakfast time. And lunch. And for snack time while she read and answered mail and needed something to wipe the crumbs off her fingers. Oh Martha! Her earth-motherly plumpness was turning to fat, after all. I remembered this as I was screaming for the children. Funny the way everything seemed to be happening at once, the way my new memories of all the skipped-over years still didn't distract me from what needed most to be done. Martha was fat. Yes. "Nora! Evvy!" Probably not buying tea towels at all but boxes of shortbread. Maybe the girls were with her! Evvy was pudgy all over, Nora smooth with a layer of baby fat sweet as icing. But the more I thought of it the more certain I was that Martha had left the tunnel by herself and headed alone for the escalator where the guides doled out the yellow rain ponchos. The children were wearing those crackly ponchos. From behind, they would resemble all the other children who had come to see the undersides of the falls.

"Nora! Evvy! Evvy! Nora!" I cried, rushing from tunnel to tunnel not daring to look at the metal grates at the ends, beyond which the water crashed past the archways. Surely the bars were close enough together then not even a monkey could have made its way between them. But they didn't reach all the way to the ceiling. I could see no yellow rain-ponchoed toddler balanced precariously on top of them. Nor any torn-off steamers of yellow plastic. "Martha!" Perhaps they *were* with her. But what if she arrived from the gift shop this minute bearing presents for both of them, then collapsed when she saw that they weren't with me? She wouldn't scream, she wasn't the type, she might simply dissolve in a puddle of scarves and skirts. The girls were not in either of the tunnels. They weren't in the elevators, weren't in the rest rooms, weren't in the too-cramped carpeted display area where guides controlled the flow of sightseers down to the underground.

"Have you seen two little girls aged two and a half, one with her hair in braids?"

"No, but if I do I'll let you know."

"Have you seen two little girls aged two and half, one with red curly hair?"

"No. Did you look in the elevators? When I was a little girl I once got stuck in an elevator."

"Have you seen two two-year-olds in those yellow ponchos?"

"No. Are they yours?"

"Have you seen two little girls?"

"No. Are they lost?"

"Did you see two little girls on this stairway?"

"No, but I saw a boy. Not so little. About ten years old. Sorry."

My new sneakers, the part of me that seemed to be most in charge of my search, were no longer as dependable as they'd been just a moment before. As if they didn't want to leave the building, then did, then didn't, fearing the children were still inside and then fearing they were out, the shoes kept bringing me ever closer to the entryway but then circled me back to the tunnels, the steps, the elevators, the entryway again, until finally they followed the revolving doorway all the way around twice before emerging outside onto the flagstone terrace. No sooner was I out there than I dashed for the wall overlooking the explosion of water, hoping to take in every inch of the scenery at once—the barge that had got itself stuck on the flat plane of rapids just a half mile short of the drop-off, the twisted limbs of the trees that somehow grew from the rocks in the frothing kettle of spray, the blunt clouds low over the New York horizon, the way the water fell yellow in some places and in some places blue and in certain, fond angles an impossible turquoise and at the bottom the pink snow still clinging to the gates of the boathouse where the sightseeing boat was moored. Gulls swooped crazily amid the sliding walls of water like shrapnel after a bomb. Earlier in the day, I had wondered how many birds died down there, struck by a droplet with the force of a thrown brick, and whether Trevor Close had ever seen anything like it and how many dead fish were snatched up by the minute to be replaced by new ones, and what kinds of fish they were and whether the water was pure or polluted and why it was that of the hundreds of tourists strolling the paved overlook and plunking coins into the telescopes and posing for photographs, only two, yes, only two, were kissing! A Japanese man and a Japanese woman, dressed identically in red cardigan sweaters and baggy blue jeans and shiny black penny loafers. Their kiss was not passionate. They appeared to be crushing their mouths together obligatorily, like two hands evenly matched in a round of arm wrestling. Still, I was jealous of the very idea of kissing, even though I'd turned down the four men who since my remission from cancer had shocked themselves by falling in love with a bald woman. They'd stood quiveringly as blossoms, wishing I might land on them and pollinate. One was a medical anthropologist who on frequent visits to Japan had been served not raw fish but nuggets of raw chicken to be dipped into mustards and sauces. Having told me that Japan was among the most rigidly conventional societies in the world, he then assured me that I didn't have to worry about ever being served raw chicken because no one in Japan would invite a bald woman into their home, not to mention someone who'd had a mastectomy, not to mention someone who'd had cancer. Then he asked me to accompany him on his next trip. I said no thanks, proudly. I had no fake hair, no fake breasts, so I'd have no fake love affairs, either. The only fakery I went in for was eyelashes.

"Evva! Norry!" I cried, my tongue as frantic and confused as the rest of me. How amazing it was, another memory I had, that came to me at that very moment, of the way Martha and I had taken pains to childproof the toilet. Kids drowned in toilets, pulled themselves over the rim and peered too far in. Household accidents being the primary cause of death among young children, we purchased a special suction-cupped toilet lock just difficult enough to open that I had once, in an emergency, been forced to use the potty. There was a clamp on the refrigerator, too, and little locks on the faucets so Nora wouldn't stick her mouth under the flow of water and drink herself breathless like a turkey in a hard rain. Evvy wasn't the type to suck straight from the faucet, but she was a climber. "Household accidents are the primary cause of death among young children," I said to myself, as if this lessened the probability of anything terrible happening so far from home. When the girls had first arrived from Mexico, Martha in tow looking as if it were she who'd been kidnapped and not the other way around, they were stockier and more mature than I'd expected, Nora already toddling at ten and a half months, Evvy crawling behind. But for days they would not leave the kitchen. Though we set up a crib in the guest room/study complete with a stuffed pig that played "To Market, to Market" when its key was wound, the girls howled every time we urged them out of sight of the refrigerator. The pediatrician had no advice. Dr. Klink, speculating that they might both be remembering how hungry they'd been in Mexico, starved maybe, especially in the weeks after their mothers were killed by the van and they had to scavenge in the maze of the court system before Martha rescued them, brought his wife over to give us advice. She was stocky and plump, her skirt and blouse a medley of unmatched colors and patterns like those of many Hmong women. She wore white pumps, and had fastened a giant plastic daisy into her tight knot of hair. Dr. Klink and she spoke in Hmong, and I was touched and impressed that out of such a strange mixture of exotic sounds should come the advice: Fill two wax paper bags with a handful of Corn Chex, Rice Chex, and Wheat Chex, then safety pin one bag to the undershirt of each girl so she can carry it with her wherever she goes.

Don't use plastic bags, they're a choking hazard. And don't tie them around the babies' necks or collars even with those edible candy necklaces. And don't use paper lunch bags; if the girls drool, the paper will disintegrate.

"I didn't know you spoke Hmong with your wife," I said later to Dr. Klink.

"She's not terribly fond of English," he answered with an ironical smile.

As if waxed paper bags of Chex cereal had been precisely what the girls had been trying to ask for all along, they beamed delightedly when we pinned the bags to their T-shirts and with a great show of relief began clamoring to get out of the apartment altogether, slapping the sliding glass balcony doors with the Chex-smeared palms of their spit-covered hands. How tenderly Nora reached into Evvy's bag, how clumsily Evvy reached into Nora's, always discarding the wheat in favor of rice and corn. Our carpet was littered with the crushed, woven squares. Which came first, Martha and I wondered later? The way the girls bounced off each other in their forays around the room? Or their curious insistence on nibbling food out of each other's bags? And was it altruism or selfishness that inspired them to do this? We didn't know. There was so much we didn't know. We should have written every second of every minute of every day in a journal. We should have taken more pictures, purchased a video camera, turned on the tape recorder every evening at bath time so we would never forget the noise of their splashing. But now we would *need* to forget, for how could we bear to recollect their wild bath times once their pummeled-clean bodies had been claimed by the falls?

"Evva! Narthie! Mora!" I cried. If only I still looked like the old Isobel Albright, everyone would come rushing over to see what they could do to rescue me.

Perhaps it was because I was bald that people remained unchagrined by my terror. Maybe they thought I was one of those exuberant people who go around singing opera to themselves. Or perhaps I just looked too good, too strong, too powerful, for anyone to imagine there might be something really bad happening. I'd been told by one of the men (a plumber) who turned wistful as flowers at the sight of me, that the tiers of dangling necklaces I draped around my collarbone, head, and forearms, served not as adornment but rather as proof that I was worthy of adornment—noble and pure and free of disease and happier than anyone had a right to be.

How I hated that word *disease,* for I had always felt *at ease* except when I was sickest from chemo. I told this to the plumber the day I refused him. To Martha I said that he left with a "wrenching sigh," but the joke only made me feel lonely. Odd, how my few bursts of romantic loneliness seemed to reside in my scars, which smarted like the patches of flesh left behind after Band-Aids have been yanked off.

"Household accidents are the primary cause of death among young children," I repeated to myself as I searched for the girls, my worried gaze trained on the parking lot, which looked nearly as dangerous as the water. Buses the size of blue whales stood so high off the ground that a two-year-old could walk upright among the wheels. From this distance, lined up in the lot, they resembled the trains we built for the girls out of chairs. We only did this when we visited Hercules in his drafty apartment, where in the absence of a normal assortment of furniture nearly a dozen folding chairs stood in for table, dresser, countertop, desk. There was even, on one chair, a miniature photo gallery of framed promo shots of his various bands and fellow musicians. If he knew we were coming, then he'd clear the chairs off and get them lined up like a train waiting at the station, but if we stopped by unannounced he let the girls gather the books and CDs and hairbrushes and apples and photos and folded T-shirts, and pile them up in a mountain in the middle of the room.

Perhaps they had wandered onto one of the buses in search of their Uncle Herky. They loved his long hair. They adored the places where his beard met the smoothness of bare flesh. They took great pleasure in caressing with their tilted faces the soft, plaid flannels of his shirts. They were frightened nearly to death the first time he took out the bass in their presence, both girls screaming inconsolably for nearly an hour even after he'd put it away.

The second time she saw the bass, Nora, who recently had learned to use the toilet, wet her pants where she stood whimpering in the doorway. Evvy had been napping. When she woke, climbed out of the stroller, and trundled in to find us, she flung herself into the safety of Martha's skirt. But then Hercules started to play. Nothing fancy. Just the sweet songs they already knew. "Twinkle, Twinkle Little Star" was the first, then "Ring Around the Rosie," then "Old MacDonald," then "Puff the Magic Dragon," "Baby Beluga," "Kookaburra," "Six Little Ducks," and "Comin' Round the Mountain." He didn't sing. He only made the bass sound as if it were singing, a little sadly at first, then with more hope, then with a kind of shy gusto as the children tiptoed closer, holding hands. Always respectful and solicitous of what they considered to be the instrument's moody but sentimental soul, the children still believed that the bass was some alien variety of living creature. Before leaving Hercules's apartment they wrapped their arms around the instrument's waist, gave it a hug, and whispered words of endearment. Sometimes, saying good-bye, they slipped into Spanish without seeming to know the difference. Now, if they were lost, if I never found them before one of the tour buses in whose backseats they'd fallen asleep carted them off to Newfoundland, then they would have taken with them their memory of their peculiarly wooden aunt, the shy one so in love with their Uncle Hercules that she wouldn't sing unless he was stroking her neck.

"Marthev! Ynor! Children! Where are they! Where *are* they! Oh help me, I can't find my babies," I pleaded with the driver of one of the buses, who sat in his driver's seat eating a bag lunch. But he rolled up the bag at once and stuffed it in a wedge of the steering wheel. Together we were off, up and down the aisles of first one bus and then another and another.

Between buses, the driver paused on the tarmac to gaze ever so quietly in the direction of the falls. I could tell he was wondering whether it had occurred to me that they might be in there. Already I'd described to him the girls' beautiful hair—Evvy's fluffy and curly with a hint of red, Nora's in a poky gathering of braids—as if we might find two *other* lost girls on the buses and wouldn't want to get them mixed up.

"Are you here with your husband?" he finally asked. "Maybe they're with him. Or is he looking for them, too?"

He scrunched his eyebrows again as he turned toward the water.

"With my friend, Martha," I told him. "Their other mother."

"Oh," he said.

"But we're not—"

"It doesn't matter," he said. "Is she looking for them, too? Over there?"

"I don't know where she is. I don't know what she's doing. Is there a bakery anywhere? I think in the gift shop was where she said she—"

"Well then, we'll go look for your babies in the gift shop," said the bus driver patiently with a touch of amusement at how silly and irresponsible I'd been not to have looked in the first place. Still, like most people, he was in such perplexed awe of my appearance that he bowed his head when I ushered him ahead of me along the narrow sidewalk, my scars burning with worry, my jewelry clinking at my brows like icicles of hair. The reason I hadn't sought out Martha, aside from the fact that my panic nearly made me forget to, was that I couldn't bear to see mirrored in her face the terror of my own. Above a fan of sassafras- and ginger-flavored candy canes she might burst into the tears I'd been holding at bay. And there was something else as well, some other, shameful reason I hadn't sought her out before. Simply, she would blame me, as she ought. For the rest of our lives, the loss of our daughters would be my fault, and we would both know it, and she would try not to say so but sometimes she wouldn't be able to help herself. At once I needed her help, her shared panic and horror, her anger, her blame, her sudden dash to the stone wall overlooking the drop-off. I rushed ahead of the driver, pushed open the gift shop door, saw the line at the cash register, and at the end of the line, Martha riffling through her wallet and at her knees—

At her knees, not even the two diaper bags with their bottles of apricot nectar. Not even a diaper. Not even a single dropped barrette or gnawed pretzel and not even a toy I'd never seen before, something the girls had picked up off the sidewalk and appropriated as their own, the way Martha and I had appropriated the babies themselves, come to think of it, a situation we'd grown adept at chalking up to a general sense of life's twists and turns and ambiguities and if no one else was perfect, why should we be?

Nothing is exactly black or white, we assured each other when beset momentarily by guilt or anguish. There are no guarantees, except that caprice is as natural a law as gravity. What's necessary is to cultivate a certain momentum, a certain resolve, a certain—

I slammed so precipitously past the line of shoppers waiting at the checkout that Martha didn't even see me before the force of my embrace overturned her wallet sending nickels and quarters and dimes all over the floor. They twinkled and spun, just like the bubbles my girls had become.

"Narvie! Mora! Ertha!"

"Isobel! What? What's the matter, Isobel! What happened?"

For I was weeping in her arms, as I hadn't wept in years. Never, as an orphan, had I shed a single tear, as if I feared that having started, I'd be unable to stop. The famous dam of courage and reserve had broken. Even my faith in the idea that life was wonderful no matter what happened, that merely being alive was more than enough, was broken.

Martha steered me through the door of the gift shop, all her unpurchased souvenirs still clutched in her arms. "Sit down," she was saying. "For God's sake, Isobel, what's wrong? But don't stop crying. Let it out, Isobel. You, of all people! Here, of all places! If only Herky could see this! Here. Sit down. Stay with the stroller. I'll go get some tissues. Anyway, I have to go to the bathroom. But here. Use this."

She handed me one of the linen tea towels emblazoned with an image of the first person ever to go down the falls in a barrel. My wailing was renewed. Around me in the foyer, at the shops, ticket counters, and snack bars, hummed the cruel air of commerce, people buying their tickets and hot dogs as if to suggest that since life was going to go on no matter what happened, there was no point in stopping it temporarily. In French and then in English the voice on the loudspeaker announced that a film was to be shown in five minutes. Maybe the children were in the theater. Maybe they had snuck into the projection booth. When Martha emerged from the rest room, I would run to her and tell her that the children were gone. In the hands of some molester or in the arms of the falls or in any case as frightened as only children can be and perhaps even separated by now from each other, Evvy alone in some dark, scary corner while Nora tumbled here and there searching and wondering. My babies. My beautiful, stolen, unbelievable babies. I could not stop crying even when I noticed them nuzzled together not six inches from my elbow in the side-by-side seats of the stroller.

They were fast asleep. Nora was drooling on Evvy's neck. Evvy's foot lay twitching in Nora's lap. They were not holding hands, but Evvy grasped one ear of the wind-up pig, and Nora the pink corkscrew tail.

What an ordinary turn of events this was. Parents lost sight of their children all the time, and panicked and imagined the very worst, and when they found them safe again felt relief just like mine, that was as shy as my worry had been at the beginning, and just as embarrassed. A full minute must have gone by before I got up the nerve to touch them. I placed the palm of one hand across both of their faces at once, then bent forward and kissed the spot where their chins met, then licked Evvy's bare knee while circling Nora's ankle with my thumb and forefinger. "Nora. Evvy," I whispered, and felt the timbre of the names reverberating in my scars exactly as I'd felt when I first held a bottle to the babies' suck, as if they were sucking the milk from my body.

But just to touch was not enough. I needed to wake them. I needed to nudge them out of their naps so they would start crying and we could console each other. When Martha emerged from the rest room both girls were in my arms and we were all three awash in tears. Through the blur I noticed with affection how frumpy Martha looked as she crossed the foyer. Not just fat, and no longer just Earth Motherly but downright frowsy. She was carrying my silly pink, scalloped umbrella; I must have dropped it in the rest room hours ago. Yes. Frumpy. She'd been growing frumpier for years but since we were such close friends, there were only isolated moments in which I could really see it. As she got nearer I took hold of the umbrella and wiped my tears in the threadbare folds.

13

And then just as suddenly, 1998. The little girls were nearly four years old, Martha weighed one hundred and sixty pounds on my bathroom scale and one hundred and fifty-eight and a half pounds on hers in her apartment down the hallway from mine and one hundred and twenty on Hercules's bathroom scale, which had been under a leaky sink in his drafty apartment when he moved in. On Hercules's scale, the little girls could stand tiptoe to tiptoe while clipping rainbows of plastic barrettes into each other's hair and still weigh less than a kitten. When he stood on my scale, Hercules liked to imagine that the small amount of weight lifting he accomplished while hoisting amplifiers onto truck beds and hauling speakers into bars was paying off. If Martha weighed herself on my scale on Monday, and on her scale on Thursday, and on Hercules's scale on Sunday, then she could trick herself into believing she was losing weight and thus treat herself to an excursion with the girls, dressing them in their matching embroidered Mexican dresses and taking them out to a Mexican restaurant for fried ice cream and honey. Although the assumption was that Martha's scale was correct and mine was high, by standing on mine I might imagine I still had my breasts. I couldn't bring myself to climb up on Hercules's scale, on which I weighed less than seventy pounds.

Like skin and bones.

Like a dead woman.

It brought back memories.

14

And then just as suddenly, 1999.

Dr. Klink and his wife and their five children, two grand-parents, and one uncle shared a small yellow house on Bong Court not far from the hospital. A vegetable patch crisscrossed by a network of ridges of turned soil on which could be seen the imprints of Mrs. Klink's knees, took up the entire front yard. A punctured garden hose, attached to a timer, made a rectangle around the whole enterprise, which smelled tangy and fragrant with mint. There wasn't much of a backyard, but on the narrow patio three shirtless men hunkered around two kettles of greasy, sludge-flecked water. On a slab of wood beside them lay a pile of what looked like possum skins. After the first man reached for a skin, which dangled from his fingers like heavy drapery, and plunged it into the first kettle of water, he passed the dripping mass to the next man, who with the blade of a putty knife scraped what looked like the fur along with some floppy membrane into a garbage can before swishing the skin around in the first kettle again and then rinsing it in the second. The cleaned flesh, which now resembled a sack of stringy white netting, was tossed onto a platter to be carried by one of four Hmong women into the kitchen, from whose propped-open windows emerged billows of sweet, oily steam.

"Gross," said one of the Klinks' many teenage nieces, who were gathered on the back steps experimenting with various shades of lipsticks.

"What is it?" I asked them.

"Guts," said one, pursing her mouth desultorily at a hand-held mirror.

"Stomachs," said another.

"No. Tripes," said the third.

There was a double garage, nearly as wide as the house. Dr. Klink's Audi and the family Volkswagen Cruiser had been backed out into the driveway behind which a score of other cars, including my own, were parked along the street. Spread out on the floor of half the garage was a plastic tarp around which four men and one boy squatted on wood four-by-fours. The men all wielded cleavers. The boy was unwinding a knot of intestines into a bucket. In a galvanized tub lay some other massive organs. Among the men's stretched-out legs on the plastic tarp lay a whole half a cow, headless and skinned, the giant, significant parts of the carcass already quartered and halved. One man butchered a leg bone, the other some ribs, the others slicing and trimming with methodical precision as if the life of the cow still hung in the balance. They had bought the cow that morning from Hillshire Farms; despite the heat of midday, the beef had a fresh, cold smell, the hunks of meat were cherry red in the dim, garage light. And there was not any blood to be seen. Across the street the other houses, as small as the Klink's, looked stark and abandoned as Monopoly houses on their own, treeless lawns, so when Mrs. Klink appeared from around the kitchen stoop bearing on her head a laundry basket stacked high with fresh-picked herbs and vines of scarlet Szechuan peppers, I could feel my own blood well up in my bald head like light in a bulb, it was all so beautiful to see. Every so often since my remission, the most ordinary places and events became luminous as temples, and here was something not ordinary at all but strange and automatically wonderful to begin with. Even the giant Sterno burners topped with kettles of simmering chopped meats that filled the other half of the garage were lovely; even when one of the men turned off the flame when the meat was still purple and dumped it all in a laundry tub to be stirred with ladlesful of pungent sliced tripe, that was lovely, too.

"Come over here, girls," I called, wanting Nora and Evvy

to see it, too, but at the same time nervous about how they might feel about all that meat. Martha would pretend to be disgusted; then for years she'd be writing poems about it. But Martha wasn't at the Klink's. It took me just a moment to remember what she was doing, what she usually was doing these days—concocting reasons to have to cross the river where Trevor Close worked the bridge. When he got off work at seven, she planned to coax him into joining us for dinner. I hoped he would come. The idea of Trevor's buttoned-up collar falling into bed with Martha's purple crushed-silk caftan would be the perfect dessert, nearly as sweet to me as to her. Or was I already excited about something or someone of my own? I couldn't tell. It felt like maybe I was, in a quiet, expectant, shivery way, the way I'd felt one day when Hercules showed me the correct positioning of my body and hands around his bass, a position that felt entirely strange yet welcome.

"Tell me, what is all of this," I asked the teenage girls. "What's all this whole cow for? What's going on?"

"Oh," one said. "Some party down at Legion Hall tonight. Aren't you coming?"

"For the Hmong Community Association," said another.

"No. For a wedding," said the first. "I think."

"Good reason not to get married," said the third, wrinkling her nose, then applying a bolt of lipstick exactly the way my mother used to do it; holding the tube straight and motionless while swiveling her face.

"As if you need a reason not to get married," said the second.

"You'll need one soon, if you don't watch out."

"I think I might shave my head, too," one said to me.

"Me, too."

"Not me. No offense. Whoever you are."

"That's okay," I said. "Who's getting married?"

The teenagers all shrugged, and popped open cans of soda.

"Mommy," said Nora, who had come up beside me carrying a sprig of yellow flowering herbs just like those in Mrs. Klink's laundry basket. "Does that hurt?"

"What, baby?" I asked.

"That," she said, pointing to the pounds and slabs of glistening beef.

"No. It can't feel a thing," I promised.

"Why?" asked Evvy. Evvy called only Martha *Mommy.* Nora only did me. Sometimes Martha and I were pleased with this arrangement. Other times it made us both terribly jealous.

"What herb is that with the yellow flowers?" I asked Mrs. Klink. She looked lovely as ever with her black hair knotted back in the stem of the plastic daisy, her checkered blouse, her skirt with a pattern of wind-tossed kites, her pumps the exact pink of ballet slippers. "Your daughters are so well behaved," she said, her plump face beaming. "I told them not to bite the Szechuans; they didn't even touch them, they just twirled the stems and admired the color. None of my children were ever so well behaved. This flower? I think you call it cilantro," she said. "Only you eat the leaves, not the flowers. We boil the blossoms in broth for flavor, then we discard them."

"Your husband told me you don't like to speak English," I said apologetically.

"Oh, he prefers to speak to me in Hmong. He's very sentimental."

There was a thumping of wood and spare automobile tires in the garage, where the men, taking a break from their butchering, were gathering around a sawhorse table to eat their lunch. There was the pop and fizz of beer and soft drinks as the men filled their plates with food, and when I stepped forward into the garage to look, they offered me some. I said no, thank you. They made the offer again. I said yes, okay, thank you, and one of the men got up from his sawhorse to give me his place at the table. I could see the chopped mint leaves and whole Szechuan peppers and slivers of garlic trapped in the sauce that clung to the tendrils of tripe. There was the smell of lime and cud, the cool spongy taste of raw meat, a faint, sharp steam that smelled exactly of sun-warmed manure, a tiny yellow flower that must have dislodged from its stem. Many Hmong people won't eat cheese, I remembered Dr. Klink having told me once. The idea of a collection of cow stomach enzymes permitted to curdle whole vats of milk was repellent to them. Somehow this knowledge allowed me to swallow those first bites of raw meat, and soon the summery flavor of tripe, like live cattle grazing in a hot meadow, when blended with an acid burst of pepper, took on a strange appeal.

I filled my plate twice more. On the kitchen stoop the teenage girls whispered and shrieked.

"So, this is a traditional wedding feast? Who's getting married?" I asked one of the men at the table.

"Yes. A cow," he said.

"No. Beef," said another.

"Beef and cow the same thing," said the first. "You like it?"

"It's delicious," I said, and took a swallow of beer. The men all laughed. I supposed it was my baldness that allowed them to treat me like one of the men, but later Dr. Klink told me it was the fact that I was American. Had I been a Hmong woman sharing their lunch without a chaperone, I'd have been considered a whore.

"You drop?" one of them asked.

"Excuse me?" I asked.

He held out one of my multitude of necklaces, a string of beads from the 1930s draped over me long ago by the Crazy Volunteer. Every time I saw it, I remembered the awkward touch of her fingers—the real hand and the fake one, lifting my hair in order to fasten the clasp. "Take this," she'd said. It was the memory of my hair, not the memory of the clumsy touch of her fingers, that gave me a chill when I took the beads from the man and slid them around my neck.

15

And then just as suddenly, back in real time, as I reluctantly called it, 1995, early one November morning as Martha, Hercules, and I were driving to the museum.

"What gets me," I said, "is that though I don't really feel tired, I don't really have much energy, either. In a way I feel more like a chair than a human being, as if my legs aren't meant to carry me around any longer, only to keep me from floating away while I recline above them. But this new lassitude; it doesn't close up my mind the way it used to when I came home from work and sat in my living room with my afghan wrapped around me and my cup of tea. All of a sudden, I can understand why old people like to sit on their front porches and watch the world go by instead of dozing in their houses. I can even almost understand the appeal of television. But thank God I can still climb the steps to my apartment. I hate the smell of elevators. Did you notice the steps leading up to the storage trailer are about a foot from the threshold? You have to practically leap across. I'd like it even more if the stairs were even farther away. Also, I have this peculiar, tart, cilantrolike taste in my mouth. If I were doing the chemo, if you two hadn't managed to convince me not to do it, I wouldn't have been able to taste it. Did you know that? That people lose their sense of taste when they do chemo? So, thank you for convincing me not to do the chemo. You know what I've been thinking, how it's funny that when we were in college, Martha, and we used to prepare those weird, supposedly ethnic meals, we used to use cilantro, only then it was called coriander, and of course we bought it dried and shook it out of the jar. It never occurred to us—I don't think it occurred to anyone in those days—that we might use it fresh. I don't even think we even knew it was a leaf. From a live plant! And parsley, too. Now if you even *buy* dried parsley—and now coriander's called cilantro! Which reminds me of when I used to go on nature hikes with this biologist I was seeing, who seemed to think I'd get a great thrill out of gnawing on plants we stumbled across on the trails. He used to pick oxalis leaves and layer them in our picnic sandwiches. Oxalis tastes a little like cilantro. The same lemony tartness. The same bite. But more mustardy. Somebody told me, I don't know who, that when cilantro matures it gets these yellow, white flowers, which can be used to make broth, along with some other things, I don't know what, but then you throw the flowers out and just use the broth in cooking. So there are three ways to use cilantro. Out of a jar, and the fresh leaves, and the broth from the blossoms. But maybe there are more ways we don't know about."

"Isobel," said Martha. "I can see you're going to make an absolutely delightful sick person. You're going to be the kind that muses and rambles. You're going to be the kind who takes pleasure in every minute."

"Do you know what happened at work yesterday?" I asked. "You know the Crazy Volunteer? You know who I mean, Martha?"

Martha had started volunteering, too. Her job for the time being was to sit at a telephone in one of the trailers and while sorting through our collection of discolored candelabra answer calls from all the people who over the years had donated objects to the museum, and now worried about their fates in the fire.

"About nine years ago my father donated some of those old hardware store calendars from the Depression," a caller might ask. "Can you tell me if they survived?"

"My sister's tatting. . . . please don't tell me it's lost."

"I brought over an old eggbeater someone made into a ballerina. And one of those acrobat toys, where the painted bear flips around. They belonged to my great-uncle. He'd be heartbroken if anything—"

To which Martha would reply, over and over, "I'm afraid we're still in such terrible disarray here we really can't say what happened to anything. No, really, we wouldn't know where to begin. Yes, I know it's been several months since the fire, but— August twenty. And now it's into November. Sorry. No. Visitors aren't insured to enter the buildings. . . . Come to think of it, I *do* think I might have seen something like that. Or at least a part of it, yes, maybe just a piece of it. Really, it's amazing to see what becomes of certain materials exposed to great amounts of heat. A corset I wrapped up the other day—it looked like a handful of crushed chicken wire, with a few of the hooks and eyes still fastened. What did you say your great-grandmother's bustle was made of?"

But there was something piquant about Martha's little fits of sympathy. This morning when we all climbed into the car she did her twice-weekly show of allowing Hercules to sit in the passenger seat instead of in back where he usually ended up all scrunched up like a pocket knife. Even in the passenger seat with the window open and his arm alert to the breeze on the road, he resembled those pictures of Alice after she'd drunk from the bottle and could no longer fit through the door. My car was a standard; every time I shifted gears my knuckles brushed up against Hercules's blue jeans, making him jump. This was our private joke on Martha, who worried about my driving. Still, lately there was something unsatisfying about my confidences with Hercules, because however much he understood, he didn't quite seem to know what was happening to me. It was true that I tasted cilantro, and true that I didn't remember exactly who had told me about the flowers in the broth, for just as some memories of the past are more vague than others, so are some memories of the future more vague than others. Even Nora and Evvy I might pass whole days and nights without seeming to remember, and then all at once I'd lay my head on a pillow as soft as Evvy's curls or fix my eyes on a window as black as Nora's braids, and know I was missing them, and feel either happy about them, or sad.

The touch of Hercules's blue jeans was soft as velvet, which caused me to shiver, which caused the car to swerve into the little island in the center of the road, from which the city had not yet cleared the papery remnants of a bed of summer petunias.

I backed down off the curb, pulled back up again, then backed down for a second time and shifted to park. The car was horizontal across the middle of the road.

"Maybe somebody else had better drive the rest of the way," I said, stepping out into the leftover stems and dry petals of the garden, wobbling just a little when Martha opened the door for me in back as Hercules circled around to the driver's seat. Both Hercules and Martha had forgotten that I had been in the middle of telling them a story about the Crazy Volunteer. I had needed to check the humidity in the storage trailer, and when I opened the door and stepped between the rows of shelves on which the dolls all lay a-tatter in their cardboard boxes, I nearly tripped across her ankles. She lay flat on her back on the metal floor, asleep, snoring in little creaks and rattles.

Somehow I thought it best not to tell Martha and Hercules, after all. Besides, Martha was trying to get my attention, once we had parked in the museum lot.

"Isobel," she said, "maybe I'll go in to work and Hercules can drive you home for a nap."

"No," I said. "I have too much to do."

"But Isobel—" said Martha.

"Mom. Just let her be," said Hercules.

Then for a moment we all sat still in the car as if waiting to see who would get out first.

16

"Have you been having indigestion, Isobel?" asked Martha on Thanksgiving morning, real time. Martha and I had decided to get up early, so I could start cooking our meal. A turkey lay nearly thawed in the sink. Already Martha had removed the giblets, dropped them into a pot of water for boiling, chopped celery for dressing, and made her own cookietraysful of herbed croutons from a couple of loaves of what passed for Italian bread in this part of the country. I was sitting on the couch in my robe and pajamas, having said I'd prepare a pitcher of daiquiris so we could get a reckless start to the day. My robe was more tightly cinched than it had been the morning before; I calculated I'd lost about a quarter of a pound.

"Indigestion? Me?"

"No joking, Isobel. Have you?"

"No."

"Do you have some kind of stomachache?"

"A stomachache? Me? Isobel Albright? A stomachache, did you say?"

"Yes?"

"No."

"Then why didn't you eat the omelet I made you for breakfast? Or the sandwich I gave you for dinner last night?"

She shook a package of cranberries into the colander, sprayed them with the nozzle, mixed them up in a pot of water and sugar, and placed it on the burner. Before me on a cutting board lay seven limes, a serrated knife, a bottle of rum, a bottle of sugar syrup, and a cocktail shaker.

"Isobel?"

"Because both the omelet and the sandwich were made with cheese," I finally answered, feeling a twinge of guilt.

"So you do get a little indigestion, when you eat cheese."

"No," I said. I cut into a lime with great diligence, sawing the knife back and forth with such shallow strokes that nearly a whole minute went by before the teeth scraped against the wood and the lime fell into halves. I held a half against my skin, measuring the colors, happy to see that my jaundice was only the palest of yellows in comparison to the brilliant chartreuse of the fruit.

I put the knife down. There was the sound of water running in the sink, then the purr of new flame in the oven.

"Then why didn't you eat the sandwich or the omelet? Are you just not hungry? Are you saving your appetite for the turkey?"

"I just don't like cheese," I answered, sitting straight up, squeezing the lime above the cocktail shaker with all of my might. Nothing happened. Not a single drop of juice emerged.

"Since when? You used to love cheese," said Martha.

"I don't know. The idea of it . . ." I said, squeezing with both hands at once. "The idea of a bunch of cow stomach enzymes mixed up in a vat of milk . . . I don't know. It repulses me," I said.

17

One afternoon shortly thereafter, I represented the museum at a televised city council meeting where the agenda of new business included a motion to investigate the fire department's inability to pump water from the nearby hydrants. While reciting The Pledge of Allegiance, I let my hand slip a little in its weariness, over my heart where my fingertips brushed against the taut, lace cup of my bra.

One of my fake breasts, a new one fashioned by Martha from a piece of nylon stocking, two rubber bands, and some bath oil beads, slid out of my bra, fell from under the silk of my dress and exploded on the floor.

I watched the bath beads skid like blue fireworks beneath the lights of the TV cameras, the dull clatter dispersing under the lectern.

Nobody moved. We all pretended not to notice. Around our obedient chorus of voices rose a dewberry fragrance, warm in the glare, that made me think of summer picnics and moonlight concerts of the sort we had each June on the lawn of the museum. Rum punch, lemonade, our whole disorganized collection of hanging lanterns casting vibrating rays in time with the too-loud music. If I was seeing a man, that year, I wouldn't bring him to the picnic, preferring my solitary blend of Victorianism, professionalism, and modern cocktail manners, and if I wasn't seeing a man that year, I'd make one up and imagine him linked to my elbow in an embarrassing white suit and bow tie.

Once, in my hearing, my mother had confessed to my father that his bow ties made her blush, but it wasn't the

thought of my father's bow ties that made me blush that afternoon before the TV cameras, nor my single remaining prosthesis that made little clicking sounds when I took too deep a
breath while describing for the public how the river had
flowed untapped within sight of the flames.

The reason I was blushing was because after the pledge was
done and we all took our seats, I'd left my hand where it was,
not on my heart but where it had come to rest instead, upon the
region of my spleen.

The cancer had spread to my spleen. When Dr. Klink had
called me to tell me the news, I'd driven immediately to
Trevor's little reference library on the bridge and asked him to
look it up. He said the spleen was flat and oblong, aubergine in
color, and that in its association with the circulatory system it
regulated blood volume and manufactured certain white blood
cells while filtering and destroying certain worn-out, useless
red ones. Also that it was considered the seat of emotion, the
wellspring of laughter, of sudden impulse, temper, passion, and
caprice.

"And here I'd been hoping I wouldn't miss it," I had said,
and took the book from Trevor's hands, and read through
what he'd told me. The book, I noticed, did not use the word
aubergine to describe the organ's reddish purple hue, nor did it
make specific reference to "passion." These had been Trevor's
innovations.

Maybe my own spleen was no longer aubergine, I thought
to myself while I spoke to the TV camera of my still-fond
respect for the fire department. But I loved that eggplant color.
And now I loved it especially in that flat, oblong part of my
body, loved it as if I'd known it were there all along! I held my
whole palm flush against the spot, as if to protect it from the
gray invading spread.

"It's important to have a sense of humor and perspective in
these matters," I related to the camera, recalling how I'd read
the definition of spleen again as if searching an old love letter

for clues to the dissolution of trust. What had gone wrong? How had we managed to fail each other? *Spleen,* it occurred to me, watching the polished toe of the city clerk's wingtip kick a bath bead all the way to the other side of the room, would be another fine name for a sprite.

18

In early December, real time, the museum flew two consultants from Maine and California to help with the wrapping and storage of our undamaged items. The first day, they gave a lecture demonstration on glassware, explaining all the things I had learned ages ago in graduate school, about how glass contains a modifying agent, often potassium, which keeps the silica malleable during construction but eventually migrates to the surface of the piece, binding with oxygen to become potassium hydroxide, which being hydroscopic absorbs moisture, resulting in the formation of that gritty, saltlike substance that clouds the surface of old glass and leads to disintegration.

All this meant, really, was that we needed to wash the glassware in a special nonreactive detergent and then dry it as thoroughly as possible before wrapping it in acid-free paper and storing it among the tubes they taught us how to make out of surgical stockings and inert foam pellets.

Which seemed a funny thing to have to fly someone two thousand miles to teach us.

But that was alright with me, because somehow deep down without even knowing it I think I'd blamed myself for my illness, as if I thought maybe if I'd eaten more carrots, or laughed more often, or loved more deeply, or seen more of the world, or thought less about things and did them instead, or *something,* then maybe I wouldn't have become sick. So to think that a piece of glass, a thing so transparent, so candid, so unambiguous, so rational as glass—to think that a thing as pure as glass might still self-destruct made me feel cleansed and pure, too.

Lucid as a goblet.

Baptized.

Innocent, somehow.
Not guilty.

NOT GUILTY, not guilty, not guilty, I kept saying to myself as I moved among the tables in the emergency annex, selecting those odd bits of glassware—chandelier prisms and faceted coat buttons—that I wanted to wash and dangle before the whirring fans to dry. The tables in the annex were too close together, their arrays of fragile, broken objects like detritus after a rummage sale. The pocket watches, I noticed, had disappeared from their spot on one of the tables during a prolonged consultation about how to fashion packing material out of unused newspaper endrolls. Hercules was nowhere in sight. David and Jayne were crouched in the hallway unwrapping sponges. The woman who used to work in the gift shop carried goblets one by one into the steaming kitchen. The Crazy Volunteer stood swaying among the close-packed tables in the center of the room, one eyelid half-closed and the other just barely fluttering. This wasn't the first time I had seen her like this, tipping forward and backward in little jerks and starts. But when I walked past, her eyes flipped all the way open as she raised herself up on the balls of her feet. "Take this," she said to me, as she had said so many times, still swaying, still a flutter, her makeup too orange in the fluorescent light.

Not guilty, I said to myself as I reached for the object she held forth in her plastic fingers.

Did I look at it?

No.

Did I even stop long enough to determine what it was, and whether or not I had the right to accept it?

No.

Did I drop it?

Yes.

19

And so, just as suddenly, the year was 2001.

What I found, when I got down on my knees and scooted along the scuffed supermarket floor beneath the produce rack to retrieve what I had dropped, was my own wedding ring. Had it slipped from my finger because it was too large? No. But I had a habit of twisting it off, sliding it back on, popping it off, sliding it back on again as with multiple avowals.

Flat and gold as it was, the ring was not entirely usual, for it had come from the museum's collection of Second World War rings worn by the brides of soldiers who had died overseas. This was rather a sad exhibit, because if it didn't make you sadder than you already were about war, then it made you sadder about marriage, instead. So I was happy with the ring, for it seemed to enclose a certain commentary which reminded me that my marriage had its own curious history, which at the moment eluded me, but it was not an ordinary marriage, of that I was certain. Not, somehow, smack in the safe solid flat middle ground of that golden institution.

We'd been married two years. The union still felt unexpected, like a bird that had flown in through an open window and was still too surprised to want to find a way out.

Astonishing, it was. But my husband was in New Orleans for a week or two, I remembered, missing him suddenly with a mighty jolt. He went there every once in a while. Why, I couldn't recall. Who he was, even *that,* I could not at that moment recall, though I remembered the taut, warm cushion of his balls against the nape of my neck as we lay in an L on our giant low futon, talking.

What we talked about, I couldn't remember.

Who talked more than whom, I couldn't calculate.

However soothing the sound of his voice, still I couldn't hear its echo in my mind.

But the sure, steady touch of his fingers, the way he laid the whole spread-open curve of his palm against the equal, bald curve of my head, the undemanding yet exacting pressure of that touch, the way he drew the palm back, away, so just the tips of his fingers slid together along my skull . . . and then poked! and then prodded! No, this wasn't my husband's touch at all! This was some impertinent pervert in the supermarket as I poked my head out from under the produce rack having rescued my wedding ring from a nest of dropped parsley.

"Not ripe," the pervert said. "A honeydew has to be just ripe."

I wrapped my arm hard around the backs of his knees and toppled him. He landed with a thump on his elbows. He was perfectly bald, like me, although his head was not as regal, not as fortunate, as mine. More tapered than domed, his head was an egg.

"Over hard," I said to him. "Now, scram."

"But I only needed to get your attention," he answered. "Surely you realize we have something in common."

"Well, not precisely," I answered.

"Why not?"

"Well, because yours . . ." I began, and then stopped, for I couldn't bring myself to say to him what I was thinking. Alongside that black turtleneck shirt, those tight black jeans, the Chinese black cloth slippers, his baldness made him look only fashionable. It seemed to have nothing to do with fear or courage, like mine did, or with the need to repudiate the idea of his own cells being expelled from his body, like mine did, or with the distinct sensual pleasure of liberation, like mine did, or with an acquiescence to a certain androgenous imperative, like mine did. But I didn't say any of this. Instead I said, rising, slapping leaves of stuck parsley off the knees of my tights, "Because your eyelashes are real. Mine aren't."

I reached forward for a pinch. He closed an eye and cocked it toward me. I gave the lashes a gentle tug, they slid off the lid in one curved, delicate piece, still bound by a moist residue of adhesive.

I yelped. Really yelped, like a trapped, humiliated dog.

"You're sick?" I breathed.

"I'll be dead before Beethoven's birthday," he answered. "That's why I wear black. Not grief, you understand, but so when people look at me and think how skinny I'm getting they might comfort themselves by imagining it's only the black that makes me look that way. Also, because black absorbs more light, which my girlfriend is desperate to believe might save me, because light, she believes, has healing properties, so I do it to comfort her. You know, to give her hope. When there isn't any hope. So, I'm deceiving her. But I suppose I might call it a white lie. Except it isn't. It's black."

"Yes," I said.

I nearly gave him the wedding ring. Nearly twisted it off for the final time, bequeathed it to him, bequeathed to him all my sudden, inexplicable bursts of longevity, my forays into the gift of the future.

With this ring I thee wed, I imagined I might recite were I to slide the ring onto his too slender finger. *With this ring I grant thee a claim to thy future, to thy rightful, lived years, to thy surprised, acquiescent, adventurous self.*

But I could not do it.

I pushed the ring back firmly over my knuckle. Around us the globes of the honeydews somberly glowed. They cost a mere dollar and a quarter a piece. It must have been a good harvest, the year 2001.

"When's Beethoven's birthday?" I asked.

"Too soon," he answered.

And still I couldn't give him the ring's promise of escape.

Before then, I'd never thought of myself as a selfish person. My selfishness was quite a revelation. I would take what I wanted. I would do what I wanted. I would have what I wanted.

Fortunately I did not want the bald man. Not that I didn't find him interesting, and absolutely down-to-earth, and even attractive in that translucent way that black is so good at revealing. I wished he might go on living, like me.

But I wanted my husband. I missed him as fiercely as if I knew who he was.

"Sweetheart," I whispered.

20

In mid-December, real time, on my way to my very first appointment with Outreach, I got off at the wrong floor in the hospital, took a wrong turn trying to find my way back to the elevator, and ended up in a dead-end hallway where instead of the elevator, two doors like spread wings opened into the hospital chapel. I'd never been there before, and since there was nobody inside whose prayers or weeping I might interrupt, I decided to go in and have a look around, conscious as I entered, of the way my body seemed to defer to the strange quiet of the little vestibule beyond the doors. I think I bowed my head, and when I took off my coat draped it carefully over my shoulders, grasping the ends of the collar. Then, since there was slush still trapped in the soles of my boots, I paused for a minute over a big welcome mat to stomp them clean in a ladylike fashion, which reminded me of how I'd always behaved myself obediently and with poise, stomping my waterproof boots, my long hair pulled back in a clasp that though it bobbed up and down with my stomping still did not release so much as a single strand of hair. I was wearing a knit sweater dress with a certain, coy cling set off by Martha's most recently homemade prostheses, of which the nipples were fashioned of whole cloves stuck into those white balls that people decorate for Christmas, but with my brooch and opaque stockings I felt like a nun in lay attire, come to dust the altar top and refresh the cut flowers.

In the corner of the foyer was a wicker chair just right for reading the kinds of magazines to be found in the hospital gift shop, but it was occupied by a potted philodendron and a stack of hymn books. Nearby on a table was a prayer request box and a ledger with the heading *For These We Pray* above a list of scrawled names. I have to say I scanned it, as apprehensive that I might find my name as at the idea of stumbling upon my own stone in a cemetery. It wasn't the thought of death that alarmed me, but of my name exposed under the queer, filtered light that made its way from the louvered ceiling to the ledger, a light the color of dulled mirrors, and all the woodwork flat and lusterless as stale chocolate, and on the walls, smooth bricks of an artificial brown drained of the essence of that otherwise complicated hue. Even the crucifixion looked brittle, for it was carved of that horrible firebrick so gritty that it left splinters of sand on whoever was unfortunate enough to touch it.

I was aware that all around me along the distant yet accessible halls of the hospital, people lay ill and dying.

I sat quietly in one of several rows of upholstered chairs facing the altar. My skin prickled in the manufactured stillness, in the dreadful, carpeted, motionless space where not a clock ticked, not a bead of moisture formed on the petals of the flowers in the vase on the table. Not even the miniature organ, upright in a corner behind a rise of two stairs, seemed cognizant of the possibility of sound.

I opened my purse, dug around for my spare pair of slouch socks, pulled them on over my hose, undid my still-long hair from its tapestry clasp, combed it, frizzed it, teased it, shook it, anything to keep the dust floating glitteringly in the otherwise empty light. But my hair was free of dust just as the sunlight was empty of sunshine; even the lozenges of colored light falling through the several stained glass windows resembled wrapped suckers.

The windows were narrow as coffins, all in a row. To each was affixed the name of a deceased. *In Memory of . . . In Memory of . . . In Memory of . . .*

Before me on the altar an incongruous microphone bowed its blunt head. Behind me an oval chorus of dimmer switches practiced a desultory hum. Above me the flat nozzles of the sprinkler system appeared vaguely alert as if sensing an untoward heat in my body, the just-burgeoning, violet, beckoning flame of anger, not at death but at the idea that such a room might pretend to make peace with death. For the room wasn't peaceful or tranquil, only dead itself, more dead than a coffin, so dead that there seemed never to have been a live soul inside it.

So I got up at once and escaped. I didn't try to find the elevator. I took the first stairway I came to, a *Staff Only* stairway leading to the parking lot where the sun turned the slush on the asphalt to runnels of singing water as welcoming to me as if I had discovered a spring in a forest. I wouldn't keep my appointment with Outreach. I wouldn't ever set foot in the hospital again. The very idea of dying there, of being *dead* there, of being wheeled down the hallway with a sheet pulled over my face and the nurses' shoes squeaking on the polished tile floors and the flowers barely wilting in the chapel before somebody whisked them away and replaced them with new ones made me indignant with horror and shame.

But the idea of dying in my bed at home was so comforting I thought I'd go there right away and have a nap, just to feel how cozy and friendly it would be with Hercules's bass tilting into the corner. By now almost carefree, I drove past my exit, took the road for the museum instead, and ended up back at work. Martha met me at the door to the office trailer, so angry with me for having driven by myself that she nearly couldn't bring herself to kiss my forehead hello, steer me to my chair, perch on the edge of my desk, and tell me the story of Cyrano de Bergerac. For days, she'd been telling me unrequited love stories while helping me sort through my mail and papers. When she finished with the story and got up to return to her own work, I opened my computer to a file I'd started just a couple of days before. It contained the word, FIRE, that was all, centered, as if it knew that more would someday follow.

I printed a single copy, and slid it into my notebook inside my bag.

21

The name of the Polish roof worker, in whom the Crazy Volunteer seemed to have taken what could only be called romantic interest, was John Grzadzielewsli. I knew this because I'd finally relented on the day I'd visited the chapel, when I was too tired to do anything else, and clomped up the off-limits stairway to the ruined attic and asked his foreman.

"You're not supposed to be coming up here yet," the foreman admonished sympathetically. Those days, everyone looked at me kindly, and offered me glasses of water and odd jobs designed to make me feel useful. The foreman handed me a drill bit no larger than a toothpick and asked if I would carry it downstairs.

"First, can you tell me that man's name?" I asked, pointing to the one with the Walkman and the sloppy tufts of blond hair that appeared endlessly tousled by small gusts of moist wind rippling under his skin. Clouds raced through his eyes as if over dark ponds, and there was an air about him of great intensity kept in check.

I dropped the drill bit on the third step from the bottom, where it rolled out of sight among small drifts of sawdust. What would my parents think of me if they could see me now, I wondered, plunked down on my bottom on the fresh cut wood of the stair, the sap tickling my nose, the sawdust so velvety under my fingers I forgot what I was looking for?

Later, I sought out the Crazy Volunteer where she was supposed to be wrapping cleaned statuary for storage, but she wasn't in sight; there was only a scale model of a Menominee Village of which the inhabitants were to be brushed free of ash with a dry toothbrush, wrapped in tissue paper, and packed in a shoebox. I picked up a thumbnail-size baby, tickled its foot with the toothbrush, blew a fleck of grime from where its navel would be if it had one, tried to feel, between my lips, the stubbornness of its miniature fists. But there weren't any knuckles, no flailing, no pushing, no grasping even at air. I felt a stab of nostalgia as suffused with sadness as it was with anticipation, then slipped the whole baby onto my tongue and swallowed it. It giggled all the way down with a mirthfulness subdued like Nora's, then settled in purring like Evvy feigning sleep. I might call it a pain pill except instead of stifling pain, it awoke it limb by limb, until I found myself curled on the pallet of burlap gazing blearily at the painted horizon beyond the tiny encampment, longing for my daughters.

It was the Crazy Volunteer who woke me, pulling poor John Grzadzielewsli along, his shirttail bunched in her mechanical hand, his crotch straining inside his jeans like a thundercloud trapped in a blue sky. For a moment I wondered if he was to be her next gift to me, and to which distant time and place I might be transported if I were to get my hands on that zipper.

But apparently such wild generosity was not the Crazy Volunteer's idea of a good, first date.

"We plan to spend the evening in my trailer and see if we feel like kissing," she brightly declared. "What do you think of that?"

"I certainly hope that both of you have a marvelous time," I answered.

John Grzadzielewsli looked stunned.

22

Next morning I had breakfast in the rooftop cafeteria in the Botanical Society building, which shared our grounds and our circular drive but which was otherwise more opulently endowed than we were; the inlaid floors were of marble, the mahogany stair rails polished every day by a student intern with serious-looking eyeglasses and a floppy yellow braid and a habit of happening to polish the outside of the front door whenever Hercules was due to show up in the parking lot, either coming or going it didn't matter how frozen the day, she was there in her Birkenstocks and nubby tights, furiously rubbing.

Breakfast was blueberries, cottage cheese, an English muffin, and my morning dose of pain pills. No coffee. I hadn't always been a breakfast person, but now the meal seemed a fine way to ease from dawn to naptime while still "at work." Not that I ate much. The thing I liked about blueberries was that I could spend a lot of time spearing them on the end of my fork and crushing the skins between my front teeth and sucking out the morsels of fruit without ever feeling how much my appetite had waned, so it didn't matter if I left the English muffin untouched after having spread it with the cottage cheese.

Between nibbles, I withdrew from my purse the piece of paper with the word *fire* on it and started writing. By the time my blueberries and juice were nearly gone I'd prepared a proposal for an exhibit documenting the fire, including a photographic history of the smoke, the flooding, the salvage and cleaning and storage and restoration efforts complementing an array of artifacts showing various degrees of destruction and repair. Scattered among everything else would be the dolls, I decided. They would hold the spent objects in their singed, melted hands, or upon the stained aprons draping their torn-apart laps, or perhaps beside them in their coffinlike boxes if we couldn't get them to sit up straight.

Beyond the window, the broad view of the frozen river sparkled with cold, and the risen span of the drawbridge was sharp against the brightness of the sky. I ate a single kernel of cottage cheese and wrote a memo inviting plans for the exhibit along with a call for journal entries, photographs, personal statements, and effects from museum staff and their offices, then blocked out a provisional design and layout. If all went well and the galleries could be got in order we might feature the exhibit when the museum reopened in what the visiting conservator had confided to me and David might be a full year and a half away, winter of 1997, when I would no longer be alive.

I lifted another blueberry onto my fork, watched it roll down the tines and into my bag. When I finally paid and left by the back service stairway, my notebook tucked in my satchel, I nearly bumped into John Grzadzielewsli and the Crazy Volunteer kissing on the landing. Shrinking back on the step a little, I stood dizzily and watched them. The Crazy Volunteer did not know how to kiss, I wasn't surprised to see, she puckered her lips and made smacking noises in his hair but John Grzadzielewsli didn't seem in the least chagrined, he was sliding his tongue along the elastic neckline of her blouse. As for her arms, one of them flapped like a bent, broken wing around his playful butting and spanking, while the arm with the fake hand had managed to undo his button and was pushing its way beyond the zigzag lightning of his fly.

"Doll," he was saying, "Yes, doll. Please, doll."

Smack, went her kisses.

23

"Does anyone know what that noise is in the parking lot?" asked Jayne as she came into the office trailer later that same afternoon carrying a load of frost-covered taxidermy specimens that somebody had discovered piled in the sway of the awning above the carport. All these months since the fire the decrepit animals must have lain there, tossed from a second-floor window by someone emptying the displays.

"Jayne. Get that stuff west of the river where it smells like it belongs," said David. He meant the cemetery. As in most towns our dead were buried in the prettiest spot, their endless gazes trained on the river as if the old cliché was right and the water marked the passage of eternal time. If someone wanted to indulge in sadness, if they needed to nurture some private grief, then they had only to lean against one of the headstones and watch the boats drift by like minutes, like hours, like years, calm and indifferent. Yes, life goes on, a funny message to be found among the broad, swaying trees of a burial ground. But like the mental hospital among the willows on the lakeshore, the cemetery sequestered its view of the water and made it consoling, a single liquid caress of space except that now the river was frozen, the water sloshing under floating, drifting barges of ice.

Having mentioned the cemetery, David slipped me one of his scared looks that were responsible for my having figured out that Martha and Hercules must have cornered him already and told him why I'd been leaving work so often, preferring to nap at home rather than with my head on a desk blotter surrounded by reams of unfinished paperwork. Their lie was designed to protect me. They knew I didn't nap when I was

home. Why waste being home on napping when I might nap at
work instead, my head cradled in printouts, my dreams awash
in a blur of dot matrix, a pen still clutched in my fingers as if I
had no intention of drifting off? At home, I courted adventure,
stood with my nose pressed expectantly against the chilly win-
dowpane as if waiting for a date to drive up in its car. Pick a
date, any date, 2001, 2002, 2020, any date would do so long as it
would drive me out of the present and carry me over that
threshold of years to some other time that was waiting for me
to join it. Just yesterday I'd plucked the silver compact from
the spice rack, pried it open with a can opener, dusted my forehead, gazed in the mirror, discerned nothing, no change, no
slight lengthening of the new furrow between my eyebrows,
no fresh cast of the mouth, no deepening of the eyes. Why so
long between adventures? I wondered day after day, longing to
meet my husband or hold my adopted daughters tight in my
arms. With frustration I took hold of the caked, leathery puff
and rubbed it more vigorously against the shiny cake of com-
pressed powder, then slapped it against my closed eyelids, my
temples, the upward tilt of my chin. Nothing. Just the gusty
clouds of powder every which way, speckling my eyebrows
and hair. The little mirror in the compact, tiny and smudged as
it was, mocked my frustration. Funny . . . slathered with powder I looked like an old lady trying to get young, rather than a
young woman trying desperately to get old. Was I surprised it
didn't work? Not really. Angrily, I tossed it in the trash can,
then picked it out carefully and carried it back to the spice
rack, a treasure still, next to the saffron, protected, rescued as it
might someday rescue me. For a moment I stood tracing the
silvery hinge, then the delicate engravings that were just like
the swirls of a fingerprint. No two silver compacts are exactly
alike, I said to myself, then grew tired of my hopelessness so
went back in the bathroom and played with my hair for a
while, twisting it into a kind of chignon but pulling harder
than I needed, trying to make it vanish under my grasp. Far
too many days had passed without any of the Crazy Volun-

teer's offerings working their magic, and I missed Nora and Evvy so much that the next time I managed to be with them I'd allow them to don their miniature berets and decorate my domed head with glitter paint, as I knew they would love to do. They'd take hold of their tiny brushes, cover my baldness with garlands of wet tinsel. But comb, brush, and pull as I might, my hair stayed a perfect gloss of chignon with not even a tendril of gray.

Sadly, I went for a walk, just a small, careful stroll around the grounds of the apartment complex át the edge of the field where the grass crunched from cold. No wind blew, but there was something else at work beneath the hoary, bent heads of the thistles, causing them to rustle and stir. I wondered if it might be a rabbit, or maybe a ring-necked pheasant, but no, it was the man who lived in the apartment below mine, dressed in his usual camouflage. Combat gear, and when he raised his square head there were the gummy black circles under his eyes like a football player's, and a gun in his hand, pointing at me.

"Got you," he whispered, but after assessing my apparent state of health, he didn't even pretend to pull the trigger, thinking better of spraying me with pellets of scarlet paint. I knew what I looked like, some days—those women depicted sewing in the backgrounds of certain sixteenth-century paintings, sensible but tragic, my mischievous expectancy cushioned all over with wise resignation.

We knew each other vaguely, me and the man from downstairs. He wasn't as imposing as he sometimes pretended. He ran a game farm outside town. On the outskirts was a camp where other men he called Ordinary Joes played war games for half- or full-day fees, depending on what time of day they got shot. Only occasionally was he out near the apartment grounds like this, testing the sights on his weapons or exercising his knees. As far as the other neighbors and I could tell, it wasn't politics that drove him into the woods with a rusty canteen full of nothing but water. He wasn't a Freeman, didn't hail from some militia in Idaho, wasn't paranoid or even jealous if someone knocked on his door at night to ask his dog-trainer wife for advice about puppies. Really, if only he'd take off those ugly green field boots and put on some normal footwear he'd look as blandly Midwestern as the rest of us. But they were such ungainly boots! Olive green canvas with black leather heels and toes. No matter what he was doing, even barbecuing in Bermuda shorts and a Lacoste shirt, he wore those boots laced like miniature corsets, the tops of his white athletic socks bunched at midcalf. His wife wore the same kind of boots, even with skirts. Until yesterday I used to think of the Miller-Fitzpatricks only as the couple with the ugly green boots. But yesterday we became friends.

"How are you feeling, Isobel?" was the next thing he said, so I knew all at once, as I had known about David, that the whole apartment complex was aware that I was ill. Perhaps it was only my impulsive new hours that had clued them in, or my nightly, jaundiced appearances wrapped in my robe on the balcony, a glass of wine shivering in one hand, the other strumming the balcony railing to the strains of whatever curious music Hercules was coaxing out of his bass. The once-stalwartly restful Isobel Albright was "out of sorts," I could practically hear them saying. "It's unlike her," they'd worry, to keep the light on after ten P.M., to keep the blinds raised and the drapes wide open, to be heard swearing at the garbage when the bag broke on the way across the lot and then to be seen furiously throwing the scattered chicken wings football-style into the Dumpster while kicking bits of wayward orange peel under the day manager's car. "It's unlike her," they'd commiserate, not to be feeding the finches but to pause instead at the edge of the dusky field in order to listen with a look of absolute delight to the howls of mating cats; unlike her to include, in the chocolate chip cookies she brings all the time to the neighborhood meetings, surprise nuggets of, what is that? ginger root?, unlike her to head for the wrong car every morning and have to be guided along by those two visitors, the young man and his mother, who have to urge her away from the driver's side into the passenger seat instead. "Have you seen how thin she's grown?" I imagine the neighbors saying. "She looks so thin, she looks so tired, she looks depleted, somehow . . .?" and then someone else saying, "Don't you know she had a double mastectomy?!" and then all of them saying, "That's terrible. That's really awful. But she looks so, I don't know . . ." "Rapturous," someone else might conclude. "She does! She *does!* But a little bit gray. Are you sure about the surgery? *Both?* She looks like she's having a vision." And someone else might interject, "I heard she wasn't doing chemo. I saw her playing with her hair. That was one thing about Isobel, you never caught her in public fussing with her hair, and yet it always looked so perfect." "I heard she's dying." "Please don't say that. They can *do* things these days." "Not for everyone." "It's so sad. That elegant woman." "So poised." "So relaxed." "And the museum fire. What timing." "Not even forty!" "No. Just forty. But there was always something a little fragile about her." "Fragile! Isobel? Are we talking about the same person? Didn't her folks die in a—" "Well, maybe not fragile, but—" "I always thought of her as being like a sail. A boat in a strong wind. Just leaning away from the wind, and moving very steadily, on a steady course, and always maintaining exactly the same—" "Until now." "Yes." "Can they really let her not do the chemo?" "I would think over Christmas we could plan some kind of—"

"How's business?" I asked Mr. Miller-Fitzpatrick. I didn't know his first name, or his wife's. When I stepped toward him onto the crunchy grass, I slipped and lost my balance for a second. Afterward I put my fingers to my brow, just gently, to see if I felt any change. He looked so stricken I thought maybe the powder was finally working—my face turning wiser but merrier, its contours shifting a little with age and with joy, my hair disappearing before his eyes. For some time now the skin under my eyes had been developing a curious sheen about which I was even a little bit vain—faint, white half-circles with a waxy cast, not as jaundiced as some of the rest of me, but now I wondered if maybe the translucence was frightening him.

"Cathy was wondering if maybe there was anything we could do for you, Isobel."

"How *is* Cathy?" Sneeze. "I haven't seen her in ages."

"Bless you. Cathy's always fine. Do you need to sit down, Isobel?"

If I needed to sit down, I would sit down, I said to myself, insulted, sneezing again from the rubbed-off powder.

And then I did sit down, as surprised as if my knees had decided to do it themselves, on the frozen, sharp stubble of grass at the edge of the parking lot. Like the times I'd gone walking because the view from my balcony seemed to command it, I sat because the vista of frosty meadow urged me to do so. Crisscrossed by high telephone wires and electric lines, the meadow made a shallow rectangular valley with the place where the supermarket was slated to go up, looking especially empty in the middle of it. Although the grass had not been cleared, the first shovel of foundation not even dug, still the broad, squat building seemed already to sit invisibly on top of it, aglow with a lunar florescence.

Miller-Fitzpatrick was as surprised as I was when I sat then and there on the frosty grass. Probably that wasn't what he had in mind when he asked if I needed to sit. But then he sat, too, and kept me company for quite a long while, delighted to answer my questions about his war games. Were the players required to fall down, when they were shot? Did the fake blood come off in the wash? Did the players forget it was only a game? Did they begin to believe they were really in danger? Did they feel the terror, the monotony, the hunger, of battle? Did they ration their cigarettes? Did the men pass around photographs of their wives and girlfriends while hunkered in rain in the fake foxholes?

At this he took offense.

"They're not fake foxholes. A foxhole is a foxhole. There's nothing fake about them."

What was it like to practice dying, was what I really wanted to know. Would he spray me so I could find out?

"Are you thirsty, Isobel?" asked Miller-Fitzpatrick around five in the evening, not having sprayed me, having pretended, to my relief, that his gun was out of paint. Because it was winter, darkness had already fallen. Though I knew—could almost feel—how cold I should be, somehow I felt untouched by the evening's drop in temperature, and when Miller-Fitzpatrick gathered some dried weeds and stole a few small logs from a neighbor's balcony, our small campfire might as well have been flickering inside us, so cozy and warm did its blue flames make us. In daylight, the passage of cars on the far side of the field made just a blur of reflective sunshine, but soon the headlights in the gray dusk were the only things we could clearly see. Ordinarily the coming of night disappointed me and made me uneasy, for with the passage of each uneventful day I chastised myself for having managed to miss my date with my future—there'd been a miscommunication, a misunderstanding, perhaps had I been sitting on my balcony instead of at the edge of the parking lot, I would have finally met my husband or held my daughters in my arms. But it was nice at the edge of the parking lot, and I was glad to be there. At five-thirty, Cathy Miller-Fitzpatrick joined me and her husband with a few bottles of nonalcoholic beer. She sat beside us with her knees raised, the bottles propped between her ugly field boots as she twisted the lids. She was young and wholesomely pretty, and smelled exactly like a basset hound. I nearly said to her, *If I had decided to do chemotherapy, chances are I would have lost my sense of smell, I wouldn't know that you smelled like a basset hound.*

"Isobel, you can lean on my legs, if you like. Are your visitors still around? Would you like a blanket, Isobel, to wrap around your shoulders?" asked Cathy.

"That sounds lovely," I answered

"Fetch her a blanket," said Cathy to Mr. Miller-Fitzpatrick, who bounded up so obediently that I burst out laughing. Finding the blanket took him a long time, as much time as if he'd climbed the extra steps to my apartment and had a chat with

Martha and Hercules telling them that I was okay, that I was high on fake beer, that I seemed not to want to go in, that in the warmth of the campfire I'd lost the peaked, jaundiced look that had made him nervous earlier. While he was gone, Cathy began massaging my neck and shoulders. How unlike Isobel, I thought, to succumb to this kind of attention, this kind of touch, from someone I barely knew. But our perch at the edge of the field was so intimate that soon the touch of Cathy's fingers felt natural, our nascent friendship sealed as if by years.

What year is it? I nearly asked her, wondering if a few had gone by without my knowing, then stopped myself with the thought of her telling the neighbors, "She asked me what year it was! It was all I could do to keep from starting to cry, but I answered her, you know, I figured, what else was there to do? It was the least I could do, to tell her it was 1995."

So instead I asked, "Is this really happening, Cathy?"

In the silence that followed I noticed that the just-rising moon was a perfect crescent showing the humorous profile of its face, fanciful as an illustration in a child's book. I lifted my hand, rotated it quietly in the dim light, watching it slide from three quarters to whole to just a sliver of illumined flesh.

"I guess I'd have to say that this is definitely happening," Cathy answered.

We sat there till two o'clock in the morning.

HAVING GONE to bed so late, I had a little trouble rising in the morning, but when Martha declared that she and Hercules were going to work without me I made them wait while I showered and dressed. At the gas station, I insisted on being the one to fill the tank. The pump was inoperable—the squeeze lever kept popping open in my hand. Each time this happened I gave a little screech of indignation, but I wouldn't let Martha or Hercules help me. I could hear Martha sighing in the driver's seat, and Hercules telling her there wasn't any rush even though it was he who had reason to be impatient. Each day before work he sat in the shelter of the museum shed sipping coffee with the Botanical Society intern with the horn-rimmed glasses and the long, golden braid. From what Martha and I could see they hadn't touched each other yet, but it was sweet how they mimicked each other's postures, both pausing at the same time to take long, shivery swallows of coffee while gazing into the start of winter. Sometimes Hercules reached forward and took her glasses off her face in order to look through them himself, a routine she found so hilarious that I began to find it funny, too.

"We haven't had any problem with that pump, least not as I heard," said the attendant when I complained about the lever. "That's twelve-ninety-one. Ma'am. Twelve dollars and ninety-one cents."

I pointed to the credit card I'd plunked on the counter.

"That's your driver's license, ma'am," he said.

"Oh, I'm sorry," I said, and reaching into my purse for my wallet pulled out some round, damp object that it took me a moment to realize was the gas cap from my car. "How did this get in my purse?" I said, then slid the driver's license back into my wallet and turned to go.

"Read my lips, ma'am," said the attendant.

"Yes," I said.

"Ma'am, that'll be twelve dollars and ninety-one cents," he said.

"Oh," I said.

"You have a credit card, ma'am?"

"Oh," I said. I took out my wallet and gave him my credit card. When he handed me the pen and the credit slip I dropped them both into my purse and snapped it shut.

"Ma'am," said the attendant. "The slip?"

"Pardon me?" I asked.

"Is everything all right in here?" asked Martha, poking her head in the door.

"She has to sign the credit slip."

"I don't see any credit slip. Do you?" I said to Martha.

"She put it in her purse," the man told her.

"Oh, God, I'm so sorry," I laughed. I withdrew the crumpled slip from the purse. "Do you have a pen?"

"She put the pen in her purse, too," said the man.

"I'll never find it now," I laughed. "Is this it?" I asked, pulling out an old pen.

"It doesn't matter," said the man.

"Here," I said.

"Isobel," said Martha. "You need to sign the slip."

I signed the slip. The signature was my own, I was comforted to see. Not a flourish was out of place.

"No. Sign here on this line," said the attendant, pointing.

"Do you know that there are people who can't sign their names in public?" I asked. "It's a recognized phobia, particularly among women. Can you imagine the things that that might say about a person, that she can't put her name to paper? The things it might mean about her self-image, her self-confidence, her sense of identity, her knowledge of who she is?"

I signed my name on the line the attendant indicated. There was not a single letter in my signature, I saw, that did not include a loop like a tiny lasso.

"I think it's time I modified my signature," I said to Martha as we walked out the door. "It's too well-behaved."

"You can do that," said Martha. She led me gently to the car. She climbed into the driver's seat. She slid the key in the ignition.

"Wait a second," said Hercules. "Here comes the man."

The attendant came running out with my gas cap, then stopped suddenly with a look of horror on his face, his skinny shoulders thrown back in their monogrammed shirt.

"Don't," he moaned.

"Don't what?" asked Hercules.

"Don't . . . don't . . . Don't start the car . . . the hose! She left the hose in the gas tank!"

"Jesus Christ," Martha whispered, removing her fingers from their grasp of the key and folding both hands in her lap.

"She *did?*" I said. "She's terribly sorry. She certainly has been a little forgetful lately, hasn't she? But she'll make amends. She promises."

I got out of the car, pulled the hose from the gas tank, hung it back on the pump where it belonged, and screwed the gas cap in place firmly and easily.

"Her profoundest apologies for her absentmindedness," I said to Martha and Hercules when I got back in the car, giving a little bow. "Is she forgiven?"

There was silence.

"Is she *forgiven?*" I repeated.

"It's not a question of forgiveness," Martha answered in a scared tone.

"But we forgive her anyway," said Hercules.

"IF ANYONE knows what could be making that racket in the parking lot . . ." repeated Jayne, removing her potted violets from under the grow lights in her corner of the trailer, then laying the taxidermy specimens on the shelves to dry. There was the albino squirrel with the appropriately red glass eyes, the weasel minus one paw, a screech owl, a kingfisher, and a bat.

"I don't remember the bat," I said.

"Me neither," said Jayne, pausing a moment to reconsider the placement of the animals as if they were flowers to be arranged in a vase. She shrugged, folded open the bat's wings, and laid it flat on its back under the glare.

"Come on, Jayne," pleaded David. "Isn't there some air freshener in the garage? Can't you put that whole grow light thing out there, please?"

"There are too many spiders in the garage," Jayne stubbornly answered, plucking a twig from the tail of the squirrel. She opened a bag of mothballs, poured several handfuls onto two saucers, placed the saucers on the shelves. The fragrance of camphor was sudden and warm. I saw the bat's wings tremble a little in response to the change in atmosphere. I saw its scrunched-up eyelids scrunch a bit tighter, like the eyes of a bat that had died one winter on my balcony and dried up like a milkweed pod, its wings so papery, as weightless as leftover autumn leaves, that it skittered in the wind. Looking now at its cousin that wasn't quite dead, I thought of myself in my coffin, under layers of earth, brittle as paper, waiting patiently for a wind strong enough to carry me someplace more romantic. Without a word to anyone I straightened my hair in its clasp, rose from my metal desk, and climbed the wood steps down to the lawn. There was no racket in the parking lot, nothing except for the top-forty strains of the workers' radios and the persistent, wonderful, muffled shrieking of the black telephone in the trunk of my car.

How slowly I approached, afraid of showing my terrible eagerness, each measured step advancing my hope and fear. And how reassured I was, when I opened the trunk and felt the familiar, blunt heft of the black receiver and the years rushing forward inside it, to a day even colder than the one I had just left behind, so my suddenly bald head smarted with the icy chill. I made a note to keep one of my hats in the trunk, having experienced, just then, a peculiar memory of six angora hoods in brilliant, deep colors. Violet. Chocolate. Emerald. Pumpkin. Cranberry. And sunflower. I'd never seen them before, had I? Yet I knew them by heart. Against my bare collarbone a hammered brass necklace held the frozen air close, and even the hooked wires of my earrings seemed to shiver in the lobes.

The month was December, the year 2006. I was past fifty years old.

"Hang on a second," I said, and carried the telephone around to the front of the car, where I made myself at home with the car's heat turned low and the fan just barely whirring. "Another second," I said, and found the knob for the seat heater, and settled Bald Queen Butterfly's muscular ass into the electric comfort of the upholstery. If all my life I'd been leery of turning fifty, leery of turning chalky and quiet and more practical even than I was already, now I reveled in the purring of my blood through my body, the expectant tingling of the nerves at the tips of my fingers, the resonant echo of pleasure between my legs.

"Why do I persist in loving a man who lives in a cave of solitude?" Martha's voice began.

For a moment I wondered if we'd arranged that she would call me and read me one of her new poems.

"Why am I in love with a man who identifies with dark rooms? Why am I in love with a man whose entire sense of personal integrity is bound up in cooking only one-pot meals? Why am I in love with a man who seems to believe that the only true way for us to be together is for me to receive even fewer phone calls than he does? Two nights in seven years we've gone out to dinner at the Mr. Cinders on the frontage road. We ate Salisbury steaks. Twice we went to a bar and had a game of pool. He won. Six times in six years he's consented to take a walk, but only in the dark when no one can see us or out on the Larson trail where there's never anyone around. I feel so sad, Isobel," Martha lamented, "I feel so very, very sad. Not for me so much anymore but for him. Because he can't break out. Because he won't let himself just be part of the world. And what I'm figuring out is, I'm one of the ways he has of doing it. I provide him with all sorts of things to retreat from. When I ask him if he wants to come over, he can say he drove past the apartment a couple of days ago and no one was home. If I want him to come shopping, he can say he bought himself a couple of things he needed just last month. If there's a movie I want to see, he can say he has a cold and since movie theaters are a prime location for the spread of germs it would be inconsiderate of him to go. If I ask him if he'd like to go for a drive, he can say he feels like sitting still, and if I say, 'Okay, we'll just snuggle somewhere and hold each other,' he says something like, 'I've been thinking of playing a game of Scrabble but I'm missing an S.' Can you imagine that, Isobel? Me saying I'd like to sit somewhere and hold each other and him saying he's missing an S? He seems to think if he's vague enough I might forget what I wanted."

"Have you talked to him about any of this since the last time you told me about it?" I asked, never wearying of Martha's ceaseless troubles with Trevor—her restlessness, her feelings of neglect, her desperate solicitude when she hoped to get through to him as to someone in a coma, as if the sound of her voice might penetrate enough to keep him from sinking further into one of his encyclopedic reveries. No matter what, I believed Martha's devotion to the reclusive Trevor was healthier by far than her old routine of thoughtless, impulsive coupling. I only hoped they were having good sex of one kind or another. The idea of Martha loving valiantly on without it made me cringe, I often told my husband, whoever he was, my face mock-cringing in the hollow behind his knee, which was my favorite toy. I liked to see if I could make my husband's knee make sucking noises by bending the leg, or by pressing parts of my own body against it, then peeling them away. Nora and Evvy were not permitted to play with this toy. I insisted it was mine alone. I told them to go play with their tape players, Ouija boards, and perfume atom-izers. But they only crouched on the far side of the door making fun of us by making the most outrageous sucking noises, which made me feel I had perverted them by introducing them at such a young age to forbidden sex games. When I said this to my husband, whoever he was, he lay for several seconds in an agony of suppressed laughter, waited until it was subdued, then turned to me and said seriously, "Isobel, just because it's a sex game for you doesn't make it a sex game for everyone else. They're just making farting noises."

To which I replied, "But is it a sex game for you?"

To which he replied, whoever he was, with the most pene-trating look of camaraderie, "You should know I'm willing to learn almost anything from you as long as you learn it from me in return. But you worry too much about the girls. Do you think you have to make up for Martha not worrying? You don't. Anyway, Martha does worry. She only does it more sur-reptitiously than most people do."

Saying this, he buried his body against mine and held me so

close that we couldn't speak, so tightly that we could barely breathe or even look at each other, our bodies so firmly entwined that we couldn't move our limbs to caress each other even when we started humming and nearly bursting with desire. It was torture. It was delight. Not for the first time I wondered if I had finally reached my prime. Nearly twenty years late, but when my parents died, I must have shoved it far ahead of me, thinking I was shoving it back. How unfair it seemed then, that they had died on the precise day I turned thirty-five, when I was *reaching my prime,* whatever that meant, except they died, so I hadn't reached it after all. I didn't want them to miss it. I supposed *prime* meant falling in love, so I fell out of love, instead, again and again, so as not to allow their deaths to deprive them of seeing my prime. Until my husband, that is. Funny, how I never cared what they were missing when my husband and I were happiest, when we knelt on the bed with our knees conjoined like two halves of an hourglass, our slow kisses full in the present. Bald Queen Butterfly, I don't know if I've mentioned . . . when I am Bald Queen Butterfly my shoulders are nearly as broad as a man's, my waist cinched in soft curves, my vanished breasts and absent nipples like shadowy ghosts hidden beneath the cotton ribbing of my undershirt. I wear a camisole style—spaghetti straps, scalloped hems, a twist of a pink rose stitched to the V of the neckline. It's like a play on words, my androgenous body against that delicate wisp of shirt. My husband plucks the straps with his tongue, tries to decide which is softer, the skin of my belly or the stretched-out cotton ribbing, and when I part my strong legs he is always shocked for a minute to see how gently I open, with a touch of Isobel's old reserve still shushing the moist folds, making them quiet and proud. But he knows what to do. Somehow he knows exactly where Isobel and Bald Queen Butterfly meet, always a different spot from the time before but he finds it and teases it, coaxes it, seduces it. He knows things, my husband, about me, I mean, things I don't even know myself. Sometimes I worry I can't return it, for there is nothing I understand about my husband half as well as what he understands about me. Far from it. But now, on the telephone with Martha, it seems my ignorance about him is as glorious as his knowledge about me. How could it not be, when it's so monumental? I don't even know his name! Or who he is! Or what he looks like!

"Sometimes I have to remind myself of what it was like before I met Trevor, when I really was single, when I was *dating*," Martha is saying. "Remember that time I kissed the car mechanic good-bye?"

I hemmed and hawed for a minute, knowing the story would come to me. She'd brought the car, my car, to the garage for repairs; instead of making her wait, the mechanic had driven her home; she'd been on so many dates that she forgot this wasn't one of them; when he glided to a halt in the driveway, she leaned over and gave him a peck on the cheek. Yes, I remembered. It kept us laughing for days before Martha fell into a funk, recognizing the rut she was in.

"I'm too old to do that stuff again," said Martha.

"You don't have to," I said. "There's no rule that says you can't love a man who's not perfect, you know."

"That's easy for you to say," said Martha, and hung up the phone before I had the chance to figure out a way of getting her to tell me my husband's name.

The second I hung up, I heard knocking on the windshield of my car. For how long it had been going on I couldn't say. It was the foreman from the construction crew.

"We need to ask you to move your car," he said carefully. "I could drive it if you want, you just move over, I'll park it. The columns have arrived."

I could see the dwarf columns stacked in the bed of a truck, layered with canvas and sheets of plastic. The fluted tops and sculpted pedastals held purple shadows. The idea of the rejuvenated splendor of the hallway in which they would stand made me contemplate all the hundreds of years to come when, barring another fire or flood or disaster, that row of columns would still exist, removed from the mortal shenanigans all around them. When all people now on earth were gone, the columns' milky gleam would still be there, like trees carved of stone. Dr. Klink would be gone. Mrs. Klink would be gone. Their five children, gone. Their bevy of uncles and aunts and second cousins and all the Hmong-American teenage girl baby-sitters, gone. Hercules, David, Jayne, Martha, the gift shop lady, the Miller-Fitzpatricks, all the Ordinary Joes with their blackened eyes and ugly field boots, gone, the gentle mammography technician, gone, all the people in all the cars on all the roads, all the nurses and priests and accountants and lawyers and striptease artists and birthday party clowns and gas station attendants, gone, even Nora and Evvy gone. And all the while, in all the years to come, the dwarf columns serene in their hallway, unfazed, untroubled by all our hilarious comings and goings.

"Pardon me, ma'am?" said the foreman, leaning a little closer through the window of my car.

I smiled at him. At last he shrugged, turned away, consulted with the driver of the truck and guided him through a series of three-quarter turns ending with the truck backed onto the frozen lawn. I sat woozily watching them unload the columns. Just as Martha and Hercules had steered clear of my sojourn at the edge of the field with the Miller-Fitzpatricks, they let me be, knowing how much I wanted just to look at things. If I gazed hard enough, if I stared with enough concentration, would that compensate for all the eons of nothingness to come?

Then the telephone rang again in my lap. The decade flipped past like a page in a book. It was Martha again, 2006, but not the same day as before. I knew this because I was wearing one of my angora hoods. Sunflower gold. The hoods were better than hair, because their color might be changed daily without mess or inconvenience, yet the softness of the lamb's wool against my temples and brow, the way the folds lay so feathery around my neck, was reminiscent of hair. Snow was

falling past my windshield, not yet sticking, just making a
frosty sheen on the glass. My wedding ring was not on my finger; I found it buried under the phone among the fringes of a
poncho that Martha had given me in exchange for a week of
cooking. Every night for seven nights I'd made a giant, eccen-
tric salad, one with shrimp and jalapeños, I remember, and
another with shavings of citrus peel, that I carried down the
hall to her apartment on a flat, wooden platter.

I didn't listen very hard to what she was saying, although I
sympathized with all of the parts about Trevor and hearkened
to the parts about the girls. They were preteen, which meant,
we supposed, that they were still children wanting desperately
to be teenagers but not knowing quite how. Right now they
were in Evvy's bedroom making snowflakes out of black construction paper, Nora petulant and Evvy resentful, for they had
borrowed one of Trevor's Clapton tapes and misplaced it. They
hadn't told Trevor yet. Like Martha, they couldn't stand the
way he'd pretend not to be bothered by it. If he didn't get
angry, he wouldn't have to forgive; that was Trevor's way, his
heart scrunched in his pocket, keeping the same old, same old
distance.

But really, what Martha was doing, by telling me all of this,
was introducing me to my husband, for as she talked about all
the other things, I daydreamed about him. I could practically
feel him inside me, his hands raised to cup the contours of my
face, my own two hands wrapped tight around his forearm,
squeezing harder than I should, my nails digging into the taut
cords of muscle as if they meant to penetrate, denting the flesh
of his forearm on which the dark hairs stood upright in soft,
sparse meadows. I was meaning to hurt him, make him cry out
and whip his arm away or at least bite my ear in return, but all
he did was level his breath in my ear and whisper, "There she
goes, there she goes," until I orgasmed.

"You talk to me like I'm a whale," I would say.

"You do breach. You do blow. But you're definitely not a
whale," he would answer, sucking and tasting the domed, bald

curves of my head. "This is my favorite part of your body, not including all the other parts I like best," he joked.

I had his words, but not his voice. I had his broad forearms and even his look of camaraderie but not his face. I had the backs of his giant knees but not his gait, height, or posture. Who was he? Whom did I love so well?

Funny, I reflected, waiting for Martha to go on talking about all the other things that would cause me to daydream about my husband. There was something about the very tenor of her voice that awakened him in me, but only in fits and starts. How frustrating it was, that all my life I'd had the man but not the love, and now at last I had the love but not the man.

"In what position are Nora and Evvy sitting?" I asked Martha, meaning, "What does my husband do with his hands? For a living, I mean. But not only for a living. I know he does something, but I don't know what."

But the phone was disconnected. The snow had stopped falling, the windshield was vivid with bright winter sun, my full head of long hair wavered in the breeze through the heating vents. There was the chalky smell of plaster. All the museum staff had gathered at David's behest to admire the slender columns as they were hoisted inside the building.

"Isobel, did you get a look at these?" Martha cried from the lawn.

"*That* noise. That ringing! What is it?" yelled Jayne.

I slid lower in my seat. The same decade flipped by, the same snow was falling, the same sunflower hood warmed my bald head. On the phone Martha rambled, "I would never have said that before. About love being wasted. I would have said, you love a man, it's over, you go on to something new with all the same amount of stuff you had before. But now I think love *can* be wasted. Love shrinks, Isobel. It knots up if you don't bestow it."

Is this a poem or are you talking? I nearly inquired. But I was too busy daydreaming about my husband's hands. I didn't like them, plain and simple. The pads of his fingers were stiff

with callus, the backs of the knuckles more hairless than the
skin on the pale insides of my thighs. But if I pressed them
softly against my closed eyelids and ran the tip of my tongue
from knuckle to knuckle pausing to flick at each tight curve of
webbing, teasing each hard nub of callus, then they began to
seem lovely to me, *his* hands and no other's. This same thing
happened every time we were together, I started out disappointed—how could such hands belong to my husband?—but
then I accustomed myself to them.

"Have I ever told you how I feel about my husband's
hands? What gets me—"I said.

Both of us giggled.

"What gets me," Martha said, "is the way you insist on
referring to him as your husband! As if you don't know his
name."

"I don't know his name," I confessed.

The phone went dead. The decade flipped backward. The
columns, twelve in all, had been carried inside.

"You don't know whose name, Isobel?" asked Martha, her
solicitous face framed in the open car window. Martha's face
had seasons like a calendar. Sometimes it was closed, sometimes remote. Today her eyes were dark as stones, her brows
drawn together in kindness and vexation.

"Would you like a muffin, Isobel? I brought some from
home. You look drained. But dreamy, too. Aren't the columns
beautiful? Why are you holding that phone? Isobel?"

"Oh, because I've always liked these old telephones. Don't
touch it," I said.

She withdrew her hand.

It struck me that she did not trouble to ask me again whose
name I didn't know. Perhaps she recognized the basic catch-22
of the question, rather like trying to learn the spelling of a
word by looking it up in the dictionary. Or perhaps she imagined that I had already forgotten saying such a thing, and that I
was drifting away. Her thinking this made me angry. She had
no idea what power I had over her. If I wanted to be reckless I

might tell her about Trevor. I might tell her that a man she hadn't met yet—who spent hours dusting the leaves of his spider plants, who would ask her, during their first conversation, which they hadn't even had yet, if she knew that the Latin word *tremendus* meant "to be trembled at"—would someday be so far under her skin she wouldn't be able to see straight.

I put my hand on her sleeve. Anxiously, she laid her wrist against my forehead, checking for fever.

"I'm just taking a break," I assured her. "Go back to work. Leave me alone now, please."

So she turned for the building to watch the installation of the columns, the hem of her long skirt rustling with cold, on her salt-and-pepper hair a dewy tracery of silver. A few of the construction workers hesitated, then swiveled to watch, embarrassed by their attraction to this fat, middle-aged lady. I wondered what they thought of me—some skinny, jaundiced creature sliding down in her car seat, muttering to herself. Or might they catch just a glimpse of my regal baldness, a glittering flash of my jewelry? At the very least I determined to look courageous, for their sake if not for my own. I sat straight in the autumn breeze, watching the windshield for signs of snow, my fingers so calm on the receiver of the telephone I feared that if it rang I might forget to pick it up. In order to remain patient I thought of my husband's hands, and how each time I was with him I would coax myself anew to fall in love with them. Every time we went to bed, when my husband slid his hand between my thighs, not even his giant fingers would seem to reach high enough or deep enough, but I'd have devised a way of settling on top of them so hungrily they nearly grazed my ribs. The best thing about our lovemaking would be how raw and susceptible we made ourselves to each other, and how we bound ourselves to each other before being flung headlong into and out of the whirlpool of sex.

I felt very lucky.

I could hardly wait to meet him.

24

It was the fur trapper's glove that finally gave me a glimpse of my husband's face. I'd forgotten about that scrappy glove; it was a hundred years old, from Lac du Flambeau, Wisconsin. Of all the museum artifacts bequeathed to me by the Crazy Volunteer, the glove was the most repugnant and yet somehow the most perturbing, a floppy patchwork of fragments of molding beaver hide held together by nothing more than the frayed remnants of the trapper's spirit. To think this was all that was left of the man, whomever he had been, this sorry excuse for a glove, this torn echo of many winters spent gathering sticks for fires and hauling hides from the tangled reaches of forest. And yet to think that this so-called glove was more than what most of us leave behind, a thing that could be touched, felt, *understood.* When I found it in the spare tire well of my car I thought maybe it was the not-quite-dead bat, who when no one was watching had roused itself under the warm rays of Jayne's grow light, and having adjusted the kinks out of its wings, flapped noisily out of the trailer on an eddy of vampire breath. From the trunk of the car, already I'd pulled the old boxy valise of cracked leather, then the giant Victorian valentine still stitched around the edges with what must have been a yard of faded ribbon, then a voluptuous blown-glass hurricane lamp that looked cousin to one of Jayne's Alice-in-Wonderland style hookahs. The valise was empty but for its thickly quilted lining. The inner flap of the valentine still held its flimsy heart of tissue paper but no love note or rhyme. The fur trapper's glove was so smelly and decayed I nearly tossed it in disgust under the wheels of the car. But first, grimacing, snarling, averting my nose, I slipped it tentatively onto my hand. Spongy tentacles of mold grew inside the sticky fingers.

"A thing doesn't have to be touched and felt in order to be understood," said my husband, for I had been thinking aloud. "What's the matter? You're shivering."

"Just a chill," I responded.

The glove was gone. I was holding my husband's hand.

No matter how much resentment I'd ever harbored for my husband's hands, he never caught on, or at any rate never *revealed* that he caught on, and for this I felt an equal tenderness. He had a comforting, meaningful grip, my husband, the tip of each callused finger so sure and precise that little pressure points of heat and responsive delight vibrated in my own.

We were walking along a beach I didn't recognize. It wasn't one of the narrow corridors of scrappy white dunes preserved on the shores of Lake Michigan close to home, or one of the West Coast beaches for whose breakers and rock cliffs I'd mourned when I'd first come midwest, or one of the cosy, high stretches of oceanfront lane along which I'd bicycled with my parents so long ago in Ireland. No, this was a flat, wet, brown stretch of seeping tide pools and tossed-up kelp and debris, made treacherous by spirals of dive-bombing terns intent on protecting their nesting sites amid the saw grass on the dunes. A mile or so farther along the beach we would come to an open air bar under a lean-to decorated with gas station flags, where we would consider tequila sunrises before deferring to our usual shots of tequila, our chasers of Corona, the wedges of lemon warm from having steeped in their own juice all day in the sun. As near as we could get to the incoming tide without being swept out to sea, that's where we would sit with our bottles of beer—our bottoms soaking in a tide pool, our bare toes trawling for hermit crabs and cool, buried clams, my bald head so shiny in the dusk my husband joked he could watch the sunset in it as if in a crystal ball.

Our steps were mismatched. To turn around and gaze back

at our arguing footprints—his speeding up while mine slowed, and mine leaping ahead where his lingered—had once been one of our private jokes.

I had a crick in one knee.

A dull, scraping sensation in one hip but nothing really annoying.

When a tern kamikazeed in such a wide arc that it nearly struck my shoulder, then shot back like a dart into the torn fabric of the sky, I felt an accustomed flicker of pride in the sharpness of my eyesight, then a momentary pang of regret for a certain dimming in the sound of the pounding of the surf, about which I hadn't told anyone yet, not even my husband.

I would tell him on my next birthday, I decided, when I would be seventy-three years old.

The year on the index card, which I had slipped into my pocket before beginning my search through the trunk of the car, was 2027. To my unaccustomed eyes, that number didn't look like a year at all. And there was something alarming in the atmosphere—a whitish glow on the horizon, the strange, snowy complexion of sky on what was clearly a summer day, that put me on my guard.

But my husband's beard was full and auburn. In the lobe of his left ear, which was the one I could see when we walked side by side as we always walked, with him to my right, was a slender hoop earring from which was suspended a single jade bead against which my husband's ample height and broad shoulders achieved an unexpected refinement. He wore wraparound mirror sunglasses and a blue cloth tennis hat although he'd never once played tennis in his life, and a pink T-shirt over gleaming black bicycle shorts in which the jut and swell of his genitals might have been chiseled from a hunk of obsidian. His nose was white with zinc oxide, for it burned easily, I remembered.

"I want to jump you," I said.

"So do it," he answered, deadpan, his voice secretive under the camouflage of his clothing.

But neither one of us slowed in our footsteps, and there was suddenly between us a nearly indiscernible tension that caused the fingers of our clasped hands to slip free of each other and fall to our sides as we walked. By the time we reached the bar, would we be holding hands again? Would I slide my hand under his butt in the tide pool, cup my fingers round his balls for everyone to see? It was okay to be sexy in public when you were senior citizens—people appreciated it. But this evening our romance felt under some strain. I couldn't say why. Nora and Evvy were fighting as usual, over the phones, long distance, party-style, with us listening in on our own conference lines. They were like those couples who argue in public at dinners in restaurants, always waiting for the most intimate moments in our four-way conversation to say something biting and cruel to each other. But this had been going on for years; it was their way of remaining loyal and sisterly even though they were so different from each other. Nora was a corporate lawyer in Los Angeles, Evvy worked for a landscaping business in a town in east Texas. Evvy was pregnant and not married, Nora married and not pregnant. Nora had sent Evvy several photos of the inside of her house, Evvy had Scotch-taped one or two of them to the refrigerator inside her trailer. Nora was slender, bespectacled, intent, Evvy as muscular as a rhinoceros, quick-witted, with a sullen enthusiasm for old-fashioned trouble. About the father of her baby she knew only that he was full-blooded Mexican like she was, that she never intended to see him again, and that if she did, she'd call the police. She still had her red curls; when she clung to the back of the moving pick-up truck her hair must have blazed in the glare from the gulf. Of the two, it was Evvy I couldn't help but care about the most, way down in my gut, not just in my bones and my head and my heart where I cared about Nora, and it drove me crazy that my husband pretended not to know this terrible secret of mine. But that wasn't the cause of the evening's strain, though my husband did say, out of the blue, as we were walking on the beach, "When was the last time we saw her?"

"Which one?"

"Evvy."

"The funeral," I answered without a bit of hesitation but not knowing quite yet whose funeral I was talking about. Funny, to know so much and yet so little, to feel so included and yet so much an alien, my bald head signaling its bemused, lofty ignorance. How we'd climbed a soggy hillside to the grave two by two, Nora and Martha, then Evvy and me, then my husband with the fury he'd nurtured in my embrace for years whenever the talk turned to Trevor.

Who had had too much to drink, the coroner had determined.

Who had merely been peering over the bridge rail to see if the osprey was still in its nest, Martha insisted.

Who had drunk more than he was used to in order to have the guts to finally tell Martha he loved her, I'd suggested to Martha in an effort to comfort her.

But her only response was laughter, stricken by the length to which he'd gone in order to avoid having to say it.

In the mist-laden sunlight his grave had looked familiarly introverted, a solitary container for the obscure body of knowledge that was Trevor himself. At the last minute, just before the burial, having looked at the hole in the dirt and how separate it was, how shabby, Martha called a sobbing halt to the tiny procession of mourners, declaring she needed to go off and find his tape player and earphones and his meager supply of favorite cassettes. Those days, Joe Cocker was his favorite. After Martha drove off, her bronzed lipstick blurry with trembling, the rest of us held a brief consultation on a slope near the grave. *What would we do,* we debated, *should Martha insist that they open the coffin so she might fit the headphones over his ears?* The answer was no. They had found him in the river. The evening before the funeral my husband had held me in the manner that was customary to him whenever there was something he was trying not to say to me about Trevor, so close I couldn't kiss him, my arms pressed so firmly against my sides I couldn't lift them to caress him. *Suicide* was the word he pressed between us so tightly it had no utterance. Trevor's last stand. The final door he'd been saving to close ever so gently in Martha's stunned face.

My husband had suspected Trevor's trump card for years before Trevor played it, but even now on the beach were I to turn to him and ask him why he'd kept it secret, he would be too angry at Trevor to talk about it.

But Trevor was not the cause of our strain this evening, either.

EVEN AFTER my husband and I tossed our shots down our throats and carried our beers to the edge of the surf, still I couldn't get a good enough look at his face except to see that it was dear to me and very familiar. I could feel our shared history surging and then retreating like background music. How slowly he sipped his beer, one swallow for every three times I arched my whole body into the froth of my own drink. Finished, I dug the lip of the empty bottle into the ridge of wet sand at the margin of the tide pool, let it fill with sand and salt-water, clamped my thumb on the mouth to shake it, and poured the gurgling mixture very slowly up and down my husband's bare legs, another habit of ours, another cog in our wheel, so he didn't flinch or jump. He was expecting it. A few minutes later he'd do the same thing to me.

"Would you take off your hat?" I considered asking him, then wondered if I might reach up and grab it myself as if in playfulness, except our mood wasn't playful this evening. It seemed we were on the edge of something more fretful than the ocean, something irksome I couldn't name, until finally he gave a sigh and leaned back as if in a big sandy chair and said, "There's something I'd like to talk about, Isobel."

"Oh, is there?" I said, because all at once I knew what it was. He did this whenever he wanted to go to New Orleans, making a bigger deal out of his excursions than they were, seeming to think I'd be hurt by his wanting to go there by himself. In a minute he would tell me that he needed some time alone, apologetically, as if after all these years he didn't realize that I liked these times as much as he did, I needed to be alone as much as he did. To grow old with another person, I often realized, did not save me from growing old by myself, as well, and every so often, it was good to face the changes with only my private self for company. Have I been sleeping less? I might ask myself. Am I less tolerant of cold? More tolerant of other people's idiosyncrasies? Am I less inclined to act impulsively? Or more?

Had my husband not gone to New Orleans, then I would have gone somewhere else and pondered these questions and others like them.

"I'm feeling," my husband confessed, "as if I'm ready for a little time to just, you know . . ."

From the very beginning I'd been shocked to hear him so tentative and so apologetic. He really shouldn't have felt this way. I gave him no reason. Besides, he was twenty years younger than I was, the wrong generation to imagine that his wife always craved his company. Who had raised him? I wondered. Who had brought up a man capable of believing he was indispensable to me?

"To just what?" I asked, humoring him the way I always did, digging my toe in the sand and kicking it forth in an arch of wet grit.

"To play around a little," he said.

I laughed. It was another of our private jokes, the way he said he was going to play around a little whenever I humored him by asking why he was going to New Orleans. Last time he'd been gone I was sixty-seven years old. Was it possible we parted only every five years? Often I went off by myself, somewhere when he was away. Maybe this time I'd rent that same bungalow in Indonesia. I wouldn't miss him. I never did, exactly, because I knew we would be together again soon. But suddenly I missed these companionable evenings on the beach and how our slowly emptied bottles of frothy, drunken sand bound our ankles and calves in wet moorings. For they wouldn't happen again, these evenings on the beach, at least not in the very same way. Our comfortable routine would be somehow altered by our having been apart, just as the tide might alter the lines of the shore. When he returned from New Orleans, we might find ourselves walking the beach at dawn instead of at dusk, we might carry a Thermos of orange juice and another of vodka, there might be a slight change in the cast of our minds and in whatever shared thoughts and moods drifted between us as we walked. Not worse. Not better. Just different. Maybe it was my age that made me sad about this; no sooner was a person *living in the moment,* as they say, than the moment changed and flung her gently just to the side of it.

A barge crossed on the water, under the harsh, white glaze of the sky.

"So that's okay?" he asked.

"When has it not been?"

"But . . ."

"What if I told you it wasn't okay? What would you do, then? Don't start playing games just because you know I'll miss you. We've never played games in the past, have we? There's no reason to start, now. Anyway it's not that terrible a thing, to miss somebody. It's just that, these days . . ."

"What?"

"I miss you more as I get older. I mean the feeling is more pungent every time. I have to get used to the flavor."

"Let me taste it, too," he said wonderingly.

He leaned forward and kissed me. All I could see was the zinc on his nose and the terrible white cast of sky. So I shut my eyes. After a minute, we could have been kissing forever. Each new kiss was the very same kiss, changeable and full of diversion, like an orchestra warming up and then delving into a piece and then stopping again to warm up for the next arrangement and then delving just as eagerly into that one. I could taste his tequila blending with mine for a more potent proof, the foregone sunrise flaming over our tongues. How young he was. Each time we kissed, I was reminded of this. Even in his fifties, he was a youth to me, his shoulders trembling around us, his fingers discovering, as if for the very first time, their accustomed places among the frets and sockets of my vertebrae.

A tern dive-bombed our feet. Behind us the cries of the other birds sounded curiously diminished, while the salt smell of the ocean was so intense that it burned our lips.

"Would you please turn your face so I can look at you?" I nearly asked my husband. Would you take off those inane sunglasses, please? Would you make up a song using only the letters of your name and sing it to me, so I'll know who you are?

Except that just then something hideous washed up against my bare foot, and I flung it back, yelping. It was a sodden clump of fur. I caught the old beaver hide glove gingerly on my big toe, hating to see it, hating to think that in less than a minute I might slide my fingers into it and leave my husband behind. Yes, how I missed him, for I knew we'd never sit in just this tide pool again with exactly this amount of tequila humming and sloshing inside us.

"I love the way you always think I'm going to go bonkers when you tell me you want a little time to yourself," I said.

"I love you, too," he said.

He blushed when I put on the glove.

25

And then just as suddenly, 2028. I hadn't rented that bungalow in Indonesia after all, when my husband took off for New Orleans. Indonesia was simply too far from my purpose. Instead, I sat perched on a sawed-off tree stump just outside the door of Evvy's east Texas trailer, feeling the whole earth seem to rock underneath me like a big rocking chair. I was singing "A Hole in the Bucket" as if it were a lullaby, my aged voice thin but insistent as wire, the taut syllables escaping through the dust to the woods above which a lone vulture circled as if waiting for the song to lose strength and collapse. The noon sun straddled the back of my neck like the jewelry I'd discarded in deference to the heat. The yellow moth that had toppled into my coffee mug had turned transparent in the dregs, and the bare soles of my feet steamed in my sneakers. But the brim of Evvy's new baby's hat was so wide that it cast the whole baby in shade, the tiny, soft cotton T-shirt soothing as milk, the fat wrists beating a fitful breeze. These new-fangled diapers were lighter than clouds and could have held all the rain from here to San Francisco, which is where I'd be headed if I ever had my fill of being a grandma. There, everyone might think me a wizened transvestite. Funny, to fit right in for being something that I wasn't. But I had a yen to shop the leather boutiques, then sit in a bar drinking Bloody Marys while writing a screenplay. Wrong city, I know, but LA has never appealed to me. It's a dark, rainy night, a young woman is driving her car, which sputters to a halt on a stretch of glistening pavement. But there's a gas station just down the block. From the pay phone she calls her boyfriend, arranges that he will come get her. She waits and waits, the worried boyfriend doesn't come, she phones again, he says he's been to the station and back and couldn't find her. She pleads, Try again, she'll wait out by the pumps, they check the address but the same thing happens, turns out she's back in the past twenty years behind the time her boyfriend shows up looking for her. Will they ever see each other again?

I felt more and more ornery just thinking about that screenplay. Somehow, the thought of being stuck in the past was one of the few things that could make me cry.

Evvy's baby's name was Jess, because Evvy had been determined to give it a name that could be for a boy as well as a girl. She hadn't told me which it was yet, boy or girl, because she meant to surprise me. Also for me to break down and change its diaper. Really I could hardly wait to get my hands on that bottom, feast my eyes on those quivering dimples, those telltale creases and folds and protrusions. Someday my own journeys would come to their rightful halt, but this baby would walk on into the years, and I wanted to know what shape it would take, and how it would love, and what voice it would use if it ever remembered the words to this song.

> But your diaper's too dry, dear baby, dear baby,
> Your diaper's too dry, dear baby, too dry

Maybe I'd be more comfortable finding something soft to lean my back against. But it was nice on that stump, full in the sun, my body a dozing circle around the baby's spot of shade. Jess had the sweetest, most oblivious grin, the ridges of pink gum like nothing I'd ever stuck my finger between, before. The gums clamped down with force, the baby sucked, bit, and mewed, then flung its eyes open, gave a little cry, and fell asleep. Still no mess in the diaper, no storm in this cloud. But I was patient as could be, only a little thirsty for some of Evvy's strong tea. My cracked leather valise was stored in the cubby under the bed, where I laid the baby gently on a pillow and loosened the string of its hat. Jess was darker than Evvy, darker even, Evvy had told me, than its father. But the baby didn't look a thing like its father. When the hat slipped back and revealed its bald head, my new grandchild looked exactly like me.

PART THREE

Pons

26

And then just as suddenly, 2010. Evvy and Nora attended the eighth grade at Flower Hill Middle School, just across the road from the technical college where Vladmir and Stanislaw, Dr. and Mrs. Klink's older sons, took some of their advanced-level high school classes. When I asked Dr. Klink why his children had Russian names, he said his wife was not fond of American names. When I asked Mrs. Klink the same question, she said the boys were named after two Russian exchange students with whom Dr. Klink had played Ping-Pong during his years in medical school.

Sometimes instead of taking the bus home from school, Nora and Evvy walked the few neat blocks to the Klinks' yellow house, not to be near Vladmir and Stanislaw, the very idea of which made them degenerate into fits of laughter or sometimes tears, but to hang around on the back stoop with the endlessly rotating supply of teenage girl cousins and sisters and friends who liked to gather at the Klinks' house. There were quite a few babies, too, and always a few grown men or women I'd never seen before who all seemed eager to have their cars examined by Vlad and Stan, as the two older boys were called. The teenagers kept a tape player and a real microphone in a corner of the kitchen, and on warm days they carried the equipment onto the stoop and did karaoke, the high Eastern tang of their voices breaking over the rows of identical rooftops that marked the Klinks' street.

But one quiet day around five, when I stopped by on my way home from work to pick up Nora and Evvy and maybe watch the news a while with Mrs. Klink, who seemed always to be crouching over something to do either with food or with laundry, the teenage girls were nowhere to be seen and instead on the back stoop stood Mrs. Klink's mother singing a Hmong prayer that seemed to go on forever, along with twin kite strings of white smoke that unwound from a bowl at her feet and climbed a perfect diagonal into the sky. In the bowl, two plucked, boiled chickens lay on their backs with their heads tilted lazily on the rim and their beaks just open, like fat men snoozing in a barber shop. Into the breast of each chicken had been thrust a spear of incense. Two eggs lay tucked under two of the wings, while in the small, bowed spaces between the legs lay two sticky offerings of clumped, white rice.

"What is she doing?" I whispered to Mrs. Klink, who with her pinkie withdrew a stray chicken feather from one of the toddler's mouths.

"You don't need to whisper. She doesn't speak English. Besides, she doesn't get offended. She's lived here long enough to know she'll never fit in," Mrs. Klink said, flicking the sodden, chewed feather into the garbage along with the rest. "That's what we do when one of the children falls. Stanislaw, you know, he fell yesterday playing football. And he bruised his arm. So she's praying for his soul to come back up."

"Back up?" I asked.

"Yes, because when the child falls, the soul remains on the ground, so she needs to coax it back," she explained, shrugging, as if to signal that the part of her that believed in such things had long since made its peace with the part of her that didn't. Then she reached for a cleaver, a chopping block, a bouquet of wilting mint leaves. "Watch. Now she'll come in and examine the bones."

The old woman shuffled into the kitchen on flat, fuzzy slippers, slid the bowl carelessly onto the table, stuck a grubby index finger into one of the chicken's beaks and, wriggling free the jawbone, lifted it into the dim ceiling light and turned it this way and that while peering at its opacity with a disgruntled expression. She did the same with a neck bone, delicately

extracting just a single vertebrae from out of the sinewy col-
umn, then searching for a clue as to the status of Stanislaw's
bruised soul—was it earthbound, still? Or had it begun its
ascent away from gravity into the freer air?

And what about my soul? I wondered. What had become
of it, since my remission from cancer? Was it floating above the
jewelry adorning my bald head, exploring the ceiling motes of
the Klinks' scrubbed kitchen? Or was it clinging by a thread of
my robe swaying from a hanger on the shower curtain rod,
caressing the porcelain shoulder of my bathtub in which it had
once lain in mournful sickness, wretched and hopeless with its
memories of nausea?

"Does it work for grown ups? Can she do a chicken for
me?" I finally asked, reaching into my satchel for the keys to
my car.

Mrs. Klink leveled on me a perplexed expression, the same
coy gaze that her husband offered whenever I turned down a
sip of his Cranapple spritzer. Between us drifted a coil of
incense smoke.

"Your soul is fine where it is, Isobel," she answered at last,
the flower she wore in her hair bobbing and quivering. "Your
soul is neither up nor down. Anyone can see your soul is in
your hands."

I withdrew my hand from my satchel to look. Entwined in
my fingers was the dilapidated, cobwebby shawl that the Crazy
Volunteer had pulled from a salvaged crate of vaudevilles one
day and draped around my shoulders. I had only to play with
the fringes to be transported back to where I'd come from, to
my darkening apartment where the smells of the neighbors'
dinners might already be wafting in the hallways as if to welcome me and my cottony, buzzing fatigue. Funny, I thought,
that when I was in my future, I missed where I had come from,
and when I was home again, sick, dying in that slow cozy winter of 1996, I longed for where I was going.

In a nutshell, that was my soul.

It wouldn't do, I thought, to want to be Isobel when I was Bald Queen Butterfly and Bald Queen Butterfly when I was Isobel.

But this was the only soul I had. It seemed to dangle before me among the slippery fringes of the shawl. I slid my fingers among them, felt the blur of the cobwebby fabric, found myself at once in my apartment with Hercules, who was playing his bass. Night had fallen. Hercules's body curved around the chords in a posture of obeisance, his nimble fingers moving quickly and surely along the neck of the instrument with gestures precise as sign language. Whatever declarations he made to it, the music spoke back in ever low, comforting tones, so I began to imagine that while Hercules was apologizing to the music for the fact of his own humanity, the notes kept reassuring him, telling him not to concern himself with such insurmountable problems and simply play. After a while, I got up and started dancing. How unlike me, I thought. How unlike Isobel, the flaps of my robe opening and closing around my coy undulations, the curtains parted at the blackness of the window, the lamp a dim spotlight on my leaping and twirling. How graceless I was—I could see this in the way my wineglass trembled on the table, and in the way Hercules bent his face closer to the strings so as to camouflage his furious blushing. Still, he did keep an eye on me, following me with the same deference he might give to the other musicians in his jazz ensemble when inviting their solos. The floor was my own. My spare socks slid around my ankles, my hair tumbled from its clasp and flirted with my face, my healed scars protested as if tightening their hold underneath where my prostheses rubbed against the margins of my bra. I closed my eyes, I opened them, I flung my hands wide apart, then back into the shadows of my loose, pink sleeves. The robe's hem caught and released me, I could do anything I wanted, then it held me, then it let me go again. Hercules's music made no demands, it only thumped in the air, there was no melody I needed to emulate or follow, only the faint ticking of the pocket watch helping my feet keep time.

Here I paused for a moment, confused. Was I dancing or only thinking about dancing? And why had Martha darted forward and apprehended me, just when I was ready to reach for my prostheses and toss them to the floor? I had thought she was asleep. Or had she been all along in the chair by the door, dressed, inexplicably for this late hour, in the voluminous purple skirt she wore every day to work, the skewed neckline of her jersey never pressed quite right? She seemed to want to dance with me. She placed her hands on my shoulders. I slid my hands around her neck, let my hair swing freely between our faces, urged her to swing past the radius of the wineglass still precariously atilt on the table. Hercules bucked with the rhythm of his playing, the bass rocked and shook against the curve of his body, he grimaced, he blushed, David grimaced and blushed, Jayne grimaced and blushed, the visiting consultants grimaced and blushed, John Grzadzielewsli grimaced and blushed from his place at the threshold of the door to the office trailer where he waited every noon for the Crazy Volunteer to wash up for lunch.

For I was not in my living room after all, and it was not late at night, and there wasn't any music save for the strains of the work crews' radio far away in the museum basement, and I was not wearing my robe, only a neat, sashed skirt and blouse.

"Isobel, honey," Martha pleaded in my ear.

"Isobel," echoed a querulous David.

"Oh, God," Jayne moaned.

Hercules looked so kind and so sorry I let Martha lead me to him, where he lifted me shyly into his arms. From inside his youthful embrace, I said to the others staring at me, "Isobel's soul hopes you will all excuse it for having embarrassed itself in this fashion."

After which Hercules carried me out to the car and drove me home to my apartment. I loved most the way he carried me over the threshold. After tucking me into bed he sat close to me while I rested and, knowing I would refuse the tea he offered, prepared it just the same.

27

Pons would make another fine name for a sprite. Not a wood sprite, and not a water sprite, either, but a House Sprite, one content to crouch behind the throw pillows on couches or cling to the undersides of coffee tables or peer out from over the tops of lamp shades. If a picture frame was off-center, if the book mark you'd slipped between the pages of your book was ahead of where you'd finished reading, if the tack you dropped ended up in the toe of your slipper and the wine sometimes seemed to vanish from the glass more quickly than you were sipping it, then that would mean Pons was restless that evening, insulted, perhaps, by having come upon his name in the sketch of the brain in the reference book open on the kitchen counter, a name just to the right of *medulla oblongata* and to the left of *pituitary. Pons,* he might have read there, *a broad mass of nerve fibers enclosing irregular masses of gray matter serving as important relay stations in the path from the cerebral cortex to the cerebellum.*

"Irregular masses of gray matter indeed," Pons mutters, and tilts the screen in the nozzle of the tap in such a way that whoever does the dishes next gets sprayed with cold water. I don't blame him. I am angered by the encyclopedia, too. Its idea of the brain is too unilaterally self-important. As if the brain is all that matters, the entry lacks compassion for the rest of the body, not to mention respect for the mysteries of the flesh itself, the yearnings of the bones, the private will of whatever the body touches. *Brain,* the encyclopedia too flatly proclaims, *supervisory center of the nervous system controlling both voluntary and involuntary functions and in higher animals the site of emotions, memory, self-awareness, and thought.*

Self-awareness indeed. The idea of the brain bearing sole

responsibility for such a thing makes me indignantly protective of how I used to stand on my balcony and lean against the railing, waiting for the evening to make itself known to me, seeming to pull me forward by the hips, and how that little spit of land I liked to visit on the river, where I so often ran into that couple in the middle of breaking up, beckoned me forth as if by some magnetic tug at my pelvis. Now that I can no longer take those walks, the thing I remember most fondly about them is that if I chose, I could shut off my brain entirely and still end up where I wanted to be. The evening gave itself to me, my legs scissored along, my body offered me into the dusk the way rock gives itself to the surrounding air.

My brain had precious little to do with it.

And I remember the mammogram, my breast squeezed between the hard plates of machinery so that my gratitude for the gentle touch of the technician buzzed in my nipple.

In my *nipple,* not in my brain.

And I remember the way I sucked my husband's fingers one by one between my lips in order to forgive his hands for so often taking him away from me. It was my lips that forgave; my tongue, my suck—not my brain. And I remember the way I imagined, not with my brain but with the watery pit of my belly, Trevor's lost, swollen body sunk in the cold river, and of the way my spine arched taut as a pulled bow when I came upon the Crazy Volunteer practicing a variety of common facial expressions in the mirror in the rest room, and of the way when I placed one of my hands on Nora's head and my other hand on Evvy's, I would feel like a planet anchored by two moons, and how buoyant I feel in those first half hours after I take my pain pills when the bed is a weightless vapor and nothing matters but the faint drifting sounds of Hercules and Martha and Dr. Klink conferring at the threshold of the living room, and how the sheets tangle around my ankles like eddies of wind upon which I'm being lifted into space which is itself a kind of self-awareness.

•   •   •

THUS THE BRAIN, I propose to Doctor Klink when at last he steps cautiously into my bedroom, is not entirely indispensable. Certainly it has its uses but it's not the whole person by a long shot and it's certainly not the whole rest of the universe, either.

"Agree?" I ask.

He gives my wrist a gentle squeeze, stealing yet another opportunity to take my pulse. Beneath the press of his fingers, our friendship stings like a trapped bee while Pons loosens the helix of sheet around my ankles only to snake it farther up between my thighs. I stretch my legs luxuriantly and give a pained smile. Dr. Klink suggests kindly that as long as I am in bed I might take off my bra and prostheses in order to feel the coolness of the bedclothes flush against my skin.

Shaking my head, I tell him I'm expecting my daily company from among the neighbors. Every day, when the visitors come and go, Hercules accompanies them across the courtyard to their apartments. On his return he brings a taste of the early spring air, which clings to the weave of his shirt until I've had my fill of it. I am always careful, after the fragrance has dissipated, to ask Hercules how things are progressing between him and the Botanical Society intern with the blonde braid. In response, he is always careful to turn pink in the face, knowing a blush is all the answer I require.

"I've told my wife about you," says Dr. Klink while feeling for swollen glands in my throat. His neck is upright as a birch tree, his eyes tenacious as knotholes. No new swelling, he determines, and no rash on the back of my tongue this morning, and nothing at all alarming about the insides of my ears. "She says she'd like to meet you."

"We've already met," Pons makes me confess.

"I don't think so," says Dr. Klink with a patient shake of his head.

"Oh, but we have," I insist. "At least we will have. We will. We certainly already did."

He bows his head, puts a finger to his lips, presses my shoulders gently against the pillow.

"She cooked my wedding," Pons makes me say.

Dr. Klink does not correct me. He doesn't say I'm not married. He doesn't pretend to wonder if he has heard me correctly. I might tell him his wife wears a flower in her hair. I might remind him of the Ping-Pong he played with the Russians in medical school. Instead, just as Dr. Klink slides the thermometer under my tongue, Pons causes my teeth to bite down very hard on the tips of the doctor's fingers.

PART FOUR

Prayer, for O Spare Me!

28

"This is amusing. This *lying-in*. It's so old-fashioned," I say to the blonde-braided girl with the studious glasses, the girl who keeps the carved front doorway of the Botanical Society building so full of gleam that she can measure the approaching sparkle of Hercules's earring even when he himself is still out of sight. One of Hercules's gifts to his mother and me was that, as if in compensation for all the attention he was paying to the girl with the floppy blonde braid, he finally relented and allowed us to pierce his ear. Thoughtlessly I held the ice against the front of the lobe instead of the back, so by the time the flesh was numb, the ear had flooded with droplets, but Martha wielded the sewing needle so expertly that Hercules's grimace lasted longer than the second it took the needle to plunge in and out. Then I dropped the gold stud in the bottle of rubbing alcohol so Martha had to fish it out with a long-handled spoon, and as she pulled the bowl of the spoon past the lip of the bottle it gave a little pop that sent the earring flying in a shallow arc ending at the bottom of my soup bowl, so I needed to finish eating my lunch before Hercules could see how he looked with the earring. Dr. Klink was enormously pleased with this story, not only because I'd eaten so much but because it was his wife's soup ladled from one of her Sunday kettles and bicycled over by one of the cousins along with a packet of herbs and sliced limes. I loved her soups, because I felt so useful and self-sufficient while tearing the mint and basil leaves into the bowl, and because the freshness of the herbs was so astringent against the steaming oils once the broth was ladled on top of the greens. Tasting that soup was like tasting health itself against my tongue before letting the hot fluorescence of citrus and jalapeño slide down the back of my throat, where it was stolen by the cancer and transformed into a gray, purposeless vapor.

The reason I'm getting a foot massage from Hercules's new girlfriend is because I know how much it frightens Martha and Hercules to think of me alone on workday mornings with only the Mahler playing in the living room and my walker right at the edge of the bed in case I want to get up and move around. How worried they were before they hired the blonde girl, phoning hourly from the museum with invented questions like whether my glass of water had spilled and whether I remembered that if I wanted to phone them, all I needed to do was press the automatic dial button on the new speaker phone, which I confess I did a couple of times because of the way the relief seemed to flood over Martha the second she heard my voice. I was pleased with Pons, who dialed the correct number every time and never turned down the speaker too low to hear. In return, Pons is happy with the blonde girl. Having curtailed his mischief after wreaking such a great deal of havoc by recently locking me out on the balcony, he's relieved that there's someone to rescue me should his tricks get out of hand. How tiny I've become! If it weren't for the fact I was pregnant I might have slipped through the rails and floated away like the absentminded player in that game of musical chairs, the weight of the plush robe just enough to keep me within plucking distance of the tops of the thistles in the sodden field. Straw thistles, black grass, blue robe, invisible me. So tiny I've become despite the pregnancy that the apartment seems entirely empty even when I am most comfortable in it, my head on big pillows, my knees upraised in the rented crankbed abrupt as the peaks of young mountains, unless my ankles are swelling in which case I have to lie Trendelenberg style, with the feet higher than the head. Interesting that a man would get pleasure out of naming for himself the posture of a sick person. The girl with the studious glasses agrees, studiously, and tells me she once knew a man named Ira Specter.

When he called on the phone and asked to speak with her, he would say, "Hello, is Julie there? Ira Specter."

After which we spend the rest of the morning before Martha and Hercules come home for lunch inventing funny names. Señor Prom. Manuel Labor. Sir Plus, Sir Prize, and Sir Mize. Sue Real, Carol Little, and my favorite, Mabel C. Rup.

"How's the ascites?" asks Martha first thing, placing her hand on my swollen belly as if to measure the day's influx of fluids through the damaged epithelium, while Hercules brings me a little dollop of real Vermont maple syrup in a teaspoon. I haven't eaten since the last of Mrs. Klink's broth, a day and a half ago, and though I'm not at all hungry I find I open my mouth to accept this new flavor, not troubling to lift my hands off my belly and take hold of the spoon myself. What a surprise, to be fed! Both of us know, as Hercules pulls the spoon from between my lips and holds it still for a final lick, that we'll do this again and again. Something Dr. Klink has been careful to let me learn by experience is that when a person is as sick as I am, everything that happens for the first time is only the beginning. Like when I fell as I was leaving my chair, the other day, and then the next day and the next. Like the time I told one of the visiting neighbors not to pray for me because I didn't believe in God but if they wanted to kiss me, that was okay. With the exception of Trevor Close, who did not come to visit but lied that he was kissing me over the phone, it's amazing how people respond to a dying person's request for kisses. Those that do it, do it on the forehead with great reverence and focus as if they think that's where you *are* when you are dying, all bunched up inside your head, waiting to be lifted out like a rabbit from a hat. All the kisses I get now make me remember how I used to keep my eyes open while making love to a person, how I locked eyes during orgasm, how I used to get nose to nose with a man and bore myself into him as if to get so close that any distance between us would be erased. But the distance never was erased, for there was never another soul I wanted to

see so much that I could bare my own to it. Until I married my
husband. Which hasn't happened yet of course, exactly. Sometimes this is so confusing to me that I shut it out of my thoughts
but mostly the truth of it washes over me with perfect equilib-
rium, translucent as wine in a glass, level and drunken at once.
"Nora, Evvy," I say to myself, feeling at once terrible sorrow
and great anticipation, knowing how if they were here now,
they'd smother me with kisses and hugs and climb back and
forth on top of my bent knees, if they were still children, or sit
across from each other over me as if I were a dinner table at
which they were having one of their famous arguments, if they
were adults. "Nevvy . . . Ora," I whisper, "Orrie . . . Nevva," as
if the parts of their names are a mantra.

BECAUSE A glass of alcoholic beverage at mealtime is said to
stimulate the appetite, I am rescued from having to ask for one
even at breakfast time, when Martha fixes me a vodka and
cranberry juice on ice so finely crushed and slivered that I can
suck it through a straw. The vodka does make me hungry, I
reassure her, but only enough that I can finish every drop of the
juice without feeling like I'm going to explode. Probably the
most upsetting thing about the ascites is that it's not gas that is
leaking into my abdominal cavity, but plasma, which finds its
liquid way through my damaged inner linings, putting me in
the irresponsible position of dying of starvation while my belly
balloons with protein, making me look pregnant. But death is
rife with contradiction, anyway. The illness makes me tired,
the lethargy soothes the pain, the absence of pain allows me to
perform mundane tasks, the ease of which invites me to think
abstract thoughts, the convolutedness of which makes me
excited, the sweatiness of which makes me thirsty, which
makes me frightened of death, which causes my mouth to go
dry requiring a piece of hard lemon candy, the color of which
makes me wonder if maybe I should try using the bathroom
before I nap, the idea of which makes me anxious to prove to
myself that I can get out of bed, convincing everyone to let me

do it on my own without using the walker, the challenge of which makes me feel full of strength even though I can barely muster enough muscle power to stand up. It makes me feel self-conscious to have to hunch over between the bars of the walker. And the cane is the same way. Instead I grip whatever wall or piece of furniture is nearest and keep my hands on it like a mime's on an invisible wall. So I suppose it might be said that I am walking on my hands, in which case it is to be expected that I fall on the floor and nothing to be ashamed of, for not many forty-year-old women can walk on their hands without falling, can they? Even so, I emit a small cry of dismay in that first instant when I feel myself tumbling and collapsing. But my dismay doesn't last. To be lying on the floor is really not that different from lying in bed, except that the view is grander because the ceiling is farther away. There's something awe-inspiring about gazing quietly around, wondering if I want to get up or not, knowing that Martha and Hercules are perfectly happy to leave me alone if I want to keep lying there for an hour or two. They bring me a pillow or blanket, and insist that I show them my parents' old photo album, with pictures of my parents from before I was born—their wedding, their honeymoon in Ireland, the first of many trips there before they moved there for good and died there, and the house they rented early on when they lived in the States, a tiny, yellow clapboard shared with a nurse who had to cut through their kitchen every time she needed to use the bathroom. Sometimes the nurse and my mother ended up doing their hair or makeup together in the mirror over the shared sink while the nurse told my mother what it was like to work in a hospital, where the things that used to upset her—the bed pans, the changing of the dressings, the sour smells and sudden eruptions—no longer disturbed her at all but appeared to her only as discrete tasks that needed her distracted attention, liked spilled milk that needed to be mopped up, or turkeys that needed trussing. While unscrewing her lipstick, while plucking her brows, the nurse described for my mother how patients near death often clutched the blankets as if they were afraid someone was going to come along and yank them away, and how when death was imminent they often ushered their loved ones out of the room so as to spare them the sight. In defiance of this observation, I pull the blanket to my chin and clutch it tight as I can with all ten of my fingers and don't die, and send Martha and Hercules out of the room and still don't die, and think how alive I am even though I am dying, which of course is the proudest and most wonderful contradiction of all.

IT'S AS IF I am kissing my husband, when Hercules feeds me. The way he fills the spoon with yogurt or tea or honey or sometimes just some fresh-squeezed lemon juice, the way he balances it between the pad of his thumb and the curve of his forefinger as if at the very apex of his body so the glint of the spoon is like the tip of his tongue ever so carefully making its way toward my own. How gentle our kisses, and how devoutly troubled and forgiving, which makes me wonder what it is for which Hercules and I need to forgive each other and why it seems we are always parting. I have learned how to suck on the spoon just so, until it seems to be sucking, too, in reciprocation, because otherwise the kiss wouldn't be real, would it? But still our kisses seem to be of apology. But for what? On some days, lemon juice is the only thing my tongue makes sense of, the tartness of it the only reality that can get through to me. Hercules seems to know in advance when it's a lemon juice day, and he always invites me to squeeze the halved fruit, a funny gesture since he has stopped asking me even if I can lift the spoon. I decline the attempt—I could no more squeeze a lemon than I could walk to that spit of land at the edge of the lake where that couple is probably still in the middle of breaking up and getting back together. Last time I came upon them, the man threw his car keys into the water rather than have to detach his copy of her house key and give it back to her. There was hardly a splash, but a flock of mallards paddling around the bend all took off at once just to land on the water again less than twenty yards out, accustomed to this peculiarly human mating display. The keys were not retrieved. In contrition the woman waded knee-deep and rummaged for them as if in the depths of a handbag, her backside nearly in her boyfriend's face, but all she found was a handful of fish eggs which she carried to him in the palm of her hand in order to change the subject and debate whether the fish eggs counted as caviar which they might take home and eat together. But how could they, without the car keys? I nearly offered to walk home myself, pick up my car and drive them, except I knew if I did, they'd never let me watch them break up and make up again. For the same reason, I never actually say to Hercules that we are kissing when he feeds me, even though we lock eyes as tight as we can. His are brown, mine are green. Funny how locked eyes feel so hard and so soft at the same time, and how there's always a question and an answer at the same time, too. But if I said we were kissing, then Hercules would be too embarrassed to continue feeding me. Even now, he blushes with every approach, his single earring winking in the shadow of his shirt collar, his face still unshaven and smooth. Dying and then not dying, I am very like the couple on the spit of land, because I know he is watching me die and yet his respect for my privacy in this matter is enormous. His mother is different. Martha is one of those special people who can be counted on to tell someone their fly is wide open, so she is always pointing out to me the ravages of the day. "You should rest, Isobel," she warns me, "You have that depressing twitch in your eyelids. But I hope you don't snort in your sleep tonight."

Martha doesn't care to discuss my pregnancy. Only the studious girl with the floppy blonde braid will massage my globed belly with cocoa butter, after Martha and Hercules go back to work. She has strong, supple hands, and a distracted air from thinking always about Hercules. I wonder if she massages him, too, with this same vat of cocoa butter of which the chocolaty color vanishes as she rubs it from navel to hip in great spirals that make me need to use the bathroom, again. I had always

imagined that a water bed would be the only thing for a pregnant woman, but now I am contented to move from the floor
to the couch in the living room. "At least I don't have to stand
on my feet all day," I tell her, allowing her to slip my parents'
photo album out of its sleeve. Every afternoon she harbors an
incongruous desire to look at the faded, color snapshots, which
seem to relax her.

Among the photos of my mother is one taken just before
she and my father departed for Ireland; she is wearing a virgin
wool suit with a fitted skirt and padded shoulders that was too
small when she tried to put it on again after I was born. I wonder where it is now, that maiden suit, and give a shout of
laughter thinking how inexplicable it is that I wonder about
the suit rather than about my mother. We never believed in
heaven or hell, and the notion of some kind of afterlife was
pointless to her, because she wouldn't be herself, she argued, so
what difference could it make? Something my mother pondered, proposed by the nurse in the bathroom who described
the way people grabbed hold of their bedclothes when they
were ready to die, was that the vast eternity of nothingness that
makes death so fearful is only the continuation of the same vast
nothingness that precedes birth. Since the thought of life going
on all those thousands of years before she was born did not
trouble my mother at all, why should she be bothered by the
years that came later? After she and my father were killed, the
only time I felt their presence was when I visited Boston while
negotiating the purchase and transfer of a portfolio of water-
colors. Before flying home I had a chance to stop at the
Peabody, where Nabokov's butterflies are displayed in a room
next to the room containing all the hundreds of blown glass
botanical specimens. While examining the little glass vials of
butterfly genitalia, I sighed as deeply as if the whole hushed
atmosphere of the room had entered and then escaped me. But
I am not a sighing person, so I understood at once that the sigh
was my mother's. She was doing my sighing for me, with
exactly the same measure of hope and regret with which she'd

used to set me up on dates with the sons of her friends. Every afternoon when I tell this story to Hercules's girlfriend, when I get to the part about how happy my parents would be if only they knew I was pregnant, she begs me to emulate the sigh, just as a child might beg me to do. "Sigh," she implores me. "Show me the sigh." So I do it, touched she would want to hear it again and again, on and off over the hours. Twenty sighs, thirty, still she wants more, it makes her so happy, so I am still sighing my parents' comfortable sighs when Martha gets home from work. Through the balcony window I watch her park the car, go around to the back and flip open the trunk. When she withdraws the cracked leather suitcase and unfastens the buckles on its torn straps and opens it and loads in the smelly beaver glove and the faded, crumpled Valentine and the crushed glass tangle of the beaded necklace, I quit sighing at once, chagrined to have neglected these things for so long. I lift my head a little higher, then sit fully upright so I can watch her contemplate the black office telephone. It's too light for a telephone, she flips it over to see that there's nothing inside; it's hollow, no bell, not even an echo of our snowy, affectionate conversations-to-be. She drops the phone, too, in the suitcase, doesn't bother to do up the buckles, carries the stuffed suitcase high like a tray in a fancy restaurant at which I am the patron waiting for a feast, then veers for the Dumpster and tips everything in, telephone, suitcase, and all.

"Did you feel it kick?" I ask the blonde-braided girl as she massages my belly, meaning to keep her from panicking in case she has seen Martha throw out my things.

"Not yet," she says. "Did you?"

"Not yet," I answer calmly. "Do you think Hercules felt the needle going in and out when his mother and I pierced his ear?"

"A little," she says, rubbing my belly distractedly. Under her touch I feel amorous, then suddenly crampy. In a moment I'll be seized with pain but even that can not make me lose hope for the Victorian valentine, the only item in the batch that never carried me into my rightful future. The more I think about it, the more I long for it, the more certain I am that the Valentine is Jess's, that whatever message might be written on it were only I to have the chance to read it would begin, "Dear Grandma."

"Can you bring me something?" I ask the blonde-braided girl, who screws the top back on the tub of cocoa butter as methodically as if winding the delicate cogs of a watch. She and Hercules are a good match, I say to myself, which makes me terribly jealous. Why, I don't know. In silent rage I watch as she retreats to the bedroom, returning a second later with the vial of pain pills.

I shake my head *no* at her offering, then take the pills on my tongue and swallow them. She's too young for Hercules, I say to myself. She's too solicitous. He needs his independence. I hear a wind in my ears, a harsh, cold whipping that slaps against the thistles in the field.

"Don't," I say.

"I won't," she promises.

"How could you?" I ask.

"I didn't," she says.

"Never," I urge.

"I promise," she says.

"Can you bring me something?" I ask again, shouting to be heard above the wheezing of the wind.

"I brought it, Isobel," she answers, flipping her blonde braid distractedly between her fingers. Flip, flip. Flip, flip. "Just a minute, just relax. The medicine will take hold. Breath deep, Isobel. Sigh."

"No, I mean, can you bring me my valentine?"

The blonde girl smiles. Flip, flip, flip. "She wants her valentine," I hear her chuckle to Martha when Martha comes in the door.

"On the spice rack," I shout, changing my mind. "Next to that Indian pollen. What's it called?"

Solemnly she brings me the cylinder of saffron. I shake my

head *no*. The wind grows ragged. It's the sound of my own breathing. A familiar crackle signals the beginning of Martha's nightly unwrapping of bakery goods. She likes to lay the fresh breads on the cutting board and admire the glazed diagonal cuts on the tops of the loaves while deciding which to eat for an appetizer and which to eat for dinner and which to save for a midnight snack or breakfast. Lately she's been talking about taking a little trip when this is over. When I'm dead, she means. My breathing deepens in my ears, steadies itself. Mexico, I think. Nevvy. Ora.

"Breathing is so simple," I say to the blonde-braided girl, who brings me a glass of water. What I want is the silver compact from the spice rack, in which just a few grains of powder still cling to the tray and to the surface of the mirror.

"I've been saving it," I say, when I finish my water.

"How are you, Isobel?" Martha singsongs from the kitchen. "How is she?" she asks Hercules's girlfriend.

"A little confused," comes the answer from behind the door of the coat closet.

"She is not," I joke.

"*Delightfully* confused," Martha asserts, lifting my hair up and sliding a cold palm over the nape of my neck to affirm the symbiosis of our relationship. She warms her hand on my neck, I cool my neck on her hand. My neck is the only part of my body left unchanged by the illness. Even the soles of my feet are spongier than they used to be. But my neck is long as ever, sinewy as ever, like a whole cat purring against Martha's caress.

"You look okay," Martha says. "I cleaned out your car. Except maybe a little more yellow in the left eye. How have you been *seeing*? Any more blurring?"

"No. Just doubling. How are yous?" I ask. "I'm fine, really. Only I want yous to give mees somethings. Not the saffrons but the—"

"That's right!" says Martha, rising for the kitchen. "I do have something to give you."

"No bread for me, please," I murmur.

"No, I have something to give you from Hercules. He left it with me. He's meeting Julie for supper tonight. 'Bye, Julie!" she calls, but Julie has already escaped down the hallway.

There is something disarming about accepting gifts while lying down, so I am glad to be sitting up when Martha brings me the package. Quite a few of the visiting neighbors have brought me gifts, which amuse me by being exactly the same types of gifts people used to give me when I was healthy and strong—books, a CD, a pen, a box of note cards, and a hair clip. How sedate I used to be! As if I were practicing! Little did I know how much athleticism is required of the sick! The other day, Dr. Klink came by with an egg crate mattress. Blue foam, and when I laid eyes on it I started shaking my head *no* and didn't stop until he carried it back out the door. I will not have that thing in my house, I declared, no matter how sick I am, I will not be that sickly, *no,* the crank-bed is bad but that mattress is horrible, it even smells like a hospital, no, no, it makes me think of old winos sleeping in doorways, get it away, I won't sit on that thing for a million dollars, no, no, *no!*

"Oh, Isobel, be quiet," Martha had scolded. "You don't want to get that raspy throat again. Remember? And you wouldn't be too fond of bed sores now, would you?"

Still I actually pushed Dr. Klink away, with enough force that he staggered backward under the floppy weightlessness of the mattress before carrying it resignedly out the door. He must have left it propped against the wall in the outside hall- way where I wouldn't see it. Then, while I slept, Hercules must have lifted me up while Martha slid the new mattress flush against the hills and valleys of the crank-bed before rear- ranging me on fresh sheets, still fast asleep. When I woke, how lightly cushioned I felt, as if I had awakened upon a carpet of moss, my bottom snuggled just right in the spongy resilience of a million trapped bubbles, my elbows deep in their private val- leys. I was settled as fog in a hollow. I could *eat* this bed, I said to myself, thinking mousse and chiffon, sponge cake, whipped cream and berries, all the while peeling the soft white hems of the sheet away from the mattress and then with every last impossible ounce of strength pulling the foam out from under me and letting it flop to the floor. So there! They had tricked me! Two days went by in this fashion—mattress off, mattress on, mattress off, mattress on—until finally I acquiesced and allowed the blue egg crate to take the place of my lost weight. "If I think of it as part of my body, it's all right," I reasoned, and laid my bones in it gently as if it were flesh ready to receive them. All my fight had been for nothing. Illness is like that; a continual fray. You rally so hard that when the fight is finally over, you think you've won no matter what you've lost.

So I am glad to be sitting upright when Martha brings me the gift from Hercules, on the floor especially, where I feel most gleefully self-possessed. So far, excepting the quiet attentiveness of his face, Hercules's gifts to me have all been intangible—his blushes, his music, his tact, his understanding, his sympathy, his ease, his youthfulness. Nothing store-bought, nothing that can be sealed in a box and delivered will ever take the place of who he simply is. So the weight of the box is a worrisome thing, for it suggests to me that having hooked up with Julie he is asking me to be content with a token of himself—a bud vase, maybe, in which I am expected to put flowers that will remind me of his tender regard. So I take my sweet, apprehensive time about opening it. There's no wrapping, no ribbon, no tape, it's just a Nike shoe box, which makes me wonder if there really might be footwear in there, not for me since I don't need shoes anymore, but for Bald Queen Butterfly, who is so enamored of her stack-heeled, yellow sneakers. Après-ski boots or snorkel flippers for Bald Queen Butterfly would be a really sweet gift, I speculate, would be exactly a Herculean kind of gesture, like the time he flipped over all the queens in the card deck the night he and Martha begged me not to do chemo.

But it's not snorkel wear, or ski boots, or even plain old sneakers.

It's the Crazy Volunteer.

The Nike box lid is loose-fitting and pops off very easily,

and inside on a bed of crumpled newspaper, there she lies. Not one of the dead dolls in burned bits and pieces but one of the live ones still damaged but rescued, her dress still visibly a dress, her blistered limbs and matted hair each in their accustomed disarray. Funny, how in her natural, plastic condition she bears a slight family resemblance to Betty Boop—the cheap cousin, maybe, her necklace of fake pearls long since misplaced. Gratefully mute, saved at last from the frightful requirements of human society, she is as reposeful as she used to be frantic, but it's a clumsy repose, knock-kneed and topheavy. She can't be stood up even though her legs are sturdy plastic in black shoes with soles flat as paddles, and her flamelicked, water-stained apron keeps inching around sideways no matter how many times I tug it straight. One hand—the right, the mechanical one—is missing, but as far as I can tell, that damage might have preceded the fire along with the dent above her eyebrow. In a way she is no worse off than I am, for she is to an unblemished doll what I am to a healthy human being, and gazing at her on her mattress of newsprint I understand that Hercules's purpose in such a gift is to demonstrate that my disfigurements have left me just as much a person as I was before and maybe even *more* womanly than I've ever been in my life—scarred as I am, expectant as I am. I feel a little ashamed, never to have realized how sentimental he is even with all those terrible Mahler symphonies he puts on the stereo.

I keep glancing away from the doll, then glancing back, then glancing away again and going about my business of lying here thinking about calling Martha back out of the kitchen so she can help me climb onto the egg crate mattress where there's a glass of water waiting, and wishing I had a pocketful of those wrapped, lemon candies and thinking how good it is that I've always liked poetry.

"Poetry books are the only really good literature lightweight enough to be held upright by a sick person," I say raspily to the doll, pointing out to her my boxful of tiny folio editions no larger than greeting cards, maybe fourteen, fifteen pages long. For days I've been stuck on the list of errata on the closing fly leaf of a pirated edition of James Joyce's *Pomes Penyeach* that in my opinion is by far the best poem in the book, and now in return for all her gifts to me, I recite it by memory to the Crazy Volunteer.

ERRATA
in 'Flood' for 'in thine' read 'is thine'
in 'Nightpiece' for 'bleak insense' read 'bleak incense'
in 'A Prayer' for 'O spare me' read 'O spare me!'

"I like especially the idea of 'bleak insense' although sense-lessness is not necessarily bleak," I say to the doll, my thirsty voice cracking with effort. In response, the doll's senselessness is captivating. She looks like she's been struck dumb before she ever quite came to in the first place, as if she knows she's missing something but doesn't quite know what it is. When she was human, her expression was much the same. But as a flesh-and-blood woman she wore too much makeup, while as a doll she's somewhat wan, drained, I see, of the crazy exuberance that used to be so disconcerting. At once, horrified, I lift her tattered, polka-dotted skirt to see if she at least has a hole between her legs. She does, thank goodness, for it would be too much of an indignity for our friendship to bear, if she didn't.

THE REASON Hercules has been putting so much Mahler on the stereo lately is because he believes that the music might make it easier for me to die. Deprived of all the usual circadian, workaday rhythms, I might instead fluctuate against a backdrop of Mahler, whose symphonies I hate for their sappy grandiosity even as I appreciate their stubbornness. "Repeat nothing but make everything develop further from itself," Hercules paraphrased the composer when, for the third time last night, he had to come into my bedroom and lift me off the floor. Night is a scary time for him and Martha to think of me falling out of bed, I've discovered, over and over again. How unhappy it makes them, to find me lying askew in the darkness, without a pillow, resting only on the bath mats they've spread on the wood. No matter how many times I do it, they are not reassured. Last night, on my fourth fall from bed, I knocked my glass of melted ice chips off the bedside table and bumped my hip harder than usual on the floor. This morning when we change my nightgown there's a bruise like smeared ink, shocking all three of us. Against the jaundiced surroundings the purple bruise looks truly healthy, so for a moment as I look at it I imagine maybe I'm going to get better, and will have to go back to work. I'll insist we go forth with my new exhibit, the one about the changes wrought by the fire. Rust on the firearms, mold on the smashed-open walls, and the torn, exploded portraits crookedly hung.

To celebrate, we decide to go out to breakfast, chatting all the while about how fortunate I am that the bruise doesn't hurt. And neither does anything else, even though I didn't take my pain pills today. Dr. Klink has been wishing for this to happen, for the cancer to kill the pain before it kills me. So really we have two things to celebrate—my new exhibit, and my freedom from pain. Of course it's a little confusing, not knowing which thing to talk about first, which accounts perhaps for Martha and Hercules's general bewilderment. From one minute to the next it seems they forget everything that's happening! But I forgive them. Careful as can be, they wrap me in one of my bygone blouses and skirts before allowing me to direct us to The Hazelnut Coffee House, where the black-and-white tile floors are so grimy we can barely distinguish one square from another and where the coffee isn't hot enough even to be felt through the paper cups, and where the help are all college students with hair in their eyes who get flustered every time they need to use the cash register. But it's the only place around for espresso. We buy scones, which I don't eat, of course, but it's nice to have one in front of me, like an anchor on which I can fix my eyes so I'll be less likely to fall out of my chair when I get dizzy from wondering whether John

Grzadzielewsli misses the Crazy Volunteer. Hercules secures me to my chair by looping a long scarf through the rungs of the ladder back, but still the other patrons gaze at me with looks of such horror and indignation that finally Martha asks them roundly to leave or face in the other direction, which a second later she doesn't remember saying, and neither does Hercules. Neither one of them in fact remembers a thing about this excursion, not even the way we all teach ourselves how to play checkers from the game we find among the other worn board games atop the out-of-tune piano. Neither Martha nor I have laid eyes on a game of checkers in nearly thirty years. The biggest question is whether or not players are allowed to jump over their own colors in order to reach a spot from which they might capture an opponent. We decide they can't. I don't win any games, of course, not being entirely awake yet and not being well enough to drink coffee, which makes it funny that I should be the one to direct the proceedings while Martha and Hercules dodder along. It's a dirty place, The Hazelnut, and maybe that's why Martha and Hercules are pretending not to be there, so they won't have to watch that young man smearing the windows with a dishtowel while somebody else misspells the day's special in pink chalk on a squeaky chalkboard. But my scone is delicious. Hercules is entirely unaware of the way he hooks his foot around the rear leg of my chair in order to keep it from tipping, and Martha doesn't hear a single thing she says about Mexico. She says, over her second cup of cappuccino without nutmeg because they've run out and without cinnamon because they can't find it, that she is planning to travel to Mexico when I am dead. When I bring this up just a second later she insists she couldn't possibly have said it, she would never say a thing like that about when I am dead, which just proves that she did say it, because she says that kind of thing all the time. That's the beauty of Martha, never to pretend anything for someone else's sake, only for her own. But later at night she declares, come to think of it, maybe she *will* go to Mexico. The room is dark, the lights off, and we've lit a few candles because Martha and Hercules like the way they flicker in time to the music. Martha needs calming down. She was a sore loser at checkers. All day, every time she touched me, her hands were either too hot or too cold. So it's a relief to me and Hercules when finally she goes off for a minute into a little riff about going to Mexico and boning up on her Spanish while working in a health clinic. She doesn't know what she'll find there, and I am able to refrain from telling her only because I'm so exhausted by our excursion that I can't take my eyes off the dancing flames in the candles. Thank goodness I can manage to keep quiet, because I have no right to rob Martha of the joy of claiming her own future minute by minute, the way I claimed mine, or it claimed me, second by second, cell by cell, so we have hold of each other entirely now, me and those years, Isobel and Bald Queen Butterfly. Martha's ignorance of our daughters is like the bud of a peony, global and hard, yet filled with promise, for someday she'll be rapturous with the knowledge of them, like I am. Keeping my secret, I go over and over the whole thing in my mind; the two Mexican women crossing the road from the clinic to the grocery, the police van careening around the corner so fast and crazy that the women can't get away, the two babies left behind in the arms of the nurses while Martha sterilizes needles for immunization, the slow Mexican court, the two drunken fathers, the baffled nuns. Nora. Evvy. And Martha gathering them up in her nurturing arms.

"The blessings of disposable diapers," Martha comments as if she hears what I am thinking. Yes, I nod, and the little Ziploc bags of Rice and Wheat Chex safety-pinned to our daughters' T-shirts, and the way, when they were teenagers, they once stowed away in the back of Hercules's car after he'd packed it for one of his trips to New Orleans. All the way to the outskirts of Chicago, they lay silent and hidden under a blanket. Then, despite his attachment to the idea that New Orleans belonged only to him, Hercules allowed the girls to accompany him the rest of the way and even made sure they were comfortably seated in the clubs where he met up with his long-lost jamming partners and settled in for the nights of playing. When they returned to me and Martha, Nora and Evvy were both very secretive, but at night we could hear them arguing about whether the plates of Cajun shrimp had been bigger in this or that club, and which sister was more often mistaken for the older one. Nevva. Orrie. The really beautiful thing is that Martha has no idea what she is stepping into by planning a trip to Mexico, no idea what will come her way, and what she will take upon herself, and how none of her expectations will apply, and how everything will absolutely amaze her! It gives us something in common, her living and my dying, because neither of us know what awaits us.

"Like a warm bath," I imagine death to be.

Hercules and Martha confer. After a moment Martha leaves for the kitchen, returning minutes later with a washcloth and the steaming spaghetti pot.

"She does like this, doesn't she," she says to Hercules when they have peeled off my nightgown and begun to soothe my scars with the moist cloth. Around and around it goes, until the rhythmic sweep of damp cloth causes my entire body to shudder and convulse, so that I vomit on my bare chest, which hasn't happened before. For a moment we all stand around watching me before Martha rushes for the phone to call Dr. Klink. Fortunately we don't need to go to the hospital, for Dr. Klink turns out to be one of those rare doctors who doesn't balk at the idea of delivering a baby in the comforts of home.

"After all, lost in a jungle for ten years," I murmur. "Bring me my makeup, please."

"Your makeup?"

"On the spice rack. Not the saffron," I tell them, but they are far too excited to leave my bedside, around which we stand and look at me a while longer while Hercules swabs me clean with the washcloth, dipping and rinsing, his great height perched on the edge of the bed. Funny, we all get so emotional to see the sheets like wilted roses underneath him that we nearly forget what I asked for.

"Please," I repeat. "I don't want to miss this. I'm so happy! So happy!"

"I promise we won't let you miss a thing," Martha reassures me as all at once the room goes bright, but it's only Dr. Klink rushing forward in his tennis whites.

"The retching didn't seem to make her too uncomfortable," Martha exclaims as we all hover delicately over me, wondering what might be making me smile the way I am when I am laboring so hard, pushing and pushing, the steep hills of the crank-bed rising higher with every effort. Below us, my smile is a delicate thing like a sliver of moon reflected in water. How secretive it is, that thin, sickle moon, as if it knows the reason for my smile. I know it, too—the reason I am smiling, the reason I'm so happy, is that there's not enough powder left in the compact to take me away from this rightful, purposeful moment. Even were I to get my hands on it and pry apart the glommed clasp, I'd find only a few granules of makeup that were I able to brush it onto my lids would make them just a little heavier, a little easier to close, my restfulness pungent with gratitude. Not many people live their whole lives through like I have, surprise by surprise. "Thank you," I whisper, looking back on the adventure of it all. Martha presses her lips to my knuckles. Meanwhile the stethoscope appears to be broken; there's no heartbeat inside it, Dr. Klink lets the ear pieces fall to his lap, the disconsolate ear of the instrument laying itself on my chest, for comfort. In the palm of his hand, Hercules's salvaged pocket watch holds every minute of the prime of my life.

Coming from Scribner in January 2000

Polly's Ghost

A NOVEL

ABBY FRUCHT

ISBN: 0-684-83589-4
Price: $24.00

SCRIBNER
A Division of Simon & Schuster
A VIACOM COMPANY

Forbes

TRAVEL GUIDE

Formerly Mobil Travel Guide

HAWAII

ACKNOWLEDGMENTS

We gratefully acknowledge the help of our representatives for their efficient and perceptive inspections of the lodgings listed. Forbes Travel Guide is also grateful to the talented writers who contributed to this book.

Some of the information contained herein is derived from a variety of third-party sources. Although every effort has been made to verify the information obtained from such sources, the publisher assumes no responsibility for inconsistencies or inaccuracies in the data or liability for any damages of any type arising from errors or omissions.

Neither the editors nor the publisher assume responsibility for the services provided by any business listed in this guide or for any loss, damage or disruption in your travel for any reason.

HAWAII
★★★★★

2

ISBN: 9-780841-61426-0   Manufactured in the USA

10 9 8 7 6 5 4 3 2 1

TABLE OF CONTENTS

HAWAII
★★★★★

STAR ATTRACTIONS

If you've been a reader of Mobil Travel Guide, you will have heard that this historic brand partnered with another storied media name, Forbes, in 2009 to create a new entity, Forbes Travel Guide. For more than 50 years, Mobil Travel Guide assisted travelers in making smart decisions about where to stay and dine when traveling. With this new partnership, our mission has not changed: We're committed to the same rigorous inspections of hotels, restaurants and spas—the most comprehensive in the industry with more than 500 standards tested at each property we visit—to help you cut through the clutter and make easy and informed decisions on where to spend your time and travel budget. Our team of anonymous inspectors are constantly on the road, sleeping in hotels, eating in restaurants and making spa appointments, evaluating those exacting standards to determine a property's rating.

What kind of standards are we looking for when we visit a proprety? We're looking for more than just high-thread count sheets, pristine spa treatment rooms and white linen-topped tables. We look for service that's attentive, individualized and unforgettable. We note how long it takes to be greeted when you sit down at your table, or to be served when you order room service, or whether the hotel staff can confidently help you when you've forgotten that one essential item that will make or break your trip. Unlike other travel ratings entities, we visit the places we rate, testing hundreds of attributes to compile our ratings, and our ratings cannot be bought or influenced. The Forbes Five Star rating is the most prestigious achievement in hospitality—while we rate more than 8,000 properties in the U.S., Canada, Hong Kong, Macau and Beijing, for 2010, we have awarded Five Star designations to only 53 hotels, 21 restaurants and 18 spas. When you travel with Forbes, you can travel with confidence, knowing that you'll get the very best experience, no matter who you are.

We understand the importance of making the most of your time. That's why the most trusted name in travel is now Forbes Travel Guide.

STAR RATED HOTELS

Whether you're looking for the ultimate in luxury or the best value for your travel budget, we have a hotel recommendation for you. To help you pinpoint properties that meet your needs, Forbes Travel Guide classifies each lodging by type according to the following characteristics:

★★★★★These exceptional properties provide a memorable experience through virtually flawless service and the finest of amenities. Staff are intuitive, engaging and passionate, and eagerly deliver service above and beyond the guests' expectations. The hotel was designed with the guest's comfort in mind, with particular attention paid to craftsmanship and quality of product. A Five Star property is a destination unto itself.

★★★★These properties provide a distinctive setting, and a guest will find many interesting and inviting elements to enjoy throughout the property. Attention to detail is prominent throughout the property, from design concept to quality of products provided. Staff are accommodating and take pride in catering to the guest's specific needs throughout their stay.

★★★These well-appointed establishments have enhanced amenities that provide travelers with a strong sense of location, whether for style or function. They may have a distinguishing style and ambience in both the public spaces and guest rooms; or they may be more focused on functionality, providing guests with easy access to local events, meetings or tourism highlights.

★★The Two Star hotel is considered a clean, comfortable and reliable establishment that has expanded amenities, such as a full-service restaurant.

★The One Star lodging is a limited-service hotel or inn that is considered a clean, comfortable and reliable establishment.

For every property, we also provide pricing information. All prices quoted are accurate at the time of publication; however, prices cannot be guaranteed.

STAR RATED RESTAURANTS

Every restaurant in this book comes highly recommended as an outstanding dining experience.

★★★★★Forbes Five Star restaurants deliver a truly unique and distinctive dining experience. A Five Star restaurant consistently provides exceptional food, superlative service and elegant décor. An emphasis is placed on originality and personalized, attentive and discreet service. Every detail that surrounds the experience is attended to by a warm and gracious dining room team.

★★★★These are exciting restaurants with often well-known chefs that feature creative and complex foods and emphasize various culinary techniques and a focus on seasonality. A highly-trained dining room staff provides refined personal service and attention.

★★★Three Star restaurants offer skillfully-prepared food with a focus on a specific style or cuisine. The dining room staff provides warm and professional service in a comfortable atmosphere. The décor is well-coordinated with quality fixtures and decorative items, and promotes a comfortable ambience.

★★The Two Star restaurant serves fresh food in a clean setting with efficient service. Value is considered in this category, as is family friendliness.

★The One Star restaurant provides a distinctive experience through culinary specialty, local flair or individual atmosphere.

Because menu prices can fluctuate, we list a pricing range rather than specific prices. The pricing ranges are per diner, and assume that you order an appetizer or dessert, an entrée and one drink.

STAR RATED SPAS

Forbes Travel Guide's spa ratings are based on objective evaluations of more than 450 attributes. About half of these criteria assess basic expectations, such as staff courtesy, the technical proficiency and skill of the employees and whether the facility is clean and maintained properly. Several standards address issues that impact a guest's physical comfort and convenience, as well as the staff's ability to impart a sense of personalized service. Additional criteria measure the spa's ability to create a completely calming ambience.

★★★★★Stepping foot in a Five Star spa will result in an exceptional experience with no detail overlooked. These properties wow their guests with extraordinary design and facilities, and uncompromising service. Expert staff cater to your every whim and pamper you with the most advanced treatments and skin care lines available. These spas often offer exclusive treatments and may emphasize local elements.

★★★★Four Star spas provide a wonderful experience in an inviting and serene environment. A sense of personalized service is evident from the moment you check in and receive your robe and slippers. The guest's comfort is always of utmost concern to the well-trained staff.

★★★These spas offer well-appointed facilities with a full complement of staff to ensure that guests' needs are met. The spa facilities include clean and appealing treatment rooms, changing areas and a welcoming reception desk.

HAWAII

ABOUT 7 MILLION TRAVELERS HOP ABOARD FLIGHTS EACH YEAR TO BASK IN HAWAII'S WARM rays and aloha spirit. Of those many visitors, nearly 60 percent are Americans from the mainland, more than 2,000 miles to the east of this paradise, way out in the Pacific Ocean.

A long list of incredible attractions lures them—gorgeous sandy beaches, lush tropical rain forests with brightly colored flowers, breathtakingly beautiful sea cliffs that soar thousands of feet into the sunny sky, the dreamiest of sunsets, some of the world's best hotels and golf courses, crystal-clear water that's perfect for snorkeling and scuba diving, world-class deep-sea fishing, and so much more. These majestic islands so moved Mark Twain that he described them as "the loveliest fleet of islands that lies anchored in any ocean."

This chain of mostly volcanic islands covering 6,443 square miles began emerging from the Pacific about five million years ago. It's believed that Polynesians from the Marquesas Group, north of Tahiti, first inhabited thpleem between the 3rd and 7th centuries AD. Then, in 1778, Captain James Cook became the first European to come across them, and shortly thereafter, King Kamehameha successfully fought to unite the islands into one kingdom under his rule.

Much change came during the next 100 years. Hawaii established itself as a player in the east to west fur trade, the whaling industry took off in the islands, missionaries introduced the natives to Christianity, and the production of sugarcane began. Immigrants from Asia were brought in to help cultivate the cane crop, which expanded the ethnic diversity.

Hawaii became the country's 50th state in 1959. These days, only 22 percent of the overall population of about 1.2 million people are native or part Hawaiian; the rest are mainly Caucasian, Japanese, Filipino and Chinese.

Of Hawaii's more than 130 isles and atolls, eight are considered major islands: the Big Island, Kahoolawe, Kauai, Lanai, Maui, Molokai, Niihau and Oahu. Six of the eight welcome visitors. Of the two that do not, Niihau is privately owned, and Kahoolawe is uninhabited.

Tourism to Hawaii has decreased as much as 30 percent in recent years, due first to the 9/11 terrorist attacks in 2001, and then later to the global recession that began in 2008. This means that these days, unusually good bargains can be found throughout the islands, from airfares to hotel rooms to restaurants. It also means that tourist services can go in and out of business quickly, so travelers should always double check their planned itineraries before heading to the islands.

All the main islands have a mixture of enticing attractions, but each one also has its own distinctive appeal. Oahu, where more than 70 percent of the population lives, is the most cosmopolitan, mainly because it's home to Honolulu and the famed Waikiki Beach. Maui, where development has boomed over the last quarter-century, is the hippest. With its many natural attractions, Kauai caters to those who love the outdoors. Given its large size, the Big Island has something for everyone, including erupting volcanoes and snow-capped peaks for skiing. Lanai pampers the wealthy in a private, secluded setting. Molokai, where time has seemingly stood still, embraces an authentic Hawaiian lifestyle.

WHEN TO GO

Hawaii enjoys a temperate climate year-round. There is little difference in weather between the two seasons: winter, from November to April, sees average daily highs in the upper 70s, while in summer, from May to October, the mercury climbs into the mid-80s. At night, the temperature drops only about 10 degrees. Temperatures are regulated by warm surface waters and cool trade winds blowing down from the northern Pacific. When the winds stop, however, hot, sticky conditions prevail. Hurricane season runs from June through November, though large storms rarely reach the islands. The islands get the most rainfall from November through March, although Hawaii's many microclimates ensure that dry weather soon follows. Water temperatures average between 74 and 80 degrees, but swimmers and surfers should be aware that strong currents can make beaches unsafe, especially in winter. The best time to visit is mid to late winter. Temperatures are ideal, humpback whales are visiting, and big surf is rolling in. However, this is also the most crowded and expensive season, so solitude seekers and the budget-minded should consider late winter or early summer. If you plan to travel into the mountains during your stay, keep in mind that the sun's rays intensify while the temperature drops (about 3.5 degrees for every 1,000 feet above sea level).

KID-FRIENDLY BEACHES

The following family-friendly beaches are some of Hawaii's safest and calmest, making them especially suitable for kids. As such, they're also sunny spots where parents can fret a little less and enjoy themselves more.

THE BIG ISLAND

Hapuna State Recreation Area: Most Hawaii experts will tell you that this is one of the Big Island's best beaches. It stretches for almost a half-mile and has calm water most of the year, although the surf can get quite high and dangerous in winter. The swimming is usually good year-round in a sheltered pool on the north end of the beach, an area that's especially good for small children. Look for the park south of the Hapuna Beach Prince Hotel on the Kohala Coast.

Spencer Beach County Park: Not only is the water shallow here, but an offshore coral reef keeps it calm, making this beach ideal for swimming. Lots of fish swim here as well, so it's a good snorkeling spot for families. The beach is located just south of Kawaihae in South Kohala, off the Queen Kaahumanu Highway.

KAUAI

Poipu Beach Park: On the island's sunny south shore, Poipu Beach is a parents' dream because it offers something for kids of all ages. Here, even the tiniest of tots can splash around in a calm, shallow cove. Older kids can snorkel out on a sandy point or go body boarding on another stretch of the beach.

Salt Pond Beach Park: Two rocky points and a reef make the water at this beach look like a swimming pool, except for the gentle waves that roll in. At low tide, kids can splash around in shallow tide pools and watch for small fish. The beach is on the island's relatively undeveloped west side, so no resorts front this beach, and it's seldom crowded.

LANAI

Hulopoe Beach: At low tide at this south-shore beach, kids can explore the wonderful tide pools, which are packed with small specimens of sea life. The beach is a short walk from the Four Seasons Manele Bay.

MAUI

Kapalua Beach Park: Offshore reefs and the lava peninsulas on either side of this beach provide plenty of protection from high surf. It's a small but lovely stretch of golden sand on Maui's west side in the upscale Kapalua Resort, up the coast several miles from Kaanapali. The views of Molokai are splendid.

Wailea Beach: The gentle waves at this gorgeous crescent-shaped beach make this another favorite with families. It's especially popular with guests staying at two of the islands most upscale hotels: the Four Seasons and the Grand Wailea. The beach is located on Maui's south side, in the Wailea Resort.

MOLOKAI

Murphys Beach Park: Many years ago, the Molokai Jaycees built this park on the island's east end so that children could have a safe place to splash around in the ocean. There is plenty of shade on the shore, plus pavilions with picnic tables and barbecue grills. The park is located just beyond Wailua.

OAHU

Waimea Beach Park: This North Shore beach isn't the place to take kids in winter, when waves can be up to 50 feet high. But it's a perfect family destination in summer, when the waves turn gentle. You'll have plenty of company on weekends, when Waimea gets especially crowded. It's located off the Kamehameha Highway, 3 miles north of Haleiwa.

THE FALL OF THE HAWAIIAN MONARCHY

Historians agree that the Hawaiian monarchy had a clear beginning. The year was 1175, when a Tahitian priest named Pa'ao arrived on the Big Island of Hawaii and introduced the concept of monarchy. He brought in a king for each island, including a Tahitian named Pili to sire a line that would last, unbroken, for hundreds of years.

There is also a clear ending. The Hawaiian monarchy ceased on January 17, 1893, when the United States Marines—at the request of the U.S. Minister in Hawaii and without the authorization of the United States government—landed in Honolulu Harbor. Calling themselves "the Committee of Safety," the Marines placed the queen under house arrest. A week later, she gave up the throne.

At that time, the relationship between Hawaii and the United States was economically based, with Hawaii's power in the hands of the Caucasians who had come to the islands as missionaries in the 1820s. It is said of the missionaries, "they came to do good and did very well." But it was really the next generation that did well, taking over land that had been meant for Hawaiians and becoming rich off the cultivation of pineapple and sugarcane. With wealth came the power that enabled them to gain influence in the Hawaiian government and then in Washington, and to bring about the fall of the monarchy.

Unlike European kings and queens, whose lineage goes back a thousand years, the Hawaiian monarchy began with a king for each island, appointed by Paao. According to the new social order that Paao established, there were ali'i—royalty—and commoners, who were required to fall prostrate in a king's presence. Pa'ao also created kapu, a series of "taboos" that were broken only upon penalty of death. Some included women eating with men and commoners crossing a king's shadow.

The system of one king per island lasted for more than 600 years. In 1791, a young warrior named Kamehameha, a direct descendant of Pili who believed himself to be the man destined in prophecy to unite the islands under one king, put an end to centuries of warfare by systematically conquering each island, with the exception of Kauai. The task of conquering Kauai and realizing a fully united Hawaii fell to Kamehameha's son, his successor in 1819.

Bringing an end to the multi-king system wasn't the only tradition Kamehameha II ended. He allowed himself to share a meal with his mother and another of his father's wives. By eating with women, he broke the centuries-old system of kapu.

Stunned that the gods did not seek revenge, Hawaiians found themselves in a spiritual void, ripe for the arrival of American Protestant missionaries a few months later. Great changes were about to take place. Less than an hour before her death in 1823, Kamehameha's wife was baptized a Christian, and thus began a long, slow shift away from Hawaiian culture and traditions toward an attitude of Western superiority.

In 1824, Kamehameha II and his wife sailed to England, where they contracted measles and died, leaving the kings 11-year-old brother, Kamehameha III, to rule the islands. In 1840, Kamehameha III drew up Hawaii's first constitution, creating a bicameral parliament in charge of legislation, with a House of Representatives elected by popular vote and a House of Nobles appointed by the king with the advice of the cabinet. Two years later, the United States recognized the Kingdom of Hawaii as an independent government. In 1848, in an attempt to restore the broken spirits of the Hawaiians—and to infuse the monarchy with revenue—Kamehameha III released millions of acres of land, intending it to be sold to Hawaiians. Instead, huge tracts were purchased by Caucasians, who had begun to experiment with the plantation-style production of sugar. For the remainder of the century, the Hawaiian economy was ruled by sugar. Plantation owners grew rich, and with their wealth came power and influence.

In 1864, King Kamehameha V issued a new constitution that strengthened the power of the monarchy. He was the last of the Kamehameha dynasty to rule the kingdom. From his death bed, he summoned Princess Bernice Pauahi Bishop and told her of his intention to make her queen. Stunned at her refusal—she wanted to lead a normal life with her husband—he died without naming an heir, leaving the Hawaiian legislature with the task of calling a popular election to crown a new monarch. A distant Kamehameha relative, William C. Lunalilo, became king. He ruled for just one year, from 1873 to 1874. When he, too, died without naming an heir, the second of Hawaii's elected monarchs took the throne. David Kalakaua set about reviving Hawaiian culture, restoring the hula to prominence and writing down chants and ancient legends for posterity. He also negotiated the Treaty of Reciprocity with the United States, in which the United States could use Pearl Harbor as a military base in return for sugar entering the United States duty free.

In 1887, feeling secure in their economic future, a group of powerful Caucasian sugar plantation owners led an armed revolt with a key provision: voting rights were to be given only to those with an annual income of at least $600 per year or with ownership of property worth at least $3,000. Those who qualified based on land ownership did not need to be citizens, thereby legally shifting the balance of power to Caucasians. The provision became known as the Bayonet Constitution.

In 1891, King David died, leaving his sister Lili'uokalani as Hawaii's first and only queen. She immediately announced revocation of the Bayonet Constitution, returning full power to the monarchy and full voting rights to native Hawaiians. But powerful foreigners revolted, and the U.S. minister brought in the Marines to ensure a successful coup. A provisional government was established with Sanford Dole as the first territory governor. President Grover Cleveland sent an investigator, who declared that "a great wrong had been done to the Hawaiian people," and Washington ordered the removal of American flags from all buildings and the withdrawal of the Marines. The president's orders were ignored.

Queen Lili'uokalani and her supporters planned a counter-coup but were discovered. The queen was arrested and found guilty of treason, for which she was fined $5,000 and sentenced to five years hard labor—a punishment that was never enforced.

The provisional government formed the Republic of Hawaii in 1894 with Sanford Dole as its first president. After the United States established Hawaii as a territory, Dole was named governor, a post he held from 1900 to 1903, when he resigned to fill a justice position in federal court.

Queen Lili'uokalani died in 1917 at age 79. She lived out her days in Washington Place, now the official residence of Hawaii's governor (320 S. Beretania St., 808-586-0240). Tours may be set up in advance.

BIG ISLAND OF HAWAII

The Big Island of Hawaii is just that: big. It covers 4,038 square miles and runs 95 miles north to south and 80 miles east to west. Even though, at 800,000 years old, it's the youngest of all the Hawaiian Islands, it's twice the size of all the other major islands combined and accounts for 63 percent of the total land in the archipelago. And it's growing bigger every day. Lava continues to flow from Kilauea, the island's fiery volcano, and the world's most active one. Since Kilauea's latest eruption began in 1983, more than 560 acres of new land have been added. In all, eruptions from five volcanoes formed the island.

Given its size, the Big Island is quite diverse. Its geography and terrain varies widely. Much of the west side looks barren, with miles and miles of black-colored lava fields that look like mounds of asphalt. The east side is more green and lush with tropical plants and trees. Sandwiched between both coasts, Mauna Kea introduces an alpine twist with its snowcapped peaks at 13,796 feet. Instead of parading around sandy beaches in swimsuits, visitors here bundle up to ski down mountain slopes. That's right, skiing in Hawaii.

Mauna Kea ranks as the tallest mountain in the Pacific, followed closely by the Big Island's other steep attention-getter, the 13,677-foot Mauna Loa. The world's biggest telescope is located atop Mauna Kea. Visitors typically arrive in Kailua-Kona, the major city on the sunny west side, and check into one of the many resorts that dot a 70-mile coastline. The island's most luxurious accommodations, dreamiest beaches, and best golf courses are north along the Kohala Coast.

Despite the allure of all the sandy stretches and green fairways on the west side, most visitors also wander off to other interesting parts of the island for half-day or full-day sightseeing trips. Must-see places include the city of Hilo and the Hamakua Coast on the east side; Upcountry in the north, especially the Parker Ranch, the country's largest ranch; and Hawaii Volcanoes National Park to the south, one of the most popular tourist attractions in all of Hawaii.

As on other islands, it's not unusual for visitors to mix sightseeing with recreational activities, such as hiking, biking and horseback riding. The Big Island also offers all types of water activities and is particularly renowned for deep-sea fishing off the Kona Coast, where many charter-boat companies operate out of the Honokohau Marina.

LEIS

Leis inevitably evoke thoughts of Hawaii. The colorful strands of fresh flowers are such a symbol of Hawaii that the state celebrates Lei Day every year on May 1. Locals throughout the islands drape the fragrant handiwork on their necks, there are lei-making contests and schools crown lei-day kings and queens. Hula exhibitions and concerts are thrown in for added pageantry.

Hawaiians can't take credit for creating leis, however. Rather, it's believed that they were introduced to the islands by the early Polynesians who made their way to Hawaii by canoe from Tahiti. And the leis weren't just made from gorgeous tropical blooms, but also leaves, shells, nuts, feathers, bone and teeth—some of which are still used in lei-making today.

To the Polynesians, leis were symbols used to pay homage to the gods, strike peace agreements, or express love. Nowadays, they typically are given to people on special occasions—birthdays, marriages, parties, even funerals—or, as in centuries past, just to show affection to those you care about.

Different types of leis suit different occasions. For example, the Hawaiian maile lei, an open lei about 4 feet long, is considered a must for brides and grooms.

If you'd like to learn this ancient art form, many hotels and resorts offer introductory lei-making classes, as do many shopping centers and other independent operations, so ask around. To watch the pros in action, head to Chinatown on Oahu, one of the best places to watch leis being made. There, at numerous stands on Maunakea Street and North Beretania, talented and well-trained lei-makers ply their craft and sell their beautiful blooming pieces of art at prices much cheaper than anywhere else on the islands.

If you decide to give someon a lei, there are some rules of etiquette to remember: Always kiss the person on the cheek; don't give a lei to a pregnant woman (it's believed that the gesture could harm the health of the unborn baby); don't give a ti-leaf lei to a politician, it's considered a bad omen.

If you receive a lei, there are a few important rules as well: Always accept a lei, as it's rude to refuse one; wear it draped over your shoulders, with portions of it hanging in the front and back; don't remove the lei in the presence of the person who gave it to you.

Maybe you would like to receive a lei upon your arrival in the islands or have some waiting for the people you're traveling with. That isn't a problem. Numerous companies offer airport lei greetings if you call and make arrangements in advance. Two companies to consider are Honolulu Lei Greetings *(800-665-7959; www.leigreeting.com)* and Leis of Hawaii *(888-534-7644; www.leisofhawaii.com)*.

14 HILO AND THE HAMAKUA COAST

Not only is Hilo on the opposite coast from Kailua-Kona, its different in almost every way. Its the county seat and more of a residential community, not a big tourist draw; its green and lush, not as dry; and its so vibrant with flora because it happens to be one of the wettest spots in the United States, with an average rainfall of about 130 inches.

Don't let the rain keep you away, though. Even though Hilo is the largest city on the Big Island, with a population approaching 50,000, its quaint and charming with a main boulevard along the bay lined with tall and lovely banyan trees (hence the name, Banyan Drive). Its downtown has been partially restored, making it an enjoyable place to do some leisurely shopping. Nearby, on the waterfront, is Likiuokalani Gardens, a 30-acre Japanese garden that is a beautiful, tranquil place.

Despite its charm, Hilo is more of a day-trip destination because it doesn't front a stellar beach, nor does it have many hotels. But it's definitely worth a trip, especially if you take the scenic drive along the dramatic Hamakua Coast, which begins north of the city and stretches for about 50 miles of spectacular scenery. The area is home to a lush rain forest, numerous waterfalls, tropical gardens and tall coastal cliffs that overlook the ocean below. The six-mile-long Waipio Valley and the fern-laden Akaka Falls are two popular attractions on this coast.

WHAT TO SEE
AKAKA FALLS STATE PARK
Highway 220, Honomu, 808-974-6200
You have to make your way along a half-mile loop trail to see Akaka Falls, but the view makes the exercise worth the effort. Here, water freefalls more than 442 feet into a stream-eroded gorge, making for a spectacular sight. Thousands of ferns and other plants add to Akaka's beauty. Before you come upon Akaka, you'll see Kahuna Falls, where the water cascades down 100 feet. The park has no facilities, just the trail.
Daily dawn-dusk.

ARNOTT'S LODGE AND HIKING ADVENTURES
98 Apapane Road, Hilo, 808-969-7097; www.arnottslodge.com
Serious hikers game for vigorous eight- to ten-hour adventures book with Arnott's, which allows you to explore remote, gorgeous areas of the Big Island. Its Mauna Kea Hike begins at 6,500 feet and climbs to 13,600 feet. On the Hawaii Volcanoes National Park and Lava Hike, a challenging trek takes you to within view of lava flows. Or go exploring the lush Hamakua Coast, home to waterfalls and deep gulches. Tours depart from the lodge, and reservations are required.
Admission: $65-$110. Daily; times vary.

BANYAN DRIVE
Kamehameha Avenue, Hilo
A canopy of banyan trees, each planted by someone famous, shades the aptly named Banyan Drive. While in Hilo to shoot a movie in 1933, filmmaker Cecil B. DeMille planted the first banyan tree. In later years, the likes of Amelia Earhart, Babe Ruth, Franklin D. Roosevelt, and King George V ceremoniously planted trees along the drive, which passes by a few of the city's most prominent hotels. A banyan trees branches spawn shoots that grow down into the soil and become supporting roots. The visible result is an eerily beautiful tangle of roots weaving their way into the ground.

BIG ISLAND CANDIES
585 Hinano St., Hilo, 808-935-8890, 800-935-5570; www.bigislandcandies.com
Everything that Big Island Candies cooks up in the kitchen is melt-in-your-mouth delicious, which explains why the place is so popular. You can watch all the goodies, including macadamia nut shortbread cookies and chocolate macadamia nuts, being made through large windows and gobble up free samples. If you want to take some home, they'll ship your treats back home.
Daily 8:30 a.m.-5 p.m.

COCONUT ISLAND
Banyan Drive, Hilo
Parents like to take their kids to this small island to splash around in shallow pools with sandy bottoms. Lots of coconut and ironwood trees also provide plenty of shade for a picnic. Locals bring their families to this park as well, often for fishing excursions. To access the island, just cross the pedestrian bridge that's next to the Hotel Hilo Hawaiian.
Daily dawn-dusk.

DAN DELUZ WOODS

Highway 11, Mile Marker 12, Mountain View, 808-968-6607

Dan DeLuz has mastered his craft, so you'll find beautifully turned bowls and other works of art on display at this homespun shop. The talented DeLuz uses koa, mango, sandalwood and many other types of Hawaiian woods to create his attractive pieces. There's a second location at 64-1013 Mamalahoa Highway in Waimea (808-885-5856).

Daily 9 a.m.-5 p.m.

HAKALAU FOREST NATIONAL WILDLIFE REFUGE

32 Kinoole Street, Hilo, 808-933-6915; pacificislands.fws.gov

Fourteen native-bird species, 13 migratory species and 20 introduced species inhabit this 33,000-acre refuge on Mauna Keas windward slope. And the birds aren't the only attraction; Hakalau is a lush forest with lovely trees, ferns and other plants.

Saturday-Sunday dawn-dusk; call ahead for permission and directions.

HAWAII TROPICAL BOTANICAL GARDEN

27-717 Old Mamalahoa Highway, Papaikou, 808-964-5233; www.htbg.com

More than 2,000 species of plants from around the world flourish at the Hawaii Tropical Botanical Garden, a privately owned 40-acre beauty in the Omomea Valley, about eight miles north of Hilo. The tropical plants you'll see here range from palms and mango trees more than 100 years old to bamboo, bromeliads, ferns, flowering vines, gingers, heliconias, orchids and many more. The various trails in this natural greenhouse take you across streams and by waterfalls and gorgeous ocean views.

Admission: adults $15, children 6-16 $5, children under 6 free. Daily 9 a.m.-5 p.m.

HAWAIIAN WALKWAYS ISLAND HIKING ADVENTURES

45-3674 Mamane St., Honokaa, 808-775-0372, 800-457-7759;
www.hawaiianwalkways.com

The guides who lead these hikes immerse visitors in nature and take them to out-of-the-way places all over the Big Island. Depending on which tour you select, you'll see volcanic summits, upland meadows, rain forests, valleys, coastlines and more. For example, the half-day Waipio Waterfall Adventure, which departs from the company's headquarters in Honokaa, about 40 miles north of Hilo, skirts this lovely valley and takes hikers across several bridges and by waterfalls and pools. The various tours range from easy to difficult, although most are moderate treks. Hawaiian Walkways supplies hikers with rain gear, lunches and snacks, beverages, walking sticks and light packs. Reservations are required, and customized tours are available.

Admission: adults $119-$600 (for personal tours; up to four guests). Daily; times vary.

HILO FARMERS' MARKET

Mamo Street and Kamehameha Avenue, Hilo, 808-933-1000;
www.hilofarmersmarket.com

Every Wednesday and Saturday since 1988, island vendors have been gathering at this outdoor market to sell fresh produce, crafts, gifts and tropical flowers. Over the years, the market has grown from a handful of vendors to more than 120. Some examples of the fruits and vegetables you'll find here include baby ginger, bitter melon, cherimoya, jaboticaba, jack fruit and white pineapple. For souvenirs, you can buy everything from bongo drums and jewelry to pareos (sarongs) and puka shell anklets.

Wednesday and Saturday dawn-noon (or until everything is sold).

LAUPAHOEHOE BEACH PARK
Highway 19, Hamakua Coast, 808-961-8311

Come to this grassy park (just past mile marker 27 on Highway 19) to watch the surf pound into large lava rocks on the coastline and to remember a sad time in the Big Island's past. Here, the Great Tsunami of 1946 slammed ashore, killing 20 students and four teachers. A monument in the park honors the victims of the disaster. The rough surf makes swimming dangerous at this beach, but Laupahoehoe has picnic tables if you want to relax and eat while you watch all the commotion in the ocean. You can also camp here with a county permit.

LAVA TREE STATE MONUMENT
Pohoa-Pohoiki Road (Highway 132), Pahoa, 808-974-6200

At this 17-acre state park, visitors can take a short, self-guided tour around a forest that was swept by lava in the late 1700s, leaving behind eerie molds of tree trunks after burning away the trees themselves. Due to an infestation of coqui frogs, state officials are working to clear some of the terrain of non-native plants that provide a habitat for these creatures, but the area represents a small percentage of the park and a visit is still worthwhile. Note that drinking water is not available at the site, although there are picnic facilities and restrooms.

LELEIWI BEACH PARK
Kalanianaole Avenue, Keaukaka, 808-961-8311

This small black-sand beach rates as your best option for snorkeling on the Hilo side of the island. Not only will you see lots of sea life, but the water here tends to attract green sea turtles and sometimes even playful dolphins.

QUEEN LIKIUOKALANI GARDENS
Banyan Drive, Hilo, 808-961-8311

At Likiuokalani, you'll find everything you'd expect at an authentic Japanese garden, including pagodas, arched bridges, bonsai plantings and bamboo patches, fish ponds and a teahouse. This 30-acre waterfront attraction, named after the last queen of Hawaii, was built in the early 1900s as a tribute to the Japanese immigrants who came to work on the sugar plantations.

Admission: free. Daily 6 a.m.-11 p.m.

LYMAN MUSEUM AND MISSION HOUSE
276 Haili St., Hilo, 808-935-5021; www.lymanmuseum.org

Newlyweds David and Sarah Lyman came from New England to Hawaii in the 1830s as missionaries and lived in this home with their children. It was the oldest wood-frame house built on the island and it has been preserved to look just as it did back in those days with furniture and other artifacts from that era. Guided tours take you back to life in Hawaii in the 19th century. The museum, just next door, has two major galleries that focus on the natural history and people of Hawaii. You can visit them to learn more about the geological formation of the islands and to get a better understanding of Hawaiian culture. Other galleries showcase special exhibits on the art, culture and the history of Hawaii.

Admission: adults $10, children $3. Monday-Saturday 10:00 a.m.-4:30 p.m.

MAMANE STREET
Mamane Street, Honokaa

On the way to the scenic Waipio Valley, you'll pass through Honokaa, an old plantation town. You can stroll along Mamane Street, where a variety of stores and antique shops are housed in old buildings painted pastel colors. While in town, be sure to sample Portuguese malasadas, sugary doughnuts without holes sure to satisfy any sweet craving.

MOKUPAPAPA: DISCOVERY CENTER FOR HAWAII'S REMOTE CORAL REEFS
308 Kamehameha Ave., Hilo, 808-933-8195; hawaiireef.noaa.gov/center

This small marine museum, which opened in 2003, enthralls young and old alike with its exhibits of creatures that inhabit Hawaii's distant atolls. A 2,500-gallon saltwater aquarium houses fish that live in these reefs, while a model of a submersible research vehicle gives kids the chance to see what it would be like to explore the ocean's depths like marine biologists do. You'll also find life-size models, interactive displays and videos that educate as well as entertain. You just might come away from here with an increased respect for our world's oceans and the life within them, and that's exactly the point.

Admission: free. Tuesday-Saturday 9 a.m.-4 p.m.

MULIWAI TRAIL
Highway 240, Honokaa, 808-974-4221; www.hawaiitrails.org

Although it's a breathtakingly beautiful hike, this zigzagging, 18-mile trail (which begins at the Waipio Valley lookout) is definitely not for weekend warriors. You climb more than 1,200 feet up the western edge of Waipio Valley to a plateau that leads to gorgeous Waimanu Valley, but at the plateau, you must cross several gulches up to 500 feet deep to reach Waimanu. In all, a round-trip hike will take you two or three days, and you must get a camping permit from the Division of Forestry and Wildlife office (call the number above), which also has trail maps. If you brave the trail, you'll be exploring lush, peaceful valleys that were once home to many Hawaiians.

NAHA AND PINAO STONES
300 Waianuenue Ave., Hilo

As you drive past the Hilo Public Library, you'll notice two large stones that are legendary in Hawaiian culture. The larger boulder, called the Naha Stone, weighs more than two tons and was supposedly moved by King Kamehameha while he was still a teenager. It was believed that anyone who could move the heavy rock would become king of the islands (which he later did). The other boulder, called the Pinao Stone, is believed to be the entrance pillar to an ancient temple once located in this area.

NANI MAU GARDENS

421 Makalika St., Hilo, 808-59-3500; www.nanimau.com

Nani Mau features five separate, well-tended gardens: the Annual Garden, where you'll encounter splashes of natural color at practically every turn; the European Garden, where herbs, roses and citrus fill the air with pleasant scents; the Anthurium Hapuu Fern Garden, where ferns provide a canopy of shade for the anthuriums to thrive in; the Orchid Garden, where hundreds of varieties of these delicate flowers blossom; and the Water Gardens, where waterfalls, streams and ponds provide just the right growing environment for lilies, bamboo and other water-loving plants. Stroll down the paths that meander through all the lushness, opt for a guided tram tour, or learn more about Hawaiian flora inside the Nani Maus botanical museum.

Daily 8 a.m.-5 p.m.

NAUTILUS DIVE CENTER

382 Kamehameha Ave., Hilo, 808-935-6939; www.nautilusdivehilo.com

Since 1975, Nautilus has specialized in shore dives on the Big Island's east side. Several of the sites it visits are within just a few miles of downtown Hilo. At Leleiwi, you'll see plenty of fish, and possibly even turtles, dolphins and whales, in season. If you're not certified, the center will give you enough training to take you beneath the surface for an awesome look at all the marine life.

PALACE THEATER

38 Haili St., Hilo, 808-934-7010; www.hilopalace.com

When the curtain first went up in this theater in 1925, the Palace was beyond a doubt the most elegant show place on the island. It has closed down a couple of times since then, but it has been open again since 1998, although restoration work continues. On the exterior, its neoclassical in design with a stucco finish and wood molding accents. On the interior, it has an Art Deco look. Nowadays, this historic venue shows art films and hosts concerts and live-theater productions.

PANAEWA RAINFOREST ZOO

Stainback Highway, Hilo, 808-959-7224; www.hilozoo.com

More than 80 animal species live at Panaewa, the country's only tropical rain forest zoo. See a white Bengal tiger, feral goats, pygmy hypos, water buffalo, spider monkeys, Amazon parrots, Macaw parrots, the endangered nene (Hawaii's state bird), and much more. The kids will enjoy following colorful peacocks through a lovely garden of orchids, bamboos and rhododendrons. More than 100 palm trees provide plenty of shade for a picnic.

Admission: free. Daily 9 a.m.-4 p.m.

PRINCE KUHIO PLAZA

111 E. Puainako St., Hilo, 808-959-3555; www.princekuhioplaza.com

With more than 65 shops and restaurants, Prince Kuhio is the largest shopping mall on the Big Island, home to Macy's and several local specialty shops. If you're in the mood for a movie, check out what's playing at the malls nine-screen cinema.

Monday-Friday 10 a.m.-9 p.m., Saturday 9:30 a.m.-7 p.m., Sunday 10 a.m.-6 p.m.

WAILUKU RIVER STATE PARK

Hilo (off Waianueue Avenue); www.hawaiistateparks.org

A short drive from downtown Hilo, the park encompasses 16 lush and scenic acres along the Wailuku River. Highlights include Rainbow Falls and a basalt lava formation known as the Boiling Pots. Water flows over Rainbow Falls and drops a precipitous 80 feet, creating a mist in which, on sunny mornings, a rainbow often appears. Legends hold that Hina, mother of the demigod Maui, lived beneath the falls in a cave. An observation area off Rainbow Drive creates an ideal vantage point for taking pictures or quiet reflection. Two miles upstream, at the end of Peepee Falls Drive, a short trail leads to the Boiling Pots. The river water bubbles and foams as it cascades through the Boiling Pots, a succession of pools formed during the gradual cooling of basalt lava.

RAINBOW FALLS

Waianuenue Avenue, Hilo

With its dramatic 80-foot drop, this waterfall is a sight to see by itself. But come on a misty morning, and the view gets even better. Then you're likely to see the lovely rainbows that gave the falls their name. The setting is pretty, too, with a pool of water surrounded by ginger and other plants. The waterfall is a very short drive west of town.

WAIPIO NAALAPA TRAIL RIDES

45-3626 Manane St., Honokaa, 808-775-0419; www.naalapastables.com

Explore the beautiful Waipio Valley on horseback through lush jungles, over streams, past taro fields and near waterfalls. The views are beautiful and the well-informed guides talk about the valley and its history throughout this scenic, leisurely ride, which leaves from Waipio Valley Artworks near the Waipio Lookout.

Admission: $88.54. Monday-Saturday 9:30 a.m. and 1 p.m. (each 2 ½ hour rides).

WORLD BOTANICAL GARDENS

Highway 19, 808-963-5427; www.wbgi.com

With more than 5,000 species of plants growing on 300 lush acres, this is the state's largest botanical garden (it's located just past mile marker 16 on Highway 19). It is also home to one of the most beautiful waterfalls, Umauma Falls, which is 300 feet tall and triple-tiered. A quarter-mile walk through a rain forest leads to the falls.

Admission: adults $13, children 13-18 $6, children 5-12 $3, children under 5 free. Daily 9 a.m.-5:30 p.m.

SPECIAL EVENTS
HAMAKUA MUSIC FESTIVAL

Honokaa, 808-775-3378; www.hamakuamusicfestival.com

This festival celebrates music by hosting concerts and workshops, offering scholarships to local music students, and funding music education in public schools. Performances include Hawaiian music, jazz, classical and more, held at a variety of venues in the area.

October.

MERRIE MONARCH FESTIVAL

93 Banyan Drive, Hilo, 877-775-4400; www.merriemonarchfestival.org

The state's largest hula festival always is dedicated to King David Kalakaua (the Merrie Monarch), an arts patron who died in 1891. Festivities include a music festival, a hula exhibition, hula competitions, an arts and crafts fair, and a royal parade through downtown Hilo. Everything is free except for the competitions. One week beginning Easter Sunday.

WHERE TO STAY

★★HOTEL HILO HAWAIIAN

71 Banyan Way, Hilo, 808-935-9361, 800-367-5004; www.castleresorts.com

In a city with very few hotel choices, the Hotel Hilo Hawaiian is probably your best bet if you need to spend the night after a day of exploring. The no-frills rooms are outdated, but they are comfortable enough, and there are good views of Hilo Bay (which it fronts), downtown Hilo and Mauna Kea in the distance on a clear day.

286 rooms. Restaurant, bar. Pool. $61-150

WHERE TO EAT

★★CAFE PESTO

308 Kamehameha Ave., Hilo, 808-969-6640; www.cafepesto.com

One of two Cafe Pesto restaurants on the Big Island, the Hilo Bay location is surrounded by a variety of small galleries in the historic S. Hata Building. The dining room decor combines a broad range of design elements, with Art Deco light fixtures hanging above rattan furnishings, and the walls adorned by framed photos of volcanic eruptions at nearby Kilauea. Locals love the calzones and wood-fired pizzas. The menu focuses on Italian cuisine, but Hawaiian favorites, such as mango-glazed chicken, are also available. Be sure to indulge in one of the restaurants scrumptious desserts, a favorite being the hot Keanakolu apple crisp, served with macadamia nut crumb topping.

Italian. Lunch, dinner. Bar. $16-35

★KEN'S HOUSE OF PANCAKES

1730 Kamehameha Ave., Hilo, 808-935-8711

At all hours of the day and night, locals and tourists alike crowd the orange vinyl booths at this popular diner. The food at Ken's is affordable, and the extensive menu runs the gamut from burgers and steaks to omelets and, yes, pancakes. To put a Big Island spin on your flapjacks, order the macadamia-nut stack with guava syrup. Fans of wrestler/actor Dwayne Johnson (The Rock) will appreciate the numerous framed photos of him hanging inside the restaurant.

American. Breakfast, lunch, dinner, late-night. $16-35

★MIYO'S

400 Hualani St., Hilo, 808-935-2273

With its satisfying food and views of Waiakea Pond and Mauna Kea, Miyo's is a restaurant that nourishes all the senses. Miyo's specializes in sashimi and traditional Japanese dishes. Favorites include sesame chicken (pieces of deep-fried boneless chicken with a spicy sesame sauce for dipping), a variety of tempuras, sukiyaki, don buris and shabu shabu. Noodle lovers will find both udon and soba selections, and vegetarian offerings are well represented. Most dishes come as a set with salad, miso soup, rice, and pickles, making Miyo's one of the best bargains on the island.

Japanese. Lunch, dinner. Bar. $15 and under

★PESCATORE
235 Keawe St., Hilo, 808-969-9090

Pescatore serves delicious, affordably priced Italian favorites. Guests feast on pasta and pizza while comfortably seated in oversized chairs with red velvet cushioning. In the dining room, ornate iron chandeliers and gilt-framed replicas of European masterworks evoke an aura of old-world elegance. The restaurant is located in downtown Hilo, across the street from the Hawaii Visitors Bureau.

Italian. Lunch, dinner. $16-35

★REUBEN'S MEXICAN FOOD
336 Kamehameha Ave., Hilo, 808-961-2552

Reuben's owes its popularity to its low-key atmosphere, reasonable prices, and extensive menu of familiar favorites such as steak tacos, chicken flautas, and carne asada, all of which are served with rice and beans on the side. The crab enchiladas and chile rellenos come highly recommended by regulars, and the huge portions, frothy double margaritas and excellent selection of beer, including a good negra modelo (dark beer), make this place a slam dunk for affordable Mexican on the island. The canned mariachi music, Mexican trinkets and bright, hand-painted murals contrast sharply with the view of Hilo Bay, but then Reuben's doesn't claim to be tasteful, just tasty.

Mexican. Lunch, dinner. Bar. $15 and under

HAWAII VOLCANOES NATIONAL PARK

The park serves as the primary motivation for traveling to the Big Island. More than a million visitors a year arrive to bear witness to the tempestuous Kilauea, the world's most active volcano. Kilauea has been erupting continuously since 1983, the volcano's longest rift-zone eruption in more than 600 years. As lava flows down Kilauea and into the ocean, new land mass is created, making the Big Island even bigger.

More than 70 million years of volcanism created the regions unique topography, diverse ecosystems and fragile animal and plant life. Recognizing its value and need for protection, President Woodrow Wilson inked legislation creating Hawaii Volcanoes National Park in 1916, 43 years before the then-US territory attained statehood. Over half of the parkland is designated as wilderness. The park has been recognized as an International Biosphere Reserve and a World Heritage Site. While driving in the park, keep an eye out for geese, or nene, plodding across the road. The nene, Hawaii's official state bird, is classified as an endangered species.

Hawaiian folklore holds that Pele, the goddess of fire, dwells in Halemaumau Crater at the summit of Kilauea. Like the volcano, Pele is considered both creator and destroyer, and as such Hawaiians regard her with awe and respect. Even today, park visi-tors often seek to allay Pele's wrath by leaving flowers along the rim of Halemaumau, where the pungent scent of sulfur pervades the air.

Most visitors arrive at the park hoping to observe flowing streams of red-hot lava. Unfortunately, Kilauea doesn't always cooperate. While molten lava is consistently visible from the sky, it cannot always be observed safely from the ground. The good news is that, lava or no lava, there's no shortage of things to see and do within the park.

If you're only here for a few hours, must-see sites include the Holei Sea Arch, Thurston Lava Tube, Kilauea Iki Overlook and Jaggar Museum. If you're here for one night, park your car at the end of Chain of Craters Road and walk east along the coast, crossing the eerie but beautiful landscape of black frozen lava, formed in recent years as molten lava flowed across the road and into the sea, disappearing with a hiss and cloud of steam. If you're staying in the park for a few days, you'll want to experience the regions diverse ecosystems by hiking the Kau Desert Trail, Puna Coast Trail, and Crater Rim Trail. Only experienced trekkers should consider tackling the Mauna Loa Trail, which leads to the precipitous summit of the world's most massive volcano.

WHAT TO SEE
AIR TOURS
Hawaii Volcanoes National Park
If you want a birds-eye view of the park, make a reservation with one of the many aerial tour operators on the Big Island. You can choose between a tour aboard a helicopter or small private plane. The helicopter tours allow for up-close observation of Kilauea's volcanic fury. Trips originate in either Kailua-Kona or Hilo.

CAMPING
Hawaii Volcanoes National Park
The park offers two drive-in campgrounds. The Namakani Paio campground, located off Highway 11, has rest rooms, water and barbecue pits. The more rustic Kulanaokuaiki campground sits in the center of the park, five miles away from the Hilina Pali Road. Camping is free and reservations are unnecessary, but stays are limited to seven nights per month. Backcountry campsites are scattered throughout the park, one of the most popular being the Halape Shelter, nestled along the coast. Backcountry campers must obtain a free permit at the visitor center.

HIKING
Hawaii Volcanoes National Park
To fully appreciate the park's dramatic volcanic landscapes and various ecosystems ranging from desert to rain forest, you need to set off on foot. The park has more than 150 miles of hiking trails—stop at the visitor center for a map. If you only have time for one hike, make it the 4-mile trek along the Kilauea Iki Trail, which descends 400 feet through rain forest, then opens up into a wide-open expanse of frozen black lava, still steaming from an eruption in 1959. Ambitious hikers should consider the Mauna Loa Trail, a 20-mile, multiday hike that ascends more than 7,000 feet to the summit of the mountain. Measured from sea level, Mauna Loa stands 13,677 feet high; but from its base on the sea floor, the monolithic mountain rises an astounding 56,000 feet.

PELE

Visit the Kilauea Volcano at Hawaii Volcanoes National Park on the Big Island and you may notice offerings on the craters rim. Locals sometimes leave these special gifts for Pele, one of the Hawaiian gods that some still worship today, even though King Kamehameha II abolished kapu, the ancient religion that recognized the gods, back in 1819. It is thought that she still lives in the Kilauea Caldera, the reason believers come to the crater bearing gifts.

There are many legends about Pele, called both the Goddess of Volcano and the Goddess of Fire. Various versions exist, all of them quite tantalizing. Factual differences aside, they all depict her as passionate, volatile and capricious.

One legend has it that a beast-man named Kamapuaa went to where she lived in the Oahus Puna district and asked her to marry him. When she refused, calling him a pig, he killed some of her family, prompting her to hide in a cavern. When he tried to force his way into her hideaway, the volcano erupted and molten rock sent the unwanted suitor back to his boat in the water.

Another legend offers up one of the explanations for how Pele came to live at Kilauea. Smitten with a handsome young chief, she came to blows with her sister, Namaka o Kahai, who also had her eye on him. The jealous sister smashed Pele's bones on Maui's Hana coast, but Pele reconstructed herself and then escaped with her lover to Kilauea. Those who still worship Pele believe her presence there explains why the volcano spews fiery lava.

Believe what you want, but consider this: some visitors disregard requests that they not remove stones from the volcano as souvenirs. Every year, park rangers say hundreds of stones are returned by the people who took them because they got spooked by all the bad luck that started plaguing them once they had the stones in their possession

KILAUEA VISITOR CENTER

Crater Rim Drive, Hawaii Volcanoes National Park, 808-985-6000

If you're looking for molten lava, this needs to be your first stop; the visitor center is staffed with rangers who can provide you with the latest information on lava flows and park accessibility. Located a quarter mile beyond the park entrance, the visitor center also has exhibits on volcano formation, native plants and animals, and early Hawaiians. A 25-minute film about volcanic eruptions is shown on the hour. Detailed maps are available for purchase, though the free park brochure contains a decent map.

Daily 7:45 a.m.-5 p.m.

THOMAS A. JAGGAR MUSEUM

Crater Rim Drive, Hawaii Volcanoes National Park, 808-985-6049

This educational and fun museum features videos of volcanic eruptions, geologic displays and functioning seismic equipment. The museum bookstore sells volcano-related books, videos and posters. An overlook offers spectacular views of the Kilauea Caldera and the Halemaumau Crater. The museum is located three miles inside the park entrance.

Daily 8:30 a.m.-5 p.m. Free

VOLCANO ART CENTER

Hawaii Volcanoes National Park, Volcano, 808-967-7565, 866-967-7565

The best place in the area to purchase high-end artwork, the Volcano Art Center is located next to the visitor center. Offerings include paintings, art

glass, photographs, koa wood items, ceramics and jewelry.
Daily 9 a.m.-5 p.m.

VOLCANO GOLF AND COUNTRY CLUB
Highway 11, just past the entrance to the park, 808-967-7331
Opened in 1920, this 18-hole, par-72 course, nearly 4,300 feet above sea level (the elevation adds bonus distance to your shots), is semi-private. Make sure to reserve a tee time in advance; rental clubs are available if you don't bring your own. Despite its location near the volcano, the course is fairly flat, although greens are elevated. No irrigation system is needed here; the areas rains keep the grass green all year-round. The clubhouse has a restaurant that's a nice spot for a simple lunch and lovely views.

PUNALUU BEACH COUNTY PARK
Highway 11, Pahala, 808-961-8311
Seek out this park (at mile marker 56) or two reasons: to see the islands only accessible black-sand beach, which is attractively lined with palm trees, and to look for Hawaii's endangered green sea turtles. Groups of turtles tend to hang out around here, eating seaweed off the rocks and resting up on the beach. Riptides make swimming at Punaluu dangerous, but people like to relax and sunbathe on the sand. A picnic area is across the road.

VOLCANO WINERY
35 Pii Mauna Drive, off Highway 11, 808-967-7772; www.volcanowinery.com
You've probably never tasted wines made of fruit blends, such as guava chablis and volcano red, a mixture of jaboticaba fruit juice and chablis. This small winery tucked between two volcanoes (located approximately three miles south of Volcano Village), the sole winery on the Big Island, is the only U.S. winery that produces such unusual vintages. Its also proud of its macadamia nut honey wine, a dessert offering. If you prefer something more traditional, however, it does make two wines with symphony grapes. Stop in for a free tasting. A nice gift shop sells a variety of wine- and volcano-related items so you can take home a souvenir.
Daily 10 a.m.-5:30 p.m.

WOOD VALLEY TEMPLE AND RETREAT CENTER
Pikake Street, Pahala, 808-928-8539; www.nechung.org
This nonsectarian Buddhist temple and meditation center sits on 30 green acres of forestland tucked away in a remote, quiet valley at South Point. Day visitors are welcome to come to this serene setting and wander around the beautiful grounds and visit the temple. Also known as Nechung Dorje Drayang Ling, the attraction opened in 1973 and was dedicated in 1980 by the Dalai Lama, who made a return visit in 1994.
Daily 10 a.m.-5 p.m.

WHERE TO EAT
★★★KILAUEA LODGE
19-3948 Old Volcano Road, Volcano Village, 808-967-7366; www.kilauealodge.com
This restaurant offers a dining experience unlike any other on the Big Island,

with a cozy and woodsy dining room that has the look and feel of the Pacific Northwest, not the Aloha State. Built as a YMCA camp in the 1930s, the lodge today serves as a country inn and restaurant. The interior features beamed cedar ceilings, koa wood tables and hardwood floors. A massive stone fireplace warms guests in the dining room. The Fireplace of Friendship, as its known, has artifacts embedded in it from around the world, including a stone from the Acropolis in Athens, Greece. On the walls, spectacular photos of volcanic eruptions and flowing lava remind diners that Hawaii Volcanoes National Park is a mere mile away. Chef Albert Jeyte, who previously worked as a makeup artist and won an Emmy for his work on Magnum, PI, specializes in continental cuisine, ranging from Pacific Rim fish dishes to European favorites such as hasenpfeffer and venison.

American. Dinner. $36-85

LAVA TUBES

Lava tubes crisscross every subterranean region of the Big Island. Lava tubes are important both to understanding the geology of Hawaii and to the culture of the Hawaiian people. With advance planning and a little luck, you can visit a secret and pristine tube in the Volcanoes National Park.

Any visit to the Big Island must include a trip to the drive-in volcano, Kilauea, where you will have a very good chance of seeing the red ooze of lava on the surface. This lava is only a very small fraction of the lava that has been flowing for more than 20 years in the world's longest continuous eruption. Under the surface, vast caverns of red-hot liquid rock pulse and flow.

To see the surface lava, you will need to drive to the bottom of Chain of Craters Road inside the park. After dark, you can see red lights twinkling high on the pali, almost like a distant city; down below on the shoreline, you will see the plume of gasses created when the lava meets the sea. In between is a vast darkness.

When lava begins its journey to the sea, it is on the surface, but it crusts over very quickly, creating an insulating layer. The lava is now under the surface flowing in a self-created tube. At some point the flow in the tube stops from above, but the lava continues to flow out, leaving a cavelike tube. These hollow tubes, like the lava fields on the surface, are everywhere.

A very interesting and easy-to-access example is also one of the most visited sites in the park, Thurston Lava Tube, where you can walk through a well-lit and paved section of the cave.

But there is also a very special tube in the park, Pua Poo Lava Tube, carefully preserved and open to just 12 visitors per week. Inside you will see all the delicate and intricate formations still unspoiled. At one point, the ranger asks that all lights be turned off and, in the absolute darkness, he explains how organisms in the cave have evolved, losing all characteristics like color and sight that depend on light. He explains how ancient Hawaiians used these caves for collecting water, burying their dead, hiding from enemies, and basic shelter.

The tour of the Pua Poo Lava Tube is led by a ranger every Wednesday and includes a 4-mile round-trip hike through rain forest. To be included you must call the park office (808-985-6017) a week in advance. The list fills up quickly, so it's best to call before 8 a.m. HST.

When you are finished with your tour, the ranger will impress upon you the importance of keeping the location of this wonderful place a secret, that should you even be tempted to reveal its location, you may well get a glimpse of the wrath of Pele, the volcano goddess.

KAILUA-KONA AND THE KONA COAST

Located on the west side of the island, the coastal city of Kailua-Kona is the center of commercial activity. Swarms of visitors stroll along Alii Drive, the main drag on the waterfront, browsing the souvenir shops, eating in one of the many oceanfront restaurants or checking out the historical attractions. Two of the city's must-sees are the Hulihee Palace, where Hawaiian monarchs came to vacation in the 1800s, and the Mokuaikaua Church, the first house of worship built by Christians in Hawaii in the early 1800s.

The Kona Coast stretches for about 70 miles north and south of the city, and is dotted by small seaside villages, a few good beaches and one of the island's best spots for snorkeling in Kealakekua Bay, which is also where Captain James Cook died in the 1700s.

The landscape along the Kona coast varies dramatically, dry and barren in some parts, verdant slopes in others (where plantation owners grow rich Kona coffee and macadamia nuts, two crops for which the Big Island is known around the world). The Big Island is also known for it's marine life, and diving and snorkeling are very popular.

WHAT TO SEE
AHUENA HEIAU
Kailua-Kona, 808-329-2911

This ancient temple, located just off the beach on the grounds of King Kamehameha's Kona Beach Hotel, served as the king's personal heiau (temple) from 1813 until his death in 1819. Guided tours are available through the hotel; check the lobby for times.
Admission: free. Daily 9 a.m.-4 p.m.

ALOHA KAYAK CO.
79-7428 Mamalahoa Highway, Honalo, 877-322-1444; www.alohakayak.com

Sea caves. Rock cliffs up to 40 feet tall. Striking coastal scenery. Playful dolphins. You'll see all this and more as you explore the Kona Coast in a kayak on one of this company's Wet n Wild Tours. You'll also dive into the ocean for snorkeling in crystal-clear water packed with fish. A morning tour lasts for four hours and includes lunch. A shortened afternoon tour (2 1/2 hours) includes snacks. The company also rents kayaks and ocean gear for those who want to paddle on their own. Opt for a glass kayak so you can see what's swimming in the water beneath you.
Monday-Friday 9:30 a.m. and 1:30 p.m.

ATLANTIS SUBMARINES
75-5656 Alii Drive, Kailua-Kona, 800-548-6262; www.atlantisadventures.com

Yes, you can go down in a submarine. Atlantis takes you down 100 feet on one of its high-tech submarines. The nearly one-hour tour will show you 25-acre natural coral reef. Who knows what will swim by—perhaps a shark or two, some eagle rays, and a school of parrotfish. Other Atlantis tours combine the submarine adventure with whale watching (December-May) a luau, or a helicopter tour.
Daily at 10 a.m., 11:30 a.m., and 1 p.m.

BIG ISLAND COUNTRY CLUB

71-1420 Mamalahoa Highway, Kailua-Kona, 808-325-5044

Expect to be wowed at this Perry Dye-designed golf course. Built at 2,000 feet above sea level on the slopes of Mauna Kea, this semiprivate course offers great views of both the Pacific and inland areas. You can also expect to be challenged. The 72 sand bunkers and numerous grass bunkers on this par 72, 7,034-yard course also demand accurate shot making. But don't be intimidated; each hole has five sets of tees to accommodate different levels of players. Amenities include a golf shop and short-game practice area.

Daily 7 a.m.-6 p.m.

BODY GLOVE CRUISES

75-5629 Kuakini Highway, Kailua-Kona, 808-326-7122, 800-551-8911;
www.bodyglovehawaii.com.

For lots of fun at sea, pack up the family and head to Kailua Pier to board this 51-foot sailing vessel for a snorkeling/scuba dive or whale-watching excursion. The boat sails to Pawai Bay, a protected marine preserve that's home to colorful fish, endangered sea turtles, and dolphins. Body Glove offers two snorkel dolphin excursions a day, and from December to March, passengers can come aboard for a three-hour afternoon whale-watching cruise on which a knowledgeable naturalist provides insight into the oversized marine mammals. A continental breakfast and deli lunch are served. You can also sign up for dinner and sunset cocktail cruises at sunset.

Check the web site for the cruise schedule.

CAPTAIN BEAN'S CRUISES

73-4800 Kanalani St., Kailua-Kona, 808-329-2955, 800/831-5541;
www.robertshawaii.com

This entertaining sail along the Kona Coast on a 150-foot double-hulled canoe at sunset includes an open-bar with tropical drinks, an all-you-can-eat buffet featuring teriyaki steak and baked Polynesian chicken, and lively entertainment including a hula show.

Check in 4:45 p.m. Admission: adults (from Kailua-Kona) $64, children $32.

CAPTAIN DAN MCSWEENEY'S YEAR-ROUND WHALE WATCHING ADVENTURES

Holualoa, Honokohau Marina, 808-322-0028, 888-942-5376; www.ilovewhales.com

Most visitors to the islands know that humpback whales hang out in Hawaii each winter, usually from about December through March or April. But other types of whales, such as the giant sperm, pilot, false killer, beaked and melon-headed whales, never leave Hawaiian waters. On his boat tours, Captain McSweeney introduces visitors to the humpbacks and all these other whales practically year-round. McSweeney, a marine mammal expert and researcher, is passionate about these sea mammals and has spent decades studying them. Tours depart from the Honokohau Marina.

Admission: adults $79.50, children 69.50. July-December 24, Tuesday, Thursday and Saturday 7:10 a.m.; December 25-April 15, daily 7:10 a.m. and 11:30 a.m.

CAPTAIN ZODIAC'S RAFT EXPEDITIONS

Kailua-Kona, Honokohau Harbor, 808-329-3199; www.captainzodiac.com.

If you want a little more adventure than quiet cruise, sign up for one of these tours. On one of these four-hour expeditions, you'll make your way through the ocean in a 24-foot inflatable raft, not a high-priced catamaran. Your destination is scenic Kealakekua Bay, a marine preserve where you'll explore sea caves and lava tubes, and swim with a wide variety of tropical fish. En route to the bay, you just might see dolphins, green sea turtles, manta rays, and, in season, humpback whales.

Daily 8 a.m. and 12:45 p.m.

DAVE'S BIKE AND TRIATHLON SHOP

75-5669 Alii Drive, Kailua-Kona, 808-329-4522

Dave's is a popular option for bike rentals in Kona. The shop specializes in mountain and road bikes, which it rents by the day, week, or month.

Monday-Friday 8 a.m.-4 p.m., Saturday-Sunday 8 a.m.-1 p.m.

ECO-ADVENTURES

King Kamehameha's Kona Beach Hotel, 75-5660 Palani Road, Kailua-Kona,
808-329-7116, 800-949-3483.

This popular dive company offers a variety of diving tours using a 50-foot double-hull catamaran, a 36-foot dive boat, and a 20-foot high-speed dive boat. Tours include a two-tank morning dive, a dive for newcomers, an afternoon-night dive with manta rays, a three-tank dive that may include stops at Au Au Canyon, Three Room Caves and Twin Sisters, and more. Lunch is served on the longer dives.

Daily; times vary.

ELLISON S. ONIZUKA SPACE CENTER

Keahole-Kona Airport, One Keahole Street, Kailua-Kona, 808-329-3441

Make it your mission to learn more about space exploration at this space center, which was built in memory of Hawaii's first astronaut, one of the seven who lost their lives aboard the Challenger mission in 1986. The center features interactive displays, including one in which you control the launch of a miniature rocket, and various space memorabilia, such as an Apollo 13 space suit.

Admission: adults $3, children and students $1. Daily 8:30 a.m.-4:30 p.m.

FAIR WIND SNORKELING AND DIVING ADVENTURES

78-7130 Kaleiopapa St., Kailua-Kona, 808-322-2788; 800-677-9461;
www.fair-wind.com

Fair Wind takes its passengers to beautiful Kealakekua Bay for snorkeling and scuba excursions on a 60-foot catamaran or a 28-foot hard-bottom raft. Take your pick, depending on which type of boat appeals to you most. Do you want to travel in style or do you prefer to be a little more adventurous? Morning and afternoon cruises are offered on both the sailboat and the rafts. Lunch is served on the morning boat cruise, which lasts a little longer than the afternoon one because it makes a second snorkeling stop. The boat cruises depart from Keauhou Bay; the raft treks from Kailua Pier.

Daily; times vary.

KONA AGGRESSOR II

74-5588 Pawai Place, Kailua-Kona, 808-329-8182, 800/344-5662; www.aggressor.com

If you're coming to the Big Island solely for the superb diving, you'll want to book a seven-day adventure on this live-aboard luxury catamaran. During the weeklong ocean journey, the 80-foot, 10-passenger boat travels along more than 90 miles of coastline on the islands west side, stopping at up to 30 top-rated dive sites teeming with marine life. Divers often make up to five dives a day, some of them at night. You'll likely see rare black coral forests, wild fauna jungles, lionfish, starfish, spotted eagle rays, coral eels, whale sharks, manta rays, and much more.

Daily.

HAWAII FOREST AND TRAIL NATURE ADVENTURES AND OUTFITTING

74-5035B Queen Kaahumanu Highway, Kailua-Kona, 808-331-8505, 800-464-1993;
www.hawaii-forest.com

This company and its outdoor-loving staff offer eight adventures that take you on tours to waterfalls, volcanoes, rain forests, and wildlife refuges. All of the trips take you far away from crowds and get you back in touch with nature and all its glory, and most involve only easy walks. See some of the world's rarest birds and plants in an area not open to the general public on the full-day birding adventure. Or, on the half-day mule trail adventure, explore gorgeous valleys and waterfalls while you leave the walking to your big-eared mount.

Daily; times vary.

HOLUALOA

Mamalahoa Highway, Holualoa

Just about a 10- or 15-minute drive up Hualalai Road from Kailua-Kona sits the charming little upcountry community of Holualoa, an artist's haven. You'll find several art galleries and arts-and-crafts shops selling creative works by island artists inside the small but spruced up plantation homes that line its two-block-long main street. Paintings, pottery, woven goods, koa furniture, jewelry, sculpture, raku ceramics and more fill the quaint shops. This is coffee country, with groves all over the mountainside leading up to Holualoa, so the town is a good place to relax with a cup of strong Kona coffee, especially at the Holuakoa Café *(76-5900 Mamalahoa Highway Holualoa, 808-322-2233)*.

HOLUALOA KONA COFFEE CO.

77-6261 Mamalahoa Highway, Holualoa, 808-322-9937, 800-334-0348;
www.konalea.com

Kona is known around the world for its delicious coffee grown on the slopes inland from the coast. See how the coffee is grown and produced by this company at the Kona Lea Plantation, where organic methods are practiced. An informative tour takes you through its orchard and mill, and then commences in the roasting room for a complimentary cup of fresh java.

Monday-Friday 8 a.m.-4 p.m.

HUGGO'S ON THE ROCKS

75-5828 Kahakai Road, Kailua-Kona, 808-329-1493;
www.huggos.com/rocksdefault.htm

At this popular oceanfront spot, live music helps keep the scene lively. Inside the bar, jazz and blues take center stage on Sunday and Wednesday after dark; piano players tickle the ivories and keep the crowd entertained most other nights. Outside, patrons can listen to Hawaiian music nightly from 6 to 8 p.m., followed by three to four hours of dance tunes, which get everyone moving to the beat. Huggo's serves lunch and light fare at night, along with an array of ice-cold tropical drinks. For heartier dining, Huggo's Restaurant is next door.

Daily at 11:30 am; closing times vary.

HULIHEE PALACE

75-5718 Alii Drive, Kailua-Kona, 808-329-1877; www.huliheepalace.org

In 1838, foreign seamen built this two-story, six-room waterfront palace for the Big Islands governor using lava rock, coral lime mortar, and koa and ohia wood. Later, Hulihee served as a vacation retreat for Hawaiian royalty. Now a museum operated by the Daughters of Hawaii, the palace is glimpse into how Hawaiian royalty lived in the late 1800s. On our last visit, the palace was closed for renovations; check to see if it's open before visiting. The palace grounds are also used for free concerts and other special events throughout the year.

Monday-Saturday 9 a.m.-4 p.m., Sunday 10 a.m.-4 p.m.

ISLAND BREEZE LUAU

King Kamehameha's Kona Beach Hotel, 75-5660 Palani Road, Kailua-Kona,
808-329-8111; www.islandbreezeluau.com

Held on the historic grounds of King Kamehameha's former estate fronting Kamakahonu Bay, this luau is perhaps the island's most popular. Festivities begin with a shell-lei greeting, followed by a torch-lighting ceremony and the arrival of the Royal Court, all decked out in traditional Hawaiian dress, via outrigger canoe. After everyone feasts on a 22-dish buffet, the drum-pounding entertainment begins. The revue features hula dancing, Fijian and Maori war dances, and the Samoan fire-knife dance.

Admission: adults $69.95, children $34.95. Tuesday and Saturday 5:30-8:30 p.m.; reservations required.

JACK'S DIVING LOCKER

Coconut Grove Shopping Center, 75-5813 Alii Drive, Kailua-Kona, 808-329-7585,
800-345-4807; www.jacksdivinglocker.com

Jacks Diving Locker provides a variety of day and night dives based on what you're interested in seeing. On its morning two-tank dives for all levels, divers are asked what they're interested in seeing and the captain selects from up to 60 sites within 25 minutes of the boat pier. Two- and three-tank dives for advanced divers may take you drift diving, wreck diving, or exploring lava tubes and caverns. At night, you may see manta rays and other sea creatures that come out only after dark.

Daily.

KONA COFFEE

Kona coffee, grown exclusively in the North and South Kona districts on the big island, has quite a reputation as one of the best javas available anywhere in the world. It's considered delicate yet flavorful, with a rich aroma that's oh-so-pleasing to the tastebuds.

What makes it so good? Experts give much of the credit to the growing conditions in the Kona region. The trees flourish on the rich volcanic mountain slopes that are drenched with sun in the morning, moistened with rain in the afternoon, and kept cool at night with mild temperatures. A meticulous cultivation process also helps ensure the high quality of the beans. From late August to late January, the beans on the trees are hand-picked, and only when they're at peak maturity, so all the trees get picked over repeatedly during the harvest season.

Don Francisco de Paula y Marin, King Kamehameha the Great's Spanish interpreter and doctor, brought the first coffee tree to the islands in 1813 and planted it in Oahu, signaling the start of coffee production in Hawaii. Fifteen years later, Reverend Samuel Ruggles brought a cutting from Oahu to Kona, which proved to be the beginning of the great tradition of Kona coffee.

Initially, big plantations grew the crop, but most went out of business when the world coffee market crashed in 1899. At that point, Japanese immigrants who were disillusioned with working on the sugar plantations started cultivating the coffee on leased parcels of land ranging in size from 3 to 5 acres. Now, more than 100 years later, more than 600 small producers are flourishing in the Kona region, and their ranks now include immigrants from China, Korea, the Philippines, Portugal, and Puerto Rico, as well as some Hawaiians and Caucasians. Some of these hard-worknig souls are fifth-generation coffee farmers dedicated to carrying on the family tradition.

Every November, these farmers, other locals, and visitors gather to salute Kona coffee during the annual Kona Coffee Cultural Festival, which runs for ten days. The fun-packed events include more than 30 activities, such as recipe contests, coffee-picking contests, growers' workshops, parades, and a cupping competition, in which esteemed international judges painstakingly choose the "best of the best" beans for that year.

Visitors who aren't on the Big Island during the festival can still learn about Kona coffee and meet some of the farmers by visiting their farms, many of which are included on a self-guided driving tour outlined at www.konacoffeefest.com. On the tour, you can sample the various roasts and buy bags of those you like best.

KAHALUU BEACH PARK

Alii Drive, Kailua-Kona, 808-961-8311

You won't have this beach to yourself because Kahaluu is the favored swimming hole on the Kona Coast, attracting crowds every day of the week. That's partly because it is excellent for snorkeling, with clear water and teems of tame fish that don't mind being stared at. Parents like coming here because shallow water makes it a good swimming spot for kids. But dangerous riptides develop in high surf, so stay out of the water when it gets rough. The park has picnic tables and grills if you want to eat beachside.

KAMANU CHARTERS

Kailua-Kona, Honokohau Harbor, 808-329-2021, 800-348-3091; www.kamanu.com

For a snorkeling/sailing adventure without the crowds, Kamanu delivers. On its 36-foot catamaran, this company takes no more than 24 people to Pawai Bay for a look at all the sea creatures swimming beneath the surface. The

small size of the group means first-time snorkelers get plenty of personal instruction. A deli lunch is served.
Daily 9 a.m. and 1:30 p.m.

KING KAMEHAMEHA'S COMPOUND
King Kamehameha's Kona Beach Hotel, 75-5660 Palani Road, Kailua-Kona,
808-329-2911; www.konabeachhotel.com
King Kamehameha I died in 1819, and he lived the last seven years of his life in this area that now includes the King Kamehameha's Kona Beach Hotel. The main attraction is the rebuilt Ahuena Heiau, a stately temple where the king tended to royal matters. Explore the temple area on your own, or take a guided tour that originates at the hotel. Also be sure to wander through the hotels lobby, where you'll find impressive Hawaiian artifacts. Guided tours: call for days and times.

KING'S TRAIL RIDES
Highway 11, Kealakekua, 808-323-2388; www.konacowboy.com
On this 4 1/2-hour horseback adventure (that starts at mile marker 111 on Highway 11), hop aboard your mount, then travel down toward the Pacific and beautiful Kealakekua Bay. Along the green-filled trail, you'll pass under ekoa, mango, coffee, tamerine and kiawe trees. At the bottom of the trail, you'll see the monument to explorer Captain James Cook, swim and snorkel in the coral-packed bay (a fish preserve), and enjoy a picnic lunch. In all, you spend about two hours of the trip riding.
Daily 9 a.m.-1:30 p.m.

KONA BREWING CO.
North Kona Shopping Center, 75-5629 Kuakini Highway, Kailua-Kona, 808-334-2739;
www.konabrewingco.com
Since 1994, Kona Brewing Co. has been producing ales and lagers that brew-lovers can buy in Hawaii, California, and Japan. Its frothy suds have names like the Longboard Lager (a must-try while in Hawaii) and Big Wave Golden Ale. See how they make them on guided tours of the facility, which are available weekdays. The brewpub serves tasty pub grub.
Sunday-Thursday 11 a.m.-10 p.m., Friday-Saturday 11 a.m.-11 p.m. Tours: Monday-Friday 10:30 a.m. and 3 p.m.

KONA COAST CYCLING TOURS
Kailua-Kona, 808-345-3455, 877-592-2453; www.cyclekona.com
Bike down Kohala Mountain. Explore North Kohala. Cycle through the lush Hamakua Coast, crossing numerous bridges and passing many streams and waterfalls. Pedal along the Old Mamalahoa Highway, making your way through pastureland and tropical rain forests. These are just some of the half-day and full-day cycling tours throughout the Big Island available from this company; see Web site for more information.
Daily.

KONA COAST STATE PARK (KEKAHA KAI STATE PARK)
Highway 19, Kailua-Kona, North of Kailua-Kona off Highway 19, 808-327-4958

A little more than a mile off the highway (between mile markers 90 and 91), down a bumpy road, you'll find this state park, just a couple of miles north of Kona's airport. It's home to two beaches, Mahaiula and Kua Bay, connected by a 4 1/2-mile trail, if you want to hike from one to the other. The swimming is very good when the oceans calm; the snorkeling is fair to good, depending on the clarity of the water on any given day. Also, there are picnic facilities at Mahaiula.
Daily.

KONA COFFEE COUNTRY DRIVING TOUR

Kailua-Kona, Kona Coffee Belt; www.konacoffeefest.com

There are more than 600 coffee farms in the Kona Coffee Belt, in towns from Keopu to Honaunau. Guided tours will give you a behind-the-scenes look at how coffee is made, while tastings allow you to find the perfect roast. One of our favorites is Kona Blue Sky *(877-322-1700)*, which is only available on the island or via web site. On a self-guided driving tour, visit farms, mills, roasters, museums, coffee shops, and retailers to learn more about this Big Island tradition. A map with detailed listings of suggested stops is provided at the Web site noted above.

KONA HISTORICAL SOCIETY MUSEUM

81-6551 Mamalahoa Highway, Kealakekua, 808-323-3222; www.konahistorical.org

Learn about the Kona Coasts history at this interesting museum located in a general store built in 1875. The museum's more than 40,000 photos, artifacts and publications take visitors back to an era when ranching and coffee farming ruled this region. The society also offers two informative walking tours. On the 75-minute Historical Kona Walking Tour, see all the main sites in Kailua-Kona and hear about their history. On the Kona Coffee Living History Farm Tour, spend an hour touring a seven-acre working coffee farm that dates back to 1900.

Museum: Monday-Friday 9 a.m.-3 p.m. Kona Walking Tour: Monday-Friday 9 and 11 a.m. Farm Tour: Monday-Friday 9 a.m.-1 p.m., with tours on the hour.

KONA PIER

Honokohau Harbor, Kailua-Kona, 808-329-7494

If you book a snorkel cruise, deep-sea fishing trip, or other water adventure on this side of the island, you'll likely be departing from this pier. But even if you decide not to venture offshore, you might want to come here late in the afternoon when the fishing charters head back into port. As the boat crews unload what anglers reeled in that day, you're sure to see some mighty large catches, such as marlin bigger than any trout or walleye you've ever caught back home.

KONA VILLAGE LUAU

Kona Village Resort, Queen Kaahumanu Highway, Kailua-Kona, 808-325-5555, 800-367-5290; www.konavillage.com

For nearly 30 years, this resort has been staging its once-a-week luau to rave reviews, with many ranking it the finest luau on the Big Island. The food is plentiful and wide-ranging. Besides the traditional roasted pig, which is cooked in the ground during the day, the menu typically includes such savory eats as chicken long rice, Haupia pudding, lomi salmon, opihi, poi, steamed taro and teriyaki beef. The fast-paced, riveting Polynesian revue that follows the filling feast features the hula, as well as a Samoan fire dancer and dances from New Zealand and Tahiti.

Friday 5:30 p.m. Reservations required.

KONA WINE MARKET

King Kamehameha Shopping Mall, 75-5660 Palani Road, Kailua-Kona, 808-329-9400, 800-613-3983; www.konawinemarket.com

Choose from thousands of wines, liquors and beers at the Kona Wine Market. Many of the wine choices are some of the best available anywhere in the world, but the shop also sells more affordable vintages, with more than 135 priced under $10. (Also be sure to check out the bargain bin, where bottles typically sell for $4.95 to $7.95.) Sample up to four wines for free on Fridays from 3 to 7 p.m. The store also sells gourmet cheeses and premium cigars.

Monday-Saturday 9 a.m.-8 p.m., Sunday 10 a.m.-6 p.m.

KULA KAI CAVERNS

Highway 11, Ocean View, 808-929-7539; www.kulakaicaverns.com

Venture into 1,000-year-old lava tubes and explore caverns that stretch for several miles. Different tours range from 20 minutes to four hours, and vary widely in difficulty to accommodate anyone who wants to take an exciting and informative walk on the dark side alongside a knowledgeable guide. On a two-hour spelunking tour, for example, you'll spend some of the your time crawling on your hands and knees as you probe the inner-cave areas. If that sounds a little too challenging for you, opt for the easy walking tour and spend about 30 minutes seeing what's inside Kula Kai. You can rest your tired feet in viewing areas with seating.

Tours by appointment only.

OCEAN ECO TOURS

74-425 Kealakehe Parkway, Kailua-Kona, 808/324-7873; www.oceanecotours.com

Does the thought of leaving Hawaii without ever riding the waves just not sound cool to you? Even if you've never set foot on a surfboard, the skilled instructors at Ocean Eco Tours will have you up and riding after a two- or three-hour private or group lesson. The company also offers a variety of diving trips, as well as whale-watching cruises, in season.

Daily.

PACIFIC VIBRATIONS

75-5702 Likana Lane, Kailua-Kona, 808-329-4140; www.laguerdobros.com

For surfers, this is the place to go to rent all types of surfboards in West Hawaii. The shop also sells all sorts of hip and fashionable beach supplies, including bags, bikinis, shorts, sunglasses and more.

Monday-Saturday 10 a.m.-5:30 p.m., Sunday 10 a.m.-3 p.m.

PAINTED CHURCH

84-5140 Painted Church Road, Honaunau, 808-328-2227; www.thepaintedchurch.org

From the outside, this looks like just another pretty little island church. But step inside this house of worship (also know as St. Benedicts Catholic

Church), and thoughts of Michelangelo will come to mind. Between 1899 and 1904, Friar John Velge, a priest who came to Hawaii from Belgium, painted colorful religious scenes on the interior to help teach the Bible to Hawaiians.

Daily 7 a.m.-6 p.m. Mass: Saturday 4 p.m., Sunday 7:15 a.m.

PUUHONUA O HONAUNAU NATIONAL HISTORICAL PARK
Highway 160, Honaunau, 808-328-2288; www.nps.gov/puho

Up until the early 19th century, Hawaiians who did wrong sought refuge here in a protective area enclosed by a 1,000-foot-long wall that was 10 feet tall and 17 feet thick. After priests absolved them, they could leave safely without worrying about being punished by death. Besides the refuge area, the 182-acre park includes coastal village sites, royal fishponds, sledding tracks, temple platforms and reconstructed thatched buildings. A self-guided walking tour takes about a half-hour. The grounds include a picnic area with barbecue grills and tables.

Monday-Thursday 6 a.m.-8 p.m., Friday-Sunday 6 a.m.-11 p.m. Visitor center: daily 7:30 a.m-5:30 p.m.

SANDWICH ISLE DIVERS
75-5729 Alii Drive, Kailua-Kona, 808-329-9188, 888-743-3483; www.sandwichisledivers.com

Sandwich Isle prides itself on personal service, since it limits its dive charters to no more than six passengers. On its two-tank, two-location morning dives, the first site is typically reached within 20 minutes, and the dives usually are in water 30- to 60-feet deep, a comfortable depth for most divers. On request, the company also fires up its boat engines for afternoon and night trips. Captain Steve Myklebust has been exploring Kona's waters for more than 20 years and has a degree in marine biology.

Daily 8 a.m.-1:30 p.m.

SEA QUEST RAFTING ADVENTURES
Kailua-Kona, 808-329-7238; www.seaquesthawaii.com

Sea Quest specializes in personalized snorkeling tours with no more than six passengers. Its four-hour morning adventure makes stops at both Kealakekua Bay and Honaunau Bay, while its afternoon trek skips Honaunau but spends more time at Kealakekua. In season, it also offers afternoon whale-watching trips three times a week. All of its tours depart from Keauhou Bay.

Snorkeling: daily 8 a.m. and 1 p.m. Whale-Watching (in season): Tuesday-Thursday 1 and 4 p.m.)

SNUBA BIG ISLAND
Kailua-Kona, 808-326-7446; www.snubabigisland.com

Snuba is a lot like scuba diving except that you don't have to swim with a heavy air tank on your back. Instead, the tank remains in a raft on the waters surface. As you explore the underwater world, a 25-foot-long hose connects you to the tank so you can breathe through the regulator attached to the hose. Learning how to use the system takes only minutes, and then you're off on your sightseeing adventure in the ocean, exploring as deep as the hose will

stretch (so 25 feet). Choose between beach dives that last about 1 1/2 hours or boat dives that range from two hours to 4 1/2 hours. All divers must be at least 8 years old. For those ages 4-7, there's snuba doo, which allows kids to float on the surface.
Daily.

UFO PARASAIL
5-5669 Alii Drive, Kailua-Kona, 808-325-5836; www.ufoparasailing.com
Get a different view of the Kona coastline from on high while soaring behind a boat for seven to ten minutes. Do your parasailing solo or with a companion; its your choice, assuming the right wind conditions. You're winched on and off the boat hydraulically, ensuring safe and dry landings.
Daily 8 a.m.-1 p.m.

WHITE SANDS BEACH COUNTY PARK
Alii Drive, mile marker 4, Kailua-Kona, 808-961-8311
In winter, the sand here disappears into high surf, the reason some people also call this beach Magic Sands or Disappearing Sands. During this time, swimming is not safe. But when the water calms down, White Sands is a popular place for swimming, snorkeling, body surfing and riding boogey boards. Unlike many Hawaii beaches, this one usually has lifeguards in summer, making it good for families. The fun never stops up on shore, where you'll find a volleyball court and picnic area with barbecue grills.

SPECIAL EVENTS
BANKOH KI-HO'ALU KONA-STYLE HAWAIIAN SLACK-KEY GUITAR FESTIVAL
Kailua-Kona, 808-239-4336; www.hawaiianslackkeyguitarfestivals.com
This lively event features Hawaiian folk music performed on acoustic guitars by the state's best musicians. Similar festivals are held on other islands throughout the year.
September.

IRONMAN TRIATHLON WORLD CHAMPIONSHIP
Kailua-Kona, www.ironmanlive.com
Each October, up to 2,000 super-fit athletes ages 18 to 80 show up in Kona with their well-trained bodies to compete in this one-day grueling race. The event unfolds along the Kona Coast and consists of a 2.4-mile ocean swim, 112-mile bike ride and marathon-length run (26.2 miles). The top-10 finishers pocket more than $400,000 in prize money. Enter to compete or join the other spectators. On the Tuesday before the race, the hard-body athletes parade down Alii Drive. Then, on Thursday night, a big pre-race party livens up King Kamehameha's Kona Beach Hotel. Finally, on the Sunday night after the championship, the hotel hosts the awards ceremony.
October.

KONA COFFEE CULTURAL FESTIVAL
Kailua-Kona, 808-326-7820; www.konacoffeefest.com
For more than 30 years, this ten-day festival has been celebrating the annual

coffee harvest. It's the oldest product festival in Hawaii and the only coffee festival in the United States. Events, which take place in various venues around coffee country, include bean-picking contests, tastings, art shows, tours of working farms and mills, and, of course, the crowning of the year's "best of the best" cup of joe.

Early-mid-November.

WHERE TO STAY

★★★★★FOUR SEASONS RESORT HUALALAI AT HISTORIC KA'UPULEHU

72-100 Ka'upulehu Drive, Ka'upulehu, Kailua-Kona, 808-325-8000, 800-332-3442; www.fourseasons.com

From the moment you enter the soaring, open-air lobby full of spectacular floral arrangements and sip the fruity rum punch offered at check-in, you will be in pure Hawaiian heaven at this resort. The Four Seasons Haulalai is meant to fit into its natural setting, and it does. Instead of a hotel tower, you'll find charming little bungalows carved into the black lava. This is one of the loveliest hotels anywhere. Tiki huts, which can be enclosed on all sides for total privacy with bamboo shades, line the saltwater pool, where the staff dotes on you all day long: Do you need water? Aloe vera? Ice cream? Your sunglasses cleaned? The other pool, which looks like something out of a Hollywood movie set with white-tented cabanas, is equally inviting. The luxurious rooms all have ocean views with a private lanai (ground-floor rooms have outdoor showers). A serene spa includes outdoor massage rooms, and a beautiful gym lines the lap pool; you'll also find basketballs courts and a rock-climbing wall. Restaurants include the beautiful Pahu i'a, where you're about as close to the surf as you can get. There's also a coffee stand and general store located right on the property that sells salads, sandwiches, cold beer and a nice selection of wine.

243 rooms. Restaurant, bar. Fitness center. Spa. Tennis. Golf. Pool. Pets accepted. $351 and up

★★KING KAMEHAMEHA'S KONA BEACH HOTEL

75-5660 Palani Road, Kailua-Kona, 808-329-2911, 800-367-2111; www.konabeachhotel.com

Some people say that this old favorite is beginning to look a bit dated, with rooms that feature typical island decor. Still, the hotel remains popular, especially with budget-minded travelers who like its affordable rates. But there's another key reason for its continued appeal: King Kam, as the locals call it, is the only beachfront hotel located in Kailua-Kona, by the Kailua Pier. Its other amenities include a swimming pool, two restaurants, a bar, a shopping mall, tennis courts, and a popular luau. The property is named after King Kamehameha the Great because he chose this same site for his residence and administrative capital two centuries ago. Throughout the hotel are images and artifacts of those bygone days, including feather capes of famed Hawaiian warriors. Wander out onto the grounds and you'll find Ahuena Heiau, the kings restored temple.

460 rooms. Restaurant, bar. Business center. Pool. $151-250

★★★KONA VILLAGE RESORT

Queen Kaahumanu Highway, Kailua-Kona, 808-325-5555, 800-367-5290;
www.konavillage.com

This 82-acre beachfront resort is made up of 125 individual "hales," or bungalows with thatched roofs. You can forget about TV, air conditioning or even an alarm clock. The point of this Polynesian village is to get away from it all and instead enjoy the many activities on-site, including snorkeling, kayaking, sailing, swimming at the beach or in one of the two freshwater pools, jogging on the resorts trails, playing tennis, and touring a historic petroglyph field. The hales are pretty bare bones—simple furnishings, tile bathrooms and quilts on the beds. In fact, the whole thing feels more like camp than a luxury resort, though you wouldn't know it from the price. Still, the rate includes all meals at the resorts oceanfront restaurants and tickets to a luau that many consider the best on the island.

125 rooms. Restaurant, bar. Fitness center. Beach. Pool. Tennis. $351 and up

WHERE TO EAT

★CASSANDRA'S GREEK TAVERN

75-5669 Alii Drive, Kailua Kona, 808-334-1066; www.cassandraskona.com

Blue-and-white-striped awnings provide a festive touch to the exterior of this second-floor restaurant. Cassandra's offers basic Greek fare, as well as a variety of hamburgers and pizzas. The open-air dining area overlooks Kailua Bay, where spinner dolphins can often be spotted performing their leaping antics above the surface of the water.

Greek. Lunch, dinner. Bar. $16-35

★HOLUAKOA CAFE

76-5900 Mamalahoa Highway, Holualoa, 808-322-2233

Holuakoa Cafe, nestled amongst small galleries and shops in the tiny, mountainside town of Holualoa, is about as local as you can get. Resembling a small wooden shack on the outside, it features a dark wood interior decorated with surfboards and local art inside. Seating is mostly outdoors beneath tropical trees, and the menu features simple soups, salads and sandwiches that change daily. The specials of the house all revolve around the coffee. Holuakoa serves only 100 percent Kona Blue Sky coffee and has a complete espresso bar capable of serving up just about any coffee drink you can dream up.

American. Breakfast, lunch. Closed Sunday. $15 and under

★HUGGO'S

Highway 19 and Opelo Road, Kailua-Kona, 808-329-1493; www.huggos.com

One of the better dining options along Kailua Bay, Huggo's serves seafood and Pacific Rim favorites. Diners in this open-air restaurant enjoy constant tropical breezes and terrific views of the bay. Anchors dangle from the ceiling, and flaming tiki torches illuminate the interior after dusk. The atmosphere is never dull either, thanks to live jazz music just about every night of the week.

American. Lunch, dinner. Bar. Outdoor seating. $16-35

★★JAMESON'S BY THE SEA
77-6452 Alii Drive, Kailua-Kona, 808-329-3195

Fresh seafood dishes are the specialty at this oceanfront restaurant. Over-looking Magic Sands Beach (so named because it disappears during high tide), the outdoor dining area at Jameson's offers splendid views and tranquil breezes. Seated at your table, its not uncommon to spot a whale breaching the waves just off the coast. The restaurant's opakapaka (pronounced oh-pah-kah-PAH-kah), pink snapper found in the waters surrounding the Hawaiian islands, is sautéed with shrimp and crab meat, and is a winner.
Seafood. Lunch, dinner. Bar. Reservations recommended. Outdoor seating. $36-85

★★KEEI CAFE
79-7511 Hawaii Belt Road, Kealakekua, 808-328-8451

This immensely popular eatery—warning: waiting times may be long and service may be brisk—is just a short drive from Kailua-Kona on a steep hill-side overlooking the Pacific. What was once a small bistro offering fresh sea-food at reasonable prices has become a sleek eatery in its new location. Some people miss the old place, but it's as crowded as ever. Fish lovers should opt for the catch of the day, smothered in your choice of red Thai curry, white-wine peppercorn gravy, or spiced pineapple glaze.
International. Dinner. Closed Sunday-Monday. Reservations recommended. No credit cards accepted. $16-35

★★★LA BOURGOGNE RESTAURANT
Kuakini Highway (Highway 11), Kailua-Kona, 808-329-6711

Though small (only ten tables) and a bit out of the way, this intimate restaurant is well worth it. The baked brie in puff pastry is a creamy, golden treat and the lobster salad with goat cheese and mango is scrumptious. Moving on, the roast duck breast with raspberries and pine nuts is a delightful mix of flavors, while the osso bucco is done to perfection. Pair your meal with a lovely wine and fin-ish with the flourless chocolate cake, and you're in French heaven.
French. Dinner. Closed Sunday-Monday. Bar. Reservations recommended. $36-85

★★OODLES OF NOODLES
75-1027 Henry St., Kailua-Kona, 808-329-9222

Located on in a strip mall anchored by a Safeway grocery store, you may be surprised to hear that chef Amy Ferguson-Ota honed her craft while working as the executive chef at The Ritz-Carlton Mauna Lani. Whether you crave Thai, Italian or Chinese, this gourmet cafe indeed has oodles of noodles to satisfy your appetite. The wok-seared ahi tuna casserole is addicting, and the miso ramen comes a close second. The menu also includes numerous vegetarian and vegan options.
Pan-Asian. Lunch, dinner. Outdoor seating. $16-35

★★★PAHU I'A
Four Seasons Hualalai, 100 Ka'upulehu Drive, Ka'upulehu, 808-325-8000; www.fourseasons.com

Close your eyes and imagine a restaurant in Hawaii, and it probably looks

like Pahu i'a: thatched-roof hut, tiki torches, a large aquarium that casts a neon glow, and an outdoor dining area with elegantly-topped wood tables that practically sit on the sand. The setting was made for honeymooners and elegant dinners at sunset, and the impeccable hospitality makes it even lovelier (the staff happily snaps photos in between serving courses). Pahu i'a means aquarium in Hawaiian and fresh fish is the specialty—the steamed local market catch with soy-ginger Hamakua mushrooms and sizzling sesame oil is light and flavorful. Chef James Babian also uses the freshest local ingredients; as a result, a simple Kona avocado in tomato balsamic reduction with a pinch of smoked Hawaiian sea salt and a sprinkle of kukui nuts is a taste treat. That's if you can stop eating the slightly sweet macadamia nut bread, which comes with an addicting porcini mushroom spread and a lemon mascarpone. Pahu i'a is also open for breakfast and serves an excellent buffet; otherwise, the lemon-ricotta pancakes are delightful. The upstairs lounge is a swell place to gather before dinner or linger over drinks afterward.
Pacific. Breakfast, dinner. Bar. Reservations recommended. Outdoor seating. $36-85

★PANCHO AND LEFTY'S CANTINA AND RESTAURANTE

75-5719 Alii Drive, Kailua-Kona, 808-326-2171; www.pancho-and-leftys.com
Situated among the numerous shops on Alii Drive, this second-story Mexican restaurant is a good place to relax and enjoy a cold drink. We're talking about Lefty's margarita, a mix of Cuervo Especial with Grand Marnier. The menu offers the usual variety of nachos, fajitas, burritos and tacos, and the setting is relaxed with beer signs as décor and TVs near the bar that broadcast sporting events.
Mexican. Breakfast, lunch, dinner. Bar. Outdoor seating. $16-35

★WAKEFIELD GARDENS & RESTAURANT

Highway 160, Honaunau, 808-328-9930
This delightful little restaurant set amidst a six-acre botanical garden and a macadamia nut orchard is a quiet escape. Owned and run by former actress Arlene Wakefield, who escaped Hollywood in 1965, Wakefield Gardens offers a small but tasty menu of sandwiches, salads and soups. Highlights include the papaya boat stuffed with tuna, the award- winning macadamia nut pie (one of 30 pies Wakefield bakes), and the rich coffee floats. Complete the experience with a free walking tour of the gardens.
Chinese. Lunch. Reservations recommended. Outdoor seating. $15 and under

SPA

★★★★HUALALAI SPORTS CLUB AND SPA, FOUR SEASONS RESORT HUALALAI

72-100 Ka'upulehu Drive, Ka'upulehu-Kona, 808-325-8440, 800-983-3880; www.fourseasons.com
This gorgeous spa practically begs you to have a massage and even to work up a sweat. The latest equipment glistens from the open-air gym lining the lap pool and there's something about Hawaii that just makes you want to get up for morning yoga. You'll also find a rock-climbing wall, basketball and tennis courts. When it's time to relax, the spa is divine. The spa has a large apothecary full of more than 20 Hawaiian ingredients that are used in

customized treatments. The outdoor area is a fantastic addition—treatments rooms have bamboo shades for privacy. Cool off in one of the outdoor showers afterward.

INTERISLAND TRAVEL

Island-hopping via air is a common practice among visitors to Hawaii. Sun-seekers who fly all the way out to this Pacific paradise want to experience more than one of its islands. But financially ailing airlines have cut back on flights and increased fares. One longstanding carrier, Aloha Airlines, ceased operations in 2008, leaving Hawaiian Airlines and lowcost competitor Go! to service the islands.

Due to heightened security, interisland carriers now ask their customers to check in up to two hours prior to their flights, compared with just 45 minutes to an hour in the past. Every minute of the additional time is needed for passengers to stand in lines to get their bags screened and to go through security upon entering and at the gates.

The good news about interisland travel: once planes are airborne, its just a matter of minutes before they land on another island again. Most interisland flights take only about 20 to 45 minutes.

Four airlines offer interisland shuttles, providing service to airports on all of the major islands:

Hawaiian Airlines: 800-367-5320; www.hawaiianair.com

Go!, 888-435-9462;

Island Air: 800-323-3345; www.islandair.com

Pacific Wings Airlines: 888-575-4546; www.pacificwings.com

Hawaiian Airlines uses jets, while Island Air and Pacific Wings do their flying in propeller-driven aircraft.

KOHALA COAST

Looks can be deceiving. From Highway 19, this coastline that stretches for about 20 miles doesn't seem all that impressive: nothing but fields of black-lava rock, mile after mile. As you drive along, you might wonder why this area earned the nickname the Gold Coast, suggesting something quite spectacular. That's because you can't see the world-class resorts from the road; they sit out of sight just a mile or two off the road at different points along the route. Each one is a world unto itself with lush grounds, multiple pools, decadent spas, restaurants and activities galore, all fronting sandy beaches. This is the island's sunny side, so rain seldom keeps anyone out of the water or off the fairways.

But the Kohala area isn't just about high-end resorts. It's also rich in history, making for some good sightseeing. You'll find many ancient petroglyph fields and the Puukohola Heiau, a temple built by King Kamehameha the Great, who was born in this region in the 1700s.

WHAT TO SEE
ACKERMAN GALLERIES
Highway 270, Kapaau, 808-889-5971; 800-484-9924; www.ackermangalleries.com
This gallery features the fine art of Gary Ackerman, an internationally acclaimed oil painter who specializes in Impressionism and Expressionism. You'll also find the exceptional work of other well-respected Big Island artists who produce furniture, hand-blown glass and more. There are two gal-

leries just blocks apart: one houses the fine art; the other is a gift gallery featuring crafts and jewelry.
Daily 9:30 a.m.-6 p.m.

ANAEHOOMALU BAY BEACH
Kohala Coast, Highway 19, mile marker 76, Waikoloa
With its long stretch of sand bordered by tall coconut trees, crescent-shaped Anaehoomalu Bay (also called A-Bay) is a lovely sight in the Waikoloa Resort. It's a good place for swimming, snorkeling, scuba diving and windsurfing, or just soaking up the rays up on the shore and having a picnic. Two ancient fish ponds and a petroglyph field near the sand provide beach breaks.
Daily.

AS HAWI TURNS
Highway 270, Hawi, 808-889-5023
If you happen to find yourself in the little island town of Hawi, take the time to browse through this fun clothing boutique. The whimsical window displays are only part of the charm; the shop sells fun accessories, gifts and resort wear.
Monday 10 a.m.-5 p.m., Tuesday-Saturday 10 a.m.-6 p.m., Sunday 11 a.m.-5 p.m.

BLUE HAWAIIAN HELICOPTERS
Waikoloa Heliport, Waikoloa, 808-886-1768, 800-786-2583; www.bluehawaiian.com
This Maui-based helicopter company also flies its whirlybirds on the Big Island, operating out of both Waikoloa and Hilo *(808-961-5600)*. One of its tours will take you over the Kohala Coast, where you'll see sea cliffs, valleys and ancient Hawaiian settlements. The Circle of Fire and Big Island Spectacular tours include rain forests, waterfalls and fiery lava flows. The various scheduled tours range from 35 minutes to two hours. You can also create you own itinerary and spend anywhere from 30 minutes to an entire day flying over the island.
Daily.

FLUM'IN DA DITCH
55-519 Hawi Road, Hawi, 808-889-6922, 877-449-6922; www.flumindaditch.com
In decades past, mischievous young Hawaiians would sneak onto plantations to go fluming in irrigation ditches. Book this three-hour tour and you can have the same fun while also learning about Hawaiian history and culture from local guides. From the company's headquarters, you're driven to a Kohala plantation, where your group then rides rafts for 3 1/2 miles along a scenic ditch. You'll pass rain forests, ravines and waterfalls, and float through tunnels.
Admission: $80. Daily 8:30 a.m. and 12:30 p.m. No children under 5.

HAPUNA BEACH STATE PARK
Highway 19, Kohala Coast, 808-974-6200
Hapuna is considered one of the island's top beaches and no wonder: it stretches gloriously for about a half-mile, is wide (up to 200 feet in summer),

and has calm water most of the year, making it good for swimming, snorkeling, diving, bodysurfing and riding boogie boards. (Note that riptides pose a danger in winter's high surf and that lifeguards aren't always on duty.) The 62-acre park also has a picnic area with a pavilion, hiking trails a camping area, and a few A-frame cabins that can be rented.

HUALALAI GOLF COURSE

100 Kaupulehu Drive, Kaupulehu, 808-325-8480; www.fourseasons.com/hualalai

Golfers rave about this par-72, 7,117-yard course, which offers plenty of challenges. Instead of water hazards, for example, this Jack Nicklaus-designed beauty relies on lava rocks to create obstacles for golfers on every hole. Also beware of the fast greens, which have plenty of subtle breaks, and the bunker that runs the length of the signature 17th hole. Only guests of the Four Seasons Hualalai can hit the fairways here. Amenities include a driving range, pro shop and restaurant.

Daily 6:30 a.m.-6:30 p.m.

KAUNAOA BEACH

Mauna Kea Beach Resort, Hualalai 19, Kohala Coast

Kaunaoa, also known as Mauna Kea Beach, isn't quite as long as nearby Hapuna Beach, but many people will tell you that this is still the island's best stretch of sand. The crescent-shaped beach offers excellent swimming and snorkeling (provided the wave action isn't too torrid); it's also a fun place to body surf (use caution in rough water, especially since the beach has no lifeguards). Green turtles like to swim here, too, so be on the lookout. The hotel owns and operates most of the facilities up on the shore, and public parking is limited.

KEKAHA KAI STATE PARK

Highway 19, Kailua-Kona

Also known as Kona Coast State Park, this small facility located less than three miles from Keahole Airport has two sections: The more developed Mahaiula section, with its sandy beach, is ideal for splashing, sunning and picnicking, while the Kua Bay section at the north end is accessible via a 4.5-mile hiking trail through the wilderness, as well as by a separate access road from the highway. In between, you'll find the 342-foot Puu Kuili cinder cone, which you can hike up for lovely views.

KING KAMEHAMEHA STATUE

Highway 270, Kapaau

Four large bronze statues memorialize Hawaii's warrior king. This is the original one that was cast in Italy in 1879. The nine-ton, nine-foot-tall statue was lost at sea for a while, before it was recovered and brought to Kapaau in 1883, near where the king was born. Meanwhile, a replica was created, which now stands outside the Judiciary Building in Honolulu. Other replicas are in Washington, D.C. and Hilo.

KINGS' SHOPS

Waikoloa, Waikoloa Beach Resort, 808-886-8811; www.waikoloaresort.com

This small, open-air shopping center includes Louis Vuitton, Macy's, Tommy Bahama, Making Waves (for swimsuits) and Blue Ginger, which sells resort wear and is only found in Hawaii. There are also several jewelry and gift shops, as well as a general store where you can pick up souvenirs, beach items and groceries. Kings Shops is also home to a variety of restaurants, including Roy's Waikoloa Bar & Grill and Merriman's Market Café.
Daily 9:30 a.m.-9:30 p.m.

KOHALA BOOK SHOP

54-3885 Akoni Puli Hualalai, Kapaau, 808-889-6400; www.abebooks.com

Literature fans won't want to miss this gem of a shop. The owners have more than 25,000 books in stock, both new and used, including prized first editions and rare reads. The shop also carries a nice selection of Hawaiiana and Oceania books, prints and maps; current bestsellers; and other popular books.
Monday-Saturday 11 a.m.-5 p.m.

KOHALA NAALAPA TRAIL RIDES

Kohala Mountain Road (Highway 250), North Kohala, 808-889-0022;
www.naalapastables.com/kahua.html

Take your pick from two rides, one on horseback, the other in a wagon, at one of Hawaii's oldest working ranches. If you choose a horse, you'll ride through green, hilly pastures and enjoy splendid views of mountains and the Pacific Ocean. The morning trip lasts 2 1/2 hours; the afternoon trip, 1 1/2 hours. Opt for the shorter tour and you'll explore the ranch in a farm wagon pulled by two Percheron geldings, while a guide tells you all about ranching in the islands.
Daily; times vary.

LEGENDS OF THE PACIFIC LUAU AND SHOW

Hilton Waikoloa Village, 425 Wailoloa Beach Drive, Waikoloa

Feast on Kalua pig, roasted chicken with mango and green peppercorn sauce, braised short ribs, fresh island fish, tropical fruits and salads, Hawaiian sweet bread and chocolate macadamia nut pie. At this luau at the Hilton Waikolia, dinner is served buffet-style, while professionals perform a mix of lively island dances and music.
Admission: adults: $95, seniors and children 13-18 $85, children 5-12 $47, children under five free. Tuesday and Friday 5:30-9:00 p.m.

MOOKINI LUAKINI HEIAU

Upolu Airport, Highway 270, Hawi, 808-974-6200

Nearly the size of a football field, Mookini Luakini is Hawaii's largest temple. It's also the oldest, having been built in AD 480 of water-worn basalt from the Pololu Valley. It took more than 18,000 workers to build it, and they used no mortar. King Kamehameha and other royal chiefs came here to fast, pray and offer up human sacrifices. You'll need a four-wheel-drive vehicle to reach the temple, which is about 1 1/2 miles down a rough dirt road off the highway.

OCEAN SPORTS

69-275 Waikoloa Beach Drive, Waikoloa, 808-886-6666; 888-724-5234;
www.hawaiioceansports.com

This beach hut on Anaehoomalu Bay rents all types of gear: snorkeling equipment, boogie boards, kayaks and more. You can also sign up for snorkeling, kayaking, windsurfing and diving trips; whale-watching cruises (in season); and sunset sails aboard on one of their catamarans.
Daily 8:30 a.m.-5 p.m.

PANIOLO ADVENTURES

Kohala Mountain Road (Highway 250), North Kohala, 808-889-5354;
www.panioloadventures.com

Go horseback riding on the 11,000-acre Ponoholo Ranch, where the views of the coastline are spectacular. You can even see Haleakala Volcano in the distance on Maui. On the 2 1/2-hour open-range ride, make your way through vast pastures with lots of room for trotting and cantering. On a three-hour picnic ride, you may eat lunch near a 30-foot waterfall or in a grassy knoll just below the rain forest. Sign up for the 1 1/2-hour sunset ride, and you'll view the sun going down from an ideal vantage point, at a spot about 3,000 feet above sea level.
Daily; times vary.

POLOLU VALLEY LOOKOUT

Highway 270, North Kohala

HAWAII ★★★★★

Visit this lookout for stunning views of a rugged, unspoiled coastline with tall sea cliffs holding court over a lush valley that was once home to many taro plantations. If you're up for a hike, take the switchback trail down to the valleys black-sand beach for some sea-level exploration of this beautiful area. While on the beach, enjoy a picnic lunch.

46   ## PUAKO ARCHAEOLOGICAL DISTRICT

Highway 19, Kohala Coast

Expect to spend about a half-hour walking along the Kalahuipuaa Trail, next to Holoholokai Beach Park. In this historic district, one of the state's largest petroglyph fields, you'll see about 3,000 ancient stone carvings believed to have been created from about AD 1200 to the AD 1800s. Access the trail from the Fairmont Orchid Hawaii Hotel.

PUUKOHOLA HEIAU NATIONAL HISTORIC SITE

62-3601 Kawaihae Road, Kawaihae, 808-882-7218; www.nps.gov/puhe

King Kamehameha I had this large heiau (place of worship) built in 1791 at the urging of a prophet. The king was told building it and sacrificing a rival would please Kukailimoku, the war god, and thus help him win control of the Hawaiian Islands, which he did in 1810. The site also includes the home of John Young, a British sailor who advised the king, and a smaller heiau submerged offshore that's dedicated to the shark gods.
Daily 7:30 a.m.-4 p.m.

RED SAIL SPORTS HAWAII

425 Waikoloa Beach Drive, Waikoloa, 808-886-2876, 877-733-7245; www.redsail.com

If you're looking for some offshore excitement along the Kohala Coast, Red Sail offers many outings such as diving charters, kayak excursions, catamaran sails, snorkeling adventures and rafting trips. Its fleet of vessels includes a 50-foot catamaran that reaches speeds of up to 12 knots, the 38-foot Delta dive boat that comfortably seats up to 18 people, and one- and two-man kayaks that just need some muscle power to ply through the ocean.

SPENCER BEACH COUNTY PARK

Highway 270, Kohala Coast, 808-961-8311

An offshore coral reef helps protect this beach, so the water is generally calm and gentle year-round. The good, safe swimming conditions attract families in particular, and snorkelers find plenty of fish. There's also a picnic area and camping is permitted with a county permit.

WAIKOLOA BEACH GOLF CLUB

600 Waikoloa Beach Drive, Waikoloa, 808-886-7888; www.waikoloagolf.com

Thanks to a spectacular oceanfront setting, you're almost certain to enjoy your time spent golfing here. Brilliant green fairways zigzag across an open expanse of black lava, while in the background a steady procession of waves crashes violently against the Kohala Coasts craggy shore. The Waikoloa Beach Golf Club consists of two 18-hole courses. The Beach Course, a creation of Robert Trent Jones, Jr., challenges heavy hitters with its narrow fairways. Tom Weiskopf and Jay Morrish designed the Kings Course, which, with its deep sand bunkers, offers a links-style golfing experience.

WAIPIO VALLEY ARTWORKS

48-5416 Kukuihale Road, Kukuihale, 808-775-0958, 800-492-4746;
www.waipiovalleyartworks.com

All of the finely crafted items sold in this gallery such as wooden bowls and boxes, koa furniture, glass sculptures, ceramic and raku creations, jewelry, and colorful paintings are handmade on the Big Island by local artists.
Daily 8 a.m.-5 p.m.

WHERE TO STAY
★★★HILTON WAIKOLOA VILLAGE

425 Waikoloa Beach Drive, Waikoloa, 808-886-1234; www.hiltonwaikoloavillage.com

With more than 1200 rooms spread among three buildings on 62 acres, the Hilton Waikoloa Village is, first things first, large. The three towers are connected by tram, boat and walkway—so be prepared to walk, or wait. But with dozens of activities right onsite, it's also ideal for families. You'll find three freshwater pools (two with water slides), a four-acre swimming and snorkeling lagoon, a tennis center with eight courts, a huge collection of Pacific art, an Italian restaurant (Donatonis) that resembles a seaside Italian villa, as well as nine other restaurants, serving everything from sushi to family-style buffets. The only thing you're really missing is a real beach but the lovely Anaehoomalu Bay is just a short shuttle ride away. One of the most popular features is the Dolphin Quest program, in which the lucky winners of lotter-

ies can swim with the dolphins in the dolphin lagoon.
1,240 rooms. Restaurant, bar. Business center. Beach. Pool. Tennis. $251-350

★★★THE FAIRMONT ORCHID, HAWAII
One N. Kaniku Drive, Kohala Coast, 808-885-2000; www.fairmont.com/orchid.
Like all of the big chichi resorts in the area, the Fairmont has a beautiful beachfront location, oceanfront pool and miles of manicured walkways, plus a spa that offers outdoor treatments surrounded by streams and waterfalls. The traditional rooms are spacious with marble bathrooms and lanais, and everything is nice enough. But can someone please clear the random dishes in the guest corridors? If only the place was a bit more cared for. That said you could do worse. It is certainly comfortable and there are all the perks of a big resort: nine bars and restaurants, kids program, and scores of activities (which cost extra). If you happen to come across a deal, and are paying less than at the other big resorts in the area (this is an expensive market), you won't be disappointed.
540 rooms. Restaurant, bar. Fitness center. Spa. Beach. Pool. Golf. Tennis. $351 and up

★★★WAIKOLOA BEACH MARRIOTT RESORT AND SPA
69-275 Waikoloa Beach Drive, Waikoloa, 808-886-6789, 800-922-5533;
www.waikoloabeachmarriott.com
The Marriott has a fresh new look to go along with its amazing location on Anaehoomalu Bay with a lovely crescent-shaped beach that borders an ancient fishpond. The resort has a fun beachy look with bright white doors and colorful stripes leading the way to the soothing guest rooms with tan walls, dark furniture, crisp white beds and private lanais. There's also a new swanky two-story spa located in front of the pool that offers Balinese-style treatments. The resort offers a range of dining options, including a coffee shop for snacks. Twice a week, the Marriott puts on one of the Big Island's better luaus.
545 rooms. Restaurant, bar. Fitness center. Spa. Beach. Pool. Tennis. Business center. $251-350

ALSO RECOMMENDED
MAUNA KEA BEACH HOTEL
62-100 Mauna Kea Beach Drive, Kohala Coast, 808-882-7222;
www.maunakeabeachhotel.com
Before an earthquake toppled the resort a few years ago, the Mauna Kea was the resort on the island, built by Laurance S. Rockefeller in 1965. Back then, no other lodging development had taken place in this barren area covered with lava rock, but that didn't deter Rockefeller. He was positive the Mauna Kea would be a winner, especially because it fronted one of the island's best beaches, a lovely crescent-shaped stretch of sand on Kaunaoa Bay. His hunch proved right, and guests have been returning to the hotel regularly, sometimes every year. In fact, since re-opening in late December 2008, almost 80 percent of the clientele are former guests. The resort is open-air, including guest corridors, with pretty Hawaiian quilts framed as art adorning the walls. The rooms resemble a chic boutique hotel, with built-in furniture, crisp white

beds and pops of bright colors. The white glass-titled bathrooms are especially luxurious (ocean view rooms have glass showers that overlook the water).
310 rooms. Restaurant, bar. Fitness center. Beach. Pool. Golf. Tennis. $251-
350

WHERE TO EAT

★★BAMBOO RESTAURANT
Akoni Pule Highway (Highway 270), Hawi, 808-889-5555; www.bamboorestaurant.info
A favorite among locals, Bamboo is located in the heart of Hawi, and like the
town, is laid back and low key. The charming interior has the feel of a grandmother's dining room. The menu focuses on Hawaiian dishes like Pacific
stir-fried noodles and pineapple barbecue chicken. Many of the ingredients
used in dishes are purchased from local farmers.
Pacific Rim. Lunch, dinner, Sunday brunch. Closed Monday. Bar. $16-35

★★CAFE PESTO
Highway 270, Kawaihae, 808-882-1071
There are two locations on the Big Island (the other is on the bay in downtown Hilo), and both prepare flavorful dishes reflecting Italian and Hawaiian
influences. The Kawaihae Harbor location sits just to the north of the resorts
along the Kohala Coast. The modest exterior includes a narrow alfresco dining area. Inside, white chairs and black tables complement a black-and-white
checkerboard floor. During the day, sunshine filters through a long wall of
windows, brightly illuminating the sparkling clean dining room. Menu favorites include seared poke with spinach, wok-fired shrimp and scallops, and
pizza margherite. With scrumptious dishes offered at fair prices, Cafe Pesto
is a good bet.
Italian. Lunch, dinner. Bar. $16-35

★★KAWAIHAE HARBOR GRILL
Highway 270, Kawaihae, 808-882-1368; www.theharborgrill.com
Housed in a historic building formerly used as Chock Ho general store, the
Kawaihae Harbor Grill prepares fresh seafood dishes using locally caught
fish. The restaurant draws a large crowd in the evenings, when locals and
tourists alike converge to enjoy flavorful dishes such as the steamed fresh
Hawaiian fish and the red Thai seafood curry. Pupus are also popular here, a
favorite being the Cajun-seared ahi sashimi. A short drive north of the Kohala Coast resorts on Highway 270, the restaurant is easy to find—just look
for the green building at the fork in the road in the small town of Kawaihae.
Seafood. Lunch, dinner, late-night. Bar. Outdoor seating. $16-35

★★ROY'S WAIKOLOA BAR & GRILL
250 Waikoloa Beach Drive, Waikoloa, 808-886-4321; www.roysrestaurant.com
Fan of Roy's will appreciate the convenient location of this restaurant (tucked
in a mall in the Waikoloa Beach Resort) where they can find their usual
favorites, including lobster potstickers, blackened island ahi and the macadamia nut crusted mahi mahi. For dessert, be sure to try to the melting hot
chocolate soufflé.
Pacific Rim. Lunch, dinner. Bar. Outdoor seating. $16-35

MAUNA KEA

Mauna Kea, or "White Mountain," is a dormant volcano in the center of the Big Island. Scientists estimate its age at 1 million years. If you measure from the base—which is about 17,000 feet under the ocean—it's the world's highest mountain. You can actually drive almost to the very top and hike the extra 200 feet to the official summit marker at 13,796 feet. There are companies that will take you up to the summit (see Mauna Kea Summit Adventures) but if you're brave enough to do it alone, here's your tour. Needless to say, it is not a trip to be taken lightly.

For some people, driving Saddle Road, which passes between Mauna Loa and Mauna Kea, is thrill enough. Built in a hurry during World War II, Saddle Road was recently repaved but it's still 53 miles of winding and hilly road, with blind curves poorly banked. (Check with your rental car company to make sure your insurance isn't voided on this road.) The landscape goes from lush to otherworldly. The road crests at 6,000 feet—almost halfway to the top. From here, the visitors center only six miles (the turnoff is Mauna Kea Road at mile marker 28).

Once you reach the Onizuka Center for International Astronomy at 9,200 feet, you begin to realize the enormity of driving to the summit. Mauna Kea still looms above, the summit invisible, while the city of Hilo is lost in clouds below. In about an hour, your body will adjust to the altitude, and you can consider going on. In the meantime, there are interesting displays, restrooms, and a fenced area out back where endangered silversword plants have been coaxed to grow.

Finally it is decision time, and here is what you need to consider: air at the summit has only about 60 percent of the oxygen content of air at sea level. Pregnant women, small children and people with respiratory problems should not drive to the summit. This also goes for people who have been scuba diving within the last 24 hours.

A four-wheel drive vehicle is not mandatory but recommended, as part of the road is unpaved and prone to washboard. The Onizuka Center stocks brake fluid, in case you need it coming down. At the summit, it is very cold and windy, so be sure to bring a few extra layers. Up there, it will be hard to move about; your limbs will feel leaden. You may experience dizziness and nausea, the beginnings of altitude sickness. Drink plenty of water to try to combat the effects.

Perhaps most important is the weather, which is difficult to determine from anywhere on the island except the Onizuka Center. Be prepared not to go. Between November and April, snow is not uncommon, and freezing fog can occur at anytime.

The rewards of reaching the summit, however, are many. From the top you look across at Mauna Loa as a sister mountain and with luck, you may see Haleakala on Maui. The clarity of the air is spectacular, great for photography. The landscape is near enough to lunar conditions that Apollo astronauts trained here. Two dozen of the world's finest telescopes are sprinkled around the summit. They are not easy to visit, although tours of the University of Hawaii's telescope are given on weekends. Call 808-961-2180 for more information.

To Native Hawaiians, Mauna Kea is sacred, and at the top it feels that way. Not only is the mountain home of Poliahu, the Snow Goddess, but three other deities as well. Also atop Mauna Kea is Lake Waiau, which is found at 13,020 feet, partly filling a cinder cone, green as a lawn in desert conditions. Below the lake, at 12,400 feet, is an ancient adze quarry, where, for generations, the old Hawaiians mined rock for axe heads so special they were traded with other islands.

WHAT TO SEE
MAUNA KEA SUMMIT ADVENTURES

Mauna; www.maunakea.com
The guides on these tours have lots of experience so you know you're in good hands. Board one of their vans with large windows for the seven- to eight-hour journey to the summit, where the world's largest telescopes are located. The trip also includes parkas, dinner and hot drinks.
Admission: $197. Daily, mid-afternoon.

HAWAII'S VOLCANIC HERITAGE

The Hawaiian Islands are crests of volcanic mountains built by magma welling up from beneath the ocean floor over millions of years. Measured from their bases at the bottom of the Pacific, these mountains are the tallest in the world. The youngest of the Hawaiian Islands is also the largest: the Big Island of Hawaii is almost twice the size of the others combined and is still growing, thanks to its two active volcanoes, Kilauea and Mauna Loa. Also on Hawaii is the chain's highest point, at 13,796 feet, dormant Mauna Kea. Southeast of Hawaii, a new island, called Loihi, is slowly growing toward the surface

---

WAIMEA (KAMUELA)

This small city in the upcountry goes by two names. Waimea (which means "reddish water") is its original moniker, but because there is also a Waimea on the island of Kauai, the postal service requested a unique referent after Hawaii became a U.S. territory. The name that was chosen, Kamuela, means "Samuel" in Hawaiian, in honor of a prominent citizen.

Today, this rapidly growing town set amid the rolling green hills of South Kohala continues to capitalize on its heritage as a farming and cattle-ranching community. One of the area's earliest ranches was established by John Palmer Parker, and Parker Ranch is still a dominant presence.

WHAT TO SEE
COOK'S DISCOVERIES

64-1066 Mamalahoa Highway, Kamuela, 808-885-3633
For gifts with a Hawaiian theme, visitors give this charming shop a big "thumbs-up." It's packed with delightful and imaginative creations including jewelry, clothing, and more, all of it handmade with care on the islands.
Monday-Saturday 10 a.m.-6 p.m., Sunday 10 a.m.-5 p.m.

COWBOYS OF HAWAII

Parker Ranch, Mamalahoa Highway, Kamuela, 808-885-7655;www.parkerranch.com
Parker Ranch, which dates back to 1847, ranks as one of the country's oldest ranches, and with about 175,000 acres, its also one of the largest. If you like horseback riding, take one of the two-hour tours of the massive spread. As

you make your way across rolling hillsides, you'll see stunning views, lots of different plants, and maybe even pheasants or wild pigs. You'll also learn about the ranch and its history from the paniolos who lead the fun outing. ATV tours are also available.

Horseback tour: $79 per person (including refreshments). ATV: $95 per person. Daily 8:15 a.m. and 12:15 p.m.

IMIOLA CONGREGATIONAL CHURCH

Highway 19, Kamuela, 808-885-4987

The builders of this church, which dates back to 1832, used only koa wood on the interior, making for a striking appearance. Also noteworthy are the calabashes that hang from the ceiling, which create an unusual look. Imiola also has an quirky layout, with the entrance behind the pulpit.

Daily 9 a.m.-4 p.m.

KAHILU THEATRE

67-1186 Lindsey Road, Waimea, 808-885-6868; www.kahilutheatre.org

This attractive 490-seat performing arts center provides some of the best cultural entertainment on the island. For about nine months each year, the theater offers a season of live performances featuring dance and music programs with artists from Hawaii and around the world. Some of the programs take a classical approach; others are quite cutting edge. On many weekends, the theater also shows first-run films.

Show times vary. Box office: Monday-Friday 9 a.m.-3 p.m.

KAMUELA MUSEUM

Highways 19 and 250, Kamuela, 808-885-4724

Though small, Kamuela Museum still ranks as the largest privately owned museum in Hawaii. It's the project of Harriet Solomon, a descendent of the influential family that founded Parker Ranch, and her husband, Albert Solomon, Jr. The displays include many Hawaiian artifacts as well as some from Japan, China and other places around the world. Especially noteworthy are six pieces of furniture from the Iolani Palace.

Admission: adults $5, children under 12 $2. Daily 8 a.m.-5 p.m.

MAUNA KEA BIKE RIDES INC.

Kamuela, 808-883-0130

Mauna Kea Bike Rides offers a variety of tours. On the Kohala Mountain Tour, beginners glide downhill while taking in the sights. The name alone of the other tour—Kamikaze Mauna Kea Downhill—lets you know it's only for serious advanced riders. On the 13-mile trek, advanced cyclists start at 13,000 feet and pedal all the way down to 6,000 feet. Breathtaking views abound. If you prefer to map your own route and ride independently, the company also rents mountain bikes by the day, week, or month.

Daily.

MAUNA KEA GALLERIES

65-1298 Kawaihae Road, Kamuela, 808-887-2244, 877-969-4852;
www.maunakeagalleries.com

For anything vintage Hawaiiana, this is the place to shop. In a tribute to Hawaii's bygone days, Mauna Kea stocks period paintings, prints and engravings, rare books, authentic aloha shirts, sheet music, luggage stickers, and all types of island objects, from hula dolls and lamps to hula girl photos. Monday-Saturday 10 a.m.-5 p.m.

PARKER RANCH

67-1435 Mamalahoa Highway, Kamuela, 808-885-7655; www.parkerranch.com

Tucked between Mauna Kea and Mauna Loa is the Parker Ranch, founded in 1847 when John Palmer Parker bought two acres of land from King Kamehameha for $10. Encompassing about 175,000 acres, it is one of the country's oldest and largest working ranches, with nearly 35,000 head of Angus and Charola cattle grazing on its green grass every year. At the Parker Ranch Visitor Center and Museum, take a self-guided tour of the facility and learn about the ranches history and revolution. The many exhibits include antique ranching tools, furnishings and clothing, a koa cabin, and many photos that take you back in time. A short drive from the visitor center are two historic homes you can tour: Puuopelu features European heirloom furniture and an impressive private art collection. At Mana Hale, you'll see native koa wood interiors, handmade furniture and Hawaiian quilts. For the active-minded, the ranch also offers horseback riding, wagon rides, ATV rides and hunting. In addition, it hosts several annual events, including a Cherry Blossom Festival in February and an action-packed rodeo in July.

Visitor and Museum center: Monday-Saturday 9 a.m.-5 p.m. Historic homes: Monday-Saturday 10 a.m.-5 p.m.

PARKER SQUARE

65-1279 Kawaihae Road, Kamuela, 808-885-7178

One of your best shopping options in the Waimea area is Parker Square. Here, you'll find a variety of pleasant stores and boutiques, including the Silk Road Gallery (Asian antiques), Sweet Wind Books & Beads (books and jewelry), Imagination (high-end children's toys), Bentleys Home and Garden (accessories for the house and yard), Gallery of Great Things (unique items from Hawaii, Indonesia, Micronesia, Polynesia and other Pacific Basin countries), and Waimea General Store (delicious edibles and gift items).

SUNSHINE HELICOPTERS

Hapuna Heliport, 62-100 Kaunaoa Drive, Waimea, 808-882-1223;
www.sunshinehelicopters.com

A helicopter tour is one of the best ways to take in all the sights of this varied and expansive island, especially if you're short on time. Sunshine's four offerings, available out of several points along the Kohala Coast, provide unobstructed views of the Big Island's waterfalls, sea cliffs and active volcanoes (often the only way to see red-hot lava is from the air).

Tours by appointment.

WAIMEA COUNTRY CLUB

Highway 19, Waimea, 6 miles E. on Highway 19, 808-885-8053; www.waimeagolf.com

This 18-hole public course is quite different from other courses on the island, and it's the only one up in cowboy country. Golfers enjoy bent greens on this Scottish links-style course surrounded by cattle ranches, while bunkers and ironwood trees keep things challenging. Carts and club rentals are available, and a snack bar serves refreshments. Greens fees are reasonable for nonresidents and even cheaper for residents.

WHERE TO EAT

★★★DANIEL THIEBAUT

65-1259 Kawaihae Road, Waimea, 808-887-2200; www.danielthiebaut.com

Housed in the historic Chock In Store, a general store that served the Waimea ranching community from 1900 to 1995, Daniel Theibaut is as much a visual delight as a culinary one. Sit in the former dress shop, the garden lanai or the green room, a beer shed building during World War II to house a truckload of beer that was delivered from Hilo once a week. The room that now houses the chef's table was a glassed-in sleeping lanai. Chef Daniel Thiebaut takes local products and prepares them according to his French cooking style. Menu highlights include cream of butternut squash soup, Hunan style rack of lamb with eggplant compote and Big Island goat cheese, and sautéed macadamia nut chicken with gingered Dijon mustard sauce, pickled pineapple and pave potatoes. Detractors rail about the "horrible service" and "overpriced food." It might be hit or miss, but it's worth a trip to find out, at least for lunch or the Sunday brunch.

Pacific-Rim. Lunch, dinner, Sunday brunch. Bar. $36-85

★★EDELWEISS

64-1299 Kawaihae Road, Waimea, 808-885-6800

This family-oriented restaurant, situated on the south side of Highway 19 in Waimea, specializes in such German favorites as bratwurst, Wiener schnitzel and sauerkraut. The exterior resembles a chalet, while the dining room has a rustic, cozy feel. Edelweiss is popular among residents of the Big Island, who make a special trip from Hilo and Kailua-Kona to enjoy the delicious, hearty fare.

American. Lunch, dinner. Closed Sunday-Monday; also September. Bar. $36-85

★MAHA'S CAFE

Highway 19, Waimea, 808-885-0693

Locals rave about the delectable dishes served at this little eatery housed in the historic Spencer House, Waimea's first frame house built in 1852. Owner and chef Harriet-Ann Namahaokalani Schutte, better known as Maha, uses locally grown ingredients in preparing such lunchtime favorites as the Maha had a Little Lamb Sandwich, made up of thin slices of roast lamb on squaw bread, with lettuce, tomato, mayo and spicy mango chutney. An afternoon tea is available from 3-4:30 p.m., which includes a delicious assortment of finger sandwiches, croissants and cobblers.

American. Breakfast, lunch. Closed Tuesday. $15 and under

★★★MERRIMAN'S

65-1227 Opelo Road, Waimea, 808-885-6822; www.merrimanshawaii.com

Nestled amid the lush rolling hills of the Big Island's ranch country, Merri-

ONLY IN HAWAII ACTIVITIES

Hawaii ranks right up there as one of the world's dream vacation destinations, and it doesn't disappoint. This tranquil getaway far out in the Pacific is packed with exciting things to do—many of which are unique to Hawaii. Here are eight only-in-Hawaii activities you won't want to miss.

Watch the sun rise from high atop a dormant volcano (Maui). Most sunrises are pretty, but witnessing the sun overtake the dark night sky from atop Haleakala Crater is breathtaking. The view of this daily ritual just doesn't get any better than from the craters summit, at 10,000 feet. After the dawning of a new day, many visitors hop on bicycles and pedal the 40 miles or so back down the volcano. Several tour companies offer this experience.

Reflect on a sad, pivotal day in history at Pearl Harbor (Oahu). The Japanese bombing of this harbor on December 7, 1941, will be forever remembered as a key day in American history. Throngs of people visit the site daily and stand atop the deck of the sunken USS Arizona Memorial. They come to pay their respects to all those who lost their lives here on the day that led to U.S. involvement in World War II.

Reel in supersized marlins (Big Island). Really, really big fish—including marlin, ono, yellowfin tuna and more—swim in the deep water off the Kona Coast, making the area a haven for anglers. Marlin that tip the scales at over 1,000 pounds have been caught, as documented on a Wall of Fame along Kona's Waterfront Row. Many charter boats take anglers offshore daily.

Sightsee along the Na Pali Coast (Kauai). This dramatic coastline, one of Hawaii's most beautiful, thrills visitors with majestic sea cliffs, fertile valleys and sensational waterfalls. Book a sailing trip or a helicopter ride to take in its tropical beauty.

Visit an active volcano (Big Island). In its latest eruption, the Kilauea Volcano in Hawaii Volcanoes National Park has been spewing lava since 1983, adding more than 500 acres of land to the islands south shore. On some days, visitors to this fascinating park can actually see the fiery lava flowing.

Ride a mule down a steep mountainside to a former leper colony (Molokai). From the top of the trail, its about three miles down to the Kalaupapa National Historic Park, home to Father Damien's famous leper colony. But the short distance entails a 1,700-foot drop with 26 switchbacks. It's an exhilarating ride with fabulous views, and the tour of the colony is a moving experience.

Snow-ski in the Tropics (Big Island). Yes, diehard skiers can traverse the slopes of Mauna Kea all through the winter, although February and March tend to be the best months for snow. There are no ski lifts, so skiers need four-wheel-drive vehicles to reach the top of the mountain, which soars more than 13,500 feet high.

Snorkel in a volcanic cinder cone (Maui). Just a couple of miles off the south coast of Maui sits Molokini, a sunken crater that's teeming with fish, making it one of Hawaii's most popular snorkeling sites. The water is so clear that visibility can be up to 200 feet. Many companies offer snorkeling trips to this great viewing spot.

man's specializes in innovative Hawaiian cuisine. Chef/owner Peter Merriman uses fresh, locally produced ingredients. Because it's hard to pick just one, a popular entrée is the mixed plate, a sampling of ponzu marinated mahi mahi, wok charred ahi and filet steak with Hamahua mushrooms. An appetizer taster platter features kalua pig and sweet onion quesadilla, crispy shrimp, lamp spring rolls, ahi shashimi and steamed Kama'aina shrimp and clams. Pale yellow walls and rattan furnishings provide a casual feel in the dining room. Framed photos of local farm scenes capture the natural beauty of the region.
Pacific Rim. Lunch, dinner. Reservations recommended. $36-85

KAUAI

IF YOU'RE A MOVIE BUFF, YOU'VE PROBABLY SEEN KAUAI ON THE BIG SCREEN. ELVIS PRESLEY romped around the island in 1957's *Blue Hawaii*, released four years after *South Pacific*, also filmed here. In more recent years, T-Rex tramped through one of Kauai's green valleys in the blockbuster *Jurassic Park*. Action hero Indiana Jones successfully plied his way through its green jungles in *Raiders of the Lost Ark*. And Ben Stiller's *Tropic Thunder* was filmed entirely on Kauai in 2007. In all, Hollywood directors have brought their actors and crews here to shoot scenes for more than 70 feature films and television shows.

Take one look at Hawaii's fourth-largest island, which encompasses about 550 square miles, and you'll know why. It's stunningly beautiful, with more than 90 percent of the land undeveloped. It overflows with breathtaking natural attractions, such as the 3,600-foot-deep Waimea Canyon; the Na Pali Coast, with jagged sea cliffs that jut 3,000 feet into the sky; and 5,200-foot-tall Mount Waialeale, one of the nation's wettest spots.

Kauai has so many scenic wonders because it's the oldest island in the Hawaiian chain. Nearly 5 million years ago, it emerged from a single shield volcano that eroded through the centuries because of eruptions and time itself, creating the spectacular landscape. It also rains a little more here than on other islands, mostly over the mountain ranges, so it's very green with fabulous-looking flora that grows profusely, thus the nickname "The Garden Isle."

Outdoor lovers take full advantage of the exciting adventures made possible by Kauai's geography. Popular adrenalin-pumping activities on the island include cycling down the twisting road that leads up to the canyon, hiking through Na Pali's deep valleys, and riding on horseback through mountain terrain, stopping at secluded waterfalls for a refreshing swim and picnic lunch. Visitors usually don't limit their exploring to land, either. They also venture offshore to sail on luxury catamarans, snorkel or dive in sparkling-clear water, reel in marlin from the deep, go rafting or kayaking, and much more.

All these high-energy activities take the adventurous throughout the island and into the Pacific. But for lower-octane fun, including hanging out at a pristine beach or sinking putts on one of the many well-manicured golf courses, visitors needn't wander all that far from Kauai's four major resort areas: Poipu on the south side, Princeville up north, and Lihue (the largest town) and the Coconut Coast to the east. Most of the hotels in these areas are just steps from good beaches and short drives—if not a short walk—from some of Hawaii's best fairways.

Kauai doesn't have the best of everything, though. Being less developed than other popular Hawaiian islands, it doesn't claim to have the hottest nightlife, the most gourmet restaurants or a shopping scene that can compete head to head with Oahu's or Maui's. To many visitors, this just makes the Garden Isle all the more appealing.

COCONUT COAST

On the east side of Kauai, north of Lihue, hundreds of coconut trees soar straight up into the blue sky, thus the nickname for this coastline. Visitors come here to see several popular attractions, including Opaekaa Falls,

Sleeping Giant and the Fern Grotto, which sits alongside the 20-mile-long Wailua River, Hawaii's only navigable river.

The Coconut Coast isn't as upscale as Princeville to the north or Poipu to the south. It's more of a middle-of-the-road resort area offering less expensive accommodations in a variety of basic hotels, condominiums, and bed-and-breakfasts. It's also an area with lots of shopping centers and restaurants, so you don't really get a sense of seclusion here, if that's what you prefer.

Kapaa, an old plantation town along this coastline, is a charming-looking little oceanside community. It can get quite busy, however, because visitors driving through town on Highway 56 are often enticed to stop and check out the many quaint shops and restaurants that line the road. It's hard to resist the appeal of the painted wooden storefronts, which sell aloha shirts and other touristy wares.

WHAT TO SEE
ACTIVITY WAREHOUSE
4-788 Kuhio Highway, Kapaa, 808-822-4000, 800-688-0580; www.travelhawaii.com
Talk about one-stop shopping. Visit Activity Warehouse and book a tour for almost any activity you'd like to do while on the island: ATV tours, circle-island tours, cocktail cruises, dinner cruises, helicopter tours, snorkeling trips, kayaking toursand many more. The prices are often at attractive discounts, something you don't see a lot of in Hawaii. Equipment rentals—everything from snorkeling gear and surfboards to golf clubs and picnic coolers—are reasonably priced, as well.
Daily 8 a.m.-8 p.m.

BAMBULEI
4-369D Highway 56, Kapaa, 808-823-8641; www.bambulei.com
It seems only appropriate that a store in a pair of 1930s-style plantation houses offer some of the coolest vintage treasures available on the island. The inventory is a wonderful mix of chic clothes from the 1930s and 1940s (including stylish aloha shirts), vintage fabrics and charming antiques from Hawaii and Asia. If you prefer new duds to precious old ones, youll also find contemporary apparel.
Monday-Saturday 10 a.m.-5 p.m., Sunday noon-4 p.m.

BUBBLES BELOW SCUBA CHARTERS
6251 Hauaala Road, Kapaa, 808-332-7333, 866-524-6268;
www.bubblesbelowkauai.com
Bubbles Below doesn't just offer dive trips; it offers underwater adventures with an emphasis on marine biology education. On its dives along the south and west shores, which you can book for the morning or afternoon, you'll likely see turtles that weigh more than 30 pounds, frogfish, lionfish, white-tip reef sharks and much more. If you prefer something a little more out of the ordinary, opt for the night dive and keep your eyes peeled for octopuses, nudibranchs, pelagics and other nocturnal sea life. From May through September, when the water conditions permit, Bubbles Below also takes divers to the private island of Niihau for an up-close look at all the marine life off that island's shoreline. While diving there, you'll see vertical walls, huge caverns and large black coral trees that will take your breath away. Most trips

leave from Port Allen.

Daily, various times.

COCONUT MARKETPLACE
4-484 Kuhio Highway, Kapaa 808-822-3641

You won't find many locals at this 64,000-square-foot shopping center. Instead, the more than 70 specialty shops and smaller restaurants are primarily targeted at visitors. The stores sell souvenirs, clothing, and other miscellaneous items of interest to vacationers. For those seeking entertainment, there's also a cinema.

Monday-Saturday 9 a.m.-8 p.m., Sunday 10 a.m.-6 p.m.

FERN GROTTO
Wailua River State Park, Kuhio Highway and Highway 580, Wailua, 808-274-3446

Most everyone who visits Kauai makes time to see this beautiful attraction, a natural, lava-rock amphitheater covered with green tropical ferns, which create near-perfect acoustics. The grotto, located in a lush jungle, is accessible only by boats, which are operated from the park's marina (on the river's south side) by Smiths Motor Boat Service *(808-821-6892)* and Waialeale Boat Service *(808-822-4908)*. It's an 80-minute ride to and from the grotto, but entertainment by musicians and hula dancers helps the time pass quickly, as do the striking scenery and intriguing Hawaii stories told by the crew. Daily; boats depart every half-hour from 9 a.m.-3 p.m.

HAWAII'S NATIVE FAUNA

The animals absent form the Hawaiian ecosystem are as interesting to scientists as the ones included within it. There are no native ants, no crocodiles, lions, tigers or other large jungle creatures. When the Polynesians arrived in Hawaii between 400 and 800 A.D., there were no reptiles, no amphibians, not even a cockroach or lowly flea.

What did exist was astonishing: more than 2,000 animal and plant ancestors are believed to have evolved in complete isolation on these remote and varied islands, forming new and distinct life forms that made Hawaii home to one of the world's largest groups of endemic species (species that exist nowhere else in the world). For this reason, Hawaii rivals the Galapagos Islands as one of the most important sites of evolutionary study.

Dogs, pigs, chickens and rats came to Hawaii with the first Polynesian settlers, and all four can still be found in the wild here today. Native animals had evolved on Hawaii to that point without the need to defend themselves against predators and they were poorly equipped to protect themselves from these foreign species. Many endemic species began to disappear, and Hawaii began a battle that it still fights today against extinction of many of its unique creatures.

Hawaii has only two native mammals—the hoary bat and the monk seal—and both are in danger of extinction. Scientists believe that the hoary bat was accidentally blown over to the Hawaiian Islands from North or South America. (Hoary means "frosted" and refers to its characteristic white-tipped fur.) Monk seals are solitary creatures that evolved without the threat of predators and as a result are naturally tame. Because of this tendency, they became a popular target for their oil and pelts beginning in the 19th century. Although they have been protected since 1976 under the Endangered Species Act, there are fewer than 1,200 left in existence today.

HAWAII MOVIE TOURS

Kapaa, 808-822-1192, 800-628-8432; www.hawaiimovietour.com

Hollywood knows a good thing when it sees it, so more than 70 films and television shows have shot some of their scenes on the picturesque Garden Isle. Take one of this company's tours, and you'll see firsthand many of the places you've seen up on the big screen or on the small screen at home: Kipu Ranch, seen in Raiders of the Lost Ark; Wailua Falls, from the opening scene of the Fantasy Island television show; Hanalei Pier, from South Pacific and King Kong, and many other island locales you've seen before. In a nod to karaoke, and to keep you in the Hollywood mood throughout the tour, your guide leads your group in spirited sing-alongs featuring tunes from the various blockbusters.

Daily, various times.

KAPAA TOWN

Highway 56, Kapaa

When you want to do some shopping on the island, hit the main drag through this charming old town. You'll find a wide assortment of funky shops and specialty stores with hard-to-resist merchandise, so it's unlikely you'll head back to your car empty-handed. Asian-influenced accessories for your home, handmade glass decorative pieces, wood carvings, aloha shirts and handmade jewelry are a sampling of the goods that independent retailers sell along this colorful shopping strip.

Daily, various hours.

KAUAI CHILDREN'S DISCOVERY MUSEUM

Kauai Village Shopping Center, 4-831 Kuhio Highway, Kapaa, 808-823-8222;
www.kcdm.org

If the kids tire of the beach, or you want to give them a break from the sun, the Kauai Children's Discovery Museum will show them a good time and teach them more than a few things while they play. In the Sea Chest Secret exhibit, several hands-on stations illustrate how difficult it was for sailors to explore the ocean in the 1700s. The Early Childhood Center features developmentally appropriate activities for children up to age 5. Youngsters play in homes scaled to their size in the multicultural Keiki Village, designed to introduce them to the various lifestyles found on Kauai. In Keiki Camp, which is offered during school breaks and all summer, kids ages 5 to 10 are kept occupied with a variety of learning adventures. On Saturdays from 3:30 to 5 p.m., the Starlab Planetarium program brings the stars to them.

Tuesday-Saturday 9 a.m.-5 p.m.

KAUAI PRODUCTS FAIR

Kuhio Highway, Kapaa, 808-246-0988; www.kauaiproductfair.com

Handcrafted Hawaii products take center stage at this weekly outdoor crafts fair. Aloha wear, bags, baskets, candles, glass art, jewelry, photography, wood art—you name it, you can probably buy it here. In addition, vendors sell tropical plants and flowers, fresh produce, and island food in case you get hungry while browsing.

Thursday-Sunday 9 a.m.-5 p.m.

POLO IN HAWAII

More than likely, nomadic warriors first played polo more than 2,000 years ago. Then, in the Middle Ages, it was played from Constantinople to Japan and became known as the Game of Kings in the East. The sport galloped its way into England in the 1850s, and tehn made its U.S. debut in 1876. These days, more than 275 clubs field teams and sponsor matches in the United States, including two clubs on the Hawaiian Islands.

Anyone who's a fan of this refined sport that's sometimes described as "hockey on horseback" can watch players compete from atop thoroughbreds on two islands: Maui and Oahu. During a game, the players race up and down the polo field at top speeds using bamboo mallets to hit the ball through the goal and score points. It's fast-paced action packed with excitement for spectators.

Here's where and when to catch the action on the various islands:

Maui: The Maui Polo Club holds indoor matches every Sunday at 1:30 p.m. at the Maui Polo Club Manduke Baldwin Polo Arena from April through June, and at the Oskie Rice Outdoor Polo Field from September through November. Admission is $3 per person. For more information, visit www.mauipolo.com.

Oahu: The Honolulu Polo Club sponsors matches every Sunday at 2:30 p.m., usually from June through mid-October. The field is located on the windward side of the island in Waimanalo. It's adjacent to Kalanianaole Highway, across from Bellows Beach. Admission is $3 per person, free for those 12 and younger. For more information, visit www.honolulupolo.com

KAUAI VILLAGE SHOPPING CENTER

4-831 Kuhio Highway, Kapaa, 808-822-4904

More than 30 stores and restaurants cater to customers at this 110,000-square-foot shopping center on the Coconut Coast. It's designed to look like a plantation village in the late 1800s, with green and white wooden store-fronts. The two anchors are Safeway and Longs Drugs. Specialty shops include the Wyland Gallery, which features ocean-inspired paintings by the painter Robert Wyland.

KAYAK WAILUA

Wailua Marina, Wailua, 808-822-3388; www.kayakwailua.com

Paddle your own kayak on this 4 1/2-hour guided tour of the Wailua River, a tour that's doable for even first-time paddlers. After about 45 minutes on the river, you'll beach your kayak for an easy hike through canyons and a rain forest to a waterfall for some splash time in the water and a picnic, if you bring your own meal or snacks. Then it's back to the river and paddling for the return trip to the marina. During the entire tour, your guide tells the history and legends of the striking Wailua River Valley.

Daily. Tours: 9 a.m., 10 a.m., noon and 1 p.m.

KEALIA BEACH

Highway 56, Kapaa

For a little solitude when you sunbathe, this beach is a good choice. It's wide, a half-mile long and frequently not all that crowded, so you'll likely have some privacy as you work on that tan. In summer, surfers and boogie-boarders like to ride Kealia's waves. In winter, the waters sometimes have strong riptides, so swim with caution.

Daily dawn-dusk.

OPAEKAA FALLS
Highway 580, Wailua

View this beautiful waterfall from a convenient lookout just about 1 1/2 miles from where Highway 580 begins. Opaekaa means "shrimp," and the waterfall gets its name because supposedly so many of them used to be seen falling into the pool at its base.

Daily dawn-dusk.

SLEEPING GIANT
Kuhio Highway, Kapaa

Just after mile marker 7 on the Kuhio Highway, look inland at the Nounou Mountain ridge, and you'll swear you see a sleeping giant. It's a sight associated with a legend involving a giant named Puni, who fell asleep after a big meal and never woke again. At the mountain itself, hike up the Sleeping Giant Trail for a stellar view. The trail is a bit of a challenge because you climb almost straight uphill, gaining 1,000 feet in altitude.

SUNNYSIDE FARMERS' MARKET
4-1345 Kuhio Highway, Kapaa, 808-822-0494, 800-883-8364

Kapaa is home to the county's largest Sunshine Market every Wednesday afternoon. If you can't make that big sell, don't sweat it. Instead, plan on buying whatever fresh produce you need at the Sunnyside market, an independently operated one that's open seven days a week. Its vendors sell fruits, vegetables, flowers and more.

Monday-Saturday 7 a.m.-7:30 p.m., Sunday 10 a.m.-6 p.m.

TIN CAN MAILMAN
Kinipopo Shopping Village, 4-356 Kuhio Highway, Kapaa, 808-822-3009;
www.tincanmailman.net

Anyone who gets lost in old books will get lost in the aisles of this unassuming but delightful bookstore, which takes you back to another time in Hawaii via the written word. It has many rare and used Hawaiiana books that will spark your interest, as well as rare prints and vintage maps and postcards. You'll also find modern fiction and some gift items, such as tapa pieces.

Monday-Friday 11 a.m.-7 p.m., Saturday noon-4 p.m.

WAILUA GOLF COURSE
3-5351 Kuhio Highway, Kapaa, 808-241-6666; www.kauai.gov

This par-72, 6,585-yard course regularly gets ranked among the best municipal courses in the country, and many locals will tell you it's the best one in the state of Hawaii. Given such accolades, you can bet Wailua presents many challenges, such as plenty of mature trees that narrow the fairways and numerous sand bunkers. The front nine holes tend to be flat, while the back nine have more elevation changes. The course parallels the ocean, which it borders on four holes, so you'll enjoy good views while on the links. Another plus: Wailua is also a bargain by Hawaii standards, with green fees less than

$50. The amenities include a pro shop, locker facilities, a practice putting green, and a driving range.
Daily 6 a.m.-dusk; last tee-off time 5 p.m.

WAILUA RIVER STATE PARK
Kuhio Highway and Highway 580, Wailua, 808-274-3444; www.hawaiistateparks.org
Encompassing more than 1,000 acres, this state park, which borders the island's only navigable river, offers a variety of sights and activities. Many people come here for a river cruise to the Fern Grotto, but the park also has a public boat ramp, kayak rentals, water skiing, hiking trails, a picnic area, scenic overlooks and more.
Daily 24 hours.

WAIPOULI VARIETY STORE
4-901 Kuhio Highway, Kapaa, 808-822-1014
If you're going to be doing any fishing on the island, this store will probably have whatever tackle you'll need to reel in good catches. It has a well-stocked fishing section that attracts plenty of anglers every day. You can also buy beach supplies, T-shirts, souvenirs and more.

WHERE TO EAT
★DUANE'S ONO-CHAR BURGER
Kuhio Hwy., Anahola, 808-822-9181
Long before fast food chains invaded the island, Duane's was a Kauai favorite for hamburgers. Operating out of a red-and-white-painted shack on the Kuhio Highway, this over-the-counter operation is a popular stop for fast food in north Kauai. Its burgers win raves for the creative toppings (blue cheese, teriyaki, pineapple) as do the thick fruit smoothies. The burger joint can be found roadside next to the Anahola Post Office, a few miles north of Kapaa.
American. Lunch, dinner. Children's menu. Outdoor seating. No credit cards accepted. $15 and under

★★KINTARO RESTAURANT
4-370 Kuhio Hwy., Kapaa, 808-822-3341
This simple Japanese restaurant is known for its creative maki rolls, including the blistering spicy tuna rolls. The eatery also has a large teppanyaki selection, with dishes such as teriyaki steak and freshly grilled local fish and scallops served with steamed rice. The full bar includes creative cocktails, sake and beers.
Japanese. Dinner. Closed Sunday. Bar. Reservations recommended. $16-35

★MERMAIDS CAFÉ
1384 Kuhio Highway, Kapaa, 808-821-2026
This tiny restaurant, which is little more than a take-out window in the center of Kapaa town with a few umbrella-shaded tables in front, wins acclaim for both its organic, seasonal menu of seafood and vegetarian dishes and its low prices (all dishes are priced at less than $11). Heaping portions of ahi tacos come alongside black beans and organic lettuce, while tofu or chicken satay is served with stir fried greens, peppers and onions with fresh ginger and

soy sauce. There's no wine list, but the tropical hibiscus iced tea more than makes up for it.

Seafood. Lunch, dinner. $15 and under

NORTH SHORE KAUAI

The world doesn't get much prettier than on the North Shore of Kauai, the island's shining star. It's superlative attractions include the Na Pali Coast, with its stunning sea cliffs; glorious beaches beautiful enough to have starred in Hollywood movies; and the Hanalei Valley, a green and lush land where the locals still grow taro much like farmers did hundreds of years ago.

All these sights will truly take your breath away as you get lost in the beauty that surrounds you on this magical shore. Here, life is good, very good.

For proof, check into the 23-acre St. Regis Princeville Resort, an ultra-fabulous facility that's fresh from a complete renovation (it reopened in October 2009). Situated high on a bluff overlooking Hanalei Bay, the hotel caters to celebrities and the privileged who can afford to spoil themselves. Matt LeBlanc and a few of his "Friends" basked in the royal treatment here when the TV star got married on the North Shore in 2003. The hotel is located in the resort community of Princeville, which also has condominium units, a bed-and-breakfast, and two recently renovated golf courses designed by Robert Trent Jones, Jr. The courses meander through the Hanalei Valley, with some holes overlooking the Pacific. The recently opened Westin Princeville Ocean Resort Villas, with its smart rooms and full kitchens, is a good option for those who want a more casual resort experience. Away from the resort, there are two commercial centers—the small towns of Kilauea and Hanalei, whose restaurants and shops help keep visitors entertained. Hanalei, with its quaint, colorful clapboard buildings, is one of the island's most alluring towns. For sightseers, Kilauea also has a historic lighthouse and a 200-acre wildlife refuge with good bird-watching.

No place is perfect, so the tranquil North Shore does have one drawback: frequent rain showers. But they cool things down and help keep the landscape all that more verdant.

WHAT TO SEE
ANINI BEACH
Anini Beach Road, Kilauea; www.kauai-hawaii.com

On the North Shore, this three-mile-long beach is the safest you'll find on Kauai in the summer because its protected by Hawaii's longest reef. Swimming, snorkeling and windsurfing are popular on this stretch of sand.The park includes picnic facilities, a boat-launch ramp and restrooms.

Daily dawn-dusk.

CAPTAIN SUNDOWN
Hanalei, 808-826-5585; www.captainsundown.com

From April through December, climb aboard the 40-foot Kuuipo—the only sailing catamaran that departs from the North Shore—for a six-hour morning sail during which you see all of the strikingly gorgeous Na Pali coast. The splendid sights include 3,000-foot cliffs, lava archways, sea caves, waterfalls and more. During your time offshore, you'll also snorkel, fish, have lunch and

HAWAIIAN LANGUAGE

The Olelo Hawaii—Hawaii's native tongue—has made a resurgence on the islands, and visitors are just as likely to hear words spoken in native Hawaiian as they are to hear them spoken in English. But it was not always that way. The oddly mellifluous and repetitive language has a rich and tangled history.

Based on a family of Polynesian languages, the Olelo Hawaii originally was a pure oral language. Protestant missionaries were said to be responsible for creating a written form of the language when they came to the islands in the late 18th century. According to island lore, the linguistically challenged missionaries could not distinguish among many of the sounds they heard in the Hawaiian language. The resulting alphabet they created contained only 12 letters: the five vowels in the English language and the consonants h, k, l, m, n, p, and w.

The limited alphabet is responsible for the distinctive sounds and syllabic reduplication in the Hawaiian language. All words end in a vowel. Every vowel sound is pronounced. Duplication of letters or syllables is common.

Pronunciation can be tricky. For the most part, vowel sounds mimic those found in English. Consonants sometimes take on the sound of another letter, particularly when they are preceded by a vowel. For example, a "w" is sometimes pronounced like a "v" when it is preceded by a vowel.

The use of several diacritical marks also adds to the difficulty of picking up the Hawaiian language. The language relies on two marks, the okina (') and the kahako (a solid line atop a vowel) to indicate a pause or the extension of a vowel sound, respectively.

The Olelo Hawaii was the official language of Hawaii until late in the 19th century, when the Hawaiian monarchy was overthrown and the new government banned the language in favor of English. While many feared that the native tongue was dead, a resurgence in interest in Hawaiian culture has brought it back to life. The Olelo Hawaii is once again an official language of the state and now is being taught in the schools.

While in Hawaii, you may hear a third language called Pidgin, which evolved from English, Chinese and Portuguese influences. Hallmarks of Pidgin include omitting or using nonstandard English forms of the verb to be, replacing a "d" or "t" sound with a "th" sound, and omitting the "l" sound at the end of a word. While native Hawaiians are happy to have you try out their native tongue, use of Pidgin should be avoided, as it is considered insulting.

Here are some Hawaiian words and phrases that may come in handy on your visit to the islands:

aloha: hello, love
aloha no: response to greeting
aloha kakahiaka: good morning
aloha auinala: good afternoon
aloha ahiahi: good evening
ahui hou: goodbye
e komo mai: welcome
olu olu: please
mahalo: thank you
mahalo nui loa: thank you very much
A ole pilikia: you're welcome
owai kau inoa: what is your name?
pehea oe: how are you?
maika i: I am fine

kala mail ia a: excuse me
kokua: help
ohana: family
kane: man
wahine: woman
keiki: child
paniolo: Hawaiian cowboy
alii: royalty
kaukau: food, meal
opu: belly, stomach
pupu: appetizer
luau: feast
imu: underground oven
niu: coconut
iamaka: raw fish
iki: a little bit
pau: finished
heiau: temple or place of worship
hale: house, building

lanai: porch, terrace
lua: bathroom
pua: flower
lani: sky, heaven
hoku: star
la: sun, day, light
moana: ocean
nalu: wave, to surf
mano: shark
mauka: toward the mountain
makai: toward the sea
kamaaina: native
malihini: newcomer
hau oli la hanau: happy birthday
hau oli la ho omana o: happy anniversary
pomaika i: blessing, good luck

listen to the stories of Hawaiian-born Captain Bob, who has spent more than 35 years sailing the waters off Hanalei. You can see all the same sights on a three-hour afternoon sail, but there are no stops for snorkeling or fishing.
Monday-Saturday 9 a.m. and 4 p.m.

CHING YOUNG VILLAGE SHOPPING CENTER

5-5190 Kuhio Highway, Hanalei, 808-826-7222; www.chingyoungvillage.com
This eclectic collection of shops offers visitors a laid-back shopping experience in the heart of Hanalei. Look for bargains on beach essentials and souvenirs at the Village Variety Store. For fun beachwear and aloha shirts, step into Hot Rocket and get yourself decked out for your island stay. Stock up on good-for-you eats at Hanalei Natural Food Store. More than 25 other retailers and restaurants will entice you, as well.
Daily; store hours vary.

GUAVA KAI PLANTATION

4900 Kuawa Road, Kilauea, 808-828-6121
Islands and guavas seemingly go together like mountains and snow. So, while on Kauai, take a self-guided tour of the country's largest guava plantation. As you stroll through the orchards to see how this tropical fruit is grown, pick some yourself for a delicious snack. After the tour, enjoy some complimentary guava juice.
Daily 9 a.m.-5 p.m.

HAENA BEACH PARK

Highway 560, mile marker 8, Haena
Haena Beach is another lovely North Shore beach where swimming is dangerous in winter, but safe in summer if the surf is down. The park has a grassy camping area as well as shaded picnic tables.
Daily dawn-dusk.

HANALEI BAY BEACH PARK

Weke Road, Hanalei
This park is surrounded by lush, green cliffs and features a crescent-shaped stretch of sand that's ideal for surfing and bodyboarding.
Daily dawn-dusk.

HANALEI CENTER

5-5121 Kuhio Highway, Hanalei, 808-826-7677; www.hanaleicenter.com
This is no run-of-the-mill strip shopping center. Its stores are housed in six restored historic buildings, including the old Hanalei School, and evoke old Hawaii. Here, you can buy surfing gear, vintage Hawaiian clothing, jewelry, resort wear for children and adults and more. Be sure to browse the Yellowfish Trading Company, where you'll find wonderful Hawaiiana memorabilia and collectibles from the 1920s to 1940s.
Daily 8 a.m.-8 p.m.

HANALEI SURF CO.

5-5161 Kuhio Highway, Hanalei, 808-826-9000, 866-426-2534; www.hanaleisurf.com

Head to this well-stocked surfing center for any of your surfing needs on Kauai's North Shore. The staff rents surfboards, boogie boards, and can also help with arranging group or private surfing lessons.
Daily 8 a.m.-9 p.m.

HAWAII FARMERS OF HANALEI FARMERS' MARKET
Kuhio Highway, Hanalei
Every Tuesday, farmers from this region bring locally grown fruits and vegetables to this outdoor market. Avocadoes, bananas, bok choy, carrots, kumquats, onions, oranges, papayas—whatever's in season, you'll find here, usually at great prices. And not only is all of the produce freshly harvested, much of it has been organically grown in this rich valley.

KA ULU O LAKA HEIAU
Kee Beach, Hanalei
Look above the boulders at this beach, and you'll see a grassy knoll with the remains of an altar of rocks. This wasn't just any altar; it was the Altar of Laka, the goddess of hula. In earlier times, this sight served as one of the most revered hula schools anywhere in the islands. Out of respect, locals still bring flower leis to the altar and remember the roots of the dance they still treasure all these years later.

KALIHIWAI BEACH
Kalihiwai Road, Kilauea
Locals bring their families to Kalihiwai in the summer, when favorable ocean conditions make for good swimming. Surfers take over the beach in winter, but strong currents challenge even the most seasoned riders. You won't find any facilities here, but plenty of grass and shade trees line the sandy beach, making it a pleasant spot in which to hang out and enjoy the ocean.
Daily dawn-dusk.

KAUAI SIERRA CLUB HIKES
Princeville; www.hi.sierraclub.org
Several times a month, local nature lovers who belong to Kauai's chapter of the Sierra Club go hiking on one of the island's many scenic trails. Visitors are welcome to join in the challenging fun. The club lists the various hikes on its Web site a few months in advance, offering a brief description of each walk, the level of difficulty, and the round-trip mileage. The list includes contact names and phone numbers, but visitors are asked not to call for information until they're on the island.
Monthly, various times.

KAYAK KAUAI OUTBOUND
Kuhio Highway, Hanalei, 808-826-9844, 800-437-3507; www.kayakkauai.com
If you like to explore by on your own, come to this shop to rent kayaks, bikes, tents and more. The staff is also happy to offer good advice on where to go paddling or hiking. Guided tours of the island's Na Pali Coast, Hanalei River, Wailua River or Poipu are also offered.
Daily 8 a.m.-5:30 p.m.

KEE BEACH

Highway 560, Haena; www.kauai-hawaii.com

You might have seen this beach even if you've never set foot on its sand: it was featured in the television mini-series, *The Thorn Birds*. The area sits at the edge of the Na Pali Coast and offers splendid views of towering cliffs. If you're a hiker, the Kalalau Trail begins here.

Daily dawn-dusk.

KILAUEA POINT NATIONAL WILDLIFE REFUGE

Kilauea Point, Kilauea, 808-828-1413

Seven Hawaiian seabirds like to nest and roost on the dramatic rocky cliffs at this 200-acre refuge, making it a particularly good spot for bird-watching. You might spot the endangered nene, the Laysan albatross, red-footed boobies and wedge-tailed shearwaters. The acreage surrounds the historic Kilauea Lighthouse, which helped many sailors navigate their ships along the North Shore from 1913 until 1976, when the lighthouse was retired.

Daily 10 a.m.-4 p.m.

KILAUEA QUALITY FARMERS' ASSOCIATION FARMERS' MARKET

Keneke Street, Kilauea

Perhaps because it's held on Saturday, this farmers' market has a real community feel, with many locals walking to and from the weekly sell. Like the Hanalei farmers' market, much of the produce is organically grown on the island. You might even see some residents out in their front yards selling what they've grown themselves.

Saturday, 11:30 a.m.-1:30 p.m.

KONG LUNG CO.

Lighthouse Road and Keneke Street, Kilauea, 808-828-1822

Nothing is particularly cheap here, but the store is packed with everything from fine wines and exquisite dinnerware to stylish stationery and jewelry sourced from around the world.

Monday-Friday 10 a.m.-7 p.m., Saturday-Sunday 10 a.m.-6 p.m.

LIMAHULI GARDEN

Highway 560, Haena, 808-826-1053; www.ntbg.org

This lovely, 17-acre garden—designed to be a living classroom—puts the focus on native plants, with botanists working to save those that are endangered. You'll also see plants brought to Kauai by Polynesians from other islands, and plants that have invaded the natural habitats in more recent times. Many of the crops are grown in the ancient tradition, including taro cultivated on lava rock terraces. You can opt for guided or self-guided tours.

Tuesday-Friday and Sunday 9:30 a.m.-4 p.m.

LOTUS GALLERY

Lighthouse Road and Keneke Street, Kilauea, 808-828-9898; www.jewelofthelotus.com

This gallery, located behind the Kong Lung Co., caters to shoppers who appreciate fine-art pieces. It features jewelry, pearls, exquisite antiques from India and other Far East locales, Oriental rugs, and other types of unique art.

Daily 10 a.m.-6 .p.m.

NA AINA KAI BOTANICAL GARDENS

4101 Wailapa Road, Kilauea, 808-828-0525; www.naainakai.com

The lush grounds of this horticulture showplace span 240 green acres. Its formal gardens feature firecracker flowers, kukui trees, rainbow and golden shower trees, red hibiscus, and more. Baobabs, prickly pear cactus, and other succulents and cacti from around the world dress up the international desert garden. Walk through the wild forest garden, and you'll see bamboo, ferns and mosses. At the beachside meadow, be on the lookout for indigenous or exotic birds, including the white-rumped shama or the native nene. More than 60 bronze sculptures scattered throughout the complex add even more beauty to the surroundings.

Walking and riding tours: Tuesday-Thursday at 9 a.m. and 1 p.m. (they run from one to five hours). Reservations encouraged.

NA PALI COAST STATE PARK

808-274-3344; www.hawaiistatepark.org

With its tall sea cliffs, lush valleys, and many gorgeous waterfalls, the 6,175-acre Na Pali Coast State Park ranks as one of the most stunningly beautiful places in Hawaii. Unfortunately, not every visitor to Kauai gets to see or appreciate this spectacular rugged coast because it's not accessible by car. Hiking is the best way to see and experience it. The 11-mile Kalalau Trail begins at the end of Highway 56 in Haena State Park, but it's a difficult trail for experienced backpackers only, who usually overnight at primitive campsites in valleys along the way. If you brave the trek, be careful about swimming in the ocean, because riptides can be strong and dangerous. If you're not up for the strenuous, multi-day adventure, you might at least consider the 2-mile day hike from the trailhead to Hanakapiai Valley. Hiking beyond the 2-mile point requires a permit from the Kauai office of the Division of State Parks (telephone number listed above). Many commercial boating companies offer Na Pali sightseeing tours, with snorkeling stops often included. Helicopter tours are another option; several companies offer them from the Lihue Heliport. Daily dawn-dusk.

OLA'S

Highway 560, Hanalei, 808-826-6937; www.olashanalei.com

Koa-wood boxes. Handmade furniture. Handblown glass. Elegant jewelry. You'll find all this and more at this inviting shop that features original creations by both local and international artists.

Daily 10 a.m.-9:30 p.m.

PEDAL 'N PADDLE

Ching Young Village, 5-1590 Kuhio Highway, Hanalei, 808-826-9069; www.pedalnpaddle.com

Stop at this well-stocked store if you're going to be camping, hiking, kayaking or pursuing any other outdoor activities in the fresh island air. Before embarking on your adventure, you can rent or buy everything from tents, hiking boots, bikes, and scooters to boogie boards, kayaks and snorkeling gear. The shop also sells miscellaneous items such as beach mats, hats and sunscreen.

Daily 9 a.m.-5 p.m.

POLYNESIAN ADVENTURE TOURS

Princeville, 808-246-0122; www.polyad.com

If you want to see all the major sights on Kauai, but want to leave the driving to someone else, reserve a seat on one of this company's island tours. Depending on which tour you take, you'll see major attractions such as the Fern Grotto, Hanalei Valley Lookout, Kilauea Lighthouse Overlook, Opaekaa Falls, Spouting Horn, Wailua Falls and Waimea Canyon. All your sightseeing is done in the comfort of an air-conditioned van, mini-coach or full-size motorcoach. Daily, various times.

PRINCEVILLE GOLF CLUB

5-3900 Kuhio Highway, Princeville, 808-826-2727, 800-826-4400; www.princeville.com

This club offers golfers two beautiful courses with 45 holes in the postcard-perfect Hanalei Valley. Both were designed by Robert Trent Jones Jr., and both have won high praise from players and the press. The 18-hole Prince Course, which unfolds over 390 oceanfront acres, is the more challenging. It climbs up and down hills, has many deep ravines and features undulating greens of various shapes. But golfers of all skills hit the links here because every hole has five sets of tees, making the Prince more manageable for even so-so duffers. The easier-to-play Makai Course has 27 holes—nine that front the ocean, nine that meander around lakes and nine that run through woodlands. Princeville's amenities include a clubhouse, pro shop, restaurant, and bar.

Daily 6:30 a.m.-7 p.m.; last tee time for 18 holes, 2 p.m.; last tee time for 9 holes, 4 p.m.

PRINCEVILLE HEALTH CLUB AND SPA

Princeville Resort, 5520 Ka Haku Road., Princeville, 808-826-9644, 800-826-4400; www.princeville.com

This full-service, 15,000-square-foot health club offers a number of fitness classes, including kick boxing, low-impact aerobics, step aerobics, tai chi and yoga. You can also pump up with state-of-the-art exercise equipment, work out in the 25-meter lap pool, or get expert advice from a personal trainer. If you're more into relaxation, sign up for a soothing massage or body treatment in the spa.

Monday-Friday 6:30 a.m.-8 p.m., Saturday 8 a.m.-8 p.m., Sunday 8 a.m.-6 p.m.

PRINCEVILLE RANCH HIKE AND KAYAK ADVENTURES

Hanalei, 808-826-7669, 888-955-7669; www.kauai-hiking.com

Mix your workout for the day with spectacular sightseeing when you take one of the four-hour tours offered by this company. On its Jungle Waterfall Kayak Adventure, youll hike through lush green valleys, kayak to hidden waterfalls, and swim in a cool, refreshing mountain pool. The Waterfall Excursion, done entirely on foot, takes you to a lookout point with a gorgeous 360-degree view of the North Shore, which boasts some of the most beautiful terrain youll ever see. At a 100-foot waterfall, dive into the water for a swim. If you prefer, opt for a custom-designed private hike. Whichever tour you choose, youll be exploring private property not accessible to the general public. Monday-Saturday, various times.

PRINCEVILLE RANCH STABLES
Hanalei, 808-826-6777; www.princevilleranch.com

Saddle up and spend the day exploring the lush green acreage of this family-owned ranch on Kauai's gorgeous North Shore. On the longer tours, you'll ride to an 80-foot, fern-lined waterfall that feeds into a mountain pool perfect for a relaxing swim. There, you'll chow down on an island picnic in this serene setting. On other tours, you can help paniolos round up a herd on a sunrise cattle drive or ride across the range marveling at the beauty of the Hanalei Mountains. Long pants and good, sturdy shoes (closed-toed only) are recommended. Children must be 8 years or older to take part, and riders must weigh less than 220 pounds for men or 180 pounds for women. Monday-Saturday, various times.

PRINCEVILLE TENNIS CLUB
Princeville Resort, 5520 Ka Haku Road, Princeville, 808-826-1230; www.princeville.com

Get a good grip on your racket and serve up some aces on one of the six Plexi-pave courts at this facility in the posh Princeville Resort. Every good tennis player knows you must keep your eye on the ball, so be sure to bring your concentration. You'll need it on the court—all the natural beauty of Hanalei and its gorgeous mountains could very well distract you. The club offers daily private and group lessons, if you want to raise the level of your game a notch or two.
Daily 8:30 a.m.-6 p.m.

SUNSHINE MARKETS
Princeville, 808-241-6390; www.kauai.gov

Buy some of the best produce available on the island at any of these outdoor, county-sponsored markets, which are held in various locales. The vendors can sell only unprocessed fruits, vegetables, nuts, flowers and plants grown on Kauai, so you're buying fresh-from-the-farm edibles with lots of taste. And you'll be rubbing elbows with many locals who do their food shopping at these markets.
Monday-Saturday, various times and locales.

TAHITI NUI
5-5134 Kuhio Highway, 808-826-6277

This small watering hole with a kitchsy, adorable Polynesian theme is a local favorite for its live music and potent mai tais. Secure an outdoor table during lunchtime and you'll be treated to local ahi carpaccio, smoked ribs with boysenberry barbecue sauce and panko crusted ono maki rolls.

TUNNELS BEACH
Highway 56/560, mile marker 8, Haena

This two-mile-long golden-sand beach gets a gold star for its excellent snorkeling in summer, when the water conditions are safe: a reef close to the beach attracts plenty of colorful fish. Tunnels is also popular with scuba divers because of the deep-water caverns close to shore. Look inland from the beach and be awed by good views of the Na Pali cliffs.
Daily dawn-dusk.

WAIOLI MISSION HOUSE MUSEUM

Kuhio Highway, Hanalei, 808-245-3202; www.hawaiimuseums.org

Visit this museum in the heavenly Hanalei Valley to get a feel for what rural life in Kauai was like more than 150 years ago. The two-story wood house was built in 1837 as a home for Abner and Lucy Wilcox, two missionary teachers from Massachusetts. The period furnishings include some made from Hawaiian koa wood, the chimney is made of lava rock, and the floors are ohia wood.

Tours: Monday, Wednesday, Thursday, 10 a.m. and 1 p.m.

WINDSURF KAUAI

Hanalei, 808-828-6838

Learn how to surf or windsurf during your stay on Kauai with a lesson from the instructors at Windsurf Kauai. Lessons include 90-minute surfing instruction on the waves in Hanalei Bay along with 3-hour windsurfing lessons in the gusts at Anini Beach.

Monday-Friday, various times.

WHERE TO STAY
ST. REGIS PRINCEVILLE RESORT

5520 Ka Haku Road, Princeville, 808-826-9644; www.stregisprinceville.com

Sprawling across 23 acres of Kauai's North Shore, the opulent St. Regis Princeville Resort sits on one of the world's most beautiful beaches. This luxury resort, situated on a high bluff overlooking Hanalei Bay, is the jewel in the crown of Princeville (a 9,000-acre community) and underwent a complete renovation and rebranding (this is the resort's first stint as a St. Regis) in 2009. The beautiful area around this resort is appropriately known locally as Bali Hai, after the idyllic island in South Pacific. Each of the 252 guest rooms and suites offers a view of the ocean, Hanalei Bay, or the dramatic cliffs through oversized windows. The rooms have been updated with cheerful, contemporary décor and flat-screen TVs. Activities abound, from swimming in the resort's infinity pool to horseback riding, sea kayaking and tennis. The golf courses, designed by master architect Robert Trent Jones, Jr., receive high marks from golf enthusiasts. Dining options run the gamut from casual poolside nibbles to high-end. Because the resort was closed at press time, check back in 2011 for its new star rating.

252 rooms. Restaurant, bar. Fitness center. Spa. Beach. Pool. Golf. Tennis. Business center. $351 and up

★★★THE WESTIN PRINCEVILLE OCEAN RESORT VILLAS

3838 Wyllie Road, Princeville, 808-827-8700; www.starwoodhotels.com

Open less than two years, this smart all-suite resort has cheerful, contemporary studio, one- and two-bedroom units with full kitchens, flat-screen TVs, laundry and Westin's signature Heavenly beds. Though the resort does not have direct beach access, the outdoor pools are expansive and lushly landscaped, and have a children's pool with waterslides. Other amenities include a well-equipped workout center, an onsite restaurant, bar and market, ample barbecue grills and picnic facilities and signing privileges at the nearby St. Regis Princeville Resort and access to the resort's golf and tennis facilities.

Restaurant, bar. Pool. Fitness center. Golf. Tennis. $251-350

WHERE TO EAT

★★BAR ACUDA
5-5161 Kuhio Highway, Hanalei, 808-826-7081
Certainly the dressiest of Kauai restaurants (thanks to its smart, tropical-modern décor, candlelight, and creative menu, rather than its dress code, which remains island casual), this tapas restaurant is a local favorite. Chef/owner Jim Moffat is devoted to sourcing fresh, local ingredients and pairing them in combinations that make flavors sing. The menu of small plates changes depending on what's in season, but might include lobster-stuffed squid with romesco sauce, grilled pancetta-wrapped sea scallops or slow-braised beef short ribs. The wine list features plenty of wines by the glass and focuses on Rhone-style varietals.
American. Dinner. Closed Monday. $16-35

★★HANALEI DOLPHIN RESTAURANT
5-5016 Kuhio Highway, Hanalei, 808-826-6113; www.hanaleidolphin.com
This small, tropical restaurant has a delightful personality. By day, it's a casual outdoor patio eatery, located beside the Hanalei River on Kauai's North Shore. Diners eat at circular concrete-formed tables topped by colorful umbrellas along the grassy riverbank. For dinner, the main open-air dining room and a small side lanai are prime spots for sampling seafood and steak dishes. (A fish market affiliated with the restaurant sits behind it.) Try the signature teriyaki ahi, or ginger and soy marinated Hawaiian chicken.
Seafood. Lunch, dinner. Bar. Children's menu. Outdoor seating. $16-35

★HANALEI GOURMET
5-5161 Kuhio Highway, Hanalei, 808-826-2524; www.hanaleigourmet.com
Located in a renovated school building, Hanalei Gourmet is both a restaurant and a deli counter—a great stop for a casual lunch or dinner or to pick up food for a picnic. The diverse menu, which reflects the restaurant's commitment to fresh, local ingredients, makes use of dolphin-free tuna, low-sodium meats, fresh-baked whole-grain breads, and homemade dressings and features sandwiches, salads, and pastas alongside full dinners. Live music several nights a week draws in a fun-loving young crowd.
American. Lunch, dinner. Bar. Children's menu. Outdoor seating. $16-35

★JAVA KAI
5-5183 Kuhio Highway, Hanalei, 808-826-6717
Though there is also a location in Kapaa, the Hanalei store is perpetually packed with tourists and locals alike who come for the fresh-roasted Hawaiian coffee, fruit smoothies and breakfast dishes like the Kauai waffle, a decadent waffle topped with bananas, papaya, whipped cream and nuts. The surfer's sandwich, a humble combo of eggs, bacon and cheese, goes well with the strong espresso shots served at the coffee bar.
American. Breakfast. $15 and under

★★LIGHTHOUSE BISTRO
2484 Keneke St., Kilauea, 808-828-0480; www.lighthousebistro.com
Tucked away in the Kong Lung Center, a small retail center about a mile off the Kuhio Highway in the little town of Kilauea, is a bright, contemporary

restaurant. Just off the road to the historic Kilauea Lighthouse and a National Wildlife Refuge, the bistro's menu features fresh-off-the-boat fish entrées, including ginger-crusted ahi with soy wasabi beurre blanc. Local original art adds color to the bright dining room, which has a vaulted beamed ceiling, terra cotta tile flooring, ceiling fans and a large wine case. Front, side and rear dining lanais provide ample outdoor seating.

Seafood. Lunch, dinner. Bar. Children's menu. Outdoor seating. $16-35

★NEIDE'S SALSA & SAMBA

5-5161 Kuhio Highway, Hanalei, 808-826-1851; www.hanaleicenter.com/restaurants

Brazilian and Mexican dishes are served at this small, casual restaurant at the rear of the Hanalei Center. A tourist favorite for shopping and dining, the center is on Kauai's North Shore alongside the Kuhio Highway. The festive dining room is painted a colorful lime green with pale yellow trim, and the furnishings are covered with island-print fabric. Additional seating is available on a side deck. Entrées such as chicken panqueca and fish tacos are served on heaping platters.

Latin American, Mexican. Lunch, dinner. Bar. Outdoor seating. $15 and under

★★POSTCARDS CAFE

5-5075 Kuhio Highway, Hanalei, 808-826-1191; www.postcardscafe.com

This restaurant, set in a quaint green cottage with white trim, has a casual, laid-back atmosphere. The décor is tropical, with hardwood floors, a beamed ceiling with ceiling fans, and rattan chairs. Seating is available inside or on front and side lanais, and the menu reflects the kitchen's use of island-grown produce and locally caught seafood—many of the dishes are vegetarian-friendly. Entrées include wasabi crusted ahi and seafood Sorrento.

Seafood. Dinner. Reservations recommended. Outdoor seating. $36-85

★TROPICAL TACO

5-5088 Kuhio Highway, Hanalei, 808-827-8226; www.tropicaltaco.com

In this small, super-casual eatery, Mexican cuisine is transported to Kauai and infused with fish from island waters. Fish tacos are the specialty of the house. The restaurant is located in the center of Hanalei, within the Halale Building on the town's main street. The proprietor ran a taco wagon for 20 years and then moved his operation indoors, keeping visual reminders of his old business on the kitchen's rear wall. Orders are taken at the kitchen window, and seating is available inside or at stools at the front porch railing.

Mexican. Lunch, dinner. Closed Sunday. Outdoor seating. No credit cards accepted. $15 and under

★ZELO'S BEACH HOUSE

5-5156 Kuhio Highway, Hanalei, 808-826-9700;

This popular casual eatery on Hanalei's main street offers pupus (Hawaiian appetizers), fresh seafood and American fare, with a thatched-roof bar that specializes in tropical drinks and martinis. The lunch menu consists primarily of burgers and sandwiches, but more substantial entrée choices are available at dinner. Occupying a plantation-style building, the restaurants décor is Hawaiian tropical, with glass-topped bamboo tables, ceiling fans and servers

dressed in colorful tank tops and shorts.
American, seafood. Lunch, dinner. Bar. Children's menu. Outdoor seating.
$16-35

SOUTH SHORE KAUAI

On Kauai, there's a very good reason the South Shore is the most popular area with visitors: the sun. It's almost always shining brightly on that shoreline, no matter what the weather is like anywhere else on the island.

The place to stay down south is Poipu, a peaceful resort with luxury hotels, several condominium complexes, and a few bed and breakfasts spread out over many, many acres of prime oceanfront property. In addition to a wide variety of accommodations, it has all the requisite amenities: two stellar golf courses designed by Robert Trent Jones Jr., a pleasant shopping center (with more stores in nearby Koloa, a quaint former plantation town), and good beaches. Families, in particular, like Poipu Beach because the usually calm water makes it safe for children.

There is one hitch: if you want to go touring, reaching the more scenic, rainier North Shore by car from Poipu can take an hour or more.

You can get about 20 minutes closer and still get plenty of sunshine in Lihue, Kauai's county seat and home to the island's airport. It isn't as tranquil a setting as Poipu, but it's a good option because a large Marriott fronts Lihue's Kalapaki Beach, another family-friendly spot. The golfing is above par at the Marriott, too, with two Jack Nicklaus-designed courses.

In Lihue, hone your knowledge of Hawaii's oldest island at the Kauai Museum, dine at one of the bargain-priced restaurants popular with locals, and check out the stores at Kukui Grove, the isle's largest shopping mall.

WHAT TO SEE
ALLERTON GARDEN
Lawai Road, Poipu, 808-742-2623; www.ntbg.org

Allerton Garden is one of two National Tropical Botanical Gardens on Kauai's south side. At Allerton, once a private estate, you'll see very formal gardens dressed up with fountains, sculptures and pools on more than 100 acres. Only 2 1/2 guided tours are offered, which must be reserved in advance. At the adjacent McBryde Garden, which covers more than 250 acres, the emphasis shifts to tropical flora from around the world. You'll see rare and endangered Hawaiian species, in particular, and learn what's being done to help them thrive. Reservations are not required for the self-guided tours, which also last about 2 1/2 hours.

Allerton: Monday-Saturday, with tours departing at 9 a.m., 10 a.m., 1 p.m., and 2 p.m. McBryde: Monday-Saturday, with tours departing every hour on the half-hour from 9:30 a.m.-2:30 p.m.

CAPTAIN ANDY'S SAILING ADVENTURES
Port Allen Marina Center, Waialo Road, Eleele, 808-335-6833, 800-535-0830; www.capt-andys.com

Board one of Captain Andy's luxury catamarans and see the verdant and mountainous island of Kauai from offshore. As you sail across the deep blue water, the view of the island is one you may never forget. The company's three tours last from 2 to 5 1/2 hours. On the snorkel tour, see all the tropical marine life that lives

STAYING SAFE IN HAWAII'S WATERS

The Pacific Ocean, which seduces visitors with breathtaking beauty and average temperatures of 74 degrees, is just one of the reasons to visit the Hawaiian islands. But the ocean can change overnight—riptides and other less-than-ideal conditions can develop seemingly at a whim. It's important to respect the sea's power and understand what to do should you find yourself in an undesirable situation.

1. Always swim facing away from the beach; rogue waves have been known to sneak up and carry unsuspecting swimmers out to sea. Should that happen, try to swim with the wave until it dissipates, which will happen in 50 to 100 yards. If you get caught in a riptide, swim parallel to the shore until you no longer feel a pull.

2. If you've never surfed before, don't begin without proper instruction, especially in the winter, when waves are rough. If the waves seem too powerful to swim, seek a sheltered beach. Above all, never swim alone.

3. Wear protective footwear, such as reef slippers, when walking in the ocean, and check for rocks and coral on the ocean floor. Wear shoes when wading in shallow tidepools, which can yield poisonous sea urchins. They will pierce your foot if you step on them, and the burn is fierce. Vinegar, wine or urine (remember the Friends episode?) will take out the sting. The tip of the sea urchin, which is the part that stays in your foot, will disintegrate in a few days.

4. Jellyfish come on shore one week to ten days after a full moon. Their long tentacles will sting if they touch you. To soothe the area, rinse with saltwater (not fresh) or rubbing alcohol, aftershave lotion or meat tenderizer.

5. More than 35 varieties of sharks patrol the island waters. Fortunately, encounters with any of them are rare. If you see one, swim back to shore quickly and quietly.

6. Finally, learn the meaning of the yellow, diamond-shaped signs that provide important warnings. They'll inform you about everything from dangerous shore breaks to strong currents. Ask the lifeguard on duty about ocean conditions, and if you're inexperienced at identifying them yourself, stick to sunbathing on beaches with no lifeguard.

beneath the surface in the waters off the gorgeous Na Pali Coast, where giant sea cliffs jut up high into the sky. On the sunset dinner cruise, see that heavenly coast while you nosh and watch the sun disappear into the ocean. For a shorter time at sea, opt for the Poipu sunset cruise and the great views of the sunny south coast. Tours leave from both Kukuiula Small Boat Harbor in Poipu and Port Allen in Eleele. Captain Andy also offers action-packed rafting trips to Na Pali.
Daily, various times.

CATAMARAN KAHANU
Eleeele, 808-335-3577, 888-213-7711; www.catamarankahanu.com
Climb aboard the Kahanu for a memorable Hawaiian experience. On these 3 1/2- to 5-hour tours, your captain takes you on a breathtaking tour to the Na Pali coast while providing insight into the history and culture of Hawaii. You'll see lava tubes, sea caves, picture-perfect waterfalls, dolphins and porpoises frolicking alongside the catamaran, and maybe even some humpback whales if you're there between January and April. Some tours include stops for snorkeling, where you can explore tropical reefs and observe some of the hundreds of species of fish found in the area. (All snorkeling gear is provided, and lessons are given to beginners.) Tours depart daily Monday through Saturday, and a buffet lunch or snack is included.

CJM COUNTRY STABLES

Koloa, 808-742-6096; www.cjmstables.com

Climb aboard a quarter horse for a tour of the Garden Isle. The scenic valley beach ride includes two hours roaming the sunny South Shore. On the three-hour secret picnic beach ride, you'll pass through ranch land and farm crops on your way to a scenic shoreline and coastal bays. For some added excitement, the ranch stages rousing rodeos every month.

Monday-Saturday, various times.

GROVE FARM HOMESTEAD MUSEUM

4050 Nawiliwili Road, Lihue, 808-245-3203; www.hawaiimuseums.org

Once, the sugar industry, not the tourist trade, ruled the Hawaiian Islands. Visit the 80-acre Grove Farm Homestead, and you'll be transported back to that sweet era. George Wilcox started operating the homestead as a full-fledged sugar plantation in 1864, but it was converted into a museum in 1978. The grounds remain much as they did in Wilcox's lifetime, with the family house, a plantation office, workers houses, beautiful gardens, poultry and livestock.

Guided tours: Monday, Wednesday, Thursday 10 a.m. and 1 p.m.

HARBOR MALL

3501 Rice St., Lihue, 808-245-6255; www.harbormall.net

For one-stop shopping, head to Harbor Mall in Nawiliwili Harbor. In addition to beachwear, arts and crafts, souvenirs, and Hawaiian shirts, the mall offers a day spa, kayak rentals, restaurants and even a wedding chapel.

HILO HATTIE

3252 Kuhio Highway, Lihue, 808-245-3404; www.hilohattie.com

Throughout Hawaii, this retail chain targets tourists, and tourists buy plenty of what it sells. Its factory-made aloha shirts, muumuus and other colorful island apparel aren't high fashion or particularly original designs, but they're appealing, comfortable and priced right. This store also sells anything and everything Hawaiian. You can buy books, jewelry, CDs, food gifts and more. To make shopping easy, the store offers a free shuttle from some resort areas.

Daily 8:30 a.m.-6:30 p.m.

HOLOHOLO CHARTERS

4353 Waialo Road, Eleele, 808-335-0815, 800-848-6130;
www.holoholokauaiboattours.com

Holoholo's various boating tours run from 2 to 7 1/2 hours. You can opt for a champagne dinner sunset sail, a Na Pali sunset sail, a Na Pali sail or a Niihau and Na Pali sail. The latter two include snorkeling stops so you can get a glimpse of the colorful sea life beneath the surface. Depending on which tour you choose, you'll ply the waters off Kauai in one of three vessels—a high-speed 65-foot power catamaran or a 50-foot sailing catamaran. All tours leave from Port Allen.

Daily, various times.

KALAPAKI BEACH

Rice Street, Lihue

For families, a beach doesn't get much better than this. Kalapaki is partially protected from the open ocean, so the water is usually calm, making for ideal swimming conditions, even for little ones (except sometimes in winter, when high surf can occasionally pose a danger). It's also a good place for novices to learn water sports, such as boogie-boarding, surfing and windsurfing. The sandy beach itself is long and wide, making it a perfect place for sunbathing. At nearby Nawiliwili Park, you'll find picnic facilities. You won't have this beach to yourself, though, as it fronts the large Kauai Marriott Resort, and is popular with locals who live in nearby Lihue, the islands main city.
Daily dawn-dusk.

KAUAI ATV TOURS

Kalaheo, 808-742-2734, 877-707-7088; www.kauaiatv.com

Climb aboard an easy-to-drive all-terrain vehicle for a revved-up, fast-paced off-road escapade. On the four-hour Waterfall Tour, you'll enjoy a picnic lunch at Kahili Falls and cool off with a refreshing swim when you're not zooming around the backcountry taking in the views. On the three-hour Koloa Tour, you'll venture along miles and miles of old sugar-cane roads, steer your way through acres of tall buffalo grass, and make stops at a popular movie site and an extinct cinder core for a 360-degree view of Kauai's sunny South Shore. All drivers must be age 16 or older, but children ages 5 to 15 can ride in a two-seater driven by an adult or a six-seater driven by one of ATVs guides.
Daily, at various times.

KAUAI BACKCOUNTRY ADVENTURES

Kuhio Highway, Hanama'ulu, 808-245-2506, 888-270-0555;
www.kauaibackcountry.com

See Kauai's lush backcountry on a 3 1/2-hour all-terrain tour, where you drive your very own ATV (led by a certified guide) through miles of isolated forests and fields. There is even a stop for a short hike to a waterfall. If the thought of getting a birds-eye view of this area appeals to you, try the zipline adventure tour. After being taken high above Kauai in a four-wheel-drive vehicle, make your way to the valley floor (with a guide) via a zip course—a series of cables to which you are attached by a harness. Another option includes a float tour down winding tunnels and open ditches—once a part of a sugar plantation—during which you'll see the amazing scenery of the coast and surrounding valleys. The tour starts at the wettest place on Earth (near the top of Mount Waialeale), so be prepared to get drenched. All tours include a picnic lunch and all the equipment you'll need (as well as thorough safety instructions for the ATV and Zipline tours). Just bring plenty of sunscreen, a towel, and your sense of adventure.

KAUAI BACKCOUNTRY WATER TUBING ADVENTURES

Hanamaulu, 808-245-2506, 888-270-0555; www.kauaibackcountry.com

In the late 1800s, workers built a very long ditch and tunnel system to irrigate the sugar crops cultivated on the Lihue Plantation. Now obsolete for watering purposes, the system has been converted into a fun excursion for visitors to the island. Parents and their kids (ages 5 and up) settle into inner tubes and spend about an hour floating along the ditches and through the tunnels, enjoying spectacular views of the ocean, coastline and valleys along the way. The scenic water ride ends with a picnic meal and swimming in a natural swimming hole.

Monday-Saturday 9 a.m., 10:30 a.m., 1 p.m., 2:30 p.m.

KAUAI COFFEE COMPANY

Highway 540, Eleele, 808-335-0813, 800-545-8605; www.kauaicoffee.com

With 3,400 acres devoted to growing coffee on Kauai's southwest side, this company ranks as Hawaii's largest coffee grower. Drop by its visitor center and gift shop for a lesson in how the company grows and harvests the beans in the island's rich volcanic soil, and how they're processed and graded. Sample some of the various brews and buy some of your favorites to take home.

Daily 9 a.m.-5 p.m.

KAUAI FRUIT & FLOWER CO.

3-4684 Kuhio Highway, Lihue, 808-245-1814, 800-943-3108; www.kauaifruit.com

This store ships everything it sells, which includes all types of Hawaii-grown flowers and fruits, from proteas and orchids to papayas and pineapples. It also stocks gift baskets, jams and syrups made with Kauai products.

Monday-Saturday 8 a.m.-5 p.m.

HAWAIIAN MUSIC

Hawaii has more to offer than sunny beaches ideal for swimming and sunbathing and gorgeous valleys perfect for exploring. Island music also hits some high notes. It features a soothing sound that's distinctively Hawaiian, with empahsis on instruments such as the ukelele, slack-key guitar and steel guitar.

No, it's not big on the mainland or in international circles, but Hawaiian music is a hot draw locally. Throughout the islands, numerous artists and groups have made names for themselves and regularly attract crowds of locals to their shows and concerts--the Brothers Cazimero, the Makaha Sons, Keali Reichel, Nathan Aweau, and Na Palapalai, to name a few. Before his death, the late Israel Kamakawiwoole had quite a loyal following, too.

The scene is big enough to warrant the Na Hoku Hanohano Awards every spring, considered Hawaii's version of the Grammy Awards. Among the categories are Female Vocalist of the Year, Male Vocalist of the Year, Hawaiian Language Peformance of the Year, Contemporary Hawaiian Album of the Year, and Most Promising New Artist.

The entertaining music is multifaceted and comes in many forms. The traditional version is just what you would expect--Hawaiian lyrics backed by one of the instruments mentioned before. But other artists lean to other styles, such as falsetto,which featueres high-pitched singing; Jawaiian, which gives Caribbean reggae a Hawaiian twist; and chants, in which sacred tunes from the past get an updated spin.

Several Web sites, including www.hawaii-music.com and www.mele.com, do a good job of orienting newcomers to this memorable island music. They review new CDs, spotlight some of the hottest artists, and list schedules of who's playing when and where. Taking in the sounds at a festival is another way to get introduced to the music. For example, each June, the Hawaiian Slack-Key Guitar Fetival sounds off at the Maui Arts and Cultural Center in Kahului. Similar events are hosted by King Kamehameha's Kona Beach Hotel in Kailua-Kona on the Big Island each July and the Kauai Marriott Resort in Lihue each November.

KAUAI LAGOONS GOLF CLUB

3351 Hoolaulea Way, Lihue, 808-241-6000, 800-634-6400; www.kauailagoonsgolf.com

Take your pick from two Jack Nicklaus-designed courses. The par-72, 7,070-yard Kiele Course, a dramatic-looking beauty, takes you alongside ocean cliffs, through lush valleys, and around many freshwater lagoons. The greens are as challenging as they are pretty, with some tough shots over ravines. By contrast, the par-72, 6,960-yard Mokihana Course is a Scottish Links gem with open fairways and well-guarded, small undulating greens. It's easier to play and more forgiving off the tees, so it's the better bet for resort players with higher handicaps. Amenities include a clubhouse, pro shop, practice greens, driving range, restaurant and snack bar.

Monday-Friday 6:30 a.m.-6 p.m., Saturday-Sunday 6:45 a.m.-6 p.m.; last tee-off at 2 p.m.

KAUAI MUSEUM

4428 Rice St., Lihue, 808-245-6931; www.kauaimuseum.org

While vacationing in paradise, perhaps you'd like to learn about the culture and history of the Garden Isle. If so, venture away from the sandy beach and into this museum, which focuses on both Kauai and Niihau, the so-called "forbidden island." The impressive permanent collection includes more than 5,000 photos that date back to 1890; myriad works of art; more than 50 Hawaiian quilts and other textiles; thousands of cultural materials, from feather work and fiber mats to drum and bark cloth; and many historical pieces, from Hawaiian saddles and World War II memorabilia to Asian dolls and scrimshaw. The onsite gift shop is a great place to pick up high-quality Hawawiiana, from Niihau shell necklaces to lauhala bags.

Monday-Friday 9 a.m.-4 p.m., Saturday 10 a.m.-4 p.m.

KAUAI NATURE TOURS

Koloa, 808-742-8305, 888-233-8365; www.kauainaturetours.com

The well-informed naturalists and scientists who lead these hiking tours open your eyes to details you'd probably never notice or know about on your own. For example, on the Sleeping Giant Mountain Excursion, they explain the role the island's geologic history plays in its climate and ecosystems. On the Na Pali Hiking Adventure, they point out coastal valleys where the island's early human occupants lived more than 700 years ago. Several other treks explore other major regions of the island. To ensure a personal touch, groups are typically kept small, with no more than ten hikers.

Tour dates and times scheduled upon request.

KAUAI SEA TOURS

4310 Waialo Road, Eleele, 808-826-7254, 800-733-7997; www.kauaiseatours.com

Experience the beauty of the Na Pali coast up close on a tour aboard a luxury catamaran. The Lucky Lady takes you on a full- or half-day tour on which you'll encounter frolicking dolphins, view ancient sites, snorkel in clear blue waters, and enjoy a meal on board or a picnic on the beach. You can also just take in the spectacular scenery while learning about the history of Hawaii and the legends of Na Pali as your captain narrates. More adventurous types may be interested in the company's rafting tours, which allow exploration of areas that larger boats can't reach. On these tours, you'll hike through an ancient village, visit secluded beach areas, examine sea caves and snorkel at a variety of sites.

Tours vary by season.

KIAHUNA GOLF CLUB

2545 Kiahuna Plantation Drive, Koloa, 808-742-9595; www.kiahunagolf.com

When Robert Trent Jones, Jr. designed Kiahuna, he used many of the ancient remnants already on the land, so you'll encounter natural obstacles such as lava tubes, a crypt, a heaiau and the remains of a Portuguese house. Nearly 70 deep bunkers, abundant water hazards, and large undulating greens also help make play challenging, but rewarding, on this par-70, 6,885-yard course. The amenities include a pro shop and restaurant.

Daily 7 a.m.-6:30 p.m.; last tee time 2 p.m.

KIAHUNA SWIM AND TENNIS CLUB

2290 Poipu Road, Koloa, 808-742-9533; www.kiahunatennisclub.com

This recreation facility is located at the Outrigger Kiahuna Plantation condominium complex, but it's open to the public for a fee. The 82,000-gallon pool includes a waterslide. Adults may prefer the 1,600-gallon spa with 10 hydrotherapy jets and submerged bench seating. The tennis club has 10 courts and a tennis shop, where you can rent equipment, buy tennis apparel, sign up for lessons, or arrange for a playing partner to try overpowering with all those dazzling shots you've been perfecting.

Pool: daily 8:30 a.m.-5:30 p.m. Tennis: daily dawn-dusk.

KILOHANA PLANTATION

3-2087 Highway 50, Kalaheo, 808-245-5608

At this eye-catching, 35-acre estate, a former sugar plantation, you'll find several quaint specialty shops and art galleries—most inside the striking 16,000-square-foot Tudor-style mansion, but a few others in cozy guest cottages scattered about the well-manicured grounds. Take time out from shopping to look around the antique-filled mansion, built in the 1930s, and perhaps satisfy your appetite with the fine dining at Gaylord's restaurant. For a fee, you can enjoy a horse-drawn carriage ride around the estate or tour a sugar-cane field.

Monday-Saturday 9:30 a.m.-9:30 p.m., Sunday 9:30 a.m.-5 p.m.

KOLOA FISH MARKET

5482 Koloa Road, Koloa, 808-742-6199

This tiny shop in historic Koloa delivers a perfect opportunity to experience a Hawaiian plate lunch. The no-frills space serves delicious platters of kalua pork with sides of rice and macaroni salad (the elements of a traditional "plate lunch") to go. Or try the many different kinds of fresh poke (salty, marinated raw fish) by the pound, including teryaki ahi, tako, spicy ahi and more. You can also load up on the fresh catch of the day at reasonable prices and pick up local desserts and pupu to complete your meal.

Monday-Friday 10 a.m.-6 p.m., Saturday 10 a.m.-5 p.m.

KUKUI GROVE CENTER

3-2600 Kaumualii Highway, Lihue, 808-245-7784; www.kukuigrovecenter.com

Visit more than 50 retailers at Kauai's largest shopping mall, just a few miles from the islands airport. Macys and Sears are the anchor department stores; the other two anchors are Longs Drugs and Star Market, a popular grocer with locals. You'll also find a cinema that showcases the latest Hollywood releases as well as several restaurants, including nationally known fast-food chains.

Monday-Thursday, Saturday 9:30 a.m.-7 p.m., Friday 9:30 a.m.-9 p.m., Sunday 10 a.m.-6 p.m.

KUKUIOLONO GOLF COURSE

854 Puu Road, Kalaheo, 808-332-9151

Nowhere on Kauai will you find a better deal on a golf course, with daily green fees of just $8. Of course, there are only nine holes, but you can play them multiple times in a day. The par-36, 3,173-yard course is good for beginners because it has wide fairways and few hazards. Kukuiolono was originally the private course of sugar magnate Walter D. McBryde, who willed it to the county many years ago. It sits atop a volcano and offers good views of the islands south side. The course is part of a larger park with a small, but attractive, Japanese Garden.

Daily 6:30 a.m.-6:30 p.m.

LAHELA OCEAN ADVENTURES

2849 Luina St., Lihue, 808-635-4020; www.lahela-adventures.com

Have you ever dreamed of catching a blue marlin at sea? Board the 34-foot Lahela and cast your line—you just might hook one, then battle to reel it in. Opt for a private or shared charter, depending on how much you're willing to spend for the adventure. You don't have to be a seasoned angler, either; the crew shows novices the tricks to catching the really big ones. The captain also takes visitors out reef fishing for much smaller catch, such as blue line snapper or squirrel fish. Or take one of the more relaxing whale-watching cruises or a snorkeling and sightseeing trek along the North Shore.

Daily, various times.

LAWAI BEACH

Lawai Road, Koloa

This small, somewhat rocky beach on the South Shore isn't anywhere near as big or popular as Poipu Beach, but it's an alternative worth considering, especially if you want to do some good snorkeling. You'll see lots of fish in the clear water. Lawai can have seasonal strong currents, however, so don't venture too far away from the shoreline when the surf is up.

Daily dawn-dusk.

LIHUE HELIPORT

Ahukini Road, Lihue

Visitors arrive and depart from Lihue Airport, but you might want to return to this transportation center even before you're ready to leave the island. From its heliport, several companies take off for helicopter tours of Kauai that feature spectacular views. And on the Garden Isle, there is plenty to see from that high-altitude vantage point—the Na Pali Coast, Mount Waialeale, Waimea Canyon, Hanalei Valley and more. Tours typically last from 60 to 90 minutes. Some of the companies include Blue Hawaiian Helicopters *(808-245-8500)*, Island Helicopters *(808-245-8588)* and Jack Harter Helicopters *(808-245-3774; www.helicopters-kauai.com)*.

LYDGATE BEACH AND STATE PARK
Kuhio Highway, Kapaa; www.kauai-hawaii.com
Families prefer this beach, and not just because it's one of the few Kauai beaches with lifeguards. It also has good, calm swimming conditions and two boulder-enclosed pools—one that's especially good for snorkeling and a smaller one that's safe for young ones to splash around in. The park also includes a well-equipped, 6,000-square-foot playground. Picnic facilities, shade trees and grassy areas add to this coastal park's appeal.
Daily dawn-dusk.

MAHAULEPU BEACH
Poipu Road, Poipu; www.kauai-hawaii.com
Strong currents and high surf usually make this beach dangerous for swimming, but Mahaulepu's striking looks makes it a wonderful spot to explore. Take in the sensational views from atop a rocky bluff on the eastern end, and you'll understand why so many people dub Hawaii paradise. To reach this remote beauty, you must travel across private land (the owner permits public access) and drive along dirt sugar-cane roads.
Daily dawn-dusk.

MEDEIROS FARMS
4365 Papalina Road, Kalaheo, 808-332-8211
Ask Kauai locals about where to buy fresh meat, and they're likely to mention this store on the island's south side. It gets raves for its farm-fresh chicken and eggs, grass-fed beef, smoked pork and sausages. Consider shopping here if you're staying in a condo with a kitchen or if you're headed out to a park for a barbecue.
Monday-Friday 8 a.m.-5 p.m., Saturday 8 a.m.-3 p.m.

NATIONAL TROPICAL BOTANICAL GARDEN
4425 Lawai Road, Koloa, 808-742-2623; www.ntbg.org
Established in 1964, the National Tropical Botanical Garden is home to a collection of some of the most beautiful and rare Hawaiian flora in existence. Its three gardens on Kauai (as well as one on Maui and one in Florida) were created not only to allow the public to enjoy and learn about these various plant species, but also to advance scientific research and conservation. The 252-acre McBryde Garden, located on Kauai's South Shore, is home to the largest collection of endangered Hawaiian plant life. It also includes research and education facilities that house more than 27,000 dried plant specimens. The adjacent Allerton Garden, situated on 100 breathtaking acres, was once a sanctuary for Hawaii's Queen Emma. Here you'll find a number of exotic flowers and plants along with exquisite sculptures, serene pools, and the

captivating Moreton Bay fig trees that were featured in the movie *Jurassic Park*. The largest of Kauai's three gardens, the 1,000-acre Limahuli Garden, is located on the lush North Shore. Due to its ongoing conservation efforts and educational and research programs, Limahuli was recognized in 1997 as the best natural botanic garden in the United States by the American Horticultural Society. Tours of the gardens depart daily from the visitor center and usually last 2 1/2 hours.

Daily 8:30 a.m.-5 p.m.

OLD KOLOA TOWN

Koloa Road, Koloa

On the road to Poipu, you'll pass through this small town and drive along its main street—Koloa Road—which is lined with more than 20 shops and restaurants in restored plantation buildings. You'll find stores such as Crazy Shirts, the delicious Lapperts Ice Cream and Sueoka Store, a local supermarket with a to-go snack bar that sells affordable breakfast and lunch meals.

Daily, various times.

OUTFITTERS KAUAI

2827A Poipu Road, Poipu, 808-742-9667, 888-742-9887; www.outfitterskauai.com

When you're ready for outdoor adventure anywhere on the island, dial up Outfitters Kauai. Its trips take you kayaking along a 15-mile stretch of the Na Pali Coast or 8 miles along the South Shore for some sensational sightseeing; biking 13 miles downhill from the rim of Waimea Canyon; or paddling down a jungle stream, then hiking into a lush rain forest for a swim under a waterfall.

Daily, various times.

POIPU BAY GOLF COURSE

2250 Ainako St., Koloa, 808-742-8711, 800-858-6300; www.poipubaygolf.com

Any course picked to host the PGA Grand Slam of Golf tournament every year has to be something special, and Poipu Bay is just that. The par-72, 7,081-yard links-style course, designed by Robert Trent Jones, Jr., sits on 210 acres of prime oceanfront property adjacent to the Hyatt Regency Kauai Resort. The course is sandwiched between gorgeous mountains and ocean bluffs, so the views are terrific, and it includes 86 sand-filled bunkers as well as water hazards on 11 of the holes. There is a GPS system available to help improve your shots and score. In addition, the golf pros offer daily clinics. The amenities include a golf shop and a grill and bar.

Daily 6:30 a.m.-6:30 p.m.

POIPU BEACH

Hoowili Road, Koloa, www.kauai-hawaii.com

Because the water at this South Shore beach is usually calm, Poipu is good for swimming, snorkeling and scuba diving. It also has some decent waves that even beginner surfers can manage. You'll find plenty of sand and grassy areas for sunbathing. In fact, Poipu is actually made up of several crescent beaches, so you have your pick of places to kick back and soak up the rays. Tidal pools at one end of the beach keep kids occupied and happy. Besides

lifeguards, Poipu Beach Park has plenty of facilities, from restrooms and outdoor showers to barbecue grills and picnic tables.
Daily dawn-dusk.

POIPU SHOPPING VILLAGE
2360 Kiahuna Plantation Drive, Koloa, 808-742-2831
You won't find any big-name chain stores in this open-air shopping center located just a short drive from Poipu's hotels and condos. Instead, the 20 or so retailers are locally owned shops and boutiques that are pleasant to browse through for souvenirs, gifts, art, jewelry, resort wear and more. Especially noteworthy is Hale Mana, where upscale gift s will surely catch your eye. The village is also home to two dining hot spots—Keoki's Paradise and Roy's Poipu Bar and Grill.
Monday-Saturday 9:30 a.m.-9:30 p.m., Sunday 10 a.m.-7 p.m.

POIPU SOUTHSHORE MARKET
Koloa Bypass Road, Koloa
Whenever you need fresh produce on the South Shore, you can do your shopping at this farmer's market. The vendors sell all types of wonderful-looking fruits and vegetables, but the market is known especially for its fresh and tasty asparagus, and even overlooks asparagus fields cultivated by Haupu Growers.
Daily 10 a.m.-6 p.m.

PRINCE KUHIO PARK
Lawai Road, Poipu
Visit this park to honor Hawaiian royalty, mainly Prince Jonah Kuhio Kalanianaole. The popular prince, the last heir to the Hawaiian throne, was born in the Poipu area in 1871. He did so much for the Hawaiian people as a Congressman in Washington, the locals still celebrate his birthday every year in March. The park includes the remnants of his royal home, his fishpond and a heiau.
Daily dawn-dusk.

PUAKEA GOLF COURSE
4150 Nuhou St., Lihue, 808-245-8756, 866-773-5554; www.puakeagolf.com
While in Lihue, avid golfers will want to play a round on this 18-hole course at the base of Mount Haupu. Because it was built around winding ravines and streams, the course is both challenging and beautiful. Tee times can be booked up to 30 days in advance.
Daily 7 a.m.-6 p.m.

SCUBA DIVING
Fathom Five Divers, 3450 Poipu Road, Koloa
Explore Kauai's colorful and exotic underwater world with a scuba dive. Whether you are a beginner or an advanced diver, you'll find a wide range of courses to suit your needs. Among the trips offered by Fathom Five Divers *(3450 Poipu Road, Koloa, 800-972-3078; www.fathomfive.com)* are a half-day introductory dive for beginners, a refresher dive for certified divers who haven't dived in more than two years, and dives designed exclusively for

advanced certified divers. In addition to courses for all skill levels, Seasport Divers *(2827 Poipu Road, Koloa, 808-742-9303; and 4-976 Kuhio Highway, Kapaa, 808-823-9222; www.kauaiscubadiving.com)* offers programs for children: in the Bubblemakers Program, 8- and 9-year-olds dive in a shallow pool with an instructor. Those who aren't quite ready to scuba dive but still want to see marine life may want to consider booking a trip with Snuba Tours of Kauai *(1604 Papau Place, Kapaa, 808-823-8912; www.snubakauai.com)*. Part snorkeling and part scuba diving, it is a shallow-water diving experience where you are attached to a raft on the water's surface by a 20-foot air line. A certified professional diver accompanies all dives and tours, and equipment is provided.

SPOUTING HORN
Lawai Road, Poipu
Gushes of water shoot up to 50 feet in the air whenever waves force water into the lava tubes just offshore Poipu Beach. But this blowhole also has a legend attached to it—Hawaiians believe the hissing sound made whenever water enters the blowhole is a lizard goddess expressing her anger at being trapped in the tube. As the story goes, the goddess tried to eat a fisherman, who escaped her by swimming under the tube. Supposedly, when she went after him, she got stuck in the tube, where she remains.
Daily dawn-dusk.

SURFING SCHOOLS
Lihue
The instructors at Garden Island Surf School *(Lawai, 808-652-4841; www.gardenislandsurfschool.com)* have been surfing most of their lives and boast a 97 percent student success rate. Kauai Surf School *(Koloa, 808-332-7411; www.kauaisurfschool.com)* is run by professional surfers. All classes are small (no more than four people), but individual lessons are offered at both schools. Although most surfing schools welcome students of all ages, some are designed exclusively for the keiki, such as Unique Technique Surf School *(808-346-0481)*. Here, kids ages 4 to 10 are given instruction in shallow water (1-2 feet) and use soft surfboards to ride the small waves of a sand-bottom beach. Lessons usually last from 1 1/2 to 2 hours, and all equipment is provided.

SPECIAL EVENT
WAIMEA TOWN CELEBRATION
Waimea, 808-245-3971
This annual two-day festival, held at the Old Waimea Sugar Mill, celebrates Waimea's multiethnic history with sporting events and other contests, a carnival, and plenty of food.
February.

WHERE TO STAY
★★★GRAND HYATT KAUAI RESORT AND SPA
1571 Poipu Road, Koloa, 808-742-1234, 800-492-8804; www.hyatt.com
This massive resort is one of the island's premier beach and golf complexes.

The lush grounds feature manicured gardens, lawns, waterfalls, lagoons, and, of course, a wonderful sandy beach. Spacious guest rooms, including 37 suites, are decorated in classic Hawaiian style and have views of the ocean or the Haupu Mountains, with outdoor lanais. Amenities include flat-screen TVs, Portico bath products and iPod docking stations. The Robert Trent Jones Jr.-designed golf course has a high-tech in-cart satellite navigation system that tells golfers the exact distance to the hole and the placement of the pin. There are also daily clinics and group tournaments. Parents can take advantage of Camp Hyatt for kids (with a special night camp option); and anyone who wants to be pampered can visit the expansive spa, which features an alfresco whirlpool and lounge area. Activities also include horseback riding, snorkeling, and kayaking, as well as the twice-weekly Drums of Paradise luau and a variety of shops. The resort's many restaurants and lounges offer an ample array of cuisines and tropical drinks.

602 rooms. Restaurant, bar. Fitness center. Spa. Beach. Pool. Golf. Tennis. Business center. $351 and up

★★★HILTON KAUAI BEACH RESORT
4331 Kauai Beach Drive, Lihue, 808-245-1955, 800-774-1500; www.hilton.com

Located ten minutes north of Lihue Airport on Kauai's east coast, this resort—a sunrise property facing east—has a broad, 3-mile beachfront. Three pools are available for those who prefer freshwater swimming. The 35-acre grounds are tropically landscaped with waterfalls, fountains, ponds, and lava rock grottos; guest rooms also feature tropical décor. Beds are topped with down duvets and the rooms have been updated with MP3 players. There are many activities and facilities for visitors, including a beachside massage cabana, tennis courts, a nightly Tahitian dancing and torch-lighting ceremony, and a twice-weekly luau.

265 rooms. Restaurant, bar. Fitness center. Beach. Pool. Tennis. Business center. $251-350

★★★KAUAI MARRIOTT RESORT AND BEACH CLUB
3610 Rice St., Lihue, 808-245-5050, 800-220-2925; www.marriott.com

Overlooking Kalapaki Bay and Beach on Kauai's southeast coast, this major golf and beach resort within the 800-acre Kauai Lagoons Resort complex includes three towers set around an elaborately landscaped courtyard. The lush tropical area—with a lagoon, waterfalls, and waterfowl—and the adjacent lobby are reached by Kauai's only escalator, which drops down from the porte-cochere. The tropical-themed rooms at the resort are ready for an update, but were set to undergo a renovation to be completed in the summer of 2009. Resort facilities and guest services are quite expansive; they include two Jack Nicklaus-designed golf courses, five pools, tennis courts, multiple Jacuzzis, a jogging trail and the ocean beach with its choice of water sports. The popular and casual Hawaiian-themed eatery Duke's is located onsite.

356 rooms. Restaurant, bar. Fitness center. Spa. Beach. Pool. Tennis. Business center. $251-350

KO'A KEA HOTEL & RESORT
2251 Poipu Road, Koloa, 808-828-8888, 888-898-8958; www.koakea.com

Opened in April 2009, this upscale boutique hotel was built on the footprint of a property that was destroyed by Hurricane Iniki in 1992, giving it prime positioning on a quiet and attractive stretch of Poipu Beach. With just 121 rooms, Ko'a Kea is intimate and luxurious with appealing and predominantly white beach-chic interior design. Rooms are loaded with top-notch amenities, from Anichini towels and linens to L'Occitane bath products, iPod docking stations, oversized flat-screen TVs and Nespresso coffee machines. Red Salt restaurant is a sophisticated spot for fine dining, and the adjacent bar is a relaxing and stylish space for after dinner drinks. The spa has five treatment rooms and offers massages, facials and wraps using local ingredients (red clay, guava, pineapple). The hotel was newly opened at press time, so check back in 2011 for a Forbes star rating.

121 rooms. Restaurant, bar. Pool. Fitness center. Spa. $351 and up

★★★MARRIOTT'S WAIOHAI BEACH CLUB

2249 Poipu Road, Koloa, 808-742-4400, 800-845-5279

Located on an appealing stretch of Poipu beach, this resort ownership property made up of two-bedroom suites with full kitchens is also available for hotel stays. The rooms are traditional in décor, but include comfortable beds topped with down duvets. Though the resort does not have a restaurant or bar, the onsite deli offers sandwiches, salads and soups at breakfast, lunch and dinner as well as Starbucks coffee. The beachfront access and sprawling pool area makes the resort a popular choice for families.

238 rooms. Fitness center. Pool. $251-350

★★★SHERATON KAUAI RESORT

2400 Hoonani Road, Koloa, 808-741-1661, 888-625-5144

This large resort fronts the beach in Poipu, with rooms spread out over several buildings that span both sides of Hoonani Road. The oceanside rooms have been fully renovated with cheerful blue and yellow décor, down duvets, flat-screen TVs and marble bathrooms; garden rooms on the inland side of the road are slated to become resort ownership rooms, and as such haven't received the same generous update. Still, the resort has plenty of activities for guests of all rooms to enjoy, from a twice-weekly luau (Monday and Friday evenings) to open-air massages by the pool. The resort has four restaurants including a sushi bar, an updated fitness center and a business center equipped with computers with free internet access.

394 rooms. Restaurant, bar. Fitness center. Pool. Tennis. $251-350

WHERE TO EAT

★★★BEACH HOUSE

5022 Lawai Road, Poipu, 808-742-1424; www.the-beach-house.com

Views of lovely sunsets and some of Kauai's best surfing conditions are available from your table at this popular restaurant on the island's South Shore. Overlooking a narrow lawn and the rolling surf of Keawaloa Bay, the Beach House has a nice lounge and a long dining room, both with large plate-glass windows to provide all tables with great ocean views. The Pacific Rim menu features such entrées as macadamia nut-crusted mahi-mahi with miso sauce and blackened ahi Caesar salad.

Pacific-Rim. Dinner. Bar. Children's menu. Reservations recommended. Outdoor seating. $36-85

★BRENNECKE'S BEACH BROILER
2100 Hoone Road, Poipu, 808-742-7588; www.brenneckes.com

Known as a great place to watch the sun set over the Pacific, Brennecke's is somewhat of an institution on Kauai's South Shore. Located across the street from Poipu Beach Park, its second-floor seating provides marvelous views across the park to the ocean. The casual menu features fresh seafood, including entrées such as ginger sesame crusted opah and charbroiled ono with wasabi shrimp.

Seafood. Lunch, dinner. Bar. Children's menu. Reservations recommended. $36-85

★★DUKE'S CANOE CLUB KAUAI
3610 Rice St., Lihue, 808-246-9599; www.dukeskauai.com

This restaurant is a tribute to Hawaii's most famous athlete and goodwill ambassador, Duke Kahanamoku. The world-renowned surfboarding pioneer and Olympic gold medal swimmer is reflected in photos, surfboards and other memorabilia on the restaurant's walls. With an appealing location at the water's edge on Kalapaki Bay adjacent to the Kauai Marriott, the open-air bar and dining room offer a laid back spot to dig into steaks, burgers, salads and fresh grilled fish.

American. Lunch, dinner. Bar. Children's menu. Reservations recommended. Outdoor seating. $16-35

★★★GAYLORD'S
Highway 50, Lihue, 808-245-9593; www.gaylordskauai.com

In the early 20th century, sugar was king on the Garden Isle. Kilohana, just west of Lihue, was a major sugar plantation when a grand Tudor-style estate house was built here in the 1930s. Today, it is the home of this period restaurant, galleries and shops set among 35 acres of tropical gardens and a working farm, which replicates life in the territorial era. Retaining a flavor of these earlier times, original art and antiques grace Gaylord's elegant formal dining and living rooms. An open, slate-floored terrace provides pleasant views of a grassy courtyard. On the menu, you'll find a blend of American and Hawaiian entreés, supported by an extensive wine list. After dinner, rides around the plantation grounds are available in a Clydesdale-drawn white carriage.

Pacific-Rim. Lunch, dinner, brunch. Children's menu. Reservations recommended. Outdoor seating. $16-35

★HAMURA SAIMIN
2956 Kress St., Lihue, 808-245-2371

Saimin is a noodle soup that's very popular throughout Hawaii. Although the recipe is Asian, it originates with immigrants to the islands. This particular restaurant, located on a side street off Lihue's Rice Street on the city's west side, is known throughout Hawaii for the quality of its saimin and its lilikoi (passion fruit) chiffon pie. This is a small, no-frills dining spot that doesn't take reservations, but the serpentine, orange-topped counters are filled with fanciers of saimin every evening.

Chinese, Pacific-Rim, Pan-Asian. Lunch, dinner. No credit cards accepted. $15 and under

★HANAMAULU CAFE
3-4291 Kuhio Highway, Hanamaulu, 808-245-2511

This historic restaurant has been on the same site for more than three-quarters of a century. It is located on the Kuhio Highway (Highway 56) in the small town of Hanamaulu, which is adjacent to Lihue. Although the menu features a combination of Japanese and Chinese cuisine, the décor is primarily Japanese. The front dining room is nondescript, but the rear of the restaurant features a sushi bar, a classical garden teahouse, and traditional private Japanese dining areas, with cushioned seating around sunken tables.

Chinese, Japanese. Lunch, dinner. Bar. Reservations recommended. Outdoor seating. $15 and under

★★KALAHEO STEAK HOUSE
4444 Papalina Road, Kalaheo, 808-332-9780

This unpretentious, upcountry steakhouse offers relaxed dining in a somewhat rustic setting. The spot is very popular with local residents, as it offers generous portions of good food at moderate prices. Steaks, prime rib and seafood are the primary items on the menu. The restaurant is located a block off the Kaumualu Highway in downtown Kalaheo, between Koloa and Waimea—an easy 6- to 8-mile drive from the Poipu Beach resort area.

Seafood, steak. Dinner. Bar. $16-35

★★KEOKI'S PARADISE
2360 Kiahuna Plantation Drive, Poipu, 808-742-7534; www.hulapie.com

Keoki's Paradise is a perfect spot for mainlanders in search of a tropical Eden on Kauai. There is a waterfall at the restaurant's entrance, and the multi-level dining areas face a small, lushly landscaped lagoon, with water rippling down lava rocks at one end. At the entry to the Poipu Shopping Village, adjacent to Poipu Road (the main byway through the Poipu Beach area), the restaurant is romantically lit with tiki torches. The fare is relatively casual for lunch, with more traditional Hawaiian and seafood cuisine served in the evenings.

Pacific-Rim, seafood. Lunch, dinner. Bar. Children's menu. Reservations recommended. Outdoor seating. $16-35

★★ROY'S POIPU BAR & GRILL
2360 Kiahuna Plantation Drive, Poipu, 808-742-5000; www.roysrestaurant.com

Contemporary décor and cuisine can be found at this restaurant belonging to James Beard award-winning chef Roy Yamaguchi. With properties throughout the islands and on the mainland, Yamaguchi's signature cuisine is universally identified as Hawaiian fusion, a blend of European culinary techniques and Asian and Pacific ingredients. This restaurant, located in the Poipu Shopping Village, across the coastal road from the Poipu Beach resorts on the sunny South Shore, has a glass-fronted demonstration kitchen in the main dining room to showcase the chef's artistry.

Pacific-Rim, Pan-Asian. Dinner. Bar. Children's menu. Reservations recommended. $36-85

★★★PLANTATION GARDENS
2253 Poipu Road, Poipu, 808-742-2216;

The entrance to this restaurant is a big part of the attraction of dining here—a

gorgeous landscaped garden filled with blooming orchids of every shape and color lines the path to the quaint plantation-style building that houses the restaurant. Inside the restaurant, which offers open-air dining on its wraparound verandas, the atmosphere is upscale and tropical, with rattan chairs, slow-spinning ceiling fans and plenty of candlelight. The menu focuses on fresh local seafood and vegetables (think curry coconut seafood stew made with locally grown tomatoes or udon noodles topped with locally-grown organic basil pesto). Save room for one of the unique housemade desserts, whether it's passionfruit cheesecake or Baked Hawaiian (chocolate and macadamia nut ice cream on a fudge brownie crust with toasted meringue).
Pacific-Rim. Dinner. Bar. Reservations recommended. $36-85

★★TIDEPOOLS
1571 Poipu Road, Poipu, 808-742-1234; 800-554-9288; www.kauai.hyatt.com
Totally tropical in décor and atmosphere, this casual Pacific Rim restaurant is quintessentially Hawaiian. Dine open air under thatch-roof hales (huts), surrounded by a free-form lagoon with waterfalls, colorful koi and extensive tropical foliage. Located on a white-sand beach on Keoneloa Bay, the restaurant is within the Hyatt Regency Kauai Resort and Spa, on the island's southern coast.
Pacific-Rim, Pan-Asian. Dinner. Bar. Children's menu. Reservations recommended. Outdoor seating. $36-85

★TIP TOP CAFE AND BAKERY
3173 Akahi St., Lihue, 808-245-2333
A Kauai tradition since 1916, this café has been a longtime source of wonderful baked goods. In a nondescript neighborhood of Lihue, one block over and parallel to Curio Highway (Highway 56), this family-run operation shares a site with a rather plain motel. Four generations of the Oto family have operated the property, and such menu items as banana pancakes, macadamia nut cookies (the first in Hawaii), and oxtail soup are quite famous around the island. The immaculate dining room, with all-booth seating, is open for breakfast and lunch and then converted into a Japanese restaurant for dinner.
American. Breakfast, lunch. Closed Monday. $16-35

WEST END
There aren't many good swimming beaches on this side of the island, and no major hotels create fantasy worlds here. Even so, there are some excellent reasons to spend at least a day touring the west end. It would be a big mistake not to.

The two major attractions on this remote side are among the biggest and best ones on the island, and they border one another. The breathtakingly beautiful Waimea Canyon stretches for 10 scenic miles, with two lookout points that offer spectacular views of its deep gorges. Bordering the canyon is the 4,345-acre Kokee State Park, an inviting rain forest with 45 hiking trails—some easy, some challenging—that give hikers plenty of room to walk and absorb nature in terrain up to 4,000 feet above sea level. From a highland lookout in the park that's accessible by car, you can also feast your eyes on the lovely Kalalau Valley.

The small towns on this side of island are sleepy, but that sleepiness adds to their charm. In centuries past, Waimea saw plenty of excitement—Captain James Cook came ashore in 1778, the Russians built a fort and missionaries set up camp in the early 1800s. Hanapepe is a low-key, charming historic hamlet that's worth a stop.

WHAT TO SEE
COLLECTIBLES AND FINE JUNQUE
9821 Highway 50, Waimea, 808-338-9855
Give yourself some time to wander through this delightful store. The owners have a lot to sell, all of it crowded into a small space. You'll get a kick out of discovering the gems hidden among all the merchandise, which includes everything from aloha shirts and glassware to ceramics and chenille bedspreads. Monday-Tuesday 11 a.m.-4 p.m., Wednesday 1-4 p.m., Thursday-Friday 11 a.m.-4 p.m., Saturday 1-4 p.m.

HANAPEPE
Hanapepe Road, Hanapepe
This little town has seen better days, but artists have discovered it and opened some inviting shops and galleries along its main street, Hanapepe Road. You can buy everything from koa wood bowls and Hawaiian tapa to oil paintings and pastels. Every Friday night from 6 to 9 p.m., the gallery owners host Art Walk, a laid-back party where shoppers can leisurely roam from shop to shop and meet some of the talented artists whose work is on display.
Daily, various hours.

KALALAU LOOKOUT
Waimea Canyon Road, Waimea
Just a few miles beyond Kokee State Park is yet another gorgeous view of Kauai that awes visitors. At this scenic spot, you'll see stunning cliffs and lush gorges that disappear into the blue sea 4,000 feet below. Mist and clouds can limit the view, but employees of the park's museum can give you tips on the best times to drive up to the lookout.
Daily dawn-dusk.

KOKEE STATE PARK
Highway 550, 15 miles north of Kekaha, Kekaha, 808-335-9975; www.kokee.org
With its 4,345 acres, 45 trails and an elevation of 3,600 to 4,000 feet, this highland state park atop Waimea Canyon ridge is a hiker's and nature-lover's dream. Within the borders of this massive rain forest live rare birds, rare plants and native mammals. You'll see some of those birds and plants, and maybe even animals, if you set foot on any of the trails, which range from easy to difficult. For maps and information about the trails, stop in at the Kokee Natural History Museum at mile marker 15. During the summer months, the museum sponsors guided hikes in the park. A grassy meadow next to the museum is a picture-perfect place for a picnic in the fresh upcountry air. If you didn't pack a meal, head to the restaurant inside the Kokee Lodge, right next to the museum, for breakfast or lunch. While at Kokee, make sure to visit the Kalalau Lookout two miles north of the museum. Kauai postcards often feature the lookout's spectacular view of the lush valley and blue ocean beyond (if fog hasn't rolled in). The lodge rents cabins for overnight stays, or

you can pitch a tent with a permit from the Department of Land and Natural Resources *(808-274-3444)*.

Park: daily dawn-dusk. Museum and gift shop: daily 10 a.m.-4 p.m.

LIKO KAUAI CRUISES

9875 Waimea Road, Waimea, 808-338-0333, 888-732-5456; www.liko-kauai.com

This company specializes in five-hour sightseeing cruises along the Na Pali coast in a 49-foot, twin-hulled catamaran. Besides the beautiful sights on shore—stunning cliffs, cascading waterfalls, lush valleys, white-sand beaches—you'll pass sea caves and likely spot dolphins or whales (in season). Because this is a Hawaiian-owned-and-operated company, every sailing trip includes lots of insight into Hawaiian history and culture. Tours depart from the Kekaha Small Boat Harbor in Waimea.

Daily 8:30 a.m.

POLIHALE BEACH PARK

Highway 50, Mana; www.kauai-hawaii.com

What you'll see at Polihale is nothing short of stunning: 100-foot-tall sand dunes and the towering sea cliffs of the Na Pali coast. The three-mile-long beach is totally unprotected, so the water conditions are usually hazardous, except at Queen's Pond on the south end of Polihale.

Daily dawn-dusk.

RUSSIAN FORT ELIZABETH STATE HISTORIC PARK

Highway 50, Waimea; www.hawaii.gov

Believe it or not, Kauai had a connection to Russia two centuries ago, albeit only briefly. In the early 1800s, a Russian doctor came to Hawaii to strike a trade deal with King Kamehameha, who then ruled all of the Hawaiian islands. On Kauai, however, the doctor sided with King Kaumualii, who wanted to rule Kauai independently, and built this fort outside Waimea (and two others near Hanalei). One big problem: the doctor did not have the support of the Russian czar, who forced him to leave the islands, and the forts fell into the hands of Kamehameha. Only the remains of this one are left, and visitors can take a self-guided tour of the 17-acre grounds. All that is left of the fort is its star-shaped stone foundation.

Daily dawn-dusk.

SALT POND BEACH PARK

Lolokai Road, Hanapepe; www.kauai-hawaii.com

There aren't any fancy resorts at this beach, home of Hawaii's only natural salt ponds. The area is a peaceful retreat with lots of grass and shade and a nice picnic area with pavilions and barbecue grills. Because a reef partially protects this beach, the water is usually calm and clear year-round, making it a good spot for swimming, snorkeling and windsurfing. At low tide, kids can watch small fish swim in the tide pools.

Daily dawn-dusk.

TOURS OF HISTORIC WAIMEA TOWN

9565 Kaumualii Highway, Waimea, 808-338-1332; www.wkbpa.org/visitorcenter.html

Several important developments in Hawaiian history have taken place in this small town: it was here that Captain James Cook first landed in the islands in 1778, that the Russians built a fort, and that missionaries settled in the early 1800s. Every Monday morning, visitors can learn more about Waimea and see some of its historic sights during a 90-minute guided walking tour. Among other things, you'll see a stone church built in 1854, the town's cemetery, a monument to Captain Cook, and turn-of-the-century buildings, some painstakingly restored after Hurricane Iniki struck the island in 1992. Tours leave from the West Kauai Technology and Visitors Center. Before or after your walk, use the center's touch-screen computers for additional interesting information about Kauai and its history. The center also has computers that visitors can use for free for any purpose, including sending or receiving e-mail.

Tours: Monday 9:30 am. Center hours: Monday-Friday 9 a.m.-4 p.m., Saturday 9 a.m.-1 p.m.

WAIMEA CANYON STATE PARK

Waimea Canyon Drive (Highway 550), Waimea, 808-274-3344;
www.hawaiistateparks.org

"Breathtaking" best describes this park, which borders Kokee State Park. The canyon—sometimes called the Grand Canyon of the Pacific because of its deep colorful gorges—is 10 miles long, 2 miles wide, and 3,600 feet deep, making for quite a spectacular sight. It was formed through the centuries by streams and faults. On the drive up, there are two major vantage points: the official Waimea Canyon Lookout between mile markers 10 and 11, and the Puu Hinahina Lookout between mile markers 13 and 14. Either offers awesome views, and at the latter, you can also see the neighboring isle of Niihau in the distance on clear days. If you want to do more than look on your drive, be on the lookout for a hiking sign just past mile marker 8, where two trails can be explored on foot. The Iliau Nature Loop takes about 20 minutes to walk, but the more difficult 2 1/2-mile-long Kukui Trail juts off and drops more than 2,000 feet into the canyon to a river and campground. For information on fishing, camping and additional hikes into the canyon, call the Kauai office of the Division of State Parks (phone number listed above). Daily dawn-dusk.

WHERE TO EAT
★SHRIMP STATION

9652 Kaumualii Highway, Waimea, 808-338-1242

This roadside shack serves inexpensive and heaping plates of shrimp tacos, boiled shrimp doused in sweet chili and garlic sauce or coconut battered shrimp. A few picnic tables and chairs provide seating, while crispy just-made French fries and papaya mango tartar sauce provide a good accompaniment to the shrimp. The location makes this a popular stop on the way to or from Waimea Canyon.

Seafood. Lunch. $15 and under

LANAI

The smallest of the accessible Hawaiian Islands, Lanai is private and intimate. Only about 3,000 people live on the island, and only about 100,000 visitors come ashore each year. At just 141 square miles, its so small and undeveloped, it has no fast-food restaurants, no shopping malls, and no stoplights. The island has only about 30 miles of paved roads.

Many visitors come to Lanai to stay in one of the luxury Four Seasons resorts on the island. The Lodge at Koele is located up in the hills at 1,600 feet, on a former Dole pineapple plantation, surrounded by tall pine trees. Its sister property, the oceanside Four Seasons Lanai at Manele Bay, fronts Hulopoe Bay, a marine sanctuary. On New Years Day in 1994, billionaire Bill Gates was married on the golf course at Manele Bay and honeymooned at the resort.

Before the resorts opened in the early 1990s, Lanai had established a name for itself as home to the world's largest pineapple plantation, but that industry has died out on the island and tourism now drives the local economy.

Today this is a place to get away from it all and enjoy the resort's gourmet restaurants, stunning golf, glorious views and quiet seclusion. Apart from the resorts, there's not much to the island. There's only one town, Lanai City, a small but friendly inland place void of all pretension. And most of the island's tourist attractions on land, including a dry-land forest, a petroglyph field and a summit from which you can sometimes see all of the Hawaiian Islands, require a true sense of adventure and a four-wheel-drive vehicle to reach. On Lanai, sightseeing usually means traveling down rugged, not paved, roads.

Except for Hulopoe, many of the beaches are tricky to access, and while good for strolling and sun bathing, many aren't safe for swimming due to strong currents and riptides. However, there are many companies that offer snorkeling, scuba, sailing, kayaking, fishing and other water-related tours.

WHAT TO SEE
CENTRAL BAKERY
1311 Fraser Ave., Lanai City, 808-565-3920

As the name aptly implies, this sweet spot is bakery central on Lanai. It supplies scrumptious baked goods—breads, pastries, ice creams and desserts—for both Four Seasons resorts on the island. Visitors to Lanai can call and place their orders (try to call 48 hours ahead), which the bakers will prepare for you.

Daily 4:30 a.m.-3:30 p.m.

CHALLENGE AT MANELE
1233 Fraser Ave., Lanai City, 808-565-2222; www.manelebayhotel.com/challenge

You're never far from the ocean at this Jack Nicklaus-designed course built atop dramatic cliffs overlooking beautiful Hulopoe Bay. On three holes, you have to shoot from one cliff to another, being careful not to land your ball in the surf below. Deep bunkers and perched greens are also a challenge, but the deep gorges and lush ravines are spectacular. There's also a driving range, putting green and a clubhouse. Tee times must be booked by phone 90 days prior to requested play dates.

EXPERIENCE AT KOELE

730 Lanai Ave., Lanai City, 808-565-4653; www.lodgeatkoele.com/experience

This course is indeed an experience. Designed by Greg Norman, the front nine holes of this upcountry gem next to the Lodge at Koele take you through pineapple fields and deep valley gorges made even more beautiful with kiawe and koa trees. Towering pine and eucalyptus trees dress up the back nine, as do sweeping views of Maui and Molokai off in the distance. And if you want to talk about a real experience, there's a 250-foot drop from the signature 17th hole into Lanai's deepest ravine. Remember, you're up high, so bring something warm to wear in case of chilly winds. Tee times must be booked by phone 90 days prior to requested play dates.

HULOPE BEACH

Manele Road, Manele

Hulope is Lanai's best beach and it's just a short walk from the Four Seasons Manele Bay. The beach is long and crescent-shaped with grassy shaded areas perfect for picnicking (the park has grills) or for taking a break from the sun. This beach is protected, so its usually good for swimming in summer and even winter if the surf's not up. Its also a Marine Life Conservation Area, so the snorkeling is A-plus, with lots of colorful fish swimming in and around all the coral not far from shore. Spinner dolphins sometimes make an appearance and, in season, whales can be spotted off in the distance. To the left of the beach, you'll find tide pools and hiking trails. If you like to sleep under the stars, you can camp here with a permit.

KANEPUU PRESERVE

Polihua Road, North Shore, 808-537-4508

The lush flora you see on this 590-acre preserve on the northwest side of the island (six miles northwest of Lanai City) gives you an idea of how native dry land forests once looked in the lowlands throughout Hawaii. Kanepuu, now managed by the Nature Conservancy, is home to 49 plant species, including three federally endangered ones: the vine Bonamia menziesii, the Hawaii gardenia and the sandalwood. A self-guided tour on a specially marked trail that forms a loop takes only 10 to 15 minutes, and you'll be glad you took this scenic walk.

Daily 9 a.m.-4 p.m.

KAUNOLU VILLAGE

Manele Road, South Lanai

Now a National Historic Landmark, this site (off Manele Road about three miles from Lanai City) atop tall cliffs used to be an ancient Hawaiian fishing village that was quite prosperous. In fact, its believed King Kamehameha would come to Kaunolu for recreation about 200 years ago. Among the 86 ruins are a temple and the remains of the king's retreat. At Kahekili's Leap, a steep drop to the ocean below, warriors would supposedly prove their courage to the king by jumping into the water from on high. The road is very rocky; you need a four-wheel-drive vehicle to reach the village.

KEOMOKU VILLAGE

East Shore

Visit this off-the-beaten-path village (located off Keomoku Road, about eight miles east of Lanai City) to see Hawaii's version of a ghost town. As the site of the Maunalei Sugar Co., Keomoku was a bustling little community of about 2,000 people until 1901, when the water turned brackish and salty, making it difficult to continue sugar production. According to legend, the gods tainted the water because sacred stones were moved to construct the village. All the buildings are decaying now except for a clapboard church, Ka Lanakila O Ka Malamalama, which has been partially restored. From here, the views of Maui are splendid, making the deserted beaches good spots for a quiet picnic.

KOLOIKI RIDGE NATURE HIKE

Lanai City, behind the Lodge at Koele, 808-565-7300, 800-321-4666;
www.lodgeatkoele.com

Head into the Koele uplands on this five-mile hike. You'll pass through Norfolk island pines and lots of wild ginger as you make your way up to Koloiki Ridge, where you'll be rewarded with gorgeous views of two valleys and the islands of Molokai and Maui.

LUAHIWA PETROGLYPHS

South Central, off Manele Road

Drive a couple of miles south of Lanai City, turn onto a dirt road, make your way to a slope overlooking the Palawai Basin, and you'll see a large field of boulders atop cliffs. On 34 of the large rocks are petroglyphs dating as far back as the 18th century. These are the best examples of the ancient rock art you'll find on Lanai. The carvings etched into the boulders depict ancient symbols, animals, and people. Luahiwa is difficult to reach and requires a four-wheel-drive vehicle.

MUNRO TRAIL

Central Lanai, off Manele Road

Get behind the wheel of a four-wheel-drive vehicle and set out on this 16-mile-long trail that takes you past beautiful pine forests to the summit of Mount Lanaihale (3,370 feet), then down to the Palawai Basin. On clear days, you'll likely be able to see all of the major Hawaiian islands from atop the summit.

POLIHUA BEACH

Polihua Road, North Shore

Swimming isn't advised at Polihua because of strong currents. Still, this beach on the northwest side of the island has much to offer: it stretches gloriously for 1 1/2 miles. The views of Molokai across the channel are splendid. And you're likely to have the place mostly to yourself, making it the perfect spot for a romantic picnic or sunset. You'll need a four-wheel-drive to get here.

SHIPWRECK BEACH

Keomoku Road, North Shore, at the end of Keomoku Road

The strong currents at this windy beach on the northeast coast make it too dangerous to swim, but those same currents make this a wonderful place for beachcombing. You'll find all kinds of shells on this beach, which stretches for more than eight miles. It's also a popular place for shoreline fishing. Offshore, you'll see the remains of a large ship and, across the channel, the island of Molokai. In season, from December through April, you might see whales. Much of the road to this beach is paved, but not the last stretch, so you need a four-wheel-drive to get here.

STABLES AT KOELE

Highway 440, Lanai City, 808-565-4424; www.lodgeatkoele.com.

Explore Lanai on horseback. Tours last for 1 1/2 to 3 hours, depending on which ride you choose. Opt for the Koele Trail Ride, recommended for beginners, and you'll make your way along a wooded trail behind the Lodge at Koele and enjoy spectacular views of neighboring islands. Wander up into hills, through guava groves and ironwood trees, on the Paniolo Trail Ride. Saddle up for the Mahana Trail ride and see the plains of the Lanai Ranch, where you'll likely glimpse plenty of wildlife. You can also sign up for a sunset ride or a private ride.

TRILOGY LANAI OCEAN SPORTS

One Manele Bay Road, South Lanai, 808-565-9303, 888-628-4800; www.visitlanai.com

This popular Maui-based company known for its A-plus trips and good customer service also offers numerous water sport tours on Lanai. The options include morning snorkel sails, sunset sails, beach snorkel classes, scuba introduction classes, scuba boat and beach dives, ocean kayaking treks, marine-mammal-watch cruises and more. Tours usually leave from Manele Harbor. Daily.

WHERE TO STAY

★★★★FOUR SEASONS RESORT LANAI AT MANELE BAY

1 Manele Bay Road, Lanai City, 808-565-2000, 800-819-5053; www.fourseasons.com

This Four Seasons perched atop red lava cliffs on the tiny island of Lanai is such a world away that Bill and Melinda Gates held their wedding here. Mere mortals will also enjoy escaping to this quiet retreat that resembles a sprawling Mediterranean villa with stunning gardens (each with a different theme) everywhere you turn. The guest rooms have private lanais and countless other amenities, plus a prime location near Hulopoe, considered the island's best beach and a marine sanctuary (guests receive complimentary snorkel gear). Enjoy days lounging by the oceanfront pool and having a massage in one of the waterfront cabanas. The rich public spaces of this resort are stunning with dark wood accents and spectacular murals depicting the history of the island (iPod tours are available). There are plenty of dining options, including an Italian restaurant and ocean grills, a delightful kids room, fantastic golf course, and a luxurious spa that you can book for your own private use after hours. Guests here also enjoy access to the Lodge at Koele.

236 rooms. Restaurant, bar. Fitness center. Tennis. Golf. Pool. Spa. Business center. $351 and up

★★★★FOUR SEASONS RESORT THE LODGE AT KOELE
1 Keomoku Highway, Lanai City, 808-565-4000, 800-819-5053; www.fourseasons.com

Located upcountry on the small island of Lanai, this English manor with Asian accents was once an old Dole pineapple plantation. Guests drive past corridors of Cook Island pines and pull up to see a large white estate with a large pineapple painted right on the front and perfectly manicured lawns where happy vacationers are playing croquet. Rooms have a cheery, homey feel with pale yellow walls, a mix of floral and plaids patterns, charming window seats and private lanais. Public spaces have soaring ceilings, cozy seating areas and wood-burning fireplaces, while the serene grounds include a reflecting pond and Chinese pagoda, and gardens of pine, bamboo and fruit. The Tea Room bar is a smart place for a drink, while the Dining Room offers some of the best dining on any of the Hawaiian islands. The resort also boasts one of the best championship golf courses in the world, designed by PGA legend Greg Norman (guests enjoy access to Manele Bay as well, where the spa is located). Other amenities include children's programs, secluded garden swimming pool, a health club, croquet, horseback riding, sporting clays and archery range.

102 rooms. Restaurant, bar. Fitness center. Tennis. Golf. Pool. $351 and up

WHERE TO EAT
★BLUE GINGER CAFE
409 Seventh St., Lanai City, 808-565-6363

There's nothing fancy about this small, nondescript eatery facing the town park, but it's quite popular with the locals. For lunch or dinner, order burgers, pizza, or stir-fry at the counter, or try the restaurant's bakery items for breakfast.

American. Breakfast, lunch, dinner. Outdoor seating. No credit cards accepted. $15 and under

★PELE'S OTHER GARDEN
811 Houston St., Lanai City, 808-565-9628, 888-764-3354;
www.pelesothergarden.com

Across from Dole Park, Pele's sits in a quaint yellow house with cheery aqua trim. Eat on the veranda out front or inside in the cozy dining room with black-and-white-checked floor and island-print tablecloths. At lunchtime, the restaurant operates as a New York-style deli, dishing up fruit smoothies, soups and made-to-order sandwiches on freshly baked bread. At night, it turns into an Italian bistro serving organic salads, pasta dishes and gourmet pizzas. If you're in a rush, pick up a picnic basket lunch and eat on the go.

Italian. Lunch, dinner. Closed Sunday. Outdoor seating. $16-35

★★★★THE DINING ROOM
One Keomoku Highway, Lanai City, 808-565-7300, 800-321-4666;
www.lodgeatkoele.com

Located within the gracious Lodge at Koele, this lovely restaurant is like being invited to dinner at someone's beautiful estate. A wood-burning fireplace warms the intimate dining room, which looks out onto the manicured lawns and a small lake. The cuisine—classic French with a reliance on local produce, poultry and seafood—is equally inviting, with entrees such as a whole Maine lobster with California Osetra Caviar and oven-roasted lamb crusted with Provençal herbs. The extensive wine list complements the fine cuisine. French. Dinner. Closed Tuesday, Wednesday, Thursday. Reservations recommended. $86 and up

MAUI

A FEW FACTS ABOUT MAUI: FIRST, IT HAS 81 ACCESSIBLE BEACHES. THE AVERAGE temperature is a very pleasant 75 to 85 degrees. You can see humpback whales splashing offshore. And many would argue that this is some of the best surfing in the world. Is it any surprise that this island is such a popular vacation destination?

This tropical playground is called the Valley Isle because of its geography. It's made up of two volcanoes: the 10,023-foot-high dormant Haleakala and the 5,788-foot-high extinct Puu Kukui, whose lava spills created a 7-mile-wide green valley between them centuries ago. This so-called Central Valley is home to the island's two major towns, Wailuku and Kahului, which are small by mainland standards and mostly cater to locals. If visitors spend much time in either town, it might be to browse through Wailuku's funky and fun antique stores. Visitors mostly flock to either side of the valley, in and around the mountainous land masses formed by the two volcanoes.

In west Maui (the Puu Kukui side), the lush, majestic-looking West Maui Mountains hover over the old whaling village of Lahaina, a hotbed of activity with its many shops, restaurants and nightclubs. North of the city are the coastal resort areas of Kaanapali, Napili and Kapalua, where several hotels provide easy access to glorious sandy beaches with good views of Lanai and Molokai not too far off in the distance.

On the Haleakala side of the island, which is much larger than West Maui, the terrain varies from lush to barren. A rain forest dominates Haleakala's north side, where most visitors make the memorable 55-mile drive to Hana, a remote haven devoid of commercialism.

On the volcano's sunny south side, the landscape looks more like a desert. Even so, you'll find several luxurious hotels in Wailea, which has been planted with lush tropical foliage everywhere you turn. The hotels here front dreamy crescent-shaped beaches.

Finally, venture up Haleakala's slopes into Upcountry Maui to experience a smorgasbord of art communities, farms, ranches, a winery and a national park. In the early morning hours, many sleepy-eyed folks huddle in the park's chilly high altitude to watch a spectacular sunrise.

EAST MAUI

When you're ready for a road trip, it's time to explore East Maui via the Hana Highway, usually described as the Road to Hana. Fifty-two miles separate Kahului from Hana (population about 700), and those 52 miles are awesome, taking you through a rain forest and some of the prettiest scenery anywhere in Hawaii. The many memorable sights include waterfalls, freshwater pools, black-sand beaches, exotic tropical flora, coastal overlooks and more. The drive can take up to three hours one-way, and not just because the sights encourage frequent stops. The road, much of it only two lanes, has 600 curves and 54 narrow bridges.

As you roll into Hana, it's soon apparent why it's touted as Maui's Last Hawaiian Place. None of the tourism-related development that has changed the landscape on other parts of the island has occurred in this small town, even though the sugarcane industry that sustained it for decades has died out. This gem of an island community, the birthplace of Queen Kaahumanu, simply borders a crescent-shaped bay with no high-rise hotels anywhere in sight. Hana's main hotel, the Hotel Hana-Maui, is a secluded retreat on 66 acres where guests savor peace and quiet in a heavenly setting. At the Hana Cultural Center and Museum, you can learn more about this remote village that preserves the Maui of yesterday.

Hana isn't the only city of interest on the east side. Way back near the Central Valley, at the beginning of the Road to Hana, sits the colorful little town of Paia. It's home to hippies, surfers, natural food stores and a string of small shops and delicious restaurants right on the highway, the town's main drag. It's a good place to fill up with gas and pick up a picnic lunch before you start heading to Hana. A little farther east of Paia, Haiku also lures visitors with shops and a few bed-and-breakfasts. But it's a few miles off the highway and up the lower slopes of Haleakala.

WHAT TO SEE
BALDWIN BEACH PARK
Highway 36, Paia

Many people rate this park the best beach on the north side, especially for family fun. The body surfing gets a thumbs-up, as does the swimming in summer, when there's less wind. Up on the shore, public facilities add to the park's appeal. Fire up a grill, then sit down to eat on one of the many picnic tables. To work off the calories, shoot some hoops on the basketball court, play a little kickball on the soccer field, or take a long walk or run along the white sand beach itself.

HAMOA BEACH
Hana Highway, Hana

Talk about a heavenly beach not far from heavenly Hana. Hamoa Beach is remote and not at all touristy, though it's maintained by the Hotel Hana-Maui (the hotel isn't located here). The peaceful, idyllic setting is just a long, wide stretch of sand backed by grass, swaying palm trees and tall black-lava sea cliffs. You'll be hard-pressed to find a much better place for sunbathing, relaxing and reading a good book, but be careful about swimming at this beach. It frequently has rip currents and the rolling surf is often quite high, which makes for dramatic viewing from the safety of the shoreline.

HANA COAST GALLERY
Hotel Hana-Maui, Hana Highway, Hana, 808-248-8636, 800-637-0188;
www.hanacoast.com

Travel magazines rave about this handsome upscale gallery, which specializes in original fine art, native cultural art, and finely crafted handwork from the Hawaiian Islands, Polynesia and the Pacific Rim. Its 3,000 square feet of display space is packed with high-quality creations that you'll want to take home: wood, stone and bronze sculptures; turned wood bowls; handcrafted furniture from rare and exotic Hawaiian woods; oil paintings; original prints from the 16th to 20th centuries. The inventory is some of the finest art you'll find anywhere on the island.

Daily 9 a.m.-5 p.m.

HANA CULTURAL CENTER AND MUSEUM

4974 Uakea Road, Hana, 808-248-8622; www.hookele.com

This facility has but one purpose: to preserve the colorful history of Hana and celebrate Old Hawaii. It does so through more than 560 artifacts (including many striking Hawaiian quilts), more than 600 old books and nearly 5,000 photographs. The cultural center includes the city's old courthouse, old jailhouse, a cooking house and a canoe building.
Daily 10 a.m.-4 p.m.

HASEGAWA GENERAL STORE

Highway 360, Hana, 800-248-8231

Two brothers opened this store for business in 1910 and it has been a Hawaiian mainstay ever since, with subsequent generations of the family running this popular retail operation. The original building burned down in 1990, but the family opened another store about a year later. Shop alongside locals and the many visitors who stop here to experience a slice of old-fashioned Hawaiiana. The aisles are packed with odds and ends, from fishing equipment and gardening supplies to all types of Hana memorabilia.
Monday-Saturday 7 a.m.-7 p.m., Sunday 8 a.m.-6 p.m.

HOOKIPA BEACH

Hana Highway, Paia

Just past the town of Paia, this is where the serious surfing takes place. Here, gusty trade winds almost always blow and winter swells often exceed 20 feet, creating ideal conditions. Even if you're not surfing, it's great fun to watch.

KAHANU GARDEN

Ulaino Road, Hana, 808-248-8912; www.ntbg.org

Far removed from the commercial side of Maui, this 472-acre garden features plants of value to people in Polynesia, Micronesia and Melanesia. One of these is breadfruit, a staple in the Polynesian diet (Kahanu Garden has the world's largest selection). The garden is also home to the Piilanihale Heiau, where islanders worshipped in ancient times. It's believed to be the largest heiau in all of Polynesia. On a self-guided tour of Kahanu, wander along a half-mile, easy-to-navigate trail to learn more about food crops that have helped sustain natives through the ages.
Admission: adults $10, children 12 years and under free. Guided tour: adults $25. Monday-Friday 10 a.m.-2 p.m.

WAINAPANAPA STATE PARK

Hana Highway, Hana, 808-984-8109; www.hawaiistateparks.org

This remote state park has a beautiful black-sand beach and great coastal trails for hiking. Camping is allowed with reservations and cabins are located nearby.

WHERE TO STAY
★★★HOTEL HANA MAUI

5031 Hana Highway, Hana, 808-248-8211; 800-321-4262; www.hotelhanamaui.com

At the end of the scenic but serpentine Road to Hana, the Hotel Hana resort promises a relaxing, restorative experience. Situated on 67 acres that span ocean beach to rolling pastureland to expansive manicured lawns, the resort is made up of 66 quiet cottages (read: no TV or Internet access) with beamed ceilings, hardwood, bamboo floors, feather beds and comfortable lanais. The full spa offers yoga and aerobics classes, tai chi lessons and a broad range of sports and recreation activities, including hiking, horseback riding, jeep excursions, nature walks, tennis, snorkeling and kayaking.

66 rooms. Restaurant, bar. Business center. Fitness center. Spa. Beach. Pool. Tennis. $351 and up

WHERE TO EAT
★ANTHONY'S
90 Hana Highway, Paia, 808-579-8340

This tiny restaurant/bake shop is the place to stop for breakfast on your way to Hana. Options include giant omelets that come with a side of rice, pancakes drenched in coconut syrup and Kalua pork Benedict, all of which taste even better when you wash them down with their rich specialty coffee. Anthony's will also pack a picnic lunch for you—there are a variety of sandwiches, as well as enormous brownies, muffins (try the pineapple coconut) and other scrumptious bake goods. Then, on the way back, cool off with a chocolate chip cookie sandwich with a scoop of Macadamia nut brittle ice cream.

American. Breakfast, lunch (until 6 p.m.). $15 and up

★CHARLEY'S
142 Hana Highway, Paia, 808-579-9453

A few historic photos dot the walls of this otherwise nondescript, family-style restaurant and bar that has been serving customers since the 1960s. (Don't believe the sign out front saying that Charley's is the "last food stop before Hana"; that's no longer true, although options are still relatively few.) At the rear, you'll find a jukebox and a dance floor, which can get pretty crowded at night, especially when live bands play here. Huge portions are the norm, even at breakfast, with standouts that include macadamia nut pancakes with coconut syrup.

American. Breakfast, lunch, dinner, late night. Bar. $16-35

★★FLATBREAD
89 Hana Highway, Paia, 808-579-8989; www.flatbreadcompany.com

Flatbread tries to use organic, local products whenever possible. The dough is made fresh every day from organic wheat, the sausage and pepperoni is nitrate-free and all the other ingredients are fresh and delicious. Pies include the Community Flatbread with wood-fired cauldron tomato sauce, caramelized onions, mushrooms, cheese and herbs; and the Coevolution with Kalamata olives, fresh rosemary, red onions, oven roasted red peppers, goat cheese, mozzarella, garlic and herbs. Specials offer up unique combinations such as organic oysters, mushrooms, heirloom tomatoes, mozzarella, macadamia nut pesto, herbs and pineapple drizzle. Yes, all that goes on one flatbread, which is the only criticism here. Pies can sometimes get overloaded. Still, the ingredients are fresh and good, making Flatbread a tasty place for pizza in Paia.

Pizza. Lunch, dinner. $16-35

★JACQUES NORTHSHORE
120 Hana Highway, Paia, 808-579-8844

The old sugar mill town of Paia on Maui's North Shore is home to this laid-back restaurant, which appeals to a younger crowd. The eclectic menu reveals Asian, European, and American influences, and for fanciers of raw seafood, there is also a sushi bar. The atmosphere is very casual, with nightly entertainment.

International. Dinner. Bar. Outdoor seating. $16-35

★★★MAMA'S FISH HOUSE
799 Poho Place, Pais, 808-579-8488

Located on Maui's Kuau Cove a couple of miles past downtown Paia, Mama's Fish House almost looks like a movie set meant to replicate the South Seas: picture a crescent-shaped cove with white sand, palm trees and canoes, and a bamboo dining room that almost spills out to the surf. The view is killer, and so is the seafood. Mama's serves fresh fish prepared Hawaiian-style: ono sautéed with Haiku tomatoes, garlic and capers, deep-water ahi seared in ginger and mahi mahi stuffed with lobster, crab and Maui onions. The South Seas theme carries over inside with bright printed vinyl tablecloths, servers in tropical prints and Hawaiian music playing in the background. If it all sound bit kitsch, be certain than it is, and despite a pretty hefty price tag, hungry patrons can't get enough of it. Be prepared to wait when you go.

Seafood. Lunch, dinner. Bar. Outdoor seating. $36-85

KIHEI AND SOUTH MAUI

Year-round good weather typifies this increasingly popular side of Maui, which runs down the south coast from Maalaea to Makena, with Kihei and Wailea located in between. The most upscale area is Wailea, a well-manicured resort along 1 1/2 miles of this coastline. Here, you can get quite comfortable in the island's most exclusive hotels. Its five crescent-shaped beaches

are about as perfect as you can imagine. At the Shops at Wailea, many high-end retailers offer top-of-the-line designer goods. And steep greens fees are probably the only complaints you'll hear about the three championship golf courses.

Just north of Wailea, Kihei is a laid-back coastal community with plenty of restaurants and smaller hotels, most of which are within walking distance of the beaches. Kihei Road, the main drag that hugs the shoreline, is packed with restaurants and little strip malls, and is usually brimming with people and activity.

Up the coast a few miles, tiny Maalaea is beginning to grow, thanks mainly to its small harbor. Visitors staying on this side on the island often climb aboard boats for all types of water fun, from snorkeling trips to whale-watching cruises. It is also home to the Maui Ocean Center, the island's aquarium.

WHAT TO SEE
ACTION SPORTS MAUI
6 E Waipuilani Road, Kihei, 808-871-5857; www.actionsportsmaui.com

Action Sports offers kiteboarding, surfing and windsurfing lessons and tours. This surf school offers classes designed to help you catch waves safely and with ease. Most of the teaching takes place on the North Shore at Kanaha Beach, near the Kahului Airport. If you're a more advanced surfer, opt for the Surfari class, where instructors unpack the boards at hard-to-get-to and secret surfing spots. A kiddie class introduces children as young as age 6 to the sport. Action Sports also offers instruction in windsurfing and kitesurfing. Monday-Saturday. Times and prices vary.

BLUE WATER RAFTING

Kihei, 808-879-7328; www.bluewaterrafting.com
For these fun-packed tours, up to 24 passengers board a motorized raft and head out into the ocean for an exciting ride and spectacular sightseeing on Maui's south side. Take the tour to the Kanaio Coast and you'll wander inside sea caves, pass through giant lava arches, and likely spot spinner dolphins at play. On the tour to the Molokini marine preserve, you're guaranteed to see scores of tropical fish when you go snorkeling at this crater. If you can't decide which of these trips interests you most, opt for one that combines the two. During whale season, a whale-watching excursion also includes snorkeling at Molokini. All tours depart from the Kihei Boat Ramp just south of Kamaole Beach Park III.
Daily. Times and prices vary.

BOBBY BAKER'S MAUI SUN DIVERS

Kihei, 877-879-3337; www.mauisundivers.com
Bobby Baker and his team of instructors specialize in classes for beginning divers and those who need refresher training. They work only with small groups, starting in shallow water right off the beach. They then move the action to depths of up to 25 feet deep, where divers can inspect coral up close, and swim with plenty of fish and turtles. For those who feel confident about their skills, an optional second dive takes a much deeper plunge, to 40 feet, where the underwater sights get even better. The dives are from beaches in the Kihei/Wailea area. For certified divers, Baker also offers cave, scooter and night dives from local beaches.
Daily. Times and prices vary.

ED ROBINSON'S DIVING ADVENTURES

Kihei, Kihei Boat Ramp, 808-879-3584, 800-635-1273; www.mauiscuba.com
This company has been in business on Maui for more than 20 years. Every day, it takes divers to Molokini and other hot spots around the island's south side. Some days it also offers trips to Lanai, night dives and a three-tank adventure. On many of its dives, the diver-to-guide ratio is as low as 4:1.
Daily. Times and prices vary.

KAMAOLE BEACH PARKS I, II, AND III

S. Kihei Road, Kihei
These three sister beaches have something many Hawaii beaches don't: lifeguards. You wont have any trouble finding the beaches, either: they line the main road through this small community that's more laid-back than Wailea. Because these parks are so accessible, locals tend to hang out at them on weekends, so don't come for seclusion; do come for the swimming, barbecue

grills, picnic tables and, if you have kids, a playground (at III).
Daily dawn-dusk.

KEALIA POND NATIONAL WILDLIFE PRESERVE
Highways 31 and 350, Kihei, 808-875-1582; pacificislands.fws.gov
This 700-acre preserve, one of the few natural wetlands left in Hawaii, attracts more than 31 bird species, including coots, ducks, stilts and many other Hawaiian water birds, as well as Pacific golden plovers, ruddy turnstones and other shorebirds. The preserve includes a boardwalk and sand dunes.
Admission: free. Monday-Friday 8 a.m.-4:30 p.m.

KEAWALAI CONGREGATIONAL CHURCH
190 Makena Road, Makena, 808-879-5557; www.keawalai.org
Built with lava rock and coral mortar in 1855, this old-time church sits alongside a quiet stretch of beach. But on Sunday mornings at 7:30 and 10 a.m., its pews get crowded with worshippers who come for something most other local churches don't offer anymore: a Hawaiian-language service heavy. In its cemetery, many tombstones feature ceramic pictures of the dearly departed.
Tuesday-Saturday 9 a.m.-5 p.m., Sunday during worship services.

KIHEI CANOE CLUB
Kihei, 808-879-5505; www.kiheicanoeclub.com
The aerobically fit members of this club take the island tradition of outrigger canoeing seriously. They practice their paddling regularly and compete in fast-paced races throughout the islands. Twice a week, however, they invite visitors to join them for a fun hour of recreational canoeing. They provide the equipment, basic training and an experienced crew to ensure you enjoy a smooth ride out on the water. It's a popular activity so get there early.
Admission: $25 donation.Tuesday and Thursday 7:30-9:00 a.m.

LA PEROUSE MONUMENT
La Perouse Bay, Makena
Captain Cook, the English explorer, may have arrived on the Hawaiian islands in 1778, but he never landed on Maui. The first Westerner to do that was Jean Francis Gallup Comte de La Perouse. The French admiral came ashore on the island's south side in 1786, after anchoring his ship in a sheltered cove now called La Perouse Bay. When you enter the bay area in your car, look for the roadside monument honoring the admiral. Its pyramid-shaped and made of lava rock. The water can be a little rough here, so the bay isn't always suitable for water fun. The hiking is good, though, so come prepared to do a little exploring of your own on foot.

MAUI CLASSIC CHARTERS
1279 S. Kihei Road, Kihei, 808-879-8188, 800-736-5740; www.mauicharters.com
This company sails two state-of-the-art catamarans off the Maui shoreline to popular snorkeling sites such as Molokini and Coral Gardens and on whale-watching treks in season. On another tour, the captain steers the boat to where friendly dolphins typically play in the water. On the Four Winds II, you don't even have to get wet to see colorful marine life—the 55-foot boat has a large

glass-bottom viewing room. Kids will enjoy the Maui Magic because they can zoom down its waterslide and make a splash in the ocean. All tours leave from Maalaea Harbor.
Daily. Times and prices vary.

MAUI DIVE SHOP

1455 S. Kihei Road, Kihei, 808-879-3388, 800-542-3483; www.mauidiveshop.com
Hawaii's largest dive shop operates solely on Maui, where it has nine retail outlets spread across the island, so you're bound to be near one. Whatever your diving needs, the Maui Dive Shop can help you. It offers diving and snorkeling trips to the island's best sites, dive courses, rental gear, rental Jeeps (to take you to out-of-the-way shoreline dive sites), and even a dive lodge (a two-bedroom apartment on Maui's sunny south side). The activity desk can also help you book a variety of other adventures on the island, from sailing and deep-sea fishing trips to horseback-riding treks and luaus.
Daily 6 a.m.-9 p.m.

MAUI OCEAN CENTER

192 Maalaea Road, Maalaea, 808-270-7000; www.mauioceancenter.com
This three-acre tribute to the Pacific highlights the beauty and wonder of Hawaii's marine life, so it's fittingly called the Hawaiian Aquarium. More than 60 interactive exhibits introduce you to the thousands of sea creatures that swim in the deep blue water beyond the shoreline and reef: sharks, jacks, squirrel fish, crabs, lobsters, sea turtles, stingrays, sea stars, sea urchins, mollusks, and much more. In the Open Ocean exhibit, you'll walk through a 54-foot-long acrylic tunnel that offers a spectacular 240-degree view of sharks and other predators swimming in a 750,000-gallon saltwater aquarium. Learn about the humpback whales that migrate here every year in the Marine Mammal Discovery Center.
Admission: adults $25, children $18. September-June, daily 9 a.m.-5 p.m. July-August, daily 9 a.m.-6 p.m.

MIKE SEVERNS DIVING

Kihei, Kihei Boat Ramp, 808-879-6596; www.mikeseverns diving.com
This company offers two-tank, half-day dives to certified divers. The locations aren't determined until the morning of the trip (though most are usually somewhere around Molokini). The divers (and the weather) determine the destination the day of.
Admission: $130, $145 (with gear). Daily 6:00 a.m.

MOLOKINI

Wailea-Makena, off the South Shore
Most visitors to Maui take one of the many snorkeling/diving tours to this marine life park, located 2 1/2 miles off the South Shore between West Maui and Kahoolawe, an uninhabited island. The small, crescent-shaped Molokini is a volcanic cinder cone whose northern rim is beneath sea level, which causes its crater to be flooded. The underwater sightseeing is spectacular, with more than 250 species of fish swimming in this area, creating a rainbow of color beneath the surface. The water depth around Molokini varies from

just 35 feet to more than 350 feet, making this site perfect for all levels of snorkelers and divers. Daily boat tours by multiple companies are available, mostly in the mornings (don't try to kayak to the island; strong currents make such a paddling trip dangerous).

ONELOA (BIG) BEACH
Makena Alanui Drive, Makena
The Big Beach—also known as Makena Beach—goes on forever and is a favorite among locals for the golden sand, sunbathing, swimming and surfing. Get here early on weekends—the large parking lot fills up fast.

SHOPS AT WAILEA
3750 Wailea Alanui Drive, Wailea, 808-891-6770; www.shopsatwailea.com
This elegant collection of shops includes Louis Vuitton, Gucci, Folli Follie, Bottega Veneta and other high-end stores, as well as more reasonably priced options including Gap, Tommy Bahama, T-shirt Factory and several locally owned boutiques and specialty shops. Dining options include Longhi's and Ruth's Chris Steakhouse. In all, the 150,000-square-foot center has more than 60 shops and restaurants.
Daily 9:30 a.m.-9 p.m.

SOUTH PACIFIC KAYAKS & OUTFITTERS
2439 S. Kihei Road, Kihei, 808-875-4848, 800-776-2326; www.southpacifickayaks.com
Maui's only full-service kayak shop offers tours on both the south and west sides of the island. Whichever tour you take, you'll paddle your way to snorkeling sights teeming with Hawaiian marine life and coral reefs. On the south side, you'll explore the Ahihi Kinau Marine Reserve, Makena Bay, Turtle Reef, or Turtle Town. On the west side, opt for a trip along the Ukumehame Valley shoreline or one that takes you from Kaanapali to Lahaina.
Daily. Times and prices vary.

WAILEA COASTAL NATURE TRAIL
Wailea
Stroll along this scenic coastal trail for fabulous views of Lanai, Molokini and the West Maui mountains. On one side are some of the state's most lavish hotels and condominiums; on the other, gorgeous crescent-shaped beaches right out of a post card. Native plants line much of this 1 1/2-mile-walk, adding to the beauty of this paved trail. During whale season (December-May), you may well see some of the big mammals playing in the water off in the distance.

WAILEA GOLF CLUB
100 Wailea Golf Club Drive, Wailea, 808-875-7450, 888-328-6284; www.waileagolf.com
Three highly rated golf courses sit above the Wailea resort area, unfurling along the lower slopes of Haleakala. If you're a confident player, opt for the Gold course, the most difficult of the three. Designed by Robert Trent Jones, Jr., it has 128 bunkers lurking beside lush fairways and fast greens, and it drops 200 feet in elevation from start to finish. The Emerald Course looks pretty with all its gorgeous tropical flowers and plants, but looks can be de-

ceiving: you'll be challenged. Every hole has four to six tee boxes, however, making the course suitable to any level of duffer. With its wider fairways and large greens, you'll likely score best on the Blue Course, which was designed for broad appeal. All three courses are visually stunning and offer spectacular views that might distract you from the task at hand. Before hitting the links, warm up at the 12-acre training facility, which has two putting and chipping areas, fairway and greenside practice bunkers, and a driving range. Also on-site are two clubhouses, pro shops and restaurants.

Daily 6:10 a.m.-6:30 p.m.

WAILEA TENNIS CLUB

131 Wailea Ike Place, Wailea, 808-879-1958; ww.waileatennis.com

For some backhanded fun, this attractive complex just above the hotel/condo strip in Wailea offers 11 hard courts and a half-court for practicing your forehand, volleys and other shots. Consistently ranked among the country's top 50 resort tennis facilities, the club serves up regularly scheduled clinics and round-robin tournaments, provides teaching professionals for private lessons, and matches up players for friendly games. A pro shop sells the latest equipment.

Daily 7 a.m.-7 p.m.

SPECIAL EVENTS

HULA BOWL MAUI

300 Ohukai, Kihei, 808-874-9500; www.hulabowlmaui.com

In early January of each year, about 10,000 screaming football fans crowd into War Memorial Stadium in Wailuku to watch 90 college all-stars do battle on the gridiron. The player standouts have plenty of incentive to do their best on defense and offense: 32 NFL team scouts sit in the stands watching their every move on the field. A full week of activities open to the public precede the game, including a fun run, team luau, autograph session, golf tournament with sports celebrities, and a theme dinner at a local hotel. But the most entertaining pre-game show is the surfing contest featuring the super-size players.

Early January.

MAUI FILM FESTIVAL

Wailea, 808-572-3456; www.mauifilmfestival.com

Each year, Hollywood comes to Maui's South Shore for five days in mid-June for this cinema spectacle. More than 50 films are screened by an array of celebrities, directors, producers, writers and movie buffs in three outdoor venues under the stars. The festival runs in conjunction with the Taste of Wailea, a culinary event that showcases Maui's best chefs.

Mid-June.

NISSAN XTERRA WORLD CHAMPIONSHIPS

Wailea, 808-521-4322, 877-751-8880; www.xterraplanet.com

In late October of each year, 400 of the world's best triathletes converge on Maui to compete against one another and take home the coveted world championship title. They swim a 750-meter triangular course in rough water,

bike more than 3,000 feet up the Haleakala volcano, then set out on foot on an 11k trail run. Visitors can sign up for fun runs and get dressed up for the Halloween bash, which doubles as the awards ceremony.
Late October.

WHERE TO STAY
★★MAUI COAST HOTEL
2259 S Kihei Road, Kihei, 808-874-6284, 800-895-6284;www.mauicoasthotel.com
South Kihei, along a stretch of southwestern Maui beaches, is the setting for this family-friendly hotel. It's across the main coastal road from the water, although some of its higher-floor guest rooms have ocean views. The decor is tropical, with rattan furnishings and private lanais in the accommodations. Although not a resort per se, it has lighted tennis courts, several swimming pools, and two restaurants, with live Hawaiian entertainment nightly at its poolside cafe. Room rates are fairly reasonable by Maui standards.
265 rooms. Restaurant, bar. Business center. Pool. Tennis. $61-150

★★★FAIRMONT KEA LANI MAUI
4100 Wailea Alanui, Wailea, 808-875-4100, 800-441-1414; www.fairmont.com
With its quiet, sophisticated vibe and Moroccan design influences, the Fairmont Kea Lani is one of Maui's best getaways. Located on the island's southwestern shore with majestic Mount Haleakala as a backdrop, this elegant escape enjoys a prime location on Polo Beach, just steps from the sand and the surf. The 22-acre oceanfront property is the island's only all suite and villa luxury resort. The roomy accommodations are decorated in a cream and white palette punctuated with island accents, and all have private lanais, marble-top wet bars, and oversized marble bathrooms with soaking tubs and walk-in showers. The villas are only a stones throw from the beach, and have spacious quarters, including full kitchens and patios with grills. Enjoy sailing, snorkeling, kayaking, windsurfing, deep-sea fishing, or simply lounging around the pool. Shuttle service is also available to nearby tennis facilities and the renowned Wailea Golf Club. The sensational Spa Kea Lani uses local ingredients in many of its treatments—a visit during your stay is a must.
450 rooms. Restaurant, bar. Business center. Fitness room. Spa. Beach. Pool. $351 and up

★★★★★FOUR SEASONS RESORT MAUI AT WAILEA
3900 Wailea Alanui, Wailea, 808-874-8000, 800-268-6282; www.fourseasons.com
Blessed with abundant sunshine and perfect white-sand beaches, Wailea is one of Maui's best destinations, and the Four Seasons Resort is its most luxurious hotel. In addition to its pristine surroundings on the Valley Isle's southwest coast, this open-air property impresses with its standard-setting service and superior amenities. The breezy style of the island is evident throughout the resort's 15 acres. Rooms are spacious and comfortable with furnished lanais, plush beds and oversized marble bathrooms. The U-shaped design of the resort means that many rooms overlook a lovely courtyard and have ocean views. Guests are greeted with orchid leis on arrival and are treated to a wide array of complimentary services, from iced tea when you come in from activities to Evian spritzes by the pool. Lighted tennis courts, a seemingly unending variety of water sports, indoor and outdoor exercise facili-

ties, and off-site golf give you plenty of options for things to do each day; that is, when you're not simply lounging by one of the beautiful oceanfront pools with a good book or enjoying a treatment at the lavish spa. Restaurants include the famed Spago.

380 rooms. Restaurant, bar. Business center. Fitness center. Spa. Beach. Pool. Tennis. Pets accepted. $351 and up

★★★GRAND WAILEA RESORT HOTEL & SPA
3850 Wailea, Wailea, 808-875-1234
Calling 40 acres of beautiful Wailea beach its home, the Grand Wailea Resort is a world unto itself. From its $50 million art collection to its nine pools on six levels, this beautiful resort appeals to the entire family. From morning to night, you can find ample activities to keep you occupied. Spend the day relaxing by the elegant adults-only Hibiscus Pool or take the kids to the theme park-style Canyon Activity Pool that is connected to multiple free-form pools complete with slides, caves, rapids, waterfalls, a Tarzan-type rope swing, and the world's only water elevator. The Grande Wailea's 50,000-square-foot Spa Grande entices with its elegant interiors, comprehensive fitness center and extensive spa menu. Humuhumunukunukuapua'a (Humu for short) is a gorgeous Polynesian-thatched roof restaurant that lets you to select your own lobster from the lagoon. In fact, there is so much to do here you not likely to spend much time in your lovely room with its wall painted in tropical colors, beautiful furnishings, and warm touches such as chenille throws and pretty pillows.

780 rooms. Restaurant, bar. Fitness center. Spa. Beach. Pool. Tennis. Business center. $351 and up

★★★MARRIOTT WAILEA
3700 Wailea Alanui, Wailea, 808-879-9122, 800-367-2960; www.waileamarriott.com
The Marriott, the first hotel built in the high-end Wailea resort complex, recently underwent a complete renovation. Built on a point of land with lava cliffs at the water's edge, the resort has two beautiful, sandy beaches on either side of it. In addition to the championship golf courses shared by all the Wailea resorts, the Marriott has five pools, including a spectacular oceanfront infinity pool, a jogging trail, a putting green, a shopping arcade and a gorgeous new spa. New rooms have a crisp, contemporary feel.

521 rooms. Restaurant, bar. Fitness center. Spa. Pool. Business center. $251-350

WHERE TO EAT
★ALEXANDER'S FISH, CHICKEN & RIBS
1913 S. Kihei Road, Kihei, 808-874-0788
Great food fast at fast-food prices is how this small seafood eatery markets itself. Highly popular, it often hosts long lines of customers waiting to place their over-the-counter orders. The restaurant is across the coast road from the beach in Kihei's Kalama Village shopping area, along Maui's southwest shore. Beachwear is always welcome (and often appreciated, according to a sign on the counter). Broiled and fried (in tempura batter) fresh fish is the specialty of the house. Eat on a small casual lanai or take it to go.
American. Lunch, dinner. Outdoor seating. $15 and under

★★GREEK BISTRO

2511 S. Kihei Road, Kihei, 808-879-9330

The only Greek bistro on Maui, this restaurant is located on the southwestern coast in Kihei, set back off the road in a small courtyard at the south end of town. There are limited ocean views from the terrace dining room. The decor transports diners from a Hawaiian island to a typical Hellenic island 8,000 miles away, with Greek scenes depicted in murals and colorful tiles to set the mood. The menu also offers dishes from other Mediterranean countries besides Greece.

Greek. Dinner. Bar. Outdoor seating. $16-35

★JAWZ

1279 S. Kihei Road, Kihei, 808-847-8226; www.jawzfishtacos.com

Born out of a single truck serving hungry beachgoers, Jawz now has a restaurant with actual seats (and televisions playing surfer movies), plus two roadside trucks in Makena, to give fans their beloved fish tacos and shaved ices. Choices include the ono, mahi mahi and ahi. Take your pick and then just try to decide which toppings to put on—the extensive salsa bar includes everything from corn salsa to sour cream with avocado.

Lunch, dinner. $15 and under

★KIHEI CAFFE

1945 S. Kihei Road, Kihei, 808-879-2230; www.kiheicaffe.com

Kihei Caffe is a local institution in Kihei town right across from Kalama Park. There are only a few tables on the outside patio; order inside and then grab a seat from which to observe the slice of Hawaiian life that takes place here each morning as locals drop in to catch up on all the latest. Start your day with a stack of the pineapple-coconut pancakes and a cup of the strong rich coffee. You'll also find breakfast burritos, French toast and cinnamon rolls topped with macadamia nuts. Specials include blackened fish and eggs, and there are a variety of sandwiches for lunch.

Breakfast, lunch (until 2 p.m.). $15 and under

★★MATTEO'S

100 Ike Drive, Wailea, 808-874-1234; www.matteospizzeria.com

When you tire of fresh fish, Matteo's makes awesome pizzas (trust us, we're based in Chicago and we know pizza). The set up is simple: order at the counter, take your number and grab a table in the open-air dining room. The wooden tables and chairs are roomy and comfortable, and there's a small bar from which servers will fetch you more drinks. Matteo's is wildly popular and it is evident why: The pizzas are outrageously good. A special goat cheese pizza with crispy onions, tomatoes and ham was aromatic and had the perfect balance of flavors, while the crust was perfect amounts crusty and chewy and tinged with smoke from the wood-burning ovens. It's the perfect spot for casual—delicious—dining. You can also pick up pies to go if you just want to head back to your hotel.

Italian. Lunch, dinner. $16-35

★THAILAND CUISINE
1819 S. Kihei Road, Kihei, 808-875-0839; www.thailandcuisinemaui.com

Hidden away in the Kukui Shopping Center, not far from the Wailea resort area on Maui's southwest coast, this restaurant offers authentic Thai cuisine. A small storefront property, its single dining room is elaborately decorated with Thai paintings, sculptures, figurines, memorabilia and nearly life-size statues. Popular with locals, it is open for both lunch and dinner.
Thai. Lunch, dinner. $16-35

★★★★SPAGO
3900 Wailea Alanui, Wailea, 808-879-2999; www.wolfgangpuck.com

Spago is one of those great spots: Yes, it's in a hotel (the gorgeous Four Seasons, no less) and yes it's fine dining. Yet the atmosphere is very relaxed (you are in Maui, after all). One could just as easily sit at the bar and fill up on the delicious sweat and sour fish lettuce wraps or everyone's favorite miso-sesame ahi tuna cones, as you could languish over a three-course meal on the romantic outdoor patio fronting the ocean. Everything at Spago is done well, from the addicting breadbasket filled with Maui onion bread to the very nice wine list to the Hawaiian flavors wafting from every dish. The menu focuses on California cuisine with Pacific Rim flavors using fresh, local ingredients. Expect dishes like the whole Big Island moi steamed "Hong Kong" style with chili, ginger and baby choy sum, and pan-roasted opakapaka with lobster-crusted potatoes.
Hawaiian, Pacific-Rim, Pan-Asian. Dinner. $36-85

SPAS
★★★★THE SPA AT FOUR SEASONS RESORT MAUI AT WAILEA
3900 Wailea Alanui Drive, Wailea, 808-874-8000, 800-334-6284; www.fourseasons.com

You won't find a better place to have a massage—and what a massage. The signature mele Wailea (the song of Wailea), which uses aromatherapy, heated towels and a blend of Swedish and lomi lomi massage, is pure bliss. A very close second is the cocoa pohaku, in which your therapist uses cocoa butter and warm stones to help loosen you up. All of the treatments here feel and smell heavenly. Scrubs use ingredients like macadamia nut, pineapple and papaya, and lemongrass. The result is everything you'd expect from a luxe tropical spa. This is also the place to have a facial—the spa uses Kate Somerville techniques and products—and there's a range of salon treatments, including manicures and pedicures.

★★★★SPA GRANDE AT GRAND WAILEA RESORT
3850 Wailea Alanui Drive, Wailea, 808-875-1234, 800-888-6100; www.grandwailea.com

The Grand Wailea's 50,000-square-foot spa has elegant interiors, a comprehensive fitness center and an extensive spa menu (there are more than a dozen massages alone). Visits begin with a complimentary hydrotherapy session, featuring five different aromatic baths to choose from, including a bubbling Japanese furo bath, cascading waterfall, cold plunge pool, Roman Jacuzzi, or Swiss jet shower; plus, there's a eucalyptus steam room and a redwood sauna to help extend your visit. Treatments pull from East and West—shiatsu (east) or Swedish (west), skin brightening (east) or hydrating vitamin C (west), as well as Hawaiian specialties such as lomi lomi and Hawaiian seashell massages.

★★★SPA KEALANI
4100 Wailea Alanui Drive, Wailea, 808-875-2229, 800-441-1414; www.fairmont.com

More than 50 treatments are available at this lovely spa inside the Fairmont, including lomi lomi massages and body wraps which make the most of local ingredients such as natural sugar cane, ginger and lime. Whatever treatment you choose, add one of the bath experiences in the 75-gallon hydrotherapy room. If you can, book a massage in the outdoor hale, where ocean breezes lull you into an even deeper state of relaxation. A full-service fitness center offers private yoga lessons or beachfront workouts.

LAHAINA AND WEST MAUI

Lahaina, an old whaling village turned visitor magnet, and several attractive resort areas hug the shoreline that wraps around the base of the splendid West Maui Mountains. This region, called West Maui, was the first on the island to be developed for tourism and it remains one of the most popular.

Visitors in T-shirts and flip flops flock to Lahaina to shop, eat and party, especially along Front Street, which can get quite busy and loud, with people pouring out of popular spots such as Cheeseburger in Paradise. Despite its commercialism, however, this village does have a lot of history, which the Lahaina Restoration Foundation has worked diligently to preserve.

To the north of Lahaina are the upscale resorts of Kaanapali and Kapalua. In Kaanapali, hotels and condominium complexes front a sparkling 3-mile-long beach with breathtaking views of Lanai and Molokai. You'll also find two championship golf courses and Whalers Village, an open-air shopping center.

Down the road, the more exclusive Kapalua spoils visitors in high style with the waterfront Ritz-Carlton and a group of comfortable villas spread out over the green mountainside. The resort has three golf courses with gorgeous views and three beaches, the most notable being Kapalua Beach, a heavenly, crescent-shaped stretch of sand with calm, clear water that's usually good for swimming and snorkeling. (Plus, the snorkeling is excellent in the summer at nearby Honolua Bay, a marine conservation district.)

Between Kaanapali and Kapalua are three other low-key seaside resorts—Honokowai, Kahana and Napili—with beachfront condominiums but not many other amenities.

WHAT TO SEE
ALOHA TOY STORE
640 Front St., Lahaina, 808-661-1212, 888-628-4227

You can cruise around in a Chevy rental—or you can visit this shop for something with a bit more vroom. Rent a Harley, or get behind the wheel of a BMW, Porche or Ferrari. The Aloha Toy Store also has rental outlets in Kaanapali and Wailea.
Daily 8 a.m.-5 p.m.

ATLANTIS SUBMARINES
548 Front St., Lahaina, 808-667-2224, 800-548-6262; www.atlantisadventures.com

Explore the depths of the Pacific Ocean in a high-tech submarine. You and 47 others will sink down 130 feet into the deep blue sea for more than an hour of spectacular sightseeing. Who knows what will swim by—perhaps a shark or two, some eagle rays, or a school of parrotfish. Other Atlantis tours combine the submarine adventure with whale watching (December-May) or a luau. Admission: adults $109, children $49. Daily 9 a.m., 10:00 a.m., noon and 2 p.m.

BANYAN TREE PARK
649 Wharf St., Lahaina
No trip to Lahaina is complete without driving or stopping by this park to see one of the city's most famous landmarks—a banyan tree planted in 1873, the 50th anniversary of the city's first Christian mission. The tree now stands 50 feet tall and has at least 12 trunks with hundreds of sprawling limbs.

DOWNTOWN LAHAINA
Front Street, Lahaina
The Lahaina Restoration Foundation has worked diligently to preserve this historic whaling village, the island's first capital, but the town has gotten commercialized just the same. Art galleries, restaurants, bars, clothing stores and souvenir shops line Front Street, along the waterfront, attracting thousands of tourists every day.

EXPEDITIONS LANAI
Lahaina Harbor, Lahaina, 808-661-3756, 800-695-2624; www.go-lanai.com
Hop aboard this inter-island ferry if you want to spend a day or two in the neighboring isle of Lanai. From Lahaina, the trip across the Auau Channel takes about one hour, arriving at Manele Harbor. On the way over, sit back and enjoy the spectacular views of both islands. If its whale season, you might also see some of the playful humpbacks that call these waters home in the winter.
Admission: adults $30 (each way), children $20 (each way). Daily: from Maui at 6:45 a.m., 9:15 a.m., 12:45 p.m., 3:15 p.m., and 5:45 p.m.; from Lanai at 8 a.m., 10:30 a.m., 2 p.m., 4:30 p.m., and 6:45 p.m.

HONOLUA STORE
Kapalua, 808-669-6128
This old general store in the Kapalua resort is a great place for a cheap and delicious breakfast, lunch or dinner. The deli in the back offers sandwiches and mixed plates and there's a veranda outside where you can eat. There's also a coffee bar, souvenirs and a variety of groceries.
Daily 6 a.m.-8 p.m.

KAANAPALI BEACH
Lahaina
Several hotels line this white sandy beach, which stretches for three glorious miles. For especially good snorkeling, put on your fins and dive into the water in front of the Sheraton Maui, where lots of colorful fish hang out around a lava-rock formation. A walkway along the beach connects several of the resorts hotels.

KAANAPALI GOLF COURSES

2290 Kaanapali Parkway, Lahaina, 808-661-3691, 866-454-4653;
www.kaanapali-golf.com

At Kaanapali, take your pick from two courses. The North Course, designed by Robert Trent Jones, Sr., debuted in 1962 as Maui's first resort course. It starts at sea level, but eventually heads up into the foothills of the lush West Maui Mountains. You must navigate lots of water at its finishing holes, so be ready for the challenges you'll face on this par-72, 6,994-yard favorite. The par-71 South Course is a bit shorter, at 6,555 yards. All levels of players enjoy teeing off at this course, thanks to its wide fairways and subtle greens. Even if the trade winds are blowing on the North Course, they may not be whipping across the fairways here because of its southern location in the resort.

Daily 6:15 a.m.-6:30 p.m.

KAHANA GATEWAY SHOPPING CENTER

4405 Honoapiilani Highway, Kahana, 808-669-9669; www.kahanagateway.com

This shopping center is convenient to the condos in Kahana, which sit halfway between Kaanapali and Kapalua. There are no big chain stores, but you'll find a variety of nice merchandise, mostly jewelry, art, swimwear and apparel. The center has several restaurants, including an Outback Steakhouse and two restaurants operated by Roy Yamaguchi, one of Hawaii's best-known chefs: Roy's Kahana Bar and Grill and Roy's Nicolina Restaurant.

KAPALUA BEACH

Lower Honoapiilani Highway, Kapalua

This crescent-shape beach isn't particularly large, but it's a beautiful spot. The water is usually ideal for swimming because two lava rock points on each side frame the beach, protecting it from strong ocean currents. The view is spectacular, with Molokai off in the distance. It's also a great place for snorkeling. With all this, the only downside is that it can get crowded.

KAPALUA GOLF COURSES

300 Kapalua Drive, Kapalua, 877-527-2582; www.kapaluamaui.com/golf

At this upscale resort, hit the links on any of three championship golf courses—The Bay, The Plantation or The Village—all of which rank among Hawaii's best. Arnold Palmer and Francis Duane designed the par-72 Bay course, which runs near the Ritz-Carlton and stretches for 6,600 yards. The par-73 Plantation course offers plenty of challenges to the best of players. As you move from hole to hole on this 7,263-yard beauty, designed by Ben Crenshaw and Bill Coore, you'll come across breathtaking natural geographic formations and lush green pineapple fields. Be prepared for a lot of twists, turns and rises when you come out swinging at the par-70, 6,317-yard Village Course, also designed by Arnold Palmer. If you want to improve your game, sign up for instruction at the resorts respected golf academy.

Daily 5:45 a.m.-7 p.m.

LAHAINA DIVERS

143 Dickenson St., Lahaina, 808-667-7496, 800-998-3483; www.lahainadivers.com

Choose from a variety of diving charters, including treks to Lanai, Molokini Crater and Turtle Reef, where endangered green sea turtles tend to hang out. The charters range from one to four dives and run from about four to eight hours. The company also offers a night dive every Thursday, as well as a snorkeling experience.

Admission: prices begin at $79 (for snorkeling), plus rental equipment. Daily; times vary.

LAHAINA RESTORATION FOUNDATION

120 Front St., Lahaina, 808-661-3262; www.lahainarestoration.org

With increased commercialism, the old whaling village of Lahaina isn't quite as historic or charming as it once was. However, thanks to the restoration work of this foundation, several old buildings in the town still take visitors back to another era. Stop by the foundation's offices in the Masters Reading Room for a map designed to take you on a self-guided tour of the key historic sights, such as the Baldwin House, lighthouse, courthouse and Wo Hing Temple. Throughout the small town, the foundation's distinctive brown signs clearly mark the must-see sights noted on the map. The group's gift shop, called the Na Mea Hawaii Store, features arts, crafts, gifts and clothing all made by Hawaiian artists.

MALUULUOLELE PARK

Front and Shaw streets, Lahaina

This may looks any community playground and softball field, but the Lahaina Restoration Foundation includes it on the city's historic walking tour. That's because the area, once considered sacred by islanders, was home to Hawaiian royalty, specifically, King Kamehameha III, who lived here in a regal royal compound until his death in 1854. In 1918, the compound was torn down and a freshwater pond filled in with dirt to convert the property into the park it is today.

★★★★★ HAWAII

117

MAUI ECO-ADVENTURES

1087 Limahana, Lahaina, 877-661-7720; www.ecomaui.com

Sign up for one of this company's hikes when you want to explore out-of-the-way parts of Maui that visitors often don't see, including remote Hawaiian villages, rain forests and secluded waterfalls. Tours also go in to the Haleakala Crater, or you can arrange a customized helicopter or four-wheel drive expedition. Hikes range from four to six hours.

Admission: prices start at $200 (plus $100 gratuity) for two guests. Daily 8 a.m.

MAUI PRINCESS AND MOLOKAI PRINCESS

Lahaina, Lahaina Harbor, 808-662-3355; www.molokaiferry.com

These 100-foot inter-island ferries operate daily between Maui and Molokai, transporting up to 149 passengers each way. During the 90-minute trip, you can stay cool and comfy in an air-conditioned main cabin, or venture out onto an open-air observation deck. Wherever you are, the views are spectacular.

In Molokai, the boats operate out of Kaunakakai. A variety of packages are available that may include narrated tours or hikes, lunch and more.

Admission: packages start at $202.75 for adults. From Maui: Monday-Saturday at 7:15 a.m. and daily at 6 p.m. From Molokai: Monday-Saturday 5:15 a.m. and daily at 4:00 p.m.

NAPILI BAY BEACH

Hui Street, Napili (off Lower Hanoapiilani Highway)

This crescent-beach slopes steeply into the water, where the swimming is good all year except during winter when rip currents can get strong. The snorkeling is okay (not as good as you'll find at Kapalua), but it's a low-key resort area with several condominium complexes and small hotels hugging the shoreline.

OLD LAHAINA LUAU

1251 Front St., Lahaina, 808-667-2998, 800-248-5828; www.oldlahainaluau.com

Some claim that this luau, a nightly three-hour oceanfront feast, is the island's best luau. The evening begins with a flower-lei greeting, a demonstration of Hawaiian arts and crafts by local artisans and relaxing Hawaiian music. For dinner, you'll fill up on roasted Kalua pig and many other traditional Hawaiian dishes, including marinated raw ahi tuna, Big Island sweet potatoes, chicken long rice, Maui-style mahi mahi, island crab salad, and banana bread. Afterward, the fast-paced production that tells the story of Hawaii is rousing entertainment.

Admission: adults $92, children $62. April-September, daily 5:45 p.m.; October-March, daily 5:15 p.m.

SCOTCH MIST SAILING CHARTERS

Lahaina, Lahaina Harbor, Slip 2, 808-661-0386; www.scotchmistsailingcharters.com

The Scotch Mist II sailing yacht finished first in the 1984 Victoria-Maui International Yacht Race, so it can glide through the water at a fast clip when the captain wants to speed things up. Book one of this company's sailing trips along the West Maui coast, take one of its snorkeling tours, or book a whale-watching excursion in season.

May-December, daily 1:00 and 4:00 p.m.

TRILOGY EXCURSIONS

180 Lahainaluna Road, Lahaina, 888-225-6284; www.sailtrilogy.com

Sail the deep blue waters off the Maui shoreline with one of the island's most popular sailing companies. On its signature Discover Lanai tour, you'll sail across the channel to neighboring Lanai, take a van tour of the isle, snorkel in crystal-clear water at Hulopoe Beach, savor a barbecue lunch and play volleyball before heading back to Maui and Lahaina's marina. Other tours take you to Molokini or Kaanapali, or set sail in search of humpback whales and dolphins.

Admission: adults, prices start at $202.54. Daily; times vary.

VILLAGE GALLERIES MAUI

120 Dickenson St., Lahaina, 808-661-4402, 800-346-0585;
www.villagegalleriesmaui.com

For more than 30 years, this gallery has been showcasing the original art of some of Hawaii's top artists. Wander through its showroom and you'll find just about any type of art on display: oil paintings, handmade jewelry, copper sculptures, ceramics, stone lithographs, wooden bowls and carvings, collages, etchings and more. You can also visit Village Gift and Fine Art at the Baldwin House at Front and Dickerson streets *(808-661-5199)* or the gallery inside the Ritz-Carlton, Kapalua *(808-669-1800)*.
Lahaina gallery: daily 9 a.m.-9 p.m. Kapalua gallery: daily 10 a.m.-6 p.m.

WHALERS VILLAGE

2435 Kaanapali Parkway, Lahaina, 808-661-4567; www.whalersvillage.com

This appealing oceanfront shopping center sits right on a stretch of Kaanapali Beach, within walking distance of the many nearby hotels. The 112,000 square feet of retail space features 65 shops and restaurants, including Louis Vuitton, Coach and Sunglass Hut. You'll also find art galleries, jewelry stores, gift shops, sundry stores, a food court, several popular restaurants, and a whaling museum.
Daily 9:30 a.m.-10 p.m.

WHALERS VILLAGE MUSEUM

Whalers Village, 2435 Kaanapali Parkway, Lahaina, 808-661-5992

From 1825 to 1860, whaling was the industry in Lahaina. This museum takes visitors back to those days with a large-scale model of a whaling ship, a collection of 19th-century scrimshaw, old photographs, antique ornaments, and more.
Daily 10 a.m.-6 p.m.

SPECIAL EVENTS
HALLOWEEN IN LAHAINA

Front Street, Lahaina, 808-667-9193; www.lahainahalloween.com

At 3 p.m. on October 31 each year, Front Street is closed to vehicle traffic for this big street party called the "Mardi Gras of the Pacific." About 30,000 ghoulish folks, many in full costume, make this a festive, crazy night of fun. Maui's biggest, wildest party of the year includes a children's costume parade, food booths, costume contests, arts and crafts, dancing and live music.
October 31.

KAPALUA WINE AND FOOD FESTIVAL

Kapalua Resort, Kapalua, 800-527-2582; www.kapaluawineandfood.com

More than 3,500 wine and food lovers come to Maui each July for this four-day culinary event. The event includes wine tastings, culinary exhibitions, a seafood festival and more.
Early July.

MERCEDES BENZ CHAMPIONSHIP

500 Bay Drive, Kapalua, 808-669-2440; www.pgatour.com

Each year in early January, the PGA Tour starts its new season with this

prestigious weeklong tournament at the Kapalua Resort. Fans come to see the biggest names in the sport, as this shootout on the fairways is limited only to tour champions from the previous year. A shuttle service is available from several locations around the island.
Early January.

OCEAN ARTS FESTIVAL
Banyan Tree Park, 649 Wharf Street, Lahaina, 808-667-9175; www.visitlahaina.com
Maui celebrates the annual migration of the humpback whales to Hawaiian waters with a marine-centered festival. The festival showcases the 50-ton leviathans and Hawaii's unique marine environment in photo exhibits, original art displays and educational booths detailing the lives of the whales. Arts and crafts booths, entertainment by local musicians and naturalists, and ocean-centered activities for kids (including the ever popular creature feature touch pool) are all part of the fun.
Mid-March.

WHERE TO STAY
★★★HYATT REGENCY MAUI RESORT AND SPA
200 Nohea Kai Drive, Ka'anapali, 808-661-1234, 800-554-9288; www.maui.hyatt.com
The Hyatt Regency Maui is located on an idyllic stretch of beach at the edge of the Kaanapali resort complex. The 40-acre resort has a lively pool area, a nice spa and a few shops (including Macy's) in the lobby. Guest rooms have platform beds with duvets, walk-in closets and private lanais. Unfortunately, it's all looking a bit tired, including the guest rooms, which look like they could be attended to a bit more carefully. Overall, you can't help feeling that this was the place back in the day, although the Hyatt continues to draw plenty of people. You can still spend your day playing golf or tennis, lounging by the pool or the beach, or relaxing at the oceanfront Spa Moana; they are also plenty of activities for the kids.
806 rooms. Restaurant, bar. Fitness center. Spa. Beach. Pool. Golf. Tennis. Business center. $251-350

★★★LAHAINA INN
127 Lahainaluna Road, Lahaina, 800-669-3444; 800-669-3444; www.lahainainn.com
If you prefer a small, intimate inn to the mass-market appeal of a large beach resort, the Lahaina Inn is a great choice. In a historic two-story property in the center of Lahaina's old whaling port, literally steps from the ocean, this charming 1938 inn has only 12 guest rooms. They are on the second floor above a small lobby and a first-class restaurant. Each guest room is individually decorated in floral patterns and furnished with antiques, period wallpaper, Oriental rugs and Tiffany lamps. The inn also offers two cottages for families and larger groups. Lahaina's shops and restaurants are outside the inn's front door, at the corner of Lahainaluna Road and Front Street.
12 rooms. Complimentary breakfast. Restaurant, bar. $61-150

★MAUIAN HOTEL
5441 Lower Honoapiilani Road, Napili, 808-669-6205, 800-367-5034; www.mauian.com.
If you're searching for a small, low-key, non-resort hotel, the Mauian could

be just the spot. Tucked away in Napili on Maui's northwest coast, this motel-style lodging is blessed with a gorgeous location on protected Napili Bay with views across the ocean channel of Molokai. The 2-acre property has an expansive lawn that stretches to a semi-private beach. Guest rooms are simply but tastefully decorated in tropical style, with bright colors and bamboo furnishings. There are no in-room TVs or phones, but there are kitchenettes for vacation stays. An island-style continental breakfast is provided in the hotel's common room, which also has a TV.

44 rooms. Complimentary breakfast. Pool. $151-250

★★★PLANTATION INN

174 Lahainaluna Road, Lahaina, 808-667-9225, 800-433-6815;
www.theplantationinn.com

Offering a variety of room types and sizes, most with balconies and all sound-proofed and individually decorated in island style, this early-1900s white-frame former residence offers a relatively quiet and intimate spot to spend a night in Lahaina. Best of all, you're right behind Gerard's restaurant, one of Maui's finest dining establishments, and a complimentary breakfast is included in your stay. A secluded courtyard and small pool frame the inn's two separate buildings which are a few blocks from all the action in Lahaina.

19 rooms.Complimentary breakfast. Restaurant. Pool. $151-250

★★★★THE RITZ-CARLTON, KAPALUA

One Ritz-Carlton Drive, Kapalua, 808-669-6200, 800-262-8440; www.ritzcarlton.com

Fresh from a complete makeover, this resort has views of the Pacific stretching all the way to Molokai. Rooms have a cheerful and homey feel with built-in dark wood furniture and Hawaiian artwork, along with brand-new flat-screen TVs and marble bathrooms. Part of a 23,000-acre working pineapple plantation, the resort also has two championship golf courses, a three-tiered swimming pool and beaches that are about 10 minutes away by foot (a complimentary shuttle transports guests to the beaches, restaurants and golf courses within the Kapalua Resort). A lavish new 14,000-square-foot spa has 15 private rooms, treatments inspired by local ingredients and several new couples' cabanas. A sleek new sushi restaurant has also been added to the hotel's collection of eateries.

548 rooms. Restaurant, bar. Fitness center. Spa. Beach. Pool. Golf. Tennis. Business center. $351 and up

★★★SHERATON MAUI RESORT KAANAPALI BEACH

2605 Kaanapali Parkway, Kaanapali, 808-661-003, 888-488-3535;
www.sheraton-hawaii.com.

This large beach resort on Maui's northwest coast has an inviting location on a semi-sheltered cove. A part of the Kaanapali Beach resort complex, the Sheraton is located next to Black Rock, a historically significant promontory in Hawaiian culture. The lobby is open to the ocean breezes, and 80 percent of the guest rooms have ocean views. Resort activities run the gamut from snorkeling and whale watching to tennis, croquet, and a full-service spa. There is a broad lawn area adjacent to the beach and a huge, tropically land-scaped, freshwater swimming lagoon, as well as a nice new spa. The rooms aren't the most luxurious but families seem to love this place.

510 rooms. Restaurant, bar. Fitness center. Beach. Pool. Tennis. Business center. $351 and up

★★★WESTIN MAUI RESORT & SPA

2365 Kaanapali Parkway, Kaanapali, 808-667-2525, 800-937-8461; www.westin.com

Within the expansive Kaanapali resort complex on Maui's northwest coast, the Westin Maui is a major beach resort and spa (and the best of the bunch in the Kaanapali resort). Situated on 12 oceanfront acres on Kaanapali Beach, its two high-rise towers provide views of the Pacific Ocean or the West Maui Mountains. The guest rooms have contemporary decor and trademark Heavenly Beds and Baths. The property features verdant tropical landscaping, including meandering streams, waterfalls and colorful gardens. There is also a huge aquatic playground complete with five pools, a huge water slide, and Jacuzzi, in addition to the soft sandy beach and its diverse activities. The Heavenly spa is a blissful retreat with 16 treatment rooms, salon, workout facility and yoga studio.

758 rooms. Restaurant, bar. Business center. Pool. Fitness center. Spa. Pets accepted. $251-350

WHERE TO EAT

★CHEESEBURGER IN PARADISE

811 Front St., Lahaina, 808-661-0830; www.cheeseburgerland.com

This wildly popular spot serves up the American classic in a party-hearty atmosphere inspired by singer Jimmy Buffett (admittedly better known for his affinity for the Florida Keys than the Hawaiian Islands), further enlivened by a rock-and-roll band that performs nightly. The thick, juicy burgers are just the ticket after a day at the beach—the Cheeseburger in Paradise is topped with jack and cheddar cheeses, sautéed onions, lettuce, tomatoes and Thousand Island dressing. Located on Old Lahaina's waterfront, the restaurant overlooks the Pacific Ocean.

American. Breakfast, lunch, dinner, late-night. Bar. $15 and under

★★CHEZ PAUL

820B Olowalu Village, Lahaina, 808-661-3843; www.chezpaul.net

Centrally located in the middle of nowhere is how Chez Paul describes its location in rural West Maui, about eight miles south of Lahaina on the coast highway (Highway 30). The West Maui Mountains serve as a dramatic backdrop for the restaurant, while the Pacific Ocean laps the shore across the street. From the outside, Chez Paul is a non-descript roadside restaurant. It is anything but. The intimate, elegant dining room is a warm spot to indulge in the superb classic French cuisine that includes dishes such as a crispy slow-roasted duck and fresh fish poached in champagne with leeks and capers. The pineapple crème brulee, served in a pineapple shell, is delightful. The food is fine dining but the atmosphere and dress are refreshingly not.

French. Dinner. $251-350

★★★★GERARD'S

174 Lahainaluna Road, Lahaina, 808-661-8939, 877-661-8939; www.gerardsmaui.com

Chef Gerard Reversade is an internationally recognized master of French cuisine, but that doesn't mean his namesake restaurant doesn't also celebrate

its Hawaiian location. Reversade uses ahi tuna in his Basque-inspired fisherman's stew, and a poha berry compote accompanies a seared duck foie gras appetizer. The flourless chocolate gateau is created with macadamia nuts and Kona coffee liqueur, while the apple tarte tatin includes tropical fruit. Gerard's décor blends perfectly with the Victorian charm of its host hotel, the Plantation Inn. Request a table on the veranda or the garden patio—they're often the best seats in the house.
French. Dinner. $36-85

★★★I'O
505 Front St., Lahaina, 808-661-8422; www.iomaui.com
This stylish and sophisticated oceanside restaurant at the south end of historic Old Lahaina has a modern, tropical flair, not to mention gorgeous views. The upscale setting features French doors, lots of chrome, a soft seafoam green color scheme, lush landscaping and swaying palm trees. The chef characterizes the cuisine as fresh New Pacific, which translates to dishes such as fresh sashimi tuna in a nori and panko crust, Maine lobster tails in a mango Thai curry sauce, and grilled baby-back ribs with a green apple confit. Specialty martinis, tropical drinks and an extensive selection of wines by the glass and the bottle pair nicely with the flavorful cuisine.
Pacific-Rim. Dinner. Bar. Outdoor seating. $36-85

★★KIMO'S
845 Front St., Lahaina, 808-661-4811; www.kimosmaui.com
Taking full advantage of its seaside location in Old Lahaina, this casual restaurant gives diners access to unfettered views of the island of Lanai across the Pacific. A two-story property, the open ground level is primarily for casual lunchtime seating at teak tables under umbrellas. With its koa wood walls and maritime memorabilia, the upstairs dining room is a bit more formal, but not much. Wherever you end up dining, the menu features local seafood at market prices, along with steaks and other island favorites and Kimo's specialty dessert, hula pie.
American. Lunch, dinner. Outdoor seating. $16-35

★★LAHAINA GRILL
127 Lahainaluna Road, Lahaina, 808-667-5117, 800-360-2606; www.lahainagrill.com
Longtime chef David Paul may be gone, but this restaurant is as popular as ever (make a reservation). The bar is buzzing and the contemporary-casual dining room filled with colorful local art and a lovely pressed-tin ceiling is often packed with pretty tanned people who come for the New American food that draws heavily on local produce. Signature items include a Kona lobster crab cake, tequila shrimp with firecracker rice and Kalua duck. Groups of six to eight can reserve the chef's table.
American. Dinner. Bar. Children's menu. Reservations recommended. $36-85

★★LAHAINA FISH COMPANY
831 Front St., Lahaina, 808-661-3472; www.lahainafishcompany.com
On Old Lahaina's historic waterfront, this over-the-water restaurant is a popular draw for seafood lovers. The vistas of the harbor and boats of all

kinds make it a fun spot to enjoy a meal. Upstairs, the dining room serves dinner only, while the ground level is for more casual dining. Nautical decor throughout the restaurant sets the appropriate mood for enjoying the catch of the day. Favorites include island fish and chips, coconut fried shrimp and Ahi Katsu with wasabi ginger butter sauce.
Seafood. Lunch, dinner. Bar. $16-35

★★LONGHI'S
888 Front St., Lahaina, 808-667-2288, 888-844-2288; www.longhi-maui.com
Located across the street from the ocean on Old Lahaina's waterfront, this casual restaurant has been a Maui staple for almost 30 years. A striking black-and-white tile floor dominates the open-air dining rooms, where the signature dish—shrimp sautéed in lemon, butter, white wine, fresh basil and chopped tomatoes and served over garlic toast—has been on the menu since 1976. A variety of pasta dishes, steaks and seafood are also offered. At dinner, guests are served upstairs in a semi-formal setting, where there's a dance floor with a live band playing on Friday nights. Additional Longhi's locations can be found in Wailea, Maui, and in Honolulu at the Ala Moana Shopping Center.
American. Breakfast, lunch, dinner, late-night. Bar. $16-35

★★PACIFIC'O
505 Front St., Lahaina, 808-667-4341; www.pacificomaui.com
Pacific'O and its sister restaurant, IO, are the only Hawaiian properties that have their own farming operation to support their kitchens. With dining rooms upstairs and on the ground floor, wonderful sunset views are available of the ocean and the island. Entrées like lemongrass-coconut fish and sesame-crusted lamb are accompanied by live jazz performances on weekend nights. Asian dishes like tempura and prawn and basil wontons are also popular here.
Pacific-Rim. Lunch, dinner. Bar. Outdoor seating. $36-85

★★★PLANTATION HOUSE RESTAURANT
2000 Plantation Club Drive, Kapalua, 808-699-6299; www.theplantationhouse.com
Host to the PGA's Mercedes Championship each January, the Plantation Golf Course at the Kapalua Bay Resort offers upscale dining. Located above the clubhouse, the Plantation House has an incredible 180-degree view of the rolling golf course, the Pacific Ocean and the island of Molokai; it's worth a visit for the view alone. The casual but sophisticated restaurant features contemporary island-inspired decor, with teak wood tables, hand-carved chairs and lovely floral arrangements. Two levels of dining rooms and terrace and bar dining provide plenty of seating options. On the menu, you'll find a nice selection of creative salads along with a variety of fresh fish preparations such as the Taste of Maui, in which the fish is given a pistachio-crust and is served atop Maui onion, local tomatoes and upcountry spinach. Weekly farm-to-table specials are also available.
Mediterranean. Breakfast, lunch, dinner, brunch.Bar. $36-85

★★★ROY'S KAHANA BAR & GRILL
4405 Honoapiilani Highway, Kahana, 808-669-6999; www.roysrestaurant.com
This popular restaurant is located in the Kahana area of Maui's northwest

coast, in the Gateway Shopping Center. The second in chef/owner Roy Yama-guchi's chain of contemporary Hawaiian restaurants, it is a sleek, upscale property with a large, attractive dining room and an impressive demonstration kitchen. The menu features Roy's classics like blackened island ahi with spicy soy mustard butter, wood-grilled Szechuan-spiced baby-back short ribs, roasted macadamia nut mahi mahi, and melting hot chocolate soufflé. Prix fixe meals are available, and the wine list includes selections made by leading winemakers specifically for Roy's.

Pacific-Rim. Dinner. Bar. $16-35

★★SANSEI
115 Bay Drive, Kapalua, 808-669-6286; www.sanseihawaii.com

When you're on vacation and you want really good food for a great value, follow the locals. In this case, you'll be joining them in line to get into Sansei right as the doors open for the half-price specials. There are two locations on Maui (the other is in Kihei), both of which locals religiously visit for their weekly serving of Sansei's creative cuisine. Favorites include the mango crab salad roll, shrimp dynamite (crispy tempura in a creamy garlic aioli) and the panko crusted ahi roll, which is flash-fried and served with a soy wasabi butter sauce. The place also fills up late night for karaoke.

Japanese. Dinner, late night. Closed Monday-Wednesday. Bar. $16-35

★SUNRISE CAFÉ
693A Front St., Lahaina, 808-661-8558

A perfect spot for a casual breakfast or lunch, this waterfront cafe is nicely situated alongside historic Old Lahaina's harbor. A simple eatery, it has several sidewalk tables, a small patio, and an inside coffee and muffin counter. Sunrise is well known for its home-baked goods, fresh pineapple juice and fruit smoothies. The cinnamon rolls and pineapple boat are particularly popular. Inexpensive and relaxed, it is also a good source for picnic lunches (order the day before).

American. Lunch, brunch. Outdoor seating. $15 and under

SPA
★★★SPA MOANA
200 Nohea Kai Drive, Lahaina, 808-661-1234; www.hyatt.com

Located in the Hyatt Regency Maui, this relaxing retreat has 15 treatment rooms where technicians deliver services such as the traditional Hawaiian lomi lomi massage or a decadent macadamia nut wrap. The salon offers manicures and pedicures (with a unique sugar scrub version for men). The Moana Athletic Club has 5,000 square feet of cutting-edge exercise machines, weights and classroom space for yoga, aerobics and more.

UPCOUNTRY MAUI

To escape the beach for a few hours, head to the upper slopes of Haleakala, an area called Upcountry, where the panoramic views of Maui and the ocean beyond are nothing short of breathtaking. It is a completely different world than down on the shoreline, and its much cooler. The familiar sights of sand and palm trees gives way to the green pastureland of ranches and tall eucalyptus trees, as you snake your way up the 10,000-foot-tall mountain. As the terrain turns desert-like near the summit, be on the lookout for silversword plants, a member of the yucca family that grows only here.

The major reason visitors come Upcountry is to make their way to the summit and explore Haleakala National Park. Viewing its crater from several overlooks is quite a memorable experience. But Upcountry also has other interesting attractions, including the Tedeschi Vineyards, which produces wine from tropical fruit, and Kula Botanical Gardens, six acres of blooming splendor at 3,300 feet. Shoppers stop in the friendly little town of Makawao, in the middle of Maui's paniolo (cowboy) country, where talented artisans have moved in and opened galleries and shops.

WHAT TO SEE
BALDWIN AVENUE
Baldwin Avenue, Makawao
Shoppers and art lovers enjoy wandering in and out of the many stores along this main street in this Upcountry community known for its artisans. Numerous galleries line both sides of the street, along with some gift/souvenir shops and a few cozy restaurants. At Hot Island Glassblowing Studio & Gallery, artisans fire up a furnace in full view of visitors and shape the beautiful glass creations you can buy here. Gallery Maui features fine-art paintings and prints, sculpture and koa furnishings, most by Maui artists. Expect to see all types of art at the Viewpoints Gallery, a fine-arts cooperative that gets raves. Many other shops will undoubtedly draw you inside their doors as well, with all the creative works they have on display. For something sweet to eat, try any of the mouthwatering pastries at the Komoda Store & Bakery, a longtime favorite.

BIKE TOURS OF HALEAKALA
Haleakala

Every year, thousands of people hop on bicycles to ride nearly 40 miles down Haleakala, Maui's dormant volcano. It's one of the most popular activities on the island, and one of the most fun and scenic. Several companies offer tours, so you'll need to call around to see which one suits you best. Many people opt for a sunrise tour so they can watch the sun come up over the summit before starting their long and winding descent downhill, back to sea level. At practically every turn, you'll encounter breathtaking views. The tours make several stops, including one for breakfast or lunch at an Upcountry restaurant. Most tours are guided, but some companies also offer the option of unguided trips if you prefer to go at your own pace. Tour companies that specialize in these bike treks include Haleakala Bike Co. *(888-922-2453)*, Maui Downhill *(800-535-2453)*, Maui Mountain Cruisers *(800-232-6284)*, and Mountain Riders Bike Tours *(800-706-7700)*.

HALEAKALA NATIONAL PARK
Highway 378, Makawao, 808-572-4400; www.nps.gov/hale
Originally a part of Hawaii Volcanoes National Park, this 30,183-acre park was established as a separate entity in 1961 to preserve the Haleakala Crater 10,023 feet at the summit (the highest point on Maui) and the surrounding volcanic landscape. Later additions gave protection to the fragile ecosystems

of the Kipaulu Valley. Visitors flock here to see the amazing sunrises and sunsets, and magnificent views. You can often see up to 115 miles out to sea from the summit area. Additional activities at Haleakala include guided and independent hiking, swimming in freshwater streams, bird watching, backpacking and camping (drive-up campgrounds, wilderness camping, cabins). Stop in at one of the visitor centers to find out what park programs are being offered during your visit.

There are three visitor centers at the park. One mile from the entrance off Highway 378, at 7,000 feet, is the Park Headquarters Visitor Center (daily 8 a.m.-4 p.m.). Near the summit at 9,700 feet, 10 miles from the park entrance off the Park Road, is Haleakala Visitor Center (summer: 6 a.m.-3 p.m., winter: 6:30 a.m.-3 p.m.). Down at sea level on the Kipahulu coast, off Highway 31, is the Kipahulu Visitor Center (9 a.m.-5 p.m.). If you'd like to visit both the summit and the coastal area, plan to spend two days here, as a single road does not connect the two areas.

Dress warmly if you plan to travel to the summit (about a 1 1/2-hour drive from Kahului), especially if you come for a sunrise or stay in the park to watch the sun set. Between dusk and dawn, temperatures regularly drop below freezing.

HUI NO'EAU VISUAL ARTS CENTER
2841 Baldwin Avenue, Makawao, 808-572-6560; www.huinoeau.com
The striking Kaluanui plantation mansion, built in the early 1900s, was once the home of Harry and Ethel Baldwin, who made their fortune in the pineapple industry. The lovely estate is now home to this charming art center, which promotes artistic impression and creativity. View the interesting art on display in the exhibit galleries, participate in hands-on classes taught by visiting artists and tour the lush and spacious grounds. The attractive gift shop sells works by local artists.
Monday-Saturday 10 a.m.-4 p.m.

KULA BOTANICAL GARDENS
638 Kekaulike Avenue, Kula, 808-878-1715; www.kulabotanicalgarden.com
This lush six-acre-garden features hundreds of tropical and semitropical plants thriving at 3,300 feet above sea level in Upcountry Maui, including bromeliads, koa trees, orchids, proteas and many other beauties. A koi pond, waterfalls and unusual rock formations enhance the scenery.
Admission: adults $10, children 6-12 $3, children under 6 free. Monday-Saturday 9 a.m.-4 p.m.

PARAGON SAILING CHARTERS
5229 Lower Kula Road, Kula, 808-244-2087, 800-441-2087; www.sailmaui.com
Both catamarans in this company's fleet were designed using the same mast technology that helped make Stars and Stripes an America's Cup winner. So these boats can move when the crew hoists their sails. From Lahaina Harbor, the Paragon I glides through the water to Lanai, a seven-hour trip that includes plenty of snorkeling and loads of beach fun. From Maalaea Harbor, the Paragon II sails to Molokini and Coral Gardens, two of the island's best snorkeling spots for eyeing turtles, manta rays and exotic tropical fish. These treks range from two to five hours. Other cruises include a coral gardens

snorkel and afternoon sail and a Lahaina champagne sunset sail.
Admission: prices begin at $56 for adults. Daily.

PONY EXPRESS TOURS
Haleakala Crater, Highway 78, Kula, 808-667-2200;
Hawaiian paniolos (cowboys) started working island ranches years before American cowboys started taming the West. Saddle up for one of two scenic rides in Maui's Upcountry. For two hours, take in gorgeous views at about 4,000 feet above sea level when you explore the Haleakala Ranch. Or start your ride at about 10,000 feet above sea level and descend deep down into Haleakala Crater.
Admission: prices begin at $95 for adults; check Web site for deals. Times vary.

TEDESCHI VINEYARDS
Ulupalakua Ranch, Highway 37 (Kula Highway), Ulupalakua, 808-878-6058;
www.mauiwine.com
Even on this faraway Pacific island, you can sample locally produced wine at Maui's only vineyard, located on a 20,000-acre ranch on the southern slopes of Haleakala. A few of the wines are made from the juice of Maui pineapples. The tasting room is located in a historic cottage built in the 1870s specifically for King Kalakaua who often visited the ranch, with a bar cut from the trunk of a mango tree. The winery is an ideal spot for a picnic lunch.
Daily 9 a.m.-5 p.m.; free tours at 10:30 a.m. and 1:30 p.m.

SPECIAL EVENT
MAKAWAO RODEO
Oskie Rice Rodeo Arena, Olinda Road, Makawao, 808-572-2076
Every Fourth of July weekend for more than 40 years, the Maui Roping Club has been hosting the Makawao Rodeo, Hawaii's largest paniolo competition. More than 300 boot-loving cowboys from around the world come to the Valley Isle to kick up plenty of dust, as they show off their cowhand skills in rough stock and roping events. The festivities also include a big Saturday morning parade, live entertainment and country-western dancing.
Fourth of July weekend.

WHERE TO EAT
★★★HALIIMAILE GENERAL STORE
900 Haiimaile Road, Haliimaile, 808-572-2666; www.haliimailegeneralstore.com
Occupying the old general store of a former sugar plantation, this unique and interesting restaurant is the inspiration of highly regarded chef/owner Bev Gannon. Signature items include crab pizza and Bev's infamous baby back ribs. The restaurant is located in Upcountry Maui in the small hamlet and former company town of Haliimaile. Set on a hillside surrounded by sugar cane, the plantation-style building has a corrugated steel exterior and a wrap-around veranda. Despite the historical context, the dining room is very contemporary, with a high ceiling, crisp yellow walls, hardwood floors, an eat-at bar, an open kitchen, and large, colorful ceramic fish adorning one wall.
Pacific-Rim. Lunch, dinner. Bar. Reservations recommended. $36-85

MOLOKAI

ONLY ABOUT 7,400 PEOPLE LIVE ON MOLOKAI, BUT MORE THAN HALF OF THEM ARE NATIVE Hawaiians, the highest percentage on any of the islands except for the private isle of Niihau. This earns Molokai its status as the most Hawaiian island in the chain.

Although Molokai is only a 20-minute flight from Oahu, you'll feel like you've taken a journey back in time to Old Hawaii when you visit. Although some of the friendliest people in the land of aloha live here—it's called the Friendly Isle—Molokaians have not actively embraced tourism. In 2008, a plan by the management of the Molokai Ranch to develop vacant land into 200 luxury homes produced such resistance with locals that the company abruptly pulled out of Molokai, closing its luxury hotel, movie theater, shops and gas station seemingly overnight, eliminating more than 100 jobs in the process and leaving the area surrounding the ranch a virtual ghost town. Unemployment on the island hovered around 13 percent in 2009, caused by a combination of the loss of Molokai Ranch, and the global recession's impact on tourism in Hawaii. In fact, tourism in Molokai was down 40 percent in the first half of the year compared to 2008. To date, there are few places to stay on the island, and restaurants are limited, quiet and decidedly casual.

The 75,000 or so visitors who explore Molokai each year don't come for mega-resorts, designer boutiques, gourmet restaurants run by celebrity chefs or the like. There aren't any. Rather, they come for the laid-back setting, nearly deserted beaches and the island's unspoiled beauty. The largest city, Kaunakakai, is quaint, but has only a few eateries and shops in a block-long downtown.

Molokai, which covers about 260 square miles, rose from the Pacific about two million years ago with the eruption of three volcanoes—one to the west, one to the east and a much smaller one to the north. Locals say that the 38-mile-long island is shaped like a shark, with its "dorsal fin" created by the smaller volcano. Many people know the island best for the tip of land called the Kalaupapa Peninsula, which sits below some of the world's tallest sea cliffs. It was here that Hawaii banished its lepers in the 1800s, and where Father Damien ministered to them until his death in 1889. This area with such a sad past remains one of the island's most popular attractions, although reaching it involves either taking an adventurous mule ride down a steep trail or paying for a pricey air tour.

Molokai's best beaches are to the west, where the climate is more arid and the landscape less stunning. For more of a tropical environ, visitors head the opposite direction, to what locals call the East End, Molokai's rainier side. The sights include dramatic green valleys, historic churches, ancient fishponds and more.

The waters off Molokai beckon many as well. As on every other Hawaiian island, there are many companies that offer an array of water adventures, including kayaking, sailing, sportfishing, scuba diving and snorkeling tours.

No matter where you go or what you do on Molokai, you won't see many other people, but those you do meet will likely be smiling and welcoming. The locals pride themselves on their aloha spirit, and with good reason: they're downright friendly folks.

WHAT TO SEE
ALYCE C. SPORTFISHING CHARTERS
Kaunakakai, 808-558-8377; www.alycecsportfishing.com

Go fishing for Pacific blue marlin, yellowfin tuna, skipjack tuna, dorado, wahoo and more when you cast out your line from the Alyce C., a 31-foot cruiser operated by Captain Joe Reich. The veteran skipper usually takes anglers into the waters off the north, south and west shores of Molokai, as well as the west shore of Lanai. In season, Reich also offers whale-watching cruises. Fishing trips last from four to nine hours, and they're small in size— the boat holds only six passengers.

Charters: upon request.

ALA MALAMA STREET
Ala Malama Street, Kaunakakai

On Molokai, the center of shopping is on this street, and the commercial area isn't much more than a block long. You'll find clothing, gift and food stores, as well as some restaurants. Some of the notables include the Kamakana Fine Arts Gallery for creations made by local artists; Imports Gift Shop for jewelry and souvenirs; Molokai Island Creations for ocean-related jewelry, such as sea opals; and the Imamura Store for aloha shirts and muumuus. And for some of the tastiest baked goods on the island, you must make a stop at the Kanemitsu Bakery, where everyone goes for delicious Molokai sweet bread.

Monday-Saturday 9 a.m.-6 p.m.; store hours vary.

ANCIENT HAWAIIAN FISH PONDS
Highway 450, South Coast

As you drive along the South Coast, be on the lookout for sheltered ponds created by walls of lava rock and coral. These are ancient ponds believed to have been built in the 13th century to catch fish for royalty. When the fish swam or washed in, they couldn't get out, so the royals were assured of fresh fish year-round, even in the winter. At One Alii Beach Park, six miles east of Kaunakakai, you'll see the Kalokoeli pond.

Daily dawn-dusk.

BIG WIND KITE FACTORY
120 Maunaloa Highway, Maunaloa, 808-552-2364; www.bigwindkites.com

For an out-of-the-ordinary Hawaiian experience, how about flying a hula girl-shaped kite in the Hawaiian trade winds? Big Wind sells a variety of fun, island-inspired kites like this, including a whales tail, sunset, and rainbow star. You can also buy colorful windsocks in numerous shapes—pineapples, hibiscus flowers, and anthuriums, to name a few. All of the store's kites and windsocks are manufactured on Molokai, using nylon, fiberglass spars, and poly tubing. If you like, tour the factory to see the workers in action.

Monday-Saturday 8:30 a.m.-5 p.m., Sunday 10 a.m.-2 p.m.

BILL KAPUNI'S SNORKEL AND DIVE
Kaunakakai, 808-553-9867

Bill Kapuni grew up on Molokai and knows all the best places to see the abundant sea life that lives in the water off its shores. He offers customized snorkeling and diving trips for a maximum of six people, using a 22-foot Boston Whaler. On one of his underwater adventures, youre likely to see scores of tropical fish, sea turtles, dolphins, mantas, eagle rays, or even whales in season.

Tours: upon request.

COFFEES OF HAWAII PLANTATION STORE

Highway 480, Kualapuu, 808-567-9023, 800-709-2326; www.molokaicoffee.com

The Arabica coffees sold in this store don't travel far before landing on the stores shelves. They're grown, harvested and processed on the Molokai Coffee Plantation, the 500-acre estate that surrounds the shop. Before or after you buy some bags of java to take home with you, take a 45-minute walking tour of the grounds (no pun intended) to learn more about how the crops are cultivated. The store also sells jewelry, soaps, pottery and other crafty items made by local artists. If you're in need of a caffeine boost on the spot, order a cup of tasty brew at the store's Espresso Bar.

Store: daily 7:30 a.m.-4 p.m. Espresso Bar: daily 6:30 a.m.-4 p.m. Tours: Monday-Friday 9:30 and 11:30 a.m.

DIXIE MARU COVE

Pohakuloa Road, West Molokai, 808-567-6083

Dixie Maru Cove isn't the best-looking beach on the west side, yet it's popular with local families, so you know it has something going for it. Indeed, because the small cove is protected, the swimming and snorkeling tends to be good and safe in summer when the water conditions are calm.

Daily dawn-dusk.

FUN HOGS HAWAII

Hoolehua, 808-567-6789; www.molokaifishing.com

Head off into the deep blue sea to fish for mahimahi, ono, ahi and other hefty fish that swim in Hawaiian waters. You'll do your reeling from aboard the Ahi, a 27-foot sport-fishing boat skippered by Captain Mike Holmes. The fishing expeditions run four, six and eight hours. Fun Hogs also takes visitors canoeing or kayaking, and on sunset cruises and bodyboarding trips. From December through April, it offers two whale-watching cruises.

Daily, various times.

HALAWA BEACH PARK

Highway 450, East Molokai, 808-553-3204

Drive all the way to the end of Highway 450 and you're rewarded with this typically uncrowded beach nestled between cliffs. Fishers and swimmers flock here—except in winter, when high waves attract only sure-footed surfers. Year-round, it's a refreshing spot to soak in some rays or enjoy a picnic.

Daily dawn-dusk.

IRONWOOD HILLS GOLF CLUB

Highway 470, Kualapuu, 808-567-6000

The name of this par-34, nine-hole golf course gives you a good idea of the surroundings—ironwood trees and hills. The Del Monte Corporation built this attractive course in the North Shores upcountry (1,200 feet above sea level) in 1928 for its executives. As you play its 2,816 yards, you'll be challenged not just by Ironwood's many hills, but also by tree-lined fairways; small, fast greens; and the winds that tend to kick up in the afternoon. Daily 7:30 a.m.-5 p.m.

HAWAIIAN FLORA

Most of the lush tropical plants you'll see in Hawaii are not native to the islands. Species like hibiscus (the state flower), plumeria, sugarcane and pineapple were brought by settles and, like most other plants that made their way here, thrived in the hospitable conditions.

Native plants thrived, too—that is, until the Polynesians first descended upon the area about 1,500 years ago. The Hawaiian islands were formed millions of years before from lava rock that sprouted from the sea, and plant life was generated from seeds brought by wind, water current and birds. The combination of its remote location and favorable climate enabled these plants to thrive without the threat of inherent predators, so they evolved without defense mechanisms like thorns, offensive odors, or other toxins. Before the land was settled, scientists say that the number of native plants in Hawaii was higher than anywhere else in the world.

But settlers brought predators in the form of animals, insects and other stronger plants. The native flora was ill-equipped to defend itself against many of these threats, and many species became extinct. Others have barely hung on, so specialized to their conditions that they can be found only in remote parts of the islands, such as the highland forest areas of Molokai and Kauai.

One of these plants is the well-known silversword, a relative of the sunflower that adapted to the high altitudes and fragile soil of the Hawaiian upcountry. These striking flowers stand 3 to 8 feet tall, with a single white spike at the center and small yellow and red flowers at its tips. Threatened predominantly by ants an humans, they can still be seen from June through October in Haleakala National Park in Maui.

Koa ("warrior") trees are endemic to Hawaii, but their abundance was threatened at the turn of the century by free-ranging cattle. Conservation programs proved successful, and today these canopy tress are a chief source of hardwood in Hawaii, used for furniture, lumber and carved art.

The best places to see the unique and fragile plants that make Hawaii so special are at Hawaii's national parks and protected nature preserves. Kamakou Preserve in Molokai is a rain forest that has roughly 220 plants found nowhere else in the world, as well as many unusual insects and birds. On Oahu, Honouliuli Preserve, which once belonged to Hawaiian royalty, has nearly 70 rare and endangered plant and animal species. Monthly hikes of the Kamakou Preserve are run by the Hawaii field office of the Nature Conservancy.

KAMAKOU PRESERVE

Forest Reserve Road, Northeast Molokai

If you appreciate the beauty of plants, then you'll want to visit this lush highland preserve near the summit of Molokai's highest peak. The 2,774-acre rain forest is home to more than 250 Hawaiian plants, of which more than 200 grow here exclusively. Rare Hawaiian birds also inhabit this green oasis, so keep your eyes peeled. You need a four-wheel-drive vehicle to access Kamakou, or you can book one of the monthly tours offered by the Nature Conservancy of Hawaii *(808-553-5236)*, which manages the preserve. Its knowledgeable guides point out all the must-sees as they lead groups along a boardwalk that runs through a portion of the forest. The views of valleys that stretch down to the ocean are stunning.

Daily dawn-dusk.

KAPUAIWA COCONUT GROVE

Highway 460, Kaunakakai

Nearly 150 years ago, in the 1860s, King Kamehameha V planted the rows and rows of coconut trees in this 10-acre grove. He planted one thousand of them (not all are still growing) to honor the men in his army and shade some sacred pools. Falling coconuts make the grove hazardous to walk through, but you can get a good view of it from Kiowea Beach Park, just to the west. The view is particularly good at sunset.

Daily dawn-dusk.

KEPUHI BEACH

Kaluakoi Resort, Kaluakoi Road, West Molokai, 808-567-6083

Come to Kepuhi to sunbathe, enjoy a picnic, or perhaps watch a lovely sunset. Be careful about swimming here, however, especially in winter when high surf and riptides create hazardous water conditions. Although the water is calmer in summer, visitors should still exercise caution because of the rocky beach.

Daily dawn-dusk.

MAPULEHU GLASS HOUSE

Highway 450 E., Kaunakakai, 808-558-8160

At this 9-acre commercial tropical-flower farm, feast your eyes on a rainbow of colorful blooms from a variety of exotic plants—ginger, plumeria and many more. The large glass greenhouse, built in the 1920s, is home to numerous beautiful orchids. A free tour of this green delight is given weekdays at 10:30 a.m. If you like what you see, have flowers shipped to your home, family, or friends.

MOLOKAI ACTION ADVENTURES

Kaunakakai, 808-558-8184

Walter Naki, an avid outdoorsman, mixes his passion for Mother Nature with his work. When island visitors get antsy to escape the laid-back beach scene, this action-loving guy takes them snorkeling, diving, reef trolling, spear fishing, kayaking, camping, hiking, or hunting for deer, goats, and wild boar (using bows or rifles, not guns).

Tours on request.

MOLOKAI CHARTERS

Kaunakakai, 808-553-5852

This charter company has been entertaining visitors with fun sailing trips since 1975. Board Satan's Doll, a 42-foot sloop, for a sunset sail, whale-watching trip (in season), or snorkeling adventure to the island of Lanai. The various tours last from two hours to a full day.

Daily, various times.

MOLOKAI MULE RIDE

100 Kalae Highway, Kualapuu, 808-567-6088, 800-567-7550; www.muleride.com

Climb atop a mule and ease your way down a 3-mile trail to Kalaupapa, the seaside village known for its leper colony, where people with the disease were banished beginning in the 1860s and continuing until the 1960s. (A few survivors still live in the village, and access to visit is restricted.) You'll descend 1,700 feet down steep sea cliffs and maneuver around 26 switchbacks before reaching the village for a guided tour sure to stir your emotions. As you explore the area, you'll learn about the colony's history, see Father Damien's gravesite, and visit St. Philomena Church. In all, this mule trek lasts about 7 1/2 hours, about four of which you'll spend riding your mule up and down the trail. Riders must be at least age 16, and advanced reservations (at least two weeks) are required. If you prefer, you can arrange to hike down or fly into the village.

Monday-Saturday 8 a.m.-3:30 p.m.

MOLOKAI MUSEUM AND CULTURAL CENTER

Highway 470, Kalae Village, at mile marker 4, 808-567-6436; www.hawaiimuseums.org

Learn more about the history of Molokai sugar plantations at this museum, a restored 1878 sugar mill now on the National Register of Historic Places. Here you'll see some of the mills original equipment, including a mule-driven cane crusher, a steam engine and redwood-evaporating pan.

Monday-Saturday 10 a.m.-2 p.m.

MOLOKAI OUTDOORS

Hotel Molokai, King Kamehameha V Highway, Kaunakakai, 808-553-4477,
877-553-4477; www.molokai-outdoors.com

This company offers a host of exciting tours both on and off land. Go hiking to Moa Ula Falls; explore a rain forest on a mountain bike; kayak along a reef; go deep-sea fishing; or climb aboard a 42-foot sloop for snorkeling fun. Molokai Outdoors also rents about any type of gear you might need for outdoor fun—snorkeling equipment, surfboards, tennis rackets, bicycles and much more.

Daily 8 a.m.-5:30 p.m.; tours are daily at various times.

MOLOKAI WAGON AND HORSE RIDE

Kaunakakai, 808-558-8132

On this step-back-in-time tour, visit Iliiliopae, a 700-year-old ancient temple. This sacred temple, one of the largest remaining in Hawaii, was supposedly made of 90 million rocks, and its stone altar stands an imposing 22 feet tall. Here, centuries ago, high priests would gather to witness human sacrifices. To reach Iliiliopae, you travel by a mule-drawn wagon or on horseback along a dirt road through a gorgeous mango grove, one of the world's largest. After seeing the temple, spend some time relaxing on a beach and eating lunch.

Monday-Saturday 10:30 a.m.

MOOMOMI BEACH AND PRESERVE

Highway 480, Northwest Molokai

At this preserve, gusty trade winds from the northeast create mile-long sand dunes that are hundreds of feet wide. But this area is significant for more than its large mounds of sand. Here, scientists have discovered remains of prehistoric birds, endangered plant species and endangered sea turtles. The preserve is difficult to access and requires a four-wheel-drive vehicle. Your best bet is to sign up for one of the monthly hiking tours offered by the Nature Conservancy of Hawaii *(808-553-5236)*, which owns and manages the preserve. Its well-informed guides can give you interesting insight into Moomomi and what scientists are learning here.

Daily dawn-dusk.

MURPHY'S BEACH PARK

Highway 450, mile marker 20, East Molokai, 808-567-6083

This is the most popular beach on the east side, especially with families—the protected water inside the reef is shallow and usually calm (except in winters), making it a good swimming spot for children. The snorkeling, diving, fishing and windsurfing are good here, too. Up on land, where palm trees and ironwood trees line the sandy beach, there are pavilions and grills for those who want to enjoy a seaside cookout or picnic.

Daily dawn-dusk.

ONE ALII BEACH PARK

Highway 450, mile marker 4, South Central Molokai, 808-553-3204

This long, narrow stretch of beach is the place to go for fun in the sand on the south-central shore. Although its not all that great for swimming because of its murky water, coral and rock, it is a good spot for kicking back and enjoying an oceanside picnic. So fire up one of the park's grills, dine in the shade under the pavilion and enjoy the beautiful views of Maui and Lanai across the channel.

Daily dawn-dusk.

PALAAU STATE PARK

Highway 470, Central Molokai

This recreational area encompasses more than 200 acres at an elevation of 1,600 feet. One of its main draws is the Kalaupapa Lookout, which offers great views of the peninsula where Father Damien ran the islands famed leper colony in the 1800s. Another trail takes you to Phallic Rock, reputed to make women more fertile. Lovely picnic areas are set in forests rich with tall eucalyptus, ironwood and koa trees. Camping with a permit is allowed in designated areas.

Daily dawn-dusk.

PAPOHAKU BEACH

Kaluakoi Road, West Molokai, two miles past the Kaluakoi Resort

Many people rank this undeveloped beauty on the northwest coast as one of the best beaches anywhere in Hawaii—it stretches for more than three miles and is up to 300 feet wide in some places. The water is usually calm enough for swimming, snorkeling and diving in summer, but high surf in winter makes Papohaku dangerous. If you notice excessive wave action, stay out of the water. Instead, go for a leisurely walk in the sand, sunbathe or

THE HISTORY OF HULA

If you think hula dancing is nothing more than pretty girls in grass skirts, think again. With its origins firmly rooted in early Hawaiian religious beliefs, hula is a sacred ritual on the islands of Hawaii. According to island history, hula began on Molokai when the Hawaiian goddess Laka began dancing to appease her sister, Pele, the goddess of fire. Laka, according to the lore, then traveled from island to island teaching the dance to the people of Hawaii.

According to island history, hula began on Molokai when the Hawaiian goddess Laka began dancing to appease her sister, Pele, the goddess of fire. Laka, according to the lore, then traveled from island to island teaching the dance. In the years that followed, hula—which refers to movement and hand gestures—played an important role in oral tradition. The people of Hawaii combined the dance movements with chants to express everything about their lives. Every movement in hula has a specific meaning; every gesture a special significance.

Despite the cultural importance of hula, it nearly became a lost art when Protestant missionaries arrived in the island in the late 1800s. Seeing only the suggestive movements of the dance, the missionaries denounced hula as heathen and banned it. But Hawaiians had a cultural patron during this time in King David Kalakua, who not only encouraged hula and other local arts to continue, but is credited with their preservation.

Out of this history, two distinct styles of hula emerged, kahiko and auna. Kahiko, or old-style hula, is performed in traditional costumes that include head and shoulder leis, grass skirts and ankle bracelets made from dog teeth or whale bones. The movements are accompanied by chanting and percussion instruments such as gourds and drums. In chant-based hula, the dance may be performed sitting or standing. Often, one set of performers moves while another group chants.

Auna is the form of hula with which most visitors are familiar. It's performed in a variety of costumes with faster, flashier moves and musical accompaniment from guitars and ukeleles.

The resurgence in interest in native Hawaiian culture is responsible for a variety of festivals and competitions celebrating hula. These exhibitions and contests offer travelers and locals the chance to see authentic hula.

The Merrie Monarch Festival: This nearly 50-year-old festival is the most celebrated in Hawaii. Held each spring, the three-day competition offers visitors a look at both form of hula along with arts and crafts fairs.

Moanalua Gardens Foundation's Prince Lot Hula Festival: Held in Honolulu on the third Saturday in July, this festival offers performances of both types of hula as well as crafts, native foods and more.

The Molokai Ka Hula Piko: This three-day festival occurs each May on Molokai and offers exhibitions of both forms of hula.

If the competitions and exhibitions have you ready to give hula a try yourself, take a lesson. Two of the more popular locales for visitors to try hula are at the Royal Hawaiian Center in Honolulu, where lessons provided weekday mornings and at the Kalani Oceanside Resort on the southeast coast of the Big Island, where free classes are held on Tuesday evenings. Many local hula schools, called halaus, also welcome visitors. For a complete listing of hula schools, visit www.mele.com.

enjoy a picnic lunch. You can also camp here. Despite all of its appeal, this remote beach is often deserted, so don't be surprised if you have it practically to yourself.

Daily dawn-dusk.

PLANTATION GALLERY

120 Maunaloa Highway, Maunaloa, 808-552-2364; www.molokai.com/gallery

If youre looking for an interesting gift for someone back home, look no further. At this jam-packed gallery, you'll find exotic items like Tibetan carpets, batik clothing from Bali and baskets from Borneo. There's also a good selection of Hawaiian books and CDs as well as silver jewelry, woodcarvings and other arts and crafts from some of Molokai's best artists. The owners of Plantation Gallery also run the Big Wind Kite Factory, located in the same building.

Monday-Saturday 8:30 a.m.-5 p.m., Sunday 10 a.m.-2 p.m.

PURDY'S ALL-NATURAL MACADAMIA NUT FARM

Lihi Pali Drive, Hoolehua, 808-567-6601; www.molokai-aloha.com/macnuts

Learn everything you ever wanted to know about how macadamia nuts are grown and cultivated at this 5-acre, 70-year-old working farm, where no irrigation methods or pesticides are used. Owners Tuddie and Kammy Purdy take visitors on guided tours, demonstrate how to crack this tough-to-crack nut and pass out product samples, all of which you can buy in the farms store.

Monday-Friday 9:30 a.m.-3:30 p.m.; Saturday 10 a.m.-2 p.m.; tours by appointment only on Sunday.

ST. JOSEPH'S CATHOLIC CHURCH

Highway 450, mile marker 11, Kaunakakai

You'll take a step back in time when you visit this quaint, but unassuming, white clapboard church, which is listed on the National Register of Historic Places. Father Damien built it in 1876, making it the island's second-oldest church. Locals frequently hang colorful leis around the statue of the priest that's outside, making for a good snapshot.

Daily dawn-dusk.

WHERE TO STAY

★HOTEL MOLOKAI

Kamehameha V Highway, Kaunakakai, 808-553-5347, 800-535-0085;
www.hotelmolokai.com

The 35-room Hotel Molokai, located about two miles outside Kaunakakai, appeals to the budget-minded, with rates less than $150 per night. Of course, for that price, guests don't get the type of cushy digs available at Hawaii's megaresorts. Here, the accommodations are beyond basic, with more emphasis on tranquility than luxury. The property fronts Kamiloloa Beach and features a South Seas motif—the rooms are housed in thatched-room bungalows and feature lanais. The bungalows don't have air-conditioning, but plenty of coco palms shade the well-kept grounds. Still, be sure to request one with a ceiling fan—and if you want to do some of your own cooking, ask for one of the kitchenette units. The hotel's oceanfront lounge is a rowdy gathering spot for locals nightly who come to see the live bands that perform.

57 rooms. Restaurant, bar. Beach. Pool. $61-150

★KALUAKOI VILLAS HOTEL

1131 Kalua Koi Road, Maunaloa, 808-552-2721; www.castleresorts.com

For spacious accommodations, rent one of the studio or one-bedroom condominium units at this complex on the west coast, about 13 miles from Hoolehua Airport. They're comfortable enough, though not luxurious, with modest furnishings and ceiling fans instead of air conditioning. The palm trees spread around the grounds give the property a tropical feel, as do the white-sand beach and heavenly sunsets. For golfers, the Kaluakoi resort area offers an 18-hole golf course, though only nine holes are currently open. The resort also includes the closed (indefinitely) Kaluakoi Hotel, making the area less crowded.

20 rooms. Beach. Pool. Golf. $151-250

OAHU

EVEN THOUGH OAHU IS ONLY THE THIRD-LARGEST HAWAIIAN ISLAND, IT'S THE MOST POPULOUS by far. Nearly 900,000 people, or about 80 percent of the state's population, live on the island, which is aptly nicknamed the Gathering Place.

So many Hawaiians came to call this island home for a good reason. In the early 1790s, a British sea merchant sailed into Honolulu Harbor and found the deepest, most sheltered port in the Pacific. His discovery changed Oahu's future forever. Honolulu emerged as Hawaii's key shipping hub, the significance of which King Kamehameha I realized. After he successfully unified the islands, the fierce king moved his court from the Big Island to Waikiki in 1804 to be near this growingly important port. His presence raised the island's stature and led the way for Oahu to establish itself as Hawaii's commercial center.

Honolulu remains the island's business capital (and state capital) and home to most Oahu residents. More than 800,000 of them live on the South Shore, in sprawling neighborhoods in and around the city. The city is also the hometown of President Barack Obama (the first U.S. president to hail from Hawaii), who grew up in Honolulu and graduated from the elite private school, Punahou. Enterprising locals have embraced the stardom of Honolulu's native son, offering tours of Obama's favorite spots.

Visitors tend to congregate here, too. Nearly 5 million tourists crowd into bustling Waikiki every year and check into the many hotels that front the shoreline. They sun and swim on the world-famous beaches, dine in restaurants that range from gritty to great, party at lively nightclubs, go on buying sprees at an endless number of shops, and still leave plenty of time for sightseeing. After all, who would come to Hawaii and not see Pearl Harbor and Diamond Head, two of Honolulu's biggest attractions? Others important sights include Iolani Palace, the home of Queen Liliuokalani until the monarchy fell in 1893; the state capitol building; and Kawaihao Church, built in the 1830s and called the Westminster Abbey of Hawaii.

Away from the big city, much of Oahu is quite rural, unspoiled, and strikingly beautiful. Many sleepy little towns and villages on the island sit between the ocean and two mountain ranges—Koolau and Waianae—formed by volcanic eruptions nearly four million years ago. The mountains and their lush forests run parallel to one another down the eastern and western coasts and entice with scenic hiking trails and other outdoor fun.

Venturing away from Waikiki doesn't mean leaving the beach scene behind. Quite the contrary, the North Shore is known around the globe for its many world-class surfing beaches, including Banzai Pipeline and Sunset. Their giant breakers pound the shore in winter, but then the water turns calm in summer, making the beaches ideal for families. On the Windward Coast, many locals consider Kailua Beach the island's best stretch of sand. Its strong gusts make it a haven for windsurfers and kitesurfers. Just up the road in Kanehoe is one of Hawaii's most gorgeous bays, where boating companies offer trips out to a sandbar for swimming and snorkeling. Farther north, several more secluded beaches add beauty to the coastline.

HONOLULU AND THE SOUTH SHORE

Honolulu, on Oahu's South Shore, is the island's undisputed epicenter. By far, it's the largest city anywhere in Hawaii, with a population of more than 377,000. It's also the state's commercial center. Important things happen here every day; it's no sleepy little Hawaiian community lost in another time.

On the east side, Honolulu is punctuated by Diamond Head, the volcanic cone that is so iconic to the islands. Hike the 760 feet to its top for great panoramic views of the city and Oahu itself. From this cone known around the world, Honolulu stretches westward for about 26 miles to Pearl Harbor, another attraction with instant recognition. Every day, thousands of people board boats and head out to the harbor to solemnly remember how and why the United States got involved in World War II after the Japanese attack on December 7, 1941.

Between these two east and west landmarks lies plenty for visitors to enjoy and explore. Roughly 5 million sun-seekers visit Honolulu every year, and most of them stay in famed Waikiki, where high-rise hotels line picturesque beaches. Who hasn't seen a postcard of that scene?

Although only a little more than two miles long, Waikiki is jam-packed with more than hotels. The surprisingly compact area overflows with restaurants, nightclubs, and shops, shops, shops galore—some of them touristy tacky, others as top-of-the-line as they get. Think Gucci, Chanel, and the like.

From Waikiki, Honolulu runs inland about 12 miles. Away from the shoreline, it features all the usuals found in any bustling capital city—a downtown area where business deals are made, a government center where smooth-talking legislators debate political issues and pass laws, a large university where ambitious students prepare for their futures, shopping and entertainment districts where people go for fun, and residential neighborhoods where the locals nest with their families.

In the midst of all that routine city life are numerous interesting attractions, including the Bishop Museum, Chinatown, Iolani Palace, Kawaihao Church, the Mission Houses Museum, and the State Capitol Building.

WHAT TO SEE
2100 KALAKAUA

2100 Kalakaua Ave., Honolulu, 808-955-2878;www.2100kalakaua.com.

A select group of high-end boutiques carry some of the world's finest French, American and Italian designer clothing and accessories. The quaint town house look of this upscale outdoor mall incorporates lava rock, limestone, and bronze into the architecture and provides an elegant showcase for flagship stores of Chanel, Gucci, Tiffany & Company, Coach, Tods and Yves Saint Laurent. This modern interpretation of classic Hawaiian architecture features open-air courtyards and tropical palms. Ongoing events promote Hawaii's arts and culture. Not to be missed is the 7-foot bronze sculpture by renowned Japanese artist Shige Yamada at the entrance. Titled The Story-teller, it depicts a Hawaiian woman who represents the Hawaiian tradition of storytelling, and preserving the unique Hawaiian identity in poems, chants, songs, and legends. Valet parking is available; complimentary validated self-parking is available next door at King Kalakaua Plaza. Taxi service upon request. Daily 10 a.m.-10 p.m.

AHUPUAA O KAHANA STATE PARK ✓

52-222 Kamehameha Highway, Kahana, 808-237-7766; www.hawaiistateparks.org

This scenic 5,200-acre park (formerly known as Kahana Valley State Park) has become an archaeological dig. Researchers have found extensive remnants of Hawaiian culture here in the valley, including religious temples, fishing shrines, stone-walled enclosures, and agricultural terraces. Most sites are inaccessible to the public. However, visitors can still take advantage of canoeing, picnicking in a coconut grove, hiking through dense rain forest, and viewing the archaeological sites that are available to visitors. Huilua Fishpond on the east side of the bay is considered the most impressive. Daily dawn-dusk. $

ALA MOANA BEACH PARK ✓

1201 Ala Moana Blvd., Honolulu

Locals and tourists flock to this urban playground, one of Honolulu's finest beaches. Located directly across from Oahu's largest shopping center, Ala Moana (meaning by the sea) comprises more than a mile of sandy coastline stretching between Waikiki and downtown Honolulu. Within its 76 acres is a yacht harbor, tennis courts, surfing areas, an events pavilion, food concessions, and expansive lawns lined with tropical palms, banyan trees and lawn bowling. At the Waikiki end, jutting out into Mamala Bay is Magic Island, a peninsula that has serene picnic areas, a swimming lagoon, and paved paths for walkers, joggers, and inline skaters.

ALA MOANA CENTER ✓

1450 Ala Moana Blvd., Honolulu, 808-955-9517; www.alamoana.com

Within walking distance of most Waikiki hotels, this tri-level 240-store mall includes stores in every price range, from the Gap to Prada. You'll also find banks, a post office, a couple of drugstores, and an Aveda salon and spa as well as a wide variety of restaurants, from casual to upscale. Plenty of stores here, like the island-wide chains Hilo Hattie and Crazy Shirts, stock Hawaiian souvenirs. Pink Line trolleys transport shoppers to the center for free from eight locations in Waikiki. (Monday-Saturday 9:30 a.m.-9 p.m., Sunday 10 a.m.-7 p.m.) Also here is Reyn's. (Ala Moana Center, 1450 Ala Moana Blvd., Honolulu, 808-949-5929; www.reyns.com). For 50 years, Reyn's has been THE place to shop for mens Aloha wear. Reyn's signature shirt line features the "reverse print" fabrics that became a classic staple in corporate offices throughout Hawaii, not just on Aloha Fridays but for every other day of the week as well. Reyn's also features women's and children's apparel. Reyn's additional locations include Kahala Shopping Mall and the Moana Surfrider hotel. Reyn's Rack in Downtown Honolulu at 125 Merchant Street houses discounted merchandise from their collections. Reyn's also has locations on the Big Island, Maui and Kauai.

ALA WAI MUNICIPAL GOLF COURSE

404 Kapahulu Ave., Honolulu, 808-296-2000; www.co.honolulu.hi.us/des/golf

Honolulu has several decent municipal courses that allow visitors to keep up with their game without spending a fortune. Ala Wai, on the perimeter of Waikiki along the Ala Wai Canal, is a flat 18-hole course that offers views of Diamond Head and the Waikiki skyline. Daily 6 a.m.-6 p.m.

ALOHA BEACH SERVICE √

The Moana Surfrider, 2365 Kalakaua Ave., Honolulu, 808-922-3111

Take advantage of all Waikiki has to offer. Located on the private beach of the Moana Surfrider hotel, Aloha Beach Service can't guarantee that you'll be ready to enter any surf contests by the end of your stay, but they will rent you a surfboard or body board so you can give it a go. Don't have your surfing legs yet? Aloha surf instructors offer lessons. If riding giants (or even gentle waves) doesn't sit well with you, rent snorkeling equipment and spend a leisurely afternoon gazing down below. Daily 8 a.m.-5 p.m.

ALOHA STADIUM SWAP MEET/FLEA MARKET √

99-500 Salt Lake Blvd., Aiea, 808-486-1529; www.alohastadiumswapmeet.net

Every Wednesday, Saturday, and Sunday, the parking lot of Oahu's Aloha Stadium is transformed into the island's largest open-air bazaar. Vendors hawk everything from bikinis to temporary tattoos, and bargains are plentiful. You'll also find tables full of jewelry, art, T-shirts, car accessories, clothing, luggage, shoes, handbags and toys. Enjoy a cool treat like Hawaiian shave ice or get a carbo boost from a fresh malasada (sugared Portuguese doughnut). Get there early for the best deals. Daily 6 a.m.-3 p.m.

ALOHA TOWER MARKETPLACE

One Aloha Drive, Honolulu, 808-528-5700; www.alohatower.com

Overlooking Honolulu Harbor, this 1926 landmark was once the tallest building in all of Hawaii. It was built to welcome boatloads of tourists arriving in Honolulu and bid a fond farewell to those making their departure, as well as to provide a harbor control and maritime communications center from its tenth-story observation deck. Today, the tower houses numerous bars, restaurants, and shops with a heavy emphasis on gifts and souvenirs. Observation deck, daily 9 a.m.-5 p.m.

ATLANTIS ADVENTURES

One Aloha Drive, Pier 6, Honolulu, 808-973-1311; www.atlantisadventures.com

For smooth sailing, nothing beats Atlantis's sleek Navatek I, which pushes off every evening from Aloha Tower Marketplaces Pier 6. The Navateks SWATH (small waterplane area twin hull) technology provides a comfortable ride on a vessel that seems to glide through the water. The evening sunset dinner cruise showcases the Honolulu coastline. The Navatek's Stars at Sea cruise includes live entertainment. For dinner, there's a steak and lobster meal. This is the only dinner cruise vessel that sails beyond Diamond Head for a view of Oahu's richest real estate—the Kahala coastline. Tour prices include round trip transportation from select Waikiki Hotel locations.

AMERICAN INSTITUTE OF ARCHITECTS DOWNTOWN WALKING TOUR

AIA Honolulu, 119 Merchant St., Honolulu, 808-545-4242; www.aiahonolulu.org

Honolulu's unique melting pot of culture is reflected in both its contemporary and historic architecture. Take a walking tour of downtown Honolulu, led by a member of the American Institute of Architects and explore Hawaii's history from this landmark perspective. Call AIA Honolulu for tour times.

ANNE NAMBA DESIGNS

324 Kamani St., Honolulu, 808-589-1135; www.annenamba.com

One of Hawaii's premier designers, Anne Namba creates contemporary women's fashions using vintage kimono and obi fabrics from Japan. Her wedding couture line is the perfect marriage of East meets West. Namba's designs also take center stage in the costuming for productions of Hawaii's Opera Theatre.

ATLANTIS SUBMARINES

Hilton Hawaiian Village, 2005 Kalia Road, Honolulu, 808-973-9811, 800-548-6262; www.goatlantis.com

The 75-minute Oahu Underwater Adventure picks up passengers at the Hilton Hawaiian Village and shuttles them out to a waiting submarine. At depths of up to 120 feet, thousands of fish can be seen along a natural coral reef formed over an ancient lava flow. The narrated tour also cruises past artificial reefs, the remains of two downed airplanes, a sunken tanker, and a sunken fishing vessel. With tickets priced at nearly $100, it's a pricey trip, but you're likely to see creatures that you'd never glimpse with just a mask and a snorkel. Children must be at least 3 feet tall to participate, and the tour is not wheelchair accessible. Reservations are required. Daily 9 a.m.-3 p.m.; check in 30 minutes prior to departure.

BAILEY'S ANTIQUES AND ALOHA SHIRTS

517 Kapahulu Ave., Honolulu, 808-734-7628; www.alohashirts.com

Baileys is a treasure cove of classic "silky" Aloha shirts made popular in the 1930s, 40s, and 50s, and today come with serious collectors price tags. Hawaiiana aficionados will love the vintage souvenirs, memorabilia, photos, house wares, apparel, and antiques that span Hawaii's history from its most sublime to its touristy tacky. Daily 10 a.m.-6 p.m.

BATTLESHIP MISSOURI MEMORIAL ✓

501 Main St., Honolulu, 808-423-2263, 877-644-4896; www.ussmissouri.com

Commissioned in 1940 and launched on January 29, 1944, this battleship served the United States for half a century before being retired and turned into a memorial. In the ship's most famous moment in history, General Douglas MacArthur accepted Japan's surrender on the deck on September 2, 1945, ending World War II. If you decide to tour the ship, be prepared to climb shipboard ladders. Daily 9 a.m.-5 p.m.

BIKE HAWAII

Honolulu, 808-734-4214, 877-682-7433; www.bikehawaii.com

This tour company, staffed by professional nature guides, offers half- and full-day rides through mountains and rain forests (you start at the top), with some tours involving hiking and sailing as well as road or mountain biking. Tours include equipment, transportation, and meals.

BISHOP MUSEUM

1525 Bernice St., Honolulu, 808-847-3511; www.bishopmuseum.org

It's worth taking some time off from the beach to ground yourself in the rich natural and cultural history of Hawaii and its people. The Bishop Museum features a wide variety of hands-on activities and programs, including a twice daily show of Hawaiian music and dance. Visit the Hawaiian, Polynesian, and Natural History Halls to see precious objects from the museum's permanent collections. Then settle into a seat at the planetarium to get a new perspective on the Hawaiian night sky. Daily 9 a.m.-5 p.m.

CHINESE CHAMBER OF COMMERCE CHINATOWN TOURS
42 N. King St., Honolulu, 808-533-3181
The Hawaii chapter of the Chinese Chamber of Commerce sponsors a two-hour walking tour through Chinatown on Tuesday mornings for $5 per person. Oahu's Lyon Arboretum sponsors tours of Chinatown's Open Markets for $17 per person and introduces you to a world of ethnic produce, herbs, and fruit used in the finest Chinese, Vietnamese, and Thai cuisines. Call the Arboretum for tour times at 808-988-0456.

CONTEMPORARY MUSEUM
2411 Makiki Heights Drive, Honolulu, 808-526-1322, 866-991-2835; www.tcmhi.org
If you're a fan of David Hockney, Jasper Johns or Deborah Butterfield, you'll find that the Contemporary Museum's artistic wonders match the natural wonders of Hawaii one for one. The only piece in the museum that dates before 1940 is the museum itself; it's housed in the historic Spalding House, which was built in 1925. Spend the afternoon pondering provocative pieces

---

EXPLORING HONOLULU'S CHINATOWN

The 15-block area of Honolulu's downtown that makes up Chinatown grew at the hands of Chinese laborers from the Guangdong Province who arrived in the 1850s to work on Hawaii's sugar and pineapple plantations. When their contracts were up, those who realized that there were better opportunities in Hawaii opened small shops and restaurants in the area around River Street.

Over the years, the area grew in size and economic strength and proved its resilience by twice rising, quite literally, from the ashes. The first of two fires occurred in 1886. The second occurred in 1899, the result of a "controlled plan" to burn down houses infected with bubonic plague, starting at the corner of Beretania Street and Nuuanu Anvenue. Due to an ill-prepared fire department, Chinatown's entire 40 acres was leveled.

Throughout the decades, the streets have seen all walks of life. In the days before air travel, cruise ships docked at a pier a block away, and well-off mainlanders headed straight for this exotic little city-within-a city. During the war, servicemen walked the streets looking for beer joints, tattoo parlors and prostitutes. Entrepreneurs were happy to oblige, creating a red light district whose legacy is still in evidence on Pauahi and North Hotel streets.

Today, a walk through Chinatown is a feast for the sense. Everywhere you turn, you'll find a new sight, a scintillating smell, a different language. Korean, Chinese, Vietnamese, Laotian, Thai, Filipino, Japanese and other cultures are represented here in stores selling baked goods, groceries, noodles, tea, duck eggs and candied fruits. You'll even find art galleries—one of the city's most popular events is the once monthly First Fridays gallery walk held in Chinatown. Every first Friday evening of the month features a different theme and includes gallery displays, restaurant specials and performances (www.firstfridayhawaii.com).

by some of the world's top contemporary artists. Once you've taken in an eyeful, wander the 3 1/2-acre sculpture and meditation garden that surrounds the museum or take a sweet (or savory) break in the Contemporary Café. If you would rather focus on works by local artists or those inspired by Hawaii itself, visit the museum's smaller downtown branch at the First Hawaiian Center. Tuesday-Saturday, 10 a.m.-4 p.m., Sunday noon-4 p.m.; closed holidays.

DIAMOND HEAD STATE MONUMENT

Honolulu, 808-923-1811

A bunch of short volcanic eruptions between 100,000 and 300,000 years ago created L'ahi, now known as Hawaii's most famous landmark, Diamond Head State Monument. Pack water, lunch and a flashlight and head out on the 1.4-mile hiking trail that ends with a 560-foot climb up stairways and through dark tunnels until you reach the crater. (Leave your flip-flops behind. The uneven terrain requires some sturdy footwear.) Your reward: a 360-degree view of the island. Along with its natural history, the 350-acre crater was also a major player in 20th-century history; it was an important lookout point for enemy activity during World War II. Daily 6 a.m.-6 p.m.

DIAMOND HEAD TENNIS CENTER

3908 Paki Ave., Honolulu, 808-971-7150

One of two tennis centers in Waikiki's Kapiolani Park, the Diamond Head Tennis Center is on the mauka, or mountain side, of the park and features nine courts in the shadow of Waikiki's famed landmark, Diamond Head. Courts are on a first come, first served basis and are limited to 45 minutes of play. If these courts are full, head toward the ocean, where there are an additional dozen tennis courts located in the park fronting 2748 Kalakaua Avenue.

FOSTER BOTANICAL GARDEN

50 N. Vineyard Blvd., Honolulu, 808-522-7060; www.honolulu.gov/parks/hbg/fbg.htm

When you walk through Foster Botanical Garden, you're truly walking through time. After a German doctor and his wife leased the land from Queen Kalama in 1853, they planted trees that still stand tall on the site today. Later, Thomas and Mary Foster purchased the land. The couple tended and expanded the gardens and, when Mary died in 1830, the land was given to the city of Honolulu as a gift. Now more than 70 years old, the Foster Botanical Garden features a wide range of plants and flowers including orchids; primitive plants; 26 trees considered "exceptional" because of their age, size, rarity, or other traits; and herb and spice gardens. Daily 9 a.m.-4 p.m.

HANS HEDEMANN SURF SCHOOL

Park Shore Waikiki, 2586 Kalakaua Ave., Honolulu, 808-924-7778; Turtle Bay Resort,
57-091 Kamehameha Highway, 808-447-6755; www.hhsurf.com

Hans Hedemann is the headmaster of the surf school that bears his name, and he's still in the waters every day sharing a love of the sport and skills that earned him a place on the World Professional Surf Tour circuit for nearly two decades. In addition to surf school, Hedemann and his instructors offer body surfing lessons and surf camps at locations island-wide with treks to Oahu's North and South shores. Private surf lessons with Hedemann are available upon request. Hedemann Surf School locations are in Waikiki at the Park Shore hotel and on Oahu's North Shore at Turtle Bay Resort. Hedemann accepts children 5 years and older, and transportation is available from Waikiki to North Shore locations.

HAWAII BICYCLING LEAGUE

3442 Waialae Ave., Honolulu, 808-735-5756; www.hbl.org

This organization sponsors group rides, with weekend rides open to the public. Check their Web site for detailed maps of suggested routes and advice about which roads are best to avoid.

HAWAII KAI GOLF COURSE

8902 Kalanianaole Highway, Honolulu, 808-395-2358; www.hawaiikaigolf.com

The 36 holes at this East Honolulu venue include a championship course, with large greens and open fairways, and a par-three executive course designed by Robert Trent Jones Sr. Every hole has views of the ocean. Clubs and shoes are available to rent, and the course has a driving range and a restaurant.

HAWAII NATURE CENTER

2131 Makiki Heights Drive, Honolulu, 808-955-0100; www.hawaiinaturecenter.org

This nonprofit center helps children become stewards of the aina (land) and offers weekend family outings and programs as well as interpretive hikes, nature adventures, and projects designed to give kids of all ages an opportunity to play caregivers to their little piece of the planet.

HAWAII OPERA THEATRE

Blaisdell Concert Hall, 987 Waimanu St., Honolulu, 808-596-7372, 800-836-7372; www.hawaiiopera.org

The opera performs famous works using visiting and local artists in a comfortable, anything-goes setting. Shows are performed January thorugh March, and in August.

HAWAII STATE ART MUSEUM

250 S. Hotel St., Honolulu, 808-586-0300; www.hawaii.gov/sfca

Explore Hawaii's rich artistic tradition in the museum's three galleries. The Diamond Head, Ewa and Sculpture galleries house a wide variety of art forms and styles, including traditional arts like quilting and pottery. The museum includes a café, gift shop, and information kiosk. Open Tuesday-Saturday 10 a.m.-4 p.m. The museum is also open from 5-9 p.m. on First Fridays, the monthly downtown gallery walk held the first Friday of each month.

HAWAII THEATRE CENTER

1130 Bethel St., Honolulu, 808-528-0506; www.hawaiitheatre.com

This historic downtown Honolulu theater first opened in 1922 and hosted dramatic plays, musical concerts, and films. Almost forsaken to the wrecking ball in 1986, a group of theater preservationists and cultural patrons spearheaded a restoration that took more than a decade to complete. In 1996, the Hawaii Theatre reopened as a 1,400-seat state-of-the-art performance venue; today it is listed on both the National and State Registers of Historic Places. It presents local, national, and international artists in music, dance, and theatrical productions. To learn more about the history, architecture, and artwork, join a weekly 60-minute guided tour, held Tuesdays at 11 a.m.

HAWAIIAN FIRE SURF SCHOOL

3318 Campbell Ave., Honolulu, 808-737-3473, 888-955-7873; www.hawaiianfire.com

"Ablaze on the waves" might be your mantra after surf instruction with Hawaiian Fire instructors, who work their off-surf time as firefighters with the City and County of Honolulu. These experienced ocean safety experts conduct classes at a secluded beach on Oahu's leeward coast. The two-hour lessons include 45 minutes of land instruction followed by 75 minutes in the water. And because they know you'll surely head back into the sea for more practice after your lesson, the instructor-firefighters help you play it safe with outstanding tips to take you over the waves. Group and private lessons provide foam-covered surfboards, reef shoes, accessories, shade tent and chair, and transportation from Waikiki. Children 12 years and younger must have a private lesson. Daily 9 a.m.-6 p.m.

HELI USA AIRWAYS

155 Kapalulu Place, Honolulu, 808-833-3306, 866-936-1234; www.heliusa.com

Many travelers opt to catch a view of Hawaii from high in the sky by way of a helicopter tour, and Heli USA is one of several companies to provide that service out of Honolulu International Airport. (Passengers are picked up at and returned to their hotels.) Tours, which start at $99, include the nighttime Honolulu City Lights Flight, the Oahu Highlights Flight and the Oahu Deluxe Island Flight. You can also sign up for a day-long tour of Kauai, a good option if you'd like to see other islands but don't have much time to island-hop.
Daily.

HOME OF THE BRAVE MILITARY BASE TOURS

Honolulu, 808-396-8112; www.pearlharborhq.com

Military history lovers salute this guided tour that begins at Pearl Harbor and continues through three U.S. military bases that have played a major role in the history of Hawaii and the country as a whole. Step back in time to learn about the days leading up to and following December 7, 1941. The tour includes a drive through the National Memorial Cemetery of the Pacific.

HONOLULU ACADEMY OF ARTS

900 S. Beretania St., Honolulu, 808-532-8700; www.honoluluacademy.org

With a collection of more than 34,000 works, the Academy is Hawaii's premier art museum, and it's the only general art museum in the state. Particularly strong is its Asian collection, which makes up almost half of the total collection, but the museum also exhibits Western art from ancient Greece, Rome and Egypt to the present. The museum is located in a historic building and spans more than 30 galleries that surround multiple courtyards. The Doris Duke Theatre shows independent and foreign films and hosts lectures, concerts and theatrical performances. Tuesday-Saturday 10 a.m.-4:30 p.m., Sunday 1-5 p.m.

PEARL HARBOR'S HIDDEN HISTORY

Before December 7, 1941, when the Japanese launched the attack that would launch the United States into World War II, the area known as Pearl Harbor was a quiet stretch of oceanfront to the west of Honolulu. In fact, the first explorers to Hawaii made little mention of Pearl Harbor, much less the island of Oahu, concentrating instead on Hawaii, Maui and Kauai. The area known as Wai Momi, which translates to "water of the pearl" or "pearl water", receives only casual mention in journals of the era through 1845. And most of these mentions are about how unsuitable the harbor's entrance was to large ships—the British ship HMS Discovery cancelled the first survey of the harbor because coral reefs made navigating the narrow entrance too dangerous.

It wasn't until 1840 that the United States sent Commodore Charles Wilkes to conduct the first U.S. survey of Pearl Harbor. Wilkes's expedition confirmed the tricky entrance, but added that if it could be deepened, "it would afford the best and most capacious harbor in the Pacific."

In 1887, as part of a reciprocal agreement, Hawaii granted the United Sates the exclusive right to enter Pearl Harbor, establish a coaling and repair station and improve the entrance. After the United States annexed the Hawaiian territory in 1898, Pearl Harbor was dredged and its channel enlarged for larger ships. The first battleship, the USS Wisconsin, entered in 1903.

Little by little, Congress acquired all the land around the harbor, divvying it up among the U.S. Navy, the Army and the Departments of Labor, Commerce and Agriculture. With the dawning of World War I, all focus shifted away from commercial interests to develop the harbor as a first-class naval base capable of taking care of the entire U.S. fleet. By the early 1940s, hundreds of millions of dollars had been spent to make Pearl Harbor a world-class port.

SHANGRI LA

900 S. Beretania St., Honolulu, 866-385-3849; www.shangrilahawaii.org

Shangri La (1937) was the home of Doris Duke, the daughter of James Buchanan Duke, who made his fortune in tobacco. After her father died, she became known as "the richest girl in the world." For 60 years she collected Islamic art, inspired by her travels throughout the Middle East and South Asia, and filled her home with the works she amassed throughout her life. She was heavily involved in the design of the house and how the works would be presented, resulting in a highly personal presentation of much-cherished objects collected for pleasure rather than monetary value. Today, the estate houses more than 3,500 works dating from 1500 B.C. to the 20th century, including ceramics, decorative arts and furniture. The tour begins with a short film at the Honolulu Academy of Art, followed by a 15-minute minivan ride to Shangri La, where guests spend 1 1/2 hours on a guided walk through the main house and grounds. Make reservations as far in advance as possible, as demand is high and tour groups are small. Tickets are nonrefundable. Wednesday-Saturday 8:30 a.m.-1:30 p.m.; closed September.

HONOLULU SAILING CO.

Honolulu, 808-239-3900, 800-829-0114; www.honsail.com

This sailing school and charter company lets visitors choose from sailboats and power yachts. Oahu trips range from two to five days in length. The company also does special charters, including weddings at sea.

HONOLULU ZOO

151 Kapahulu Ave., Honolulu, 808-926-3191; www.honoluluzoo.org

You may not have expected to see giraffes, chimpanzees or Indian elephants in Hawaii, but they're waiting for you at the Honolulu Zoo—along with the birds and reptiles of Hawaii and other Pacific islands. Ongoing exhibits include African Savanna, Tropical Forest, Islands of the Pacific and a children's zoo. Go beyond a simple look-see at the animals: the "Snooze in the Zoo" program gives you and your kids the chance to have a sleepover party at the zoo. Other programs include "Breakfast with a Keeper" and "Twilight Tours." Daily 9 a.m.-4:30 p.m.

HOOMALUHIA BOTANICAL GARDEN

45-680 Luluku Road, Kaneohe, 808-233-7323;
www.co.honolulu.hi.us/parks/hbg/hmbg.htm

This 400-acre botanical garden contains endangered and rare plants as well as a network of trails for hikers, bikers, and horseback riders (bring your own horse). Its name means "to make a place of peace and tranquility." Stop in at the visitor center to find out what programs are being offered on the day of your visit and to secure passes and car permits for camping (Friday-Monday). Daily 9 a.m.-4 p.m.

INTERNATIONAL MARKET PLACE

2330 Kalakaua Ave., Honolulu, 808-971-2080;
www.internationalmarketplacewaikiki.com

More than 130 shops and artisans' carts draw shoppers to this kitschy, touristy, but longstanding Waikiki fixture for Hawaiian gifts and souvenirs. Jewelry, clothing, and handicrafts make up the majority of the offerings; you'll also find a variety of options for snacks and quick meals. On many evenings, local musicians perform. Daily 10 a.m.-10:30 p.m.

IOLANI PALACE STATE MONUMENT

King and Richards streets, Honolulu, 808-522-0824; www.iolanipalace.org

A National Historic Landmark, this magnificent building served as Hawaii's capitol until 1969, as well as the home of Hawaiian royalty from 1882 to 1893, when Queen Liliuokalani was overthrown. (After the coup, she was held in one of the second-floor rooms for eight months.) Its grand koa wood staircase, throne room, and other lavish spaces have been restored to their former opulence, and many original furnishings were tracked down from around the world and brought back to the palace. The galleries tour, which does not include the palace itself but does include jewels, regalia, and photographs, is self-guided. A 90-minute grand tour is also available; reservations are recommended, and children under age 5 are not permitted. Open Tuesday-Saturday 9 a.m.-4 p.m.

ISLAND SEAPLANE SERVICE INC.

85 Lagoon Drive, Honolulu, 808-836-6273; www.islandseaplane.com

Soar like a seabird over Oahu on these flight tours conducted by pilot Pat Magie and his staff. Pat's planes are film-famous, as seen in the Adam Sandler movie 50 First Dates. Tours range from a half-hour to one hour and offer a spectacular birds-eye view of some of Oahu's most famous landmarks as well as its stunning topography and coastlines. Complimentary van transportation is available from Waikiki Hotels.

ISLAND TREASURES

Koko Marina Center, 7192 Kalanianaole Hwy., Honolulu, 808-396-8827

Tucked away in an East Oahu residential shopping complex on the way to Hanauma Bay, this jewel of a store is filled with handcrafted items created by artists in Hawaii. Finds include beach glass jewelry, koa wood home accessories, Hawaiian quilts, tropical ceramics, feather lei, beauty products, artwork and photography ready for framing. Open Sunday 10 a.m.-4 p.m.; Monday-Thursday 10 a.m.-6 p.m.; Friday-Saturday 10 a.m.-8 p.m.

KAHALA MALL

4211 Waialae Ave., Honolulu, 808-732-7736; www.kahalamallcenter.com

If rain threatens to ruin your day, you can always go shopping. This 90-store mall includes a Macy's and a Barnes & Noble, along with typical finds like Gap and Foot Locker. Monday-Saturday 10 a.m.-9 p.m., Sunday 10 a.m.-5 p.m.

KAWAIAHAO CHURCH

957 Punchbowl St., Honolulu, 808-522-1333

The first permanent Western house of worship on the island, this 1842 church was built by Christian missionaries and Hawaiians. Designed in New England colonial style by the Reverend Hiram Bingham (1789-1869), the church was a massive effort by workers, who dove for and dragged ashore tons of coral and then chopped, shaped, and smoothed it into 14,000 thousand-pound blocks. Kawaiahao (which means water of Hao) is where Hawaii's monarchs were baptized, wed, crowned and buried. Twenty-one royal portraits hang in the upper gallery, and the pews at the rear are still reserved for royal descendants. The public is invited to Hawaiian-language services, complete with song, every Sunday. Tours follow the services. Sunday 10:30 a.m.

KO OLINA OCEAN ADVENTURES

92-100 Waipahe Place, Ko Olina, 808-396-2068, 866-456-6666; www.koolinaoceanadventures.com

Whether you want to watch whales, swim with dolphins, snorkel the reefs or head below the surface and try your hand at Snuba (a hybrid of snorkeling and scuba diving), this tour operator probably has a trip to accommodate your interests. Catch your boat at the Ko Olina Marina, about a 45-minute drive west of Waikiki. Daily.

LYON ARBORETUM

3860 Manoa Road, Honolulu, 808-988-0456; www.lyonarboretum.com

This nearly 200-acre arboretum receives an average of 165 inches of rain annually, making it a terrific place for trees and plants to grow. The colorful foliage draws a number of birds, including cockatoos, doves and the native amahiki. On the grounds you'll find Aihualama Falls, reachable via an easy four-mile hike. Guided tours of the gardens are given on Tuesdays and Saturdays; call for reservations. Monday-Friday 9 a.m.-4 p.m.

MAGIC OF POLYNESIA

Waikiki Beachcomber Hotel, 2300 Kalakaua Ave., Honolulu, 808-971-4321,

877-971-4321; www.magicofpolynesia.com

Illusionist John Hirokawa and a cast of dancers and chanters entertain audiences in this family-friendly stage show that combines magic with Polynesian lore. Packages include dinner, cocktails, or show only. Daily at 6:30 p.m. and 8:45 p.m.

MAITA'I CATAMARAN

Honolulu, between the Sheraton Waikiki and Halekulani on Waikiki Beach,

808-922-5665, 800-462-7975;www.leahi.com

Billing itself as "Hawaii's fastest, wettest ride," the 44-foot Maita'i takes up to 47 passengers on a cruise around Waikiki. The sunset sail includes cocktails, including the namesake mai tai. Advance reservations are required, and private charters are available. Daily at 11 a.m., 1 p.m., 3 p.m., 5 p.m.

MAKANI KAI HELICOPTER TOURS

Honolulu International Airport, 110 Kapalulu Place, Honolulu, 808-834-5813;

www.makanikai.com

View Oahu by air with some flightseeing on Makani Air. The 30-minute tour covers the south and eastern shores, while the 60-minute Sacred Falls Alii Tour whisks you above Oahu's famed North Shore. Peer down at famous surf spots, private valleys used in the film Jurassic Park, the worlds largest pineapple maze, and the Arizona Memorial, where you get an aerial view of the USS Arizona in her final resting place below the waters of Pearl Harbor. For an extra fee, take home a personalized video of your tour, complete with sights, pilot commentary, and your own comments made while in the air. For a romantic evening, Makani Kai offers a Honolulu City Lights night flight with dinner included. Free transportation from Waikiki hotels is available with all tours.

MANOA FALLS TRAIL

Honolulu; www.hawaiitrails.org

When you dream of Hawaii, what do you see? If a waterfall is in the picture, then the Manoa Falls Trail is a must. Not even a mile long, the trail provides a 100 miles' worth of sights, including a grove of fragrant Eucalyptus trees and a lush rain forest, before you arrive at the 100-foot-tall waterfall. Though it's a fairly easy hike, wear sturdy shoes and pack some drinking water. Join the trail just shy of the entrance to the University of Hawaii's Lyon Arboretum.

MARTIN AND MCARTHUR

1815 Kahai St., Honolulu, 808-845-6688; www.martinandmcarthur.com

Traditional island living is handcrafted in furnishings made from one of Hawaii's rarest and most beautiful woods—Koa. Specializing in pieces that reflect the richness of Hawaii's 19th-century Monarchy Era, Martin and MacArthur's collection ranges from koa rocking chairs to living and dining room pieces.

MISSION HOUSES MUSEUM

553 S. King St., Honolulu, 808-531-0481; www.missionhouses.org

To put it mildly, 1820 was quite the turning point in Hawaii's history. That's the year American Protestant missionaries established their headquarters. Step into that pivotal time at the Mission Houses Museum. Walk the grounds on your own or take one of four daily guided tours. On the last Saturday of the month, museum interpreters dress in period clothes and give guided tours of the museum, which includes the oldest frame house in Hawaii. Don't miss the museum's quilt collection—it features some of Hawaii's oldest quilts and patchwork bedcovers. If the designs inspire you, order one for yourself at the museum gift shop. Open Tuesday-Saturday 10 a.m.-4 p.m.

NATIONAL MEMORIAL CEMETERY OF THE PACIFIC

2177 Puowaina Drive, Honolulu, 808-566-1430

At once somber and serene, the National Memorial Cemetery of the Pacific (also known as the Punchbowl) is the most-visited national cemetery in the United States. The site, which opened in 1949 with the interment of 776 servicemen killed during the December 7, 1941, attack on Pearl Harbor, gets its name from its shape: it sits in a crater formed by an extinct volcano. In addition to more than 13,000 soldiers killed at Iwo Jima, Guadalcanal and other World War II battles in the Pacific, the cemetery holds casualties from Korea and Vietnam and other U.S. servicemen. Among the interred are war correspondent Ernie Pyle and Ellison Onizuka, one of the astronauts aboard the ill-fated Challenger space shuttle. Daily; closed federal holidays except for Memorial Day and Veterans Day.

QUEEN EMMA SUMMER PALACE

2913 Pali Hwy., Honolulu, 808-595-3167; www.daughtersofhawaii.org

Even Hawaiians need to get away from time to time. In the late 1800s, Queen Emma, wife of King Kamehameha IV and mother of Prince Albert Edward, inherited this royal retreat from her uncle, John Young II, an advisor to King Kamehameha I. Run by the Daughters of Hawaii, the gardens and Hawaiian-Victorian home offer a relaxing way to spend an afternoon. Gaze out on the lily pond, take in the blend of Hawaiian and British treasures that Queen Emma collected, and ander the grounds as Queen Emma did more than 100 years ago. Daily 9 a.m.-4 p.m.

REEF TREKKERS SCUBA DIVING TOURS

Honolulu, 808-943-0588, 877-359-7333; www.reeftrekkers.com

Shipwrecks, downed fighter planes and lava tubes are just a few of the things you might see during a dive with Reef Trekkers, which strives to find the best dive spots and conditions around the island. Dives, costing $95 and up, vary in length and skill level; just explain what you're looking for and they'll do their best to accommodate your interests and experience. Private and semi-private PADI scuba diving and certification courses are also available.

ROYAL HAWAIIAN AHA A'IANA

Royal Hawaiian Hotel, 2259 Kalakaua Ave., Honolulu, 808-931-8383;
www.royal-hawaiian.com

Underneath the stars on Waikiki Beach and in the shadow of the legendary Pink Palace of the Pacific, this tasteful evening of Hawaiian song and dance is held on the Royal Hawaiian hotel's oceanfront lawn and includes an elegant multi-course dinner and plenty of tropical drinks. Monday nights.

ROYAL HAWAIIAN CENTER

2201 Kalakaua Ave., Honolulu, 808-922-0588; www.royalhawaiiancenter.com

This 150-store mall is within walking distance of Waikiki's hotels. Upscale designer boutiques like Bulgari, Fendi, Ferragamo and Hermes rub shoulders with more budget-friendly local shops selling handicrafts, Hawaiian apparel and fresh leis. The mall also hosts free cultural events, like hula lessons and a torch-lighting ceremony put on by the Polynesian Cultural Center. Daily 10 a.m.-10 p.m.

SANDY BEACH

8800 Kalanianaole Highway, Honolulu

This is one of the best body surfing beaches on Oahu and also one of the most dangerous. Strong rip currents and shallow shore breaks have left many adventurers severely injured. Still, Sandy is a hub for the teen and 20-something crowd, who congregate here to sunbathe and socialize. The grassy area attracts kite flyers who fill the skies most weekends with colorful kites.

SNORKEL BOB'S

700 Kapahulu Ave., Honolulu, 808-737-2421, 800-262-7725; www.snorkelbob.com

Rent snorkeling and scuba equipment; take snorkeling and dolphin-watching tours, downhill biking tours, helicopter flights and attend luaus. Daily 8 a.m.-5 p.m.

SOUTH SEA AQUATICS

2155 Kalakaua Ave., Honolulu, 808-922-0852; www.ssahawaii.com

Ready to go deep? Pay a visit to this full-service dive shop. Whether you're in the market for new gear or somebody to teach you how to use it, South Sea Aquatics has the goods. The shop also runs a daily dive trip that leaves from Honolulu Harbor. While the final destination depends on the day's conditions, most trips feature a deep wreck dive and a reef dive. Daily 10 a.m.-9 p.m.

SUNSET ON THE BEACH

Honolulu, Waikiki Beach; www.sunsetonthebeach.net

On weekend evenings, recent and classic movies are projected onto a 30-foot screen right on Waikiki Beach. Locals and tourists alike gather to enjoy live music before the show and settle in for the main event, which usually begins at 7:30 p.m., after the sun sets. Food vendors provide snacks during the festivities. Saturday-Sunday at 4 p.m.

USS ARIZONA

Kamehameha Hwy., Honolulu (from the Honolulu/Waikiki area, take either Ala Moana
Blvd./Nimitz Hwy. or H1 W, exit 15A), 808-422-2771; www.nps.gov/usar

This memorial is the final resting place of many of the 1,177 crewmen killed on December 7, 1941, when the battleship USS Arizona was bombed by Japanese naval forces. The interpretive program features a talk followed by a 23-minute documentary film about the attack on Pearl Harbor. Afterwards, visitors board a Navy shuttle boat for a trip to the memorial, which spans the hull of the sunken ship and contains the ship's bell, as well as a shrine room with the names of the dead carved in stone. Although their numbers are dwindling, survivors of the attack still come to tell visitors their stories of that tragic day in American history. Prepare to face huge crowds at this popular tourist attraction that sees more than 4,000 visitors per day—arriving early in the morning is your best bet, as tickets are given out on a first-come, first-served basis. The last program of the day begins at 3 p.m. Daily 7:30 a.m.-5 p.m.

USS BOWFIN SUBMARINE MUSEUM AND PARK

11 Arizona Memorial Drive, Honolulu (adjacent to the USS Arizona Memorial),
808-423-1341; www.bowfin.org

Get a small taste of what life was like for the 80 men assigned to the USS Bowfin submarine during World War II. Now a National Historic Landmark, the sub was used for nine war patrols after its launch on December 7, 1942. Take a tour of the sub, view sub-related artifacts in the 10,000-square-foot museum, and watch a video about submarine history in the 40-seat theater. After learning your fill, spend some time at the waterfront memorial on Pearl Harbor; it honors the 3,500 submariners killed during the war. Children under age 4 are not allowed on the submarine. Daily 8 a.m.-5 p.m.

VICTORIA WARD CENTERS

Ala Moana Blvd., Honolulu, 808-597-1243; www.victoriawardcenters.com

Four square blocks from Auahi Street to Ala Moana Boulevard and between Queen Street and Ward Avenue comprises Victoria Ward Centers. Stroll through six retail complexes housing 120 shops, 23 restaurants and a 16-screen movie megaplex. Food, fun, bargains, and a farmers market can be found here. Check out the concierge located in the Ward Entertainment Megaplex lobby for assistance with shopping, movie, dining reservations, or taxi services.
Daily.

MAMO HOWELL DESIGNS

Ward Warehouse, 1050 Ala Moana Blvd., Honolulu, 808-591-2002;
www.mamohowell.com

Mamo Howell took the Hawaiian woman's love of the muu muu and made it fashionable to wear in the most stylish of settings. Check out her Alii Nui collection created in her own signature prints. Men's and children's apparel as well as gift items can be found here. Monday-Saturday 10 a.m.-9 p.m., Sunday 10 a.m.-5 p.m.

NATIVE BOOKS/NA MEA HAWAII

Ward Warehouse, 1050 Ala Moana Blvd., Honolulu, 808-596-8885;
www.nativebookshawaii.com

A hui (group) of local artists began this cooperative venture as an outlet for those items that truly are made only in Hawaii. Here you can find rare Niihau shells, hand-painted fabrics, calabashes, fine art and prints, ceramics, musical instruments, and one of the islands' most extensive Hawaiian book collections. Monday-Saturday 10 a.m.-9 p.m., Sunday 10 a.m.-5 p.m.

WAIKELE PREMIUM OUTLETS

94-790 Lumiaina St., Waipahu, (15 miles west of Honolulu off H1, exit 7);

808-676-5656;www.premiumoutlets.com

These 50 factory outlet stores include Barneys New York, Coach and Polo Ralph Lauren. Monday-Saturday 9 a.m.-9 p.m., Sunday 10 a.m.-6 p.m.

WAIKIKI BEACH WALK

Lewers Street, Honolulu, 808-931-3593; www.waikikibeachwalk.com

What was a tired stretch of Lewers Street has been transformed into Waikiki Beach Walk, a two-story stretch of shops, restaurants and coffee shops lining the street that leads to the Halekulani hotel and Outrigger Reef. The new luxury high-rise hotel Trump Waikiki opens at one end of the walk in late 2009.

WAIKIKI HISTORIC TRAIL

Fountain Courtyard, 2201 Kalakau Ave., Honolulu, 808-841-6442;

www.waikikihistorictrail.com

While wandering Waikiki, look out for bronze surfboards—they're markers for most of the sites along the 2-mile trail. The area's history features rich cultural traditions and royalty of both traditional and surfing varieties. The trail's 23 sites include the estate of Hawaii's last reigning monarch, Queen Liliuokalani; the Healing Stones of Kapaemahu at Kuhio Beach; and a bronze statue of Duke Paoa Kahanamoku, an Olympic champion swimmer, movie star, and the "Father of International Surfing." Wander the trail on your own or take a tour with the Native Hawaiian Hospitality Association; there are two daily tours Tuesday, Thursday and Saturday.

WAIKIKI TROLLEY TOURS

Honolulu, 800-824-8804; www.waikikitrolley.com

Waikiki Trolleys have been dropping people off around the island for 20 years. The electric cars—reproductions of San Francisco's well-known open-air trolleys--make it easy to tour (and shop) Honolulu from the Bishop Museum in the west all the way to the Sea Life Park in the east. Buy tickets at the Waikiki Trolley Ticket Booth at the Royal Hawaiian Shopping Center, the Ala Moana Shopping Center stop, Victoria Ward Centers stops, or many of Waikiki's hotels. Then, just hop on and off anywhere along the trolley's four different routes.

X-TREME PARASAIL

Honolulu, 808-737-3599; www.xtremeparasail.com

Soar high above the Pacific—600 feet high, as a matter of fact—with this family-owned operator out of Waikiki Beach. Transportation is included from major Waikiki hotels, and flights range from 9 to 15 minutes, depending on how "X-treme" you want to get. Flights cost $40 and up; observers who want to ride along in the boat and snap photos pay a lesser fee. Daily 8 a.m.-dark.

SPECIAL EVENTS
ALOHA FESTIVALS
Honolulu, on all islands, 800-852-7690; www.alohafestivals.com
Parades and other events celebrate Hawaiian culture during a week-long festival throughout the islands. September

FESTIVAL OF LIGHTS ✓
Downtown, Honolulu, 808-547-4397; www.honolulu.gov/csd/citylights/
Catch the glow of a Hawaiian-style Christmas. Honolulu glitters with lights all through the month of December. Head down to the waterfront to see one of the best displays: boat owners deck out their decks and light up the night with fun themes for the Hawaii Kai Marina Festival of Lights boat parade. December.

HAWAII INTERNATIONAL FILM FESTIVAL
Honolulu, 808-528-3456; www.hiff.org
Crouching Tiger, Hidden Dragon. The Piano. Shine. Shall We Dance? These are just some of the many critically acclaimed movies that have premiered at this film festival, which promotes understanding and cultural exchange among the peoples of Asia, the Pacific, and North America. It's actually two festivals in one. For the Spring Festival, held the first week of April each year and featuring 20-plus independent flicks, the lights dim at several venues only on the island of Oahu. The fall festival, held the last week of October, showcases up to 200 films at venues on every island in Hawaii, making it the country's only statewide festival. Early April and late October.

HAWAII INTERNATIONAL JAZZ FESTIVAL
Honolulu, 808-941-9974
Oahu is in full swing when the festival hits town for two days every summer. Whether you choose one of the free public events or pay your way to a concert at the Hawaii Theatre Center, you'll get the chance to mellow out or liven up with some of the world's best jazz talents, including local favorites like the Honolulu Jazz Quartet and the 17-piece Territorial Big Band. July.

HAWAII STATE FAIR
Aloha Stadium, 99-500 Salt Lake Blvd., Honolulu, 808-486-9555
Auto show, petting zoo, carnival rides, and concerts. May-June.

HAWAII STATE FARM FAIR
Aloha Stadium, Honolulu, 808-682-5767
Breathe in the fragrance as you pass through the fair's native plant sale. You'll probably want to keep the sweet smell of orchids and other Hawaiian plants in mind when you move onto the fair's animal exhibits, including a petting zoo that tots love. Plenty of stomach-churning rides await on the fairway. Top off your day with samples of tasty Hawaiian treats and typical fair junk food. Early-mid-June.

MADE IN HAWAII

If Hawaiian canoe makers were honing their craft today, they no doubt would be set up in a studio surrounded by the latest tools. But in old Hawaii, they had little more than a pump drill and a stone adze with which to work. Using skills and knowledge passed from generation to generation, they crafted magnificent canoes, some that carried 100 villagers at a time and some that simply carried their families. And just as with their knowledge, the canoes, too, were passed down from generation to generation. The crafts of Hawaii are rich in tradition, stemming form a time when everything was fashioned by hand, textiles and objects were made with great pride, and those who made them were well were revered.

Hawaiians were great weavers. They split leaves from hala trees, removed the thorns and spine, soaked them, and then dried them over fire. The leaves were woven into baskets used for picking coffee beans, plaited into mats, or made into pillows. Hawaiians also worked with raw bark from the mulberry, or wauke, tree; it was pounded into pulp, formed into strips, dyed with colors form sea animals and plants, and painted for texture and decoration. Flowers and herbs were pounded or sewn into the cloth to add fragrance and the material—kapa cloth—was frequently made into bed covering.

Koa wood, used for its density, strength and luster, was crafted into woodware and furniture for the ali'l (royalty or aristocracy) and used for small idols, mirrors and poi pounders.

Lei making is an ancient tropical art form, the leis formed by hand in a traditional pattern. Sometimes twisted, sometimes braided and sometimes sewn together with shells, leis have always been made with flowers native to the islands on which they are made. Smooth, ivory shells called pupu are found only on the island of NI'ihau and were strung together into leis of multiple six-yard strands and presented to royalty.

No less important to royalty—and no less painstaking to create—were the adornments, idols and cloaks created from the feathers of brilliantly colored red and yellow birds. Featherwork was a highly prized art. By attaching the feathers to a net of olona cord, workers created helmets and capes worn by men during battle. Feathered adornments, idols and cloaks were acquisitions of only royalty and aristocrats.

With the resurgence of Hawaiian pride in native culture, many of these crafts are re-emerging. Handcrafted bowls of koa, mango and monkeypod wood can be found, as well as koa hair ornaments, chopsticks and key chains. Weavers are still making hats and purses out of hala leaves and are now also using coconut leaves, still lovely although not a match for hala's quality. Kapa cloth is hard to find. If you do find something of kappa, read the label carefully; much of it is important from Samoa or Tonga.

Beautiful Ni'ihau leis of pupu shells can be found but are very expensive, a traditional multi-strand lei may cost around $25,000. Smaller pieces of Ni'ihau jewelery can be found at much lower prices.

HONOLULU FESTIVAL

Honolulu, 808-596-3327; www.honolulufestival.com

This large cultural festival celebrates cooperation and harmony between the people of Hawaii and those from the Asia-Pacific region. Events, which take place at the Hawaii Convention Center, the Ala Moana Shopping Center, the Honolulu Academy of Arts, the Royal Hawaiian Center and Kalakaua Avenue, include a float parade, music and dance performances, demonstrations, and educational seminars. Early March.

HONOLULU MARATHON

Honolulu, 808-734-7200; www.honolulumarathon.org

One of the world's largest marathons, the Honolulu Marathon hosts some 32,000 runners on the second Sunday each December on a marathon course designed to accommodate both the novice and elite runner. Racers begin at Ala Moana Beach Park, travel through downtown Honolulu, wind their way past Waikiki along the ocean to Hawaii Kai and return back to Kapiolani Park for a glorious finish and a coveted Honolulu Marathon Finisher tee shirt. Included in the fun is a week of activities that features an all-you-can-eat carbo-loading luau. Second Sunday in December.

KING KAMEHAMEHA CELEBRATION

Honolulu, downtown and Honolulu Harbor, 808-586-0333; www.hawaii.gov

King Kamehameha was the most famous—and best loved—king in Hawaii's history. Join all of Hawaii in the celebration of his life and accomplishments, including the growth of local industries and agriculture, and trade with foreign nations. This state holiday features a floral parade complete with marching bands, parties, and much more. The parade starts at King and Richards streets and ends at Queen Kapiolani Park. The best photo op of the day is, without a doubt, the king's statue in downtown Honolulu, which is draped with some of the biggest leis you've ever seen. June.

LEI DAY

Honolulu, 866-888-6284

One of the most recognized symbols of Hawaii, leis are given at celebrations or just to welcome people to Hawaii. In 1927, Hawaii's poet laureate decided that leis deserved a celebration of their own and Lei Day was born. Join in the fun on May 1 by exchanging leis with friends or family members. Wear them while watching the Lei Day parades or contests. On May 2, help place the leis on the tombs of Hawaii's royalty following a 9 a.m. ceremony at The Royal Mausoleum on upper Nuuanu Avenue. Early May.

MOONLIGHT MELE ON THE LAWN

Bishop Museum,1525 Bernice St., Honolulu, 808-847-3511; www.bishopmuseum.org

This annual summer concert series is held underneath the stars on the Great Lawn of the Bishop Museum and features music and dance from Hawaii's top local recording and entertainment artists. June-August.

NFL PRO BOWL

Aloha Stadium, 99-500 Salt Lake Blvd., Honolulu, 808-486-9300; www.nfl.com/probowl

This all-star pro football game, which has been held in Hawaii for 30 years, pits the best players of the NFC against the standouts of the AFC. Tickets are available through Ticketmaster. Early February.

TINMAN TRIATHLON

Ala Moana Beach Park, Honolulu, 808-732-7311; www.tinmanhawaii.com

Join the fun for an 800-meter swim, 40-kilometer bike ride and 10-kilometer run around Oahu's south and east shores. July.

TRANS PAC YACHT RACE

Honolulu

Every odd-numbered year, boats of all shapes and sizes set sail from the Palos Verde peninsula, south of Los Angeles, and travel the 2,225 nautical miles to the finish line in the waters off Diamond Head Lighthouse in Waikiki. Spectators line Diamond Head Road to view the continuous parade of yachts as they glimmer in a moonlit sea or sweep by in the sunshine.

WORLD INVITATIONAL HULA FESTIVAL

Waikiki Shell, Kapiolani Park, Honolulu; www.worldhula.com

Dancers from around the world flock to Honolulu to take part in this annual event celebrating Hawaiian culture. Tickets are available through Ticketmaster and at the Blaisdell Center Box Office. Early November.

WHERE TO STAY

★★ASTON WAIKIKI BEACH HOTEL ✓

2570 Kalakaua Ave., Honolulu, 808-922-2511, 808-923-3656; www.astonhotels.com

This hotel (formerly ResortQuest Waikiki) has two main selling points: low rates and a location right across the street from Waikiki Beach. All of the hotel's guest rooms, located in two high-rise towers, are decorated island-style, with tropical colors and new flat-screen TVs, and all are small, ranging in size from 225 to 300 square feet. Like the guest rooms, the hotel's two restaurants won't break the bank. Tiki's Grill and Bar, an open-air dining room with a retro South Pacific design, features island cuisine. The chefs at Wolfgang Puck Express whip up sophisticated fast food in a sidewalk café setting. The hotel has a pool, but few other resort-type amenities.

713 rooms. Restaurant, bar. Pool. $$

★★★★HALEKULANI ✓

2199 Kalia Road, Honolulu, 808-923-2311, 800-367-2343; www.halekulani.com

Halekulani, or "house befitting heaven," has catered to well-heeled guests since 1917. Located on the western side of Waikiki Beach, this hotel is a calm oasis in otherwise chaotic Waikiki, offering understated elegance and top-notch service. Rooms are housed in several low-rise buildings that surround the historic house at its center, which now houses one of Honolulu's top special occasion restaurants, La Mer. (Downstairs is the more casual Orchids and the ever-popular House Without A Key). Many of the touches that make a stay here special (handmade chocolates at turndown, gorgeous floral displays throughout the hotel) are due to the fact that Halekulani has everything from a bakery to a laundry and floral studio onsite. Rooms may not be as trend-conscious as others on Waikiki, but they're comfortable and include flat-screen TVs, MP3 docking stations and DVD players. Spa Halekulani is petite, but offers intensely personalized service and a range of treatments.

455 rooms. Restaurant, bar. Fitness center. Spa. Beach. Pool. Business center. $$$$

★★★HAWAII PRINCE HOTEL WAIKIKI

100 Holomoana St., Honolulu, 808-956-1111, 866-774-6236; www.princeresorts.com

This hotel looks sleek, with its guest rooms housed in twin 33-story towers. All of the rooms have floor-to-ceiling windows that offer great views of the Ala Wai Yacht Harbor and the Pacific Ocean. Unlike at many other Waikiki hotels, the rooms aren't decked out in tropical décor; rather, they're more modern with neutral palettes and streamlined furnishings. To help keep guests fed and entertained, the Prince has three restaurants and two bars, including the Prince Court, which specializes in contemporary island cuisine, and Hakone, which attracts diners with sushi and other authentic Japanese dishes. The hotel is the only one in Waikiki with its own golf course, but its about 45 minutes away by shuttle bus. Waikiki's sandy stretches are a five-minute drive away, as is good shopping at the Ala Moana Shopping Center. 521 rooms. Restaurant, bar. Fitness room, spa. Pool. Business center. $$$$

★★★HILTON HAWAIIAN VILLAGE BEACH RESORT & SPA ✓
2005 Kalia Road, Honolulu, 808-949-4321, 800-445-8667;
www.hiltonhawaiianvillage.com

With a whopping 3,000 guest rooms, an action-packed stretch of beach, numerous shops and restaurants, and spa facilities, you'll never have to leave this sprawling resort while you're here. Vegas-like in size and scope, the Hilton Hawaiian Village caters to vacationing families, with kids' programs and a kids' pool. Rooms are spread throughout six towers tailored to different types of travelers—for example, the beachfront Rainbow Tower with its soaring rainbow mosaics is great for families and vacationers, while the Ali'i Tower is meant for a more upscale business and leisure clientele. More than 50 varieties of exotic plants and flowers mingle with waddling penguins, pink flamingos, talking parrots and other wildlife on the lush 22-acre grounds, and the resort's more than 90 shops run the gamut from inexpensive t-shirt stores to pricey boutiques carrying high-end jewelry. There's even a

THE WORLD OF WAIKIKI

Who hasn't heard of Waikiki? It's one of the world's most famous beaches, which explains why it's always so crowded. Every day, about a quarter-million people work and play near this stretch of sand.

That's a lot of people for the relatively small size of Wakiki, which reaches only a little more than two miles along Oahu's sunny South Shore. The beach is bordered by Diamond Head (the volcanic cone that serves as the area's landmark) and the Ala Wai Yacht Harbor to the east and west, and the Ala Wai Canal to the north (which separates Waikiki from Honolulu). To the south, Waikiki's sandy beaches line the Pacific.

The entire Waikiki coastline is often referred to as Waikiki Beach, but it's actually split into seven stretches of sand. The other six are Duke Kahanamoku, Fort DeRussy, Gray's, Kuhio, Queens and Sans Souci beaches.

About 90 percent of the rooms available on Oahu are found in Waikiki. Some of them are large, like the 1,695-room Sheraton Waikiki; others are luxurious, such as Halekulani, where the generously sized rooms average 620 square feet.

Besides the beaches and hotels, Waikiki has plenty more to offer, including shopping that ranges from kitschy to elegant. Much of the retail activity centers around Kalakaua Avenue, where visitors swarm to International Marketplace for open-air souvenir shopping. The area's many attractions include Diamond Head, Kapiolani Park, the Honolulu Zoo and the Waikiki Aquarium. This is not the place for peace and quiet, but for those who seek excitement there is more than enough entertainment to go around.

Harley-Davidson accessories shop with a great selection of island-inspired biker wear. The 22 restaurants and lounges provide a wide range of dining options, from the Euro-Asian Bali by the Sea to a New York-style deli to Italian, Japanese, and Chinese. Fitness classes and snorkeling lessons are included in the room rate; hula and surfing lessons, water aerobics and lei-making classes are also offered. On Friday nights, the Super Pool (so named because it's 10,000 square feet) is the setting for a Polynesian show that concludes with a fireworks display over Waikiki.

2,860 rooms. Restaurant, bar. Fitness center. Spa. Beach. Pool. Business center. $$

★★HILTON WAIKIKI PRINCE KUHIO

2500 Kuhio Ave., Honolulu, 808-922-0811, 800-445-8667; www.hilton.com

A recent update added colorful, contemporary décor and new amenities (flat-screens, down duvets) to this quiet hotel two blocks from Waikiki beach. All of its guest rooms, housed in a 37-story tower, are attractively decorated with a Hawaiian touch and offer good ocean and mountain views. The executive rooms, where the amenities are a step above, features special services such as a private lounge. The hotel's amenities include a restaurant, lounge, 24-hour workout room, and tenth-floor outdoor pool with a large sundeck and Jacuzzi. For business travelers, it offers lots of meeting space, high-speed Internet access in every room, WiFi connections in the lobby, and a full-service business center.

606 rooms. Restaurant, bar. Fitness center. Pool. Business center. $$$

★★★HYATT REGENCY WAIKIKI RESORT ✓

2424 Kalakaua Ave., Honolulu, 808-923-1234, 800-633-7313; www.hyatt.com

With 1,230 rooms in two 40-story towers, this is one large hotel. You'll realize that it's no intimate hideaway as soon as you walk into the huge lobby with its cascading waterfalls and tropical plants. The location is just across the street from Waikiki Beach, on the side nearest Diamond Head. The hotel has five restaurants and bars, including the Colony, where chefs prepare steak and seafood dishes; and Ciao Mein, where you can opt for Chinese or Italian cuisine. The stage near the Elegant Dive bar features live entertainment daily. The resort houses more than 60 shops selling everything from apparel and jewelry to art and specialty gifts. Send the kids off to Camp Hyatt (the children's program), and then relax with one of the massages, facials or wraps available at the 10,000-square-foot No Hoola Spa. Book one of the rooms on the Regency Floor, and you'll have access to private rooftop sun decks with whirlpools. All of the guest rooms are extra roomy and have been modestly updated with down duvets and flat-screen TVs (read: the rest of the room still needs attention), but those on the Regency Floor are a step above the rest with special services, such as complimentary continental breakfast and afternoon appetizers.

1,320 rooms. Restaurant, bar. Fitness center. Spa. Pool. Business center. $$$

★★★JW MARRIOTT IHILANI RESORT & SPA AT KO OLINA

92-1001 Olani St., Ko Olina, 808-679-0079, 800-228-9290; www.ihilani.com

Located 17 miles west of Honolulu International Airport, this elegant 17-

story Marriott is far removed from the bustle of touristy Waikiki. It's located in the secluded, upscale 640-acre oceanfront Ko Olina Resort and borders a lovely crescent-shaped beach, with the Waianae Mountains visible in the distance. All of its guest rooms are large, with more than 640 square feet of space. They're also well appointed, with marble baths, deep-soaking European tubs, large-screen televisions and private lanais with great mountain and ocean views. The 35,000-square-foot spa offers an array of decadent treatments, including numerous types of massages and a variety of water therapies, body scrubs and body wraps. Among the hotel's four restaurants is Azul, which serves up steaks and local seafood in a sophisticated, white-tablecloth setting. Watch the sunset from the Hokulea Bar, which serves appetizers and cocktails. Other amenities include a Ted Robinson-designed golf course, tennis courts and an extensive children's program and a marine life program that keeps youngsters busy and smiling.

387 rooms. Restaurant, bar. Fitness center. Beach. Pool. Golf. Tennis. Business center. $$$

★★★★KAHALA HOTEL & RESORT ✓

5000 Kahala Ave., Honolulu, 808-739-8888; www.kahalaresort.com

There are plenty of reasons why celebrities check into the Kahala when visiting Honolulu. Its quiet location, on the opposite side of Diamond Head from Waikiki in a lush, upscale neighborhood fronting a gorgeous stretch of sand, delivers North Shore-style relaxation only 10 minutes from downtown (which has been lure enough for notables such as Kanye West and George H. W. Bush). Conceived and originally opened by Conrad Hilton in the 1960s, the resort still maintains the tropical chic meets Mid-Century modern look it did on opening day (including in the vaulted lobby with its massive colored glass chandeliers). The recently refreshed rooms, updated with elegant pastel décor, local art, and thick mattresses topped with crisp Italian linens, are stocked with spacious bathrooms, flat-screen TVs and gorgeous views of the mountains or beach. The grounds include a coral reef-protected beach, six resident bottlenose dolphins (who participate in the hotel's unique encounter program) and two turtles, a completely updated fitness center, and five restaurants. The Spa at the Kahala offers a pampering experience that's a notch above others: treatments take place in your own spacious suite, complete with full bathroom, soaking tub and shower (there's also a quiet tropical garden outside for post-treatment relax-ation). With a pleasant sandy beach, outdoor pools, fully equipped fitness center, there's no need to leave the resort, but for those who wish to, there's a complimentary shuttle that can take you to Waikiki and Honolulu's shopping centers.

306 rooms. Restaurant, bar. Fitness Center. Spa. Pool. Beach. Business Center. $$$$

★★★MARRIOTT RESORT WAIKIKI ⌡

2552 Kalakaua Ave., Honolulu, 808-922-6611, 800-367-5370; www.marriottwaikiki.com

Big is best seems to be the concept behind most Waikiki hotels, and this sprawling Marriott with two guest towers is no exception. The resort, located opposite Waikiki beach, is spread over 5.2 acres, and offers some of the island's best views of Diamond Head and the Pacific Ocean. The 1,310 rooms are housed in two tall towers—one 33 stories, the other 25 stories—

and have been updated with cheerful, colorful island-style décor and down duvet-topped beds. The hotel has two rooftop pools, plenty of stores and boutiques in the shopping arcade (including a bridal boutique with attire for last-minute ceremonies), an updated fitness center, and the Spa Olakino and Salon, which has 12 treatment rooms. The restaurants and bars include the Kuhio Beach Grill, which features continental cuisine spiced with flavors of Hawaii and the Pacific Rim, and the poolside Moana Terrace, which also serves up live entertainment nightly.

1,310 rooms. Restaurant, bar. Fitness center. Spa. Pool. Business center. $$$$

★★★MOANA SURFRIDER, A WESTIN RESORT & SPA

2365 Kalakaua Ave., Honolulu, 808-922-3111, 800-937-8461; www.moanasurfrider.com
They call this historic hotel the First Lady of Waikiki for good reason—it was the first hotel on this famous stretch of sand, having opened way back in 1901. Although the Moana eventually merged with the neighboring Surfrider, guests checking in still access the hotel lobby via the original colonial porte-cochere. The rooms, most of which have ocean views, are divided into three wings. Nostalgiacs prefer the Moana Banyan Wing, the original rooms, all of which have been recently updated with new marble bathrooms and Westin's signature Heavenly beds. These rooms aren't all that big, but they're elegant and comfortable. The hotel fronts the beach, but there's also a pool; both are a stroll away from the classic Beach Bar, an open-air spot situated under the hotel's signature, massive 100-year-old banyan tree. The Moana Lani Spa was added with the recent renovation; the men's and women's relaxation areas include open-air lounges with beachfront views. The Beachhouse restaurant is popular with locals and guests alike for its contemporary, seasonal seafood, while the Veranda remains the place to go in Honolulu for traditional afternoon tea.

795 rooms. Restaurant, bar. Beach. Pool. Spa. $$$

★★NEW OTANI KAIMANA BEACH HOTEL

2863 Kalakaua Ave., Honolulu, 808-923-1555, 866-765-8336
In a market packed with mega-resorts, the New Otani is a welcome respite. It's a small boutique property with just 124 rooms—and although the rooms aren't all that big or luxurious, they're clean and comfortable, with pastel colors and blond wood furniture. The hotel is located on the quiet end of Waikiki in the shadow of Diamond Head, and it fronts lovely Sans Souci Beach. It's also just across the street from Kapiolani Park. At the waterfront Hau Tree Lanai restaurant, savor a romantic evening while dining alfresco underneath large hau trees. The ocean views are also good from the second-floor Miyako Japanese Restaurant, where the menu features traditional kaiseki dinners.

124 rooms. Restaurant, bar. Fitness room. Beach. $$

★★OUTRIGGER REEF ON THE BEACH

2169 Kalia Road, Honolulu, 808-923-3111; www.outrigger.com
It's hard not to like the Outrigger Reef, especially given its prime spot on the beach in Waikiki. Its spacious rooms, which are divided among three towers, have contemporary tropical décor and updated bathrooms. The hotel also boasts plenty of amenities, including an extra-large swimming pool with

hundreds of lounge chairs; lots of activities, such as catamaran sails, surfing lessons and canoe rides; onsite shopping; a children's program packed with activities; and a spa with a variety of treatments. Every Friday, the Outrigger serves up island culture with classes in lei-making, craft demonstrations and talented locals performing Hawaiian music and dancing the hula. The Ocean House Restaurant is a popular spot for fresh seafood, but the hotel's busiest dining venue might just be the onsite Starbucks café.

858 rooms. Restaurant, bar. Fitness center. Beach. Pool. Business center. $$$

★★OUTRIGGER WAIKIKI ON THE BEACH

2335 Kalakaua Ave., Honolulu, 808-923-0711, 800-688-7444;
www.outriggerwaikiki.com

This hotel is Outrigger's flagship property in Hawaii, with a location directly on the liveliest stretch of Waikiki beach. The comfortable rooms feature Hawaiian touches, such as nostalgic photos of Waikiki's past and lamp bases in the shapes of hula dancers and pineapples. The many restaurants and bars include Duke's Canoe Club, one of the most popular gathering spots on Waikiki, and Chuck's Steak House, which serves up prime USDA beef and fresh seafood in a pleasant beachfront dining room. Numerous stores and boutiques are located onsite. But the biggest draw, of course, is the beach, where you can swim, take surfing lessons and ride in outrigger canoes.

530 rooms. Restaurant, bar. Beach. Pool. $$$

★★★THE ROYAL HAWAIIAN

2259 Kalakaua Ave., Honolulu, 808-923-7311, 866-716-8110; www.royal-hawaiian.com

Since 1927, this grand Waikiki hotel, known as the Pink Palace of the Pacific for its pink stucco exterior, has been the stylish place to stay in Waikiki. After closing for several months for a full renovation that was completed in April 2009, this Starwood Luxury Collection resort is reopened and refreshed, with interior design that showcases the hotel's signature rosy hue. Rooms are colorful and contemporary, with pillow-top mattresses and flat-screen TVs. Bathrooms got a makeover, too, with luxe touches such as marble vanities and salon-quality tourmaline hairdryers (as well as pink Frette bathrobes). The hotel's signature restaurant has been reborn as Azure, a beach-chic dining room where the chef showcases fresh seafood sourced from Honolulu's daily fish auction. The Mai Tai bar remains the beach's prime gathering spot, and it overlooks the lawn where the weekly Aha Aina (Waikiki's most sophisticated dinner and traditional Hawaiian dance show) takes place. For first-class pampering, sign up for one of the treatments in the Abhasa Waikiki Spa, a heavenly place for relaxation.

528 rooms. Restaurant, bar. Spa. Pool. $$$$

★★SHERATON PRINCESS KAIULANI

120 Kaiulani Ave., Honolulu, 808-922-5811, 800-325-3535; www.sheraton-hawaii.com

With 1,150 rooms, this is one large hotel that's divided into a 29-story tower and two wings. It offers a good location just across the street from the beach, on the former estate of Princess Kaiulani, Hawaii's last princess. Though the range of services at this hotel surpasses others, the rooms and public areas are ready for an update; as such, rates are a shade lower than at other hotels on Waikiki. Amenities include an outdoor pool, fitness facility and business center. Among the many dining options are Momoyama, where chefs prepare Japanese dishes tableside; Pikake Terrace, an open-air dining room that features sumptuous buffets; and the Princess Food Court, where guests can chow down on burgers, pizza, sandwiches and many other international favorites. Hawaiian performers entertain with island music nightly by the pool, and in the Ainahau Showroom, a talented cast presents Creation—A Polynesian Journey, an exciting show with fire-knife dancing, illusions and ancient and modern dances.

1,152 rooms. Pets accepted. Restaurant, bar. Fitness center. Pool. Business center. $$

★★★SHERATON WAIKIKI

2255 Kalakaua Ave., Honolulu, 808-922-4422, 800-325-3535;
www.sheraton-waikiki.com

This hotel, located right on the beach in the heart of Waikiki and adjacent to the Royal Hawaiian, is massive with 1,695 rooms in two 30-story towers. A complete overhaul in 2009 (that at press time was still underway) refreshed all of the rooms with colorful tropical décor, flat-screen TVs and duvets. The charmingly vintage 1950s hotel was built in such a way that more than two-thirds of those rooms face the water and offer some sort of ocean view. Like the hotel itself, the rooms tend to be spacious, and they have lanais. Given this Sheraton's size, it's not the best choice for those who want lots of peace and quiet in an intimate setting—particularly with the addition this year of a kid-centric "Superpool" complete with fountains and waterslides. (An adults-only infinity pool fronting the ocean is under construction). The hotel has plenty of restaurants, the most elegant of which is located on the 30th floor: Twist at the Hanohano Room, which dishes up Continental dishes and flavors from Hawaii along with one of the city's most stunning views from both sides of the floor-to-ceiling window enclosed space. The new ocean-front restaurant Rumfire has a creative menu of small plates plus plenty of specialty cocktails. The adjacent Royal Hawaiian Center provides even more dining and shopping choices.

1,695 rooms. Restaurant, bar. Fitness center. Spa. Beach. Pool. Business center. $$$$

★★★WAIKIKI PARC HOTEL

2233 Helumoa Road, Honolulu, 808-921-7272, 800-422-0450; www.waikikiparc.com

This casual sister to the upscale Halekulani delivers streamlined, Asian-influenced style in a quiet pocket of Waikiki adjacent to Waikiki Beach Walk. The modern hotel tower has streamlined, comfortable rooms with flat-screen TVs, iPod docking stations and an in-room wine bar. A rooftop pool provides a spot for sunning as well as an outdoor lounge (on Wednesday nights it hosts "Dive-In Theater", a fun take on alfresco movies), while the guest laundry and concierge lounge with computers and free internet access make the hotel a home away from home. The Waikiki branch of star chef Nobu Matsuhisa's Nobu restaurant, located on the first floor for the hotel, serves up sushi and Latin American-influenced Japanese fare in a low-lit stylish setting. The unique Lotus program lets you take the hotel's neon orange and yellow sports cars for a spin. Surfing lessons are available through Hans Hedemann School of Surf and begin in the hotel's pool before moving on to Waikiki. 297 rooms. Restaurant, bar. Pool. Fitness room. Business center. $$$

WHERE TO EAT

★★★3660 ON THE RISE

3660 Waialae Ave., Honolulu, 808-737-1177; www.3660.com

This restaurant is appropriately named, as it's situated near the top of a hill on Waialae Avenue, a thoroughfare that rises sharply on Honolulu's east side. The eatery offers an eclectic blend of European and Pacific Rim cuisine, spotlighting fresh, local ingredients. For hearty appetites, the 3660 Medley deserves consideration; this eye-opening, stomach-filling entrée includes sautéed ahi, grilled beef tenderloin medallion and baked stuffed chicken breast. The restaurant has multiple banquet rooms, making it a good choice for private parties.

Pacific Rim. Dinner. Closed Monday. Bar. Reservations recommended. $$$

★★★ALAN WONG'S

1857 S. King St., Honolulu, 808-949-2526; www.alanwongs.com

One of Hawaii's most acclaimed chefs, Alan Wong is often credited with helping to establish contemporary Hawaiian regional cuisine as a foodie genre, and it's what he still serves nightly to rave reviews at his unassuming namesake Honolulu restaurant. Housed on the third floor of a non-descript office building in downtown Honolulu, the space is casual, with an open kitchen and white-linen draped tables. The food is seasonal and locally sourced, with dishes such as ginger crusted onaga (red snapper) served alongside soy braised twice cooked spare rib with gingered shrimp. Dinner service features five- and seven-course tasting menus served with or without wine pairings.

Hawaiian. Dinner. Reservations recommended. $$$

★★★AZURE

2259 Kalakaua Ave., Honolulu, 808-923-7311; www.royal-hawaiian.com

This newly-opened restaurant inside the Royal Hawaiian has three great things going for it: unparalleled views of Waikiki and the Pacific, a stylish dining room and even more attractive local clientele, and an approachable menu of fresh, local seafood. Chef Jon Matsubara oversees the constantly changing menu, adding whatever's in season to create dishes such as ginger steamed opakapaka and black and blue seared ahi (with a spicy nori crust). The service is casual and friendly, but attentive, and the wine list is as down-to-earth as the menu.

Seafood. Dinner. Reservations recommended. $$$

★★★BALI BY THE SEA

2005 Kalia Road, Honolulu, 808-941-2254

With an elegantly appointed dining room overlooking Waikiki Beach, Bali by the Sea has a setting (inside the Hilton Hawaiian Village Beach Resort and Spa) that can't be beat, making it a popular option for special occasions. The menu emphasizes Pacific-Rim cuisine, with signature dishes such as scallion-crusted ahi tempura and sautéed island opakapaka.

Pacific-Rim. Dinner. Closed Sunday. Bar. Children's menu. Reservations recommended. $$$

★★★BEACH HOUSE AT THE MOANA

808-921-2861; www.beachhousewaikiki.com

Locals love to dine at this restaurant inside the Moana Surfrider, with its ocean views, casual chic décor (think cozy sofas loaded with pillows and pulled up to white-table cloth topped tables), and creative island-inspired menu. Sample dishes such as kona lobster bisque laced with sherry to filet mignon with fois gras, and then save room for desserts such as dark rum crème brulee. The menu is designed steakhouse style, so you can pair your New York strip or ahi with sesame ginger glaze with whichever side you like, including pineapple fried rice and whipped parmesan potatoes.
American. Dinner. Reservations recommended. $$$

★★★★CHEF MAVRO

1969 S. King St., Honolulu, 808-944-4714; www.chefmavro.com

Offering one of Honolulu's finest dining experiences, this restaurant is the creation of award-winning chef George Mavrothalassitis, who mastered cooking in the French towns of Marseilles and Cassis. Mavrothalassitis moved to Honolulu in 1988, and since then he has focused his talents on perfecting a cuisine that couples French preparation techniques with fresh Hawaiian ingredients. The restaurant has no wine list; instead, each menu selection is paired with a wine. Menus change often depending on what's in season, but might include lobster pot au feu or wagyu beef with no-butter béarnaise. For special occasions, opt for the six-course meal, priced at $175 with wine pairings. The restaurant is a five-minute drive north of Waikiki Beach.
Hawaiian. Dinner. Closed Monday. Reservations recommended. $$$

★★DORAKU WAIKIKI

2233 Kalakaua Ave., Honolulu, 808-922-3323; www.dorakusushi.com

This stylish Royal Hawaiian Center sushi bar is the creation of Kevin Aoiki, the son of restaurateur and Benihana founder Rocky Aoiki. With a dark, clubby atmosphere and windows that open to Kalakaua Avenue, it's a trendy spot for digging into unique maki rolls (Cuban beef, for example, made with grilled rib eye and asparagus) or sipping the creative cocktails (including the potent watermelon lychee martini). The restaurant is a particularly good value during lunch, when sushi combos are offered at attractive prices.
Sushi. Lunch, dinner. $$$

★DUKE'S CANOE CLUB WAIKIKI

2335 Kalakaua Ave., Honolulu, 808-922-2268, 808-923-4204; www.dukeswaikiki.com

This every-popular casual restaurant sits in the heart of all the action, directly across the street from the International Market Place and just a few steps away from the soft sands of Waikiki Beach. The atmosphere here is vibrant, with locals and tourists alike flocking to Duke's nightly to enjoy live Hawaiian music. Dig into heaping portions of baby back ribs or fresh grilled local fish. The restaurant's namesake, surfing legend Duke Kahanamoku, mastered his sport by ripping the curls off Waikiki.
American. Breakfast, lunch, dinner, late-night, brunch. Bar. Children's menu. Reservations recommended. Outdoor seating. $$

★★HAU TREE LANAI

2863 Kalakaua Ave., Honolulu, 808-921-7066; www.kaimana.com

This restaurant derives its name from the 150-year-old tree that spreads out over its dining area, shading the surrounding tables. Situated on Waikiki's quieter eastern side at the edge of Diamond Head's Gold Coast, Hau Tree Lanai offers Pacific Rim-inspired dishes, such as mango-marinated pork chops and twin lobster katsu. The restaurant overlooks Sans Souci Beach, a favorite place of the Scottish writer Robert Louis Stevenson.

Pacific-Rim. Breakfast, lunch, dinner, brunch. Bar. Children's menu. Reservations recommended. Outdoor seating. $$

★★INDIGO

1121 Nuuanu Ave., Honolulu, 808-521-2900; www.indigo-hawaii.com

This Chinatown eatery, situated a door down from the magnificent Hawaii Theatre, prepares inspired Hawaiian-influenced cuisine under the guidance of chef Glenn Chu. The lunch menu offers a variety of dim sum, one of the most popular being the goat cheese won tons with four-fruit sauce. The dinner menu appeals to a wide range of tastes, from the miso-marinated salmon fillet, to the Mongolian lamb chops, to the grilled island breast of chicken. In the restaurant's Green Lounge and Opium Den and Champagne Bar, the young and young at heart gather to enjoy live music and dancing Tuesday through Saturday nights.

Pacific-Rim. Lunch, dinner. Closed Sunday-Monday. Bar.Reservations recommended. Outdoor seating. $$

★★KEO'S IN WAIKIKI

2028 Kuhio Ave., Honolulu, 808-951-9355; www.keosthaicuisine.com

Tiki torches and an array of colorful flowers greet visitors to this popular Thai restaurant, located on the west end of Waikiki a few steps north of Fort DeRussy Park. The restaurant's owner and namesake, Keo Sananikone, has published over 100,000 copies of his cookbook, entitled Keos Thai Cuisine. Many of the restaurants fruits, vegetables, herbs and spices are grown locally on farms owned by Sananikone. A signature entrée is the Evil Jungle Prince, an extra-spicy dish featuring your choice of shrimp, chicken, or tofu, served with basil, coconut milk, and red chili on a bed of chopped cabbage.

Thai. Breakfast, lunch, dinner. Bar. $$

★★★★LA MER

2199 Kalia Road, Honolulu, 808-923-2311; www.halekulani.com

Regarded by many to be the premiere fine-dining restaurant on Oahu, La Mer is located in the luxurious Halekulani hotel, directly above the restaurant Orchids. Beginning with the gorgeous fresh floral displays at the restaurant's entrance, the space exudes elegance, with tables arranged to make the most of the ocean views. Sample sophisticated dishes such as dorade baked in rosemary salt crust, or wagyu with truffle Madeira sauce and baby vegetables. The menu is offered as two-, three- and four-courses with dessert, and can be paired with wines from the extensive list.

French. Dinner. Bar. Jacket required. Reservations recommended. $$$$

★MEI SUM DIM SUM
65 N. Pauahi St., Honolulu, 808-531-3268

This eatery offers Hong Kong-style dim sum in the heart of Honolulu's Chinatown. Dim sum means "from the heart" in Cantonese, and dim sum are typically bite-sized pastries, such as fried dumplings, served with tea. A delicious specialty at Mei Sum is the barbecued pork half-moon pastries. Those seeking a healthier—and perhaps more adventurous—option should consider the seaweed tofu soup.

Chinese. Breakfast, lunch, dinner. $

★★★NOBU WAIKIKI
2233 Helumoa Road, Honolulu, 808-237-6999; www.noburestaurants.com

Star chef Nobu Matsuhisa now has 21 branches of his namesake restaurant spread around the world (with several more Matsuhisa restaurants to boot), so sightings of the Japanese chef at this branch tucked inside the Waikiki Parc Hotel are a rare treat. You will, however, be able to sample the same delicious creative Japanese fare and sushi that you can find at any Nobu location. The dark and amply sized lounge and bar is a good spot for cocktails, while the stylish dining room with its open kitchen is a comfortable space for digging into king crab tempura with ponzu sauce, black pepper cod with balsamic teryaki, plenty of sushi and sashimi and Nobu's signature black cod with miso.

Japanese. Dinner. Reservations recommended. $$$

★★★OCEAN HOUSE RESTAURANT
2169 Kalia Road, Honolulu, 808-923-2277

This seaside restaurant has the look and feel of a turn-of-the-century plantation house. Situated in the Outrigger Reef hotel, Ocean House enjoys a great setting right on Waikiki Beach, with views to the east of Diamond Head. The atmosphere in this open-air restaurant is elegant but casual, and the menu features everything from crab-stuffed mahi mahi to pulehu prime rib.

American. Dinner. Bar. Children's menu. Reservations recommended. $$$

★ONO HAWAII
726 Kapahulu Ave., Honolulu, 808-737-2275

Locals stop in for authentic Hawaiian cooking without pretense and stream through for picnic and party take-out; tourists get a lesson in island cuisine. The name Ono means delicious, and the generous combo plates feature dishes—kalua pig (pit-roasted pork) or lau lau (pork cooked in taro leaves)—typically available only at a family luau. Casual, quick, warm service and very reasonable prices allow experimentation and sharing.

Pacific-Rim/Pan-Asian. Lunch, dinner. Closed Sunday. Bar. Outdoor seating. $

★★★ORCHIDS
2199 Kalia Road, Honolulu, 808-923-2311; www.halekulani.com

Creative and fresh seafood dishes are the specialty at this oceanfront restaurant, located at the Halekulani hotel. An Orchids favorite is herb-crusted opah, served with a light citrus curry butter. True to its name, the restaurant is decorated with a variety of colorful orchids. The restaurant boasts panoramic views of Diamond Head and Waikiki Beach. Orchids' acclaimed Sunday brunch attracts a large crowd.

Seafood. Breakfast, lunch, dinner, Sunday brunch. Reservations recommended. $$$

★★PINEAPPLE ROOM
1450 Ala Moana Center, Honolulu, 808-945-6573; www.alanwongs.com

A creation of chef Alan Wong, the Pineapple Room, tucked behind the dresses and denim on the third floor of Macy's, is one of the most popular dining options at the Ala Moana Shopping Center. The restaurant features a spacious dining area with high ceilings and contemporary décor. The cuisine here has been described as soul-warming comfort food with a local twist. Two of the tastiest dishes are the pineapple-barbecued baby back ribs and sweet chili-glazed red snapper.

Pacific-Rim/Pan-Asian. Breakfast, lunch, dinner. Reservations recommended. $$$

★★★ROY'S
226 Lewers St., Honolulu, 808-923-7697; www.roysrestaurant.com

Celebrated chef Roy Yamaguchi, known for his blending of European preparation techniques with the flavors and ingredients of the Pacific Rim, opened Roy's, his flagship restaurant, in 1988. The restaurant was an immediate success, leading to a franchise of Roy's that today numbers 36 locations, including one in Yamaguchi's native Japan. Roy's Hawaiian fusion cuisine focuses on seafood dishes, such as hibachi-style grilled salmon, flavored by citrus ponzu sauce and served with Japanese vegetables; to try a variety of flavors opt for the pupus, which include wood-grilled Szechuan-spiced baby back pork ribs. The restaurant has a prime spot at the end of Waikiki's Beach Walk, sandwiched between Halekulani and the new Trump Waikiki.

Pacific-Rim/Pan-Asian. Dinner. Reservations recommended. $$$

★★SAM CHOY'S BREAKFAST, LUNCH & CRAB
580 N. Nimitz Highway, Honolulu, 808-545-7979; www.samchoy.com

Bright neon signs glow and buzz above the entrance to this casual, budget-friendly restaurant. Located just west of downtown Honolulu in the Iwilei industrial district, Sam Choy's is home to the Big Aloha Brewery, which handcrafts a variety of beers onsite, a favorite being the intensely hoppy James Cook IPA. Bring a big appetite to Sam Choys—large portions are the standard here. Popular entrées include crabmeat stuffed island fish, and seared garlic shrimp with udon noodles.

American. Breakfast, lunch, dinner. Bar. Children's menu. $$

★SIDE STREET INN
1225 Hopaka St., Honolulu, 808-591-0253

Locals claim that the Side Street Inn is where the chefs go to eat when they get off work. The restaurant's low-key interior, with cafeteria-style, laminate-topped tables, will not appeal to those seeking an upscale experience. But the throngs of people who crowd these tables confirm that the food here is exceptionally good. Menu favorites include the teriyaki rib eye, pan-fried

island pork chops and Chinese-style crispy chicken. The Side Street Inn is, true to its name, tucked away on a quiet side street, a few blocks northwest of the Ala Moana Shopping Center. The restaurant can be difficult to find, so first-time guests should either bring a detailed map or arrive in a taxi.
Pacific-Rim/Pan-Asian. Lunch, dinner, late-night. Bar. No credit cards accepted. $$

★★★SUSHI SASABUNE

1419 S. King St., Honolulu, 808-947-3800
Allow master sushi chef Seiji Kumagawa to guide you on a tour of impeccably fresh Pacific fish. Perch at the sushi bar for the best seat in the house. There's no menu, so order a flight of sake or a Japanese beer and enjoy the parade of perfectly crafted sushi and sashimi. Follow the rules (one piece, one bite) and tell your waiter when you are pau (Hawaiian pidgin for finished) (leaving food on your plate is a big no-no). The experience justifies the large bill: extraordinary quality and authenticity.
Sushi. Lunch, dinner. Closed Sunday. Reservations recommended. $$$

★★TIKI'S GRILL & BAR

2570 Kalakaua Ave., Honolulu, 808-923-8454; www.tikisgrill.com
With a prime second-story location overlooking Waikiki Beach, Tiki's Grill & Bar comes alive each night, energized by live music, tropical drinks, and a clientele that's predominantly young. Hand-carved tiki masks adorn the walls, and a 30-foot man-made volcano holds a commanding presence in the bar area. Local bands and solo artists perform contemporary music nightly. The menu reflects Pacific Rim influences, examples being the guava-glazed grilled pork ribs and macadamia nut-crusted mahi mahi. If you seek a drink that packs some punch, consider the ocean potion, a blend of light and dark rum, triple sec, melon liqueur and orange and pineapple juice.
American. Lunch, dinner, late-night. Bar. Outdoor seating. $$

SPAS

★★★★SPA SUITES AT THE KAHALA

5000 Kahala Ave., Honolulu, 808-739-8938, 800-367-2525; www.kahalaresort.com
Each of the luxurious, 55-square-foot private spa suites at this spa is decorated in elegant, island-influenced style. Treatments begin with a welcoming foot bath and massage that uses Hawaiian sea salts and aromatic water. A signature treatment includes the 'oli 'oli therapy, which begins with a body brushing followed by a honey scrub, lomi lomi massage, mamaki mud wrap and scalp massage. The warm pohaku stone massage melts knotted muscles with strategically placed warm stones. New and unique services include tooth whitening (perfect for brides preparing for a wedding) and the men's suite where deluxe shaves take place in a comfortable chair perched in front of a wall-mounted mirror with a TV inside. The recently added relaxation garden is a pretty spot to enjoy a spa lunch post-treatment.

★★★★SPA HALEKULANI

2199 Kalia Road, Honolulu, 808-931-5322, 800-367-2343; www.halekulani
The healing traditions of the Pacific Islands inspire this spa's authentic treatments, which use only fresh island ingredients such as coconut, orchid, hibis-

cus, seaweed and papaya. All of the spa's massages, body treatments and facials begin with a ritual foot pounding, an exotic way to treat neglected feet. In addition to traditional Swedish and shiatsu massages, Samoan-inspired nonu, Japanese amma and Hawaiian lomi lomi, hapai and pohaku massages are offered. Therapists will even customize a massage based on your needs and preferences. Facials are individually crafted for specific skin types, and the body scrubs and wraps come complete with a steam shower and mini massage.

CRUISING THE ISLANDS

If you've already explored Oahu and are looking for an easy way to see the rest of the state (including the sprawling cattle ranches of Kona; the historic Front Street of Lahaina, once the capital of the kingdom of Hawaii; and the lush rain forest, cascading waterfalls, and rainbow-tinted Waimea Canyon of Nawiliwili), consider a Honolulu-to-Honolulu cruise.

Norwegian Cruise Line (NCL) operates year-round interisland cruises lasting seven days aboard the Pride of America. The ship stops at Hilo and Kona on the Big Island, Kahului on Maui and Nawiliwili on Kauai, with optional tours to Molokai and Lanai. NCL cruises are geared toward families, with a number of on-board activities to keep multiple generations happy, including a fitness center open 24/7 and a huge children's activity center. The company also promotes its freestyle cruising, with no fixed seating at its restaurants and no dress code. As for shore excursions, they're all optional. Take a tour in a horse-drawn carriage or ride a mule through a grove of guava trees in Kona. Tour Kauai by helicopter, kayak down the Huleia jungle stream featured in the films Raiders of the Lost Ark and Jurassic Park, or drive through quaint towns and sugarcane fields to spectacular Waimea Canyon, where Captain Cook first landed.

Another opportunity for island-to-island travel comes by way of Ocean Voyages, which offers fully customized journeys. You pick the destinations, route and length of your stay in each location. You can also select a sailboat or a motorized boat. The smallest number of passengers an Ocean Voyages vessel accepts is six; however, if a couple or a family of four wants to join an existing charter, they're more than welcome. With Ocean Voyages, you needn't start in Honolulu, and you needn't end where you start. However, you do need to create your own shore excursions. If you have sailing experience and are certified, Ocean Voyages will help you find the perfect boat for your own journey.

Other interisland options exist, but they are not round-trip and usually travel from Honolulu to Los Angeles; San Diego; Ensenada, Mexico; or Vancouver, British Columbia (or vice versa). Carriers include Holland America, Princess Cruises, and Royal Caribbean. Several luxury cruise lines, such as Crystal Cruises and Radisson Seven Seas, include Hawaii as part of their around-the-world cruises. Call or visit their Web sites for details:

Crystal Cruises, 800-804-1500; www.crystalcruises.com
Holland America Line, 877-724-5425; www.hollandamerica.com
Norwegian Cruise Line, 888-625-4292; www.ncl.com.
Ocean Voyages, 800-299 4444 (U.S. only); www.oceanvoyages.com
Princess Cruises, 800-774-6237; www.princess.com
Royal Caribbean International, 800-398-9819; www.royalcaribbean.com

LEEWARD OAHU

Oahu's Leeward Coast is often called the Waianae Coast after the mountain range in this area on the island's west side. It isn't a big hangout for visitors, and not just because it's relatively undeveloped. The ethnic Hawaiians who live in its coastal towns—primarily Nanakuli, Waianae, and Makaha—prefer to protect their region and heritage, keeping the coast from getting too touristy or less Hawaiian. And this striking coast is worth seeing, with its slow-paced towns, pretty beaches, soaring sea cliffs and expansive stretches of unspoiled rural territory.

Every winter, plenty of outsiders do indeed converge on Makaha Beach for the annual Makaha International Surfing Competition, a popular international event because of the giant waves that roll into the shore. Surfers also like to wander over to this coast to ride the big breakers at Yokohama Beach, the northernmost one on the west side.

A little north of Yokohama, another attraction tends to bring some visitors over to this coast—Kaena Point State Park, home to Oahu's westernmost tip. It's a rugged area that rewards hikers with gorgeous views of jagged cliffs and deep gulches.

The Leeward Coast's only lodging option, the JW Marriott Ihilani Resort & Spa, delivers first-class pampering in an elegant, waterfront setting on the coast's southern end, less than 20 miles from the Honolulu International Airport. The resort is part of the exclusive Ko Olina Resort, which includes a Ted Robinson-designed golf course.

WHAT TO SEE
CORAL CREEK GOLF COURSE

91-1111 Geiger Road, Ewa Beach, 808-441-4053; www.coralcreekgolfhawaii.com

This 18-hole, 6,808-yard, par-72 course was designed by Honolulu-based course architect Robin Nelson. The layout features coral reef structures, six lakes and a coral creek that makes its way down the middle of the course affecting play on 13 holes. Hole 2 plays right into the winds of the Ewa Plain. Native Hawaii plants and foliage add to the color commentary of this course. Instruction, pro shop, grille and restaurant facilities are available. The $130 greens fee includes cart.

HAWAII PRINCE GOLF CLUB

91-1200 Fort Weaver Road, Ewa Beach, 808-689-2213

The Hawaii Prince Hotel is the only Waikiki hotel with its own golf course, although it's located 40 miles from the hotel on Oahu's sunny Ewa plains. Covering 270 acres, this course features three nine-hole layouts and a variety of play experiences for golfers at all levels. Facilities include an all-grass driving range, PGA instruction, pro shop, putting green, rental clubs and shoes, tennis courts, clubhouse, restaurant and snack bar. Dress code is collared shirts and Bermuda shorts, and denim is not permitted.

HAWAII'S PLANTATION VILLAGE

Waipahu Cultural Garden Park, 94-695 Waipahu St., Waipahu, 808-677-0110

This outdoor history museum, set on 50 acres, tells the story of Hawaii's sugar plantations through restored and replica buildings, demonstrations, and exhibitions. Guided tours are available on the hour, with the last tour of the day beginning at 3 p.m. Monday-Friday 9 a.m.-4:30 p.m., Saturday 10 a.m.-4:30 p.m.; closed holidays.

HAWAIIAN RAILWAY

Ewa Station, Ewa Beach, 808-681-5461; www.hawaiianrailway.com

The only active railroad on Oahu takes passengers on 90-minute narrated tours at 15 mph. You can catch bus 431 in Waikiki; it stops at the station's front gate. Sunday 1 p.m. and 3 p.m.

HAWAIIAN WATERS ADVENTURE PARK

400 Farrington Highway, Kapolei, 808-674-9283; www.hawaiianwaters.com

Hawaii has water everywhere, but if you're up for a bit of water park action, the only game in town is Hawaiian Waters Adventure Park. Whether you have kids in tow or not, the park features 25 acres of keep-you-cool fun. Take an 800-foot tube cruise or a six-story free-fall down a speed slide. Let your kids lead the way down family water slides or into the wave pool. Drip dry while you chow on pizza, hot dogs or other tasty treats. Daily from 10:30 a.m.; closing time varies by season.

KAENA P

Farrington Highway, Mokuleia

This 5-mile, two-hour hike runs along the remote and rugged leeward coastline of Kaena Point State Park. You might spot nesting albatross, seabirds and, in the early morning, schools of dolphins that frolic offshore. During winter, you might see whales at play. Don't plan on swimming, as currents here are treacherous; however, check out the tide pools for a peek at Oahu's marine life.

KO OLINA GOLF CLUB

92-1220 Aliinui Drive, Kapolei, 808-676-5309; www.koolinagolf.com

This popular 18-hole Ted Robinson-designed course is known for its stunning landscaping, replete with waterfalls, pools and multi-tiered greens. Located adjacent to the JW Marriott Ihilani Resort & Spa at Ko Olina in West Oahu, this 6,847-yard, par-72 course is a former host site of the Senior PGA and LPGA Hawaiian Ladies Open. Services and facilities include a driving range, putting green, lessons, carts equipped with GPS systems, pro shop, day spa, and clubhouse.

MAKAHA BEACH PARK

Makaha

In summer months, the waves at Makaha are gentle enough to host keiki (children) surf competitions, but in winter, crests reach heights of 15 to 20 feet. Off shore, divers enjoy exploring the numerous coral reef caves, while on the beach, local families gather for picnics, fishing, and recreation.

MAKAHA RESORT GOLF CLUB

84-626 Makaha Valley Road, Waianae, 808-695-9544; www.makaharesort.net

In scenic Makaha Valley, this William Bell-designed course offers both ocean and mountain views that could be a golfer's biggest challenge. The par-72,

7,091-yard course offers hidden greens, 107 bunkers and terrain that seems to be sloping up when it's actually sloping down. Don't be surprised if a wild peacock struts across the fairway to join the play. Facilities include lessons, pro shop, and restaurant.

OLOMANA GOLF LINKS

41-1891 Kalanianaole Highway, Waimanalo, 808-259-7926

This public 18-hole golf course gets tricky with water obstacles on the front nine holes and hills and tight fairways on the back nine. The signature 8th hole features an elevated tee overlooking a whale of a water hazard that leads to a green lined with native Hawaiian koa and Honduran mahogany trees. Reserve tee-time up to 30 days in advance. Facilities include driving range, chipping green, bar, restaurant and snack bar.

PARADISE COVE LUAU

Ko Olina Resort and Marina, 92-1480 Aliinui Drive, Ko Olina, 808-842-5911, 800-775-2683; www.hawaiianluau.org

Paradise Cove's luau setting on a postcard-perfect oceanfront lagoon is more than a traditional luau buffet; it's an extravaganza of interactive activities. Try your hand at pulling in the fishing net hukilau style, learn the art of imu (underground oven) cooking, test your gamesmanship in the ancient Hawaiian arts of Oo hie (spear-throwing) and Moa Pahee (dart sliding), and stroll through a marketplace of Pacific arts and crafts. You can even go home with a temporary Polynesian tattoo. Dinner packages include the luau buffet and an evening show featuring the dances and music of Hawaii and Polynesia.

VALLEY OF THE TEMPLES

47-200 Kahekili Hgihway, Kaneohe, 808-239-8811

Tucked into the back of Memorial Park in Kaneohe is the Byodo In Temple, a complete full-scale replica of the 18th-century Temple of Eternity that can be found in Uji, Japan, just outside the city of Kyoto. Erected in Hawaii in 1968, it commemorates the 100th anniversary of the arrival of the first Japanese immigrants to Hawaiian shores. Today, the grounds include a meditation building; a 2-ton, carved wooden Buddha at the entrance; and a 5-foot-tall, 3-ton brass bell, which visitors ring for good luck. Peek into the ponds, filled with 10,000 Japanese koi carp. Daily 8:30 a.m.-4:30 p.m.

YOKOHAMA BAY

Waianae

At the end of the road on the Waianae Coast, this sandy stretch of beach is actually Keawalua Beach, but earned its nickname Yokohama from the Japanese immigrants who made their way here from the plantations to spend their rare time off pole-fishing. Today, this narrow, rocky beach is still most popular as a fishing spot, with waters calm enough for swimming only during summer, if at all. There are no lifeguards or concessions.

NORTH SHORE

Mention the North Shore, and one word comes to mind: surfing. This coastline is known around the globe as the Surfing Capital of the World because of its big, powerful waves in winter. Just how big? The swells sometimes soar as high as 30 to 40 feet.

Any serious surfer in the world can name the North Shore's best-known surfing beaches: Banzai Pipeline, Sunset, Ehukai and Waimea Bay. They're legendary in the sport, and most every professional wave-runner dreams of riding their high surf. These beaches aren't for the inexperienced from about October through April, when they pose serious danger because of their big breakers and strong currents.

Come summer, however, the coastal scene changes dramatically. Amazingly, these fierce beaches turn calm, making them good for swimming, fishing and all types of other water activity.

While the beaches are the North Shore's biggest draws, but the area also has some noteworthy attractions. Puu o Mahuka Heiau State Park, near Sunset Beach, is home to Oahu's largest temple, believed to have been built in the 18th century. And the Waimea Valley Audubon Center, near Waimea Bay, attracts nature lovers with all its native flora and fauna.

West of Waimea is Haleiwa, the area's main town, a quaint place with lots of plantation-style buildings dating back to the early 1900s. For visitors, it has many restaurants, boutiques, gift shops, art galleries and, naturally, surf shops.

Those who want to bed down on the North Shore don't have a lot of choices. There's only one major hotel, the Turtle Bay Resort, a few bed and breakfasts, and some vacation rentals, such as cottages, condos and private homes. The lack of accommodations is one reason most people stay in Waikiki and make the North Shore an exciting day trip.

WHAT TO SEE

BARNFIELD'S RAGING ISLE SURF AND CYCLE

North Shore Marketplace, 62-250 Kamehameha Highway, Haleiwa, 808-637-7707;
www.ragingisle.com

You'll spot this shop, located in the North Shore Marketplace, by its exterior of gray with yellow trim. Find custom surfboards by Bill Barnfield, as well as everything you need for a day of mountain biking Oahu's scenic North Shore. Barnfield's also carries sports apparel and accessories for guys, gals, and kids from Billabong, Oakley, and Rip Curl. Daily 10 a.m.-6:30 p.m.

DOLE PLANTATION

64-1550 Kamehameha Highway, Wahiawa, 808-621-8408; www.dole-plantation.com

This former fruit stand is home to the Pineapple Garden Maze, claimed to be the world's largest maze. Covering 1.7 miles, the 2-acre maze is made up of more than 11,000 native plants, including hibiscuses. Visitors can also take a ride on the Pineapple Express, a 20-minute train ride during which narrators describe the history of pineapple and other agriculture in Hawaii and the life of pineapple pioneer James Dole. Or try the Plantation Garden Tour, whose highlights include bromeliads, ti leaf and other native flowers. Informal displays and presentations teach the more than one million annual visitors about the history of the pineapple and the Dole Company. Naturally, fresh pineapple can be purchased onsite to be eaten right away or shipped home. Daily 9 a.m.-5:30 p.m.

HALEIWA
Kamehameha Highway, Haleiwa

At the turn of the 20th century, this sleepy seaside town was at the end of the railroad line—Oahu's first getaway retreat destination. Not much has changed in 200 years. Haleiwa still exudes laid-back living. Body clocks here are set by the sun, moon and ocean tides. In winter months, Haleiwa swells with surfers who take on some of the world's largest and most powerful waves, right down the road at Waimea Bay, Sunset Beach and the Banzai Pipeline. In summer, Haleiwa earns its keep from shoppers exploring its bounty of eclectic galleries, boutiques and cafés like Matsumoto's shave ice. A historic district, Haleiwa boasts several building on the Hawaii State Register of Historic Places, such as the 1921 structure now housing Surf N Sea Ocean Sports.

HAUULA LOOP TRAIL
Hauula Homestead Road and Maakua Road, Hauula

This 2 1/2-mile hike (about three hours) features a fairly steep climb through fields dotted with ironwood trees and Norfolk pines and marked by switchbacks through fields of wild flora and fauna. When you come to a fork in the trail, go right and continue climbing up the ridge until you cross the Waipilopilo Gulch. The path then loops around toward the ocean overlooking Kipaupau Valley and offers panoramic views of Oahu's windward coast and coastal waters, shimmering in five shades of blue. Mountain bikers also ride this trail, so stay to the right to avoid collisions.

KUKANILOKO BIRTHING STONES
Haleiwa, off Kamehameha Hwy. between Wahiawa and Haleiwa

The most sacred ancient site in Oahu is a group of stones strewn about this clearing in a grove of eucalyptus and coconut trees. It was here, more than 900 years ago, that wives of high-ranking chiefs came to give birth. Today, historians think that the Kukaniloko Birthing Stones might also have served as an astronomy site.

MALAEKAHANA STATE RECREATION AREA
Kamehameha Highway, Laie, 808-293-1736

This recreation area is a favorite camping site for local residents. Camping is permitted Fridays through Wednesdays. The mile-long slash of crescent sand is excellent for strolling, and during low tides, you can wade out to Goat Island, a bird sanctuary just offshore. April-Labor Day: daily 7 a.m.-7:45 p.m.; rest of year: daily 7 a.m.-6:45 p.m.

NORTH SHORE CATAMARAN CHARTERS
Haleiwa, 808-638-8279, 888-638-8279; www.sailingcat.com

Depending on the time of year, this tour company will either take you snorkeling or take you out to watch for humpbacks, Hawaii's favorite marine mammals. From January to May, 2 1/2-hour whale-watching tours to Waimea

Bay depart both in the morning and in the afternoon; in the mornings from May to October, the catamaran takes passengers out into the bay to snorkel, with a picnic lunch included. Tours depart from Haleiwa Harbor. Daily.

NORTH SHORE ECO-SURF TOURS

Haleiwa, 808-638-9503; www.ecosurf-hawaii.com

Stan Van Voorhis takes time out from designing custom longboards to lead guided surf tours of Oahu's North Shore, and private and group surfing and windsurfing lessons. Learning to surf with Stan begins on the beach, discussing theory (comprised of science and experience), safety, surf riding skills, and on-land exercises.

NORTH SHORE MARKETPLACE

66-250 Kamehameha Highway, Haleiwa, 808-637-7000

The North Shore might be country living, but the shopping here will tantalize the most sophisticated city slicker who has an eye for specialty shops. The Silver Moon Emporium features vintage-style clothing, jewelry and accessories. Patagonia goes tropical for active sportswear, Jungle Gems sparkles with gemstones, crystals and bead jewelry. You can mix and match your bikini or get one custom made at North Shore Custom and Design Swimwear. Quench your thirst with a mango smoothie at the Coffee Gallery or celebrate surviving the North Shore swells at Cholo's Homestyle Mexican.

NORTH SHORE SHARK ADVENTURES

Haleiwa, 808-228-5900; www.sharktourshawaii.com

If you dare, let Joe Pavsek take you 3 miles out to sea, put you in a cage, and drop you into the water (the cage floats), where you're bound to come nose-to-nose with 5- to 15-foot sharks. During the two-hour tour, you're also likely to see green sea turtles, dolphins, and humpback whales in season. Daily 7 a.m.-3 p.m.

PACIFIC SKYDIVING CENTER

Dillingham Airfield, 68-760 Farrington Highway, Waialua, 808-637-7472;
www.pacific-skydiving.com

If freefalling from 13,000 feet sounds like your idea of fun, then the Pacific Skydiving Center has just the adventure for you. Departing from Dillingham Airfield on Oahu's North Shore, a turbo-prop plane takes jumpers into the sky in about ten minutes; if you can bear to look, you can see the whole island on your way down. Newbies start with a tandem jump with one of the center's Tandem Jump Masters. Daily.

POLYNESIAN CULTURAL CENTER

55-370 Kamehameha Hwy., Laie, 808-293-3333, 800-367-7060; www.polynesia.com

With its multiple villages, each depicting life on one of the Polynesian islands (Tahiti, Samoa, Fiji, etc.), the Polynesian Cultural Center is the place to immerse yourself in native culture—an experience you just can't get on the mainland. People from these islands demonstrate ancient practices, like coconut cracking and spear tossing. In addition to the seven villages and an Easter Island exhibit, two live shows provide entertainment: the 30-minute Rainbows of Paradise canoe show in the afternoon and the 90-minute Horizons at night, featuring a cast of 100 dancers and musicians. There's also an IMAX theater showing ocean-related films on its giant screen. Because the center is Hawaii's single most popular attraction, reservations are recommended. Visitors purchase ticket packages with varying levels of service, amenities, and dining options, including the Alii Luau; some include ground transportation from Waikiki as well. Monday-Saturday 9 a.m.-6:30 p.m.

POLYNESIAN CULTURAL CENTER ALI'I LUAU

Polynesian Cultural Center, 55-370 Kamehameha Highway, Laie, 808-293-3333, 800-367-7060; www.polynesia.com

Take a 15,000-square-mile tour of Polynesia and end the trek with a feast created in the spirit of ancient Hawaiian Alii (royalty) at the Polynesian Cultural Center, Hawaii's number one paid visitor attraction. One of Oahu's most authentic luau presentations, this luau adds in the option of an all-day luau package, which includes admission to the Center's seven Polynesian villages, the long canoe pageant, an IMAX film presentation, tram tour of the Laie town, the luau feast and show. This Polynesian revue is one of the world's largest, featuring more than 100 native Pacific island performers, most of whom are students attending the neighboring Brigham Young University Hawaii.

PU'U O MAHUKA HEIAU

Pupukea Road, Haleiwa; www.hawaiistateparks.org

Rock walls and stone floors mark the ruins of what was once the largest sacrificial temple on Oahu. In the 18th century, Kaopulupulu presided over the heiau (temple), which stood the length of two football fields. Built on the bluffs overlooking Waimea Bay, the heiau's altar has been restored, and visitors who come to pray and pay homage to the mana (spirit) of the ancient gods often leave offerings of lei.

SHARK'S COVE

Haleiwa

Legend has it this cove got its name from a white shark that used to regularly visit this protected reef located between Pupukea and Haleiwa. No one in recent memory has ever seen a shark here. Instead, any fins you'll see are attached to snorkelers and scuba divers who come to check out the cove's undersea wonders during the calm-water months of summer.

SURF-N-SEA

62-595 Kamehameha Hwy., Haleiwa, 808-637-9887, 800-899-7873; www.surfnsea.com

In addition to being a great place to purchase beachwear or rent equipment for a variety of ocean activities, this surf shop offers lessons and tours. Learn how to surf, windsurf, bodyboard, scuba dive, or snorkel, or head out into deeper waters to sportfish or get up close with sharks (in a protected cage, of course). Daily 9 a.m.-7 p.m.

TURTLE BAY RESORT GOLF CLUB

57-091 Kamehameha Hwy., Kahuku, 808-293-8574; www.turtlebayresort.com

Two of Oahu's top courses reside here. The championship 18-hole Palmer Course designed by Arnold Palmer and Ed Seay, offers traditional Scottish links play and a course designed around a wetlands bird preserve. The 18-

hole Fazio course is the only George Fazio-designed course here in the islands. This course saves the best for its final hole—a 160-yard carry over the Punahoolapa Marsh right into the prevailing trade winds. Facilities include a pro shop, driving range, putting and chipping greens and a snack bar.

WAIMEA VALLEY

59-864 Kamehameha Highway, Haleiwa, 808-638-9199; www.waimeavalley.net

This 1800-acre area includes natural habitats, botanical gardens and waterfalls. Meander along paths through the gardens and archaeological sites, or set off along the trails where you'll see many rare and endangered native Hawaiian flora and fauna. Daily 9:30 a.m.-5 p.m.

SPECIAL EVENTS
VAN'S TRIPLE CROWN OF PRO SURFING CHAMPIONSHIPS

North Shore; www.triplecrownofsurfing.com

Male and female professional surfers from around the world gather on Oahu's North Shore each winter to compete in three different surfing competitions including the famed Bonzai Pipeline Masters and the Women's Roxy Pro. November-December.

WORLD FIRE-KNIFE DANCE CHAMPIONSHIPS AND SAMOAN FESTIVAL

Laie, 808-293-3333; www.polynesia.com

The Samoan tradition of fire-knife dancing heats up the night skies at the World Fire-Knife Dance Competition held as part of the Polynesian Cultural Centers annual Samoan Festival. Junior competitions feature fire dancers as young as the age of six. May.

WHERE TO STAY
★★★TURTLE BAY RESORT

57-091 Kamehameha Highway, Kahuku, 808-293-6000, 800-203-3650;
www.turtlebayresort.com

For people who stay on Oahu and want to escape the crowds in Honolulu, this North Shore property is the best bet. It's situated out in the country, as the locals say, on the northern tip of the island, on the opposite side from Waikiki. The setting is gorgeous—so attractive that the resort was the location of the 2008 film Forgetting Sarah Marshall—with lots of unspoiled beauty, not to mention 5 miles of beaches, including some of Hawaii's most famous surfing spots. All of its rooms, suites and beach cottages have good ocean views, so you're guaranteed sensational sights without leaving your room. The beach cottages, which feature Brazilian walnut floors, 15-foot ceilings, king poster beds, large marble bathrooms and freestanding glass showers, are hard to beat for those not on a budget. They're also roomy, ranging in size from 740 to 850 square feet. There's not a lot of development on this side of the island, so there aren't a lot of attractions, but the hotel offers a wide assortment of activities—play golf on two courses designed by Arnold Palmer and George Fazio, hit some winning shots at the tennis center's 10 courts, go on a buying spree at the resort's shops, get spoiled at the spa, take a hike on the resort's 12 miles of oceanfront trails, swim in the ocean or one of two pools, and more. The hotel's dining and entertainment options are plentiful, with onsite restaurants and lounges, including the 21 Degrees North, which serves contemporary island cuisine in an upscale setting.

443 rooms. Restaurant, bar. Fitness center. Spa. Beach. Pool. Golf. Tennis. Business center. $$$

WINDWARD COAST

As its name telegraphs, Oahu's Windward Coast serves up plenty of Hawaii's cooling trade winds. It is also an appealing region of stark contrasts: the coast is home to the island's largest population concentration outside of Honolulu, as well as Oahu's lushest rural areas.

The area is much more urban on its south end, where more than 70,000 people live in the two cities of Kailua and Kaneohe. The two towns are ripe with the commercial activity one would expect in areas filled with locals—restaurants, shops and other businesses. But visitors seeking a tropical vacation don't let that deter them; rather, the many bed and breakfasts in this area attract tourists with room rates much cheaper than in Waikiki.

Many consider Kailua Beach, which runs for nearly two miles along the funky Kailua coastline, Oahu's best beach. It has become a real favorite with windsurfers and kitesurfers, who can get some mighty good rides out of its strong winds. Just up the coast, Kaneohe fronts one of the loveliest bays anywhere in Hawaii. Residences, condominiums and a few private yacht clubs and marinas line the bayfront. Boating companies take visitors to a sandbar offshore for swimming and snorkeling. From there, the views of the Koolau Mountain Range back on shore are spectacular.

North of Kaneohe, the rural country begins. On one side of the highway are majestic-looking mountains; on the other side, a shoreline dotted with several more picturesque beaches. Near the northern tip of this coast, in the Mormon settlement of Laie, is one of the island's top tourist attractions, the Polynesian Cultural Center, which the Mormon Church operates. The PCC, as locals call it, teaches visitors about life in Fiji, Hawaii, Marquesas, New Zealand, Samoa, Tahiti, and Tonga. The PCC is as popular as the other most-visited attraction on the Windward Coast: Hanauma Bay, one of Hawaii's best snorkeling spots.

WHAT TO SEE
AARON'S DIVE SHOP
307 Hahani St., Kailua, 808-262-2333; www.hawaii-scuba.com

One of Oahu's oldest and largest dive outfitters, Aaron's offers both beach and boat dive excursions and takes dive charters in waters around the entire island. Whether you're a novice or expert diver, there is a course that will get you in the water, including intro dives, refresher classes and three-day certification courses. The fleet of vessels accommodates 6 to 12 passengers and can bring you to sites such as the wreck of The Mahi, a 186-foot World War II US Navy Minesweeper that sank in 90 feet of water off Oahu's Waianae coast, and the wreck of a Gull Wing Corsair fighter plane, which crashed in 1945 in the waters off East Oahu. Daily from 6:30 a.m.

CAPTAIN BOB'S ADVENTURE CRUISES
Kaneohe, 808-942-5077, 888-222-3601

Captain Bob's Adventures begin with a ride on a 42-foot glass bottom catamaran named Barefoot, which glides through the seas off Oahu's stunning Windward Coast. Board at the Heeia Pier for a lazy day sail that gets you close-up views of the coral reefs and marine life. The catamaran also breaks at Ahu o Laka Sandbar for some serious snorkeling in waters full of tropical fish and honu (Hawaiian sea turtles). As a reward for your sea excursion, there's a lunch barbecue. Shuttle transportation is available from Waikiki hotels, with pickup between 9 and 9:30 a.m. and return at 4:30 p.m. Daily except Sundays.

HANAUMA BAY NATURE PRESERVE

Hanauma Bay Beach Park, off Hwy 72., Hawaii Kai; www.honolulu.gov

Hanauma Bay (curved bay) was formed by a series of underwater volcanic eruptions more than 30,000 years ago that blew up steam, rock, hot gases, coral and ash. Over the years, the ash chemically hardened to create a sunken volcanic crater that opens to the sea on its outer edge, creating an almost perfect crescent stretch of sand and an ocean playground teeming with colorful marine life that enthrall throngs of snorkelers. Hanauma's coral reefs protect the 50 species of fish here from their natural predators. The fish are so tame that they swim right up to you, making Hanauma the most visited (and crushingly crowded) snorkeling destination in Hawaii. All visitors must enter through the park's marine education center and view the seven-minute video created to both educate and enlighten visitors about this delicate eco attraction. From the visitor's center, walk or take a tram ride (50 cents a ride or $2 for a day pass) down the steep road to the beach, where you'll find snorkeling equipment, pontoon wheelchairs and beach wheelchairs for rent at the beach kiosk. Food concessions are also available. If you're there on a Saturday around the time of the full moon, consider a moonlight swim, when the park remains open for family night until 10 p.m.

HEEIA STATE PARK

46-465 Kamehameha Highway, Kaneohe, 808-247-3156

This hillside park is known for its sacred sites that were once centers of aquaculture for ancient Hawaiians. Hawaiians built these fishponds by using lava rock to enclose natural bays and creating slotted gates where fish could move into the ponds, but not find their way out. Several of those gates are currently being restored. Snorkel cruises leave from Heeia Pier, which juts out into Kaneohe Bay. Daily 7:30 a.m.-6:30 p.m.

KAHANA BAY BEACH PARK

Kailua

Families with young children enjoy Kahana's shady ironwood and pandanus trees, picnic tables and shallow waters protected by offshore reefs that create a perfect swimming spot. The remains of two ancient Hawaiian fishponds are still visible nearby. The ponds are being restored, so as time goes on, you'll be able to see more of the ancient aquaculture structure designed by Hawaiians many ages ago.

KAILUA BEACH PARK

Kailua

Steady year-round breezes from almost every direction make this beach Oahu's wind- and kite-surfing capital. Windsurfers, kiteboaders and kayakers share the waters with snorkelers and swimmers. If you rent a kayak, paddle out to the tiny Mokulua islands, a bird sanctuary. Volleyball courts, food concessions, lifeguards and parking are also available.

KIMO'S SURF HUT

150 Hekili St., Kailua, 808-262-1644; www.kimossurfhut.com

Rent both surfboards and body boards, along with skeeboards, fins, leashes, wax, board bags and everything a surfer needs to get into the curl. While you're here, check out the classic surfboard collection displayed on the walls throughout the store. For board stories and surfing tips, chat it up with Kimo and his staff of knowledgeable surf hut hui. Monday-Saturday 10 a.m.-6 p.m.

KUALOA RANCH AND ACTIVITY CLUB

49-560 Kamehameha Hwy., Kaaawa, 808-237-8515, 800-231-7321; www.kualoa.com

Hollywood has called on the Kualoa Ranch & Activity Club plenty of times. The setting for films including Jurassic Park and Pearl Harbor, Kualoa is a 4,000-acre working cattle ranch. Try a horseback ride complete with views of the Kualoa Mountains and the Pacific Ocean, an all-terrain vehicle ride into the Ka'a'awa Valley, kayaking along the shore of Secret Island, or an easier-on-the-bones afternoon spent touring the ranch by bus. Daily.

KUALOA REGIONAL BEACH PARK

Kaaawa

Stretches of grass border this thin, straight line of beachfront, which offers a front row panorama of Kaneohe Bay, with Mokolii islet taking center stage. There is a view of the dramatic Koolau Mountain Range, covered with trees, foliage, and lava rock that has been carved by centuries of wind and rain, creating the look of rich, green velvet. The park's Windward Coast location means winds blow from every direction, making it a favorite of windsurfers year-round. Campers, picnickers and beachgoers love it for the natural beauty.

LANIKAI BEACH

Lanikai

The town of Lanikai is known for its expensive real estate and the creamy slip of sand that you reach through the public access pathways along Mokulua Drive. Head here for swimming, boating, snorkeling and sunbathing, or simply to catch a picture-perfect Hawaiian sunrise.

MAKAPUU BEACH PARK

41-095 Kalanianaole Highway, Waimanalo

Fronting Sea Life Park and sitting below the Makapuu Lighthouse on the cliffs above, Makapuu Beach's blue waters beckon, but navigating the unpredictable ocean currents and strong surf here is best left to the most experienced of water enthusiasts. Volcanic cliffs ring this stretch of coastline, making this one of the more photogenic beaches on Oahu.

MAUNAWILI TRAIL

Pali Highway, Maunawili

This hike meanders along the base of the windward coastline and ends up in Waimanalo, and makes for an 11-mile hike one way. The trail begins just beneath the Pali Lookout, about a quarter-mile down from the Pali Tunnels on the windward side of the tunnel, where you'll be treated to views of the Koolau Range, Mount Olomana, and paths that travel through ohia and koa wood rain forests. You'll need to park cars at both ends of the trail or arrange for a pickup in Waimanalo Valley upon completion of your hike.

NAISH HAWAII

155A Hamakua Drive, Kailua, 808-262-6068; www.naish.com

This family-owned and operated business includes world championship windsurfer Robby Naish. The company offers extensive windsurfing and kiteboarding lessons, board rentals and sales, as well as lodging advice for those eager to stay near Kailua Beach. Both private and group lessons are available. Private lessons last 90-minutes and include an additional 90 minutes of rental equipment use immediately following lessons at no extra charge.

NUUANU PALI LOOKOUT

Pali Highway, Kailua

You'll be swept away by the views from this vantage point 1,200 feet above sea level and amid the majestic Pali (cliffs) of the Koolau Range. The natural beauty lies in stark contrast to its history as the site of one of Hawaii's most violent battles. It was here that Kamehameha I, in his desire to unite the islands, pushed Oahu forces back into this valley. Refusing to surrender, many of the warriors either jumped or were pushed to their deaths. The lookout is also infamous for its powerful winds, but still loved for its lush tropical views that span the entire windward coastline. Daily 9 a.m.-4 p.m., weather permitting.

SEA LIFE PARK HAWAII

41-202 Kalanianaole Highway, Waimanalo, 808-259-7933, 866-365-7446;
www.sealifeparkhawaii.com

If you saw the movie 50 First Dates, you're already familiar with some of the lovable creatures that make their home at Sea Life Park, located about 15 minutes from Waikiki. Dolphins, stingrays, sea lions, monk seals and sea turtles are among the featured attractions here. Pay $25 to enter the park, see the shows and tour the exhibits, or splurge for a dolphin swim, a stingray encounter, an underwater photo safari, or one of several other interactive programs, which require advance reservations and top out at more than $100 per adult. You can even get married at the park, which is set on the lovely Makapuu Point, with the help of an onsite wedding coordinator. Daily 9:30 a.m.-5 p.m.

SENATOR FONG'S PLANTATION AND GARDENS

47-285 Pulama Road, Kaneohe, 808-239-6775; www.fonggarden.com

Hiram Fong was the first Asian American to serve in the U.S. Senate. In 1950, he purchased a small plot of land that eventually grew to its present-day size of 725 acres and once supplied local markets with bananas. Today, trams take visitors on tours of the expansive gardens, which contain five areas named after U.S. presidents. Rushing waterfalls, tropical birds, delicate native flowers and exotic fruit and nut trees make for lovely viewing. Lei-making classes are available at the visitor center. Daily 10 a.m.-4 p.m.

TWOGOOD KAYAKS HAWAII

345 Hahani St., Kailua, 808-262-5656; www.twogoodkayaks.com

Follow kayak enthusiasts to Kailua's calm and reef-protected aquamarine waters. At Twogood Kayaks you can sign up for a variety of tours, including a guided ocean kayak tour led by a trained naturalist, and a turtle safari where you'll swim with turtles and have lunch on famed Kailua Beach. The all-day Adventure Package tour is self-guided and begins with a kayak lesson sea orientation and includes your kayak rental, a picnic lunch, and hotel transportation.

WHERE TO EAT

★★BACI BISTRO

30 Aulike St., Kailua, 808-261-2857; www.bacibistro.com

If you begin to tire of island-style cuisine, have a meal at Baci Bistro, cozy neighborhood spot in Kailua. Hot and cold antipasti, risottos, a wide variety of pasta dishes, veal, pork, chicken, and fish pair well with the restaurant's nicely varied selection of wines. Top it off with a traditional tiramisu, a glass of grappa, or limoncello.

Italian. Lunch, dinner. Bar. Children's menu. Reservations recommended. Outdoor seating. $$

★★CROUCHING LION INN

51-666 Kamehameha Highway, Kaaawa, 808-237-8511

Popular among tourists visiting the beaches and lush mountains along Oahu's western coast, this restaurant, named for the rock formation just north of the town center, serves classic American fare. The outdoor dining area overlooks the Pacific while the more refined interior dining room features vaulted ceilings and a large stone fireplace. The food here is satisfying, if unexceptional. Crouching Lion Inn is known for its fresh pies, perhaps the most popular—and decadent—being the Mile High Coconut Pie.

American. Lunch, dinner. Bar. Children's menu. Outdoor seating. $$

★★HALEIWA JOE'S SEAFOOD GRILL

46-336 Haiku Road, Kaneohe, 808-247-6671; www.haleiwajoes.com

Fresh seafood is the focus at this casual tropical-themed restaurant. The open-air dining room overlooks the gorgeous Haiku Gardens (a popular spot for weddings) and dramatic mountains. Dig into small plates such as tako poke or tempura crab rolls, or big plate of ahi teriyaki topped with beurre blanc.

Seafood. Lunch, dinner. Bar. Children's menu. Reservations recommended. Outdoor seating. $$

INDEX

M

★★★★★ HAWAII

191

★★★★★★ HAWAII

HAWAII

MAUI COUNTY

450

30

360

378

31

31

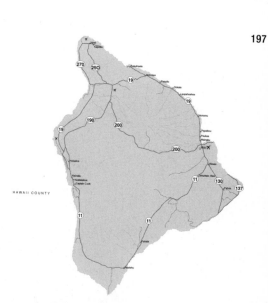

270 25O

19

190 200

19

200

HAWAII COUNTY

11

130 137

11

11

KAUAI

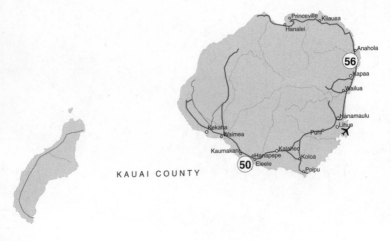

KAUAI COUNTY

Princeville
Kilauea
Hanalei
Anahola
56
Kapaa
Wailua
Hanamaulu
Kekaha
Lihue
Waimea
Puhi
Kaumakani
Hanapepe
Kalaheo
Koloa
50
Eleele
Poipu

OAHU

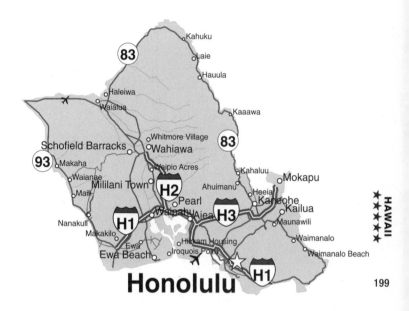

Honolulu

HONOLULU COUNTY

199

HAWAII
★★★
★★★
★★★

MAUI

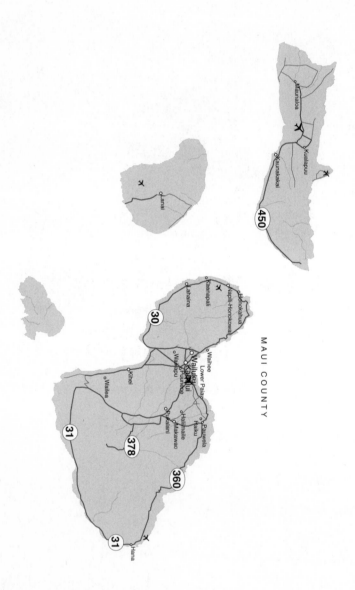

MAUI COUNTY

BIG ISLAND OF HAWAII

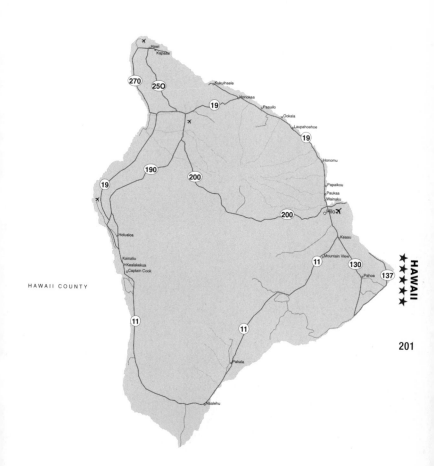

HAWAII COUNTY

HAWAII
★★★
★★★

201

NOTES

NOTES

NOTES

NOTES

HAWAII
★★★★★

NOTES